LIGHT OF THE FIRE'S-EYE

ROBERT WILLIAM GROFE

Light of the Fire's-Eye by Robert William Grofe

ROBOT REEF
An imprint of Robert William Grofe, Publisher

Light of the Fire's-Eye copyright © 2018, 2013
by Robert William Grofe, Publisher

Address comments and inquiries to:
ROBOT REEF
c/o Robert William Grofe
600 Dolmens Ln.
Malvern, PA 19355

spacegrofe@yahoo.com

ISBN-13: 978-0615808314 (Robot Reef)
ISBN-10: 061580831X

Printed in the United States of America

Second edition: 2018

For my Dad

LIGHT OF THE FIRE'S-EYE

"The distinction between the past, present, and future is only a stubbornly persistent illusion."
— Albert Einstein

"Technology is not a question of what one can do; it is a question of what one wants."
— Teodor Monroe

baetyl ('bēt-əl) *n.*, *pl.* baetyls, baetyli ('bēt-əlz, 'bēt-ə-lī). 1. A sacred stone. 2. A meteorite or similar-looking rough stone of legend thought to contain magical powers, described variously by antiquarian mythographers and lexicographers as being of divine origin, animated, and possessed by demons, and associated individually with different gods. [< Lat. *baetulus* < Gk. *baitylos*, meteoric stone < Heb. *bethel*, house of God (*beth*, house + *'el*, God).] — Also **baetylus** ('bēt-ə-ləs) *n.*, *pl.* **baetyli**, **baetylia** ('bēt-ə-lī, bē-'tĭl-ē-ə)

pyropite ('pī-rə-pīt) *n.* 1. Any of the various iron-magnesium-aluminum garnet gems belonging to the pyrope-almandine series ranging from deep red to violet in color. 2. A specific solid-solution mineral variety of garnet that is five-sixths pyrope $Mg_3Al_2(SiO_4)_3$ and one-sixth almandine $Fe_3Al_2(SiO4)_3$. [< ME *pirope* < MF < Lat. *pyropus* < Gk. *pyropos*, fiery-eyed (*pyr*, fire + *ops*, eye).]

fire's-eye ('fīrz-ī) *n.*, *pl.* **fire's-eyes** ('fīrz-īz). 1. PYROPITE. 2. Any deep red garnet gemstone resembling pyrope, particularly with a characteristic radiating asterism resembling a human iris. 3. A stone of legend in various galactic cultures said to exhibit unique radioactive luminescence and believed to contain rejuvenating powers in its natural state.

Excerpted text from "Expostulum Cillius": Transworld Bareilli HC IA, R&D; Special Projects, confidential transcript file set JPDL81FO9Y30, auth B14-062; compiled by C.P. Faro (ID 0620046); highlights.

File JPDL81FO9Y30.29: Sanchuniathon
ref Philo Byblos, ca 110 ce; sourced Sanchuniathon, ca 1340 bce; "Phoenician History"; key "creation of sky", "uranus", "baetylia"...
/The universe began as a blast of wind and cloudy air and a turbid chaos dark as Erebus, and these were boundless and for long ages had no limit. But when the wind became enamoured of its own parents and a mixture took place, that connexion was called Desire. This was the beginning of the creation of all things, but the wind itself had no knowledge of its own creation. From its connexion Mot was produced, which some say is mud and others a putrescence of watery compound, and out of this came every germ of creation, and the generation of the universe. So there were certain animals which had no sensation, and out of them grew intelligent animals, and were called Zophasemin, that is, "observers of heaven", and they were formed like the shape of an egg. Also Mot burst forth into light, and sun, and moon, and stars, and the great constellations. [citation text removed]
/There were gods who dwelt in the neighborhood of Byblos, and from among them was born Epigeus or Autochthon, whom they afterwards called Uranus, so that from him they named the element above us Uranus because of the excellence of its beauty. [citation text removed]
/The god Uranus devised the Baetylia, having contrived to put life into stones.

File JPDL81FO9Y30.21: Pliny
ref Gaius Plinius Secundus "Pliny the Elder", ca 79 ce; sourced Sotacus Carystus, ca 400 bce; "Naturalis Historiae", key "mineralogy", "magnets", "baetuli"...
/Sotacus classifies magnets into five varieties: the first found in Aethiopia, the second from the Magnesia which has a common boundary with Macedonia and lies on one's right hand as one makes for Ioclus from Euboea, the third found at Hyettus in Boeotia, the fourth from the neighborhood of Alexandria in the Troad, and the fifth from the Magnesia which is in Asia. [citation text removed]
/Sotacus distinguishes also two other varieties of the stone, a black and a red, resembling axe-heads. According to him, those among them that are black and round are supernatural objects, and he states that thanks to them cities and fleets are attacked and overcome, their name being "baetuli", while the elongated stones are "ceraunia" ("thunder-stones").

File JPDL81FO9Y30.02: Messenger
ref Zer-Fu Ep-Tun-Ak "The Zirer Land Messenger Journal", gp 136-224-523/139; sourced Po-Sat-Loc-Nid, Lum-Kel-Te, gp 136-224-411/621; article SAR 07837-42 "reprint of working status report, TOR12936880", key "cillian minecraft", "teledura documents", "a-pic-lit-roy belt"...

/Inspecting A-Pic-Lit-Roy 214896, surface scans of the crater at 57-98-01-55 yielded a single, distinct mineral that initially appeared to reflect the search lights of the probe as a splendent metal or highly refractive crystal; focused examination revealed unique garnet botyroidal presentation of iron magnesium aluminum silicate with resinous, semitranslucent luster and reduced diaphaneity. Specimen contained visible asterism, atypical conchoidal face, and internal luminescence observed in extremely rare stratified virtual nonradioactives of the Sac-Taw region. Impervious to fracture by industry-standard technique. Unreadable using available on-site screening equipment; telemetrics failed to obtain measurable data. Additional qualifiers were confirmed through robotics and visual inspection.

File JPDL81FO9Y30.03: Demodocus
ref Demodocus Smyrna, ca 515 bce; sourced Pygmalion Tyre, ca 1000 bce; "Vitae Phoenicia", key "travels of pygmalion", "orestes story", "byblos baetyl"...

/I saw a baetyl in Byblos [citation text removed], borne in the hands of the servant who called himself Orestes, and swaddled in rags that failed to cover its glow; it was like an uncut gemstone covered round with small protuberances and imperfections but smooth like glass to the touch, with a diameter the width of a palm. He showed us the orb uncovered, and it was luminous, and its light changed when he moved it in his hands, sometimes appearing larger, then smaller, and its colour would turn in kind, from the deep red of cinnabar to Tyrian purple, changing with the light of the room. [citation text removed]

/He told me it came to him in the East, where a great and violent desire had drawn him away from his village. He hastened to an ancient place at the foot of the mountain where no other person had walked, and rested there, and at that moment he saw a ball of fire fall from the sky and land before him. Orestes saw that the fire had cooled, and he beheld the baetyl in its earthly form, and he took it in his hands and asked it to convey the name of its god, who was Ouranos, the beautiful lord of the heavens. Orestes carried it to his home and kept it always thereafter.

/Orestes said he was not the master of the baetyl, but it was his charge, and he would pray to it often; and the baetyl would answer his prayers and direct him in his life.

File JPDL81FO9Y30.11: Inquirer
ref Philadelphia Inquirer, 1992 ce; article Tuesday 9-29-92, Local News
"Strange Airport Disappearance Mystifies Travelers and Officials", key
"philadelphia", "blaze-of-light man"...

/A local man disappeared spontaneously just before midnight yesterday at Philadelphia International Airport in what witnesses described as a "blaze of light."

/John Walker, 48, of the Tinicum Island area was waiting for Delta Airlines Flight 152 to Los Angeles at the boarding terminal when he vanished during an unexplained surge of light that seemed to originate where he was standing, according to police. Security cameras recorded the incident and airport officials are reviewing the film. Walker is now officially listed as missing.

/At least 10 people witnessed the event. Delta flight attendant Mindy Thompson was on duty at the check-in counter at the time.

/"He was there one second, and then there was a flash, and then he was just gone," Thompson said. "It was like a magic trick."

/Officials did not comment on whether they believe the incident was a prank or hoax, but witnesses are still being interviewed, according to Detective Brad Randall of the Chester Township Police. The investigation is ongoing, Randall said.

/Walker was last employed by a printer manufacturer in Wilmington, Delaware. No friends or relatives were available for comment.

File JPDL81FO9Y30.47: Arnaud
ref Antonin Arnaud, 1934 ce; essay "Heliogabale ou l'Anarchiste Couronne",
key "emperor elegabalus", "meteorite reverence"...

/But there are stones that are alive, like animals or plants, and like, one may say, the sun, with its spots that move about, inflate and deflate, and dribble into one another. [citation text removed]

/The spots are born in it like a cancer, like the effervescent buboes of the plague. [citation text removed]

/All this is alive; and one may say that some stones are alive; and the stones of Syria are alive, like the miracles of nature; for they are stones hurled from heaven.

File JPDL81FO9Y30.07: Sende
ref Sende Kerellen Almedan, gp 136-224-572/458; essay "Exhibition of
Yveianna", key "scinti lore", "teledura documents", "fire's-eye"...

/When isolated from ambient light, the mineral would simulate a burning ember in the center of a raging fire, rough-hewn around the surface and with its traces of coarse outcropping mingled with the glow of emanating heat. For the poet cognizant of the breath of life endowed our long-lived race by the energy of the stars, the find evokes images of Home Volier in its nascence, even the cooling moment that ensued the Origin itself, if physics allowed it to be seen from an outside standpoint.

From HIPA MATS GEO DB:

Proposed acceptance of mineral "pyropite" based on explicit and extensive information from United Colonial Society Realm Historical Authority; additional complementary supplements from Prano-Donan Collective Union, Volieran Science Association, and Teledura Group of Astrogeologic Research Organizations; no sample supplied; extremely rare exception basis confirmed by given historical record.

Entry submitted by C.P. Faro, 3609.

ENTRY FILE: 07829467392PYOX   AUTHOR: CPFARI06712   DATE: 03103609
CODE: CT-AB-G3-042029 \ CLASS: iron magnesium aluminum silicate \
COMPOUND: "pyropite" \ AKA: (hum) pyrope rubidicoronis = baetylite = ambrosite; (an) laa'ssiq ta'hranaq; (cil) ap-sat-oc = tep-tak; (drb) glnrc; (gul) rampas; (ico) makkar-lanador = shorlach-teyo; (key) shrevyndyr = illfyr; (pro) embon; (rax) hstoaxatcorat = ratarat = toctinac; (sc) eyv-yeveret; (tel) isilisili = taca-teh \
FORMULA: $(Mg_3Al2(SiO_4)_3)_5(Fe_3Al_2(SiO_4)_3)$ = Pyr_5Alm; solid-solution pyrope-almadine series \ COLOR: red var. \ HABIT: botyroidal-massive; euhedral \
CRYSTAL: cubic; hexoctahedral \ FRACTURE: uneven; conchoidal \ STRUCTURE: 0.000; cleave neg; twin neg \ SOLIDITY: 1667 kg/mm^2 \ BULK MODULUS: 337 GPa \
TENACITY: brittle; superhard \ SPECIFIC GRAVITY: 3.498 \ LUSTER: vitreous; resinous; pearl \ DIAPHANEITY: subtranslucent \ PARTICULATE: colorless \
REFRACTION: 1.775/1.775.0.000; isotropic; pleochroism neg \ DISPERSION: 98.75 \
ABSORPTION SPECTRA: 562–450 nm \ SOLUBILITY: H_2O neg/HF pos \ PHASE POINTS: UUUU/3640 K \ RA DECAY: UUUU dpm \ ABUNDANCE: 0.000 ppm; extremely rare \ MINERAL ASSOCIATIONS: no known trend

LIGHT OF THE FIRE'S-EYE

* * *

ROBERT WILLIAM GROFE

PROLOGUE

A

The trees of the forest towered above, forming a ceiling of blue-green as high as an ancient earthly cathedral. Marigold looked up as she darted through the forest. The leaves and branches were all far, far up the trunks—too high to reach by climbing. They didn't build homes in trees that high.

Loud chattering animal noises were growing louder. She was the deep forest… the land of the spirewood, the tallest trees in the area for hundreds of kilometers around. And for now, they were all hers. There were no houses in these trees. Here, the woods were her own personal hideaway, a massive blue-green blanket of protection under which no one who happened to be flying overhead could see her.

She imagined she was a tiny white flea hopping through a patch of bristly body hair. Perhaps the body hair of one of her sheridans. There was a novel idea—to have the ability to make Shey Deiga or Shey Aful-Kiron itch at will. Drive one of them crazy for a change.

She laughed, then suddenly stumbled, landing face-forward with her arms outstretched. She blew pine needles out of her mouth and stood, looking back and dusting off her clothes. A giant wooden root was sticking out across the trail.

Blast! Why couldn't she just have wings, like everybody else?

The shiny blue pouch around her waist was squashed and covered with loose dirt. She frowned as she rubbed her scraped elbows and knees. Right when she had just washed all her clothes, right on the same day. Double-blast!

She was less than a kilometer from the Circle of Trees now, but if she didn't hurry up, she wasn't going to get a good seat for the Viewing. She broke into a full run, keeping her eyes on the trail.

Shey Aful-Kiron had said that this Viewing was important, and that no one should be late. She had never missed a Viewing, but Shey Aful-Kiron had still singled her out and told her to make sure that she was there… the sheridans were always saying things to get people to go to the Viewings. Why not? They were fast, easy ways to educate everybody in the dormitory at the same time. The stories always had some scinti historical significance. Usually they were legends about scinti heroes, or the forests of Home Volier, or the adventures of scinti trade ships. And usually parts of the stories turned

1

up later in class.

Of course, they had a Viewing every quarter-volimoon, and she had already seen a lot of the stories at least twice, but they were always a nice break from classwork. Even watching the reruns was definitely more interesting than studying local flora and fauna on the dormitory computer banks.

The forest was getting dark now. The double-sun would be down soon, and the Viewing was going to start immediately after nightfall. There was a very good chance she was going to be late, which would mean she would wind up sitting at the outer rim of the circle while others enjoyed the full effects of the show. It wasn't something she really wanted to do.

If the sheridans wanted everybody to be there at the Circle of Trees so early, why did they assign so much work? It wasn't fair. She had done all her work for the next day, changed her clothes, and then headed for the Viewing straight from the dormitory. It took an hour for her to cover that distance, at least, and the sheridans all knew it. Sure, she had taken a couple of hours to relax and unwind after class, but how could they expect her not to relax?

She was going to be late. She dove through a hole in a hornbrush thicket that was hanging into the trail. The entire trip from the dormitory to the Circle of Trees didn't take anybody else more than ten minutes. It wasn't fair at all.

The opening in the trees was just ahead. She broad-jumped a nasty stretch of snaggleweed and jogged to the edge of the clearing. The trail led between one last pair of straight-trunked spirewood trees and up a gentle, grassy hill, rising out of the underbrush. She puffed, continuing up the path more slowly.

The hill continued to climb until she came to the Circle—12 trees spaced evenly around a field large enough to seat everyone from the three dormitories. 11 of the trees were lofty shadowlines, straight as arrows and thinner than the spirewoods. Their branches were trimmed so that they reached only toward the other trees of the Circle, braided together to give the trees the look of a single, gigantic basket.

A fire lit up the middle of the field, and directly across from it was the twelfth tree. The twelfth tree was the exception, a single, black giant rockwood twice as tall as the others and wide enough for a scint to make a comfortable home within its base. The twelfth tree was the nerve center of the Circle. It was there that the sheridans would conduct the show.

Fortunately, only about a fourth of the seat cushions laid out on the grass were occupied, mostly by the younger students. The sky was still fairly well-lit to the east. The Viewing probably wouldn't begin for another half hour.

Marigold smiled and flushed as she passed onto the field. She wasn't late at all. There were plenty of people who hadn't yet arrived.

She was never late. When was she going to learn that?

The field was alive with conversational scinti chirping as she moved toward the center. Students paused and stared at her as she approached them. They always stared, even though they all knew her by now. They stared right into her mind, and then they looked away...

The fire flamed high at the center of a wide, circular marble hearth stained the color of dirt. The compression lamps at the hearth's rim were already lit. There were available seats in the front, probably because the fire was a little too hot, but the sheridans would shut down the fire when they started the holograms.

She chose a seat and unstrapped the pouch from around her waist, placing it on a cushion as close as any to the fire. Then she turned and headed toward the giant rockwood.

The tree loomed into the darkening sky above the others. The branches and the top of the trunk had been removed, and the tree had been carved to make room for the elevators, the holo-projector, and a stage for those who were conducting the Viewings. From the outside, it wasn't much more than a massive, dead husk. But it still looked natural, with its knotted, gnarled, twisting bark and its gargantuan, spreading roots.

She squinted up at the platform of the stage, a converted protrusion in the bark from where an old limb had once sprouted. All evidence of scinti technology was camouflaged, just as in any other scinti forest home. Supposedly, they did it to preserve the integrity of the forest.

She shrugged and walked through the opening at the bottom of the tree. The scinti didn't like flaunting their technology. Not like humans. On the human worlds, technology was everywhere. Bustling cities, all kinds of spacecraft, dazzling laser-generated works of art. Humans didn't hide their achievements.

There was barely any technology to see at all near the dormitories— only the information stored in the computer banks, and the holograms at the Viewings.

The inside of the rockwood was lined with rows of diode displays, monitors, keypads, and controls. Several sheridans were busy setting levels and pressing buttons. A lady sheridan saw Marigold enter. She turned and perked her angular ears up, touching her slender hands together. It was Sheya Hamay Paran-Heya.

The rings around her large eyes widened. "Sese vayla, Marigold."

"Sese, Sheya Hamay. Where is Shey Deiga?"

The sheridan bowed her head. "He is on the platform." She extended her arm, unfolding her wing at one of the elevators. "You may see him there, if you like."

Marigold nodded back at her. "Fiya-maray." She waved as she stepped into the elevator.

Bon Sheridan Deiga Karavia-Sharla was the eldest elder of the dormitory, and it was no surprise that he was going to be conducting this Viewing. He had always been active, telling stories and overseeing the teachings of the other sheridans. He always seemed to know what was going on. He still knew the names of every student in the dormitory, and he knew exactly how to tantalize each one of them.

Marigold stepped off the elevator and looked around. The hollow of the tree was completely dark, but the sky was visible through an opening at the top of the trunk. The bon sheridan didn't appear to be there at first glance… maybe he was waiting to scare her. He knew she was there. He always knew when she was there.

The air was scented with the smell of an aromatic wire buried somewhere among the computers in the wood. Alkad, the thought stimulant. It always smelled like alkad at the Viewings. The scent rose and fell with the soothing sound of wind washing over the treetops.

Marigold immediately thought back to the first time she had been in the house high up in Deiga's tree, in his pyramid-shaped green room, with an open skyway at the peak designed to filter the moonlight. He had invited her to join him in Seselada, the periodic rite of tranquility. Really not much more than an hour of sitting on pillows, doing absolutely nothing. Very boring. She had turned down the next invitation.

The outside view caught her attention. She walked out through the opening in the wood and onto the platform, leaning on the thin polyglass railing.

Kad Lalimbra's double-corona was just setting behind the trees to the east. Purple clouds were spreading across the horizon. One of Kad's moons was becoming clear just above the clouds, and stars were rapidly blinking into view. It was breathtaking. It had been a while since she had last been up in the rockwood.

A high-pitched voice filled the air. "Marigold Frisby Josefson. So, I see your assignment for tomorrow is finished."

She turned around. "Yes, it's finished, Shey Deiga."

He was stooped, holding a cup of ferrel stems and wearing an orange woodling tunic that would shine impressively under the floodlights. He was older now, but he still looked the same as he had when Marigold had first arrived on Kad, with his large, olive green bristle-haired head and its out-of-proportion alien features, his light, bony body, and his wings.

The thin diamond pupils of his gigantic eyes were long in the growing darkness. His nostrils were crinkled in mischievous fashion. "You do know that you still have other work to do. Shey Fayverra has given you a week to complete Fourthmoon High Point climate analysis. And there will be more assignments. Do you think you can handle such a workload?"

How did he know that? "Rillic-ti-rillic. Of course I can, Shey Deiga. You aren't saying you want me to go back and miss the Viewing, are you?"

The sheridan trilled back in a practiced tone. "So. You choose to neglect your studies. To procrastinate. Are you managing your time the way you have been instructed, Marigold Frisby Josefson?" He cocked his large, bristly head to one side.

Marigold felt herself clenching her fists. "But Shey Aful-Kiron said this Viewing is important, and no one should miss it! He even told me specifically to make sure I was here! Shey Deiga, everything that has to be done tomorrow is done—believe me, it is!"

He clicked his callused lips together. "So much fire! I am glad you are here, Marigold. You will enjoy it, I know. In fact, I think you will find this Viewing particularly interesting."

She exhaled. He was getting to her again. He was so good at getting to her. She looked out at the field. The seats were filling up now, and the sky was getting dark even to the east. "They're always interesting, as long as they're not about Kad. I like it when they show the other planets."

Deiga nodded. He stooped to set his cup on the wooden floor then stood up and stretched, fanning his wings through the jagged slashes in his tunic. Marigold was nearing his height now, and soon she would be taller than he and all the other scinti sheridans. Maybe then he wouldn't tease her so easily.

He looked out at the crowd and light reflected off his eyes. "So. You like the other planets. Well. It doesn't surprise me, Marigold... you have travel in your blood. Do you have a favorite place of all the places in the sky?"

She smiled, closing her eyes momentarily. "I'd like to know more about Scalaway. I've never been there, but my father used to say there were a hundred perfect coves on every island, and that the ocean was as clear as the spring near Gailey Calora."

Deiga's thin diamond pupils suddenly seemed to lose focus. "Your father made many lands sacred."

He was right about that. Her father had brought her on a few of the trips to Earth, and each of them had been a new adventure. She remembered her sixth birthday, when she had been introduced to all the exotic looking ambassadors in London—furry people with lots of eyes, people that looked like lizards and insects, and people that didn't look like anything she had ever seen. And her father had always said that as amazing as everything was, none of it compared to the beauty of his home planet.

As soon as she was 40 volimoons, she would be done with her education. Then she could get registered, and she would be able to fly to Scalaway herself.

But for now she would have to endure the drudgery of the green and brown forest, and the green and brown scinti, and their green and brown clothing, and the green and brown way they decorated every little thing they could get their skinny little hands on.

Deiga bowed at her. "You will be old and away from us soon enough, Mageveila."

Marigold grimaced, suppressing a whine. Mageveila was a Sralo-Varsea word for a Volieran brush flea. Deiga was probably never going to stop calling her "Mageveila." Sheridans could be so unbelievably irritating.

"It is said the groundling is happier than the sky-glider, because the groundling cannot see the places he could otherwise be." He blinked with a small smile. "Just enjoy the Viewing. There is experience in the Viewing."

She sighed. "That's easy for you to say, Shey Deiga. I'll bet a lot of the old legends aren't even true." She looked away from him, touching her hair, testing the band that held her braids together.

Deiga's ears pricked up, and his longer, whiter bristles stood out. "Ah, but the Viewing is real life, Marigold. You will experience nothing less than the truth here."

She raised an eyebrow. "Oh come on, Shey Deiga. They've had millions of years to add to the stories and change things around. It seems to me it's always about the drama. I'm sure even you exaggerate just a little." She smirked, clasping her hands behind her back and rocking on her heels.

The rings around Deiga's eyes expanded. "Well. Some details are subject to interpretation, and often color is added by the storyteller for dramatic effect, but any good story based on true events must be rooted in truth. The words themselves will vary with time, but not the greater message—not at all. Every story has its own message, and the message does not change. Conveying truth in a meaningful way… this is the storyteller's sacred responsibility." He paused. "And facts can always be checked. You should not guess at these things. The lake-fisher is adept in a boat, but less so if the boat wanders into the ocean. Remember this, Marigold... the old legends are never rewritten. They endure." He held up his hand. "Yveianna."

She stepped to the railing and leaned on it, touching her chin with a finger. "What?"

The bon sheridan aimed his pupils at Marigold. "Yveianna," he repeated. "Translate, please."

She frowned. Sralo-Varsea usually made as much sense to her as English. "Do you mean 'eyveian'? Doesn't that mean 'full'? Like a cup of water?"

"Yes. So. A derivation. In the Old Tongue, the word 'Yveianna' meant the beginning, the end, and everything in between. From birth to death. The full cup of water, or the full sky of stars. An equivalent human phrase is 'Alpha to Omega.' Before it meant, 'the complete picture'; now it simply means 'complete.'"

Marigold pressed her lips together. The rings around the bon sheridan's eyes were at their full extension, spread across the better part of his face, and his hardened lips were drawn taut above his small, pointed chin. He was worked up about something. It was as if he were back in the dormitory, raving over trade history.

"There is order in completeness, Marigold. There is serenity. If a legend is not complete, it should not be told. The legends are all for the most part in their original form, as they always have been. We are careful when we repeat them for new listeners... this is our tradition. Year by year, century by century. Do you know the graystone bridge over Kavarai Creek?"

She nodded quickly. "I cross it every time I come here. It's on the main trail." Of course she knew the bridge. She knew it better than anyone else— she was the only one who had to use it.

"That bridge is as sturdy a bridge as you will find this far from the cities. If all the fellian in the three dormitories crossed it at once, it still would not fall. But the bridge is made up of jagged stones, angled so that they support each other. Great care was taken in fitting the stones together just so. True enough, there is more than one way to assemble a pile of jagged stones, and if the bridge were put together differently, it could possibly be as strong, but in every bridge there are keystones, and for a bridge to stand the keystones must be securely set. And when a bridge is sturdy, there is no reason to take it apart and reassemble it. The old legends are like the bridge; when they are remembered, it should be like pictures chiseled on slates of graystone. When

7

we rearrange the pictures, we risk the legend's strength. And if we remove the most important pictures, the legend will not stand. Take heart, Marigold… there is the certainty of the legends, and the great care in which they are told. Keep that in mind during the Viewing."

A white light came on inside the hollow of the tree, and the crowd murmured. Shey Fayverra Vinete stood by the elevator, gesturing nervously at the controls hidden in the inner bark. Marigold looked up. There was only a rim of reddish light over the eastern treetops now. Everywhere else, the sky was the deep indigo of night. The Viewing was about to begin.

She turned back to Deiga, raising her eyebrows. He blinked slowly and bowed his head. She hurried off the stage and Shey Fayverra ushered her quickly into the elevator.

She laughed, shaking her head as she descended. Of course Deiga wanted everyone to believe the legends were accurate—he didn't want to spoil the magic. But some of the legends really had been passed on for thousands of years. They had to have been exaggerated at least a little bit. There wasn't a way to make sure every single storyteller in history never exaggerated—it wasn't possible. Someone was bound to have made some improvements.

She jogged through the crowd until she reached the fire. There was a gap in the seat where she had left her pouch. She smiled, moved the pouch, and crossed her legs as she sat.

The light in the giant rockwood had gone back out, and nothing could be seen on the stage. In the other direction, the moon was getting higher up in the sky. Everywhere else, the stars were standing out. The bugs were getting louder now, along with the murmurs of anticipation. Marigold bit her lip and stared at the fire.

The flames licked at the sky, just as they had before, making the night look blacker than it was. They weren't changing. Marigold frowned. Then, just when she was about to look away, they began to shrink. The center of the hearth was sinking. Marigold beamed.

The fire lowered until the tips of the flames were below ground level, leaving a hole filled with rising smoke. Marigold felt a subtle vibration below her seat, and a low whirring noise began. A panel of clear, white lookingstone slid across the opening, and when it stopped, the giant rockwood lit up. Shey Deiga was standing on the stage with his wings outspread.

The section of the crowd facing the rockwood began to cheer, and quickly the cheering spread around the circular field. Marigold opened her pouch and took out her earknobs and her translator box. She fitted the knobs in her ears, but left the device off for the time being. Deiga remained motionless, glowing in his bright orange tunic. Then he dropped his arms.

"Avan!" He looked around the crowd. *Hush,* Marigold thought.

The crowd immediately fell silent.

"Ona layah! Pah issia fea Kry Sokryaha ti Gamate-Passa!" *Welcome. Let us begin this Sacred Night of the Fourthmoon.* Deiga's voice was everywhere, as if carried by a swirling wind. There were computers under every square centimeter of grass in the Circle of Trees. There were huge sound-speakers hidden everywhere. The acoustics were as good as they could get. Scinti engineering was never more apparent than it was during a Viewing.

Of course, Marigold wouldn't be hearing the story through the big speakers. She pressed a button on the translator box, and heard a faint, momentary hiss as the signal hit the knobs in her ears. She put the box back in her pouch. The translator would mimic the sound and pitch of the storyteller's voice. It wasn't as good as the real thing, but it was better than hearing the story in Sralo-Varsea. Somehow, the stories just weren't the same if they weren't spoken in English. She touched her ears, testing the knobs.

On stage, Deiga held up a finger. "You have heard the tale of the shell-fisher who spends his life dreaming of finding a pearl in his day's draw, who one day comes upon a pile of diamonds and mistakes it for broken window glass."

He sounded fine. She looked up at the stage.

"So. We can sometimes forget the reasons why we do the things we do. Most of our legends have been passed down by our ancestors for more lifetimes than we can count. These legends tell us who we are, why we live in the trees, why we built ships to take us here and to the other planets. But there are other stories besides these old legends of ours, other stories that we can learn from. This we sometimes forget."

Marigold sat up. This wasn't beginning like any of the Viewings she knew.

"On occasion, legends from other parts of the Galaxy come to our attention. The legends of the Fissica. The Ynereia. And the Deiassa."

Marigold opened her mouth. The Deiassa. Humans. Deiga was looking in her direction. Was that why the sheridans were telling her she was going to be interested? Were they actually going to do a Viewing devoted totally to humans? They couldn't. No, they wouldn't do that, would they?

Deiga spread his wings again. "The museum at High Point does not contain many artifacts from other worlds. But there is one item there that was left by the scint Deya Bershevia 106 years ago. Now see…"

An upside-down cone of blue light rose through the lookingstone, fanning out from the hearth so that it covered a wide circle in the sky. Then, in the wood of the stage, just below Deiga's taloned feet, a small red dot appeared. The holo-projector was on.

Marigold focused her attention on the projection cone that now glowed above the hearth. Ghosts swarmed through the light for a moment, then the image steadied. A large rectangle with rounded corners appeared in the light, slowly revolving so that everyone could see. It looked like some sort of very old registration card, enlarged so that it was at least 20 meters across. A two-dimensional picture of a grim, human face was set on what was probably the front side. A man's face.

The man had apparently been resisting any sort of expression at the time of the portrait, and it made the flat reproduction seem all the more lifeless. His jaw was set and his mouth was drawn wide and flat across pale skin. His hair was brown and tousled. His eyes had a greenish tint. Green eyes… that was different.

The picture had a dim, sky blue background, and above the man's head, the word "Pennsylvania" was written in thick English letters. To the right of the picture, more English words and numbers were printed within a square of faded pink and white boxes. Marigold squinted. The words were in capitals, but they were smaller, and some were hard to read. A lot of it was abbreviated gibberish, but the bottom section looked like a man's name and address.

```
ZACHARIAH HERSCHEL WYLER
1717 CALLOWHILL ST 407
PHILADELPHIA    PA 19103
```

The card was laminated, with an orange inlay of five symbols: a series of fat, inverted trapezoids, each one with a smaller squashed trapezoid stacked on top of it. The inlay flashed, reflecting imaginary light as the hologram turned. The symbol looked vaguely familiar.

Marigold shook her head, frowning. Pennsylvania. It had to be somewhere on one of the human worlds. It looked really primitive—the picture was rough, and it had no depth to it at all. Maybe the man was from Ustinov. According to file, the people of Ustinov weren't as concerned with appearances.

The symbols flashed again. Shey Deiga had given a class about general symbolism recently… Marigold suddenly smiled and nodded. It was a keystone, of course. Deiga could never resist dropping little hints in conversation, especially before a Viewing. It was on the bridge sign at Kavarai Creek, and it meant "completion." According to Deiga, it was an old symbol adopted from the humans. Marigold sat forward, pursing her lips.

Deiga called out from the stage. "This is a license card issued on Dessa many centuries ago. The Deiassan you see in this picture was born before his race's Space Age, before the Deiassa had the technology to travel among the stars. This Deiassan was born in a time when the Deiassa knew only of what could be found on their own planet. Yet this man was destined to become involved in a quest for an ancient talisman, one of the great quests in recent Galactic history. This man was destined to touch one of the fire's-eyes." Deiga lifted his arms above his head, and his wings fanned out like two halves of a parasol. "This is the legend of the ancient talisman that crossed his path."

Marigold's eyes widened. Dessa. The origin of the Human Race. But there was obviously more to this story than just the man on the license card. Scinti were sure to be involved with these talismans somewhere down the line. Still, it would be nice to get a look at Dessa on the big projection cone.

The license card disappeared. A hole opened in the center of the blue light and grew to fill most of the blue projection cone with the image of space, a black void filled with stars. Then the stars swam, and turned into a cloudy whirlpool. Yellow letters indicated that the universe was in its primordial period, just after the Great Explosion. The letters disappeared, and the swirling trails of cloud began to thicken.

Deiga paced from one end of the stage to the other, looking in the direction of the gaseous image. "So. The fire's-eyes. To understand the power of these talismans, one must go back to the very beginning, when all matter in the universe formed from plasma in the cauldron of creation. Most of it became the matter we see every day—the land and water of the planets, the air we breathe, and the gas of the stars. But a very small fraction of the matter formed after the Great Explosion became the fire's-eyes, scarce within the vast reaches of space. Somehow, the material of the fire's-eyes was different. They were simple silicate compounds, but when they cooled they were harder than diamonds. Unbreakable. Some were tiny as microbes, some as massive as space stations. They were translucent, like gemstones, and they varied in color. But unlike even the most precious gemstones, they gave off their own light—they glowed from their own fire, and lit up the sky. They were almost alive. The fire's-eyes. Priceless in their aesthetic appeal. Beautiful enough to cure the sick, some would say." Deiga leaned forward

11

against the invisible railing. "But the fire's-eyes had more than aesthetic appeal. It is said that each fire's-eye was a small piece of immortality. It is said that a person who touched it had the power to see into the mind of another, and the power to live forever. The power of a god."

By now, the cloudiness in the cylinder blotted out the blackness of space. But the clouds ran bloodshot, and peeled away to reveal scarlet light so strong it seemed to leap beyond the bounds of the projection cone. The source of the redness hovered in the exact center of the Circle of Trees. It looked like a shiny salla berry.

Then the light shrank until the fire's-eye shimmered like an old star. "They were discovered by the Fissica millions of years before our people evolved on Home Volier. Many were sought. The Fissica considered them to be space's greatest treasure. But the fire's-eyes' time in the universe ended, and they self-destructed. They dematerialized, and their power disappeared from existence. The fire was extinguished. That was almost two millennia ago. The brighter a star burns, the faster it burns out."

The shining orb grew faint, then exploded in a flash of brilliant white light. Then it was gone, and an overhead view of the Galaxy emerged in its place. A gradual zoom toward one of the Galactic Arms began. Soon the view plunged into the plane of the Galaxy, spun, and sped forward until it came to a nebula. Tendrils of orange and red dust swept rapidly past, as a wall of cloud slowly approached. Then the view came through the cloud wall, out into the depths of starry space.

"But before they were gone, the fire's-eyes made their mark. So many had been collected by the Fissica and the Ynereia during deep space trawling expeditions that the power of the fire's-eyes was widely known throughout large regions of the Galaxy." The view swung right, and a star with a yellow tint stood out more prominently than the rest. "Most of the fire's-eyes remained in space, but we know of one that did not. This fire's-eye fell on Dessa. This was the fire's-eye that Zachariah Herschel Wyler touched."

The stars were replaced by the image of a lone blue planet, large as a travel balloon. Marigold blinked silently, grinning. Dessa. Earth. Her own race's homeworld, floating in the middle of the field. Her mother's homeworld. Four times she had been there. The view was as fantastic as the view from orbit, as far as she could remember.

"This is the story of how this single, ancient talisman caused a handful of people to alter the very course of time. To change what had already passed.

"One man found the fire's-eye. He learned of its powers through long years of experience. He hid from the outside world, attempting to conceal the powers of his find. But despite his efforts, others eventually learned of the talisman. They sought to take it from him, and as a result, purely by accident, the fire's-eye landed very briefly in the hands of Zachariah Herschel Wyler, a man who knew nothing of its powers. From then on, chance would determine the fate of the fire's-eye, and of a great many other things."

Deiga was hesitating, letting the excitement build. Marigold exhaled loudly, looking through the blue light at the sheridan's short figure. She noticed the loud chirring of the deep forest again—the night was in full swing now.

"The contest for the fire's-eye of Dessa was a struggle among many people and it spanned many years. But it began quietly, on a dry mountainside…"

The projection cone swam, and the bright light of a single sun lit up the field. Marigold pressed her lips together, trying not to squeal. She wasn't going to get much sleep this week.

*　　　　　*　　　　　*

I   SEEDS OF SECLUSION

"Time is like a river, ever flowing relentlessly toward the sea, pulled by the force of the current. For the leaf fallen on the surface, there is but one inevitable direction... a gradual descent downhill, lasting only as long as it remains afloat. But the river turns as it descends; it may die to a murmur as a brook, then build to the strength of roaring falls. So the path may turn.

"For the fire's-eye that fell on Dessa, the path through time begins and ends as the path of the fallen leaf. But to understand its course between those points, one must go beyond the figurative river. For the luminous stone passed to the Deiassa at the dawn of civilization and gave steady of its light, shining true until they made their fledgling forays into space, but its fate was not determined until much later, amid the surrounding stars."

Humania. GCL AE.001
Phi 00 00 00.00 / Theta 00 15 37.33 / Rho 00.00 / JD 588943(E)
Alpha Confinii: EARTH; "Elam"; circa 9 June 3101 BCE

The searing eye hung high in the midday sky, bleeding its relentless heat and casting an orange pall over the eastern mountains. Uru'ishtim squinted upward and sighed raggedly as the onager trudged forward, leaning into the incline of the trail.

The gods were with him, evidently. Sometimes it was more a curse than a blessing. Utu held sway at the moment, glowering down from his celestial perch and treating the mountains and anyone traveling among them with the usual helping of punishment before the soft highland breezes settled in. The priests would say that Enlil, the god of wind, was more powerful because it was he who carried Utu's chariot through the heavens, but chances were that none of those priests typically walked the trail into the mountains at noon.

Uru'ishtim frowned at the heat rising off the natural path in front of him, a fairly level shoulder along the pale, salt-dusted mountainside. For the moment, it was about as hot as the mountains had ever been—hot enough to make miners head back to Susa. People were gathered at the marshes along the way, waiting for the cooler air. Some had already given up, heading back into the city with empty bags and looks of beleaguered disgust.

The onager brayed, and Uru'ishtim relaxed his grip on the pack animal's mane. He dismounted and peered over the edge of the pass, looking back to the west behind him. A rigid drop-off banked toward uncompromising rock at the foot of the mountain. The city was still just visible on the horizon, beyond the foothills.

This new northern pass was unfamiliar territory, and the loose, crumbling limestone of the initial slopes had already tested his agility. The main passes to the south were generally wider and lower to the ground, and consequently more heavily traveled, so there was little metal left along the adjacent walls of rock. The more precarious way was the more promising. But it wouldn't always be so... there would always be miners to brave the dangers, as long as treasures lay waiting to be found. Eventually the northern reaches of the mountains would be spent as well. Now was the time to move, if ever.

The experienced miners in town liked to tell stories about balancing on stretches as narrow as a rope, sheer, slippery cliffs and jagged rocks—they spoke of tempting the will of the gods. But they always headed back up those rougher pathways, despite their words of fear and warning. The veterans of the mountains liked a comfortable living, and they knew how to get it. They were concerned with competition, not the gods.

Uru'ishtim inhaled the hot air, nodding, dropping his eyes to the trail. The vegetation of the plains and lower hills had thinned, with the dry yellow grass now cleared away to the edges of the level area, mingling with the twisted roots of broken, long-dead trees, but weeds still sprouted underfoot in tiny clots, tough as the surrounding rock and frequent enough to force extra caution. Mountain passes were mountain passes. This one would have its narrow stretches, and like the other trails it would eventually lead to a negotiable open area wide enough to mine. The treacherous drops would be a little less precipitous than others would have him believe, and the faces a little more accessible. And here there would be a much better chance of finding what he needed. The smiths would offer a full gur's worth of barley for a handful of silver and gold... and these hills might have held lapis lazuli, or carnelian. Who knew what they would give for a fair-sized precious stone?

He turned and rubbed his neck, glancing around at the craggy surface of sun-bleached rock. Here to the north, the layers of salt were thinner, just a mere film over the embedded mud and stone, but the effect was a muted shade of ginger brown that hid any traces of the darker patches that indicated the presence of valuable metal. Alone and without the supplies to set fire to the rock, he was limited to the lodes at the surface, but the ridge held many visible shears... it was just a matter of finding them. Higher up there would be breaks in the wall where the dirt and stone had already been carved away, worn down by the elements of nature. There the veins of metal would be exposed. If there was no silver and gold, copper and tin would suffice—

farther north, they were likely in greater abundance. Now that bronze was in demand among the cities of Sumer, the duller metals brought value as well... if he could load the animal down with rocks full of copper and tin, he would eat heartily for a month.

He glanced at the empty bags slung in rows along the onager's neck, then looked back to the horizon and wiped the sweat off his brow with the back of a hand, flinging it in the direction of Susa. Moving east to mine the mountains had never promised to be easy, but it was better than a life of serfdom in Eridu. Alalgar, the new ensi, would have him earning his shekels while he tended to the temple grounds with no hope of escape regardless of the work his father had done for Alulim, the founder of the city. In Susa, life was harder to be sure... the quarters were smaller and the meals lacked flavor. But Susa wasn't run by a despot, at least for now. The smaller city didn't offer many rewards that weren't hard-earned, but it did offer freedom.

A flat band of clouds stretched low over the horizon as if pressed beneath the weight of the haze. Uru'ishtim exhaled, letting his gaze drop to the yellow, grassy hills that separated the city from the mountains. Tiny streams nurtured the valley, feeding the Karun River that hung off to the left, arching out of view as it snaked its way into the mountains farther east. A natural version of the irrigation canals his father had engineered around Eridu. Pleasant enough, but not nearly the lush green paradise that existed in rumor.

Uru'ishtim smiled to himself as he crossed to the onager and climbed back onto the animal's back, patting it on the side. He could always run again. There was bound to be a real paradise somewhere.

He kicked the onager gently with his heels, and it gradually resumed its trot, picking up speed as it rounded the bend to the left. His eyes lingered over the landscape beyond the mountain for a moment more as he stared southwest, the direction of Eridu. The first city of Sumer was just a day's journey away, but it seemed much farther. It had not yet been two years, but it seemed like another lifetime long removed.

A trick of chance. It could have easily gone differently, his father with the ear of a much stronger and more just ensi. His father had virtually built the city himself, with skill and ingenuity, laying the foundation for generations to come, setting up his family to live comfortable lives basking in the glow of his innovations. Then death had come to his father and the ensi in the space of a few months, and Uru'ishtim, son of Tibira-Sik, had watched his future disappear.

So it was. And just as always, all hailed the glorious ensi, voice of Enki, interpreter of the will of the gods and their unquestionable edicts. Uru'ishtim snorted as the onager led him through the shade of a cock-eyed tree flaring upward from below the edge of the cliff. Alalgar had wasted no time in taking credit for the work of his predecessors. If the people chose to open their eyes and apply common wisdom, they would see that this ensi was nothing more than a mortal overlord, and at that, a bare shadow of the men who had built Eridu. But the heirs of Eridu were apparently content to remain in the dark.

Uru'ishtim shook his head as he moved back out of the shade. Enki, the patron god of Eridu, was said to be the god of crafts. The new ensi would do well to listen if the gods truly did have his ear. As it was, the ensi of Eridu would fail to see fine craftsmanship if it were dropped on his head from the sky.

Uru'ishtim leaned lower on the onager as the incline increased, testing the ties on the water pouches at the onager's neck. He would need to quench his thirst early if the winds delayed much longer. The heat was intense, beating forcefully against his back through the thin flaxen cloth of his shirt. Not unlike the overwhelming oppressiveness of a fever, threatening total incapacitation. The words of a medium floated back to mind from five summers before, when the sickness had taken him and his spirits had been at their lowest. *Take heart… you will find what you seek at the end of your days.*

His father had believed the woman had cured him that day with her odd techniques and the help of the gods. Uru'ishtim glanced up at the sky. Kneeling before a lamb's liver wouldn't help him now. And if he died today, the woman would be proven wrong.

The shoulder of the mountain abruptly leveled out, widening to a span that would have accommodated at least four travelers riding abreast. Then the slope fell away, and traces of rubble became evident along the mountain wall, spreading across the trail as it continued to descend. Uru'ishtim scanned the face of rock, nodding. He had risen to the looser stone… he was moving into the range of workable surfaces. The path narrowed again. It was much more uneven now, shifting without warning… it was rapidly becoming too treacherous for man or beast.

The onager slowed down and nearly stopped on its own, tossing its head, wrestling against the bridle in its mouth. Uru'ishtim dismounted carefully and leaned against the mountain wall. In front of him, the way was suddenly no wider than the length of his pick. Loose rock was everywhere, and the mountain had become surprisingly steep—a misplaced step could lead to a fatal fall. He took a water pouch and held it beneath the onager's muzzle. The animal drank noisily while he waited a few moments, frowning down the path. He exhaled heavily, grabbed the reins by the animal's head, and advanced on foot.

Perhaps a fall wasn't the worst thing in the world. Death on the mountain would be quick, and it would mean freedom from the mining life, freedom from any temptation to go cowering back to Eridu to serve at the whim of the ensi. He would behold the mystery of the gods once and for all, if they existed as the priests and their followers claimed.

The shoulder appeared as if it would disappear into the very mountainside, then opened up once again, allowing him to walk comfortably beside the animal. Ahead, the path veered left around a bend in the mountain. Uru'ishtim sighed. It was difficult to imagine the way getting much more difficult, but apparently, the miners who had come this way before had not been exaggerating as much as he had guessed. They had managed it, though, after all. It was passable—that was all that mattered.

He took a glance over his shoulder. Susa had slipped behind the brown bulge of mountain. The invigorating sense of being in tune with the natural surroundings had been a pleasant surprise among the grim aspects of a miner's life. As hard as the work was, to be completely independent, relying only on his own wits was thoroughly rewarding. Here among the mountains he was completely separated from the commotion of the city, immersed in tranquility. The only sound was the crunch of fragmented stone beneath his feet and the hooves of the animal, as if he and the animal were the only living things for leagues in every direction.

The animal broke the silence with a plaintive bray. Uru'ishtim froze, refocusing on the path ahead. Just past the turn, the shoulder had crumbled away. The mountain side looked as if it had been lifted away with a great shovel, leaving a gap too wide to cross, with or without a beast of burden in tow. Large chunks of rubble lay strewn along both edges of the rift, thrown up onto the path like water splashed from a pond.

Uru'ishtim shook his head, rubbing a hand across his forehead. It had happened recently. If the other miners had spoken the truth, they had reached the workable parts of the wall and made it well past this point... there had been no mention of a break in the trail like this. They had seen their share of wealth from this mountain; he would not. He would have to turn back. He stepped around the onager, glancing over the down the slope of the mountain as he sidled past.

He gasped. Far below the shoulder, a vast patch of blackness had enveloped the foot of the mountain—an enormous circular depression that stretched out across the ground and up onto the wall of rock. It seemed to reach well up the mountainside, though the angle made the exact height hard to judge. The black stain spread outward around the edge of the rim, like the spill of ash around a dead fire. In fact, it looked very much as if it had been charred by a great fire—scattered wisps of smoke rose lazily, suggesting the mountain had been cooked at its foundation, and in the center a single ember still glowed, bright as a star.

He stepped closer to the edge, keeping his hand on the onager. Within the broad rim, the texture of the blackened dirt and rock looked smooth, reflecting the light of the sun with a sheen that was almost metallic. The circle was so perfect... it was as if the gods themselves had reached down from the skies with an enormous branding iron.

Uru'ishtim blinked, looking back up. In Susa two nights before, there had been talk of a blazing light as big and bright as the moon that had fallen from the night sky. Some had spoken of a great earth-rending crash that had accompanied it—the light was said to have fallen to the east, beyond the mountains. Most had not seen anything, and those who had heard it had believed it to be thunder. It had all but been forgotten by the following evening.

Suddenly, the onager bucked and wrested the reins from his grasp. The animal screamed and came forward, kicking out with its front legs. Uru'ishtim stumbled, flailing his arms and frantically trying to maintain his balance. His heart raced, and the prospect of death flashed before him, the image of his broken body lying in the rubble... he wanted to live. Now, in the space of an instant, whether it meant working the mountains or tending the ensi's temples for the rest of his days, there was nothing he wanted more. Then the rock beneath his feet gave way and he toppled, lashing out with his arms, grasping at empty air. He fell, and for a moment he was descending freely, and then he felt the rough edges of the rocks. He rolled, battering his arms and shoulders, and then slid—the rocks beneath him were sliding, falling with him. He felt an explosion of pain in his upper right arm and then began tumbling violently. Rocks jabbed and pounded his body. Something cracked roughly against his head, snapping his neck back. He closed his eyes.

Then he was motionless, staring up at the sky. He lay inverted on his back, his arms and legs spread wide. The upper rim of the depression lay beyond his feet, and above it, the wall of the mountain loomed.

He was done for. Even if he was somehow able to scale the incline, the onager would surely bolt back down the pass, or otherwise work itself into a frenzy and fall off the cliff. It was a wild animal, free to leave him stranded in the heat. He would never make it back to Susa on foot with no water.

Cruel fate. The callous gods had waited until his moment of death to show him the value of life. He had nothing to return to, and now, more strongly than ever, he yearned to return.

The aroma of smoke filled his nostrils, and almost in the same instant he felt the increasing sensation of heat beneath him. He tried to move, and a wave of pain rocked him back. Every muscle of his body seemed on fire, from his neck to his legs, but it was his arm where the pain was the most intense. He winced and rolled on his side, looking down at himself, suddenly nauseous as another flood of pain shook him. His right arm was broken, bent at an awkward angle, and bleeding. He had gashes on both legs, and a separate ache was growing in his neck. He looked blearily back up at the mountain, trying to focus, but the view seemed blurry and distorted. A faint noise was descending from somewhere above... far above. It might have been the onager braying. It hardly mattered.

His skin was beginning to burn beneath him. He gritted his teeth and struggled to his knees, fighting the agony firing through his limbs, now feeling the burn of the smooth, blackened rock sharpen against his left palm. Gasping, he tried to stand, but fell back against the slope of the pit, reeling from the impact, rolling over his mangled hand as he slid downward.

Then light flooded his vision. Death... he was passing to the world of the gods, seeing the firmament of An unfiltered for the first time. Then he heard the braying of the onager, faint but distinct. So the onager had remained on the pass. It was still alive, and so was he.

His eyes adjusted slowly. The light was coming from beneath him. He sat up, steadying himself with his unharmed arm, and turned, squinting. He was almost at the very center of the black pit. Just below him was an object he had seen from high above, something he had mistaken for a dying ember. From up close, it was nothing like an ember. It was a glowing stone the size of a peach, embedded in the surrounding rock, but it glowed not from heat— its color was not the color of heated rock. It was a deep, rich, penetrating red, like the skin of an apple. Or like blood. The stone was translucent, somehow lit from within. Its brilliant core seemed to reach outward, bathing its dark surroundings in a pure, steady, red-tinged halo.

Uru'ishtim felt his pulse quicken. The stone seemed to be beckoning him to take it in his hand, but he was almost afraid to touch it. There were stories of sparkling red and purple gems in mountains of the north, and great, beautiful diamonds from the west, but never of any mineral that emanated light like a star.

Take it in his hand! He was a fool to think of it. His pick was up the mountain—this stone might have been the most precious find of all time, but he had no way of freeing it from the surrounding rock. Never mind that under the present circumstances, he lacked the strength he would need to escape the mountain.

He looked again at the glowing stone. There was nothing he had seen or heard that would have explained it—a thing that held the light of Utu and Nanna, an object of the sky, borne to Earth by the gods. It had been placed there for the taking, and fate had landed him within reach of it. He had been meant to experience this thing that was clearly new to Earth, this thing that was unlike all other things.

He touched it, and felt as if he had dipped his arm in a stream. The stone was a mix of varied textures, like other gems… with flat, angular facets of translucent, clean fracture emerging out of a rough agglomeration. A smooth, effervescent sensation seemed to flow out from it and fill his body. It was exhilarating.

The pain in his other arm subsided. He looked at the arm and watched as his muscles seemed to work instinctively, guiding the limb back into place. The blood that spilled from the many tears in his skin suddenly ebbed, and stopped. His wounds were healing… all of his injuries were healing. He stared at his hand, flexing his fingers, then looked back into the reddish glow. Visible though the translucent surfaces like a flame seen through thick, warped glass, spreading outward into its surroundings… it felt as if the light itself was coursing into his body, filling him with the power of the gods.

The stone came away from its nest of rock as if he had placed it there himself. It was warm in his palm. He stood up and felt as if he could leap out of the pit. The air felt cooler, and the face of the mountainside no longer looked as menacing. Suddenly, the prospect of scaling the distance to the shoulder seemed like nothing at all. So the gods were with him after all; he had been slated for rejuvenation, not death.

Or perhaps he had defied the gods.

He stared steadily at the mountain. His vision had improved, along with his strength. He could now see the onager clearly, standing exactly where he had left it, bleating loudly and kicking out. Unsettled, but rooted there at the edge of the drop off as if tethered to the wall.

He tramped up the black slope of the depression and hauled himself over the upper rim with ease, feeling only strength in the arm that had been broken so soon before. He looked again at the stone, appraising it as he started up the mountainside, using only one arm to steady himself against the incline as he climbed with his legs. In his hand the stone had the look of many of the worthless shards of rock discarded by miners, and its luster and translucence were not unlike the gems he had heard talk of in the tavern in Susa. It was the light that made this stone unique… but this was more than just some natural lantern, some rare and curious variety of mineral.

Uru'ishtim felt his pulse slow as he climbed, moving as smoothly as if he were strolling along a city street. No sum of oxen could equal the value of this find; it was too valuable an object to exchange for profit. There were other rocks in the mountains that would bring him food and comfort, and the trinkets of wealth, and somehow, the prospect of turning up enough metal day after day to survive didn't seem so daunting.

He reached the path, and dusted off his clothes. The onager continued to bray, staring at the stone through one eye with its head turned to the side. Uru'ishtim loosened one of the bags lashed along its side and dropped the stone in, tightening the strings.

He guided the onager around and headed back toward the city.

*   *   *

Tarantula Nebula, Large Magellanic Cloud. GCU LMC GE.078
Phi -90 41 23.06 / Theta 36 49 48.00 / Rho 44377.53 / JD 2708341
30 Doradus: OS, "R136 Vicinity"; 1 February 2703 CE

Salaman Nevis coughed. The cabin air had a putrid tinge. He could almost feel the tiny particles of dirt brushing his lungs as he inhaled. There was something wrong with the life-support systems, something very subtle and insidious.

He let out a quick laugh. Yet another failure. Nothing designed on Earth or Scalaway ever worked right, not completely. But none of that would matter soon enough.

He stared at the blue-skinned human intermediary unit seated on the transom in front of the circuitry of the command terminal access panel. The android was wide-eyed, at full attention.

"Tell me why we're doing this, Salaman."

He nodded at the fabricated woman. "Call up the program and run a final check."

The intermediary unit cocked its head. "I really don't understand this."

Salaman frowned. It was tentative, impressionable, but not as blindly obedient as he would have preferred. The android had been constructed barely more than two years before. Completely inexperienced.

22

He scratched nine months' growth of bristling red beard. "I don't need you to understand anything. If you were responsible for planning and interpretation, you would need to understand, but you aren't the facilitator of this expedition, are you? I'm the xenobiologist; I'm the facilitator. You are the IU." He cleared his throat, rubbing his chest. "You're responsible for making sure the on-board doesn't malfunction while storing and compiling information. That's it."

The android gave him a blank stare with sapphire, acrylic eyes. The model was unassumingly small in stature, with an idealized, taut figure... the aesthetics were unnervingly accurate. The designers had synthesized the mind of a fascinated young child and placed it in the perfectly sculpted body of a 20-year-old woman, with a hairless scalp and the color of the cyan thermoset to serve as an instant visual reminder that it was the product of manufacturing. Twisted anthropomorphism, as envisioned by irresponsible corporate marketeers—evidence of the human ego on display.

He grunted to himself. And they said these intermediary units could potentially remain operational indefinitely.

As long as this particular model lasted some 900 years.

The android still wasn't showing any indication of calling up the program. Salaman rubbed his fingers together and glanced at his hands. "This should be simple, not difficult. Any inconsistencies in the program should be completely obvious. If you're having problems translating it to your memory, we can have the on-board check your systems again." He looked up, raising his eyebrows.

With its right hand, the intermediary unit fingered a wire that connected its opposite arm to the circuitry of the hull. A section of thermoset was neatly rolled back along the forearm, exposing the small interface socket beneath the imitation skin that was bleeding data directly into the ship. "I understand the procedure, Salaman. The program is secure, and everything is in place in my memory."

Salaman cleared his throat again. Truly impressive that he had managed to put up with the situation for as long as he had. "Good. Call it up."

The android shifted in its seat and looked in his direction without making eye contact. "Correct me if I'm wrong." It paused. "These instructions are specific. Intended for a specific individual. When this is recovered, assuming the recipient follows through with everything... the person is liable to proceed. There won't be a reason for the person to run a preliminary test, or consult a contemporary expert in the field for guidance."

Salaman nodded. "Make your point."

23

The android shook its smooth, blue, feminine head and focused on his eyes. "Don't you think you could increase the success potential by providing testing information? This is all theoretical. There's a lot of risk, and you haven't really offered any incentive..."

Salaman frowned and scratched his nose. "IU. Call up the program."

The android twisted its kinematic links, shifting its back without contacting the panel immediately behind it and turning its head in the same direction like the drill at the end of a cam-profiling remote miner. "Salaman, I realize this is your project, and you don't want my input. But I think my point is valid—the program has inconsistencies. You're asking someone to travel into a virtual dimension and implement a 4 billion-year flight pattern using reactive subroutines and no coordinates... there's no record of anyone ever attempting something like this in D5 or D6. How can you expect someone—"

Salaman raised his voice, cutting the intermediary unit off. "Technically, the time period is not 4 billion years. Time accelerates more slowly in entelechial space. In this case, it's a 1.2 million-year trip, and to anyone aboard the spacecraft, tau gamma dilation at maximum readdressed sublight will result in an apparent 878 years. But I don't expect you to process those details. They are irrelevant, and so are your concerns."

The android frowned at him. "Salaman, this isn't even your field. This is continuum theory. You came here to study alien plant and animal chemistry, not cosmology. I realize you've been researching the ytaoans for a long time—"

Salaman growled and sat forward. "You don't realize anything! The only reason you're here is that I need to make sure the program feeds properly." He exhaled heavily, turned on his heels, and paced along the cabin, stopping at the angular window toward the rear.

The single red dwarf star was almost at the center, and around it, invisible in the distance, was the throng that had brought him to the Tarantula Nebula. He nodded. "They know how things work. The ytaoans are familiar with the ways of the universe; the people who programmed you are not. Your programmers know nothing, and you are essentially a walking recorder of their misguided nonsense. You're a molded mass of silicon and plastic— about two years ago, you were being pieced together in a London assembly plant. You think you have something enlightening to say to me? I'm not interested in anything your logic circuits tell you to spit back out at me from your pool of so-called human cosmological knowledge." He sighed and looked at the circular lights that ran the length of the ceiling. Pointless. "I'm

24

done talking. Call up the program and run a check."

The android's small mouth shrank almost to a pout, and it closed its eyes as if it were preparing to cry. It was looking down at the floor grid.

Petulant mock-humans. Just what the universe needed. Salaman sniffed loudly and caught another whiff of the acrid air. He grimaced, peering back at the android. As far as he knew, those London designers had been sensible enough to overlook the installation of tear ducts. "Are we clear? Let's go— call it up right now."

The android nodded once and stared into space. Salaman turned back to the window.

The glorious purple and orange dust trails of the nebula spread in the background of the tiny star. It suddenly looked like the fruit of a silky pagla tree on Tagajal. The memory of its tangy pungency made him stifle a sneeze.

Experimental test flights into the eigenspaces were hardly new territory. Human engineers had sent dozens of pilots to their deaths with half-baked notions of exploring the virtual spaces. There was a new rash of pioneers every century, every time there was a navigational breakthrough—the initial widespread fascination with hyperspace at the onset of field propulsion, and renewed interest with virtual kinetic energy potentiators, arc reflectors, and guided neutrino communication. They had never come close to working out the physics for maintaining integrity above D6, and neither had any of the other sentients, despite the cumulative millions of years they'd had to perfect their evolving technologies. They saw themselves as masters of the universe, and they effectively regarded the ytaoans as interstellar plant life.

They weren't even close.

Salaman glanced back at the intermediary unit. The android had apparently gone into a meditative state, unable to be compliant without shutting down the higher functions of its neural net. Pathetic.

He shook his head, frowning as the bitter, metallic taste of the unclean ventilation ducts made its way to his mouth. It was all the same, on every planet. The universe was full of ignorant minds producing uninspired technology. The ytaoans knew that. They saw the way the humans and the other sentient species wasted their potential. Humans had never managed to employ the full extent of their brains; even the scinti were operating at a limited capacity.

He was ahead of all of them now.

The people of Earth were like the android, locked in their linear thinking, unable to recognize a fresh idea when they were handed one. For a time, the Independent Human Scientific Alliance had accepted much of his research, sponsored several publications. He had seen his share of support from the Society for Advancement of Nature, the Astrobiologists' Guild, and various groups from the nonhuman spheres—they'd had no choice. His work had been solid and well-documented. But no one was really interested in the parallel evolution of microbes in remote regions of the Galaxy or genetic similarities among isolated groups of sentients. They cared about inventing ways to exploit one another. Terraforming and weaponry. Imperialization. Maximizing credit, and improving economic means. Independent Human Scientific Alliance! They were like little birds mucking around in the dirt, pulling up a random worm and calling it innovation.

He closed his eyes and let his mind relax, and he sensed the ytaoans in the emptiness. The tapering elliptical bodies hung silently, drifting in the dusty space thousands of kilometers from the Homeworld Dusk Cruiser, never hiding themselves from his mind's eye, and it was as if he were floating with them, free in the darkness. The ytaoans had been a mystery to every scientist in the Galaxy for thousands of years, but now they had decided to bring him here. Out of everyone in the Galaxy, they had chosen him. And they were excellent teachers.

He smiled to himself. In time, the people of Earth would all know his name. He would be the one that they remembered long after the Earth had been scorched dry by its expanding sun. He would be the first sentient being in history to direct a man into the past—that alone would serve as evidence that he was more brilliant than the circular-thinking peons who populated the Galaxy. It would need to be kept quiet for a time, but in the end he would be rewarded. A human man would go back to the beginning, back before the formation of stars. The man would bear witness to the phantasmagoric beauty of multicolored, swirling plasma streaks left after the explosion of Genesis, and eventually the ytaoans would spread word of it, after news of it was no longer a threat to the integrity of the universe. Eventually all the people would know, and they would revere the name of Salaman Nevis.

"The program is intact."

Salaman blinked. The intermediary unit was standing by the terminal, poised to remove the connection to the on-board. He squinted. "Good. Initiate on my mark." He stared out the window, concentrating. The ytaoans would let him know when to begin. They would give him the sign.

The ytaoans had contacted him flawlessly from the nebula, across the expanse of more than 190,000 light-years, and he had heard their beacon loud and clear, guiding him as if a port transmission receiver had suddenly gone on inside his head. It was ironic. He was the only nontelepath among his father and three brothers, but now he could see far more than any member of his family had ever seen.

They had always looked down on him for not having their gift, even though he had always been the most intelligent. They had never respected him, just as the flighty little birds of the scientific community had never respected him. Jealous of his ingenuity. He closed his eyes, frowning. The Independent Human Scientific Alliance would one day regret rejecting the commission for this ytaoan study.

Out of the darkness, a bright red speck appeared and grew quickly larger. It was round at the center, tapering to two points at the sides. The shape of a human eye—one of the ytaoans. They were signaling him. It was time.

"Mark."

Two bell-tones sounded in the cabin. The timer had started. The on-board computer was responding to the program. Soon, everything would be set. Salaman stepped to the open berth opposite the android and sat down, nodding and rubbing his hands. The familiar sensation of tiny insects sprang up on the open areas of his skin, slowly creeping beneath his clothes. The cabin air was getting worse, and he was letting his concentration lapse.

Even now, he knew so little of what they knew, but it was already more than he would have guessed his mind could contain. At first, the flood of knowledge and near-instantaneous uptick in acuity had been staggering—it was as if a permanent drunken stupor had been shaken off with a splash of ice water. Now it was impossible to imagine himself before his time in the nebula. In minutes, he would know infinitely more.

"Salaman?"

He raised his eyebrows.

The intermediary unit was blinking distractedly. "Why did you place an override on my functioning?"

He stood and looked at the android momentarily, then started into the aisle that ran between the berths in the passenger compartment of the ship. In moments the would-be person would lose its inquisitiveness.

"Salaman, the on-board just set my CPU to lock into my field-effect relays. Why are you shutting me down?"

He stopped and turned around, raising an eyebrow. "Because you're annoying. You have to ask?"

The android frowned. "Why would you have the on-board run an auto shut-down? You already have my functions slaved to the CTA. Salaman?" It blinked, looking past him down the aisle. "What's going on—where are you going?"

He stared back for a moment, then turned and continued toward the stern.

"The chamber is programmed for repressurization and reoxygenation, and it's set to look like part of the natural fusion-ignition sequences." The android raised its consumer-tested voice. "You can't go outside without letting me run prep—we're not set up. Salaman, tell me what you're trying to do—I'm supposed to help you."

Salaman turned as he approached the inner door and rested his hand above the keypad on the lock console. "How does the song go? I was blind, but now I see." He pursed his lips. "That's basically the gist. The on-board will have more for you after I finish this. Right now, I just need you to tune out."

The android's sapphire eyes flashed under the overhead cabin lights. "Can I point out that your behavior is erratic? There's no logical reason for you to leave the ship. On top of that, you've been behaving abnormally since we came into contact with the ytaoans... you should consider you might be under their influence."

Salaman nodded, waiting. The android moved to stand. It froze, and its eyes became distant. It stalked along the cabin floor and turned, finding the crease outlining its berth and lowering it from the hull. It settled onto the berth and began strapping itself down, moving slowly and purposefully, as if under hypnosis.

Salaman thinned his eyes, scratching his cheek. The android was right. He was clearly under the ytaoans' influence. But the android couldn't comprehend what was in his mind any more than a typical human content to live out his or her life in banal mediocrity.

It was over now. His dealings with androids and the other trappings of human society had concluded. The minds of the ytaoans were already strengthening within him.

He closed his eyes as a tingling sensation entered his hands and feet. There was no more use for rage and disgust. The ytaoans saw everything, but they separated themselves from the anguish, as he now would. There were too many meaningless problems. The Galaxy was in turmoil—even after the end of a devastating war, the raxatots and the kyhyvvhrs were still unofficially raiding the territories of the other races, and the gulak still abusing and discriminating against the drbdu of the neighboring sphere. Proteid isolationism was closing off that race's trade routes to those outside its sphere, and resentment and jealousy of the advanced and ungenerous cillians were rapidly reaching new heights.

Noise. Nothing but noise. But maybe the peoples of the universe would follow his example. Maybe they would be inspired, and the ignorance would pass away.

The android was secured. The five-minute countdown to initiation of the fusion-hyperspace cycle began with a single, low chime that filled the ship. Everything was set.

The 6-meter aisle between the berths in the passenger compartment appeared to stretch out longer and thinner. And the ship seemed suddenly bright—the ruddy brown tinted-chrome interior was almost glowing under the flood of the white photo-panels. None of the fear he had anticipated was there.

He tapped the emergency code into the lock, and the inner door slid open. Everything had flowed so smoothly since he had come to the nebula. Now it was time. He would exit the ship, and he would have perhaps a second of consciousness before the sudden depressurization shredded the tissue of his lungs. It would be quick.

He stepped into the airlock chamber and stared at the rear hatch as the inner door closed behind him. He touched a control near the seal and the horizontal photoband at the top of the hatch became yellow. Then green.

The hatch parted at the middle as the shutter doors slid open, disappearing quickly into the hull. There was an instant of roaring air and then a rush of vertigo as Salaman's body moved out of the range of the artificial gravity. At the last second he caught a glimpse of the Dusk Cruiser hanging amid shadowy, orange-brown dust, already impossibly far away.

*   *   *

... GCL RN.016

Phi -99 50 12.40 / Theta -20 51 45.34 / Rho 56.11 / JD 3038318

Tau Puppis: DEMTEEDUM; "West Teegarden Plateau"; 14 July 3606 CE

Applause echoed off the high ceiling of the enclosure, drowning out the hum of the humidifiers. Above it, 100 meters of sandstone separated the facility from the dry air of the plateau, and the only way up was an assembly lift with a two-way code lock. Departing might have nominally been an option, but the company people certainly hadn't made it easy.

The enthusiastic response by the small throng of specialists was a bit much. Felix Prado bit back a frown, keeping his eyes low as he clapped in tandem. It was as if Teodor Monroe had personally funded each of their institutions with a year's worth of personal grants. Not a proud moment for the scientific community.

The charismatic head of Brackens Merida moved out from behind the podium, crossing to the edge of the dais, his eyes narrow in the warm lighting. His black thobe and the shallow Galinan cape that trailed from his shoulders looked like cocktail lounge attire.

He smiled and nodded as the ovation tapered off. "Thank you." He nodded again. "Thank you, everyone." He raised his voice and held up a hand emphatically. "We are at the forefront, ladies and gentlemen. The forefront. I fully expect that what we accomplish over the next few weeks will endure, and you will know you were a part of greatness. History is built on a series of singular pivotal moments when we as a people seize the opportunity to advance." He held up a fist. "Technology... it's the lifeblood of our civilization. Technology conceived by visionaries. People like you." He waved his hand lazily around at the people in the banked seats. "I'm grateful that you've chosen to participate, and I'm confident in your success. Welcome to the team." He flashed another smile and placed his hands on his hips as the crowd erupted again, then turned and headed left in the direction of the project lead.

Felix adjusted his sitting position, glancing toward the chemical engineer to his right—Janus Harlowe, relatively well-respected among his peers. Apparently the man was a true capillary-exhibitor genome mu, though the clean scalp certainly didn't make him stand out among this group. It was said the man had gone into lab work to blend in with all the clean-shaven fusion specialists with alopecia universalis. Harlowe nodded back at him, seemingly impressed at Monroe. Felix looked back at the dais.

At least Monroe had made well-informed decisions about his staff. Cristan Faro was a competent project lead, formerly a consultant at Exoworld Thermal. Faro had now been with Brackens Merida for several years... Monroe had to have offered him a royal ransom.

Faro moved to center-stage, glancing after Monroe. "Thank you, Mr. Monroe." He cleared his throat and leaned low over the podium, adjusting his round, distinctive spectacles with two fingers. "Our sponsor will be monitoring our progress closely." He paused, inhaling audibly through his nostrils, then looked around at the audience. "I just want to run through the highlights before we break this session. We will start by focusing on the cillian historical documents in the reference materials; from there, we will map out a complete atomic structural iteration set, identify all classifiable properties and potential power sources, and ultimately reproduce the mineral with similar properties."

Harlowe leaned toward Felix. "This has the inherent potential of becoming a much larger project."

Felix nodded, keeping his eyes on the podium. "Demarcation issues arise if we fail to predict quantifiable properties."

Faro took a breath. "We know Mineral X is aluminum silicate within the iron-magnesium almandine series, and our initial assumption is that these extreme power sources are related to chain decay from the extinct radionuclides AL-26 and FE-60. The initial plan is to simulate early-stage Genesis, circa 4.6 billion Julian years before present, by containing reconstituted laboratory compounds in a specialized compression chamber and flooding them with cosmic rays in controlled proportions." He paused, clearing his throat. "If you'll direct your attention to the tablets in front of you, you should be cued to Section 2.4, titled 'Critical Event.'"

Felix glanced down at the desk and tapped the flat, white-framed screen lying in front of him. A red chemical formula appeared, with a series of specs trailing beneath it in green phosphor.

Faro's voice droned on, losing its inflection. "We have evidence the mineral underwent a spontaneous phase change in JD 2448894, in a universal-scale event, after which it has no longer been found. The phase change held enough power to convert matter in the immediate surroundings to pure energy, somewhere on the order of 50 gigawatts. Based on the estimated evolutionary frontier, we have a measurable half-life of 2.3 billion years, which puts molecular stability between K-40 and U-238 on the table of common isotopes. However, the materials of this mineral are, as you know, not known to be radioactive. The fact that decay to the atomic structure seems to have occurred in natural synchronicity on a universal scale violates the principle of nonstochastic quantum-level behavior, and that will have to be accounted for as you build your hypotheses." He paused, looking up. "Yes?"

A man in the front row of seats raised his voice. "Have you accounted for the discrepancy in the output? Even with this synchronous decay, there isn't anywhere near enough binding energy to add up to that amount of power."

Faro nodded. "Yes, the power level is another complication. The only way to get the sufficient amount of power at the atomic level is a total mass-to-energy conversion."

The man responded quickly. "But doesn't this imply nonnatural causality? If someone manufactured this construct before, we should be able to replicate the process once we put together the methodology."

"We're going forward under the assumption that this event is part of a fundamental natural process that we're discovering for the first time." Faro glanced off toward right stage and nodded at the crowd. "All right, you should have all the data you need for now on your tablets. We'll reconvene next week. That's all."

The room was again abuzz as people fussed to get out of their seats, murmuring to one another in dozens of not-so-private sidebars. Felix waited a long moment, then stood. Harlowe flashed a crooked smile as he gathered the tablet along with his own personal devices. "This should prove interesting, whatever we find. Don't you think?"

Felix raised an eyebrow. "Interesting, yes. Possibly foolish." He nodded, adding a wink. "But that remains to be seen."

Harlowe seemed satisfied and moved off, side-stepping along the row of seats. Felix looked back at the stage. Monroe stood with Faro, by the bound decorative curtain at the right edge of the dais. The mogul media darling was beaming broadly, shaking hands as the subject-matter experts approached. Rumor had it Teodor Monroe had designs on political office; he certainly looked the part. But the man was said to have a darker side as well. He exacted tight control over his projects, and much of the purpose behind them remained hidden. His outlet affiliates had been linked to the Foundation of Deneb and their acts of piracy, among other suspect businesses. The man had even been implicated in a scandal surrounding the death of a company product spokesperson, though he had evidently managed to put it behind him.

Felix reached the edge of the seats and took a glance in the direction of the security guards standing at the end of the corridor that led to the assembly lift. This project indeed fit the mold of some of those others… there was little practical application for power generated by a natural rock, fascinating as that notion might have been. And there was no real evidence in any of those historical documents that this was suggestive of a new fundamental force. Without an enormous amount of credit as backing, a project like this would never have come to fruition, nor would it ever have likely been proposed.

Credit was something Monroe had in abundance, whatever his motives.

*   *   *

... GCL AE.001
Phi 00 00 00.00 / Theta 00 15 37.33 / Rho 00.00 / JD 2448887
Alpha Confinii: EARTH; "Philadelphia"; 21 September 1992 CE

Locals and college kids choked the misshapen slope of intersection between Geno's and Pat's Steaks. Monday evening, and the congestion at 9th and Wharton was nearly as thick as South Street on the weekend.

Zack Wyler stood under the roofed patio in front of Geno's. He flattened himself against the wall as a group of people pushed past, keeping his eyes on a pair of large men.

The crowd was making it easy to blend.

One of the men wore an overstuffed, cream-colored blazer. He turned and glanced around, flipping a French fry into his mouth and chasing it with a fountain drink. Joey Imperato.

His companion was in a charcoal gray suit, with slicked-back hair. The man nudged Imperato and both of them headed away from the food bar.

Zack squinted, focusing past the darting heads as the two men broke away from the main thrust of the crowd and out of the lights of the intersection. He tore off a mouthful of bread and cheese-soaked meat, tossed the rest of his sandwich in a trashcan, and pushed away from the wall, licking his lips.

There was an off chance the two of them were looking to get their rocks off on a double-date with a pair of prostitutes, but it was starting to look more like poker night, or a drug pickup. If it was significantly sordid, it might have been enough to satisfy Samuel Goldstine, women or not.

Zack adjusted the strap of his backpack as he slipped around a pair of slow walkers. Hopefully it would be quick. Finish off the job, make his days as Goldstine's personal gofer a thing of the past.

Imperato and his friend turned at the corner, away from where they had parked. They clearly hadn't come for the cheesesteaks. Zack stayed on the opposite sidewalk. He reached the curb and leaned on the stop sign, peering after them, giving the spiked, alien fuzziness at top of his head a quick pat.

There was a good chance the case would be open and shut. If Imperato had a gumar, he would give himself away in a day or two, hopefully sooner rather than later. Based on past experience, Rachel Imperato wasn't getting what she needed out of the relationship, and there was a possibility both of them were stepping out on one another. Of course, Goldstine didn't want to know what his daughter was doing. Either way, Joey Imperato definitely fit the unfaithful spouse profile.

If Imperato wasn't messing around, the case would take longer, prolonging the privilege of tailing a gigantic, hot-headed, unpredictable thug for an extended period of time. But the big man was probably exercising his mojo, just as Goldstine thought. Imperato was a predictable, careless lunkhead, and the case would probably turn out to be a cinch. Probably.

Zack tugged at the top button of the imitation military fatigue shirt, trying to air out his skin. Sweat was beginning to prickle his neck beneath the long hair on the backside of the acrylic mullet, and the discomfort was starting to feel conspicuous, as if he would have been better off going without a disguise. He waited until the two men were a block away, then followed. The two were still walking at a normal pace. They hadn't noticed anything yet. Even though it was around midnight, there were still plenty of people milling around, walking home and going to their cars. Good environment for a tail.

Zack side-stepped around a pair of women in their early twenties. One smiled in his direction as they passed—a skinny, long-legged brunette in a tight red skirt. Probably more amused at the ridiculous punked-out roadkill on his head than anything else. He avoided her face, keeping his eyes ahead.

Rachel Imperato was a ritzy, blue-eyed heat-seeking missile with a rebellious streak about as long and contrived as her glistening, product-treated black hair. Zack had met her once, back at Samuel Goldstine's house on the latest suspected embezzlement case. They had been alone together for a good solid half hour of blatant flirting... her marriage to Imperato hadn't exactly seemed to be the foremost thing on her mind.

Zack snorted, scratching his jaw. Nice idea, but Rachel Imperato was definitely off-limits. Raging gorilla for a husband, aside from the obvious fact that Samuel Goldstine was a connected control freak with a legendarily low tolerance for assholes trying to shtup his daughter.

The men turned left onto a side street. Zack made his way to the edge of the small alley, sneaking a glance as he passed. The men were standing at a metal door lit up under a red light, apparently waiting for someone to let them in. Invite-only. Overall, it wasn't a lot of lighting—to catch them on their way in, he was probably going to have to overexpose the film and make some magic with the developer.

No cars were parked along the sidewalk directly in front of the alley, but there was a trashcan and telephone pole just off to the left. He circled back around, moving into the street, then stopped in an unlit area behind the trashcan and looked again into the alley.

The two men were apparently content to wait. Imperato tugged on his jacket and muttered something. The other man laughed and nudged him. No obvious anxiety about whatever it is they were up to.

Zack grabbed the strap slung on his shoulder and slipped the Nikon F4 out of its pocket with the opposite hand, squinting up at the building. He frowned, moved the viewfinder in front of his eye, aimed at the men at the door, and hit the shutter release, then stepped back around the trashcan and pressed against the wall, taking a quick look around. People were walking by, shooting a few curious looks in his direction and moving on. Not a problem. He sidled up to the edge of the wall and snuck a glance inside the alley, measuring the shadows. It was darker toward the street, and the two men were probably 20 feet away. Plenty of background street noise. They weren't going to pick him out.

The door opened, and a man almost as big as Imperato stepped out. Shoe-in for a bouncer. The man was bald, and his head looked like a block of granite. He gave Imperato and his partner in crime the once over and ushered them inside. Zack snapped another shot before they were through the door.

He waited several seconds, then lowered the camera. Poker night, most likely. So it was a waiting game… so much for quick and easy. He was going to have to head back to Passayunk Avenue lying low in his car and sitting on Imperato's Trans Am, possibly all night. He shook his head and muttered under his breath. "Crock of shit."

He lowered his face and pulled the mullet wig off his head, glancing around as he headed back up 9th Street. He reached Wharton and rounded the corner, looking up at the dark rooftops of the scrunched row houses along the city block. No clear indicator of what might have been inside that door— nothing stood out in his memory of the area. He was going to have to cash in another favor with the 0-9 and get them to run the address.

He slowed his pace as he approached a group of women moving toward one of the cars parked along the sidewalk on Wharton. One of the women stared at him as she opened the passenger side door. "Zack? Zack Wyler?"

Zack blinked at her. She looked vaguely familiar… thin, frizzy-haired blonde, sharp features. She glanced around at the other three women standing around the car. "Hey, guys, look—do you believe this? It's Zack Wyler!"

Zack glanced around at the other three women and his eyes stopped on the brunette standing in the street by the driver seat. Melanie Katsoulis. Homecoming—the five-year reunion for the Class of '84. Her class. Her hair was a lot shorter than he remembered, but the distinct beauty mark below her right eye was a dead giveaway.

A small girl with short, dirty blonde hair stood on the curb opposite Melanie. She was nodding her head. "Wasn't he on the football team?" She looked less familiar. It had been a long time since Penn State.

The frizzy-haired blonde was smiling, showing her teeth. "He was the star running back sophomore year." She raised an eyebrow at Zack. "What are you doing with yourself these days, Zack? Staying out of trouble?"

Melanie raised her eyebrows. "That would be a first." She paused. "Is that a wig in your hand?"

"Costume party." Zack flashed a smile across the car. "Hi, Melanie." He placed the wad of hair back over his scalp, holding out his hands theatrically, then took it back off, glancing over his shoulder and wiping his forehead.

Melanie shook her head, smiling. "I never took you for the back-woods Pennsyltucky type."

"The short-hair look is definitely better." The frizzy-haired blonde's eyes stayed on Zack. "We're on our way up to Vinny's on Washington Avenue. You want to join us?"

Odds were Imperato was going to be in that house until he felt it was necessary to go back home, and he wasn't going to be cueing himself up for any more worthwhile incriminating camera shots. Zack nodded and glanced at Melanie. "You have room in the car?" The car was a compact Honda Accord.

Melanie smiled. "It'll be cozy, but I think we can fit you in. What do you think, Jen?"

The frizzy-haired blonde nodded. "Absolutely."

Melanie shrugged. "Hop in, Zack Wyler." She ducked into the car and settled behind the wheel.

The frizzy-haired blonde stepped back and gestured at her door. Zack winked at her and climbed inside, moving next to another dark-complected brunette. Very pretty. All of them were very pretty. The blonde squeezed in next to him and he felt the muscles of her leg press against his.

Melanie pulled the car away from the curb and into the street. Zack craned his neck, glancing back toward the row houses, and exhaled heavily.

The blonde leaned into him, grinning. "You aren't being followed, are you?" Her eyes danced playfully. Her neck smelled like citrus fruit.

Zack caught Melanie's eyes in the rearview mirror. "Who'd want to follow me?"

Melanie shook her head.

II   THE INTERLOPER

"The unique quality of the stone was astonishing to the few who beheld it... a glimpse of the unknown for the scientific, even evidence of the supernatural. Yet the stone was slated to fade into obscurity, lost in the stretches of time with the forgotten curiosities of life on a lonely planet.

"But hundreds of years after the end of its existence, its legend was heard again, extracted from amid the echoes of the past like a floating leaf plucked from a stream... a rediscovery that coalesced around the activities of a man with a particular talent for drawing attention, sparked by the infusion of memory stored in the circuits of a cybernetic mind."

```
... GCL BZ.012
Phi 15 03 00.20 / Theta 69 06 40.70 / Rho 11.04 / JD 3040381
Alpha Bootis: SCALAWAY; "Barrier Island"; 6 March 3612 CE
```

Shimmering swaths of infrared flashed in staggered bursts over the isotachic surface grid, feeding optical lidar data into the satellite photogrammetry algorithms like a pulsing heart. The many thousands of islands broke down the huge masses of homogenous ocean air and prevented cyclogenesis over most of the planet, but not along the extended coastline of Barrier Island. A wall of cliff ran at a southward angle from the north pole into the temperate latitudes, creating permanent wind shear that spanned the top third of the planet—a natural convection generator that a 7,000-kilometer row of transformers used to power the Human Sphere's largest station complex.

According to the remote sensors, the waves along the coast were reaching 20 meters, tugged by Scalaway's twin moons, stirred up by the front minima and the press of Coriolis force. Typical night. But it was the waves that brought people to the lookout posts in droves during the day; at high tide, the impossibly long solid curl of surf would rise kilometers away and race toward the lip of the cliff, crashing some 10 meters below the edge of land in a thundering explosion of white ocean foam and phosphorescent vegetation. To the human mind, the low moan of the wind was like a mythical angry spirit. Supposedly, the experience was spectacular.

Optics continued to scour the landscape. The satellites were fully operational, and the com systems were flooded with links from the ground, but none were encrypted with messages. Every one was strictly closed-ended, observation-only. Nothing but a bunch of confused artificial-intelligence units trying unsuccessfully to find out what was going on; no one was actually soliciting a response.

Jajqrt170 killed the connection to the satellite, frowning as she shifted her attention back down to the massive commercial technology station. Three time zones of topside docking bays, and now not a single ship was landing or taking off—the labyrinthian superstructure was suddenly a lead-walled robotics mausoleum. A million catacombs stacked 30 stories deep in the planetary crust, as silent as if the place had been buried and forgotten for a thousand years.

Her pupils dilated beneath her eyelids as her multiplexers signaled her peripheral interfaces, calling up the regional ops partition of the complex's gargantuan mainframe. The mainframe was offline, and there were no available data pools or active channels in anything she could access, no real clues to what was going on. Just nonresponsive circle-hex, as if every memory cell in the complex had been fried by x-rays.

A network of security cams with available visual feeds ran through the partition, but there wasn't much to see. The metal corridors were dark, lit only weakly by the eurostroxal photo-panels in the ceiling, holding their residual charges while the emergency protocols left all nonessential auxiliary systems powerless. Integrated kinematic units remained motionless, frozen midway through their rotation. The technicians had stopped working, leaving the halls empty, lined with cells of sealed and unsealed portals.

Jajqrt170 opened her eyes as the reconstituted images of the outside world gave way to the input from her own visual sensors. The portal of her own cell happened to be sealed, and if there was an override to the lock, it was off-limits to her. Security of the facilities was apparently a higher priority than the emergency evacuation needs of the clients. Above her head, the small green channel-balance light was blinking as if everything were status quo.

She had an immediate impulse to get to her feet, but a secondhand image of herself flashed in her primary mnemonic registers as if it had been burned in her field cells for decades. She was naked, prone on the tilted operating bed and attached to the local terminal with heavy teraflop cables affixed to the four lateral interface conduits along her sides, and a bug cleaner wire behind her right ear. Her heels were locked in place on the chargers set at the bottom of the bed, and both her arms were detached at the clavicle cross-socket. She was more or less immobilized, caught in the middle of the procedure.

She tipped her head up and glanced around. The Scalamex Standard autodoc was positioned at one of the computer consoles, holding her disembodied right arm. The left arm was apparently being rewired elsewhere.

She ran a quick, superscalar internal scan, focusing on her memory die core. She frowned, and for an instant the sensation of microstrand flexors manipulating the resilene skin around her mouth felt oddly alien. She blinked and banished the feeling, frowning more deeply.

The field cells were functional, and there were no corruptions in the file address banks or the cache hierarchy, but most of 2703 was still missing. The extended blackout was still there. If the autodocs had already worked on her neural net, they had been unable to fix the problem. Which would indicate the problem wasn't fixable.

Maybe they hadn't had a chance to work on it before the systems had gone offline.

A series of field cell snapshots flooded the conscious region of her central processing die core—choppy memories of her first on-board experience, broken up in useless brief intervals as if her mnemonics had never recorded the visual input data in a steady stream. A C27 Homeworld Dusk Cruiser docked at the edge of a landing bay in London. The bearded face of the ship's pilot, and various glimpses of him seated in the cockpit and standing around the cabin, performing unknown activities. There were a few extended periods of clarity, scenes from a xenobiological expedition in the Proteid Sphere, discussions of data samples. Then it all fell away, and she was again alone in the pilot seat, drifting in orbit around Sol just outside the aphelion of Pluto.

Everything from then on was clean. There had been ten more pilots and six different ships. 909 years of flawlessly recorded experience. Salaman Nevis was dead by now; whatever had actually taken him out of the picture was long past the point of being critical. The bigger issue was the fact that in 909 years of internal scans, she hadn't managed to source out a nine-month hole in her memory. Either something in her mnemonics was preventing her from calling up those field cells, or the field cells themselves had been irrevocably damaged.

So the possibility of a terminal polymorphic metastasis corruption still existed, even though most cases of TPM resulted in rapid proliferation of cognitive breakdown. The statistics weren't good—in 84.67+ percent of all cases of mnemonic system failure in human-make androids, the problem was a cache hierarchy glitch, essentially self-correctible as soon as the android became aware of it. The rest of the cases were either caused by hard circuitry burnout in the neural net, external tampering, or TPM. Burnout and tampering were easily detectable and fixable. TPM was not. And in 100 percent of all cases, TPM eventually attacked the android's control die core; when that happened, it was either lobotomy or the scrap heap. Either way, the personal functionality that uniquely identified each android mind was destroyed.

In TPM, the lost memory was unrecoverable. If she could come up with a single piece of missing information, if the thoughts of the past had been misfiled and not completely erased, she was probably curable.

Salaman Nevis might have been responsible for the problem himself. From the readable field cells prior to the memory gap, he had been an arrogant egomaniac, and he hadn't been remotely respectful of androids in general, habitually slaving her to the ship's on-board. Maybe he had wiped her memory on a whim. Something in the broken bits of data suggested his behavior had been increasingly erratic, illogical. Maybe the self-proclaimed most brilliant scientist in the Galaxy had ended up fuguing in a fit of hyperspace narcosis, left her and the rest of civilization for his own peace of mind. Or maybe an on-board malfunction had killed him.

For all she knew, she might have killed him herself.

She strained, sorting through the broken images. The complete data sequences should have been right there. It was as if her mnemonics were stuck in an endless feedback loop, forcing her to skip over a critical line of code.

Her transistors were sluggish, and the pulse of radiation through her microcapacitors seemed to pound at the insides of her head. It was exactly how Dexter had said she was going to feel, as if he really knew anything about what it was like to have an electromagnetic circulatory system.

The thought of her energy control die core popped into her head, and she looked back down at her feet. The chargers were offline, along with most of the systems in the complex, which meant she was draining energy. The autodocs would have taken her transducers offline to perform the operation, and there wasn't enough light in the room to effectively feed the solar cells in her photovoltaic array, so she was going to lose consciousness if the station didn't reopen for business soon.

She twisted her neck, looking again at the cell portal. It was just as closed as it had been before. The corridor outside was visible through the small polyglass head panel, incrementally brighter than the cell. She could have probably managed to disconnect herself from the operating bed, get control of her energy systems, and stop the power drain with a quick dynamic recycling sequence, but she wasn't going to get through that portal until the complex went back online. And it probably wasn't such a wise idea to disengage in the middle of a surgical procedure.

Obviously, something out of the ordinary was going on. Barrier Island Station didn't have full-scale power outages, and it never shut down. Ten minutes of down time would have cost Scalaway millions—it was the hub of interstellar commerce. The island might have been under attack by extortionists, but Barrier Island was protected better than Interplanetary Authority headquarters on Irina. There were pirates with some serious firepower in the Human Sphere, but the complex had an entire division of Scalawegian planetary defense standing by. The station was essentially a gigantic, impregnable bunker, built to withstand a military assault, underground and shielded from cosmic rays by a 10-meter-thick roof of lead. And it was essentially sabotage-proof. The counter-terrorist software was state-of-the-art, and if someone did manage to get a virus through to the mainframe, there were firewalls upon firewalls to prevent it from spreading. If the station was somehow compromised and shut down internally, there were remote-link failsafe overrides on three other islands spanning the circumference of the planet. The governments of the Human Sphere didn't want the complex down for a nanosecond.

Remote links… calling Dexter through the Zenith Explorer's on-board was one thing she could do. He was light years away, and there wasn't anything he could do about it directly. But he might have known what was going on. At the very least, he could find out.

She scanned for the guided neutrino com and found it. Still functional. The primary transmitter was seated in her left forearm, but if the autodoc had left her enough neural wherewithal to roust herself from a surgical procedure without external stimulation, she should have had no problem with a transmitter conversion at another interface. The backup relays were in place. She initiated a conversion sequence at the left anterior interface, transcribing the configuration algorithm and channeling residual power to the corresponding dye's fluidic microarrays. She smiled. She was groggy, but she wasn't completely useless.

She closed her eyes and ran the Explorer's code sequence. The on-board didn't respond.

She double-checked her com system… nothing wrong on her end. The ship was 28 light-years away, but distance wasn't a factor with guided neutrino arc-reflector technology. Access should have been virtually instantaneous as long as the Explorer's code receiver was still functioning. She wouldn't have been able to get through if Dexter had the ship in

41

hyperspace, but he wasn't due to leave until after her surgical procedure, and she was supposed to be offline for another six hours. Without a com, Dexter would have to coordinate a new flight pattern to Scalaway manually. He wasn't likely to leave early if he didn't have to.

There was a possibility nothing on the ship worked. Dexter could have left early for reasons unknown, laid in a bad flight pattern, and crashed—there was a greater incidence of critical error in flights with no navigational help from an intermediary unit.

Doubtful, knowing Dexter's piloting skills—not to mention his ridiculous luck. More likely, the problem was limited to the ship's com system. Either a component had failed on the flight to Beta Lyrae or someone had overridden the codes on the ground on Valentina. A basic com lockdown was typical in ship detention... Dexter had probably aggravated the wrong gaming official and gotten himself in more trouble than usual.

Jajqrt170 sighed. Dexter would probably enjoy being stuck in that system. More time to gamble, more time to win.

She ran the sequence again. Still no response from the on-board. "Bugs."

There was nothing else she could do but wait until she went below the low power threshold. Hopefully, nothing had gone wrong with Dexter or the ship.

She was probably not considering everything there was to consider. Maybe there was a problem with her own circuits, damage she couldn't detect. Any number of things might have gone wrong when a surgical procedure was abruptly interrupted. Guidestars, there was obviously something wrong with her circuitry—she hadn't gone to the station for nothing. Things were haywire on Scalaway... there was no reason to think there were problems aboard the ship as well. Too much of a coincidence. Besides, nothing ever went wrong with Dexter.

She closed her eyes and tapped the satellite a second time. The other androids in their cells were still activating the com system, the same as before. But there was a difference in the flow of power now—the satellite was picking up a new signal. An unencrypted radio signal... local transmission. Contingency protocol for a resolution support crew when dealing with a disaster recovery emergency; someone was broadcasting a situation report. The frequency information was filtering into the satellite databank.

Jajqrt170 zeroed in on the databank and began converting the information for her aural decompressors. Maybe she wasn't in a position to do anything about it, but as long as she was awake, it couldn't hurt to know what was going on.

* * *

```
... GCL GZ.031
Phi 100 41 44.00 / Theta 65 19 20.80 / Rho 30.97 / JD 3040382
Eta Ursae Majoris: GALINA; "Marquis Mountains"; 6 March 3612 CE
```

Q'um Lharaa Saaj stepped into the jam-packed lift box. Despite the lack of space, the humans pressed away from him as if physical contact would have a toxic effect.

Saaj shot his trifurcated saurian tongue out and back in, tasting the foul but familiar aroma of the fleshy aliens. On Galina human arrogance was at an extreme; the rich reveled in their elevated status, barely making an effort to disguise their abhorrence of the poor, and of anyone nonhuman.

The wealthiest planet in the Human Sphere stood as an emblematic symbol of its frail-bodied overlords and their unwavering ability to humiliate other sentients by downgrading the importance of strength and power. On Galina, climatological and atmospheric conditions were mild—good for thin skins, and ideal for the sensitive, widely sought-after halapa clover that had credit rolling into human bank accounts. There was none of the jagged drama of the anadon worlds. Even the mountains seemed measured and peaceful.

Halapa thread was smoother than other fabrics; to humans, it was comfortable to the touch, and thus, more valuable. They fed their inane appetite for fine clothing and filled their pockets with the proceeds, thanks to the curiosities of the more advanced sentients who should have known better than to involve themselves in the ways and activities of an infantile race.

Now Galina was the home of the decadent and the superficial, many of the wealthiest people in the Galaxy. The latecomers. They had moved in after the halapa industry had taken off, supplanting the blue-collar culture of terraforming frontiersmen. The latecomers had monopolized the economy, redefining the social structure of the planet and effecting a caste system as primitive and unbalanced as a feudal fiefdom of ancient history, comparable to nothing in the spheres of civilized, interstellar species.

The lift was unnecessarily slow. A man in a purple tunic inadvertently brushed against Saaj as he watched the glowing level indicator above the door. Saaj snarled at him, and he cringed.

Humanity was a race of irrational, short-sighted parasites; it was amazing these sentients had managed to work out the schematics for faster-than-light travel before dying out in a cesspool of their own negligence.

The door glided open and the people poured into the penthouse. A combination of the evening twilight and glare-proof walls of transparent quartz-acrylic composite created the illusion that the party was going on in open air beneath a hovering roof. The floor fanned out around the elevator shaft in a large octagon. Groups of people in varied colorful dress littered the rug, standing idly and lounging on scattered curving couches, conversing in cliques, gesturing dramatically and carelessly. Luxurious food and drink stations were visible in every direction, round bars of apparent marble and gold, adorned with racks of carefully arranged glassware.

Saaj shoved his way past a pair of green-clad humans and flashed his eyes around looking for the eminent host. Senator Teodor Monroe had as much credit power as any Galinan latecomer, but his wealth derived from a different source. His CU was also substantially inherited, but Monroe was a full-blooded Anastasian, raised on a planet of farmers and food engineers. His family's assets had been amassed through more legitimate industries. And unlike most who held residence on Galina, Monroe had taken steps to increase his fortune through his own achievements, rather than indulgently spending it down. Speculating on technology, building his own corporate empire as he forwarded a career in politics.

"Saaj—welcome to Rocas Grisos." Monroe was behind a circle of couches by the virtually invisible wall, standing with a white-haired woman in a sparkling blue gown. The senator himself wore a ruffled, maroon caladine blouse held tight by laces that ran through the neck and waist, trailing a black, shoulder-length cape. Clearly he had made an effort to stand out even among this fashion-obsessed crowd. He nodded at the woman. "I hope you'll excuse me, Ms. Tayner."

The woman touched him on the arm and scanned Saaj from the chest down without making eye contact, as if she had interest in his mustard yellow multipurpose suit. She sipped a drink and seemed to settle on his surface boots. "Of course, Teo." The distaste was apparent in her tone.

Monroe bowed politely and moved toward Saaj. "Follow me." He swept past, heading for an unoccupied area of the floor.

The guests seemed to sense his presence, making way as he stepped through the crowd. He moved at a long, striding pace with his head held high, fluttering his cape conspicuously behind him. The man had made a practice out of exhibiting his wealth and power, attending to every detail of his look. His hair was a well-coifed bed of steeled curls, darkened with silver-oxide spray, with calculated touches of lighter gray at the sides, most likely to suggest experience. A short, even mustache reflected the darker color in his hair, and chemically treated skin gave his face the effortless, healthy hue that he needed for his public appearances.

Saaj eyed the senator's regal profile from the right as they crossed to an open area near another face of the wall. The man's true complexion was most likely pale, judging by the grim determination motivating his behavior. Like other humans, he had a weakness for superficial aesthetics, but his seemed more a means to an end. In reality, Monroe was as cold-blooded as any sensible anadon.

Monroe stopped in front of the wall, seemingly admiring the sunset. Saaj followed his lead. The view was agreeable—a green and red valley of flowers trailed off toward the nearby ridge, where low-angle sunlight from the blue star bathed the mountain tops in lavender.

"You're earlier than I expected." Monroe kept his eyes on the wall.

An attendant approached, walking along the curve of the wall with a tray of tiny appetizers. Monroe held up a pair of fingers as if to halt Saaj's voice like a conductor commanding his orchestra, then glanced back at the attendant, redirecting the man with a subtle shake of his head.

Saaj gurgled quietly as the muscles of his throat filtered the building moisture away from his windpipe. Working for humans was objectionable but necessary; regulatory enforcement measures in the Anadon Sphere were more effective, increasing risk and limiting the truly lucrative business opportunities.

And the opportunities offered by this man were more than lucrative.

Monroe nodded as the attendant circled away. "Go ahead. Bottom-line it for me."

"We hit our target. Data transfer ended at 37:45 Lyuda Zulu." Saaj paused. "No major setbacks, but the ground control AD had plausible deniability concerns. I made an adjustment."

"Yes, I saw that in your report." Monroe smiled thinly. "I assume this assistant director is on board now. If he continues to be skittish, we may have to monitor the situation and follow up with him."

Saaj nodded silently.

Monroe brightened abruptly. "It seems the reactive cluster containment field worked."

"All incoming and outgoing neutrino communications were cut off from the satellite station, as we expected. Our assessment results were replicated exactly."

45

Monroe stared out the window. "Then this Higgs boson predictability Mr. Faro was concerned with—it wasn't a problem after all." He turned to look up at the anadon. "This is going to revolutionize communication security, you realize. They are going to have to revamp the defensive schematics for Trojan belljar networks across Humania. And they will. All because an exclusive team of physicists were able to coordinate the behavior of a few infinitesimal particles in just such a way as to effectively trap neutrinos... all because of technology. But I already have my reward for solving the puzzle."

Saaj grunted silently to himself. The engineering achievement had more or less been pioneered long before by the scinti, and perfecting it on a large scale had been a matter of purposeful focus and little innovation. The success of the mission had more to do with compromising ground control on Lambda B Fornacis 6, and the subsequent reconfiguration of the GN receiver and infiltration of the system that had allowed the team to set off a global EMF pulse—but the senator would not be sympathetic to the point.

Monroe took several steps away from Saaj, gazing at the majestic view. "Staying a step ahead in technology is the key, you understand. That and maintaining cohesiveness. The governments of the Galaxy, the Interplanetary Authority, all of the would-be obstacles of this empire I'm putting together are operating at a distinct disadvantage. They aren't united in thought like my organization. While they struggle to communicate with one another and debate over jurisdictional issues, hamstrung by bureaucracy and provincial bickering, I'm free to expand my power base unopposed, and virtually unnoticed."

Saaj stood by the window, shifting his weight from one foot to the other. The senator tended to indulge himself with the sound of his own voice, but he was a busy and efficient man. The party was just a stopover before he headed for his processing facilities in Merida; the musings would end soon enough.

Monroe spun, stroking his silver-tinged mustache in an intentionally contemplative pose as his cape fluttered around his arms. "It's ironic, Saaj. I'm a respected citizen in these parts of the Galaxy, and it's all because of wealth. Staggering wealth, granted—and adding in a measure of acutely cultivated style doesn't hurt—but it's all about having sufficient bank, ultimately. Sentient beings are shallow, be they human, drbdu, raxatot, or proteid. The trait is universal in this Galaxy of ours—every one of us is impressed at the core of our varied anatomy by raw power, despite whatever pretended values we boast. Show others you have a little credit, and you've bought yourself instant, irrepressible respectability. They'll start to overlook the little indiscretions. Show them that you have credit like I do and they'll overlook a lot more than that."

He laughed, scanning briefly to make sure no one was listening in. "Understand this—the universe is full of things there for the taking. Outside this Galaxy lies an infinite untapped resource, too large to exploit in one lifetime. Life is short, Saaj, but for now, I am in a position to reap."

Saaj glanced at the floor, shifting in his stance. Monroe held up a finger. "Of course, every brilliant plan needs muscle to put it into effect, and the man in charge of the muscle plays an extremely valuable part in that plan. You've played a pivotal role for my organization once again, Saaj. How do you feel about the work you're doing? I've been asking quite a bit of you lately—do you feel you're being compensated adequately?"

Saaj hesitated. There would be more assignments with increasing rewards for a field operative who knew his place. He straightened. "I am curious why the secured data aboard a hyperdrive contractor is of such interest to you… I could work more effectively if I knew more about the purpose. But our contract is clear. 400,000 proteid gana upon success, plus continuing dividends at eight basis points in CU. I deserve what you agreed to pay."

"I see." Monroe leaned close to the anadon, and seemed to momentarily gain in height. "It should be enough, I'd say. You could probably retire comfortably on Ekseniya with that portion alone."

Saaj stared back at him. "Retirement is not in my thoughts at this time, senator. Neither is Ekseniya."

Monroe flashed a grin, thinning his eyes. "I see." He took a quick scan around the room, then looked back at Saaj. "You're aware I consider myself a student of history… I'm not sure whether the stories of the past are in your wheelhouse, but I assume you know a bit about the development of the human race, considering you've now immersed yourself in our culture. Is that correct?"

Saaj paused. "I know some of human history. But it is not an area of focus in the Anadon Sphere, and what information we receive about the humans is often filtered."

Monroe raised an eyebrow. "I'm sure it is. We tend to leave out the less flattering details ourselves. A passive education never guarantees a complete picture, which is why I value proactive research, as I'm sure you do as well. Particularly while assessing the accomplishments of those considered nefarious."

Saaj took a step closer to the window panel as a pair of women brushed past, one tall and broad-shouldered in a black twist of a garment that matched her hairstyle and color. He hissed. "I rely mainly on personal experience."

"Have you heard of the Medellín Cartel?"

Saaj took in a breath, trying not to taste the air. He exhaled slowly through his nostrils, sweeping the open room with his eyes. Typical human gathering, purposeless conversation at elevated volumes, uneven lighting. Very little movement; most seemed to be content remaining in their scattered clusters, as if they intended to remain in their soft lounge seats and on their arbitrary spots of carpet all night. He shifted his attention back to Monroe. "The name is not familiar. A political confederation of some sort?"

"A business empire. Arguably the most powerful of its kind in pre-stellar Earth history—an exception in a world dominated by competing national governments. It traded in what was universally considered contraband, but it functioned outside the scope of international law."

Saaj straightened. "It sounds similar to the Foundation of Deneb."

"That it was. It was run by a man named Pablo Escobar. He carved out his place in history with acumen and cold-blooded determination, seizing control of the criminal enterprises of his city, then building his own effective nation, winning public support and amassing an army. His asset base and cash flow outgained that of his surrounding country... he even held a seat in his country's congress." Monroe winked. "There are parallels to the Foundation, to be sure, but I believe there's a better comparison closer to home. This organization you've joined has already eclipsed anything those pirates on Olga have managed."

"So it would seem."

The senator flashed a smile. "The key thing to remember is that as brilliant as this Escobar was, he couldn't have done it completely on his own. He developed a solid brand to carry out his plan as the cartel grew. Perhaps his wisest practice of all was the way he managed his expansion—the way he took care to select his people, people who shared his simple, clear-cut vision for success. He formulated the plans, but it was his soldiers who brought them to life. I'm particularly interested in a man named Rafael Avila, one of his closest confidants, and a most effective agent."

Saaj grunted. If the historical accounts were remotely accurate, pre-stellar Earth was a melee of squabbling tyrants and waves of wholesale genocide. It was hard to imagine that any criminal opportunist would have had difficulty carving out his place in that environment.

Monroe gave him a hard look and cleared his throat pointedly. "Avila was one of the Sicarios of Mesoamerica, a group of legendary assassins. He had a singular excellence for professional killing that was only matched by his demonstrated loyalty to the head of his organization. He managed to escape two of the deadliest prisons of the day, and made a name for himself while he was with the cartel. He oversaw the execution of over a thousand of Escobar's enemies, and he became known as 'El Mano Blanco.' The White Hand. Resourceful, disciplined, icily resolute. And loyal. He had ample opportunity to retire in luxury, yet he returned time and time again to the man who had made him rich." He paused. "The strength of an organization depends on the integrity of its people, Saaj. You can't be successful in any business if allegiance is in question."

Saaj looked down at the carpet and flicked his tongue. The senator's words now sounded less like arbitrary chatter about primitive, long-dead Earth criminals and more like an orientation speech. The man liked to talk, but he rarely ended a conversation without making his meaning completely clear. "I agree."

Monroe nodded once. "Good to know." He exhaled audibly. "I'd like you to make arrangements to join me at the Buchanan office. We hold strategy sessions every week, and I'd like you to get a look at how things go in our inner sanctum. Gain a new perspective on our business. We meet in a few days—I'll make sure you get the details by tomorrow."

Saaj turned back to the sparkling view of the mountain valley. Professionalism and loyalty. Strength. Teodor Monroe had every reason to be wary of a weapons specialist from the corporate sector of the Anadon Sphere—there was little tolerance for humans on Yabahta, let alone deference to a criminal overlord. But the senator had done his research, and he knew the quality of individual he sought in a command consultant. Good fortune for an exile from the Anadon Race.

Saaj bowed his head in assent. "I will be there."

Monroe turned and held up an arm, drawing instant attention from the rest of his guests. He nodded back at Saaj. "Now, I believe a drink of celebration is in order, if you'll join me. No sense trying to keep a low profile in this mix." He smiled broadly. "I know you're not exactly keen on mingling with humans, but you might even enjoy the conversation today. Everyone's abuzz about this information heist at the Stasya Hyperdynamics Trojan complex… you might want to render an opinion."

Saaj watched the senator step toward an attendant holding a tray of glasses and signal several others to join him, transitioning flawlessly to a more public persona. Saaj grunted. Impossible to tell whether the man was joking. If a man's ultimate success was proportional to his nerve, Monroe was going to be every bit as successful as he believed.

*   *   *

```
... GCL EE.271
Phi 63 11 15.36 / Theta 14 47 00.47 / Rho 270.42 / JD 3040381
Beta Lyrae: VALENTINA; "Sheliak City"; 6 March 3612 CE
```

"Tell me something... what's it like not being able to see in color?" Dexter shook his head, widening his eyes brightly. "I can't imagine what this place would look like without all this pizzazz."

The proteid stared at him through the polyglass window. The veins visible in its semitranslucent membrane seemed to get larger. It stretched out an appendage to press a button on the translator, and let out a low moan. The display box on Dexter's side read, "Do you have more tokens to credit, Mr. Massengill?"

It probably wasn't good practice to hold conversations with tellers while still playing, but it was an opportune time for a spell. The sentients at the table were tediously close-lipped on this particular day. Dexter glanced absently at his empty coin purse and waved in the direction of the loqaqi stations. "No, that's fine—they're holding my place back there. I'll have quite a bit more to ring up in a little while, when I'm done." He paused, peering at the single off-center pit that served as the gelatinous sentient's eye. "So as I understand it, your species is completely monochromatic—you have no conical photoreceptors, you have a keen sense of differentiating light intensity, but everything is in black and white. I understand all that, but I'm curious about whether you see things differently—are the lines blurred, do you see the same shapes as humans and other sentients?"

The proteid made no response. The unformed bulge at the top end of its body that seemed to serve as a stand-in cranium heeled slightly to the left.

Dexter stared back for a long moment, then nodded and flashed a smile. "I mean, it seems you never hear very many personal accounts from you proteids." He shrugged. "I know sentients generally like to be able to look one another in the eyes when they converse, but I don't see why I should avoid talking to someone solely because of depressed optical ganglia."

The proteid tapped the translator. "Mr. Massengill, you should be aware that the Blue Topaz has changed ownership since you were last here. The new manager does not wish for his customers to loiter at the teller windows.

50

If you have no tokens on your person, please leave the window."

Dexter frowned, raising his eyebrows. In truth, he did in fact have a blue-and-red tenpiece on his person, but there was no sense in debating the point. He nodded again and pushed away from the window. Not as if he hadn't asked for it—proteid gruffness was as much a constant as the speed of light.

He glanced down and patted the left pocket of his slacks as he moved out from under the dimly lit, low ceiling of the credit alcove and back into the glittering brightness of the casino complex. The tenpiece wasn't representative of a particularly momentous occasion; essentially it was just a leftover coin that had gotten somehow separated from a handful of tokens in his pocket and then managed to escape detection during a stopover at a small port in the Gemma System. It just happened to be the only one he had never cashed in for CU, and toting it around without turning it in had informally become part of the ritual. His "lucky tenpiece," as it were. Though as with every other newly introduced factor in his life, carrying the token or not had never seemed to affect his luck in the least.

He made his way back to the gaming floor. Beta Lyrae casino decor was considered to be on the fringes of good taste by many, but he had long since gotten used to it. The gaudiness was a staple in Beta Lyrae, and when it came to gaming there was no place in the Galaxy like Beta Lyrae.

The ground-level promenade was more or less the same as the other gaming floor areas in the Blue Topaz Casino, on a larger scale. A wide hall funneled foot traffic into a spacious, cylindrical cathedral chamber, its curved wall befitted with extravagant gulak designs. Swirling splotches and zigzags surrounded the room—alleged abstract representations of alien vistas, blending magenta, chartreuse, and turquoise shades. A multitude of crystal chandeliers hung above the hexagonal tables, over an ocean of spongy rubber carpeting.

A polyglass pillar-aquarium at the center of the vast cylinder ran up through the floor and out the mirrored ceiling toward the roof of the building, exhibiting some of the more exotic marine life of the planet. Dexter shouldered his way past as a Valentine cleaner used a pair of tentacles to pry a suckercup from the inside surface.

Some of the harsh color effects were softened by a constant smoky haze. Ventilation ducts along the walls kept the air just clear enough to see the entire room. As always, the place was thriving. The numbers booths that lined the curving wall were packed, and people were pulsing in through the double-door entrance, coursing through the room and clustering at the tables.

Along one edge of a six-sided loqaqi ring just past the pillar-aquarium, a yellow diode blinked above the coin pocket, where some 5,000 CU was unceremoniously piled. A new dealer was in place at the center of the ring, an albino human with thinning hair. Probable Demteedum man.

Dexter smiled at him. "Can I get in on this hand?"

A few of the sentients shot sullen glares in Dexter's direction. The dealer began flinging triangular tiles at five of the six frames embedded in the faux-obsidian table surface. "Next hand, sir."

Dexter bowed as he sat down. "Of course—worth a try. Soon as you're willing, then. Consider me in." He peered over a particularly short gulak's shoulder at the dealer's darting hands, watching as the tiles landed in rapid succession. In moments the requisite four were dealt to each player. Dexter looked up at the man. "Pleasure. I'm Dexter Massengill."

The dealer didn't look back. "I know who you are, Mr. Massengill." He pointed to the gulak, who passed.

Dexter blinked. Fair enough. "Well, I haven't seen you before. Obviously you've got a talent for tossing the tiles. Where are you from?"

The dealer remained expressionless, pointing to the next player. "Clipperville."

The next player was a man with a ruddy complexion wearing rather uncomfortable-looking beige suit, complete with neckpiece, windbreaker, and gloves. Pressure suit goggles dangled from his lapel, as if he was taking a break from a desert surveillance duty shift. He grunted. "Two." The dealer flipped him two more tiles with the flick of a wrist.

"Demteedum—I thought so. I was in Clipperville once. They make a great spicy udon."

The dealer turned away from the table and glared at Dexter. A man several seats away yelled in an unmistakable accent—no doubt he was from the Vera System. "Go on, fred, you're holding up play!"

The Veran man was practically shirtless, sporting a pair of wide, blue suspenders and virtually invisible webbing over a curly-haired chest. No dress code in Beta Lyrae—the clothing tended to be as varied as the gulak color scheme.

Dexter held up a hand, smiling and bowing his head toward the dealer. "Oh, don't stop on my account. Please continue."

The dealer let his glare linger for a microsecond more, then turned to a sharply dressed, tall, green-skinned anadon—female, judging by the height.

The anadon held up a clawed hand. "Baqaq." Two tiles tumbled into her frame, and she leaned forward. "Ssaya—afaal mejah!" A display of her tiles flashed briefly in the air showing the purple glow of the muqaqi tile—the taboo sixth color. The anadon's hand was compromised.

The dealer passed new tiles to several others as they grumbled their requests. A large, bearded man in a green, elastic yarmulke sat up. "Loqaqi."

Even the tone of the winner seemed subdued. The dealer adjusted unseen controls, and the hologram confirmed his claim: four yellow among the seven tiles in his frame; no purple.

The dealer rolled his head. "Winner." The hologram blinked away, and the tokens in play around the table disappeared into their pockets and filtered to the winner. The man grabbed a handful of black-and-white thousandpieces from his coin pocket and began stacking them overtly on the tabletop. The suspendered Veran man made a huffing noise and departed.

The diode above Dexter's coin pocket went from yellow to green. The dealer raised his eyebrows expectantly. "Sir, you need to remove any tokens you aren't betting."

Dexter nodded. "Yes. No, I'm fine. Go ahead."

The dealer looked around at the other players and paused. "Bets are off." The diodes went red. He dealt the tiles.

Dexter watched as the seemingly nondescript plastic triangles tumbled into his frame and looked up. A new image of an inverted triangle hovered above the table, this one exclusive to him. The representations of the tiles shimmered in unison. He smiled as the dealer pointed at him. "Loqaqi."

The dealer raised an eyebrow. His hand moved under the table. The image of Dexter's tiles was replaced by a larger one visible to the others. "Winner."

Dexter patted the table. "Four blue. Well, that was quick, wasn't it?"

The smallish gulak next to him stared at the tiles with five tiny eyes. Possibly a female... hard to distinguish differences in gender under the matted brown fur, but the primary males were generally much wider across the shoulders. Of course, there were three gulak sexes. The second-stage fertilizers had the same build as the females, but they tended to avoid crowds of mixed species.

The gulak spoke with a thick, halting accent. "He gets dealt loqaqi on first hand with credit down? Clear as Keynindra night of seven moons, this person is working inside angle for house."

Dexter shrugged. "I understand your concern, but trust me, it's nothing untoward. It happens more often than you'd think." He turned to the dealer. "I'm actually going to have to step up the betting a bit from here on if I want to make my usual 50 K—hopefully it won't cause any major cash-flow problems at the table. My android gets out of surgery in about a half hour, so I'm going to have to jump away sooner than I'd like."

The dealer looked at him blankly. "It's not a problem, sir." He raised his voice. "Bets are off."

Dexter glanced at the diode above his tokens as it flipped to red. "I wouldn't think so." He nodded at a newly arrived slender woman with a wild, glossy mane of indigo hair who seemed to be appraising him across the table. "After all, this is a fine establishment here. I don't go anywhere else anymore, you know. I mean, if you gamble at just any old place, there's always the chance they'll run out of money." He flashed a grin.

The man in the yarmulke let his fist fall to the right of his stack of tokens. "Is there a chance you'll stop running your mouth so we can play?"

Dexter frowned. The ruddy-complected, beige-suited man stood and moved away, replaced immediately by a broad-shouldered male gulak not much taller than the fellow species member already seated.

The anadon in the lead-off position raised her brow and hissed. "Aren't you pushing your luck?" Her three-tipped tongue flitted briefly out of her flat muzzle.

Dexter shook his head. "That's just it. I'm always pushing my luck. I don't know what it is—I'm not a particularly talented player—but I've never come out of a gaming situation in my life with a lower credit cache. Believe me, if I lost now, I would be very surprised."

The fourth tile landed in Dexter's frame. Four different colors this time: red, yellow, blue, and green. No purple bust tile, as usual. He scanned the eyes of the other players. Not one of them looked happy to be there; the table was clearly in need of an energy injection. He cleared his throat as the dealer looked his way. "12, please."

There were mumblings and more than a few gaping looks in his direction. The dealer stared for a moment. "All right, Mr. Massengill, anything over eight takes everyone else out of play. You're aware."

Dexter sighed. "I understand."

The dealer handed Dexter 12 more tiles. "16 out."

Dexter squinted at the holographic triangle as it filled up with color. Three more reds, yellows, blues, and greens. Beautiful. No duqaqi busts—no fifth tile in any single color, and no oranges, keeping the total number of different colors to the allowable four. And, of course, no purple. He beamed.

The dealer had a sardonic look on his face as he watched Dexter's expression. "Checking on a hand of 16."

"You're supposed to assume it's a winner, aren't you?" Dexter widened his eyes at the coin pocket as the tiles went up on public display. "Loqaqi. Quads, right? Four payouts should put me somewhere north of 54,000 CU. But I suppose it wouldn't hurt to play just one more hand." He turned to the other players. "I'll leave you to it after that. There's really nothing quite like Shel City, is there?"

The others showed a variety of dumbfounded and annoyed expressions before gathering their coins and leaving the table. This time no one else jumped in, although there was a small group of onlookers gathering who pressed inward as the space became available. Dexter raised his eyebrows at the dealer. "Well, I guess it's down to you and me. Don't worry—I'm sure you'll be able to reach your table quota after I leave. It usually fills right back up as soon as I stop." He paused, waving a hand in the air. "No need to ask… let it ride once more."

"Mr. Allister, please hold the table for a moment." The brusque female voice was coming from somewhere behind Dexter's right shoulder. "Mr. Massengill?"

Dexter turned around to see a virtual wall of brown fur. Two broad-shouldered gulaks wearing maroon staffer vests were taking up most of the area immediately behind his seat, training their oddly clustered eyes on him. Larger than the two previous gulaks, and definitely male. A dark woman in a neat black suit stood between them. She cleared her throat and spoke again. "My name is Ritsa Rabani; I'm the personal assistant to the general manager. Mr. Malgovar would like to speak with you."

He nodded. "Oh, certainly. I haven't met the new manager yet. What is this about, if I might ask?"

"If you'll just come this way." The woman started toward the rear exit of the room, and the gulaks moved their shoulders to let Dexter through. He stood and headed after her.

Rabani had dark skin and jet black hair. Her accent was distinct, but hard to place, so it wasn't immediately clear as to which of the many planets in the Human Sphere she hailed from. Perhaps it was someplace he hadn't yet visited… it was always good to get new leads on a stopover.

Dexter caught up to her. "You know, Ms. Rabani, I'd only just heard about the management change today. I had a chance to meet Gustin Yazov on several occasions—very personable man. I suppose he's moved on to bigger and better things."

She glanced back at him, allowing her sleekly styled hair to remain over one eye. "Mr. Yazov is no longer with the company."

Dexter took a look over his shoulder. The unsettling feeling of being the center of two many-eyed sentients' attention prickled the back of his neck, as the gulaks were now bringing up the rear, keeping pace as they followed along. "You know, Ms. Rabani, I appreciate the special attention, but I'm not sure an escort like this is necessary. I'm fairly well-known here."

They reached the exit and the opaque hologram door disappeared. Rabani turned around and looked at him sternly. "It's standard procedure, Mr. Massengill. If you'll just follow me, I'm sure everything will become clear."

Dexter frowned. The gulak muscle were clearly new; casino management typically checked in with him every once in a while—it was in their interest, as he was costing them credit. But the previous management team had skillfully avoided ever leaving the impression they suspected him of any wrongdoing. This new policy was a bit of a concern.

They walked into a hallway, and the door sealed itself off behind the gulaks. Rabani led them to the end of the hall. Another doorway was open at the rear wall of the casino, seemingly waiting for them. Inside was a lift; the cylindrical box looked as though it should have been big enough to carry ten sentients, though it seemed uncomfortably crowded when the gulaks filed in, bristling and hanging just off his shoulders. The curving brass-plate door slid open to the left. Dexter looked up at the round, mirrored top as he stepped inside.

The initial bump of the lift stabilizers caught him off-guard, and the muscles of his legs tensed. He frowned sourly at the subtle pressure change in his ears as the lift shot upward, then turned, glancing at the gulaks. The frozen masks of fur on their faces were difficult to read, but one seemed to be working his jaws in anticipation. The central trio of eyes were fixed on him while the peripherals were shifting between the other gulak and Ritsa Rabani, who remained as impassive as a statue.

A few seconds later, the stabilizers abruptly bumped again, and the door opened to reveal purple sky. They had to be at the administration level, at the very top of the building.

Rabani stepped off the lift and motioned for the others to follow. "This way, please."

The gulaks ushered Dexter out into a short corridor that opened onto what looked like a vast, circular outdoor plaza that must have spanned the roof, with a maze of hedge-lined walkways, trees, and benches, lit by scattered plumes of soft lighting rising from the floor. The ceiling above was clear polyglass, virtually invisible under the Valentina night and given away only by red reference tags that rimmed the outer edge, seemingly suspended in midair. Apparently the top floor doubled as an observation deck.

Surrounding the plaza was a long row of evenly spaced office doors, separated in places by the lift corridors. Rabani led the group down a broad walkway that ran along the wall of offices, then stopped at an open office. Dexter glanced up at the tag; it read, "TEMP STOR 20B." He frowned. Temporary storage?

Low-angle lighting and broken shadows made the inside of the office difficult to see. Strange place for a meeting.

One of the gulaks shifted his stance and eyed Dexter, apparently signaling that it was time to enter. Dexter hesitated, glancing at Rabani, then obliged and stepped through the doorway, soaking in the surroundings. Not much more than what met the eye through the open doorway—essentially it was one big room with no decoration and a single window that took up the entire back wall, more like an abandoned office than a storage area. Two people were standing by a small table near the back. One of the men stepped forward, small in stature but rather rotund; he wore a starch white suit that fit him a bit too tightly.

The man nodded vigorously. "Mr. Massengill." He cleared his throat and sniffed. "Dion Malgovar. Sit down." He pointed at a small chair in front of the table.

Dexter hesitated momentarily and immediately became aware of the two Gulaks breathing behind him. He stepped to the chair and sat. Malgovar moved around the table and sat in front of him. The other man remained silent with his arms folded, a dark-haired, expressionless man in a monochrome flatsuit. A bodyguard, maybe. Possibly, the new manager was a touch paranoid.

Malgovar smiled tersely, leaning forward. "Are you having a nice evening?"

Dexter nodded. "I was, yes." Behind Malgovar, the window looked out on the lights of Sheliak City; multicolored speckles of compressed gas lighting blinked from the nearby casinos, their rooftops lit under a pair of brilliant control towers that marked one of several adjacent landing pads. Dexter shifted in his seat. "The evenings are always nice on Valentina."

Malgovar glanced toward the window. "Yes, around here, we like to call it the Muqaqi Sky." The man seemed to be frowning, with a jutting lower lip that gave the impression of mild disgust. "It seems apropos to me. Wouldn't you agree?"

Dexter raised his eyebrows. "I hadn't heard that. So they named it after the purple taboo color. Interesting." He shrugged. "It seems odd to denigrate the beauty with such a negative connotation."

"Muqaqi isn't negative, if you're the house." Malgovar laughed briefly.

Dexter smiled. "I see your point."

The general manager thrust his chin forward and scratched his jowls. "So you are familiar with the taboo color. I wasn't sure." He shot Dexter a hard, challenging stare.

Dexter paused, studying him. "Well, yes, I make it a point to be fully familiar with all the casino games. It's what I do. I suppose you could say I don't see the purple tile turn up very often when I play loqaqi." He shook his head. "I guess that's why I like gaming here so much."

Malgovar nodded. "In fact, you never get dealt muqaqi when you come here. You've been coming here for five years without ever losing at loqaqi, roulette, cards... everything we have." He stood and strutted toward the window, circling back and nodding, dangling his arms at his sides, wrapping his knuckles against his legs. The man wasn't all that physically imposing, but there was a natural menace in the way he moved. Veiled aggression. "It's unusual. Wouldn't you agree?"

Meetings with Gustin Yazov had always been congenial and positive. This had a decidedly different tone. Dexter cleared his throat. "Well, I do remember losing a hand here and there. I've never netted a loss overall, but it's not really accurate to say—"

"Mr. Massengill, you're a consistent winner, and as the general manager of this establishment, it's my responsibility to investigate all potentially fraudulent activities." Malgovar waved a hand and squinted, nodding at Rabani. "Ritsa, if you would? I'm needed elsewhere."

"I'm not involved in any fraudulent activities. If this is about an ongoing investigation, I'm afraid I can't help you." Dexter turned in his seat. Rabani stepped smoothly around the table as the gulaks moved in behind him. Dexter half-stood, looking back at Malgovar. "I think I'd like to head back down, if you don't mind. It's a pleasure to meet the new manager..."

One of the gulaks placed a clawed hand on his shoulder and guided him roughly back into his seat. Malgovar held up a hand. "Relax, Mr. Massengill. We're going to need you here a little longer. Ms. Rabani should be able to answer any questions you might have; meanwhile, I'd suggest you answer hers." He took a sidelong glance in Ritsa Rabani's direction, tugging at the front of his slacks, then headed out of the room.

The man in the flatsuit remained. Apparently he was not one of the manager's bodyguards, and the thought of that was somehow unsettling. Rabani moved into position across the table from Dexter. "If you answer honestly, your cooperation will be taken into account."

Dexter sat forward, shaking his head. "I can't answer any differently. As I said, I'm not involved in any fraudulent activities—really, this isn't necessary. Mr. Yazov and I have already been through all this... it's never been a problem before."

"Our first order of business was a thorough investigation of Mr. Yazov's books." Rabani stared at him flatly. "Your success stands out. You've maintained a continuous above-average rate of return over an extended period in a venue where the probabilities are carefully controlled. Either you're working with an accomplice on the inside, or you have a particular advantage over the other patrons in your ability to predict things—these are the only reasonable conclusions. Either scenario constitutes fraud. You should be aware there are strict penalties for fraud on Valentina."

Dexter closed his eyes, laughing to himself. The suggestion had been made before, albeit more delicately. "Well, I'm not working with anyone, and I've been tested many times for telepathic abilities. My CRP always comes out at around 55. Right on the average." He shook his head. "I'm not a grifter, I'm just lucky. Things usually work out well for me, and I have no idea why." He paused. "Mr. Yazov had me tested himself, actually. I wouldn't mind doing it again, although I don't really see the need."

Rabani nodded. "We're familiar with the cortical tests, Mr. Massengill. According to our files, you've been netting roughly 510,000 CU on the gaming floor per year. You've been here 38 times and never once left with less credit than you started. We calculated the probability of that success rate at 2.14-minus-8. That's one in 46.8 million."

Rabani had no reference notes in front of her, but she was rattling off numbers like an android. In fact, it was possible she was an android. Dexter pursed his lips, raising his eyebrows. "Well, you can't really blame me for wanting to continue to play, can you? I mean, if you had that kind of luck, you'd keep coming back as well—don't you think?"

Rabani straightened in her chair. "We're prepared to waive formal charges if you provide specific details about your methods, and you agree to reimburse us in full for your winnings."

Dexter blinked. "Reimburse you? Well, I see no reason I should have to do that—I won that credit fairly."

Rabani glanced toward the man in the flatsuit. "Then I need to inform you that the law allows us to keep you incarcerated for a period of up to 60 days, at which time we will initiate criminal prosecution and recommend maximum sentencing before a local municipal justice." She paused. "You'll have an opportunity to defend yourself against the charges at that time."

Dexter gasped. "60 days—you can't be serious." He twisted in his seat and stiffened as he again felt the heavy gulak claws on his right shoulder.

Rabani sighed, seemingly bored. "Under these circumstances, we have the authority to temporarily recoup your CU and impound your ship, with or without your consent. But it will go much better for you if you cooperate now. I'll ask you one more time. How were you able to defraud this casino? We'll need the names of anyone else involved, whether or not they actively assisted."

It was difficult to digest—this sort of treatment might have been conceivable on Vera and in some of the other seedy areas of the Galaxy, but in Beta Lyrae? What could he tell this woman? He hadn't swindled anyone. He had been beating the odds at a tightly run casino for five years; curious, for sure, and absolutely a cause for concern on the part of the casino administrators, but how was he supposed to come up with an explanation if he didn't have the foggiest notion himself?

Of course, Jayjay would probably find the situation highly amusing, tell him he had had it coming. She would likely remind him of it every time he decided to go gaming. Assuming he actually did have the desire to go gaming again, when this business was in the past.

Rabani stared for a moment longer, then nodded at the man to her right. She stood, looking back at Dexter. "I'll need you to give me your wristcom."

His wristcom. Dexter frowned. There was no logical reason to antagonize these people further, but the wristcom was his one link to the ship, not to mention Jayjay and life beyond Beta Lyrae. It was a little thing, but the notion that they felt free to commandeer it, his rightful winnings, and anything else of his at will was too much. He paused, raising his eyebrows. "I will not."

Rabani signaled the gulaks with a subtle flick of her eyes, and they simultaneously grabbed him by the back of the shirt and hoisted him to his feet, handling him as easily as if he were a tiny child. Together, they promptly took hold of him by the forearms. Then the gulak on the right shifted his hold, working its grasping, thick-haired claw toward the wrist band.

Dexter squirmed, struggling against the hold. If he didn't get off a call to Jayjay now, chances were he wasn't going to talk to anyone for the full 60 days. Apparently Valentinan law didn't offer much in the way of courtesy to an accused grifter. But he only needed a brief distraction… if he was able to contact Jayjay even for a moment, signal his location, she'd figure something out as soon as she was out of her surgery.

The gulak again adjusted its grip, and Dexter tore his arm away, wrestling his hand into the side pocket of his slacks and groping upward with his fingers, straining for the clip on the wristcom strap. A small object fell into his palm, and for an instant it felt as if the round face of the com had come loose in his hand—he closed his fist around it, then frowned. He was holding a single plastic token. The tenpiece.

The gulak ripped his hand free of the pocket and forced it high in the air. The other gulak growled something at his partner, and the one on the left worked its long claws on the wristcom. The sentient increased the pressure, and Dexter's hand sprang open like a mechanical device. The tenpiece and the com hit the deck surface simultaneously. The gulak kicked the wristcom with a stump-like, unshod foot, and it skittered away toward the right wall.

Rabani stepped briskly across the floor and scooped up the com. She sighed and turned to the man in the flatsuit. "Keep him here." She stalked to the door and disappeared.

Dexter rubbed his wrist, looking back at the other man. "This really isn't necessary, if you'll listen."

The man nodded toward the door. "You should sit down. We're going to be here a while."

"I mean, I'm happy to cooperate, really. But I'm being honest—I'm just not sure what I can tell you."

One of the gulaks jabbed him sharply in the ribs, and he stumbled forward against the table. "Trag frarra, grifter! The man told you to sit down."

Dexter steadied himself and climbed back into the chair. Pain cascaded over the right half of his torso. He breathed, trying to focus on the window ahead, something outside the scope of this sudden nightmare.

"Try not to look so uncomfortable. It is impolite to look uncomfortable with sentients of another race." The graveled voice came from the other gulak, close behind. It sounded like an unoiled motor.

The gulak to his right chimed in. "No worries. He will have plenty of time to get used to us."

They both began barking out an exchange of explosive, guttural laughter like a pair of alpha male predators vying for control of their pack. Then outside the window, the lights across the city went out. Seconds later, everything went dark.

One of the gulaks lurched clumsily into his chair, and he jumped up, spinning out of the way, then felt a jolt across his shoulders as he stumbled roughly into the other gulak, who fell away, apparently caught off-balance.

61

Suddenly the room exploded with blood-curdling shrieking and scrambling as the gulaks attempted to react. Shapes began to form as his vision adjusted—bulky alien torsos looming to his left and right, one of them moving in, raising its thick, treelike arm.

Dexter ducked, then tripped over the fallen chair and fell forward against the floor. Both gulaks were converging on him, slashing at him with their wickedly sharp, needle-like claws, though they seemed to be having trouble landing their blows. Gulaks were known for having pinpoint nocturnal vision, but perhaps it was taking time for their eyes to adjust. He rolled, covering his face with his arms, then felt skin open up along his collar bone—one well-placed swipe was likely to rip his head off, and the gulaks seemed poised to do it.

One of the gulaks got a grip on his arms, pinning him momentarily, but he wrestled free and rolled clear, finding his feet and making a mad dash for the doorway, which stood unbarred. He headed through without looking back, rounding to the right.

The only light in the building was the dull glow of the sky overhead, a hangover of the prolonged, diffuse twilight trailing from the expanding dust spiral around the double-star. General grid power overload, possibly; reserve power would likely be up in seconds.

He ducked into the first outer passage he reached, sprinting for the lift chamber, then slowed. The lifts weren't going to be any more functional than the field barriers. Blast!

Noises emanated down the corridor from the main walkway. Voices. He was trapped. He glanced behind him. The voices were getting louder.

Maybe no one had seen him enter the passage… there were dozens. He pressed against the wall, holding his breath, then started as the streamers along the corridor walls flickered and went back on, followed by brightness overhead as light flooded across the entire deck. He hesitated briefly, then spun and dashed to the end of the passage, slapping the wall console several times to signal the lift.

He looked back again, breathing heavily. With any luck, there were still enough of a crowd to make it easy to blend in, if he could make it to the ground floor. He stared impatiently at the brass-plate door, looking repeatedly over his shoulder as he waited.

The door slid open, and he took an apprehensive step onto the carpeting of the lift platform. His eyes went immediately to the diode panel. He cleared his throat. "Ground level."

The ground level diode lit up, and the door slid closed—no one had rigged the boxes to override his voice command. Dexter closed his eyes and exhaled, then staggered left as the lift began its descent. A stinging sensation was spreading from his chest and shoulders. He frowned down at himself, dabbing at his shirt where the fabric had been torn away, and winced as his hand came away with blood. He blinked as he tried to focus his vision, shaking himself. The gulaks had done some damage after all, and he was apparently starting to get dizzy from blood loss. Not ideal.

The door slid back open, and Dexter peered out. A large hall led out to one of the arteries that ran around the entire facility, most likely connecting to various side exits. If casino staff had an eye out for him, the safest path out might be to pick his way toward one of the smaller doors and then snake back around the perimeter of the building to his ship. Of course, he wasn't familiar with the intricate side passages of the complex, and there was a chance the casino had locked down the nonessential exits. And straight ahead, beyond the larger cross-passage was the promenade that split the casino floor. A direct route to the outside, and a much more direct route toward the ship.

Dexter straightened and started down the hall. There were a few people visible milling around. He kept his head low, taking in as much as he could as he crossed the larger path. The crowd had thinned, but it seemed to be business as usual.

He swallowed as he approached the gaming floor and quickened his pace, weaving his way past the credit alcove. There, right in the center of the row of booths, Ritsa Rabani and two men in gray security uniforms were talking to one of the tellers. No guns were visible, but these were security staffers, sure to be armed.

The lobby was about 10 meters away, and the front entrance another 20. If he ran, he was going to attract attention, but he didn't have far to go. The landing pad was right outside. He closed his eyes and shook his head, heading into the open.

He kept a steady pace as he crossed in front of the alcove. Out of the corner of his eye, he saw Rabani move, openly signaling to the other two.

He broke into a run without looking back. There were no doors at the front—just a gigantic opening in the wall. Of course, they might have had a large emergency field barrier, something security could throw on to seal people in. It would have been hard to implement considering all the people constantly traversing back and forth, but an emergency was an emergency. Not something he had ever really had to worry about before…

He hit Spiral Sky Boulevard without slowing down, then glanced back as he crossed to the landing pad. The men in security garb were getting into a car with another man. Now at least one refractor was visible—an enormous-looking Hessdalen rifle. Dexter swung his attention back in front of him. If they knew where his ship was, they could have easily disabled the drive to keep him from leaving. Of course they would know where his ship was.

The Zenith Explorer was straight ahead, stationed another 20 meters away. The long ship was as he had left it, poised on its landing skids, facing its tapered cab toward the casino. Hopefully, there wouldn't be any trouble getting it into the air.

The car behind was already airborne, gaining on him fast. Jayjay would probably still be in surgery, so getting the ship rolling was going to take some doing on his part, but he would be safe for a little while as soon as he had the ship sealed up with him inside.

If Jayjay were available, she could feed the calculations to the ship in a second, and he would be off the planet before anyone was able to remotely disable the ship. That is, if they hadn't already disabled the ship.

Plasma blasts exploded on the pale pavement to his left and right— possibly warning shots, possibly not. He hit the platform of the gangway without slowing down, then tripped over his own feet, barely maintaining his balance as a bolt of superheated liquid energy sliced past him, hitting the ship centimeters from the control pad at the hatch. He dashed the rest of the way up the gangway and bolted inside as the security staffers leapt out of the car and started sprinting toward the ship. Plasma rained on the hull. Dexter shot through the main compartment to the cockpit, diving around the pilot seat on the left and positioning himself in front of the secondary CTA interface, closing the gangway and tapping quickly through the self-diagnostic as he sat down in front of the built-in dash monitor. The ship was responding, apparently unmolested. The com connection had cut out, presumably due to whatever had caused the general blackout, but the casino people hadn't gone to the trouble of commandeering his access... apparently they had assumed he wouldn't make a break for, or at least that he wouldn't make it all the way back to the landing pad.

"All right, Jayjay, it would be great if you're up." He leaned forward and punched up the com at the center of the control shelf. Jayjay didn't respond. He double-checked the event timer, set to Scalaway time. 04:16 NZS. The procedure hadn't been scheduled to finish up until the 0800 hour, but there was always a chance they might have gotten her problem worked out early. He shook his head. No such luck.

Without Jayjay, he wasn't going to be able to bypass the fusion ignition sequence for the IXE lift cannons… getting the ship off the ground would be significantly less instantaneous. He gritted his teeth and looked out the front window. A cargo rig was entering the landing pad with a massive industrial rock-cutter suspended above its belt chain.

He held up his hands, looking up. "But I didn't do anything!"

These people were going to render the ship permanently unflyable if they could.

His eyes fell on two controls in the lower left corner—arm and release keys to the double-turret at the bottom of the bow. If Jayjay didn't get online soon, he might actually have to shoot at someone.

No. Pulse plasma volleys from the modest turret cannons wouldn't work fast enough to disable a huge rock-cutter—maybe a couple of people would go down, but the one working the cannon would be protected by the thick shielding. Engaging the gunmen wasn't going to solve anything. He shook his head and glanced at the opaque panoramic display glass that wrapped the front half of the cockpit beneath the glareshield, brushing his left hand over the trio of MUDI touchpads and swiping the Tier 1 thumbwheel. The primary flight windows popped up around the pilot station, flashing glowing navigation data that matched the color of the green-on-green monitor phosphor. He keyed in a flight plan interrupt, barely conscious of the text log as it appeared in the monitor, and reached forward with his left hand, sliding the throttle to escape mode as the engine rumbled to life beneath the floor panels. There was a chance he could lay in a basic command stream and override the power flow protocols, get himself off the planet on a short hop and have the ship stand by for destination coordinates. It was going to be close.

The monitor blinked and Dexter leaned over on the com. "Jayjay?"

"Did you get your money's worth?" The voice was crisp and clean through the guided neutrino decoder. Angelic, on this particular occasion.

"Guidestars, I thought you were going to be in surgery four more hours. Never mind, Jayjay, just get me out of here—I need you to bypass ignition, I need ice cans right now." The cargo rig had positioned itself with the barrel of the cannon aimed directly at the cockpit. The gunmen were already moving out of range behind the rig.

"So you finally wore out your welcome. I won't say I didn't warn you." Jayjay sounded inappropriately amused. "You're all set."

Dexter unhooked the helm from its recess in the control shelf and jabbed at the console, activating the gravitonic field and IXE lifters. The Explorer rose, and he moved both hands to the butterfly grips of the helm, pressing it forward and surging away from the Blue Topaz in a loose upward spiral. A reverse view appeared in the window near the PDG's right extreme, showing the landing pad 100 meters below in the space of a second, beneath a spray of ionized xenon. The rock-cutter was already invisible in the distance.

He switched to on-board control, glancing down at his ruined clothes, then sighed and sat back as the purple-tinged atmosphere faded to black emptiness.

III   PROFANE INDENTURE

"So the fire's-eye was held on Dessa for a span of 80 Deiassan lives, all the while hidden away by the one who held it—a mortal man changed by this source of undying energy, a man both blessed and enslaved by its power. But in the stone's twilight, it would be offered up to a potential heir as its keeper tired of his burden, and in this way the man compromised his long solitude... the decision would color the fate of the stone, but not in the way he had intended.

"For some who toiled in the dark, unaware of the brilliant light hidden in their midst, the effect of the stone on their lives would be like a drop of blood in a pool, unraveled and boundless in a space of an instant, irreversibly blended within the environment, spreading outward... ever more conspicuous."

... GCL AE.001
Phi 00 00 00.00 / Theta 00 15 37.33 / Rho 00.00 / JD 2446198
Alpha Confinii: EARTH; "Caracas, Venezuela"; 13 May 1985 CE

Raindrops hammered the roof of the prison compound, somewhere above the mold and lichen of the dirty cell's untended ceiling. Rafael Avila sat in the corner, smoking a kretek cigarette. The only openings were a barred hole at the eye-level of the iron door and a slot near the floor for food. Rain was the only evidence of how near he was to the outside.

The ceiling lamp buzzed with electricity, casting just enough dismal light to keep a man from going insane. It was an isolated jail cell, not far from the road but hidden by the jungle growth, a small metal box of a building originally designed for short-term incarceration. But enemies of the state were locked away across the countryside in similar fashion, jailed and forgotten, with little more than a rusted cot, a toilet hole, and an occasional bowl of dog-food. Rafael took the cigarette out of his mouth, pinching the black paper between his thumb and forefinger and watching the trail of smoke for a long moment. It was no different here in this supposed democracy, this self-proclaimed place of law and order. Panamá, El Salvador, and Colombia, now Venezuela. It was all the same.

The American prison would be far more sophisticated. If he reached America, escape would be nearly impossible. But the American agents would have a hard time getting him to the federal penitentiary in Miami—there were always opportunities during prison transfer. He only needed a small window.

67

He stood and crossed to the door, taking another long drag of clove-sweetened tobacco and nicotine. He peered through the barred opening at the young Venezuelan soldier standing guard and exhaled, letting the smoke bleed into the outer chamber. The man saw him and looked away, stiffening as he moved a hand to his belt, brushing his sidearm. Rafael frowned and turned, stalking back toward the tattered cot.

The difference now was that the eyes of the U.S. government were on him—he was no longer another failed recruit of the Army's covert training school in Panamá, someone easily buried in the anarchy of Central America. To the Americans, he was an embarrassment, maybe enough that they had plans to silence him before he was able to give his own accounts of the Army's exploits in El Salvador, possibly before he ever reached Miami. Now that he was well-known to the press, he was sure to be regarded as a threat to some powerful decision-makers.

But now that he was with the Cartel, the Americans knew that they had more than just Rafael Avila to contend with. El Patrón had freed prisoners before... the don had proved that no one was out of reach. Those who could not be bribed could always be killed, as Escobar liked to say in describing the policy that had made him one of the richest and most feared men in the world. *Plata o plomo.* Take silver or take lead. The Americans were strong, but they had already taken their share of the silver.

A loud clank interrupted the drumming of the rain as the lock was released, followed by the squeak of the outer door. Rafael moved back to the barred opening as one of the American agents entered the chamber. Hendricks, the point man.

The agent brushed past the guard and nodded without looking directly toward the cell. "Smoking's bad for your health, Avila. Don't you know that?" He spoke in English; the cabrón didn't even bother speaking Spanish around the Venezuelan police. Hendricks coughed into his fist and rested his other hand visibly on the butt of his gun. "Wouldn't want you to spoil your appetite." He stepped to the thick iron door, nodding and glancing up toward the ceiling.

Rafael grunted. "They are late with the food again."

"I guess you've gotten used to better accommodations since Isla de Coiba." He sniffed and looked around, moving around the chamber like a circling predator. "If it makes you feel better, you'll be out of here sooner than you think." He grinned, exposing the gold upper tooth at the left side of his mouth. The man looked like a goblin.

Rafael removed the cigarette and flicked it on the concrete floor. "You are moving me early?"

Hendricks nodded. "Operation Snowman just got bumped up. We move you out tomorrow." He knocked on one of the side walls as if he were testing it for weakness. "With any luck, the concierge service will be better in Miami." He paused. "Of course, in the U.S.A., the better conditions tend to go to the people who are more cooperative."

Operation Snowman. It was impossible to tell whether the Americans were using the true code name for the extradition or whether they were making a feeble attempt to aggravate him. He ran his tongue over his upper lip, tasting the beaded sweat, then rubbed a forearm across his mouth and spat toward the corner of the cell.

Hendricks exhaled and scratched the back of his head. "You know how this works, Avila. Help us with the don and things go a lot easier."

Rafael lowered his brow. The Americans were no better than El Patrón, descending on Central America with their Army and their CIA trainers. They applied as much pressure as necessary to get what they wanted. They preyed on the lost young of war-ravaged homes, molding them to do their bidding, using death squads and murder to achieve their politically motivated ends. The father of the Cartel was nothing more than a business man who had followed the CIA's blueprint for success. And they had shown no honor. El Patrón did not abandon his people... a friend of Pablo Escobar was a friend for life. The CIA had already demonstrated how easily they discarded their human assets when their initiatives led to disaster.

He lifted his arms and twisted, stretching his shoulders. "I have said what I mean to say."

"Your choice." Hendricks headed back to the outer door, then stopped as the guard moved out of his way. The agent shrugged. "We leave for the transport 0-600. Give us trouble and we take you down. Consider yourself warned. Nothing personal." He leveled his eyes at Rafael.

"Keep your warnings." Rafael crossed the cell and pressed his face to the tiny bars in the door. "I was trained at your school in Colón. I know what your warnings are worth." He breathed. "Tell me, agent. Do you lie to yourself so you can sleep at night, or do you actually find pleasure in watching men pay for the crimes you made them commit?"

"Made them commit?" Hendricks lingered at the chamber's exit, glancing at the guard. "My dossier says you were in trouble plenty without our help before we pulled you out of prison on Coiba. You were a Casco barrio rat and a murderer." He crossed the floor, meeting Rafael's eyes. "You were also in the Atlacatl Battalion. We consulted with Special Forces on a few Salvadoran counter-insurgency units, but we didn't tell you and your alumni friends to go into El Mozote and slaughter an entire town. Hundreds of women and children, raped and burned. That was you, Avila. You were on your own, just like you are now."

Rafael stared coldly back through the bars as the muscles of his jaw tightened. El Mozote! The Americans had washed their hands of the blood, but the battalion had done exactly as their CIA trainers had intended, letting loose a band of armed murderers to subdue the leftist Salvadoran population, then sending their Special Forces to hunt down their monstrous creation, making them disappear one by one. The soldiers of the CIA's school in Colón were either left dead or left to rot back in their scattered jungle prisons.

The agent's face broke into another demonic, glinting smile. He narrowed his eyes. "We have you tied to 72 deaths, and we both know that number should be a lot higher. We have footage of you entering the Palace of Justice in Bogotá last month, just before the rebel raid that left 11 justices dead and the fire that destroyed federal evidence against your friend, Pablo Escobar. So let's be honest… you're a dangerous man to have out there. Makes sense to me why society would want you locked away for good."

"Qué broma! Me quieres muerto. You want me dead, not in one of your hediondo jail cells."

The agent scratched his chin and frowned, nodding. He took out his gun and tapped the barrel against the bars. "If we wanted you dead, you'd be dead. Remember that, Avila." He paused. "Operation Snowman is cut and dried. Frosty goes to America, until we hear different."

Rafael growled, leaning close to the barred opening. "Hijo de puta! Todos estaremos muertos muy pronto." With the door gone, no sidearm would have stopped him from attacking. Hendricks was trained to kill, but that did not mean he would react in time. For the American agents, facing death was an exception, not routine. All it would have taken was a split-second of fear and indecision. A moment of doubt.

"I'll see you at 0-600." Hendricks flashed another smile as he backed toward the outer door. "Sleep well, Avila. I know I will." He turned and headed out, side-stepping past the guard. The door slammed behind him with a bang.

Todos estaremos muertos muy pronto… we will all be dead soon enough. Rafael frowned down at the dirt-smeared concrete, nodding to himself. Yes, ultimately they would all be dead—he, Hendricks, and everyone else, whether or not they thought their lives were worth more than that of a bloodsucking mosquito. But some would die sooner than others. He stared at the sealed outer door a moment more, then spat at the floor and turned, pacing toward the cot.

*   *   *

```
... GCL AE.001
Phi 00 00 00.00 / Theta 00 15 37.33 / Rho 00.00 / JD 2448870
Alpha Confinii: EARTH; "Philadelphia"; 4 September 1992 CE
```

The law firm was immaculate. The building had looked smaller from the outside—here was an interior decorator's masterpiece. A trio of elevators hummed at constant attention along a short hall outside the glass wall that enclosed the rest of the 15th floor.

Beyond an inscription on the door that read "Halpern, Sutherland & Kovach," the ceiling hung over a sprawling room. Men and women sat bunched in islands of desks on the open floor, typing and talking. People buzzed from one office to another, keeping the doors in constant motion and giving the place the air of a live coral reef. The focus of attention seemed to be on a conference room, where people disappeared through the door and emerged with new steaming cups of coffee and Danishes.

Light filtered in through windows half-dimmed by vertical blinds, playing patterns on a photocopier. The carpet looked as if it had never gone unbuffed.

The room was almost exactly it should have been, as if exported from a dream. All the dreams seemed to bleed into life eventually.

The room was crowded. Today was the day for job applications—visitors sat in chairs randomly scattered around the room, among the lawyers and secretaries, waiting for their respective interviewers. Everyone wore the same standard grays and browns, conservative suits and dresses. Everyone was anxious. It was the ideal environment for anonymity.

John Walker glanced down at his own suit and stepped away from the elevator. He would be able to stay hours without being noticed—more than enough time to familiarize himself and develop an approach plan. And with any luck he would see the woman. It had been almost five years since he had last seen her in person.

He looked through the glass panel, scanning the floor without moving his head. For the moment, Cassandra Prescott was nowhere to be seen.

Inside the room, a gray-haired man emerged from behind a door and beckoned one of the applicants inside.

Attorneys. They were the perfect manifestation of civilized law in the modern world. The codes of Hammurabi and the strict bureaucratic modifications of Rome had long since been perverted to a profit-making machine, a playground for rich merchants and power-hungry politicians, and a tool of manipulation and oppression, where immaculately dressed sirens lured their prey with promises of wealth and happiness and watched as their victims dashed themselves on the rocks by the boat load. There had been a time before the laws had been written down, when the community had functioned successfully on its own, and personal rights had been understood. Now, people were kept in fear of the law—fear of fines and imprisonment, and character assassination. Too often, the people were right to be afraid.

Still, there were those in the field of law who practiced the ancient profession with honor, who held their responsibility to the public in the highest regard. Walker closed his eyes and exhaled a long, even breath.

Cassandra Prescott had always been one of the special ones... it had been clear from the moment he had first seen her, feeding the squirrels in Rittenhouse Square as a teen-age girl. He had seen her smile, and he had seen her eyes, and he had traveled to the suburbs west of the city to hear her laughing with her friends. She had been born into privilege, but she had not relied on it. Her career ascent had been rapid and well-deserved, and her many accomplishments admirable. She had devoted herself to helping others, in her profession and in her charity work, and she believed in the health of the body and mind. She had long since demonstrated her strength of character, but one look into those dancing eyes on that day in the park had been enough. She had an inner light that few people had, and none of the trivialities of the secular world could obscure it.

Walker pushed his way past the glass door and looked around, searching the faces of the people in suits as he moved into the room. The mindset in the aspect of their eyes was as easy to discern as the bright colors of their power ties.

Too many people were content in these charmless surroundings, driven only by money as a means for consumption. They made machines to take them to further heights of convenience, becoming reliant on their continued technological advancement. The laws that had been created to make justice now worked against it. The planet had been so promising for so long... it was a shame.

He kept his eyes low, conscious of the thoughts that played on his expression, and headed for a gray, prefabricated wall next to a pair of chairs where applicants were sitting.

The world had reached new heights of corruption, and the spectacle had grown tedious. History was a repeated pattern of expanding human blight. Western civilization, in all its glamour and majesty, was little more than a modern version of the hordes of Asia that had exhausted the resources of their home and fanned outward, plundering Europe and spreading ruin in their drive for supremacy.

Walker risked a mild frown. It was at an end now. The conquerors had reached around the world and run out of land as their population grew. Perhaps they would one day move to the seas... or the stars. Perhaps they would just subsist in their polluted and strife-torn hovels and decay as the natural world died around them. Of course, there was always hope that the pattern would be broken. Enlightenment shined through every once in a long while, and there were many who still believed in a bright future. Regardless, the world of Humankind was no longer rewarding to be a part of, and life was no longer a blessing. For others, perhaps it was. Not for him.

It was time to give away the stone.

The 5,000-year-old secret had become a tedious burden, and something deep in the core of his being told him he could afford to wait no longer. He would face the consequences of emerging out of seclusion and divesting himself of the stone, and perhaps, he would live out his life normally, in the company of others.

It was an old fantasy—he had taken steps to end the long journey before—but now was truly the time. All the preparations were underway. Perhaps he would die in the process, but if not, he now had a purpose— another person worthy of the gift. He now had an iron-clad reason to walk away from it.

A large woman in a pink dress had noticed him. She got out of her chair and offered it to him. One of the applicants. He sat down and the woman stared at him, drawn by his eyes, subconsciously sensing his wisdom, his deep-seated power. The reaction was common. She was preparing to address him. There was room for idle conversation, but nothing needed to be said.

He looked at her sternly. The spell was cast—she turned away, and he was free of any interference. Then he heard a voice.

The years had only improved his hearing, as well as his other senses— he quickly blocked out everything else in the room. It was the woman's voice, and it was like music amid the coarse noise of the workplace, coming from the direction of one of the offices. Unmistakably the same voice he had heard nine years before... Cassandra Prescott had added to the natural, pleasant melody of her speech, developed a measured, direct cadence owing

73

to her confidence in her environment. Her words were sure, unfaltering. No question she had come into her own as a lawyer. She would be perfect.

There were compassionate people in the world, probably many who had led pure lives, deserving of reward. But there were few with that unique combination of passion and spirit, few who challenged the capacity of their intellect while retaining their humanity, who maximized the quality of life for themselves and those around their own unique way. If they still existed, he had not yet seen them. No one was quite like Cassandra Prescott.

Masquerading as a colleague would not work. He would need to approach her as a client, with a ruse that would draw her in slowly. Play on her compassion. A ruse veiled in honesty...

He stood and stepped away from the wall. The woman's office door was ajar, and as he looked it swung inward. The woman stepped out of the office and began consulting with one of the secretaries. Lustrous auburn hair was bunched behind her head, draping down the nape of her neck and back behind her shoulders. She wore pointed, angular glasses and a tan skirt suit, and she held a cup of coffee, standing casually as she emulated her words with her free hand.

His eyes widened. It had been a few years since he had seen her, and as familiar as her face was in his mind, it was never an adequate depiction. Less so now—she had become a truly breathtaking woman. Her success in her profession was apparent, but she might just as easily have done anything else she wanted, regardless of affiliation or acumen. It was a rare, powerful beauty, the sort that inspired art and legend.

He saw her eyes, and it was as if he were back in the park, nine years before, looking on as she fed the squirrels, smiling back at him with pure openness. She was comfortable with the people around her; she enjoyed life in a way that few did.

Every instinct was confirmed. He would do it today—he would bring the stone into the open air and deliver it to its temporary hiding place, and it would belong to Cassandra Prescott within the month. He would use the knife.

She was perfect.

*   *   *

Zack pushed open the door of his apartment and threw his car keys on a coffee table under the mirror. He looked at himself and grimaced, rubbing his eyes, then trudged into the kitchen and set his backpack on the counter. He rotated his head, cracking his neck, and glanced at the clock above the cabinet. Just before 8 a.m.

Sleeping through the daylight hours tended to make a person depressed, not that skulking through the backstreets of South Philly was a hell of a lot less depressing while the sun was up. Not such a good career choice for people who gave a damn about not getting their biochemistry all out of whack.

Of course, this time the all-nighter had been a choice. Not the worst decision he had made in the last week, but it definitely wasn't the best.

Six days since the last time he had put in serious time on a tail, but apparently he needed a larger recovery window. His lower back felt as though someone had been wailing on it with a two-by-four. His eyes fell on the cabinet above the sink.

The girls had stopped at a bar five blocks from where his car was parked; he could have just taken off, walked back there, and driven home. There hadn't really been a good reason to go back to Melanie's apartment.

Melanie Katsoulis. Homecoming all over again. There were probably a thousand different legitimate ways he could have engineered a smooth exit from the bar, and he had somehow managed to stay. He could have easily told the girls he would meet them at the bar, and then wised up while walking back to his car instead of horning in on a ride he didn't need. Now the night was shot to hell, and any chance of catching Imperato in the act and getting off this jackpot case was effectively blown.

Zack frowned, shaking his head. The lantern-jawed dipshit had probably just packed it in and buried himself in cards all night, but not necessarily. And it was going to be tough to account for the time if a certain lantern-jawed dipshit's father-in-law decided to ask.

He opened the cabinet and took out the single, half-empty Jim Beam bottle, setting it in front of him. Out of sight, out of mind… bullshit. He scanned the countertop briefly for a shot glass, then gave up and twisted the lid. He winced as the liquor stung his dry throat.

The other three women were already foggy. All three were Penn State grads—two from Melanie's class, and one from the class behind her. Danielle, the other brunette—she was the younger one. He hadn't known her

75

at all. The one frizzy-haired blonde definitely stirred up some memories, and the details should have been a lot clearer than they were. They were clear to her, anyway.

But why should he have been able to instantaneously remember a random handful of women from college? It wasn't as if they had spent the entire night reminiscing—the three girls had stayed for a couple of drinks at the bar, smiled and said goodbye, and left. He had known a hell of a lot of people at Penn State, and he had spent the last two years at a completely different college. Not to mention he had plenty of other things to think about.

He rubbed his back. Melanie was in better shape than he was.

He took another swig and left the bottle on the counter. The buzzing in his ears was dying down slowly.

He made his way to the office at the back of the apartment and blinked as he tried to focus on the old steel desk. Painful morning light was already creeping through the skewed blinds. A stack of overstuffed manila folders had slumped across the scribble-covered blotter. An overturned pencil holder was seeping ink onto a single crinkled newspaper page, and the desk lamp had fallen in the wastebasket.

He stretched and scratched the mask of beard growth on his face. "This is a crock of shit."

He glanced at the empty gun rack on the wall and instinctively patted his right side. The Beretta was in its holster under his jacket, tucked in the shoulder strap against his ribs, where it was supposed to be. If he actually started leaving his gun around he was going to have to seriously think about a day job.

He rolled his right shoulder and frowned at the clutter on his desk. Pinned under a dried-up rocks glass where the other folders had been shoved away were the only two active case files. One was active in a strictly technical sense—the folder had been collecting dust for nearly a week. A dead-end, pointless infidelity case that deserved to be flushed down the toilet and forgotten about forever. Long overdue for a wrap-up phone call, despite the limited amount of time spent on it and the marked lack of material for the write-up. Of course, another day of surveillance would make it look a little better on paper, even if it was a complete waste of time. Hell, the client had expected him to run a month-long investigation—no one was going to go up his ass with a microscope about one more day of billable hours.

He spotted a bottle of Tums next to the file, removed the lid, and popped a handful of tablets in his mouth, swallowing them down after a few cursory munches.

Outside, somebody's brakes screeched, followed by a chorus of honking. Zack glanced dully at the blinds. Somebody in the city had somewhere to go.

He reached for the answering machine playback button and paused his hand in midair. The light was off. The building power had gone out again. Crap.

The phone rang as he looked. He winced, recoiling. "Goddamn it!"

It rang a second time, and he jumped again. He moved around the desk, grabbed the receiver, and shoved it in his face. "Zack Wyler." He stared toward a file cabinet in the darkest corner of the room.

"Yes, Mr. Wyler, this is Hannah Adams. I believe we have some unfinished business."

Shit. The infidelity client, for the first time in two weeks. Like a goddamn demon invoked by thought. Zack rubbed his left eye and squinted. "Hannah Adams. Sorry, you're going to have to help me out here. I don't remember your name." His eyes went straight to the folders beneath the rocks glass. The Dunbar case was on the bottom, now buried under the Imperato file.

There was a pause. "I see. Okay, Mr. Wyler, I'm calling on behalf of Halpern, Sutherland, and Kovach. We retained you to do some work for one of our clients in a divorce case. Does that help?"

Retained. The word had a large amount of baggage attached to it. Zack frowned. "Yeah, right—the Dunbar case." Next to the file cabinet, the closet was open. Several hangers and a large pile of cotton shirts were clumped on the floor.

"Yes, well, we haven't heard anything from you in over two weeks. My firm gave you the advance you asked for and to put it bluntly, we haven't really seen a return on our investment yet. I would have thought your people would have had something for us by now."

Zack nodded. "I usually wait until the end of the billing cycle to do the wrap-ups."

"My firm is paying you a lot of money, Mr. Wyler—don't you think you should be keeping us up-to-date on your progress?" The woman's voice seemed to be intensifying.

Zack sighed. "You want a progress report. Okay, let's try this… I think you're barking up the wrong tree."

The woman sniffed loudly. "Barking up the wrong tree. Very colorful. We're a respected law firm, Mr. Wyler. Dogs bark up the wrong tree, not us."

Zack smiled and glanced at the ceiling. "Look, I did some digging, and I was on this guy something like 30 hours. Based on what I've gathered so far, Les Dunbar isn't shtupping anyone. Not currently, anyway. He's probably a bad husband, but you and your lawyer friends might want to try another angle if you're planning on pumping up the alimony."

"Oh, is that so? I find that hard to believe. I'm guessing you haven't had a lot of experience with married life. My client has been married to this man for nine years. I think she might know her husband better than you do based on a couple of nights, don't you? I assure you, we've got a very strong case."

"Then you don't really need my help, do you?"

Hannah Adams' voice got louder. "Excuse me—what kind of a response is that? I thought I was dealing with a professional—do you want my firm's business or don't you?" There were sounds of rustling and a creak, suggesting the woman was pushing herself away from a desk, standing up. She cleared her throat. "You don't really seem to have a good handle on this case... I think I'd like to speak to your manager now. Put me on with your manager, please."

Zack raised his eyebrows and yawned. "Sorry, ma'am, I definitely can't help you there. You hire Private Island, you get me—this thing's a one-man show." He suppressed a belch.

"Well that's obvious." The woman laughed. "Okay. I think I'm starting to see how this works. You collect your money up front, then do nothing and say you weren't able to find any evidence."

The light through the blinds was getting brighter. Zack rubbed his eyes and exhaled heavily. "Just trust me on this. I was there, okay? This guy had plenty of time to get his rocks off, and he didn't come close. Typically, cases like this, these guys take me on a midnight tour down Market Street hitting about three strip joints an hour, and I get enough eye-candy myself to satisfy about 90 percent of the male population. This guy... I'm telling you, he holes up in this tiny local dive with his buddies and spends his nights in a beer mug. There wasn't a female within five blocks of that place—he didn't get one sniff in there."

The woman was silent for several seconds. "Oh, good—now I know what I'm dealing with. I suppose you're going to show me receipts that prove how hard you've been working the case, how expensive everything is. Is that it? You have some system worked out for turning your personal entertainment into fake invoices?" She hesitated. "All right... let's just suppose you did do 30 hours of legitimate detective work. 30 hours is what, two, three nights? Really, that doesn't seem like an awful lot of work for an entire month, Mr. Wyler."

Enough. Apparently the woman was content to keep the conversation going until she heard what she wanted to hear. Time to shut it down. "All right, listen. That's not how it works... Ms. Adams, was it? You think because you paid up front you can push me around? Doesn't matter how much money you give me, it's not going to make me like this guy any more for a cheater. I do surveillance, I don't manufacture bullshit."

"Now look, I never said—"

"You paid me to check up on this guy, and that's exactly what I did. It is what it is. If that doesn't help you win a big settlement, tough shit."

"Excuse me, what gives you the idea—"

"And for the record, a $500 retainer covers the initial consultation plus the first 20 hours or so. You still owe me for another full day of surveillance, and you're lucky I stopped running the tab when I realized I wasn't going to find anything."

"You must be out of your mind if you think you're going to get additional money out of this firm."

"You don't have a choice, sweetheart—you signed the contract yourself."

The woman inhaled sharply. "I am not your sweetheart, you pig!" Her voice went up an octave. "You think that contract entitles you to be a bastard?"

"No. The contract entitles me to cash, as you know if you really do have a law degree. Wasting 30 hours of my life tailing a sorry-ass sap and then catching shit when I try to collect for my trouble, that's what entitles me to be a bastard."

That did it. The woman's voice trembled. "If you think I'm going to let you get away with talking to me like that... I could have your license. It would be so easy."

Another satisfied customer. Zack raised an eyebrow, shaking his head. The woman was a venomous, egotistical, spoiled little baby, probably from somewhere on the Main Line, maybe new to the job, not used to dealing with the city folk. And he was next-morning drunk and tired. And why was he still talking to her? "Look, lady, find yourself another detective, or go through the garbage on your own time. And next time try not to be such a bitch about it. I'm not listening anymore." He coughed into his hand. "I'll try to get that bill in the mail before the end of the month, if it makes you happy."

"Low-class asshole—"

Zack hung up the phone and put his hand to his forehead, turning away from the window. His temples were throbbing. The hangover had begun. "Goddamn crock of shit!"

He stepped to the desk and pulled out the Dunbar file. It had been utterly blown-off for a full week now, largely because he had been about as sloppy as ever in compiling the receipts. The photos were lame, and could have been thrown together in a single night. Under the circumstances, if he did manage to patch together a semi-decent-looking invoice, it wasn't going to hold water.

He glanced back at the phone. Hannah Adams might have still been talking, since the woman clearly didn't get the concept of phone closure. Probably could have been handled better.

I thought I was dealing with a professional...

He sighed and shook his head. He might not have been at his best for the Dunbar case, but he could have been the most thorough, competent, anally retentive private detective in the world and it wouldn't have made the slightest difference. Truth was truth. Unfortunately for Fiona Dunbar's lawyers, the woman had nothing on her husband. The man was a golf addict and he liked to hang out in bars with his friends. Three days and nights of tailing him had proven it beyond a reasonable doubt, and one night would have done it. Fiona had been away for the weekend—guys like Les Dunbar who had a woman on the side didn't waste opportunities like that. Not to mention there had been no hits on his credit card—no hotel stays, no expensive dinners, no flowers or gifts. The lawyers had been on a fishing expedition, nothing more, nothing less. Hannah Adams had been looking to win favor from the partners of her firm by going with a cut-rate detective agency and saving them some labor expenses.

After all was said and done, she had probably done just that.

Zack smiled and abruptly laughed out loud. Good old trusty Yellow Pages ad. Highlighting the words "unfaithful spouse" in a $1,200, 6-square-inch rectangle had boosted business, but it sure as hell hadn't made business any easier.

He scratched his head as he exited the office in the direction of the bedroom. Infidelity was about the most debasing kind of case there was, and it was also the most common. It was the bread and butter of the detective service industry. Every person in a relationship had fears at one point or another that he or she was being cheated on, and most of them were right. No one was ever going to dispute pictures of his or her philandering significant other, and on those instances when it turned out there was nothing going on, the clients were usually too relieved to question the evidence.

Usually.

And then there were the lawyers.

Zack threw himself on his mattress, then noticed that the shade of the only window in the room hadn't been drawn. The bars on the outside were showing clearly in the early morning light.

He flipped his head so he was facing the other way.

Lazy.

He closed his eyes and felt his muscles relax. Jennifer. The frizzy-haired blonde's name was Jennifer. Jen McMillan. She had been in his Macroeconomics class that last semester before the transfer. At one point in time, they had known each other well. Her hair had been a little different without the perm, but she looked basically the same; she could still have passed for a college girl.

Jen McMillan. If he had stayed at Penn State about a month longer, that name might have been a lot harder to forget.

*   *   *

A great herd of people bustled along the wide hallway. Hannah stood in the doorway to her office, tapping a finger against her hip as she waited for a hole in the traffic.

Unbelievable. How many people worked in this building now? The place was turning into a zoo.

She realized she was holding her breath and slowly exhaled, stepping into the hall in front of a slow-moving intern. He clutched an armful of papers to his chest and stopped. "Oops, excuse me, Ms. Adams."

She ignored him, pumping her arms and picking up her pace. Idiot. The 20-year-old bootlicker pretended to be courteous, but he was probably just as chauvinistic as the rest of them, gay or not.

Craig Halpern was coming in the other direction, walking slowly along with one of the newer hires—a perky little brunette, probably 40 years younger than him. The senior partner was waving his arms around, making a big display of it as he showed her around. The man looked almost gleeful.

Typical. Hannah pressed her lips together and stared straight ahead, avoiding eye contact as she passed them. She weaved her way through the group strolling in front of her, veering left to the other side of the hall. Ahead, Cassie's office door was open. Good.

Hannah rounded into the office without slowing down, knocking twice as she passed the door. "Cassie, I need to talk to you... oh."

81

Cassie was sitting at her desk, on the phone. She looked up and held up a finger. "Uh-huh. Okay… I'll probably be there in about an hour. All right, thanks." She hung up and raised her eyebrows. "Hey Hannah. What's up?"

Hannah looked tentatively at the phone. "Am I interrupting? You're going somewhere?"

Cassie leaned forward and put her palms on the desk. "I have some time. Sit down—something wrong?"

Hannah glanced at the pair of black wire-frame guest chairs at the wall by the desk. "Well, I was hoping I could ask you for a favor." She turned one of the chairs toward her and sat.

Cassie shook her head. "Shoot."

Hannah cleared her throat. "I think I'm in trouble."

Cassie stared back at her. "Go on."

"You know the divorce case I'm on—Fiona Dunbar?"

"Yes. I don't know much about it, and I don't usually deal with divorce cases." She moved her chair closer, sitting up. "What kind of trouble?" She spoke slowly, deliberately, like a parent probing a distraught child.

Hannah frowned and squinted, nodding. "You know… maybe I should just go to one of the partners with this."

Cassie sighed and smiled. "Obviously something made you think of me. Why don't you just tell me what happened, and I'll help you if I can?"

Hannah glanced at the name plate on the desk: "C. PRESCOTT, LL.B, J.D., ATTY AT LAW." As formal as anyone in the firm—just like the name on the door pane, the plate left no hint the office was a woman's. Just as Cassie liked it.

Next to the name plate was a set of yellow and black bicycle trunks, neatly folded on top of a light blue sweatshirt. Cassie was making a show of looking busy, but evidently there was room on the agenda for exercise.

Hannah leveled her eyes at Cassie. "It's the detective I hired to investigate my client's husband. I'm having an issue with his methods. I think he's ripping me off."

Cassie paused. She cocked her head. "We have a regular service set up for detective work, don't we? There should be a standard contract."

Hannah wriggled in her seat, trying to get comfortable. "I went with a different agency. I thought I could save the firm some money."

Cassie shook her head, raising her eyebrows. "Okay. But… you do have a contract with the agency, I hope."

Hannah pursed her lips and looked down. "I'm not stupid, Cassie. Of course I have a contract. The problem is that this man didn't do the job and

82

he still wants his money, and now I'm still stuck on square one with my client, and I'm going to have to start over with the investigation on top of paying this shyster." She exhaled and held up her arms, still looking in the direction of the desk. "I don't particularly like the idea of having to explain to the partners why my expenses on this case are double what they should be."

Cassie cringed empathetically, sitting back. "Yeah, I've heard about problems like that before. You have to be careful about some of the smaller detective businesses; a lot of them aren't too concerned with their reputation among clients."

Hannah frowned. Cassie couldn't possibly have thought of something more patronizing to say. "Obviously I'd like to avoid having to pay this man additional money. His contract obliges him to account for his time, so we'll see what he comes up with as far as that goes. He's apparently putting together some nonsense evidence saying how much work he's put into the case, but I'm confident that if I don't pay him, he won't legally be able to collect." She shook her head. "I'm not worried about that so much, but I'd like to get back the money I've already paid him, and I was hoping you could help me with that."

Cassie glanced at her bookshelf along the wall. "I see." She clucked her tongue and looked back at Hannah. "So… it sounds like you're saying you haven't actually seen an invoice from the detective agency."

There it was. Hannah folded her arms and raised an eyebrow. "That's right."

Cassie's desk phone rang. Cassie flashed a big smile and drummed the fingers of both hands against the desk. "Excuse me one second, Hannah." She picked up the phone and rotated sideways in her chair. "Yes, yes this is she—are you calling about the baby grand? Yes, that's right. Uh-huh—the Sound Palace, on Fifth and Sansom. They had a Steinway available there for a hundred dollars less. Yep. Go ahead and check it—that's fine. Great. No, I can tune it myself…"

Hannah rolled her eyes at the ceiling. A Steinway! Cassie probably had an arrangement to have her assistant put calls through whenever she had a visitor in the office so she could make a big fuss about her latest shopping spree. She probably couldn't even play "Chopsticks."

Hannah peered across the desk at the delicate angles of Cassie's profile. She was sporting the cold, professional look, as usual, with her narrow designer frames over her eyes and her hair up in a tight-bound professional do. Cassie liked to talk about how she frowned upon using her femininity to her advantage, but that was easy for her to say. She could go out of the house with whatever look she wanted, with make-up on or without, wearing clothing more conservative than a nun, and men would look at her the same way every time. Her beauty was completely effortless, and she knew it.

Hannah laughed to herself. Cassie could pretend all she wanted that the idea of manipulating men repulsed her; it wouldn't change the fact that she did it every day. She was working it just as much as anyone.

Cassie hung up the phone abruptly and smiled again. "Sorry." She squinted. "Okay—you were saying you haven't actually seen the invoice. So, if you don't mind my asking... what makes you so sure this agency isn't doing its job?"

Hannah rubbed her neck, meeting Cassie's stare. "It's obvious. He says he's certain, based on 30 hours of surveillance, that my client's husband is not having an affair, which is ridiculous on its own. But my client is certain there is an affair going on, she's overheard phone conversations and found plenty of unexplained receipts. She knows, Cassie." Hannah leaned forward. "This detective didn't get back in touch with me for a week after I hired him, and he didn't even seem to remember what case I was talking about when I followed up with him. He sounded disoriented; he might have still been in bed, planning to sleep until noon for all I know. He was completely unprofessional, believe me—I can tell when a man is bullshitting me. He says he spent time on the case, but I think he hasn't even started on it yet." She straightened, tossing her hair. "On top of that, he insulted me several times. He used highly offensive, sexist language. He called me 'sweetheart,' he accused me of not being a real lawyer, and he actually called me a bitch before hanging up on me. This man has no business taking money from anyone. Maybe he's gotten away with this around other people, but I think it's time someone put a stop to it."

Cassie was sitting calmly in her chair with her hands flat on her desk, reserving any immediate reaction. "Well, you definitely hired the wrong detective agency. You're right—no one should have to put up with abuse like that. Where did you find this person?"

"He had a big ad in the Yellow Pages. Supposedly he specializes in divorce cases. And he was much cheaper than our firm's agency. You get what you pay for, I suppose." Hannah glanced at the ceiling, shaking her head. "Private Island Detectives. Apparently, there's only one actual detective... how this caveman manages to keep a business running on his own I have no idea." She looked at Cassie. "Zack Wyler is the man's name."

Cassie nodded silently, staring back for a moment. Hannah studied her eyes. Skepticism. Cassie was extremely sharp, and she would assume there was a certain level of exaggeration woven into the story. Cassie knew her well; Cassie had listened to her complaints more often than she would have preferred, despite protestations to the contrary. Cassie believed that the other women in the office were histrionic and overdramatic—as if she were above feminine behavior herself.

Cassie swiveled in her chair and stood, stepping toward the bookshelf. "What exactly do you want me to do—what are we talking about, here?"

Hannah shrugged. "I'm thinking you could call him for me and scare him into giving me… giving the firm… its money back."

Cassie turned to Hannah, frowning. "You want me to threaten him."

"That's right. I can't say anything more convincing than I've already said—he's not about to listen to anything else I have to say—but if he hears it coming from someone else, he'll know we mean business." Hannah moved closer to the edge of her seat, placing her hands in her lap, and widened her eyes. "Really, Cassie, I need someone who isn't afraid to go after this bastard, and you were the first person I thought of. If you don't do this, I don't have anyone else to turn to."

Cassie rested her elbow in the opposite hand and looked away, rubbing her forehead. "You could turn to the partners." She looked back at Hannah, waving a hand in the air. "I'm sure you're making much more of a big deal about this than they would. Look, I know you want to get back at this guy, but I really think you should consider letting this go. It might not seem like it right now, but you really are better off in the long run cutting your losses. Why don't you just bounce it off Craig—he's not as much of a monster as you think."

Hannah rolled her eyes, tipping her head back. "Oh, sure, just bounce it off Craig. Are you kidding? That is not an option, Cassie." She shook her head, clamping her mouth shut and exhaling through her teeth. "You might get away with a stupid mistake that costs the firm money, but you've been here longer than I have, and you make them more money. Do you realize how many people they've hired around here just in the past month? They don't need me. So you're telling me you would have me risk my place in this firm because you don't want to stoop to making one phone call."

Cassie folded her arms and sighed, looking down at the floor. "Hannah. You don't have any real evidence the man didn't do his job—I can't go after someone no-holds-barred and threaten his practitioners' license based on speculation." She paced across the padded carpet, rubbing her hands together. "You realize that if I did what you're suggesting and he smelled a bluff he would have standing to come after the both of us with a malpractice suit? I would have no leverage, and this man is sure to know it's not cost-effective for a law firm like this to go after his license."

Hannah glared at her sourly. Coming to Cassie for help had been a mistake. Cassie had no intention of helping her; Cassie clearly felt that a person—particularly, a woman—who had made such an egregious lapse in judgment deserved to suffer the consequences. Cassie would have never made such a dire error herself and wouldn't dare deign to help someone who had… no, certainly not her. Not Cassandra Prescott.

Cassandra Prescott had no idea what it was like to need a job.

Hannah turned back to the window behind Cassie's chair and rose, smoothing her suit skirt as she stood. She turned to Cassie and raised an eyebrow. "I think you're right. I think I would have stood a better chance garnering sympathy from the partners." She turned toward the door.

Cassie moved in front of her and held up both hands, nodding without looking directly at her. "All right, hold on, Hannah." She cocked her head. "I'll look into it for you. I'll see what I can do."

Hannah raised her eyebrows. "Good." She paused. "Thank you, Cassie. I appreciate it."

Cassie folded her arms. "I'm not going to threaten him, and I'm not making any promises. But I will look into it. Maybe you're right… maybe he just needs a nudge from a third party." She glanced at her watch and stepped subtly out of the way of the door. "I probably won't be able to do anything today… I'll let you know before the end of the week. I'll do a little poking around, see what I can find. And then we'll go from there."

Hannah stared at her. The light was reflecting off the lenses of Cassie's glasses, hiding her eyes. Impossible to know for sure if she was being up-front…

Hannah smiled. "All right, then. Hopefully you'll have some good news for me before the end of the week." She moved past Cassie, stepping through the doorway, and turned. "If you're looking to dig up dirt on the man, I wouldn't think it would take too much effort. Remember… Zack Wyler."

Cassie nodded, holding the edge of the door. "Right. Private Island Detectives."

"Exactly. Good. Thanks again, Cassie. You're the best!"

Cassie bowed her head briefly and closed the door. Hannah dropped her smile, spun, and stalked back down the hallway.

*   *   *

Cassandra Prescott exited the big, brick nursing home building in the same outfit she had been wearing when she had entered—a snug periwinkle sweatshirt over yellow spandex. The outfit was new, and she had left the office building much earlier than usual, but the routine was the same. As always when she was in running clothes, she wore no glasses. The daylight was beginning to fade, but for a brief, enchanting moment, a break in the clouds set off her face as if she were standing before an open flame, animating her brown eyes even from across the wide street like a pair of magnificent, glistening stars.

She had gone straight west across town, taking Walnut Street all the way, moving slowly, pacing herself, and jogging in place when the traffic and the lights had stopped her, heading over the bridge and into University City. The path from her place of work to her brother's home. Always the same route, always on foot.

She hesitated next to one of the trees that flanked the building's entrance, looking back and forth. For a moment, her gaze angled straight back across the street, lingering. She sensed something… but there were too many others. Across from the nursing home, there was a bench, and there was a pick-up zone to the right. There were loiterers and passersby. Her eyes never settled on the tiny public seats in the shadows along the wall.

Staying close seemed so effortless now. It would have been easy to arrange another look at her face along the way, but the risk was too great. Above all other things, she could not know she was being watched.

Now she moved southward, heading away along the opposite sidewalk, walking for several steps and looking down at her electronic device, then starting into her jog, shrinking amid the shifting throngs. She was on the path home to her grand apartment building, most likely to retire until early the next morning.

Her life was truly full, surely more than she knew. Changing that life would risk tainting her purity, but it was a necessary risk. She could do so much more. She was the one—there was no one else.

It was imminent now.

The man stood, scraping the iron wire of the chair against the cement below, looking down the street for a long moment. Then he turned and headed in the other direction.

*   *   *

Rittenhouse Square was a brisk 40-minute jog across town from the Philadelphia Nursing Home, not long enough for a decent dose of classical music on FM. 15 minutes of ads and then a set of the same crappy, overplayed songs she had heard in the morning.

The ornate gold-plated railings around the Regency Building's expansive marble front steps were visible from halfway down Manning Street, nestled between the sycamores just off the corner of the park. Cassie glanced behind her as she angled into the street, cutting across in the middle of the block. She sidestepped between the fenders of the tightly packed cars on the other side and picked up her pace as she neared 18th Street.

She paused at the corner and adjusted her headphones, frowning. Another bad station. Good radio was getting scarce… she was going to have to stay on classical music or find a decent portable CD player.

She removed the headphones and put them back in her pack as she waited for a pair of cars to zip by, then crossed before the light changed green, rounding onto the sidewalk and jogging up the steps.

The doorman was sitting in a chair by the wall under the overhang with a book in his hand that had the markings of a romance novel. He stood and set the book down as she reached the landing.

"Hi, Paulo."

He nodded at her as she moved through the door. "Ms. Prescott."

A well-dressed old man was seated on one of the couches in the lobby as she entered, and he gave her a steady, open stare that was borderline lewd. She shot him a quick frown before glancing in the direction of the reception desk. Janiqwa was smiling back at her. "Hello, Cassie, how you doin' this evening?"

Cassie smiled back without stopping. "Hi, Janiqwa, I'm good." She looked back without stopping. "How's it going here?"

"Can't complain, can't complain. Will you be taking the stairs today?"

Cassie padded across the checkerboard floor toward the stairwell, turning and walking backwards. "You got it."

Janiqwa shook her head. "Crazy white girl."

The buzzer sounded. Cassie cranked the steel door handle, leaning into the stairwell door with her shoulder, and shoved it open, moved inside, and started up the gray steps. The door banged closed behind her.

She took a deep breath of the stale air and laughed to herself. Sure, she didn't absolutely have to climb stairs after jogging across town, but it was six flights—it wasn't as though she lived on the penthouse floor.

She slowed her breathing as she ascended, making herself relax in the dim light of the stairwell as her footsteps echoed around her. Just an extra ten minutes out of the day. Less than an hour, counting the jog. It was the least she could do for her health, considering the mental stress and sleep deprivation she put herself through every day. There were a lot of people who spent a lot more time on personal fitness than she did—most people in the city spent more time on their commute. Realistically, it was a minimal effort. Not even close to being obsessive compulsive, as Janiqwa seemed to think. Of course, Janiqwa wasn't exactly an expert on personal fitness; the woman was 50 pounds overweight and was barely able to make it up the front steps without breaking a sweat.

Cassie frowned. Fulton would have said she was being obsessive compulsive, for sure. He would have said something about being locked into a pattern of behavior, creating a metaphorical prison for herself as a result of weirdness between her and the rest of the family, punishing herself for trying to assert her independence.

Somewhere between the time of the accident and the present, Fulton had managed to adopt a collection of perfectly annoying tidbits of advice that he seemed to love to toss out at any given opportunity. Losing his mobility and becoming the sounding board for an unending series of visitors had apparently added the dimension of smarmy radio psychologist to his personality. And he was fully aware of the torment he was now unleashing on the rest of the family. He loved it.

Cassie shook her head, breathing through her teeth, glancing up at the 12-story stairwell framed by the dark, square underside of the next landing up. She was pounding her feet against the pavement every day, but she wasn't getting any farther away from the Philadelphia Prescotts. Fulton, on the other hand, was a quadriplegic, but he was having no trouble distancing himself from the family. Despite the best efforts of their mother and father.

Cassie rounded the landing between the fourth and fifth floors. If her mother and father had gotten their way after the accident, Fulton would never have been free to make a decision on his own for the rest of his life. The original plan had been to set Fulton up in a plush permanent care room at Devon Manor, in the suburbs. Much closer to home. At Devon Manor, he would have been surrounded by doting servants and monitored every minute of the day. He would have been moved to one of the rooms of the Strafford estate for every family gathering—their mother would have seen to that. He wouldn't have been neglected, by any means, but there was no chance he would have been happy.

He was still every bit as sharp as he had been before he had smashed his

Porsche into a lamppost, even though his talking was labored and it took a concentrated effort for him to carry on a conversation. He still had the same philosophies, and the same opposition to their father's pocket politicians. The same aversion to being near their father. Fulton had always hated living in the house.

But one could never completely escape. In an effort to demonstrate control, their father had recently taken it upon himself to have Fulton transferred within the Philadelphia Nursing Home to a much larger room on the first floor, where he would have more direct access to facilities, and, potentially, to the outside. Fulton had objected vehemently, but this time, the words hadn't held the same tone of sincerity as protests of the past. Of course, if he did happen to secretly love the new room, he was never going to admit it to another living soul, probably not even to himself.

Cassie smiled, looking down at her feet. The room was beautiful. Bradford Alan Prescott, eminent patriarch of the Philadelphia Prescott family, was an overbearing control freak. He could be offensively intrusive and completely insensitive, sometimes blatantly insulting. Every once in a while, he did manage to do something right.

Of course, there would be baggage attached. Fulton would probably be obliged to play a prominent role in some public event in the near future.

Cassie reached floor six and sighed, retrieving her keys from the tiny pouch strapped to her hip. She jiggled open the lock and slid her way through the door and onto the posh, soft carpeting in the hallway.

She glanced up at the big, crystal chandelier as she headed for her apartment. Fulton would have to do a lot more than secretly enjoy a bigger room in the nursing home before he was as much of a sellout as she was.

She let herself in and closed the door behind her, turning the deadbolt and latching the chain. The foyer was dark, as it generally was by early afternoon. No trace of the incredibly annoying orange low-intensity tint of the lighting from the outer hall. She stooped and removed her shoes, setting them in the small basket to the left of the door, pausing for a moment, touching her toes and letting the weight of her body stretch the muscles in her legs and arches. She closed her eyes and straightened slowly, rolling forward on the balls of her feet and exhaling in a steady, even stream. She turned, rolling her head around her neck and dropping her arms to her sides, shaking them out as she rounded into the soft, ambient light of the expansive area that doubled as a living room and dining room, stepping down from the foyer and moving from the rigid solidity of the hardwood floor onto the thick Persian rug. She skirted the cushy loveseats and couches around the big glass coffee table and crossed the dining room, making a direct line for the kitchen.

She turned on the light, found her hand bag on the side table, and collected the headphones and radio, unclipping her pouch belt as she glanced at the phone on the counter. Five messages, according to the blinking red display on the answering machine. She slid her cards out of the pouch and stuck them in the hand bag with her keys, then crossed to the phone and hit the play button.

"Hello, Cassandra, I tried to reach you at work… your father wants me to tell you we'd like you to help us out at the wine tasting at the Convention Center… some important sponsors will be there, and Larry Rosenthal has been in my ear about making sure the family is well represented… there will be cameras, and we could use your face, dear… all right, love you, good-bye. Call your father."

Mother. Cassie looked at the floor. The second message was from Elsa. "Sorry to bother you at home, Cassie. Mr. Kovach just stopped by and said to tell you your 8:30 tomorrow with Walden-Kohler is cancelled… they want to reschedule for next week."

Cassie raised her eyebrows. She would need to be at the office early anyway, but the extra time would come in handy. The next message was from the Sound Garden, asking for confirmation that she was interested in purchasing a Steinway.

She pursed her lips. She didn't exactly need a baby grand piano, but she had put off doing something with the room long enough. The room looked empty with nothing but a keyboard stand, and the stool wasn't particularly comfortable; as it was, she barely played anymore. The big bay window was the perfect access point for a piano, and visions of a music room were the reason she had agreed to take the apartment in the first place.

That, coupled with the fact that her father had made an enormous stink about the idea of anyone in the Prescott family living in smaller accommodations. To him, anything less than the Rittenhouse Regency had been unacceptable. Not that it had been up to him…

The next message was a follow-up from the Sound Garden. A salesperson was trying to sweeten the pot by offering various package deals. Unfortunately for the Sound Garden, the people at Center City Music had already agreed to match the price, and their delivery service had a much better reputation. Cassie hit the fast-forward button.

She glanced back through the open doorway. On the other side was a pristine, immaculately carved mahogany dining room set with enough room for a party of ten. She had used it twice in three years.

There were a lot of things she didn't exactly need.

The last message was from Hannah. "Hi again, Cassie. Hannah here. Just checking up. I was planning on stopping by again—I know we all work flexible hours, but I hadn't realized you were planning on leaving early…"

Cassie stopped the tape. Just checking up! In fact, she had made it clear at the morning meeting the previous Friday that she had planned on leaving early on this particular day. She had also fully expected to have to work 16-hour days for the rest of the week on the Walden-Kohler merger… Hannah probably hadn't realized that either.

Cassie glanced sideways at a second doorway just to the left of the kitchen counter. The swinging door was propped open, showing the small adjoining room she had converted into an office.

She sighed and glanced at the ceiling. She was sweaty and in dire need of a shower, and she was under no obligation to be in any hurry. Hannah wasn't a client, and she was barely a friend on a good day.

Cassie dabbed at her forehead with the back of her sleeve. Of course, now her time had been freed up, and she couldn't rightly say she was busy if Hannah happened to call again.

She took a glass out of the drying rack, turned to the refrigerator, filled the glass with cold water, and took a long drink, looking back at the phone. She shook her head, paced back across the linoleum, and headed to the swinging door, backing her way through.

The laptop computer was on the middle of the desk, as she had left it. Her own personal little window into the world of information. It was fairly state-of-the-art—a much smaller version of the personal computers at work, a flat, square slab of plastic designed to open and close like a clamshell for easy portability, though it wouldn't have done her much good disconnected from the network she had set up in the office. She set the water glass on a coaster, and slid open the narrow drawer directly beneath the computer, locating the thick, black glasses that never left the apartment and fitting them over her face, sliding the drawer back in as she sat down.

To the immediate left of the computer were a traditional black desk telephone and a much sleeker-looking steel gray modem box. She reached behind the phone and unclipped the cord, attaching it to the outlet on the modem. She opened the laptop and turned it on, waiting for it to boot up.

There were two definite advantages of having an industry maven for a father: one was the safety net, not that she had ever needed it; the other was technological access. In the course of running his various textiles enterprises, Bradford Prescott was exposed to every business-related technological breakthrough that occurred, and he always had the news before the most of the public.

The latest advancement—and potentially the most significant one to affect her life—was an application called the World Wide Web, which was being put together on the Internet and was eventually going to unite every computer consumer on Earth via an instantaneous, user-friendly interface. Her father was already saying that the Web was going to have a bigger impact on the world than television, and he might well have been right. It had only been public for a year; it was in use, but even now, most people didn't have access to it. For the time being, its users were mainly commercial; there were various user fees that made it inconvenient enough to discourage a lot of the general public. Thanks to her father, she knew better.

The textured, blue pattern of her desktop background appeared on the laptop screen. She clicked the Internet connection icon and listened as the modem dialed up the local server, imitating the sound of a phone. There were several seconds of white noise, followed by music, as the connection went through. Good. No problems today, hopefully.

For a lawyer, it was a miracle. There were enough independent stores of information linked up already to provide details about almost any topic. Research that in the past had taken her long hours in the library now often took her no more than 30 minutes. There were glitches that still needed to be worked out—the software was primitive, and the hardware would have to improve a lot before it allowed people to take full advantage of the time savings—but it was infinitely better than having to slog through stacks of paperwork by hand.

The computer seemed to be laboring indefinitely, showing a blank, white page while a tiny animated bird cursor flapped its wings up and down despondently, and then the screen abruptly changed, showing her home page on the Web. She moved the cursor to the search field and entered "private island detectives."

A short list of references appeared, most of them sponsored commercials for Caribbean resorts. There was one article about the disappearance of a girl vacationing on Corsica. Nothing about the agency. She tried modifying the search and again got nothing. She shook her head. Apparently, this particular outfit wasn't up on the hot new way to advertise. Not really that much of a surprise.

She entered "zack weiler" and waited while the computer searched again. One reference appeared about a nuclear physicist living in Edmonton, Alberta. Probably not the same guy. She frowned. Spelling was key in a Web search. She dropped the first "e" from the last name, added the word "philadelphia," and tried again. She could always look it up in the phone book, of course, but that would require opening the desk drawer to the left of her ankles...

The computer found nothing again, but this time, a line appeared along the top of the screen: "Did you mean zack wyler philadelphia?" The name appeared as a link, highlighted in blue. She clicked on the link and waited again.

This time, the screen filled up with a new list of references. There were various links to Penn State football stories, but the one at the top was an article in a *Philadelphia Daily News* archive file about a police detective named Zack Wyler who had been terminated from the Philadelphia P.D.

Bingo. She moved the cursor and opened the link. After several seconds, the screen was replaced by a long, narrow block of naked, unformatted text under the heading "PDN CITY/REGION 07-89." She scrolled downward, scanning for the name. The page was huge; it apparently listed every article that had run in the paper for the entire month. She gave up and ran a word search for "wyler," and the text on the screen changed.

PDN 07-25-89 CITY/REGION
"COP GETS THE BOOT"
Ed McCauley
PHILADELPHIA DISTRICT COURT—Detective Zack Wyler of the 9th District was dismissed Friday from the Philadelphia Police Department, according to a public statement issued by Deputy Commissioner Harold Martin. The dismissal occurred 3 days after allegations of courthouse misconduct in which Wyler was accused of corrupting the testimony of a material witness in a murder case.

Wyler was an 8-year veteran and had served his district's Homicide squad for over 3 years.

In a press conference held outside the courthouse Tuesday morning, defense attorney Frank Ocala claimed that Wyler had had sexual relations with Larissa Blanchard, a witness for the prosecution against Jonas Sample. Wyler had also testified against Sample. A mistrial was declared after a lengthy recess, and Sample was released late Tuesday afternoon pending further charges.

Sample had been incarcerated since May 14, when he was indicted for stabbing Dantwane Elliott to death in Overbrook.

According to Deputy Commissioner Martin, Wyler's dismissal was an "internal decision based on job performance." Martin declined to comment on whether or not the action was the result of Wyler's conduct during the Sample case or in any way influenced by the defense attorney's press conference.

Cassie smiled thinly. Hannah really knew how to pick her private detectives. The woman had said it best herself: *You get what you pay for.*

Zack Wyler may or may not have been the bastard Hannah claimed he was, but if what the article was suggesting was true, he was definitely guilty of being less than professional.

Cassie ran a hand through her hair and clicked back to the list of links. Five minutes and she already had leverage on this guy. It would have taken her days scrolling through microfiche to find the same article.

A link further down made reference to the dismissal in a Harrisburg paper. She clicked the link.

> SPORTS/STRIKE 2 FOR FALLEN FOOTBALL STAR
> State College, PA—In 1979, Zack Wyler was breaking records. Now the only thing he breaks is the law.
> After promising freshman and sophomore seasons at tailback for the nationally ranked Nittany Lions, Wyler was on the radar of football scouts all over the NFL. He gained an eyebrow-raising 689 yards in 4 games, posting a phenomenal 172.3 yards-per-game average over the 2 seasons that still stands as a record for the school's storied football program. He followed up his debut season by gaining 1,235 yards in 10 games while sharing backfield duties with James Finley, averaging 8.4 yards-per-carry and compiling 307 all-purpose yards in an October game against Cincinnati.
> But Wyler's gridiron success ended 3 games into his third season. He was brought up on statutory rape charges in October of '80, and immediately cut from the team. The case was settled out of court, and Wyler avoided jail time, but it effectively ended his football career. He transferred to Temple University, where he failed to land a starting position in the backfield and eventually quit before the start of his senior season.
> He remained in Philadelphia and joined the police force, but after seemingly putting his past behind him, he has again plunged his life into disgrace. In an unprecedented act of public reprimand, police announced that Wyler had been summarily discharged after 8 years..."

Cassie stopped reading. She backed out of the article and sat back in her chair, shaking her head slowly. Statutory rape. Mind-boggling. It was basically a painfully stereotypical case of the big-shot college meathead letting his Johnson screw up his life, but unlike most misguided males this man apparently hadn't learned a thing with age. This man had probably gone through his entire life taking woman for granted, running roughshod over them as much as it suited him, worming his way into positions of power. Now he was running ads saying he specialized in hunting down unfaithful spouses. Preying on the distraught, vulnerable female like a spider snaring bugs.

He wasn't the only one. Cassie squinted at the screen, frowning. In New York several months back, there had been a case involving a bogus job offer in the classifieds—a man had actually rented out office space and lured a crowd of applicants there under the premise that he was hiring for an entry-level position. The man had meticulously presented a professional appearance, scheduled separate private interviews one at a time, and managed to expose himself to 12 different women before the police arrived. Any abusive misogynistic schizophrenic with a little extra cash was free to run an ad.

Private detectives didn't generally mince words; it was no stretch to imagine someone with Zack Wyler's reputation calling Hannah a bitch, as she had said. Not that there was anything anyone could do about abusive language. Even the most vicious verbal attack could be defended as perfectly legal. Of course, if a man's words did happen constitute an unquestionable, valid assault it was possible a judge would be compelled to hold him accountable. Technically. If it was provable; if it hadn't happened to be a private, unrecorded conversation. And if the entire world wasn't so completely desensitized to the idea of nonphysical abuse.

Cassie took another look at the references containing Wyler's name before closing the application and shutting off the network connection. Seven different hits about the Penn State team of '78-'79. The list of Wyler's minimal football exploits still dominated his subsequent transgressions.

It was completely unfair. Men got away with being ignorant pigs on a daily basis. A latent level of hostility toward woman was evident everywhere, even in a supposedly urbane, civilized culture. It was evident in the workplace dynamic, no matter how white-collar the atmosphere, despite all the so-called equal opportunity and diversity initiatives. Women were discouraged against filing sexual harassment suits because most of the time, they didn't win. Most incidents were never reported, and when they were, the women were invariably ridiculed, sometimes overtly. In the few pockets of enlightened society where sexist behavior wasn't prevalent, it was still accepted, whether the general public wanted to believe it or not. Even at Halpern, Sutherland & Kovach—one of the more litigation-conscious, fiscally responsible employers in Corporate America—there were men who had trouble controlling their behavior, repeatedly finding excuses to stop by, occasionally tossing out a lewd proposition and then lamely pretending it was just a joke. There were a couple of self-proclaimed alpha males at the firm who fit that profile.

Cassie abruptly yawned and stretched out her arms, and the dampness of her undershirt suddenly sent a chill along the small of her back. She turned off the laptop, snapping it closed and detaching the phone cable from the modem, then stood and stretched again, gritting her teeth as the gooseflesh sprang up along her arms. She exhaled loudly and pushed her way back through the swinging door, stepping quickly across the kitchen and dining room and heading to the right, toward the bedroom.

Leverage. She had plenty of ammo for a conversation with Zack Wyler, thanks to his sordid past. With any luck, he would back off without a fight, maybe even agree to reimburse the firm in the interest of mutual commerce, considering he probably preferred to avoid any new negative press. It might not have been completely appropriate for her to sort out Hannah's mess, but it wasn't malpractice to spend a little spare time acting in the interest of the firm.

Women deserved to win the battle every once in a while. After all, 1992 was "the Year of the Woman," according to the political pundits, referring to the "barrage" of women running for office in the upcoming election. Even though male senators would still hold 95 percent of the seats in the Senate if every woman running was successful. Even though a presidential candidate with a woman on the ticket didn't have a snowball's chance.

She entered the bedroom and pulled her sweatshirt over her head, tossing it on the oversized, faux-antique bed. She stopped in the middle of the wide credenza and caught her reflection in the dressing mirror as she slid her legs out of the running tights. Glasses. She frowned and stepped closer to the credenza, scooping her tights off her foot and looking again at the mirror.

We could use your face, dear.

Slightly less stylish than the glasses she kept at work. Maybe she would wear the thick horn-rims to the wine tasting. Her parents would have been thoroughly dismayed if she dared to show up wearing glasses at all. She smiled and turned toward the bathroom, peeling off her socks.

She should have gone exactly as she was now—thick horn-rims and sweaty underwear. Let the society paper cameras go to town. She shook her head at the carpet.

Of course, the only reaction that would have come from her father would be the same disapproving look—that single furrow of his brow and pout of his lips that had the power to melt away seven years of school and three years of living on her own in the heart of the city, all the experience, better judgment, and common sense that came with being an independent adult. A look that he never seemed to direct toward anyone else.

Cassie frowned flatly. She could have spent six hours in the salon and then shown up in the sleekest, most elegant gown she owned. Her father would inevitably end up giving her the look regardless of what she did or said; if it wasn't because of her dress, it would be for some other baseless reason. It was always baseless, and she always saw it coming, and there was no legitimate reason it should have bothered her, and yet, somehow, it always did.

She put her glasses on the credenza and headed into the bathroom, closing the door behind her.

IV   THE PROPRIETOR

"It has been said that the Deiassa have a tendency toward being wastefully aggressive, that they are defined by naked gluttony… greedily fulfilling whatever whimsical desire enters their minds as they feed an insatiable compulsion toward self-aggrandizement. This is not an altogether fair characterization, considering the fight for survival forces a species to be ruthlessly effective in its effort to be successful. Indeed, there are no true genetic pacifists among the 12 sentient species that came to dominate the Galaxy we know.

"But there are extremes in every culture, and certainly there have been Deiassans who craved power and glory. For some, it is their sustenance… they seek power and glory at all costs, and often, their endeavors lead inadvertently to the advancement of the greater species.

"By century 37, new sources of power were scarce indeed."

```
… GCL FN.036
Phi 78 24 37.00 / Theta -20 39 56.90 / Rho 35.26 / JD 3040382
Kappa Pegasi: OS, "Ustinov Vicinity"; 7 March 3612 CE
```

The soft earth tones of the cockpit's ergonomic resin surfaces were rather overwhelmed in the exaggerated glow of the photo-panels. Dexter Massengill leaned forward in the pilot seat, rested a hand on the caramel-smooth gloss of the dash, and stared as a set of atypically skeletal fingers seemed to blend with the keys and displays in a flowing pattern of twisting, unfocused lines. He watched for a long moment, then sat up and rubbed his eyes, returning his attention to the sloping plane of transparent quartz that now literally served as a window to another dimension. A spectrum of symmetrically balanced bands of color was on display, dull red at the edges, brilliant blue down the center. A perfect view of the Rainbow Road.

The structural subspace light shift was as familiar as an old painting, comforting in a way, though it was always coupled with a helping of the less pleasant effects of perceptual distortion. According to the human brain specialists, prolonged periods of exposure in hyperspace could potentially lead to neurological damage and, in extreme cases, schizophrenia. But the point was essentially moot, since in D6, it took under an hour to cross the entire Galaxy, and the diameter of the Human Sphere could be covered in about 90 seconds. There were those who thought the effects were cumulative, of course. If that was the case, most of the human population had been progressively wailing away at its collective mental faculties for centuries; whether present-day spacefarers had yet managed to render themselves feeble-minded was certainly debatable, based on some of the nonsensical ways so-called sentients conducted themselves.

Dexter ran his tongue around in his mouth, testing the odd shapes of his teeth. If the purveyors of panic were right about cumulative brain damage, his on-board hours definitely put him in the high-risk category. Not much he could do about it; he wasn't going to stop flying, so there was no point in worrying. With gravitonics filtering out all the truly taxing elements of space travel, the Rainbow Road was a quick, smooth, relatively painless ride. Once a person knew what to expect, the weird, subtly disconcerting effects of the Rainbow Road were barely noticeable, and if any real damage was occurring, it was on too small a scale to register on the repeated physicals. Life essentially depended on the on-board, so if the autodocs said everything was copasetic—if Jayjay said everything was copasetic—that ought to have been as good as truth for anyone.

Jayjay sat upright in the starboard seat watching code stream down the primary monitor embedded in the dash at her command station. In the suggestive warp of the hyperdrive, the color seemed to leap off the plastics of her skin and clothing, bathing her deceptively dainty form in a sky blue aura, mingling with the platinum brightness of her short, charmingly mussed hair. A silver fairy cast aglow under an argon lamp. In reality, she looked marginally less waiflike, but no less angelic. Aside from the cobalt tint of her skin, her designers had left no evidence she was anything other than a beautiful woman, no obvious hint that contained within her soft, petite frame was an inferno of ultraviolet radiation and self-perpetuated nanomechanics, a 900-year-old composite of silicon and nickel-titanium and a masterwork of densely woven circuitry that was still among the most intricate in modern application.

Jayjay was from one of the early lines of biologic-derived-anatomy humanoid, but the novel development of dynamic recycling with energy control accumulators and emission converters had enabled the androids to adapt themselves and function indefinitely, leaving no real need to improve the design. That and the onset of self-awareness for forms of artificial life meant the androids with the most experience tended to be the most skilled in their varied professions. They also tended to have the most interesting personalities.

Dexter shifted in his seat, raising his eyebrows and tipping his head in an overt stare. Jayjay was ignoring him. He smiled and turned back to the spread of color bands in the glareshield. Also hiding under that innocuous human façade was the lightning-quick neural capacity of several hundred thousand brains, with a resulting temperament that leaned toward the impatient. Sometimes she was downright ruthless.

The on-board computer shut off the hyperdrive, and the shapes and colors in the cockpit began to solidify.

Dexter blinked and lowered his gaze to the splayed handles of the helm jutting out of the pilot station directly in front of him, immediately noticing the cool smoothness of the authentic lacquered twisted-root, the scinti trademark in their line of human-oriented spacecraft. The idiosyncratic pictogram engraved in the wheel hub might have been artistically woven script or the stylized map of a local nebula. Each ship they put together held discrete insignia, it was said. But most of them were wind metaphors... the scinti had about a million phrases to describe the wind.

The intricate lines seemed fixed in place once again. Reality was back to being reality. Dexter looked at Jayjay. "I'm curious about hyperspace perceptual distortion."

Jayjay blinked. She shook her head. "What about it?"

Dexter shrugged. "Do synthetic minds get those effects?"

"Synthetic minds?" Jayjay shot him a flat stare. "Yes." She looked back at the CTA monitor and tapped in a command, presumably a query to confirm location.

Dexter paused, frowning. "I'm just wondering if the things you see are similar. Skewed visuals, overly intense lighting... or do androids have their own unique set of sensations, something a natural human wouldn't know anything about. I mean, do your photovoltaic arrays flare up, or do you get caught in a feedback loop—some data processing-oriented thing?"

Jayjay turned toward him and ran a hand through her milky, light-soaked bangs. "You really can't tell that you're being ignorant, can you? The input mechanisms are the same—my algorithms are based on a human neural map. Stimuli and receptors, just like yours. You know this." She sighed. "Yes, it's mainly visual effects. And so you know, it's not accurate to describe the android mind as synthetic. It's artificial, not synthetic. 'Artificial' means manufactured. 'Synthetic' means imitation."

Dexter nodded. "My apologies."

"Humans put the parts together, but each neural network is different." She batted her eyes. "You never know what you're going to get when hypermutation kicks in."

Dexter looked at the floor panels. "I never meant to imply you aren't original." He turned to the glareshield, now a frozen panorama of stars. "Where are we?"

"Sector Foxtrot November 0-3-6. Should be free and clear of the commerce lines." She stood up and dusted off her clothes as if she had just been tending to the engine. She leaned past Dexter and tapped the EMF indicator. The circular crystal proximity display remained devoid of light, and the tiny diode below it blinked green. "And we are alone. The ship seems to be working fine. Guess you managed not to break anything." She smiled and straightened, then side-stepped through the companionway to the passenger cabin.

Dexter rotated his seat backwards and watched her through the rounded portal as she moved along the aisle toward the stern. She was wearing new attire—a navy tank top and thigh-length shorts she had apparently picked up on Scalaway. Standard fare—utilitarian for someone who might need access to the conduit panels on her limbs. A mite slinkier than her usual garb, perhaps.

Dexter looked back at the stars. One yellow-white dollop stood out at dead center: Kappa Pegasi A. The Ustinov-Jih System, home of one of the more no-nonsense governments in the Galaxy, and a good place to air grievances without having to deal with a lot of red tape. It also happened to be a planet that wasn't particularly embroiled in the gaming industry.

The familiar pale blue brilliance of the Northern Triangle hung compressed in the upper left corner of the glareshield, with distant Deneb at the apex, making it fairly easy to gauge Jayjay's unconventional approach. "We're above the plane, I see. Coming in at a sharp ESE descent. I'd put us around minus-80 theta, plus-85 alpha, I'm thinking 3.5 lights. Still a long way out. You're thinking we should stay adrift until we talk to someone, I take it." He glanced over his shoulder. "What are you up to back there?"

She raised her voice. "Giving you some space. Take off your bandages—I want to see if those wounds are healed."

That figured—the sensation of gulak nails tearing his skin had just about left his memory. Dexter peered down at himself and gingerly touched the tape over his neck and chest. He opened his shirt found the edge of the tape, grimaced, and peeled it off, wincing. He rolled his head back and exhaled. For some inexplicable reason, having the autodoc dope a person up for bandage removal was considered excessive, despite the fact that they had more lidocaine on supply than they were ever going to use, along with all their other med stores. The sadistically apportioned adhesive on the tape was easily as painful as a garden-variety flesh wound.

"Dexter, did you take your bandages off? Come on back here."

He shook himself, zipped up his shirt, and walked back into the passenger cabin, rubbing his chest. He sighed. Stepping out of the more confined space of the cockpit into the main area of the Explorer was typically relaxing, particularly after the intensity of hyperspace. The interior of the scinti-made craft had been designed with an eye for human comfort—the ambiance was like that of a high-priced city cell on the ground. Cozy couchettes lined much of both hulls, ending at a semicircular lounge and dining alcove that led into a small, brightly lit galley bar toward the stern. Access panels were camouflaged expertly within the rustic, pleasing decor; metal surfaces were hidden under styrene molding and a taut, supple carpet. Plush, low-density urethane cushioning was everywhere forward of the galley bar. Everything was in warm shades of sienna and beige, lit with dimmer lines almost invisible along the edges of the ceiling. The scinti engineers had even managed to deemphasize the critical features that were typically more conspicuous on an FTL ship—gravitonic distributors, ventilation recycling, climate control mechanisms had all been flattened out and spread against the hull, completely covered by the molding. And all the emergency evac and prolonged suspension apparatuses were tucked away in compartments below the floor panels, amid the engine access crawlways.

Dexter made his way to the lounge area and plopped down on the soft seating. Jayjay was active in the galley; she had already opened a panel in the hull and removed the autodoc, essentially a short spindle surrounded by tightly folded spider arms and topped by a stack of rotating disks that served as the device's control head.

He spread his arms along the top of the couchette, looking back toward the bow. He nodded, sniffing the familiar simulated fragrance of cedar and juniper. The only real evidence that he was sitting in an interstellar vehicle were the three circular portholes along the overhead and the dug-out ladderwell in the starboard hull with steps leading down to the boarding hatch. But the ever-present proximity of the stars only added to the charm.

It also didn't hurt that the Zenith Explorer had been built to sustain a crew of eight. The ship was some 32 meters from scoop to burners, and a full 6 meters at the beam—a lot of ship for just two people, although Jayjay probably didn't see it that way. Of course, most people didn't actually live aboard their ships full-time.

Jayjay glanced at him. "How are you feeling?"

Dexter shook his head. "Wonderful until I pulled the bandages off." He yawned and rubbed the back of his head. "So when are we going to make this call? I thought the idea was to get this business with the casino taken care of sooner rather than later."

Jayjay frowned, cocking her head. "Excuse me. I thought I might deal with your injuries first, if that's all right with you."

Dexter squinted at her, sitting up. "All right, Jayjay—I don't really care about it. I was only asking because you seemed to think it was rather important before. I'm actually feeling tiptop, thanks to you, and I think I've had enough medical attention for the time being. Listen, I'm happy to make the call myself, if you want. Jayjay?"

Jayjay was facing the autodoc, touching her temples.

Dexter frowned. "Jayjay—are you all right?" He stood slowly. Another spell. The operation was supposed to have fixed the problem.

Jayjay shook her head. She focused on him, dropping her hands. "Fine. I'm fine." She blinked and turned back to the autodoc. "Let's worry about you. Demodiscosis is common in gulak subunguis lacerations."

Dexter moved around the bar, stepping onto the smooth flooring of the galley. "Jayjay, I'd like to run a quick check of your systems before we do that."

She whirled at him. "I don't need you run a scan on me—I already ran a complete self-workup through the on-board. I'm perfectly capable of issuing commands to the on-board." Her eyes were intense.

Dexter studied her expression. When agitated, her pupils tended to dilate a touch unnaturally wide, one of the oversights of her makers in their effort to replicate the human eye. It wasn't a look she held often.

She was lashing out, overreacting... possibly because she was scared about it herself; it didn't mean the Barrier Island technicians had failed to fix the mnemonic glitch. Not necessarily.

She waved at the cockpit. "Dexter... you think I wouldn't have the ship specifically look for recurring problems after what happened down there?"

He exhaled at the floor. "I suppose not."

"No. Trust me, if I still have this thing, I want to know about it." She looked back at the autodoc as one of its needle-tipped appendages unfolded from the spindle. "Now go lie down... we need to check your auto-immune response. Then we'll make the call."

Dexter nodded. "Fair enough." He patted the bar and crossed the lounge to an adjustable section of seating on the starboard side of the passenger cabin, where the hull molding was slightly recessed within a rounded groove. One of the eight berths. He tapped a small sensor just above the groove, and the couchette rotated into the floor, replaced by a slat of denser, more evenly distributed cushioning that extended farther into the aisle. "Well. It has been a crazy day, hasn't it?" He sat heavily, and a tingling thrill ran along his spine as all the muscles in his back seemed to simultaneously relax.

She raised her eyebrows. "That it has." She moved to the slat, and the autodoc glided after her, riding on its hidden maglev pad. It extended its jointed spider-arm toward Dexter as Jayjay stepped to his shoulder. "Take your shirt off and hold still."

Dexter pulled his shirt roughly over his head and hugged himself against a chill that was probably nothing more than imagination.

"Lie down."

He kept his eyes on Jayjay as the needle found his wrist and sank in. She was giving him a calm, reassuring smile now. Acting like herself, for the most part. Her spells before the surgery on Scalaway had been more pronounced, sometimes occurring midsentence. Sudden onset trances. She had shut down for as long as nine seconds, then resumed function as if nothing had happened. And there had been no memory of the event. But she had always been adept at detecting the problem afterwards. She had always known something was wrong.

Jayjay was nodding, lightly touching his neck. "The hotstitches look good."

Dexter glanced down at his bare chest. Hotstitches usually had a ghastly radiating burn that made them seem to stir in place and brought the thought of burrowing insect larvae into mind, but he had barely noticed these. "Yes, no one does skin stapling like this particular autodoc. On my ship, it's all the best kinematic effectors that CU can buy."

Jayjay smiled down at him. "You better not be talking about me like an inanimate object again." She frowned suddenly. "You know, I don't understand why you have a problem with med tape—it's not as if you have any body hair to rip off."

"It still hurts." Dexter made a fist as the autodoc withdrew the needle. Jayjay was definitely still herself. The snappiness was probably just post-traumatic anxiety, nothing more.

She looked at the display on the autodoc's control head. "This should take a minute or two."

The much larger, preexisting gap in Jayjay's memory may or may not have still existed. She hadn't mentioned anything about it yet, and she might have said something to him if the occurrences of 909 years before had come flooding back—the nine-month blackout surrounding her trip to the Large Magellanic Cloud. But the issue was a sore spot, and she would only share what she was comfortable with, when and only when she was ready. It would have been nice to know what the technicians had found; hopefully the details would be available when they filed their final report. For now, irritating her by broaching or pressing the subject wasn't going to make her any more likely to talk about it.

It stood to reason that her latest memory problems were somehow tied to that incident. From what Jayjay had imparted, the circumstances of that trip and Jayjay's pilot at the time were highly suspect. There was certainly a good possibility the pilot had tampered with Jayjay's functioning himself, removing stored memory and introducing algorithms to cover his tracks. The new hiccup might have been the result of a simple flaw in his programming hidden somewhere in an adaptive command register under layers of obfuscated code.

Jayjay spoke again. "Almost done."

The techs at Barrier Island could have missed a tampering-related corruption. It was possible the damage was irreversible; if so, it wasn't the worst thing in the Galaxy. Jayjay could live with a hole in her memory; any tampering-related flaw was containable—perhaps she would need additional surgery, perhaps not. As long as it wasn't TPM. For a TPM corruption, there would be no need for additional surgery.

Dexter closed his eyes. She didn't have TPM. No reason to think that, not now.

"All right. Autodoc says you're fine."

He rolled his head toward her. "I told you."

She smiled, and the organic composite elastoresilene skin crinkled at the corners of her almond eyes. "Now, let's go straighten out this Beta Lyrae thing." She stood and stalked toward the cockpit, calling over her shoulder. "I'll be surprised if there isn't a mark out on you."

Dexter sat up, glanced after her. True enough, the android face was an imprint of prototypical, measured beauty, with variety ranging within the limits of a defined set of mathematic proportions, but something about that sassy, dimpled smile of hers outdid the makers' run-of-the-mill model.

He put his shirt back on, pushed himself to his feet, and headed through the companionway, frowning. "A mark, as in they flagged my ID? You really think they would want the IPA involved in this?"

She situated herself in the co-pilot seat. "They might. It's your word against theirs, and the Blue Topaz has more clout than a nomadic gamer with no employment and no references."

Dexter waved a hand as he sat. "Well I have you to vouch for me, don't

I?" He paused, watching her fingers fly over the keys as her monitor came back alive. "I mean, I suppose I've been a bit of a gadabout for a while now, but you've known me for over five years—you must have noticed a couple of good character traits."

Jayjay shook her head as she tapped the com. "Don't count on having access to your CU anytime soon."

"Ouch."

Jayjay's eyes were on the CTA monitor. "I'm going through Eo-Nowar Port Com... see if they'll put me through to Municipal Control. I figure there rather than Bentonburg; in Bentonburg we'd have a better chance having our signal picked up by IPA surveyors."

Dexter glanced at the secondary monitor as it flashed the code Jayjay was currently streaming. He looked back at her. "You want to avoid the IPA? Jayjay, I didn't do anything wrong."

She nodded. "I know, but it's better if we contact them first."

"So why don't we just do that?"

She sighed and held up a hand. "Because they won't take you seriously unless you have an advocate. Trust me, there's a process here." She paused. "Okay, I'm through, and they are patching us through to the munis. We might be here awhile."

Dexter sat back, folding his arms and looking at the glareshield. "I see. Well, you seem to know what you're doing. One is almost forced to think you've been in trouble with the authorities before."

She raised her eyebrows. "I've been around a while." She frowned at her monitor.

"Maybe Salaman Nevis got you into trouble at some point? You said he was a bit of a maverick."

Jayjay didn't look back at him—a surefire indication he was treading on thin ice. Then again, a discussion of her old ship pilot might possibly shed light on the memory block. And they were liable to be drifting awhile; no better time for an interesting discussion than the present, and nothing was more intriguing than the mystery of those nine missing months. He rotated his seat to face her. "You think it's possible Salaman got you mixed up in something and then had your memory erased, maybe leaving some trace of experience about it? Maybe talking it out could jog your memory..."

Jayjay rolled her eyes. "I've told you everything I know about Salaman Nevis." She looked back at him. "When they find you floating alone in a spacecraft with the pilot missing and no knowledge how you got there, authorities do take an interest. As far as that goes, yes, Salaman did lead me into a run-in with the law. Beyond that, there's nothing to talk about, so let's drop it, shall we? Salaman Nevis is not my favorite conversation topic. Seven years, I'd think you might have picked up on that."

Dexter nodded. "As you wish."

"Good."

He looked at the console, trying to think of something useful to do. Her response was predictable—she hated revisiting old topics of conversation, particularly when they were about that part of her life. He had asked for it, and it was probably a good sign that she had reacted in typical fashion. Most likely, neither of them would ever know what had happened in the Tarantula Nebula in 2703, just as they would probably never learn anything more about the current mnemonic glitch. But no news was good news—most AI glitches tended to fix themselves through the examination process. With the randomness of an android's adaptive cognition factoring in, people often never learned anything about causation postmortem. The Barrier Island people had been extremely meticulous, reexamining Jayjay's procedures step-by-step, reviewing all the documentation with the two of them. There was no better place in the Human Sphere to take an ailing android, and there was no better test of an institution's effectiveness than how its staff handled themselves during a contingency situation.

Dexter's eyes fell on Deneb in the upper left corner of the glareshield, home of the Foundation, safe haven of free pirates. Foundation pirates had a reputation for causing chaos, targeting centers of commerce and holding them hostage for basis points off the profit margin. The pirate mindset seemed to be in favor closer and closer to home—the draconian laws on Valentina were a case in point. Apparently no system was safe. Just a day before, a band of marauders had managed to sabotage the Trojan belljar network on Stasya, a place that had been previously acclaimed by many to the most secure establishment in the Human Sphere.

He sighed. Sometimes chaos wasn't such a bad thing. Natural phenomena were just as much of a threat to standard operating procedure as anything the pirates could come with, and one particular phenomenon had just worked very much in his favor. The apparent cause of the blackout in Shel City and wide-scale system failures on Scalaway, two timely events that had effectively allowed him to escape imprisonment, was a surge of cosmic ray activity. Beta Lyrae B and Arcturus were among hundreds of star systems that had experienced electromagnetic disturbance. Not as lucky for most of the people in those population centers, to be sure, but chaos notwithstanding, the stars were quite literally with him.

He shrugged and smiled. "Well. I'm just glad they were able to get you fixed up in the midst of all that craziness." He peeked at her; she remained silent, avoiding his eyes. He lowered his chin and swung back toward the console, nodding.

The com diode flashed. The pilot station monitor switched to communication mode, replacing the mess of command circle-hexadecimal code with a single line identifying the neutrino arc source. A clean digital representation of a nasal, monotone voice filtered through the cockpit speakers. "Read... Scinti Zenith batto, Explorer Class, model Zoo-Hot-4, serial I-Lee-Go-Al-Bev-1216. Bu-shue, ENMC; qua fare?"

No picture. Apparently, the Eo-Nowar patrols didn't have a viable cam feed. Jayjay leaned toward the com, glancing at Dexter. "Read. We have an incident to report."

"Trey-bu... state the nature, please."

"Recreational practice violation, nonjurisdictional." Jayjay seemed to be focused just above Dexter's eyes, as if script was written across his forehead.

"RPV." There was a pause. A deeper, throatier voice took over. "Bu-shue, Explorer. ENMC Rec Branch, you have Escort Constable Dig Balboa... qua fare for you set day?"

Jayjay cleared her throat. "We had a run-in with the casino management in the Beta Lyrae system."

"Casino issues. And who is we?"

"Jajqrt170—I'm the IU aboard this ship, speaking on behalf of Dexter Massengill, the pilot. Dexter is here; he's a little shaken up from the incident."

Dexter raised an eyebrow. Jayjay bit back a smile and looked away.

"Massengill. Set incident fare happened in open space?"

"No."

"Trey-bu... so, set incident fare happened onside the planetary jurisdiction of your most recent harbor, and circumstances were such, reporting the incident to local authorities over set-la jurisdiction was ney feasible?"

Dexter frowned. Jayjay shook her head. "No—I told your operator this was nonjurisdictional."

"We have our own criteria on that, set-la. Just a few more questions..."

Dexter cut in. "Excuse me, Mr. Balboa, the incident took place in Beta Lyrae, but I needed to leave the system..."

"You're Massengill?"

Dexter nodded, glancing at Jayjay. "Yes, I'm Massengill. Now look, I had to put down on Scalaway to pick up Jayjay, but the authorities there are preoccupied with another incident, and they didn't have time to bother with this…"

"Ah, wey, Barrier Island. Set some shoze, la. So you know, we general recommend reporting all incidents at the prem location when your body is ney in immediate danger. Set fare shoze mey-yer easy for us patrolmen if information relays timely and by the proper channels, with respect to Barrier Island. Too, set is mey-yer for the advocate. Helps with the tempo. So next time you fare wait out the locals and make them hear your report, wey?"

Dexter sat forward, squinting. The Ustinovie patwa was a bit jarring on the heels of the clipped, rarefied English of a cosmopolitan nucleus like Beta Lyrae. Jayjay might have thought to flip up the transcription text. "Are you telling us we have to go back to Scalaway to report this?"

Balboa laughed. "Perdone, mo-nome. Par-yen—ney fare set-la." He paused, then spoke more slowly, as if the dialect difference had just dawned on him. "Ah, I will not make you do that. I can process you in-system."

Dexter brightened. "Good. That's a relief."

The patrolman's voice resumed its boisterousness. "Couple more things, so I fare know what we have, see. Kell type… ah, what's the nature of the violation?"

Dexter glanced at Jayjay. She looked as though she had no idea what he was going to say in response. He nodded. "Well, it seems they think I was doing some long-term grifting—I go there fairly often. I'm not a grifter, but I do win, well, more or less always. I have this luck; I can't explain why, really, so I can't say I blame them for the initial reaction…"

"You're genome psi?"

Dexter rubbed his hands together. "No, no, I've been tested a number of times, average CRP, negative for pineal indicators, no spikes. I've done nothing illegal, and I'm happy to submit to verification."

"Wey, par-yen fret—no worries, we can fare test set-la, if need be. Go on."

"They argued that the odds were too small for a person to win at that rate, over an extended period, and therefore, I had to have rigged the game. I wouldn't even know how to rig a game of loqaqi—everything goes through the hands of the dealer."

Jayjay made a loud exhalation sound. "Okay, this isn't relevant. Bottom line, casino management is demanding all his credit winnings, and they threatened to process him as a criminal unless he explained his methods of success. He escaped while they were preparing to move him to a holding cell for the maximum 60 days prior to trial."

"Wey? Set-la, that's a petty twist. So we have a possible bonafide cap case?"

Dexter looked from Jayjay to the com on the dash in front of her. "That's right. They assaulted me, and fired on me and my ship as I ran. I could have been killed. I barely made it off Valentina."

Balboa paused for a long moment. "Par-yen rey loqaqi, I don't know bu-cue on this gaming or how they fare do things at the grand casinos, but we have some few riffraff card joints don-see on the lower levels. They let some few bodies win occasional and keep the losers to think they have a shot. Hire others to fuss in public like they win continuous. If a body complains, maybe those business-runners give up a spot of CU, or maybe they ghost the om-bu. Bu-cue mal shoze, Massengill. Sey gone to fare do some time searching up evidence for set-see." Low, incoherent mumblings of at least two individuals came through the speaker. "Guarantee. You have clearance to put don-see in-city—we are sending you the port call letters present-time. Come don-see soon as you coordinate."

Jayjay sat forward, shaking her head. "We're not putting down until we know where we stand with the scarabs. If there's a warrant, we're going to need protection assurances."

"Set ney… it won't help your situation. I'm no advocate, but the slower your tempo, the bigger the hit on your Massengill's CU, and the mey-yer the chance of prison time."

Dexter frowned at the monitor. Obviously, the best possible scenario was still going to cost him CU—the Blue Topaz would make sure of that, no matter how well he tested. Somehow that knowledge didn't lessen the sting of hearing the words spoken by a law man.

Jayjay responded carefully. "Our concerns are legitimate. We're not turning ourselves in if there's a chance of being sent back to the casino's custody. You have our statement and our information, and we're not running; that's going to have to do it for now."

More mumbling. "Set coom, set fare… fare qua sey fare. Stay on, and we'll dip the IPA channels, check if your Blue Topaz Casino is elevating your name and locking you down. We can fare get you protected when we get toot-shoze gar-bozz on the table, but we need you in port soon if you want to avoid been tagged for a fugitive."

"Okay, understood. Let us know."

"Right. Out." The monitor went blank.

Jayjay turned to Dexter. "That's about it. We're in the munis' hands now."

Dexter pursed his lips and looked out the glareshield at the tiny yellow ball. "So now what? He works out the details of settlement?"

Jayjay sat back and touched her neck. "The preliminaries. He'll compile all the information and turn it over to an advocate. If the casino has anything reported, the advocate will contact them and make the arrangements pending your official testimony. With any luck, you'll probably end up with a huge fine and a clean slate." She flashed a smile.

"I could do without paying a huge fine to an outfit that took shots at me." Dexter raised his eyebrows at her. "So that's the end of it for me—all of this will now be negotiated by a complete stranger?"

"We're probably going to be here a while." She stood and patted him on the shoulder. "Easy come, easy go." She headed out of the cockpit.

"I suppose, yes." Dexter popped out of the pilot seat and followed her across the passenger cabin. "Live by the sword, die by the sword. And preferably not by gulak claws and plasma refractors."

Jayjay moved into the galley and stopped at the galley counter that wrapped from the bar to the starboard side of the bulkhead. She opened the cupboard panel with a touch and frowned at a honeycomb of jigsaw-fitted appliances and packs of organic cubes for the Protopac synthesizer. "You probably shouldn't joke about it just yet."

Dexter stepped to her side, leaning on the counter. "You know, it amazes me that these fancy, civilized establishments still feel it's necessary to conduct business this way. You'd think the frontier behavior would have died down by now." He glanced over Jayjay's shoulder at the cupboard. "I mean, early 2400s I could see. A few scattered worlds, no real government off Earth, settlers flocking to planets only half-terraformed. Pirates galore. But now we have the Bank and the IPA—we've got tabs on just about every sentient in the sphere. What is wrong with my species? How does something like this happen?" He paused. "Jayjay, are you thinking of making food?"

"I need an energy burn; I was going to take some solution. Why, you want some algan or silicone oil?" She took a small, flat cartridge from out of one of the lower cubby holes and turned. "You know, you should be trying to get some sleep right now."

"I'm fine, Jayjay, really. Still going on adrenaline." He stepped to the sink in the corner of the counter and tapped open a pantry drawer filled with tins of natural food spread. Authentic taste was preferable to a hydrogenated fusion concoction from the Protopac at the moment, but he wasn't inclined

112

to go through the process of peeling open a container and creating trash to dispose of. "Maybe not algan or silicone oil, but I might want a nip of alcohol before I try a siesta."

He shrugged and closed the drawer, then looked back at Jayjay. She was staring blankly in his direction, not quite at his eyes. Frozen as if immersed in deep thought or running an abrupt internal scan. Or incapacitated in some way. "Jayjay... are you all right?"

She remained frozen as a mannequin. Something was definitely amiss. "Jayjay?" He stared for a moment, then grabbed her by the shoulders and gave her a firm shake. "Jayjay?"

She blinked and focused on him, at once looking more amused than anything else. "Dexter?"

He nodded. She appeared fine. The spells before the procedure had consistently left her looking stricken, morose. None of that was evident now. Brief periods of internal recalibration were common after tune-ups; this was probably just surgical hangover.

She peered dubiously up at him. "What are you doing?"

She was right in front of him, well within arm's length. The height differential was more apparent than usual—she was a full head shorter than he. Personal space zones aboard the ship had become somewhat more relaxed over the past five years, but he was clearly in violation now. For some reason, she was making no move to pull away.

What was he doing? Dexter opened his mouth and closed it again. He suddenly realized his hands were still on her shoulders and quickly dropped them to his sides, taking a half step back. "Oh, me? Nothing. You... we were talking."

"Talking, huh?" She half-smiled, fixing on his eyes, looking from one to the other. She shook her head. "You're bloodshot." She stared at him a moment more, then opened the cartridge in her hand, poured the fluid into her mouth, and dropped the container into the hole next to the sink, stepping around him on her way out of the galley. She raised her voice. "You should really think about getting some rest."

Dexter kept his eyes on her as she headed for the main terminal access at the other end of the cabin. "Maybe you could use some rest yourself. Where are you going?"

She raised her voice. "Realigning the tokamak. Lot of wear and tear on the ring lately—we could have used a total reconstitution of the Droescher-Hauser. You had ten down hours without a co-pilot at the best place in the sphere for ship maintenance, but you preferred to go gaming again."

Dexter sighed raggedly. Clearly, she was fine. "It was a tough decision." He stepped to the lounge and sat on the couchette. "Really, Jayjay, it's not as if I go all the time. I was looking forward to that trip—you know that."

Jayjay shook her head and opened the access panel. Dexter watched her for a moment more, then looked back in the direction of the stern. If she had any concerns about a residual malfunction, she wasn't interested in talking about it. No sense beating her over the head about it now, while there wasn't anything that could be done. Soon enough they would be docked, where it would be easy enough to find an android specialist if she did show additional signs of a problem.

He stretched, leaning back. His eyes were starting to feel heavy. Possibly an effect of the thoroughly comfortable polyfoam, but a nap suddenly didn't seem like such a bad idea. The situation seemed to be under control—maybe if he sealed off the long day with a self-administered night, the stressful events would become problems of the past. Maybe, with a little luck. He was no stranger to a little luck.

He rolled his head back and looked up at the porthole on the ceiling. No stars appeared above the ship within the small circle, just empty blackness. There was something pleasant about the idea that in all the noise and tumult of the universe, there might be one small portion of spacetime completely free of commotion. Of course, the vast stretches of the universe were for the most part lifeless and empty; it only seemed the other way around.

Sometimes more so than others. He let his lids fall closed as Jayjay's fingers pattered softly against the MTA keypad like raindrops.

*   *   *

... GCL FZ.111
Phi 79 34 44.24 / Theta 33 18 36.92 / Rho 110.38 / JD 3040382
Beta Draconis: ANASTASIA; "Buchanan"; 7 March 3612 CE

Teodor Monroe swept off the gangway of the Scintivar Nova Archangel toward the man in the orange flak jacket of a customs officer. The man stood alone at the bottom of the ramp with his hands clasped behind his back. A gesture delivered by the spaceport director, no doubt.

"Welcome to Buchanan, Senator Monroe. Can I take you to your office?"

Certainly not the duty of a customs officer. Cyrus Gelkirk was probably peering down through his binoculars from the director's tower at that moment. The man was to be commended for his effort, but a boldfaced pretense like this was just embarrassing. Monroe feigned a smile and stepped past the man to scan the thoroughly crowded landing bay for a much more impressive individual.

He frowned and turned back to the officer. "Have you seen a dark-skinned woman with long, straight black hair? I was expecting to meet her here, not you."

The man seemed to shrink. "I'm sorry, sir, I don't know anything about that. You might want to come with me to get checked in. Follow standard procedure."

Teodor ignored him and scanned the landing bay again. A hand went up not far to the right. He waved off the officer as he hopped from the sloping platform. "Check the hold if you like, but you can tell Mr. Gelkirk I'm not in the mood to be searched today." He plunged into the mass of darting people.

Buchanan was an advantageous spot as a center of commerce, but the city had grown beyond the point of being useful. The spaceport itself was now clearly the busiest place on Anastasia, and while the heavy traffic helped to feasibly circumvent import laws, it was now drawing unnecessary attention to the Royal Planet.

And from an individual standpoint, traveling through Buchanan had become extremely unpleasant. One was compelled to race away from the landing bay immediately to avoid the press of the crowd once the area cordon was lifted; the 5 square kilometers devoted to the embarkation zone was too small to handle the relentless flow of traffic. The solution conjured up by previous directors was no more than a sorrowfully inadequate workaround—a pathetically small troop of Port Authority guards assigned to usher pilots and passengers away from their ships as fast as possible to make room for the incoming. That and a ridiculous, unenforceable ceiling on the number of people per ship. As it was, people sprinted from their various crafts, in any direction that would take them away from the crowd. During peak hours, it was a free-for-all; if a careless person fell, there was a serious possibility of a trampling.

Only fools landed at Buchanan during peak hours. Of course, there were many fools in the Human Sphere. Teodor kept his eyes level as he wound his way among the darting bodies, varying his pace as less experienced flyers hurried past him. At the moment, the crowd was not a serious concern. People were rushing as always, moving at a good clip, but the crowd wasn't thick enough to cause danger. Ahead, the unmistakable willowy figure of Ritsa Rabani emerged in a black, form-fitting Khalil Alcazar, stepping toward him.

He raised his hand, signaling her to stop. "Ms. Rabani. You're looking smart."

She bowed her head. "And you, senator." Her look was excellent—her black hair was supported by a silver barrette, pouring down either side of her head in a curving, symmetrical wave that reflected her figure. The hair, dress, and narrow, angular sunspecs emphasized her razor-sharp sleekness, setting off the smooth perfection of her caramel skin and drawing on her dark, understated sex appeal. She had been paying attention to the image consultants in his absence. Of course, she always paid attention.

Teodor exhaled. "Beautiful day. All things equal, I'd rather have stayed on in Galina another night… I was in the middle of an enterprising evening." He scratched his mustache. "Let's have it, Ms. Rabani. You have some news for me?"

She stared at him through the shaded mirrors of her sunspecs. "Information is limited. Massengill was raised on T Eradini 6 Station, in an orphanage. Born in 3562, but complete birth records are not available. He's had a gaming VIP status since 3588 and is on record at 12 different systems, mainly Valentina. He purchased an Interstar Skyhawk in 3582 and his current Zenith Explorer in 3606, and he's been working with the same IU since then. CRP tested by protocol in 3565 and 3567, and again at the Blue Topaz medical facility in 3607, ranged between 54.47 and 54.56; negligible telepathic potential. Aptitude testing rated him very high in logic and mathematics, placement in semiotics and cognition curricula through the Crescere Scientia program. He has no record of offenses, and his Lyuda account is clean." Her voice was flat, as always; beneath the specs, the dark brown eyes would be equally devoid of expression.

Teodor pursed his lips. "Malgovar is here?"

"Yes, senator."

He placed his arm across her shoulders and gestured toward the cab strip at the edge of the landing bay. "That man is becoming unpleasantly predictable. What about blowback?"

Rabani kept pace on his right as he led the way to the cabs. "The story seems to have died in the local outlets, but the intersystem media are investigating casino psi screening processes and Lyuda Humania has opened an investigation into incidents of violence at the Blue Topaz." She breathed. "Malgovar had described Massengill as 'psychologically disturbed' in the initial interview."

"Yet another mistake. Never make the story more interesting than it needs to be… it should have been dismissed as a typical internal casino matter that we regret was not controlled." Teodor rubbed the thumb of his left hand against the forefinger. "I see. One would think he would have been getting better at this sort of thing, having exercised so many similar initiatives over such a short tenure." He paused momentarily, then resumed his stride. "How many of these initiatives is that now, since he took over management? I'm remembering five now."

"That's right. Four others over the last 87 standard days. One death."

"All those we know about." Teodor nodded, concentrating on maintaining his composure. "Malgovar may be exercising initiatives outside the premises that have yet to be discovered. What we do know with great certainty is that the public are being shown the face of a casino manager who has no qualms about assaulting his clientele with extreme prejudice. And worse—extreme incompetence." He stared at Rabani as he walked. "Your counterpart was present, I assume?"

"Yes." The woman's eyes were scanning the view in front of her, possibly counting the number of people between the two of them and the cab strip. No hint of reaction to indicate she had taken the comment as a slight. Of course, she wouldn't have made that mistake even if she had been capable of an emotional response.

"And yet she failed to ensure our manager's initiative was properly executed. Very unlike her."

She said nothing.

"I hold you blameless, of course." He shook his head. "Obviously the circumstances were beyond control, this time. But I'll have to zoom in on Beta Lyrae from here on out, whether I'm embroiled in an affair like Stasya Hyperdynamics or not. Ritsa Rabani… will have to take note. Never let Mr. Malgovar out of her sight."

"Of course, senator. I will see to it."

He patted her on the small of the back. "Are the others here?"

"They're all in your office."

Teodor nodded. "Was there any trouble in transport?"

"No story has emerged. There was no Port Authority interference, and there is no chatter on the IPA coms."

As usual. This Ritsa Rabani knew his mind better than everyone else. It was no secret that he was connected to the Beta Lyrae casino establishment, among his many other business interests. He was on the Board of Directors and other oversight committees for corporations and collective guilds on 20 different planets. Like the widespread, veritable army of individuals much less nefarious than the casino managers themselves, the managers were clearly employees of his, based purely on his majority ownership of a holding company on Vera. But the connection was complex, and he was sufficiently insulated in the unlikely event the IPA ever uncovered evidence of any wrongdoings on Beta Lyrae. As it stood, the IPA scarabs were not only lacking the motivation to flesh out the true nature of his organization—the levels upon levels of expertly laundered funding, the extent of his involvement, and the control he truly exercised—they were virtually incapable of doing so. His organization was far more efficient than the supposed powerful galactic police force. Efficiency alone was too much for the scarabs and their mismanaged technology budget. Their bureaucratic hierarchy was ancient, and their surveillance was outmoded—he had built more effective reconnaissance after six years of focused direction. Spending time trying to follow up on crackpot theories that a wealthy senator might be connected to unproven criminal activities in various sectors wasn't, and would never be, a priority, not as long as the nebulous, disjointed police force was scrambling around the Human Sphere trying to put out the little fires—skirmishes among pirates and prospectors, joy-riding space pilots trying to duck the grid, hackers trying to change their credit balances—and meanwhile devoting more resources than they could afford to the unceasing, useless diplomatic missions among the other sentient races. The scarabs in their current state of incompetence were never going to be a threat to those who knew how to avoid being blunderingly obvious.

Dion Malgovar was apparently not among those capable of treading delicately. Malgovar had excelled in a smaller bet-booking outlet on Vera, spearheading an eyebrow-raising two-year profit margin in an almost unmanageable wasteland of robbery and murder. The man had had a solid background, with military training and expertise in security. He had been elevated to a finer life in Beta Lyrae, served there strongly as a lieutenant in the Velvet Sky, and seen to the permanent disappearance of a problematic systems infiltrator. He was skilled in eliminating the enemy, and his résumé had seemed reasonable enough in a pinch: tenacious fighter from a rough neighborhood with steel nerves and substantial management experience. Unfortunately, good judgment had not been borne out as one of his finer qualities. A critical shortcoming... possibly a fatal one.

Teodor stepped off the landing bay, and a cab landed in front of him almost immediately. The drivers in Buchanan knew the blue diode glow of a senator's hailing beacon.

He waved a hand in front of the driver's window. "District Chambers, as fast as possible." He opened the door of the car to let Rabani inside. "Ms. Rabani, I take it Mr. Faro is working on the report with our new data from Stasya Hyperdynamics?"

"As you requested, yes." She climbed in and removed her sunglasses. The whites of her eyes glowed out at him.

He ducked into the car after her, and smiled for the first time. "Now, feel free to brief me on any additional specifics you may have uncovered, and I'll work on you."

The long-skirt came away from her legs with a single stroke of the static seal along the left side. Teodor leaned forward and thumbed the inside curves of her thighs. Rabani tipped her head back and stared expressionlessly at the soft lighting of the overhead.

*   *   *

Teodor stalked into the large, rustic room. The high walls towered above the elongated octagon of authentic glass, the only one of its kind among the human worlds and possibly among the largest single finished pieces of glass left anywhere. The three general managers from Beta Lyrae were seated around the long right-central side of the octagon; they looked his way immediately and stood as he crossed the woolen sea-tone rug and took his place at the head of the desk.

Dion Malgovar was nearest to Teodor. No trace of concern stood out on his corpulent face, but he looked less than comfortable, his arms held stiffly against his bloated flanks.

Teodor filled his chest with air. "Thank you for being punctual, gentlemen. I'm glad you were able to meet with me on such short notice, and I'm sorry about any inconvenience." He glanced at Malgovar. "I assume we all know why we're here."

Malgovar nodded silently, and the others followed suit. Thero Esperanza and Clavitus Gaffer, also relatively new in their respective Beta Lyrae establishments. Both were smallish in stature, both with the darker skin-tone, Gaffer a pigment-treated Demophonian albinoid and Esperanza from the orange spectra-soaked Kishka system. They were both replacements from within who had been installed on an interim basis at the accession of their casinos, both with financial backgrounds. They were useful enough for now, but they were essentially unmemorable, unaccomplished men, lucky to have secured their current positions and around only until the next shining star appeared.

Rabani entered the room and stepped to the left side of the desk.

"Ms. Rabani." Teodor smiled thinly and placed his hands on the desk. "Let's get to the point, then. A client of the Blue Topaz was doing rather well. Mr. Malgovar decided that the best way to deal with the situation was to confront the man and threaten imprisonment. In fact, I'm told, Mr. Malgovar, that you went so far as to announce that you would be detaining him for the maximum duration, and pressing charges to the full extent of the law. However, the man escaped. Do I have that right, Ms. Rabani?"

Rabani nodded once, clasping her hands behind her back. Malgovar frowned and shifted, passively adjusting the cumberbund wrapped around his large abdomen. "Mr. Monroe, the situation is being dealt with. My people have already contacted the IPA, and I'm happy to tell you the man has reached out to local authorities on Ustinov. We should be able to come to an arrangement that satisfies everyone."

Teodor leaned on the desk and set his jaw. "Mr. Malgovar, I don't believe I asked you to speak."

"I'm sorry, Mr. Monroe—"

"Please! 'Senator Monroe,' or just 'senator' will do." Teodor smiled, rubbing his mustache. "Really, we've known each other longer than that. Enough." He sighed and looked up at the ceiling. "First things first. I find it unfortunate that this needs to be stated, but I do realize some of you haven't been with me that long and, thus, may not be familiar with the way I do things. So I will extend all of you the courtesy of offering a fundamental bit of organizational advice just this once. I suggest you take it. When somebody makes a mistake in an operation at this level, it jeopardizes everything the operation has ever accomplished. Everything. And this operation of mine has accomplished quite a lot. One mistake has the potential to undo it all. I trust all of you understand that, and I will not repeat it." Teodor trained his eyes again on Malgovar. "Unfortunately, Mr. Malgovar made a mistake. An egregious one. Now, let's hear what you have to say."

Malgovar glanced at the managers standing next to him. "It was a fluke, senator. I followed our normal procedures for handling special-case repeat offenders. We brought him to a secure room guarded by three trained staffers, we offered him leniency if he would give us information on the grift... he didn't budge, so we were obliged to hold him. And we would have held him, but there was a city-wide power failure, and that's apparently when he got free. Slipped away when the lights went down, and we couldn't get to him before he reached his ship."

Teodor raised an eyebrow. "Bad luck?" He paused. "But Ms. Rabani tells me you only have inferred evidence that this man was violating the rules. Nothing concrete. Despite a five-year window to draw from."

Malgovar sighed. "Hey, I did what I thought I had to do. This is a man who's been on our list for years… steady winner, off-the-charts success rate. He's got to be an offender. Yazov gave him all the boilerplate warnings, but the man wasn't getting the message. He kept coming back, even though he had to know we were onto him. I could have continued to monitor his account, but this man was going to keep coming back for more until I stopped him. There's something off about this guy." Malgovar licked his lips. "As I said before, it's all taken care of. It's all worked out now."

Teodor nodded in Malgovar's direction. "I've delegated a great deal of responsibility to you, and I expect your level of judgment to be irreproachable, whether you're handling an everyday problem or something unusual, like this. Where I think your instincts to act were correct, your choice of resolution seems short-sighted—you chose to follow standard procedure in a situation that called for more imagination. But even more disturbing is the clumsy execution." He paused, cocking his head. "By my account, there have been four other incidents within your purview since you've been installed, and in each case the situation was allowed to become unmanageable. Damage to casino property in several attempts to secure clients in violation, ugly scenes that appear in the news outlets. And one case of a man being shot in the back as he ran from your staffers—and the same thing might have happened again. I pay my people to ensure that these incidents do not become public spectacles. You agree, yes?"

Malgovar shook his head. "I'm sorry, senator… every situation is different, and we do keep things under control most of the time, but we've had a lot of people causing large problems at the Topaz over the past year, some within the organization, and I've always taken the viewpoint it's better to cause a scene to catch an offender than to let one go—that's the way of Valentina, and it's only way to reinforce a no-tolerance policy. I've never had a problem with situations like this before, and I thought you were on board with my methods."

Teodor nodded once. "Four very public displays of aggression toward the clientele, and now this. That's a lot of potential questions for any independent observer who might be keeping an eye on the Blue Topaz. I am not a big fan of knee-jerk reactions. An organization cannot survive without reserve." He glanced around at the others. "This situation we have now is creating risks I don't care to take. I've always considered it smart policy to keep myself isolated when it comes to this sort of thing at the casinos, but you've now effectively made that impossible." He pushed away from the desk, pacing as he looked up at the array of paintings that adorned the walls, clasping his hands behind his back. "I take no issue with impromptu personal interrogations when fraud and casino security are threatened; along those lines, feel free to do what you feel is necessary—I'm not concerned with individuals who complain about inconveniences. Casino managers are given a lot of latitude, and I expect you to take advantage of this as you see fit. Beyond that, I expect you to run your businesses as though your every move were being recorded for posterity, as though you were at all times being watched by the eyes of the public, by the IPA, and by me. As for the management of casino funds, use your discretion, as always. Do what you need to do to ensure the profits continue to filter through the traditional channels. Just remember whose profits they ultimately are. My casinos, gentlemen. My rules." He turned and held up a hand. "Are you exercising you're authority in other ways I'm unaware of, Mr. Malgovar? Meting out retribution outside casino grounds, off the books?"

Malgovar's eyes were locked open. He shook his head quickly. "Senator Monroe, no. I follow the plan." He frowned. "Your people are all over Shel City—there's no way I would get away with doing that even if I was inclined. If you thought I was that stupid, I'm not sure why you signed off on my hiring."

"That is a good answer." Teodor stepped closer. "But you'd better hope I don't choose to check it out, because if I did, I'm confident I'd find some other practice of yours that would force me to remove you. Listen to me, Mr. Malgovar, the next time somebody defrauds that casino as thoroughly as in this case, I want to hear about it from you. I'll decide how to handle it, and if conventional means don't resolve things, I'll take the necessary steps." He walked behind Malgovar and leaned over his shoulder, breathing on the back of his neck. "I'm sure you'll figure things out." He smiled. "Now you're excused. Go back and work on reasserting some legitimacy there—the character assassination angle is a good start, but you let me worry about your grifter from here on. Keep me posted on your media polls, and stay clean... I want to hear good news by the end of the week."

The manager smoothed his overstuffed clothing, visibly irritated. "Thank you, senator. I'll be in touch soon." He backed toward the door.

Teodor shot him a glance before he got there. "Mr. Malgovar?"

"Yes, sir?"

"I don't want to see you here again." He winked. Malgovar exited, and Teodor looked at Rabani and gestured at the door. She crossed to it and closed it behind the manager.

Teodor let his gaze linger on the woman for a moment, then placed his hands on the backs of the remaining two managers' chairs. "Mr. Esperanza. Mr. Gaffer. I trust we don't have the same sort of thing going on in the Society or the Pantheon."

Esperanza shook his head. Gaffer spoke up. "No, sir."

Teodor patted the men on the shoulder before stepping away. "Of course not. It's very tedious to go through the process of replacing men in your position. None of us want that." He turned and looked at an old human impressionist painting on the wall. "It was a most unpleasant ordeal when I had to replace Mr. Yazov. I'm sure you remember, Mr. Gaffer... you were with him, I believe."

Gaffer coughed. "Yes, sir. I remember."

"Yes. Very unfortunate. We certainly don't want a repeat of that." Teodor sniffed loudly. "Ms. Rabani is my eyes and ears in Beta Lyrae. She has done an exquisite job keeping me apprised of all goings on, and she will be continuing in that endeavor. Mr. Gaffer, I happen to know that at the end of the last inventory period, the Pantheon was missing... how many credits, Ms. Rabani?"

"496,724."

"You are unceasingly amazing; thank you, Ms. Rabani." Teodor smiled, turning to look at Gaffer. "Almost a half-million CU. In an industry where many billions change hands daily, I believe that amount happens to be just below the negligible margin of error differential, according to the banking regulations set down by the good people in Lyuda. But I won't ask you to explain it—let's just say we're operating on a clean slate, starting right now, shall we? Consider yourselves warned. Ms. Rabani will be on hand if you need any further assistance in your recordkeeping. Are we clear, gentlemen?"

Gaffer stared at him. "Yes, senator." Esperanza nodded slowly.

Teodor returned to his chair and sat down. "Fantastic." He looked up, frowning at the two casino managers. "I'm about done with you two now."

The men disappeared through the door. Rabani turned to him. "Should I see them to their transports?"

Teodor nodded. "Please do. That would be good of you, Ms. Rabani." He paused as she turned back to the door. "Oh, and Ms. Rabani? Let's stay close to Mr. Malgovar. I may need you to deliver a message to him in the near future."

She nodded and headed after the others. Few words were needed with Ritsa Rabani. Indeed, if he was soon in the market for a new general manager candidate, he wasn't going to find anyone who exhibited more control and discipline than she. Except perhaps this grifter.

Teodor tapped the table, then sighed and stood, shaking his head. Malgovar had been successful outside of his dalliances, much more so than the other two managers. The situation now seemed to be salvageable, but that was small consolation. The truly unforgivable thing was the failure to identify a potential opportunity. This was an uncommon grifter with inexplicable success. He had earned a healthy, steady profit for a long time, he had left no clear evidence of his methods, and he had done it all with an unremarkable psi rating. This was a man who needed to be brought close to the fold, but instead, Malgovar had done his best to alienate him, and very nearly kill him.

Whatever Malgovar's value, giving him a chance to make another blunder like that was something he could ill-afford to do.

*   *   **

... "Ustinov Vicinity"; 8 March 3612 CE

Dexter stared at the comlink as he straightened in the co-pilot seat, smoothing the fabric of his shirt. "All right, I just want to be sure I understand. As of now, I'm unable to access my account at all?"

The comlink buzzed for a moment, as if the officer at the other end was pounding something against his speaker. "Wey. You are purveying stolen assets, where the IPA is concerned—you're official status EV. In violation. Set-la is unfortunate standard procedure." Constable Balboa was apparently the one and only case representative for Eo-Nowar Municipal Control, and he sounded bored. Perhaps empathy didn't translate well through the Neo-Franco accent.

Dexter rubbed his neck, frowning. "But you're saying the Blue Topaz won't press charges if I submit to the IPA, and I don't cause any further trouble."

"Correct. The casino manager contacted the Bank; it's his prerogative as to alleging criminal prosecution. Set coom set fare; that's how it works. This manager, he seems agreeable enough... about as agreeable as he can be."

The images of the small room on Blue Topaz Casino's upper level sprang up as if playing on a monitor. Agreeable was not an adjective that

124

seemed to fit Dion Malgovar or anyone else in that room. Dexter shook his head. "But you still think I should come down and talk to you in Eo-Nowar before I go to the IPA?"

Balboa cleared his throat raucously. "Correct. If you're telling truth, the accusations are par-yen nothing and you are ney fare stealing CU, you will need an advocate to hear your side on toot-shoze, to back you up. Without an advocate, you might not get your account access back for an extended duration, par-sham, sey po-sabe."

Dexter squinted, glancing at Kappa Pegasi A in the glareshield. "Why? Why would they do that if the Blue Topaz doesn't press charges?"

"Vrey, sey ney simple, set-la. The custodians of the Lyuda Bank are under obligation to follow the IPA's lead. The scarabs may so choose to open their own separate investigation if they judge you might conduct future criminal activities. If so, they may lock up your account for a standard year or longer. And even if you fare take an advocate, you still may end up with frozen credit, if the Blue Topaz chooses to fight you on it."

Longer than a year! Dexter blinked. "Well, that's a bit excessive, isn't it?"

There was a pause. "Perdone, Massengill, set coom set fare. Unfortunate, these are the facts."

Frozen credit. Very bad news. Clearing a mark off his registration status wasn't much good if the computer network on Lyuda locked up his account indefinitely—he would be relegated to the fringes of society either way, scrounging for food and fuel, forced to barter or gamble off the books to earn lot slips from day to day. Of course, not having a mark on his name did offer the added bonus of not being constantly monitored by the IPA.

"Your move, Massengill."

Dexter turned and checked for Jayjay in the main cabin, but she was out of sight, somewhere among the rooms and holds that separated the galley from the burners. The door at the back of the galley was closed. "So whether I go along with what the casino is asking me to do, I'm in it for a while."

"Wey. Unless you get lucky."

Dexter grunted to himself, patting his lips as he leaned low over the console. He was depending on luck a little too much lately. "I'm going to need some time to think about this, Constable Balboa."

Balboa sighed. "IPA has no jurisdiction over you when you are in Eo-Nowar. You drew me, so as long as you are in-city, I have custody. I won't bring in the scarabs until you give me the go-ahead. Just down the batto and let me handle everything; sey gone fare plu-fass, set shoze." The voice paused. "Plu-vrey, you don't want to be hanging in space for the rest of perpetuity, and you can ney fare go back to Beta Lyrae. As far as landing your batto goes, you can fare put her don-see or plot a course for the Jade Planet."

Irina. The blue-green pearl of the 70 Ophiuchi System wouldn't have been a bad destination under other circumstances, but heading for the IPA's home base into the waiting arms of an inquest committee wasn't a particularly attractive prospect.

Dexter shook his head. "What about the fact that they opened fire? It can't be legal for them to fire plasma weapons at casino guests without complete evidence of wrongdoing... what if I make a counter-accusation? Won't that have any effect?"

"Wey. Most likely you would have your account locked up even longer. No witnesses, no evidence... your chances are slim against a big institution on Beta Lyrae. And you run the risk of making them mad. If they almost ghosted you before, maybe they think finishing the job is worth their while."

There was another choice the constable hadn't mentioned: Dexter could run. Let the mark stand and credit be damned. He could go for a couple of years in space before he ran out of cubes for the Protopac, and he could fill it back up with anything organic. There were plenty of uninhabited, bioactive planets charted among the sentient spheres—50 kilograms of prime humus from any one of them could ideally feed him for another five years, and he and Jayjay could take care of the on-board systems without any help. If he really wanted to, he could avoid civilization for the rest of his life.

After another five years or so, the events at the Blue Topaz Casino would blow over, and the IPA would stop looking for him. New credit could be established under a new name. A slight hassle, but very possible. Gaming at the big casinos would be out, but there were smaller venues off the beaten path.

Balboa yawned and cleared his throat. "I will look into it, but don't expect miracles, pa-fare. The way the in-house laws are written set-see, the corporations fare do whatever they want, whenever they want, toot-shoze, toot-quan. Meanwhile, you need to land so we can sort all this out."

And as soon as he landed it was completely out of his hands. He nodded. "I'm going to think about it a bit more, Constable Balboa. I need to discuss this with the IU. I'm not ready to come down just yet."

The constable sighed heavily. "Trey-bu. Let me know when you decide, and don't take long. Out."

Dexter dropped his hands to his thighs, standing slowly. He paused, frowning at the glareshield, then ducked through the companionway. The dimmer lines in the passenger cabin were dialed down to a dull glow. Sit-down lighting, usually reserved for more formal dining. The table was in fact set up, with cloth napkins, plates, and utensils piled together near the edge. A pair of crystal wine flutes and the stout, nearly formless shape of a kyhyvvhr grog bottle stood on the galley counter. So Jayjay was prepping real food after all. Not a bad idea—they both sorely needed to unwind.

Dexter's eyes lingered on the grog. "Well, this Constable Balboa seems to know what he's doing... sounds like our best bet is to turn in here and let the munis work things out, like you said, although he doesn't seem to think those murderous thugs are going to be held responsible for anything they did in Beta Lyrae. I have half a mind to head straight out of the Galaxy and leave it all behind." He squinted at the door. "This has all the earmarks of a fine feast, here. Something interesting on the menu?"

No response from sternward, though Jayjay shouldn't have had any trouble hearing him. The indicator light on the touchpad was blinking green, which meant there was no air seal in effect and no need to use the com. It generally wasn't necessary to lock things up unless there was tinkering to be done on the burners, something that would make life-support more vulnerable. Typically they reserved the back half of the ship for privacy, each taking turns sleeping or unwinding in one of the four personal cabins while the other enjoyed the extra space of the main cabin and cockpit.

It seemed an odd moment to call it a night. Dexter frowned. "Jayjay—everything all right?"

The light went solid green and the door slid open. Jayjay stepped into the galley in a white cocktail dress. Scalawegian island wear, from the look of it, a simple, one-piece garment sashed tight at the waist and ending at a flat hem just above the knees. Casual chic... definitely elegant.

Dexter raised his eyebrows. "Well. That's new."

"I did a little shopping." Jayjay flashed a thin smile. "I was thinking this might be a good time to celebrate your birthday. We don't exactly know what's going to happen from here on out." She stepped to the Protopac and took out a platter containing two steaks that could not possibly have been manifested by the synthesizer.

The Terran Vernal Equinox wasn't for another month or so, but she did raise a good point. He sniffed, keeping his eyes on the steaks. "Well, it isn't as if we know what the actual date of my birthday really is." The steaks were thoroughly seasoned with black and red pepper shavings, and the smell of garlic and tarragon filled the cabin.

127

"Sorry. I know how you like your traditions."

He shook his head. "I couldn't possibly turn down a meal like this, Jayjay. You know that." He paused. "Are they augmented freshwater oyster?"

She nodded. "That's what you like, isn't it? The spices were premixed, but the steaks are the real thing, straight from the fru-de-mare labs on Pike. I've had them stashed in vac-pacs for three months." She raised the platter and held it tantalizingly close to his face for a moment before rounding the bar and setting the steaks on the table.

Dexter stared at the dress as she stooped to organize the place settings. She didn't tend to wear attire that emphasized her femininity; for whatever reason, she had never really embraced that aspect of her character. Not that her femininity wasn't blatantly obvious, regardless of what she wore. It was more convenient for her to keep the accesses on her limbs accessible, so her clothing was generally on the sparse side, utilitarian but not really hiding her figure. But this dress certainly did more to compliment it, softening her curves, tracing the lines of her thighs...

She peered back at him and raised an eyebrow. "Are you going to sit down?"

"Of course, yes, right away." Dexter cleared his throat and looked immediately at the ceiling, making his way to the table. He positioned himself in front of one of the steaks. "You're having one too, I see."

Jayjay nodded. "I could use the energy boost. And liquid solutions get old after a while, even for androids." She moved back to the galley, presumably to punch up more food. "Seaweed salad and succotash all right?"

"Of course, absolutely." He found himself staring at the dress again and fixed his attention on the genetically engineered slab of cloned oyster meat. "You seem to be pulling out all the stops. Fancy dinner, new dress... I'm thinking I might need to go get myself one of these tune-ups on Barrier Island."

"It's really no big deal, Dexter."

He filled the two flutes with the grog and eyed the dark blue liquor in the glass. True enough—it didn't take a lot of planning for a simple birthday dinner, and she had done similar dinners previously. But she generally didn't make a fuss about what she was wearing; her outfits were all similar tank tops and jumpsuits, and she wore the same sorts of clothing on or off the ship, special occasion or not. Allegedly, she had gone for years before she had even bothered to acquire hair, a lot longer than the typical android. This dress suggested she wanted to look nice for him.

If that was the case, it was definitely a first. He took a sip of the liquor, and it buzzed on his tongue.

Jayjay tended to take a more no-frills approach to just about everything, possibly because she had lived through a period during which androids weren't taken seriously by many, viewed as subservient. Maybe Salaman Nevis's attitude toward her had influenced her personality in that regard.

Dexter snuck a glance toward the galley, then turned back to the cask of grog. He had known her over five years, and they had certainly established a close friendship, but there had never been any suggestion the relationship might progress further. She was unquestionably beautiful, competent, and strong, and he was by no means a person who had a prejudice against relationships between sentients and artificially intelligent beings. Jayjay cared more about him than any of the handful of women with whom he'd had liaisons in his travels.

And he was obviously getting carried away with presumptions when all she had done was put on a simple dress. He was clearly being an imbecile. He took another drink.

Jayjay put a large salad bowl in the center of the table and a smaller bowl next to Dexter's plate and sat down in front of him, flashing another smile. "Dig in." No succotash for her. Apparently she didn't want to attempt to digest the corn kernels, synthesized or not—something about a systemic problem with lipid transfer proteins in the particular grain.

"Thank you, Jayjay. I'm honored, really." He held up his flute. "Cheers."

Jayjay nodded and clinked glasses with him. "Cheers. Happy birthday." She set hers down without taking a drink. Odd habit, but she tended to avoid eating and drinking while engaging in social rituals, possibly because she relished any opportunity to take a break from multitasking. Of course her fuel cycles were much more protracted than a biological human's; she often sat down at the table without eating a bite.

Dexter nodded and took another sip. "Excellent. Mm." He cleared his throat. "You should have brought out some methanol."

She shook her head. "Maybe later. I'll get a better burn off this steak if I don't mix it with the high-grade stuff."

Dexter began slicing up the thick, diamond-shaped cut of meat. "Well, I'm glad you're partaking. It's not as easy to enjoy delicious food like this when I'm the only one getting the benefit out of it." He hunched over his plate and scooped a fork-full into his mouth, immediately closing his eyes. The complex flavors of roasted, spicy succulence exploded across his tongue.

129

There had been many days of instant, weak-textured pseudo-meals. "It's nice that we managed to find something that we both like. It can be a little disconcerting when you drink those tiny cans of solution as you watch me stuffing my face. Makes me feel like an animal at the zoo." He took another bite. "Mm. This is incredible... so for you, not as efficient as an electrolyte wash-through, I would think, but you still like this sort of food, yes?"

Jayjay slid herself closer to the table, staring back at him. "Organic food isn't that functional for me, but yes. It takes longer to break it down, and that's a plus. Lots of metals and creatine... it's a good mix." She sliced her cut evenly into six elongated strips.

Dexter swallowed a mouthful of succotash. "So it's more the particularities of the fuel burn than a taste thing, per se."

"Something like that." Her gaze appeared to linger on his mouth for a long moment.

Dexter looked down and dabbed his mouth with the napkin. Animal at the zoo. "So you're feeling well, I take it."

Jayjay stared for a moment more, then blinked at him. "Yes. Sure."

It might have been as good a chance as he was going to get. "You know, if you don't mind my asking... is your long-term memory functionality any better?" He paused, looking down at his plate. "You'd think on a full mnemonic diagnostic they'd be able to nail down that gap in your records."

The corners of Jayjay's mouth slowly dropped. She fiddled with her utensils. "I was interrupted midway through that full diagnostic—I'm lucky I didn't get any more mnemonic failures." She stabbed a strip of meat with her fork and bit it cleanly in half, swallowing it without chewing. "Don't you think I would have told you if they corrected the memory gap?"

A reaction he should have expected. Dexter ran his tongue around the inside of his mouth. "So you haven't had any additional losses of memory since the tune-up. That's a good sign, I'd say."

Jayjay dropped her fork on her plate and straightened in her seat. "Why don't you just say what you mean? You think I have TPM, don't you?"

Dexter took a swig of grog and gulped down a mass of food. "Well, no. Of course not. It's just we should try to keep on top of things, if the techs found anything of note or did any repair work in that area. That's all."

Her frown deepened. "I am on top of things."

"I know you are." Dexter sighed. "I'm sorry. I just worry about you." He reached for the grog and cracked a smile. "Clearly, your mastery of the Protopac hasn't been affected, as everything here is phenomenal."

Jayjay was shaking her head. "It's three buttons. You can master three buttons as well as I can—when you make dinner it's exactly the same. You think I'm going to have trouble remembering a three-button sequence?"

Dexter laughed. "Well, at least you still remember the important things, like my birthday."

"Your birthday." She squinted at the filled flute glass in front of her and abruptly drank it down. "You didn't even say anything about my dress." She half-smiled at the empty glass.

Dexter sat back and rubbed his neck. "I did notice. I think I did make a brief comment…"

Jayjay suddenly seemed to be staring blankly across the table, her head tilting slightly to the side. Dexter stood slowly. "Jayjay?"

She shook herself and focused on him, blinking and stabilizing herself with her hands on the table.

Dexter realized he was holding his fork. He put it down. "Jayjay, you just froze. Are you aware of what just happened?"

She leaned forward, frowning. "We were talking about… food. And then you brought up the memory gap. Not my favorite subject."

The spells were back, and judging by the two headaches she had already had, the frequency was increasing. "Jayjay, let's go hook you up to the computer for a second."

Jayjay opened and closed her mouth. "I'm fully capable of… self-diagnostic exam…" She trailed off and shook her head, then slid her legs from underneath the table. "Don't you like my dress? You didn't say anything…"

Dexter stepped back from the table. He had spoken too soon—her mnemonics were still buggy and now it was affecting her emotional responses. "Jayjay, listen to me… you're not rational right now. We need to find out what's wrong, so let's just get you connected to one of the terminals and let the on-board sort this out. I'm going to have to insist." He took a tentative step around the table.

She rose, scowling. "Oh, and you're the expert on being rational—a nomad loner who goes from planet to planet avoiding meaningful interactions with all other sentient beings and makes his living as a gamer because he believes he's incapable of losing CU. So I should listen to you, an insensitive, undernourished shut-in, tell me what's good for me? Why are you pretending to care—are you worried that the big, woman-shaped block of semiconductors won't be able to fly your ship to the next casino?"

Dexter stumbled backwards, raising his hands as if to fend off a physical attack. "I'm not pretending to care, Jayjay—don't say that."

Jayjay stopped yelling almost immediately, and she stared at Dexter as if she had gone into shock. She blinked and shook herself again. She was having trouble focusing again.

"Jayjay?"

Her stance became wobbly, and she reached for her face with both hands, brushing distractedly at her bangs. Her eyes fixed on his mouth. "You can't... fix it..."

She collapsed sideways and slumped face-down on the floor.

"Jayjay!" Dexter dropped to his knees and nudged her. He rolled her onto her back. Her eyes were open, staring blankly toward the ceiling.

Guidestars! His mind raced. He would have to move her to the main terminal if he couldn't get her awake, but the first step was to flood her microarrays with the manual override at the base of her skull. He rubbed his hands together and reached beneath her neck.

She stirred before he found the nodule beneath the skin. Her eyes darted around in a circle. She touched his hand as he withdrew it. "What happened?"

He exhaled heavily. "You gave me a scare. You became erratic, and you passed out."

She relaxed and looked up at him. The low light played in her eyes as if they were liquid. "I'm not right, Dexter." She was herself again, calm and controlled. That ever-pleasant, innocent face of hers had been almost unrecognizable during the spell, and now she looked as fresh again as if he hadn't laid eyes on her for a decade... the unique, magnetic illusion of softness that so flawlessly hid all the lightning-quick competence and cast-iron strength. She was particularly radiant at the moment.

On impulse, he stooped lower and brushed her cheek. "I've been trying to tell you. What do you remember?"

She seemed to be looking at his mouth. "You were talking to Eo-Nowar, and I was putting on a dress." She paused. "Erratic is an understatement. I don't remember the words I used, but I think I said some things I didn't mean."

Dexter nodded. "I know. Par-yen fret. No worries." He cleared his throat and flashed a smile. "Come on, we need to get you to the on-board before this happens again." He helped her to her feet and turned, but she grabbed his hand, stopping him.

"Dexter... I'm sorry." She stared at him for a moment, then leaned forward and gave him a quick kiss on the mouth.

For an instant, it wasn't entirely clear whether she was entirely coherent. But her eyes were completely focused now, staring right back at his. The affection was apparently genuine, even though on some level deep down she also apparently felt he was an insensitive, undernourished shut-in.

She seemed to read his confusion. "Just in case I don't remember later, I appreciate your help."

He nodded slowly. "And in case I don't remember later, I very much like the dress. You look quite lovely."

She smiled.

He raised his eyebrows. "Let's just get you better. Come on."

He turned and led the way to the main terminal access at the head of the main cabin. He unfolded the seat and stepped back as she sat down. He reached for the connection cable but she waved him off.

"I'll do it." She paused. "Thank you."

Dexter bowed his head and stepped back. She secured the feed and smiled back at him as the on-board began scanning.

She was fine for now. The on-board could keep things under control temporarily, repairing any peripheral damage and maintaining biorhythms. But if the ultimate problem was fixable, the solution wasn't going to come from the on-board. She was going to need a neocortical specialist.

So that was that. He turned and headed for the cockpit.

Jayjay called after him. "Eo-Nowar?"

He positioned himself at the console and tapped in a command, dropping in the Kappa Pegasi A coordinates and starting the sequence for an autopilot approach pattern. He turned in the seat, glancing over his shoulder. "Eo-Nowar. We'll get you checked out while I deal with the munis."

He switched on the com; the monitors were still defaulting to the ENMC call code. Dexter tapped in a quick hail sequence, but Jayjay's voice came through the speaker before he sent it. "Dexter, I think letting the munis handle this is the right move, but don't do this for me. I don't think you're going to find anyone on Ustinov who can do a better job than the people at Barrier Island."

Dexter's eyes narrowed. "We'll see. Your symptoms weren't like this when they screened you before."

"You need help on the approach?"

"No, I'm fine—just sit tight for now. I need the com." He frowned and sent the hail.

The fact that the best repair station in the Human Sphere had failed to locate the problem was not a good sign. But large-scale operations like Barrier Island did have a way of overlooking atypical items on occasion, and the blackout probably hadn't helped their attention to detail.

TPM wasn't a fixable problem, but Jayjay didn't have TPM. There were a thousand other things that might have been affecting her, all resolvable. Someone would fix the problem, if not on Ustinov, then somewhere else. Things would work out. Things always worked out.

Dexter caught a glimpse of his reflection in the angled portside pane of the glareshield, a distortedly elongated image of his upper torso.

Undernourished. He was by no means undernourished. A little on the thin side, perhaps, but maintaining body mass was no easy task for someone living aboard a spacecraft. Jayjay obviously hadn't meant all the harsh words, but she had still spoken them as if there were some semblance of truth behind them. Did she really view him like that, like he was a scrawny malnute? Insensitive was understandable—his social graces were sorely lacking and people often tended to despise him upon meeting him, for one reason or another—but to describe him as undernourished was completely unfair. No surprise people found him insensitive—they were often impossible to figure out, and Jayjay was no exception.

He took another glance toward the cabin. As long as her personality wasn't obliterated by a degenerative corruption, she could be as complicated as she liked.

The com diode flashed. "ENMC, read one Explorer, Zoo-Hot-Fox, I-Lee-Go-Al-Bev-1216. Qua fare?"

Dexter sniffed and leaned toward the speaker. "I need to make arrangements for a landing."

V   RETROSPECTION

"Time and space... the physical nature of our universe holds an endless supply of treasures for those who study with keen eyes the great tapestry that surrounds us, for those who are patient and perseverant. The educated know that they can learn from the events of the past, and that a wealth of information with decisive action is a recipe for power.

"In this way, the legend of the fire's-eye was not learned purely by chance, though chance would play a role. For the man who knew what to look for, discovering the legend was a product of drive and direction over time... an unwavering focus on the singular goal of power.

"Power through information and action. Never would the reward be greater."

```
... GCL AE.001
Phi 00 00 00.00 / Theta 00 15 37.33 / Rho 00.00 / JD 2446198
Alpha Confinii: EARTH; "Caracas, Venezuela"; 15 May 1985 CE
```

A line of cars clogged the road leading back from the Caracas International Airport. The long black sedan sped in the other direction, toward the region of darkness that was now clouding half of the early morning sky.

Rafael Avila shifted, trying once more to keep the hand-cuffs from digging into his lower back. The two CIA escorts to his left and right left no space on the back seat, despite the size of the car. He pointed his chin in the direction of the driver. "Ésta es locura. El aeropuerto estuviere estupefacto si no cerrarese."

Agent Hendricks smiled at Rafael from the jump seat against the partition. "You afraid of a little rain, Mano Blanco?"

The agent to Rafael's left nodded at Hendricks. "You gonna ride him the whole time? You guys sound like my parents."

The driver glanced across at the escort in the passenger seat. "Everyone is leaving the airport for cover from the storm. This is not a safe place to be when the coastal weather is like this."

The man in the passenger seat looked around at the retreating cars in the left lane. "We have our own plane to take him out of here, marshal. A minor squall might close down your airport, but it's not going to keep us from doing our jobs."

Rafael glanced at him. The man was in a military uniform. Probably not

135

CIA. A captain in the American Air Force, by what the driver had said, not afraid of his captive like the cabrón in the jump seat. This one had conviction.

Rain began hitting the roof of the sedan as the airport came into view, silhouetted momentarily in flash of lightning. Soon it would be faster and harder than the constant drizzle of the interior jungle at the prison. Mid-September tropical storm… this was going to be a powerful one.

All the better. A distraction could become a great ally.

The driver slowed the car. Rafael looked at the back of his head. The Venezuelan federal mariscal was PTJ, a member of the Cuerpo Técnico de Policía Judicial, the national security force. The Venezuelans were familiar with the layout of the airport and they knew how to handle themselves in a tropical storm, but the Venezuelans weren't running the operation. They were a tangled, uncoordinated mess of frayed organizations, mostly PTJ and Bolivarian intelligence working with corrupt local police who would have poor aim and be quick to run if trouble broke out. The Venezuelans truly wanted no part of El Patrón or the cartels, and they wanted nothing to do with Rafael Avila. They were just going through the motions.

Rafael lowered his brow, staring ahead at the windshield past the open partition. All he needed was a hole—one moment when the Americans weren't paying complete attention.

He looked out the window as the car approached the long building that housed the terminals. Outside, the walkways were choked with people scampering for shelter, redirected after trying to leave the country before the forces of nature struck. Surely it was more congested than the Americans had imagined. The military teams were trained to be efficient and effective under adverse circumstances, but this was chaos. Many of these people were young, with limited, specific information and almost no real experience—the CIA man seated to the left could have passed as a college student. These Americans were confident, but they didn't really know what to expect, and they couldn't know how they would react if they were forced off the itinerary.

People were spilling into the road, panic-stricken. Buses crowded along the sides of the row of airlines, overstuffed with those who didn't have their own transportation, or didn't have time to get to it. Now, the rain was pouring faster than the sedan's windshield wipers could handle.

The Air Force captain spoke up. "Keep going. We'll use the luggage cart route. Turn in up there."

The driver obliged, coming to a stop in front of a passage that divided the terminal building in half. A Venezuelan guard with an assault rifle tapped the glass of the captain's window. The captain rolled it down and raised his arm as the water showered in.

The guard looked past him. "Buenodías, mariscal. Qué pasa?"

The driver wiped a thick black mustache. "Tenemos control de seguridad." He pointed his thumb at Rafael. "El Mano Blanco."

The guard glanced at Rafael and nodded. "Uno momento." He stepped away from the car and took out a two-way radio.

The captain turned to the driver. "Did you tell him we have security clearance?"

"Sí, capitán. I'll say again, this is not a good idea. The storm will not pass before tonight."

The captain frowned. "He's not your business anymore, marshal. He's mine. I have orders to get this man to Miami six hours from now, and I'll be damned if I don't do exactly that."

Rafael glanced at Hendricks. The agent wore his typical amused expression. The gold tooth glinted in the odd play of light through the tinted windows; the man's face looked like a twisted mask during Carnival in Río.

The guard leaned back inside the window and pointed inside the passage. "Mira, mariscal, directo delante a las pistas."

The driver held up his hand. "Graci, señor." He pulled the car to the right and into the passage, crossing to the other side of the building. Ahead, the planes were barely visible through the rain on the airstrips across the tarmac.

The captain shook some of the water off his sleeve and pointed to the left. "It's up there at the end of those runways." The man knew no Spanish, but somehow it didn't make him any less formidable; he obviously took his job seriously. He was going to be a difficult obstacle.

The driver nodded. "Sí."

The captain peered ahead. "Aw, great big balls of shit!" Reporters and camera crews in foul weather gear were scattered just off the ramp to the runway.

The car stopped in front of a gigantic C-130 plane, the heavy artillery and troop mover. There had been a time El Patrón had hoped to see a plane like that of his own. The United States government hadn't always been the enemy.

Several military policemen stood around the plane's open cargo bay door, some Americans, some Venezuelans. There were probably more inside—if the escorts got Rafael on board, escape would become nearly impossible. It would have to happen soon.

The captain got out of the car and saluted the nearest American MP. Hendricks nodded at Rafael. "Almost time to leave all this behind. Hope you're ready."

The reporters moved in, shoving microphones at the captain and pressing toward the windows of the car. The MPs held them back. A British voice at the forefront carried above the others. "Captain, is the extradition still on schedule?"

"Son, I think you better get the fuck out of my face before I take a shit in your mouth, and you can quote me on that."

The wave of reporters subsided slightly. The captain plunged forward. "I got a job to do. If you ass-licking fuck-nuts get in my way, I'm going to have you shot in the eye. Is that clear?"

He circled to the opposite side of the car and motioned for the driver to roll down his window. A Venezuelan officer opened the door and the CIA man to the left got out and ushered Rafael into the rain. The reporters fell back.

Raphael weighed the shackles on his feet, adjusting his stance, and swept his eyes in a circle while another burst of lightning offered a glimpse of the surroundings. There was little cover in the direction of the airport buildings, and they were probably too far, but there was a stretch of thicket along the edge of the airstrip, much closer.

The driver opened his window a crack. The captain pointed at the plane, shouting above the howl of the wind. "You see that? That's a Lockheed C-130 Hercules. It can heft a payload of over 20 tons, and it'll fly through anything. We'd be safe in a goddamn hurricane. Now stop worrying about your piss-ant storm—we'll be through it in less than an hour."

The driver wasn't impressed. "It's not your plane I worry about." His eyes went toward Rafael.

The captain glanced at Rafael as two MPs took hold of his arms. "We can take care of ourselves, marshal. Thanks."

He stepped away from the long car and the driver closed the window. Hendricks and the younger CIA man were already out on the other side, standing at the edge of the airstrip as the sedan backed away.

The captain motioned to pair of soldiers under the tail of the plane and nodded at the MPs with Rafael. "All right, let's get this show on the road."

Hendricks crossed to Rafael, stepping in front of him. "Hope you have a safe flight."

The captain grabbed him by the shoulder. "Knock it off, Hendricks. Your work is done here. Now get the hell out of my sight and let me do my job, all right?" He paused as Hendricks walked away, laughing to himself. "Oh, shit, now where's the goddamn spotter? Goddamn Company assholes insisting on being involved and now we have to stand here with our thumbs up our asses."

A low beating noise suddenly began sounding lightly around the airstrip. It rose quickly.

The captain drew his gun from its holster and checked the cartridge. "Goddamn Company bullshit. Goddamn, motherfucking sonofabitch! Get Avila on board!"

A spotlight hit the two MPs as they dragged Rafael into the open, toward the plane. The beat of rotor blades thundered rapidly louder, and the pooling water on the ground rippled away. Rafael kept his head low as a helicopter moved overhead, a glaring halo of white light, otherwise invisible through the sheets of rain. His pulse quickened.

He closed his eyes and spun out of the two men's grip, turned on the one to his left, and cracked him on the bridge of the nose with his forehead, then pivoted and threw himself at the other MP, splashing onto the flooded pavement on top of him. He twisted and squeezed his legs back through his arms, bringing the hand-cuffs to the front, then hit the other man in the face with his elbow and snatched his sidearm.

The peal of a single gunshot sounded from somewhere near the car, followed by several short bursts of machine gun fire. There was yelling, barely audible over the noise of the rotor blades. Rafael rolled, shot down the first MP as he was staggering to his feet, then fired up into the spotlight until it went out. The helicopter veered left as the sound of its engine changed pitch.

Rafael squinted, glancing around wildly as he moved into a sitting position... nothing was clear in the swirling mist, but vaguely there was discernible movement around the massive plane, some 10 meters away. More armed men were coming out of the back hatch. He hunched forward, slipping the flimsy prison-issue shoe off his left foot and setting it upside-down over the chain between his shackles, braced himself, and fired twice into the soft rubber sole. The shock of the blast shot through both ankles, but the chain came free.

He rolled to his feet, ducked, and sprinted in the direction of the thicket, gritting his teeth as the waves of pain rose through his legs. Another gunshot came from the right, at close range. He whirled and fired the sidearm's last shot, threw the gun at the shooter's head as it came into focus, then leapt after it, kicking the pistol from the man's hand, moving behind him, and wrapping

139

his hand-cuffs around the man's neck. He pulled the man slowly away from the area of the plane, backing up, searching for signs of movement.

The man struggled as Rafael dragged him onto a patch of grass at the edge of the airstrip, and Rafael tightened his grip. Then three shots hit the man in the chest, and the force knocked Rafael backwards. The man landed on top of him, momentarily pinning him. Rafael shoved the man's body aside, jumped to his feet, and froze. Hendricks was standing in front of him, grinning, with a gun aimed at his head.

The agent shrugged. "End of the line, Frosty."

Somewhere in the distance, a siren went off. Hendricks turned. Rafael ducked and dove at him. Hendricks fired, and a bullet tore through Rafael's shoulder, but he didn't slow down. He ripped the gun from the man's hand easily, spun and landed a foot on his jaw. Hendricks went down fast, hitting the ground with the back of his head.

Now the gold-toothed cabrón would realize his fear. Rafael stayed off him for a moment, letting him roll on to his stomach and start to crawl. Then Rafael struck, straddling the man's back, pinning the man's shoulders with his knees, and sweeping his hand-cuffs below the neck. He pulled back until he heard the crack of the cervical vertebrae.

The area suddenly lit up under another spotlight. He looked around, blinking. A truck was moving in behind him. Then he felt the cold, wet muzzle of another gun touch the base of his neck.

"It's over, Avila." It was the Air Force captain.

The siren's low moan rose, sweeping over the airport. A clap of thunder sounded in the distance. Rafael turned to face the massive plane at the end of the last runway as another group of MPs rushed forward.

*   *   *

The plane swerved as a pocket of turbulence shook the interior. Six United States Air Force airmen shifted uncomfortably against the hull of the cargo bay.

Captain William Braddock stared at them, looking from one face to the next. Damn fucking chaos. The pick-up shouldn't have been attempted during the storm. The flight back wouldn't be a problem, but Washington seriously needed to get its agencies on the same page the next time they tried to take someone out of South America.

He looked at Avila. The bleach white skin made him look like a damn ghost. Hell of a thing, trying to keep a ghost locked up.

He tilted his hat back over his eyes. Avila was securely cuffed to the bulkhead at the back of the cargo bay. The White Hand wasn't getting away again, not while there were no secret-agenda Company boys on board to skull-fuck the Armed Forces.

The whole thing stank on ice. The CIA had crashed the party with their seven spotter helos and then not even managed to get more than one mustered for the walk to the plane. Last-minute, need-to-know bullshit—the Company helos had to have been prepped and ready on La Tortuga for days. They had obviously come with an abort order at the first sign of trouble, which had probably included picking off Avila from the air if he tried to escape. Hell, they might have been planning to take him down whether there was an escape attempt or not. No surprise the CIA would want to keep the man's mouth shut. They had allegedly been the ones who trained him in Panama.

Stan Hendricks had sure as hell been ready to pull the trigger.

Braddock grunted to himself. The airmen in the plane were new— assigned to the captain's command from above. Missions like this, it was never a good thing work with people who were question marks. They all looked nervous to a certain extent, and they were all trying to hide it.

The airman sitting closest to the cockpit was doing a particularly good job of hiding his emotions, avoiding eye contact, staring at his rifle.

The captain leveled his eyes at the kid. "What's your name, son?"

The airman met his eyes for a moment, then drifted back to his gun. "Morrison."

"This your first mission, Morrison?"

He looked back up and studied the captain. "Second. I was in Beirut for a year. Nothing exciting, like this."

The captain nodded and looked back at Avila. He was getting antsy. Two hours on the plane in shitty weather that had damn near stretched to Cuba. It had been a long ride. He sighed loudly. "Don't worry, airman. The excitement's done. From here on out it's just a ride to the next prison."

He squinted, leaning his head against the metal hull. Nobody had told him anything. All he was supposed to do was make sure Avila made it to the airport in Miami. Make sure nothing else happened. That was the job.

Avila looked back at him as if he was reading his thoughts. He twisted against the bulkhead and raised his head. "They will not let me live. You know that."

Braddock raised his eyebrows at Avila. "No one's talking to you, dishrag."

Avila lolled his head loosely as if he was about to pass out. "Those

141

pendejos do not want me alive. Make no mistake. You are not delivering me to my next prison, you are delivering me to my death."

"You think I fucking give a shit what happens to you?" The captain crossed the cargo bay, running a hand through his hair. "Everybody's going to sit the fuck back, relax your fucking legs, and we're all going to have a nice and fucking peaceful flight to Miami!" He rubbed his eyes and pushed his way forward into the cockpit.

The co-pilot was half-standing, craning to look over his shoulder. "What's going on? Sounds pretty loud back there."

"This mission is too damn long, that's what's going on." Braddock let a trickle of sweat drop past his eye. CIA bastards, making him jump at shadows! "Let's try to keep on our toes the whole way through."

The pilot glanced at him from the other seat. "Everything okay?"

Braddock scowled. "I'd like to avoid another shootout, if that's possible." He exhaled heavily. "Can we transmit yet?"

The co-pilot settled unsteadily back into his seat and jammed his headset on. "We're just coming out of the storm."

"It's about fucking time. See if Colonel Pine is at the goddamn airport yet. We need new orders… I'm thinking we might need a redirect."

The co-pilot cleared his throat. "Homestead, this is Osprey, we have a Tango-Romeo-one-one-four… Homestead, this is Osprey, Tango-Romeo-one-one-four…"

Braddock looked out the front window. A gray cloudbank seemed to dissolve as he looked on, and a wave of blinding sunlight hit the plane, flooding the cockpit like a flash of lightning. Braddock winced and blinked. He rubbed his eyes and tried to shake off the red tint of afterimage on his retinas. It was going to be a long, ball-busting, smacked-ass of a day.

"Homestead, Osprey, Tango-Romeo-one-one-four…"

*   *   *

… "Philadelphia"; 28 September 1992 CE

The uneven fluorescent lighting flickered. For an instant, the square panels of the bathroom ceiling blurred, and the bland pale gray had the look of crude, pre-Roman stone masonry. A house on some lost hill in the middle of the Greek peninsula. The same pain had coursed through his body there, made him nauseous—the feeling of impending death. It had not happened since. It might have been the same moment, separated by a vivid dream.

Walker... that was the name now.

John Walker blinked and reached for his face, wiping the sweat from his eyes. The line tracing the bottom of his ribcage was on fire. It had not felt that way nearly a month before, the day he had reopened the ancient region of the wound and taken the stone out of his body—the day he had first parted with it after so many years. While still nestled in its place, the stone had dulled the nerves of his skin, calmed his body's revulsion to the blade. Not so, this time. For an agonizingly long minute, he had held the stone in his left hand as he crudely forced the blade with his right. His body had resisted as if he had never done it before, as if he were as prone to suffering as at the day of his birth, and grasping the stone by hand had done nothing to remove the sting. It was as if the stone had withheld its rejuvenating power as punishment for temporarily parting with it.

But the stone was back in its place now; the wound was already starting to heal beneath his fingers. His pulse began to slow, and the familiar warmth crept back over him. It was done.

He sat up carefully and exhaled. He was naked on the floor, wedged in the corner next to the toilet, looking at the blue plastic door of the special-needs stall. The men's room was locked with a deadbolt, in a corridor out of the way of the airport bustle. Well-chosen. Tending to the stone had taken longer than expected, but as he had guessed, the few who had tried to enter had not bothered to find a custodian with a key.

He picked the box-cutter knife from among the bloody washcloths scattered between his legs and used a railing to pull himself to his feet, patting himself dry with the clean towel on the top of the toilet. He picked up the soaked rags, bunching them together with the knife and binding them all in the towel, then opened the stall door.

He crossed to one of the tiny sinks fitted to the wall and tossed the bundle in the trash receptacle directly beneath the paper towel dispenser, then splashed a handful of water on his face, staring at himself in the mirror.

His eyes were red—he had become excessively fatigued while detached from the stone. Now his strength was returning... and along with it, a strange sensation. A mild euphoria, separate from the warmth in the blood, and the general sense of physical health and mental acuity. Perhaps he had not been as prepared to part with the stone as he had surmised.

Perhaps it was just as well the woman had refused.

Someone rattled the outside door. The noise stopped, then started anew, louder and more prolonged. John Walker looked sharply left, then calmed himself. It was over... the person was already gone. John Walker turned,

143

stepped to the far stall, and took his fresh clothes off the hook on the door.

He dressed quickly, then stepped into his shoes and slipped back into the trenchcoat, cinching the belt tight and brushing himself off. He nodded as he felt the edges of the envelope in the inside pocket—the will listing his possessions, and the key that had so recently been the only link to the world's greatest prize.

He turned again toward the trash receptacle and removed the envelope, weighing it in his hand as if to estimate the value of its contents. The stone had been separated from him for almost a week... it had been left unattended, secured by only a padlock that could have been breached with a simple cutting tool, a quick shuttle ride away from one of the busiest places in the Northeast Corridor. Very easily, the stone could have been snatched up by some fortunate, opportunistic soul, someone driven by avarice and aggression. Someone much more typical of the Human Race, and much less worthy than the likes of Cassandra Prescott.

John Walker frowned at his reflection. If it had been stolen, he would have been forced to live without it, regardless of Cassandra Prescott and her whims.

He had not handled it well. She was too much of a professional to agree to be named as an heir to a client she barely knew; he had been too impetuous. She would never have accepted a gift from anyone other than a true friend, and befriending her would have required opening up to her. And in all his travels, personal relationships were perhaps his greatest failing.

In truth, he had never needed to complicate the matter as much as he had. There was no need for the woman. If he had ever truly had the willpower to live out the end of his life, all he would have had to do was walk away. Instead, he had chosen to plunge the knife back in and return the stone to his abdomen, and now he was moving on once again, as if nothing had changed, as he had done so many times before.

He was no more worthy than anyone else.

He threw the envelope in the trash slot on top of the bundled knife and rags and exited the bathroom, heading along the long, tubelike corridor toward the metal detector.

There was a slight line at the conveyor belt. John Walker glanced around, focusing on the other people for the first time—there were at least 20 people in the immediate area, sluggishly hauling their luggage, moving in both directions and lingering at newsstands. The airport was more active than it should have been during the 11:00 hour on a Monday. There had to have been weather problems in other parts of the country—a number of the flights had been listed as delayed.

John Walker found his boarding pass and flashed it in front of the security guard as he approached the cordoned barrier. He bypassed the conveyor belt and stepped through the threshold of the metal detector, waited for the second guard to nod, then continued.

A large monitor board stood ahead at the center of the aisle. Flight 152 to Los Angeles was on schedule.

He stepped around the sign and continued toward the terminal. No matter if it ended up delayed. Time was no longer a concern. In a relative blink of an eye, he would be in Tahiti. Perhaps there, the time would not pass so slowly.

The corridor ended at an open area that extended indefinitely in both directions, with various shops and eateries spread among the terminal benches. He headed left, past a coffee bar. A good third of the tables were occupied, and every face seemed etched with tired irritation. For some reason, the prospect of an unanticipated number of people wasn't as discomforting as it should have been.

He stopped suddenly, looking down and touching his abdomen. The stone was nestled in its place, as perfectly placed as if it had never left his body. But there was something stirring at the back of his mind, like a distant memory...

He had chosen his path, and he was at the mercy of destiny. The thought had occurred to him long, long before. He had watched a man starving in the street in Corfinium, struggled to put himself in the man's place.

Suddenly, it no longer seemed to matter—none of it. His decision to carry the stone, his failure to give it away. His continued weakness. There was a driving force behind it all... something that had driven him to part with it. But parting with it was not what was meant to be. It belonged with him, not with the lawyer.

He had chosen his path, and he was at the mercy of destiny...

"Excuse me."

He shook himself. A woman pushed past him, on her way to one of the seats in the terminal. He walked to the check-in desk. A lone flight attendant was helping a young, sharply dressed couple. The attendant was a dark, attractive woman; most of the airport staff seemed to have been selected based on pleasant appearance. Some things never did change.

He stopped behind the man who was speaking to the attendant and caught the woman's eye.

Attractive, yes. Not nearly as attractive as Cassandra Prescott.

145

An oddly severe sensation spread through his belly, almost like a sharp pang of hunger, but not originating from his stomach. He vaguely felt the boarding pass slip out of his hand.

The flight attendant seemed to be looking in his direction, saying something to him, but there was no sound. Others were looking as well. Everyone seemed to be getting farther and farther away.

Walker looked up. Suddenly all he could see was an overhead fluorescent light panel gradually shifting from its natural white to a soft, pinkish tint.

Tahiti was not to be. No life on the new ocean, no tropical island paradise for the time-worn soul. But there would be mercy. Peace, at long last. An ancient prayer wound its way to the forefront of his mind.

"Sir?" Mindy shook her head. "Sir—can I help you? Are you all right?"

The small man in the brown trenchcoat continued to stand motionless, without trying to pick up his pass. He looked upward.

The couple in front of her turned to look, as did a few others hovering at the counter. There were murmurs; a salt-and-pepper-haired gentleman in a blue suit began looking around at others in the crowd. "Is he all right?"

The man in the trenchcoat might have been having a stroke or a heart attack. "Sir?" Mindy reached for the intercom.

Brilliant light exploded across the terminal. Mindy gasped and covered her face. There were shouts... one person screamed. She squinted. The light seemed to center directly on the point where the man in the overcoat had just been standing, completely obscuring him like a giant, blazing dagger. Then, an instant later, the light was gone.

A dark pile of clothing lay on the carpet in the man's place.

*   *   *

... GCL FZ.111
Phi 79 34 44.24 / Theta 33 18 36.92 / Rho 110.38 / JD 3040382
Beta Draconis: ANASTASIA; "Buchanan"; 8 March 3612 CE

The office was a large room, decorated with a gigantic, dazzling overhead orrerium showing Beta Draconis and the planets of the Anastasia System, in addition to a number of painted artworks from preinterstellar Earth. The door was the only break in a row of old teak bookcases that surrounded the room, completely packed. Above them, the walls were painted to look like they were made of wooden slats wherever they weren't shielded from view by the gallery of paintings. Four sculptures stood on pedestals in the corners, and an enormous glass conference table with an unusual elongated octagonal shape stretched the length of the back wall, covering half of the rug.

There were none of the telecommunicators, none of the robotic waiters that could be found in any high-class conference room of the day. Nothing was automated here. Monroe had managed to keep out any evidence of modern technology. Apparently at the Anastasia District Chambers building, the office holder could do with the room as he pleased. Monroe's office was timeless. Inside, the only sign of modernism was the clothing and exotic guests who had the privilege of making their way inside.

Saaj stood in one corner of the room, surveying the others through his peripheral vision, pretending to examine a marble statue of a winged baby. Monroe stood at the head of the conference table, in front of the chair with the highest back in the room. The dark-complected Ritsa Rabani stood by his side.

Seated around the table were four of the senator's closest confidantes, immediately recognizable to anyone well-schooled in corporate affairs, though they kept a low profile. Kamil Nasr-Rakh sat on the left, hunched forward and examining a tablet with his one functional eye. He looked up and acknowledged Saaj with a nod. Nasr-Rakh had been the point man leading the landing party on the Trojan satellite at Lambda 2 Fornacis 6, a dermal-exhibitor genome mu, with cracked, blistering skin that apparently covered most of his face, more or less sealing up his right eye; he looked like the victim of a chemical explosion or UV flare-up. Former Foundation man and capable primary, he had long been seen as the fist of the organization's shadow operations.

Marco Tevecher, the executive officer of finance, was next to Nasr-Rakh, striking a contrast to the genome mu with his tall, thin frame. Jan Harlowe sat opposite them, the hairless lead engineer and head of the research division, and next to Harlowe was Len Razdorian, the legal XO.

The man on Harlowe's other side, nearest to Monroe save for Rabani, was Cristan Faro. Faro had served as the lead consultant on several terraforming projects in the outer Human Sphere. Some ten years earlier by human measure, he had been well sought-after by corporations across the Galaxy, but his name had quickly sunk beneath public radar. Faro was possibly the senator's closest advisor; officially he headed up operations, but he maintained oversight of all special projects on the research team.

Saaj hissed softly. This was an inherently privileged meeting. The fact that Monroe had included him was a significant step forward.

Monroe spread his arms. "Shall we begin? I'd like you all to welcome our friend, Q'um Lharaa Saaj."

Nods toward Saaj circulated around the room. Monroe glanced in the anadon's direction. "Saaj will be joining us in critical discussions going forward. Saaj, feel free to chime in any time you have a question. Please, take a seat."

Saaj nodded slowly, taking a place next to Nasr-Rakh. He was the newcomer. Proper protocol demanded that he remain silent until he was specifically directed to speak. Monroe would expect adherence, despite his words. Monroe was always measuring, testing.

Harlowe snuck a Saaj a nervous look across the conference table. Saaj looked back at him and flicked his tongue, brushing it over the calcified outer edges of his mouth.

Monroe nodded. "Excellent. Business at hand... Mr. Razdorian, have we secured the patent on reactive cluster containment?" He sat, glancing at Saaj. Saaj settled onto the uncomfortably soft seat.

Razdorian's eyes dropped to the table's glass surface. "Sir, we have. It's on the ledger in Harperton for the next wave of approvals."

Monroe gave Tevecher a sharp look, tapping the table with a finger. "And we are responding with the investments in on-planet security systems?"

Tevecher nodded quickly. "We are. All funding had Bank confirmation by 03:00 LZS."

Monroe inhaled a long breath. "We have effectively made Trojan belljars obsolete." He smiled. "Information enrichment compounded by profit. Let's make sure we increase our exposure sufficiently in field generators as well."

Tevecher sat forward. "Yes, we're weighing our selections there, as well as the other areas where we're projecting a bump."

Monroe patted the table, looking down. "Very good. Legal and finance, I'm done with you, and Mr. Nasr-Rakh, you are dismissed as well—thank you for your fine work at Stasya Hyperdynamics. The organization owes you its gratitude."

Nasr-Rakh stood, along Razdorian and Tevecher. Tevecher bowed his head. "Just carrying out my role, senator."

Monroe glanced back at Saaj. "They know me so well." He swiveled to his other side. "Ms. Rabani, will you show them out, please? And secure the lobby and all com channels."

Rabani nodded as the three men headed for the door and briskly followed them out. Saaj examined her as she exited. With her suit and slicked-back shock of hair, she could have passed for a typical business executive, ruthless in mindset, but formidable only as far as she drew power from a credit-rich asset portfolio. But her gait was stiff and purposeful, more the look of military than a corporate power-broker reliant on a shield of credit. She needed no hired help to defend herself.

"Ms. Rabani excels at making things go smoothly for me." Monroe stared at Saaj. "And that's saying quite a bit. The business of being eminent is a very rocky road."

Saaj turned back to Monroe. "Her reputation precedes her."

Monroe raised his eyebrows. "Yes, she is quite difficult to ignore, isn't she?" He nodded at the door. "Efficient and ever-present. Priceless qualities for those of us who value our assistants."

The senator leaned forward and surveyed the room, seemingly poised to continue, but he remained silent. Saaj shifted, straightening in his seat. "There is a rumor she is engineered."

Monroe's gaze settled again on Saaj. "Very little escapes your attention, Saaj. In fact, she has a number of secrets." He sat back, clasping his hands. "Yes, I expect you'll eventually learn most of these little-known tidbits of ours. Ritsa Rabani is actually one the prototypes developed by our R&D special projects staff."

Some details of the senator's eccentric obsession with science and technology had filtered out into the industry news postings, particularly among those who kept a close eye on corporate activities, but nothing very substantive. He was careful about leaks, and the press releases were vague, with most of the specifics left confidential, though initiatives like this were plainly Faro's primary role. Monroe would not have been sharing organizational secrets lightly.

Faro's expression was unreadable. Saaj popped the liquid mucus seal that separated his trachea from his larynx and felt the stagnant air stream through his sinuses as the pressure released. The room held an odd flavor, some sort of sweetened smoke. The senator's eclectic tastes were apparently multisensory. Saaj suppressed the reflex to test it further, bracing his tongue inside his mouth as he turned to Monroe. "A human prototype. I wasn't aware you had exposure in genetics."

Monroe massaged his mustache. "One of the advantages of maintaining a private status is that you aren't required to publicize every project. Mr. Faro put it to action—why don't you enlighten our associate, Mr. Faro?" He stood up abruptly and stepped to the nearby bookcases along the back wall.

Faro looked more like a politician than a head of tech operations. He was Monroe's age, but his boyish face made him look at least 20 human years younger—easily comely enough to win plenty of votes in a human election, by human standards. He wore a gray flatsuit, with a bright white necktie against a flawless black shirt. His hair was full and silver-black, styled as a man who spent a career in the face of media cams. An outmoded pair of round eyeglasses was the only overtly scientific thing about him.

The operations XO peered at the anadon. "We were conducting a series of experiments designed to maximize biological longevity, with a focus on extending human life. We took fertilized eggs from subjects who had exhibited the characteristics we were looking for, and we injected a cocktail of lignoceric acid and metabolomic cytotoxins in various combinations; the idea was to build structurally stronger cell mitochondria while we worked on figuring out the right combination for a self-sustaining catalytic reaction that would lead to a steadier, more durable metabolism." He took a small cloth out of his breast pocket, removed his glasses, and began rubbing the lenses, shaking his head. "We cloned the trial samples, and we had some notable successes with one of the subject sets."

Saaj eyed Jan Harlowe, seated silently next to Faro. The bald man offered no sign that he was expecting to speak. Clearly he was the front man for research in name only.

Monroe was looking up at the large painting that dominated the back wall, an angular stylized image of a winged creature, white and distorted out of realistic proportion. He raised his voice. "The so-called Rabani set—named for the Earth clinic that supplied us. Yes, the process of manipulating the growth of the fetuses in this way had the unfortunate effect of causing defects that our people were unable to correct, but this one group of fertilized eggs was particularly resilient despite the damage to the cellular mechanisms. Of course this was the group that contained our associate, Ms. Rabani." He swung around on his heels and looked to Faro, folding his arms.

Faro nodded. "We were able to guide the coding the way we had hoped for most of the target maturation genes, but we couldn't keep the reactions stable. We hit all our marks in the Rabani clones, and they showed much higher stability, but the cellular breakdown caused by an imprint of our manipulation was terminal, effectively ending the possibility of longevity, even though the coding was perfect for an extended life span. Theoretically, without the given damage, the Rabani clones might have potentially lived

800 years or so. As it was, we estimated the surviving zygotes would be capable of living five or ten years at maximum." The operations XO glanced at Harlowe. "We're now projecting the Rabani clones will live for 48.6 Julian. As it turns out, our initial estimates of the dynamics were off; her cellular structure was more resistant to the pattern corruption than we anticipated." He paused. "There were some other side effects we didn't predict. The exogenous chemical infusion affected the clones' tropic hormone production, causing sterility and dampening their emotional responses. The test subjects were unable to reproduce, and inhibited serotonin absorption in the neurotransmitters gave them a low ceiling on excited sensitivity when reacting to stimuli."

Monroe frowned disdainfully at Faro as he returned to the table, remaining on his feet behind the curving high back of the oversized vanguard chair. "In our original plan, the samples were to be preserved in stasis while we ensured we were able to replicate the process; it was never our intent to allow them to reach maturity. The Rabani set failed to meet our control group specifications, but its characteristics were still interesting enough that we deemed continued study worthwhile. Fortune was smiling on Ms. Rabani."

Saaj shifted his eyes, keeping his head as still as possible. The atmosphere in the room was getting thick with human entitlement. Rabani was just outside, yet these men were discussing her like a disposable laboratory animal. He cleared his throat with a loud crackle. "When were these experiments conducted?" Faro had not been with the organization for ten human years; if he had jumped into the project the day he had joined, Rabani would still barely be old enough to look like a mature female.

"Very good question, Saaj." Monroe's eyes gleamed. "Ritsa Rabani has only been alive for seven years. Four rotations, by the Ul'an Hatranass calendar you're familiar with. We fell short in our efforts to maximize life, but Ms. Rabani is an example of our main success in this venture—to maximize maturity. The surviving fetuses treated to Mr. Faro's recipe were uniformly resistant to disease, and they developed a much stronger musculoskeletal system."

The achievement had apparently not been considered worthy of a public announcement. There were myriad implications toward the lucrative industry of army-building... Monroe had possibly sold the patent privately to the IPA or some other isolated military group. Saaj growled quietly under his breath. An obvious question hung in the air; the senator was apparently baiting him. "Have you done further testing along this line of research? It would seem a worthy venture, considering you came so close to your initial objective."

151

Faro exchanged glances with Monroe, who patted his chair and pushed away again, moving to another area of books off the near corner of the table. The senator seemed content to act as though he were spending a quiet, leisurely evening perusing his library while the others sat rigidly for the duration of the meeting.

The senator was making it more difficult for his audience to watch him, forcing them to make a choice between straining uncomfortably to keep their eyes on him or risk missing the nuances of the human visual cues. It was a gamesmanship tactic, a means of keeping the audience in a position of inferiority, and it might have been directed specifically at Saaj—yet another reminder to an anadon not used to being subservient to a human. Saaj flicked his tongue, lowering his brow. If he wanted to taste success, it would be on the senator's terms.

Faro spoke slowly. "We think we already have the blueprint for a genetic arrangement that would extend the human life span several thousand years… it was just a matter of putting it into place without disturbing the metabolic process." He looked toward the senator. "We set up an environment where the problem essentially corrected itself organically using strains of pure DNA."

Saaj rotated toward Faro. "You are referring to genetic material from other individuals?"

Faro nodded. "A new set of uncorrupted zygotes, yes. We spliced various samples of DNA with selected target genes from the Rabani DNA using only isolated structural patterns, mitochondrial metabolic decay rate, and certain imprinting mechanisms. Among other things, the genes we added were optimized for universal compatibility in bonding scenarios, so we expected a negligible fail rate, and we got it… everything went as our simulations predicted." He paused. "We've only taken our initial samples through the first stage, but we're ready if we want to initiate a round of second-generation clones."

Monroe held up a hand, twisting around to face Faro. "Of course Mr. Faro is correct—we can take the new DNA from anywhere, so we can be selective when we choose a candidate to follow in Ms. Rabani's footsteps. And we're prepared to move forward when the time is right, but for now, the project is on hiatus." He ran a finger against the binders of the books in the shelf, then spun and headed along the length of the conference table, skirting the line of seats. He paused to lean low as he passed behind the anadon. "You have other questions, Saaj?"

Saaj exhaled, staring blankly across the table in the direction of

Harlowe. "I wonder why you would discontinue a successful project such as this, with your objective in sight. By waiting, you delay any benefit you could collect, if I understand you correctly. And without licensing your methodology and biochemical proportions and making your findings fast with proof, you jeopardize marketability. It would seem there is more to this story."

"Indeed." Monroe appeared at the empty front edge of the conference table. He raised his eyebrows. "We have secured the exclusive rights to the methodology... we own the process, and this means of extending human life is ours alone to pursue. We won't move forward with it until I am convinced the benefits are worthy of bringing such a thing to the attention of the public. Besides, there are matters of posterity to consider." He paused, smiling darkly. "After all, we're talking about granting the luxury of extended life that goes beyond the usual preservatives and medical regenerative stimulants, beyond all records of human existence. The gift of many lifetimes is not something to idly grant to the first random clone that happens to show sufficiently nondefective genetic material. Before I extend that privilege and crown this newer, better version of Humanity, I'd like to have a suitable candidate for the honor."

Saaj sat frozen in his seat. Monroe's eyes were locked on him as if this suitable candidate he envisioned should hold some sort of personal significance. Clearly the senator couldn't have been considering anadon DNA—the logistics of splicing interspecies genetic material would have obviously presented unnecessary complications. More likely, it was the look of a man unwilling to compromise in his convictions, despite reason. A look of defiance. Monroe would withhold his scientific breakthrough for exactly as long as he chose. Perhaps he would withhold it until he uncovered a way to take this so-called gift of life for his own.

Monroe sighed. "In any event, we've already been rewarded for our trouble. Ms. Rabani has developed into one of my greatest assets." He continued to fix his attention on Saaj.

The anadon snorted quietly and shook his head, sliding his eyes toward Faro. "Have you attempted to correct the flaws in the Rabani DNA, to further improve it?"

Faro sat up, speaking quickly. "We did some preliminary testing in that area before the project was tabled. We think we know specifically what caused the defects in sterility and brain chemistry. We do think it's possible to better control those factors without affecting the accelerated maturation, so that option is available if we decide to run another test."

Monroe shot Faro a sharp glance, and the advisor became as inanimate as the furniture. But the senator smiled again in Saaj's direction, apparently more amused than annoyed. "I have every confidence in Mr. Faro's abilities to make other rewarding creations, but his talents are of more use to me in a different area. I like Ms. Rabani's DNA just as it is. There are currently 76 surviving clones at my disposal, indistinguishable from one another, and each one as efficient as the next. It suited my purposes to keep them separated, use them more or less as an information network spread throughout the points of contact in my organization." He arched an eyebrow. "You seem quick to point out flaws in a such a clear-cut blessing."

Yrissor! Injecting unsolicited opinion had been a mistake, and Monroe was making him squirm intentionally. Saaj exhaled hotly. "Apologies, senator. I meant no disrespect and regret any offense."

Monroe flashed a smile, exaggerated in the spotty, uneven lighting emanating from the ornately camouflaged photo-panels above the conference table. "Not at all, Saaj. I'm impressed that you aren't afraid to speak your mind. It's one of the things that makes you attractive as a potential lieutenant of mine." His facial expression was backlit—dark, and for a moment, impossible to read.

Saaj bowed his head. Despite the words, there was a hint of veiled hostility in the arrogant, patronizing tone of the senator's human voice. It was a tone reminiscent of the haughty ignorance of his Galinan party-goers.

Monroe continued around the opposite side of the table to the long edge where Harlowe and Faro were seated, putting a hand briefly on Faro's shoulder as he reached him. "It's thanks in part to these flaws, as you call them, that every one of Ms. Rabani's incarnations is completely loyal to me. No heightened emotional response, no need for personal actualization, ambition. They are as selfless and dedicated as a low-grade, nonsentient computer apparatus. I've never been partial to AIEs and their inevitable susceptibility to outside manipulation. It's difficult to find good, loyal help in my business, but I do expect a very big commitment from the individuals I choose to invite into my inner sanctum. I hope you can appreciate that, Saaj."

Saaj nodded slowly. "I can." He paused, selecting his words carefully. "Your investment in these experiments has borne good returns."

Monroe smiled broadly. "Indeed it has. Information is power; I make it my business to compile information that no one else currently has." He glanced at Faro and gave him a quick pat on the shoulder, then stepped away from the conference table and circled back toward the front wall of the room, stretching his arms as he looked up at the paintings. "These simple clones have infused this organization with new life—they might only have one-fourth the time we humans are normally endowed, but it would be a mistake to dwell on the matter of their limited life span. The manifestations of Ritsa Rabani are a shining example of our ability to triumph over death." He straightened. "She is my eyes and ears, and she is everywhere, ubiquitous until her time expires. I named her Amritsa, after the Hindu pool of nectar that fueled the gods' immortality. Remember it, Saaj… immortality is the ultimate goal. It's always in my mind."

Saaj stared back at him. Studies of boosting longevity had been thoroughly saturated, and research into it had essentially been dead for over three centuries. Clearly the senator had forged new inroads, in addition to reaping the benefits of this ready-made army. But Monroe not only believed he could extend human life, he literally believed he could defeat death. Exaggerated ego and frivolous glorification were common traits among humans, but this man had taken it to a completely new level. Where most in his position focused on amassing personal wealth, the senator had apparently bent his will on this immortality fixation. Was it possible all of the legendary organizational trade secrets were actually just exercises in a falraaq human's misguided attempt to transform himself into a god?

Somehow, it was not surprising. In a way, as distinguished and imposing as the senator was, this fit his profile perfectly. A brilliant, insatiable strategist with a violently impulsive edge. The man was an adept, calculating entrepreneur, visionary in the veiled architecture of his empire, but it was increasingly obvious this rumored volatility of his was more than just the exaggerated bluster of political enemies. Stories of the man's explosive rage had circulated in the past… hints of improprieties, even links to a few deaths under questionable circumstances. It was naturally difficult to believe a man of his stature was capable of setting aside his cultured pedigree and immersing himself in the filth of killing—strangling a mistress in her home, or slitting the throat of an isolated worker in the heat of the halapa fields. The senator had consciously reinforced the record of his success as a competent, cerebral leader at every opportunity, but there was something beneath the expertly rendered social graces, something familiar among those who were close to him. Deep down, this human was guided by a driving, ruthless, visceral desire for personal aggrandizement. He had no qualms about breaking the laws when it was in his interest, even ordering sentients killed while he was far away and insulated with an alibi. There was a much darker side to the senator than his public could have imagined, and

155

the single-mindedness of an obsession about immortality was a reminder.

Monroe clasped his hands behind his back, pitching his voice like a practiced orator. "There's a bit more to this that you might be interested to know. Ritsa Rabani is pure-blood Dravidian, hailing from the Indian Peninsula on Earth, a strand that presents a heavier pigmentation, if you're unfamiliar with the many colors of the Human Race." He inhaled sharply, stepping to the wall, toward a dark portrait of a woman. "Do you like that smell, Saaj? Dravidian incense. I find it exhilarating."

Saaj let the scent of the spiced smoke drift back into his sinus cavities, and his eyes momentarily blurred as the long, narrow slits of his pupils dilated. Monroe was going to continue to prompt predictable responses, orchestrating the conversation like a puppeteer. "I rarely notice aromas that are not offensive. This air is not offensive to me."

Monroe smiled. "I'm so pleased." He looked down and rubbed his chin with a finger, as if posing for a portrait.

Saaj felt the membranes at the corners of his mouth twitch. The senator assumed he had everything lined up exactly as he wanted, his whims indulged, his subordinates programmed like maintenance androids. He was accustomed to manipulating throngs of people with the twitch of a facial muscle or the simple fluctuation in his voice, articulating calls to action with the gesture of a hand, tugging the emotional level of the weak-minded human crowds in any direction he desired.

Saaj grunted. The senator knew exactly what he was doing. He had risen to the pinnacle of society on Anastasia through his carefully crafted public speeches. Eventually, his skillful communication had made him a senator, though his money had influenced his planetary government long before he had held an elected office. Now he wielded power from within that government, snowing the public while he reaped profit behind their backs.

Saaj glanced at the other two companions at the conference table. Faro was wearing the pained expression of a man with indigestion and no drugs to take for it, while Harlowe looked resigned and listless. The two seemed to have no fear of reprisal for their outward disinterest.

Monroe seemed enthralled with the portrait above him, staring at it as if memorizing its position. "Yes, smell the Dravidian incense... soak it in. The spice of life. It was no accident that I chose Dravidian DNA to take the first step toward realization of the first undying soul." He turned and focused on Saaj.

The first undying soul. It was fortunate the senator knew well enough to keep his ravings to the privacy of his conference room... the man would find his public much more difficult to manipulate if he allowed them to see him as a madman. Saaj leveled his eyes at Monroe and made no response.

"The Dravidians have a fascinating religious background, the most endearing to me of any of the religions from Earth. The ancient Hindu faith places the sanctity of life above all, to a greater extent than any other religion. Every living thing is sacred; we pass from one life to the next, each time taking on a new form reflecting the way we've previously lived. Karma. Balance. Rebirth. Incredibly attractive to me as a concept. Really, is there a belief system in history that better reflects the symmetry of the universe as we know it in modern society?"

Clearly a rhetorical question. Saaj bowed his head and waited.

Monroe looked back at the painting. "Are you familiar with the *Mona Lisa*, Saaj?" Faro removed his glasses a second time and pinched the bridge of his nose between his thumb and forefinger. Without turning his head, Monroe stifled the man's stirrings. "I realize you've heard this before, Mr. Faro, but I want Saaj to hear this and I need you here to explain a few things to him." He raised his voice a notch. "Do you know the painting?"

Saaj stared at the bust of the black-robed, dark-haired human female. The woman seemed to stare at him with a wry, slightly disturbing smile. "I have never seen it."

"It's possibly the most famous painting in human history to date. You are looking at a copy, of course, although the replication process I undertook to obtain this makes it indistinguishable from the original without a molecular examination. The original was painted in 1503 by Leonardo da Vinci of Firenze."

Saaj adjusted his chair, repositioning himself to face Monroe. The painting was still visible in the corner of his eye, plain and somewhat small among the other works on display. "Ss. I know little about human art. It seems ordinary for a famous work."

Monroe frowned, hesitating, then crossed the room and resumed his place at the head of the glass table, this time seating himself. "Thank you again for your candor, Saaj, but Leonardo da Vinci is one of the most important artists in human history, and he was much more than an artist—he was a great thinker, a mathematician who had a love for technological advancement, as I do. Now I understand it may be difficult for an anadon to appreciate the significance of a human artist and his work... you've been brought up with your own anadon-oriented perspective, more or less ignorant of human accomplishments. Your cultural biases are really none of my concern, but I need you to trust me in what I'm telling you. Can I count on you to do that?"

Saaj lowered his brow. "Yes, senator."

"Listen to me carefully. An artist is survived through all eternity by immortalizing himself with a painting. Symbolically, the ultimate immortalization is in a self-portrait. The artist's own face glorified and sent down through the ages, reminding everyone of the artist's years of life." He glanced at the *Mona Lisa*. "That painting is Leonardo's self-portrait. He painted his own face on the maiden's body so that his eyes would always return the gaze of those who looked at his art."

Saaj snuck another glance at the painting, and the rendered human eyes stared helplessly back. Strange that a male sentient would choose to impose his face on the body of a female, and stranger still that his people would later revere him for it.

The anadon's jaw tightened. Centuries before, it would have been possible to pursue a purer career within the Anadon Sphere and avoid humans and their idiosyncrasies, but now everything was connected to interspecies commerce. The last truly lucrative opportunities that did not involve humans or other distasteful sentients had disappeared in the distant past. His fate was intertwined with humans, and there were no opportunities more lucrative than the promise offered by Teodor Monroe. The musings of the senator were important, whether they appealed to anadon ears or not.

Monroe was holding a finger in the air. "I fancy Leonardo knew something about the Hindu religion. Perhaps the *Mona Lisa* is a painting of himself embodied as the two-faced goddess of motherhood and destruction, known as both Uma and Kali, good and evil. The all-encompassing and everlasting. I'm convinced Leonardo wanted life and power as much as I do." He leaned forward, pressing against the glass surface like a crouching predator. "I have been investing heavily in my own personal advancement of technology in an effort to find the key to eternal life. I'm not satisfied with life as it is now, Saaj. We progress further and further, pushing the human life expectancy gradually closer to 200 years, but in the end, death is inevitable. We may yet push it further, but it will never be satisfactory until we can guarantee continuous life for as long as it's desired. Understand—I don't want to live on symbolically, like Leonardo in the painting. I could be the most powerful sentient ever to grace the Galaxy, but as it stands, I'm nothing more than that. After my death, someone will come along who surpasses my accomplishments, obscures my name. I don't want that to happen, Saaj. I want it all. I want to be the strongest, and I want it to last until I decide I've had enough. I want every intelligent being to fear my name for centuries on end. I want to be known as the first immortal.

"In Hindu belief, all life is respected—every insect, every plant—because everyone is reincarnated, and every form of life has a chance of becoming human. Endless life. An enriching story, perhaps, but nothing more than mythology. The scientific disciplines are the only set of guiding principles that can be tested and do not collapse under scrutiny. Science. Technology. Uma and Kali are as symbolic as the *Mona Lisa*. The Hindus may believe in endless life, but that belief, as endearing as it is, is nothing more than the result of wishful thinking. Convenient myth, created in the imaginations of mortal beings. Judaism, Christianity, Islam, and the different sects of your own people. Fantasies. Death is the only true reality."

Saaj grunted. There were still those who believed there was truth in religion, and there were many of them among the anadons. Most sentients in the presence of an anadon would have chosen their words more carefully. The senator had his own set of rules.

Monroe seemed to be reading from the pages of an invisible textbook floating in the air above the opposite end of the octagonal table. "We've become reliant upon technology, and I say this is good. Technology is our only true salvation. Without it, a species is doomed to die out with the death of its star... we've already achieved the capability of immortality as intelligent races. In fact, it isn't a stretch to imagine we can attain immortality on an individual level, as impossible as that may strike you. Life is a powerful force, but like any other resource, I believe it can be harnessed. In fact, the idea doesn't even fly in the face of nature, for nature has already provided us examples to emulate."

He paused for dramatic effect. Saaj took a measured breath and listened to the air thunder through the two craniolateral cavities at the joints of his jaw. He glanced at Faro as the man lightly scratched his cheek.

Monroe looked at Saaj expectantly. Saaj squinted into the senator's stare. "You are referring to the ytaoans?"

Monroe smiled. "The ytaoans!"

The legendary spaceborne race of beings held a singular, passive existence, drifting and feeding off the starlight, scarcely more animated than a species of plant or exomicrobe. Sporadic studies had established them as intelligent, capable of telepathic communication, and they were supposed by some to wield telekinetic powers, though evidence had yet to be obtained to confirm that hypothesis. Perhaps Monroe's people had finally pioneered a new breakthrough.

"We know nothing about the ytaoans, Saaj. No one has ever so much as collected a tissue sample, or done any sort of extended close study. And I would love to study them—if xenobiologists' theories are correct, the ytaoans have indefinite life spans. I believe the ytaoans have achieved a golden plateau of evolution, perhaps a greater height of intellect than seen in any of the other sentient races, thanks to the advantage of not being at the mercy of any one star's life span. If the ytaoans can do it, then so can I." Monroe paced around the table, passing behind the backs of the two XOs and crossing the rug toward the other side of the room, then whirled back around. "I don't have the benefit of billions of years of uninterrupted evolution, but I have something better. The sentient species have frozen the course of our natural progression by seizing control of it, taking it into our own hands. If I want to become immortal, I'll need to manufacture it myself. But it's in my hands." He returned to the far end of the table and focused on Saaj. "Technology. Information and ingenuity. We have the means, and we are limited only by what our imagination can conceive of. Saaj, I intend to use technology to my advantage. It is an old truth among the people of the Anadon Sphere. To quote Jaldab'r of Aaq 'Uladin: 'Balarh-daqa urla Hass-tap'r.' The Conqueror sees the farthest."

Saaj felt his back stiffen. It was rare that a human dared to speak the name of the Great Truthsayer, let alone attempting to pronounce the ancient Ul'an words. The blasphemous violations of etiquette were mounting, and they were obviously intended. The senator apparently wanted to know the limits of anadon patience. He would soon learn it if he pressed the point much further.

Monroe looked from the anadon to Faro and back. "It is my intention to dominate the Galaxy. This is my birthright as an intelligent being with the means to acquire power—you know as well as I that the history of the Galaxy is no more than a series of conquests. Domination and conquest... these are the legacies of intelligent life. Ever since the rise of the iconath, the race with the strongest technology has exerted ruthless control over the other races. Even today."

Monroe's words rang true. The threat of alien technology had been the direct cause of the unification of the Anadon Empire on Ul'an Hatranass. Ages before, the iconath had risen in the Hub, at the center of the Spiral. They had evolved quickly and dominated the entire Galaxy until their power waned, and they were forced to retreat back into the Hub by the vorines, the next rising force. The vorines had spread like fire, surrounding the diminished Iconath Sphere and moving into every Spiral Arm, extinguishing every inferior form of intelligent life they came across. Then they had gone,

160

and the cillians had emerged—those crawling half shells, with their fragile claws and tiny stub-legs. They had the pathetic look of small herd animals, but with the disappearance of the vorines, they had inherited the Galaxy. And they had managed to establish a firm galactic trade monopoly with their superior technology long before anadons or humans ever existed.

Monroe's fingertips were white against the table top. He seemed completely absorbed in his vision, his eyes burning with intensity, as if he were bent entirely on this one singular passion and he had lost sight of all else. But Monroe was a businessman, and he was aware of everything in the room at all times. The man was putting on a show because he wanted everyone in the room to have the impression that he was capable of anything, including the ability to become some sort of immortal Galactic overlord. Whether or not it was a remotely realistic notion, he could make anyone believe that it was. And that might have been all that mattered.

Monroe pulled himself out of the apparent trance and glared at the anadon. "We discovered hyperdrive over a thousand years ago. If we can break the barrier of light speed, I say we can break the aging process. We just haven't found the formula yet… but we do have a lead. Mr. Faro?"

Faro composed himself quickly. "You may know Jin Fong and her experiments on rejuvenation. She was able to isolate gravity as a factor affecting the production of free-radicals that cause chaotic long-term mutagenic damage in mitochondria."

Saaj nodded slowly. "And this is what controls the aging process, I assume."

Faro nodded. "Right—mitochondrial metabolism is the accepted key factor driving senescence. Aging." He paused. "Essentially, Fong showed that death is accelerated by external forces… gravity is a form of physical erosion on the body. Her findings explain the jump in the human life span at the start of mass interstellar transport—less gravity, longer life span. She effectively offered up a tidy explanation for the inevitability of death—gravity exists throughout the universe at some minute level, so no one can completely escape it."

The senator stood and returned to the shelf of books to the left, this time quicker and more purposeful in his movement. He removed a large, well-kept tome, and began leafing through the pages.

Faro went on. "The implication is that if an external force can accelerate the production of free radicals, it stands to reason that a force exists which could do the opposite. There were follow-up tests involving the various manifestations of matter and energy, but none of them yielded results. In most cases, the forces had a similar effect to that of gravity… free-radical production went up, not down."

Monroe continued to leaf through the book, then hesitated. "Mr. Faro was able to locate an archive containing documentation acquired from the cillians that was not released at the Conference of Kad, last millennium." He looked up. "'To those who are constantly devoted and worship me with love, I give the understanding by which they can come to me.' From the *Mahabharata*, specifically the *Bhagavad Gita*. More from Hindu. Words to remember." He flashed a smile in Faro's direction, closed the book, and slipped it back onto the shelf, turning to Saaj. "The epic states, 'What is found here may be elsewhere; what is not here is nowhere else.'" He returned to the table and sat next to Saaj, raising his eyebrows. "That said, what we did find in the cillian files were numerous citations of a particular compound that seemed to have the qualities we were looking for."

Saaj blinked the nictitating membranes of his inner eyelids, moistening his lenses as he focused on Monroe. "An impressive accomplishment. I am not aware of any other cases of a latter-generation sentient breaking cillian file encryption."

Faro cleared his throat unpleasantly. "The archive was compiled by the teledura sometime before the era of interspecies exchange. They used basic long-term position-point surveillance techniques to identify com sources and siphon sensitive information as it was being encrypted."

The daalfin-taaq! Saaj snorted despite himself. Strange that Monroe would believe he could rely on information delivered by teledura spies—the amphibious bipeds were the most incompetent race among the 12 sentient species, repeatedly challenging the much more powerful cillians in attempts to expand their colonial realm, repeatedly failing. A race with a history of unwarranted arrogance, displayed in acts of pointless defiance against the other sentients and especially against the anadons. They deserved no better than their anadon label, a term adapted from the humans—*daalfin-taaq*. Helpless beasts of the water; foolish squanderers of the gift of higher intelligence.

He swallowed a growl, keeping it low in his throat. "It seemed unlikely the cillians would have allowed such valuable information to fall into the possession of daalfin-taaq." He was careful to direct the remark toward the two XOs and away from the senator, but Faro sucked in his lips and let Monroe handle the response.

The senator flared his nostrils. "Daalfin-taaq… reconnaissance… is apparently better than our own. They seem to have devoted themselves toward avenging the long history of cillian economic suppression they saw during their colonial period. Single-mindedness can be a powerful weapon." He smiled. "To the point. The cillian records contain details of a unique form of matter. They called it 'ap-sat-oc'—'beautiful fire-like object'—and also 'tep-tak'—'life-giving stone.' This is not an unfamiliar story to humans... we have similar descriptions of special, sacred stones in human history, passed down to us from long before the age of interstellar commerce. They were known as 'baetyls,' often associated with meteorites, attributed magical powers and associated with mythological gods. Pliny the Elder, a well-known Roman historian and naturalist, named these baetyls among his categories of classified magnetic minerals in his work, *Naturalis Historiae*, reserving two separate classes for them and describing them as 'supernatural.'"

The senator's interest had to have been based on something more substantive than these ancient tales. Saaj glanced at Faro, shifting in his seat, then turned back to Monroe. "And you believe that this cillian documentation is more accurate than these unscientific accounts from human antiquity?"

Monroe seemed unflustered by the pointed doubt. "Yes, that's right—but I am also establishing that the story itself is universal among the sentients. Each sentient has its own version of the story of the sacred stone—even the anadons. Perhaps these stories, wild and unreal as they sound, have a foundation in truth. This new documentation from the cillians came from much further along in the sentients' path of scientific advancement. It offered a layer of modern scrutiny to the claims and descriptions not seen in anything in our history." Monroe looked from Faro back to Saaj, cocking his head. "In fact, tales of this cillian material had apparently reached human consciousness prior to our rediscovery of the records found by the teledura. We found these minerals had been known unofficially among human geologists in the 2300s as 'postulare material cilliae,' which simply means 'theoretical matter of cillian claim.' We've readdressed it as 'pyropite.'" He smiled. "According to the cillians, it is a basic variety of garnet gem along the pyrope-almandine series with a specific proportion of magnesium to iron. An aluminum silicate... just regular matter, the same as any matter found in the universe today. A crystal. But it is said that this material glows with a light of its own." He smiled. "Pyropite, Saaj. The fire's-eye stone."

Saaj was impassive. His knowledge of physics was murky, but simple rock did not produce visible light without some other form of stimulation. "Uqaa. You are suggesting this aluminum silicate compound is somehow generating its own nuclear energy, as a star does?"

163

Monroe straightened, taking a deep breath, and his chest seemed to swell. "Nuclear energy, yes, but not like a star. This mechanism would have to be something entirely new."

Faro exchanged glances with Harlowe, and Harlowe eased himself forward and sighed quietly, then spoke for the first time. "Cillians hypothesized a new quantum dynamic that would be required for material with the described properties. This matter would have to be undergoing a process causing a steady rate of fractoluminescence, something that would break down the molecular bonds to sufficiently excite the electrons in a very slow-acting, arithmetic chain reaction. Radioactive decay is stochastic—it doesn't occur at a steady rate, so if the cillian records are accurate, this material is being acted upon by something our physical laws haven't predicted." The man's voice was hollow and meek. Either he doubted what he was saying, or he was too overly familiar with the story.

Faro nodded. "An exotic force that hasn't been tested. And there was evidence suggesting this force might have the desired effect of reducing free-radicals and preserving cell mitochondria."

Saaj looked from him to Monroe. Monroe pursed his lips, his eyes sparkling in the soft light. "When a cillian touched the pyropite, the individual would be infused with new life... a sense of exhilaration and uncommon strength. Cillians who kept the pyropite with them enjoyed unprecedented life spans. Some are documented to have lived for tens of thousands of years." He tapped the table and leaned closer. "And there is one more bit of evidence." He frowned at Faro and raised an eyebrow.

Faro motioned to the tablet in front of Harlowe, and Harlowe tapped at it briefly and slid it over to him. Faro sniffed and straightened his eyeglasses. "According to the cillians, in JD 2448894, all of the known matter of this kind underwent a spontaneous phase change and disintegrated in what seems to be a sudden total matter-energy conversion." He leaned over the tablet screen. "Quote: 'All accounts of observed samples describe consistent disintegration by complete and immediate phase transition to broad-spectrum energy, with a short-lived carryover effect to proximal organic material ranging outward in proportion to the size of the given sample.' End quote. It goes on about how these intense energy emissions engulfed and essentially annihilated cillian technicians in a number of laboratories where they were working with the samples at the time... also that there were reported instances of simultaneous energy flares in space that measured hundreds of kilometers in radius. At the same time, there are reports across the Cillian Sphere of power blackouts and widespread mechanical failures as well as spontaneous cases of symptomatic seizure, all occurring within minutes over an expanse of roughly 8,000 light years—that much we do have corroborated by scinti source documentation. Apparently the cillians didn't attempt to hide that part of it, though they blamed it on a gamma ray burst." He cleaned his throat. "Here, they attribute all of these anomalies to the wide-scale eruption of this matter."

Saaj looked down at the clear glass of the table. The chronicling tasted of folklore. "It sounds to me like misinformation. Material like this has value in warfare… the cillians would be motivated to record that it was destroyed to prevent pursuit by another species."

Faro nodded. "I did some cross-checking and found something in an unexpected place. There was an unusual death on Earth in JD 2448894, the same time the matter disintegrated."

Saaj sat forward. "Earth, in the Human Sphere?"

"The death was reported in the news. A man by the name of John Walker disappeared in a flash of light at a public transport facility. Witnesses said the light consumed the man, though there were apparently no other casualties among the people who saw it. The flash was simultaneous with interference in radio transmissions all over the planet… the event was recorded, which is no doubt why it wasn't dismissed out of hand."

Monroe cut in, projecting his voice as if Saaj was seated in a far corner of the room. "John Walker. A very unobtrusive man who led an unusually quiet life. He became known as 'the Blaze-of-Light Man' and was celebrated for a time. Over the years, the story became more of a footnote and was ultimately forgotten. One of the many unexplained phenomena in the annals of human history, relegated to the status of myth and legend." He turned in his seat, raising his eyebrows at Faro.

Faro looked down and took a breath. "Right. And back then we didn't have the technology to unbind a person at the molecular level, so the recording that confirmed the witness accounts was at the time quite remarkable and was heavily scrutinized, but never explained. The recording equipment failed several seconds after the incident occurred, and it initially appeared that the flash of light and erasure of the man's image was the effect of damage to the visual medium, but close examination of the footage uncovered no discontinuity; otherwise, I'm sure the story would not have survived. To the science of the day, it was impossible for a man to simply disappear. Nothing like this had ever happened before, and nothing has happened since. The only thing we have today that could have done something like this on such a specific level is a particle weapon, like a proteid cap-slinger. Back then, we didn't even have handheld lasers."

Saaj crackled his throat. A strange story. But sentients had always loved to revel in the unexplained. Strange things happened every day according to the Hjaalzoa, the tabloid news network of the Anadon Sphere.

Monroe cut in. "For me, the mystery around John Walker doesn't begin and end with his reported death. A follow-up investigation revealed that this man had no living relatives and no known acquaintances, he was apparently unemployed, and his history was dubious. There were records of several bank accounts in his name, unusually spread out around the world, but there was even a question about the identification number he was using with these accounts; he was apparently using the number of another man with the same name. He seemed to have lived virtually off the grid. This was viewed at the time as something that cast doubt on the veracity of Walker's death—the idea that he might be using an assumed name suggested that he was a grifter who was perhaps motivated to fake his death. Certainly there were magicians capable of pulling off a disappearing act that would fool a video recorder. I, on the other hand, chose to believe there might be more to it than that. There were several other curious details that the reporters of the day failed to emphasize." He stared at the anadon.

Clearly he meant to continue. Saaj looked back at him, waiting silently.

Monroe cocked his head. "The name Walker used on his bank accounts was 'John Ulysses Walker.' He was careful to leave out the middle name in any other business he conducted, perhaps to make it easier for him to use another man's name, but I wondered if the middle name was a clue to his true identity. Found among his things were an assortment of antique trinkets from different time periods that one might have expected to find in a museum, and also, most significant of all, a bounded journal containing handwriting in various transliterations, largely in the archaic scripts of the ancient Mediterranean… a virtual chronology of human history's lettering systems, starting with cuneiform, the script of the ancient Sumerians." The senator's eyes gleamed. "Evidence that this man had an uncommon interest in Antiquity, perhaps indicative of nothing more than a fervent historian, or an opportunistic expert with an understanding in how to convert archaeological artifacts into profit. But perhaps Walker was living his life in the shadows because he was motivated to keep his age out of the record books. I found the name 'Ulysses' to be a particularly interesting choice, if indeed he chose it. With his bank accounts, he associated himself with the Roman adaptation of Odysseus the Wanderer, of Greek myth."

Saaj lowered his brow. The senator was actually suggesting this human carried a sample of the matter himself and had been subject to the same fate that had befallen the cillians, that this 'Blaze-of-Light Man' had hidden his age because he had experienced a freakish expanse of longevity. Ancient Greece and Sumer... how long did Monroe suppose this man had been alive?

Monroe seemed to read his thoughts. "It's incontrovertible, Saaj. This man disappeared at the precise moment the event swept the Cillian Sphere— he had no friends or relatives because they died thousands of years before him, and he knew cuneiform because he was alive when the writing system was in use. I would have his power if the pyropite existed today. I assure you, Saaj, if I had one of those crystal gems, I would never die."

Abruptly Harlowe spoke again. "The cillians' specs say the pyropite was resistant to all forms of erosion. The crystals wouldn't burn up entering a planetary atmosphere, and they wouldn't melt even at stellar core temperatures. Lasers, refined plasma weapons, nanonuclear surgery, and any other technique they tried were all ineffective. This material was indestructible. But we think that if a sample had been enclosed in a specially engineered fusion-filter at the time of the disintegration, we could tap the power of this matter in the form of pure energy at a tempered level. Theoretically, it might be possible to safely direct the energy into a living sentient organism before it degrades."

Saaj raised his head and looked across the open table at the paintings spaced along the wall. It was hard to dismiss the possibility that the senator had lost touch with reality, but the man was being completely sincere not only because he coveted extreme personal aggrandizement, but because he had a good reason to believe that it could be achieved. The universe yielded rewards to those who took the time to understand it. A disintegrating man would seem magical to a culture that had never seen a laser-assisted-plasma refractor, but in retrospect, such an incident was easily studied and exploited.

He glanced at Faro, who was now looking down, completely nonchalant. Self-assurance, maybe. If Monroe got his way, anyone close to him would benefit. His conquest would bring the Galaxy to bear... to his friends, he would offer the fruits of a galaxy at his mercy, and to his enemies, he promised to exercise the vengeance of an angry god.

Monroe brushed his mustache, suddenly conjuring again. The indoctrination appeared to be coming to a close. Saaj hissed quietly to himself. There was probably no role for him in this particular initiative; the purpose of this presentation was clearly to show him that he was a trusted member of the senator's organization.

Monroe was watching his eyes. He inhaled sharply and stood. "That should do for now, gentlemen." He waved at the XOs and they stirred and stood after him. Saaj waited until they were both up, then swung his legs out from under the table and rose himself.

Monroe turned to him. "Saaj, I need you a moment more, if you will."

"Yes, senator."

Monroe stared at him for a long moment… briefly it felt as if the senator was trying to read him, as if he fancied himself as the one human truly capable of reading an anadon expression. Then his face broke out in a roguish smile. "Why don't we concentrate for a moment on matters we can control at the present time? I want you to track down this Dexter Massengill for me. My ham-fisted GM at the Topaz failed to recognize that what Mr. Massengill can give us is far more valuable than any damage he's been able to do. I want to know where a man with no ties or connections, an orphan from virtually nowhere, gets his resourcefulness. I want you to extend him an offer."

Saaj straightened, cracking his stiffly calcified spine. "I'll get it done."

"Good. Make sure you do. I believe you'll find him in Eo-Nowar." He paused. "If you recall our discussion about the Medellín Cartel, I believe one of the first assignments Pablo Escobar handed down to Rafael Avila was to neutralize a group of local government authorities causing problems at one of his airfields. Avila was to persuade the group with an offer of profit-sharing. They insisted on remaining true to their obligation as elected officials, and he ended their terms in office. Avila understood that gaining their support was the cartel's priority, but he also understood that improvisation is a necessary component of the job."

Saaj hissed quietly. "I am aware of your priorities, senator."

"I'm confident you are. Shall we go?" Monroe started for the door and gave a quick shout. Rabani opened it from the other side, and he promptly passed through. Faro and Harlowe stood in place and signaled Saaj to go ahead. Saaj treaded out, taking a last look at the *Mona Lisa*.

He snorted. Uma and Kali. Good and evil. Even humans had gone through their days of holding religion above all other things, as had every sentient species at different times. The various chronologies were littered with examples of reverence to false prophets cluttering truth with their lies about mythical gods. Teodor Monroe strove to have the Galaxy believe that he was the one to be revered, as had individuals before him. But the way Monroe wielded power, there was no need for inventing stories of omnipotence.

"Ultimately, disorder rules our universe, from the vantage point of the observer who lives within it. Structure unravels as time progresses, and chaos abounds, more and more. It can be seen in the decay of an atom, or the gradual exhaustion of mitochondria in a living cell... the settling of ripples in a pond... the collapse of civilization. Some struggle to organize their lives, only to have the reins of control wrested from their grasp.

"But the law of entropy is not a constant. Our universe is rife with perturbations, and as it blasts apart, eddies of symmetry are created... the swirl of galaxies... the synchronized dance of a moon around its planet. There are moments of perfection amid the disarray. Natural thermodynamics notwithstanding, order can manifest by chance... and it can be asserted. A straighter, measured path can be forged, if one is willing to put forth the effort."

```
... GCL AE.001
Phi 00 00 00.00 / Theta 00 15 37.33 / Rho 00.00 / JD 2448890
Alpha Confinii: EARTH; "Philadelphia"; 24 September 1992 CE
```

Cassie Prescott held her menu high in front of her face without reading the words. Across the café patio and right on the other side of the railing was an odd little man. The man had been walking back and forth on the sidewalk for almost a half an hour, staying directly in her line of sight. He was nowhere near a bus stop.

She lowered the menu slightly. The man was still there. He didn't look like a vagrant; he had on a beige trench coat, clean, and not disheveled. He had to be waiting to meet someone, but he didn't have the air of someone who was being stood up, or inconvenienced. He was strolling in slow, even paces, and he didn't seem interested in anything around him. He wasn't looking around at the people passing by, trying to identify faces—he wasn't looking for anyone. He seemed resigned, content to stay there in front of the café all day if he had to.

Cassie shifted in her seat. He was perfectly positioned to casually observe her, although he hadn't looked in her direction once, as far as she could tell. She hadn't caught him, anyway. If he was eyeballing her, he seemed to know exactly when to withdraw his stare.

It couldn't have been Wyler. The man was too small to be a football player, and he didn't have the build. Of course, Wyler could have had an associate.

She frowned and glanced at her watch. Wyler was now 20 minutes late. He had left a curt message saying he would be there; he had made no attempt to negotiate a different time, and he had left no indication he wouldn't show. Now, apparently, he was blowing it off. Probably something she should have counted on.

She raised her eyebrows and sighed, focusing on a picture of the Hollywood Café's grilled chicken Caesar special. She could always use the time to actually eat lunch. She dropped the menu on the glass table and squinted again at the man on the sidewalk.

There was something weirdly familiar about him, but if she had ever seen the man before, there was no way she would have forgotten it. His face was dynamically distinctive, dark and creased with sunken shadows. Murky. He had appeared not long after she had been seated, and she had noticed the face almost immediately.

She looked in the other direction, toward the door that led inside the café. If the man was just a creep hanging around to stare at her, he wouldn't have been the first. It was a big city, and there was definitely no shortage of creeps.

As she looked, a waiter in a green apron emerged through the door, followed by a larger man in a green bomber jacket and jeans. The waiter gestured in her direction. She sat up and removed her napkin from her lap, dropping it on the table. This would have to be Wyler.

She half-stood and raised her hand, and the man made eye contact. He seemed to hesitate for a moment, then lowered his head and started loping toward her table.

She sat back down and took a glance around at the other tables, as if she were scanning a jury. The strange man with the dark face was gone, and for some reason, that was an enormous relief. She turned her attention back to Wyler.

The jacket was tattered and dirty, worn loosely over a wrinkly plaid flannel button-down that was open enough at the top to see a sizable chunk of the black T-shirt underneath. The man's brown hair was short and relatively unbrushed, parted loosely at the side of his head.

He was rugged looking—a short, roughly trimmed beard added to the effect. He looked like a typical aging football jock: bigger than the average man, broad-shouldered, and maybe a slight hint of little extra weight around the neck. Definitely past his prime. He could have been decent-looking if he cleaned himself up a little, not that he was at all her type. He certainly did fit the profile.

He wasn't someone her parents would have wanted her to consort with, either. She pushed the thought out of her head and raised her eyebrows at him as he approached. "Mr. Wyler?"

The man scratched his bristly chin and nodded. "At your service." He stepped to her chair and extended his hand. "You're the one who left the message, I take it?"

Cassie smiled coolly. "Cassandra Prescott." She leaned forward and took his hand briefly.

He smirked back at her, raising an eyebrow. "Pleasure's all mine." His eyes seemed to be lingering on the area of her neck.

"I'm sure." She looked down at the table and waved. "Have a seat."

He cleared his throat and kicked out the chair opposite hers. "So, you work with Hannah Adams. I take it you're familiar with the case... what are you, second chair?"

Cassie cocked her head, studying him. "Actually, no. I'm here to represent the interests of the firm. I'm sure you're aware Ms. Adams has concerns with the agreement of service, and I want to make sure we all walk away from this feeling okay about things. Fair enough?"

Wyler rubbed his mouth, nodding. "Sure, sure. So... help me out here. I'm a little confused. Is there somewhere in the contract where it says Hannah Adams doesn't have to pay me if she doesn't feel like it? I must have missed that." He tapped the table with a finger, shifting in his seat and leaning slightly forward.

Cassie patted her leg beneath the table. The man's voice was slightly raised, and his manner was brusque. It was subtle, but he was posturing for an offensive. This wasn't going to go down smoothly. "Not at all, Mr. Wyler, we think you should be paid for any time and effort you put in—we just want to make sure you've held up your end of the deal." She pursed her lips, looking around at the empty tabletop. "We'll want to review your invoices... did you bring anything with you? We just want to make sure we can substantiate all of the charges we get billed for."

Wyler paused. "Tell me something, does your firm often have situations like this, where an employee sets up a contract of service and then decides not to honor it?"

Cassie shook her head and sighed. "Mr. Wyler, it's not an unreasonable request, and this doesn't have to be a problem—we just want to know what we're paying for."

Wyler shrugged and leaned forward. "We're talking about a big firm, here, right? Your time must be pretty valuable, I would think. But they send you out here to meet with a guy that's not even charging the going rate for a little detective work. My total bill's probably going come in at around $700. Almost seems... not cost-effective at all."

Cassie stiffened, biting her lip and scrunching the fabric of her skirt in her fingers. "Look, Mr. Wyler—"

"Not to mention the added costs and publicity problems you might run into if someone like me sued your firm for breach of contract. I don't get why a firm like yours would want to deal with that headache." Wyler lowered his brow and leaned back in his seat. He shrugged and waved a hand in the air. "Maybe you could explain that to me."

Cassie widened her eyes. Publicity problems? Did this guy really want to get into it about publicity problems? "Maybe we wouldn't, under normal circumstances, but based on Ms. Adams' statement about her follow-up call with you, it's probably not a good move on your part to pretend you've conducted yourself in a professional way since the initial agreement."

Wyler frowned and folded his arms, shooting her a sharp look. "Is that right?"

Cassie worked her jaw. She nodded. "She says she received no progress reports from you, even though you led her to believe there would be—as of today, she still hasn't received any documentation from you—and when she called you to check up on things, you gave her a hard time. A really hard time. She said it got pretty ugly." She shook her head. "Is any of that not true?"

The man's expression didn't change, but a crease appeared in his forehead. "What's your point? Contract doesn't say I have to make nice phone conversation."

Cassie raised her eyebrows. "What's my point? Are you asking me that because you can't understand why she would be upset about it, or because you just don't care?"

Wyler snorted. "You tell me—you seem to think you know all about everything."

Cassie narrowed her eyes. "All right. According to her, you used some extremely abusive language. Contracts can be voided, Mr. Wyler. One could argue that Ms. Adams shouldn't have to subject herself to abuse by you or anyone else. One could also argue that someone prone to explosive outbursts who can't keep his temper under control shouldn't be allowed to conduct business professionally. Who knows? A judge might decide someone like that shouldn't have a license. Licenses can be voided too."

Wyler forced out a single laugh. He shook his head, leaning forward and tapping his finger hard on the tabletop. "Explosive outbursts, huh? Lady, you think you know me? You don't know me." He looked off toward the traffic, then turned back, licking his lower lip. "You know what, counselor? Yeah, I said some things, but your friend said some things too. The truth is, the woman was asking for it. She doesn't like it, she should try not to be such a goddamn bitch to people."

Cassie nodded slowly, letting the words soak in. This wasn't going to be productive—Wyler wasn't going to be agreeable to anything, no matter what she said. He was a stubborn, macho jerk who didn't like losing arguments, so he probably avoided people who were strong enough to defend themselves verbally. For him, it was now about not backing down. He probably wasn't going to give her the satisfaction of making any monetary concessions, and he definitely wasn't about to listen to any other opinions a female lawyer had to offer. But the idea of seeing him lose face was irresistible. He was right on the edge now.

Cassie cracked a pair of knuckles with the thumb of the same hand. She steeled herself and shot him an icy stare. "You should really be more careful about what you say in front of a lawyer. You keep running your mouth, and you will get sued, I promise." She paused and tossed her hair behind her shoulder. "But I'm not here to lecture you about your behavior."

He grunted. "Yeah, huh? You could have fooled me."

She smiled. "Ms. Adams would be well within her rights to make a big stink out of this—and believe me, she's fully equipped to do that—but I think I can convince her to drop this if you'll agree to forget you ever did business with our firm. You forgive the debt that you haven't substantiated yet, return the $500 retainer, and everything goes back to the way it was before. And then no one has to go to court over this, or drag anyone through the mud."

He nodded, leaning forward and pointing in the air. "Uh-huh, sure. Except that 30 hours plus is an awful lot of time. I put a lot into this case, and, although this might be difficult for you to understand, I actually do need the money more than a multimillion-dollar Center City law firm."

"Then where's your documentation?"

Wyler scratched his chin. "I didn't know this was a court appearance." He grumbled something inaudible under his breath. "The documentation is in my file cabinet, where it belongs. Ms. Adams will get it when I send the bill. I sure as hell don't need to show it to some lawyer I've never met before." He shifted in his seat, shaking his head and glancing sideways. He scratched the back of his neck. He was breathing loudly now.

Cassie watched him. He wasn't stupid, but he wasn't good at hiding things either. If he had a file, it must have been in sorry condition, and it probably wasn't going to justify his charges. "I'm going to put it to you again, because I'm not sure you get what I'm saying here. Forget about this case, and give us back our money, or we will go to court. We will show that you have a long history of demonstrating questionable character. The judge will hear about your rape case in college, and about how you were kicked out of the Philadelphia PD. And, because you played tailback for the Nittany Lions, I'll bet it will get some play on the news." She squinted. "Of course, we would prefer to avoid that, and I'm guessing you would too."

Wyler looked down at the table and started laughing silently. "I guess pissing people off is okay as long as you're a lawyer." He nodded. "Are you done now? Is that it?"

Cassie glanced to her right and watched a bus pull along 16th Street. She sat up. "No harm, no foul, with no restitution attached… that's about all I can offer. Just so we're clear… you're turning down the offer?"

"Offer?" Wyler laughed again, then abruptly stood, shoving his chair backwards. He half-turned and glared back at her. "You want to know what I think, counselor? I think you're full of shit."

Cassie folded her arms and sat back. "Really, that's such a surprising remark from you."

Wyler pointed at himself. "I think your friend was trying to cut costs by hiring me, she freaked out when she realized she was in over her head, and she went to you to bail her ass out because she's afraid of looking bad at the next meeting with the partners. I think you set this meeting up hoping no one else in the firm ever hears about it, and you know damn well there's no way in hell any sensible judge is going to void the contract. You figured you could scare the money out of me, so your friend doesn't have to run up the firm's expenses on another detective. Might as well try, right? No harm, no foul." He shrugged. His green eyes were boiling.

Shit. Cassie opened her mouth and closed it again, looking away briefly. He had seen completely through her, and now, from her expression, he was going to know he was right, and there was going to be no way to back him off. So much for a graceful exit.

She suddenly became conscious of her fingers digging into her thighs through the skirt. She moved her hands to the table and pressed her palms flat against the cold glass. Strength and calm.

Wyler glanced in the direction of the single door leading back through the restaurant. "So no, counselor, I won't be taking you up on your offer to have me give the money back. And if you were hoping for some sort of compromise, like, say, waiving any additional fees, you can forget about that too. You want to sue me, you take your best shot." He located his chair and dragged it back to the table.

He remained standing there, glowering, making no move to leave. Cassie sighed and locked eyes with him. "You know… if you had been just a little bit less of a complete asshole, none of this would have happened. We wouldn't be here right now."

"Asshole, huh?" He nodded, raising his eyebrows. "Oh, I see—I orchestrated this whole thing. That's the way you see this."

Cassie stood slowly, stepping away from the table. "Yeah, that's the way I see this. All this because you couldn't keep your mouth shut. You know, you're right about this meeting—I'm not here on behalf of the firm, I'm here as a favor to Hannah Adams. And you're right that Hannah worries about what the firm thinks of her, but I'm not Hannah, and you know what? Now, instead of owning up to how obnoxious you were over the phone, you blatantly disrespect me to top it off." She folded her arms. "Now you have my attention, Mr. Wyler, and, so you know, I can make this lawsuit fly, and the firm will back me on it. Based on what I've seen so far, you're not going to look so good in front of a judge. I, on the other hand, look amazing in front of a judge. So I'm going to ask you one more time—give me a reason not to go forward with this. Make me a counteroffer, or face me in court."

Wyler stared at her. He shook his head. "Why the hell should I?"

Cassie cocked her head, looking at the stone patio. "Come on, Mr. Wyler. You blew off your client. You may have invoices, but I think we both know you didn't do your best work here."

Wyler squinted. "Let's be honest, counselor. None of that shit really matters here. All that matters to you is that I'm a man."

"You would think that, wouldn't you?" Cassie tipped her head back. "I'm not so sure you qualify."

"Face it. You wouldn't be standing here ripping me a new one if I wasn't a man. You don't really care about the facts." He shook his head, holding out his arms. "You bring me out here and antagonize me, you dredge up all this shit from my past and throw it in my face. You have all of your convenient stories, you have me pegged as your basic woman-hater, and you see no reason to bother yourself about what my side of the story might be. It didn't matter what I was going to say here. You have it all worked out, your opinion, your nice little mental picture of what a complete bastard I am—it's all set. End of story, let's string this guy up. Am I wrong?"

Cassie pursed her lips, glancing down. "Maybe not. But to be fair, legally speaking, you did rape a girl."

Wyler growled through his teeth, pointing at the ground. "Statutory. Statutory. Okay? The girl was 17 by about two months. I was two years older than her. Two years. It wasn't like I knew about it—you think I was looking for that kind of trouble?"

"Oh yes, I'm sure you were a great guy."

Wyler waved his hand in the air recklessly. "You want to know something else? That girl was a freshman at Shippensburg. She was a college girl. Did you uncover that little detail in your research?" His voice was easily loud enough to be heard across the patio.

Cassie raised an eyebrow. "Oh, I see. So it was her fault, not yours."

"It wasn't like I found her by trolling through the elementary schools—what was I supposed to do, check her ID?"

Cassie sniffed, flaring her nostrils. "It's amazing, you know… hearing you talk about it, it's like you don't even view it as a mistake." She shrugged and shook her head. "You'd think a person who's been burned on this before might have taken something away from the experience, but you, you keep plugging right along until they drum you out of the police force."

Wyler fell a pace away from the table, running his fingers through his hair. "Goddammit, that does not make me a bad person! When is this shit going to go away?" He rubbed his eyes.

Cassie rolled her neck and patted her sides, smoothing her skirt. There were plenty of people seated at the patio tables, and they didn't seem to be making very much noise. They were whispering if they were talking at all, and the clinking bustle of the wait staff had all but stopped. The sounds of the café had almost slipped beneath the surrounding hum of tires against pavement. Like it or not, she and Wyler were the center of attention.

Wyler looked at her, then glanced around, seemingly reading her thoughts. "Well, congratulations, counselor. I guess you managed to prove what a jerk I am after all."

Cassie sighed. "That's not why I'm here." She took another glance around. People were pretending not to look, but it was obvious they were watching the conversation now. The situation was completely out of hand.

Enough. She had plenty of witnesses to skewer while she was being paid to do it. "All right, look. Maybe I did prejudge a little, but that's beside the point. Bottom line, I'm here representing Hannah, and she has legitimate issues with the way you did business with her. That's why I'm here." She frowned and shook her head, avoiding eye contact. "Your past history is not my problem."

Wyler looked down and scratched the back of his head. He took in a deep breath and exhaled loudly through his nostrils. His face was twisted in a dark scowl, and the veins of his neck were bulging.

Cassie raised her eyebrows and nodded. "Look, I think I've said enough here. I have to get back. If you want this to go away, you give us a call." She found her handbag on the table and slipped the strap over her shoulder. "Otherwise, you'll get the official notice on the court date within the week. I'll be in touch." She frowned. It was a complete bluff and he probably knew it. But if there was a graceful way to end the conversation, it wasn't coming to her.

Wyler didn't respond. He remained motionless, staring intensely at the glass table like he was going to put a fist through it.

Cassie hesitated. Wyler was on the other side of the table, directly between her and the door that led through the restaurant and out of the café, and it was going to look obvious if she went out of her way to avoid going near him. Maybe she had pushed the man too far—he had a short fuse, and he had demonstrated some arguably antisocial and self-destructive behavior, and it was absolutely possible he was capable of doing something dangerous. If he did, he was going to find out she knew how to defend herself.

It was also possible he was a perfectly normal guy whose life was being unexpectedly held under a microscope, who was justifiably angry at walking into a wholesale ambush. She cleared her throat and nodded again. "That's that, then." She lowered her head and stepped around the table, brushing past his shoulder.

Wyler spoke up behind her. "Hold it."

She held her breath and spun. Without thinking, she rolled her right hand into a tight fist, keeping it hidden against her handbag.

Wyler swung around to face her, still scowling. "Fine, you win. I'm done with this. Tell your friend she can forget about the rest of the bill—but there's no way in hell I'm paying back the retainer. You want that, you're going to have to go ahead and sue me."

Cassie relaxed and dropped her hand from her bag. She shifted her stance, cocking her head. "That's $500. The total bill was going to be something like $700, right? That's not much of a concession—it's still a substantial portion of the charges."

Wyler scratched his cheek and squinted. "Do you have any idea what it's like to tail a guy all night?"

She stared back at him, bright eyed. She shook her head. "No. Do you?"

177

"The work I did on that case is legitimate, whether you and your friend believe it or not. I'll get you the invoices when I get my shit together. I might be slow with paperwork, but that doesn't mean I didn't do my job. I'm a one-person business, and I get a little backed up sometimes. I don't blow off cases. I did every bit of those 30 hours of surveillance, and the contract says I get compensated for it, so trust me, this is a good deal for your friend."

Cassie brushed a strand of hair away from her face. "I'll talk to her. We'll have to see how she feels about it."

He nodded. "Another thing. Your friend didn't want to hear the truth, but 30 hours of surveillance don't lie. The man I was following is not messing around on his wife. If you really do care about your friend's expense report, you might want to tell her to think about a different angle for her client's divorce proceeding. Unless she wants to throw away her money on a detective for real."

Cassie exhaled, digesting the words. "I think Ms. Adams can judge for herself how she should prepare her case."

Wyler nodded. "Let me tell you something about your friend. She took some serious shots at my integrity for not telling her what she wanted to hear. She was every bit as insulting as I was. She treated me like a piece of shit, and you know, I kind of got the impression I wasn't the first person she ever talked to that way."

Cassie said nothing.

Wyler raised an eyebrow and shrugged. "Hey, you know what? Maybe she's right. I basically am a piece of shit. I think that's been clearly established here today. I mean, I lead a shit life, don't I? You want to know what it's like to tail people all night? It's like tailing a goddamn neighborhood dog-walker. Total shit." He stepped toward her, pointing at the ground. "I deal with nothing but shit—shit that's really none of my business. I live in a shit apartment, and I eat shit food. I breathe shit, I sleep on shit, and when I need to stay awake, I drink shit coffee. Contrary to what you might think, I do not enjoy dealing with shit, because it makes me feel like shit. The only reason I do this shit is because I'm good at doing this shit, and I don't mind coming out smelling like shit every damn time. So excuse the fuck out of me if I'm not perky when a client calls me at 8 in the morning and tells me I'm doing, pardon my French, a shit job."

Cassie's lips parted. She stared at him, blinking. "Are you done?"

"Yeah, I think so." The volume of Wyler's voice went down precipitously, as if the air had gone completely out of him with his last salvo. He breathed, shaking his head, and his eyes found Cassie's. He shrugged again. "Just do everyone a favor and get Hannah Adams to back off on the retainer. She's getting off easy. There are a lot of people in my business who would have kept the tab going a long time after they were convinced they weren't going to turn up anything."

Cassie frowned and rubbed her arms. "I said I'll talk to her. If she agrees on no more money changing hands, you can consider this dropped. That's all I can do." She paused. "I should go."

Wyler gestured at the door.

Cassie cleared her throat. "If Hannah wants to go ahead with a suit, I'll let you know by tomorrow." She glanced at Wyler. "But I think I can convince her we've all wasted enough time on this." She turned and crossed the patio. An older gentleman stepped out of the way, holding the door open for her as she approached. She flashed a brief smile and heading through without slowing down.

Inside, the café was alive, as if nothing had happened. People were talking at a normal conversational volume, and servers were moving around as if the kitchen had just opened.

She made a beeline for the exit, glancing down at her handbag and adjusting the strap on her shoulder as she pushed her way back outside, then slowed and took a breath, glancing back in the direction of the patio as she rounded toward the crosswalk, shaking off her right hand. The people sipping soup in the café had gotten a good show as it was, but a well-placed blow to Wyler's solar plexus would have made the scene a lot more memorable.

Wyler was still standing there, staring off into space. Without warning he turned and looked straight in her direction. She looked away immediately. Definitely not a good fit for the firm of Halpern, Sutherland & Kovach. Too bad… the man did seem to have some impressive observational skills for an antisocial burnout. Unfortunately he also had the ability to speak.

The walk sign lit up. Cassie frowned up at her building as she started across the street. The idea that a detective had to be some crass, boorish brute was ridiculous—the whole persona was tired and unnecessary. Obviously there was more to it than that with Zack Wyler, some deeper pathos that he wasn't ready to deal with. The man was clearly not happy with himself.

Of course, frivolous lawsuits and underserved attacks on a man's personal life probably didn't do much to improve his self-image.

Cassie sighed as she stepped onto the sidewalk and headed for the wall of tinted glass along the outside the lobby. Hannah Adams was no picnic herself. It wasn't hard to imagine her insulting a man like this, setting him off. Wyler's charges weren't exorbitant, and assuming he had the invoices, there wasn't really a good reason not to pay him what he was asking. Going after him for the money had been a mistake, whatever his personality issues were and whether or not he deserved it.

Cassie stopped in front of the revolving door and cleared her throat, fishing in her handbag for her security card. Hannah owed her big for this.

The lawyer appeared on the sidewalk and looked back at Zack momentarily, then quickly turned away and headed across the street. Damn good-looking woman, and she used it to her advantage. Not much point in trying to fight her; she wasn't about to give in to someone like him.

Goddamn big-mouth assholes from college. So much for the district justice's order that the case be sealed. That crock of shit had played out over a decade ago, and the sex offender rap was never going to die now that he had fucked up as a policeman. Students had yapped, their parents had yapped, and the media had sniffed out the story, sunken their teeth into it, and ripped the case file wide open after the departmental discharge broke. And he wasn't the only one who had to live with it.

Angela McAfee's name had been circulated around campus as much as his, and it had come up again when the media had dug in. It was legal bullshit—she wasn't any more or less naïve as any college kid looking for a one-night stand. Girl or boy. Of course, nobody gave two shits about it if it was the boy who was underage.

Zack scowled. Matter of a couple lousy months. Angela McAfee had known what she was doing, and she had done it before.

The smile on Angela's face had been huge. The memory was in an alcohol-soaked haze, but it had stayed. She had grinned like a cat, kneeling spread-legged on the double-bed, looking down at him with her brassiere in her teeth, dangling it vertically between her breasts. The light from a neon Miller Lite sign in the corner of the room had captured her face perfectly. He had said something, and she had smiled a little wider, and her eyes had danced at just the right moment.

There might have been a lot of women who didn't know what they were doing when it came to sex, but Angela McAfee was not in that category. And if she hadn't been as experienced as she was, so what? He would have had no way of telling her from any of the other college girls. She had gone to the party, had a little to drink, and openly shown interest, just like anyone else. She had played the game. Her choice. Maybe some of them had regretted it later on, but it had always been their choice. And his.

Moral gray areas. He had a talent for moral gray areas. He was definitely guilty of blatant unprofessionalism—he was a chronic, repeat offender in that area. It didn't necessarily make him a morally reprehensible person, despite what some lawyer thought based on an at-a-glance assessment.

Cars moved through the street, erasing any trace of Cassandra Prescott. Zack looked at the brown, fitted stones that made up the patio. Apparently, it was all pretty clear-cut to the good counselor. Ms. Prescott was obviously not the type of person who let facts get in the way of a good opinion.

One more person to add to his growing list of fans. Zack glanced at a menu propped up on an empty table, frowning for a long moment. The food in the kitchen smelled good; probably immaculately prepared, with all of the trimmings fit for a yuppie power lunch.

He grunted. He was hungry, but if he was going to eat something now, it was going to be at a place with a liquor license.

He shouldered his way to the door and headed for the exit.

*   *   *

Cassie stepped quickly past the reception area and angled for her office, skirting the pantry and avoiding eye contact with the three people lingering at the coffee maker. She threw open her door without slowing down and jumped as it hit the wall with a bang.

The venetian blinds in the office were closed, leaving the room shielded from the outside light. Nice and dark... good. She put her hands on her hips and exhaled, waiting a few seconds, then stepped around her desk and flopped into her chair. She glanced at her name plate and leaned forward, turning the rosewood wedge around and looking at the gold and black lettering. She frowned and put it back in position.

Zack Wyler probably hadn't listened to a word she had said. He might not have been an outright misogynist, but he was a self-abasing, small-minded, unpleasant ass who had all of the social graces of a baboon and evidently wanted her to think as much. Still, he had been right—the lawsuit was a waste of time. Beyond that, he hadn't acted like a man trying to cover up for not having done the job. She had no real reason to believe he hadn't earned the money he was owed by contract, and if what he was saying about Hannah's case was true and there was no affair going on, Wyler could have easily continued to charge Hannah until she stopped him herself. Now the man wasn't even going to get paid the small amount he was asking for.

Cassie opened a drawer in her desk and took out a bean bag, squeezing

181

it rhythmically in her hand. Maybe if Wyler had been remotely decent at the café, the subject of his contract might have never been broached. And she wouldn't have had to wonder whether she had just possibly bullied a man out of getting the full payment he rightfully deserved.

She picked up the desk phone and punched in Hannah's number. The call went to voicemail. Cassie bit her lip and hung up at the beep.

Ultimately she had no one to blame but herself. If it had been left alone, Hannah would have forgotten all about it the moment the next drama popped up. Probably before the week was out.

Cassie frowned. Not much she could do about it now. She examined the bean bag in her hand. Throwing a bean bag at the wall and watching her diploma crash to the floor was a possibility. Of course, the frame would have probably just plopped onto the soft carpeting without a sound. Not very satisfying.

There was a quick knock. Cassie turned to the doorway as Elsa Lyme leaned into the office. Cassie raised her eyebrows. "Yes, Elsa—what's up?"

Elsa nodded, and a shoulder-length shock of maroon-streaked, bottle-blonde hair fell across the left half of her face. "I'm sorry, Cassie... there's a man who'd like to see you? He doesn't have an appointment, but he says it's important." She took a tentative step into the room, frowning up at the shadowy ceiling tiles. "Should I turn on the lights?"

Cassie wrinkled her nose. "That's okay." She dropped the bean bag back in the drawer, stood, and stepped to the blinds, flipping them open. "Did he say what it's about?"

Elsa shook her head, folding her arms.

Wyler, maybe? Now what? Cassie stared at her. "I guess he has something against setting up an appointment by phone?"

Elsa shrugged. "I offered him a card and asked if he would leave a message, but he says he'll only talk to you." She sighed. "He seems very insistent." Her subdued vocal fry was practically a purr... if she had a sense the matter was urgent at all, she wasn't showing any signs of it.

Cassie moved back to her desk. Nothing else that required immediate attention came to mind. "Do I have anything besides Mr. Howard at 3?"

"Just those corporate resolutions." Elsa paused. "Should I clear one of the conference rooms?"

Cassie nodded. She was way ahead of schedule on all the paperwork. "No, that's okay—I'll just see him in here." She flashed a smile. "Thanks, Elsa, you can go ahead and send him in."

Elsa nodded and turned away, ducking back through the doorway.

Cassie brushed a strand of hair away from her eyes and sat back down, glancing around at her desk. Everything appeared to be more or less in order. She sighed and placed her hands on the desk, straightened in her chair, and focused on the doorway as Elsa returned with a small man in a brown sweater.

Cassie froze. The odd-looking man from outside the café patio was suddenly standing in her office. He had his coat draped over his right arm now, and wasn't immediately recognizable in the sweater, but there was no mistake—it was definitely him.

Elsa placed a hand on the doorknob. "I'll be in reception if you need me. Do you want the door closed?"

Cassie shook her head absently. "No, that's all right." She paused. "Leave it open."

The man nodded to Elsa, and she backed out of the room. The man turned to face Cassie and smiled warmly.

Cassie stared. He was smaller than he had seemed before, maybe 6 inches shorter than she was, and he had no bulk. But he wasn't particularly thin either—in fact, from appearances he was fairly well-proportioned, but small. A scaled-down version of a normal-sized man.

His current impression was not at all like the one he had given off outside the café. He had seemed somber, standing alone on the sidewalk. Troubled. Now he looked completely at ease.

Up close, he looked Eastern Mediterranean. Probably Greek, or Arab. His skin had a tint that was almost an olive green, and his hair was thick, black, and neat. Now, the deep, hardened lines that had seemed to darken his face outside on the sidewalk looked more like permanent dimples.

And the clothes he wore were bright and new. A starched white shirt collar folded perfectly out from under the sweater. Either he had just been shopping at a department store or he was unbelievably meticulous with the iron and the fabric softener. The spiffy look hadn't come across at all with the coat on.

He looked all around unthreatening. Smile wrinkles accented the corners of his dark brown eyes as if he wore make-up.

Cassie pressed her hands flat on the top of the desk. The man had obviously followed her from the café. As warm and positive as he suddenly seemed, there was something extremely unsettling about him. It was the way he was looking at her... it wasn't a lewd or hungry look, nothing alarming or creepy, but it was as if he was passively confident in her presence, as if he knew all about her. Like an old friend.

There were two likely possibilities: he had seen her at the café and gotten the impulse to ask her out, or he was legitimately looking for a lawyer. Hopefully, he was looking for a lawyer.

He stood silently, apparently waiting for her to say something.

She tapped the desk with her finger and stood, smoothing her skirt. "Yes, how can I help you, sir?"

A strong smell seemed to surround him—not offensive, or necessarily bad. It was a completely unique scent... spicy, like an unbalanced musky cologne, but not as sharp. It was possible it was just his natural body odor. He turned and took a long, hard look at the open door.

Cassie sniffed. The man was going to have to give her a clue about what he was doing there before she agreed to any closed-door meetings. She cleared her throat lightly, raising her eyebrows.

The man smiled, glancing around casually. "Yes, hello. I understand your name is Cassandra Prescott. It's a pleasure to meet you." He spoke with an unnerving clarity, pronouncing every syllable like a man officiating a spelling bee. Something a second-language speaker might have done.

Cassie nodded at her name plate. "That's me."

He smiled and stepped forward, extending his hand. "My name is John Walker."

Not an Eastern Mediterranean name. She leaned forward and shook his hand, smiling back at him. His skin felt as dry as paper. "Nice to meet to, Mr. Walker." She stepped back, pressing her hands against her thighs. "What can I do for you?" She gestured toward the chairs at the wall near the desk.

He stared at her for a moment more, then turned and studied the chairs as if he had never seen wire-frame furniture before. "I'm in need of a lawyer, and I would like to enlist your services." He pulled one of the chairs tentatively across the carpet and sat in front of her.

She sat down after him, cocking her head. There was something strange about his eyes. Something intense... soulful. She glanced at the doorway and suddenly felt the sensation of being shut inside her office, cut off from the rest of the world.

She blinked and cleared her throat, looking down and sliding her chair a few inches closer to the desk. She exhaled and patted the top of the desk, looking back at the man. "You need a lawyer. Mr.... Walker, was it?" She shook her head. "I'm sorry, it's been a long day."

He shrugged. "Not at all."

"I guess I'm not used to unscheduled visits." She raised her eyebrows. "Usually we get a phone call first."

He looked brightly back at her. "I understand."

Cassie nodded slowly. She caught herself staring at his eyes a second time and immediately looked down at the desk. She frowned. She was being an idiot. This was ridiculous. She looked up and focused on the rubber tree plant in the corner. "You'll have to excuse me... I don't know what's wrong with me today." The man probably thought she was a complete airhead.

He was hiding it well. "Please, don't worry. I have certainly had my share of long days." He paused. "It's my fault for barging in here like this."

She sighed. "Thank you, but it's definitely not your fault."

He sat up, holding up a hand. "Of course, if this is a bad time, I could always come back."

"No, no." She shook her head, keeping her eyes low. "So you need a lawyer. Who referred you?"

He bowed his head. "Well, I've seen you work. I had three days of jury duty, and spent some time at the courthouse." He paused. "I was never picked, of course. But I've always been fascinated by the justice system... anyway, I ended up sitting in on a bunch of trials, and I happened to catch you in action."

Cassie nodded. "Really. I haven't done any trial work in a while—do you remember the case?"

"I don't believe I caught the name, and I didn't see enough to get the full picture." He shook his head. "In any case, among many lawyers, you were the only one who seemed to take a real interest in the wishes of your clients. Now that I need one myself, I thought I'd ask you first."

"That's very flattering, Mr. Walker." She raised an eyebrow. "Were you also watching me at the Hollywood Café?"

He laughed. "Yes, I admit, I did see you there. I didn't want to disturb you during your lunch. I was on my way here from my home, and when I saw you, I knew I'd have to wait. I apologize if I made you uncomfortable."

"Well, thank you, Mr. Walker. I appreciate that." Cassie sat back, resting her elbows on the arms of the chair. She was starting to relax, thank God. What the hell was wrong with her? "I think that's why most people set up an appointment beforehand."

He closed his eyes. "Yes. You're right. But I was hoping to talk to you directly."

"You were being optimistic." She smiled flatly, folding her arms. "We're pretty busy around here most of the time, and talking to a lawyer directly without trying to make arrangements ahead of time is not a luxury most people get."

He nodded, unfazed. "I suppose I should be grateful." He didn't look as if he was ever fazed.

She leaned forward. "So let's start by finding out what the problem is, and I'll see what I can do." She opened the top desk drawer and took out a small stationery pad, dropping it on the desk in front of her.

"Very well." He sighed. "I'm in the process of drafting my will. I'd like to have you examine it to make sure that I have everything in good order. This has become very important to me." He stared at her, and his dark eyes didn't blink once.

She frowned. "I see." He definitely hadn't seen her litigating about a will issue. He might have seen her in front of one or two witnesses, possibly as second chair on a patent dispute… it could have been about her legal skills, but it also might have been about how she looked in her court attire.

She rolled her lips inward, shifting in her chair. Not exactly a fair assumption by her, and his criteria for choosing a lawyer weren't any of her business. She found a gold ball-point pen and tapped it against the pad. "So it's just a matter of formalizing your will?"

"Yes. Essentially." Walker paused, opening his mouth as if he was deliberating about how he was going to proceed. "How long would something like that take?"

Cassie shook her head. "It depends on your provisions, but if it's already more or less drafted, I'd say… probably no more than two weeks."

"I was hoping to have this done sooner than that." He was still smiling, but his eyes showed concern. The change in his outward mood was subtle, but the mirth in the atmosphere seemed to disappear abruptly. It almost felt as if the temperature of the room had dropped.

He was waiting for her to respond. Cassie wiggled the pen in her fingers. "I'll tell you what, Mr. Walker, I do have some spare time early next week. If you give me the will I can look at it and make sure you have all the essentials, and I can have it redrafted if necessary. Then all you'll have to do is approve it."

Walker's eyes changed focus, looking past her, and the man seemed to lose his resolve. For an instant, his steady calm disintegrated. His expression became pinched, and creases appeared around his mouth.

The look was an uncomfortably familiar one. Cassie stared down at the desk. She had seen it on too many faces in her visits to the Philadelphia Nursing Home. Fulton had shown that look a few times himself.

Then the expression was gone, as if she had imagined it. Walker's face was as composed as before.

There was a good chance this will had a short time horizon. Cassie put down the pen and coughed lightly into her fist. "Maybe we can get this started for you today." She swiveled and opened the large bottom drawer, slipping one of the contract forms out of its hanging folder and positioning it on the desk. "This should give you an idea of our rates. You'll want to make sure you're okay with what we charge. Mr. Walker?"

The man seemed lost in thought as he stared at the form on the desk. He nodded slowly. "There is more. I'll also be needing someone to handle my affairs when I'm gone, and I'd like it to be you." His eyes were wide and powerfully earnest.

Cassie squinted back at him. "You want me to be your personal representative based on seeing me for a few hours in the middle of a court case?"

He nodded again. "Yes. I've looked into your career, and I've done some research on a few other lawyers. It's you I want."

Cassie scratched her head, half-smiling. "Mr. Walker, far be it from me to turn down a new client, but really, you hardly know me. When people need to name a person to execute their will, they usually ask a friend or relative." She paused. "Are you sure about this—doesn't anyone in your family know a good lawyer?"

"I have no friends or family left in this area, Ms. Prescott—I really don't have anywhere else to go. I was hoping that you'd be able to accommodate me." His tone was soft and steady, almost inappropriately objective, as if he expected nothing at all and would completely understand if she refused to help him.

She gave him a hard look. "I could do this for you, if that's really what you want. But I have to tell you that my expertise is in contract law. There are a couple of lawyers at the firm that I can recommend who have more of a probate background."

"I'm not interested in other lawyers, Ms. Prescott."

She sighed. "In order for me to do this, I'd need you to keep this firm up to date on your contact information. You'd have to let me know whenever you move or change your phone number."

Walker paused for a long moment, clasping his hands together in his lap. "That won't be necessary. Your services will be required soon."

Cassie glanced at the vent in the far corner of the room. The air seemed completely stagnant. "May I ask why?"

"I have pancreatic cancer. I was diagnosed late and have chosen not to undergo treatment." He looked blankly back in her direction as if he were staring straight through her head to the wall behind her.

She grimaced and was immediately conscious of her expression. She kept her eyes toward him. "I'm sorry."

"I don't have long. I would like to make all the arrangements as soon as possible."

She shook her head, looking down. The man wanted her assistance, not her pity. She straightened. "Of course. I'm sure we can work something out."

She exhaled, glancing around her desk. The only other writing implements visible were a red marker and a blue editor's pencil. She grabbed the pencil and set the ball-point down on the contract. "As far as costs, we'll bill you for the time spent. You should also know the executor gets a percentage of the estate, depending on the assessment of the value of the estate, and we have a standard $600 retainer for ongoing legal work, which, if I remember correctly, will be deducted from the proceeds as part of the executor fee when your estate closes." She paused, glancing down at the form on the desk. "Do you have the will with you, or anything showing the assets you have? I could give you a better idea."

Walker shook his head. "I'm sorry, no. I didn't bring it with me. But I'll sign a contract of service, whatever the cost." He stared at her. "I'm prepared to make a down payment today."

A quick look at the paperwork now would have made it a lot easier to expedite the legal work. Too bad. She frowned. "That's fine, Mr. Walker. You can pay Elsa at the reception desk on your way out, if you like. If you're okay with everything I've told you, we would just need you to sign the contract of service and we'll be good to go."

He nodded. "Thank you, Ms. Prescott."

"Just have Elsa schedule an appointment with me for early next week, and make sure you bring with you the draft of your will. And it would help if you included a list telling me where all the property you intend to leave behind can be located, and bring whatever other documents you have—bank statements, property information, or anything else that you'll be including." She slid the contract and pen across the desk toward Walker. "I'll need you to sign this form accepting our terms of service before I can start working on this. Take a moment to read it, or you could take it home with you if you want to think about it some more."

His face was showing concern again. He leaned forward and stood slowly, making no move toward the contract. "Ms. Prescott, I should tell you... I'd like to keep this between the two of us until the time of my death, as much as possible. I don't want the workload to be shared with any other lawyers or paralegals." He looked down and found the chair, setting it back against the wall. "I'd prefer you didn't share my name with any other people at the firm.

Cassie stood after him, shaking her head. "We can keep everything as private as possible, but... Mr. Walker, I hope you realize that other people will need to be involved once the assets go to your estate. Even if you don't name any beneficiaries, there are taxes that need to be filed, and we'd need to send out a public notice after your death in order to give any creditors the chance to make a claim. We'd also need a disinterested third party to attest to your signature on the will itself. We'd need to have someone here in the office do it if you were unable to bring a person yourself."

Walker's dark eyes somehow seemed to become even more intense. "Please, Ms. Prescott. I know it's asking a lot. I understand you need to account for your time, but it's very important to me that my name isn't mentioned. I'll sign your form, but I ask that you keep it in a private file, and that you don't share any of my information with anyone else until after my death. As I said, I don't expect it to be very far in the future." He bowed his head. "After that, you have my permission to share the necessary details."

How altruistic of him. Cassie frowned, tapping the desk with the fingers of both hands. She cocked her head, shifting in her stance. "But we'd still need your name and address in order to bill you."

"I will pay in cash."

She folded her arms in front of her. The man had planned ahead enough to bring $600 cash, but he hadn't bothered with any documentation? He was starting to sound like a fugitive. Everyone had a right to representation, but that didn't mean she had to represent him.

He was watching her expression, and apparently reading her thoughts. "I see you have misgivings. I realize this would have gone more smoothly if I had brought everything with me today, but please try to understand... the will is a catalog of everything in this world that has any meaning to me. I'm not comfortable at the thought of passing out on the bus and having someone take it away." He paused. "You understand I don't have much time. I'm hoping you'll be willing to meet with me in my own neighborhood for any future business together. Lately, I'm much more comfortable near my home, and I prefer not to venture this far away. I need to be in familiar surroundings for my last moments."

Cassie scratched her ear. "I'd be willing to work with you to a degree, but you should understand we bill in 15-minute increments. If you need us to handle this outside the office, we'll have to charge for travel time. It could be considerably more expensive for you."

"I'm not concerned with the cost."

"But you understand that I would have to take it back here when I work on it."

Walker shrugged. "Yes. That much is necessary, I understand."

Cassie looked down at the stationery pad on the desk, still completely blank. For a review of a single legal document, this case was starting to feel like going down a rabbit hole.

To get the documentation ironed out and properly prepared, she was going to have to sit down with a probate textbook, and if there were any complexities or anything unusual, she was probably going to have to get help. Barry Fryth dealt with probate, and he was reasonable enough; he would probably be willing to give his opinion without giving her a hard time, if necessary. It could be done without sharing the man's name. But Walker wasn't making it easy.

"Ms. Prescott, if I may." Walker's eyes were less intense now, and he almost looked different, though he had barely moved a muscle in his face.

Cassie motioned for him to continue. "Go ahead."

Walker closed his eyes and let out a long breath. "I have a difficult time trusting people. It's difficult for me to interact with people at all, though I've learned to hide my social discomfort. And now I find myself at the mercy of the people I've always tried to avoid. I need to do this my way, or I won't do it at all. I'll understand if it's too much trouble." He took a step back as if to reinforce the idea that he was willing to withdraw.

The man was nothing if not sincere. He absolutely fit the part of a man who suffered from social phobias; his situation was extreme, but he wasn't the first high-maintenance client to walk through the door.

He cracked a hint of a smile, keeping his eyes on hers as he stood in the middle of the office. He held up a hand. "Ms. Prescott, I chose you because I get the sense you have rare compassion. But I really do appreciate that I'm asking you to go a long way for my own convenience. I hope I haven't wasted your time, and I thank you for listening to me, whether you're willing to help me or not."

Enough. She sighed and nodded, picked up the pencil, and started a quick list of the highlights. "That's not necessary, Mr. Walker, but thank you. I can try to keep the case off the books for the time being." For a man who had trouble communicating with people, he certainly had no problem reading the jury.

Then again, she wasn't about to enter this man's home. "Is there somewhere not too far from where you live that we could meet? A public library, or something?"

He crossed back toward the desk. "There's a children's playground very close to my home."

"Perfect. What if we meet there? I can't do it tomorrow, but I guess I could squeeze it in on Saturday—is that all right?"

"Yes." He widened his eyes. "But I wouldn't want to force you to work on one of your days off."

She flashed a smile. "It's fine, Mr. Walker. All right, good. I'll pick up your documents Saturday, and then we can make arrangements to meet a second time for your approval… we should be able to wrap this up in a couple of meetings. Where do you live?"

He seemed to ponder the question then nodded once. "I live at 8328 Tinicum Boulevard. Should I give you driving directions?"

"Sure—go ahead."

"Take Broad Street south until it turns into Route 291. Take the exit that leads to the airport. Go north on Island Avenue. Turn left at the second traffic light after the overpass, at Tinicum. The building is called the Langford Hotel. It will be one block farther, on the right. The playground is on the next block, at 82nd Street. On the left. After you enter, you'll see a white, dome-shaped climbing frame apart from the other playground apparatus. I'll be nearby, at a bench by the water fountain; I can meet you there." He paused. "From here, it should take you about 40 minutes."

She scribbled the directions on the pad. If he wasn't going to ask her why she wouldn't meet him at his home, she wasn't going to ask him why he lived in a hotel near the airport. "Can you give me a number where you can be reached, so I can call to confirm the meeting?"

He smiled weakly. "I'm afraid I don't have a phone." He cleared his throat quietly. "And I should tell you, please don't try to mail me anything at my street address. I don't accept mail there, so you'll have to bill me in person."

She nodded. That figured. She stooped and took a business card from the stack in the tiny wooden trough at the front of her desk and looked up. "How does noon sound?"

"Noon is fine."

She jotted the appointment on the back of the card. "Okay, meeting at playground, Tinicum Boulevard, Saturday, noon. So you remember." She raised her eyebrows and handed it to him.

He took it without looking at it. "I won't forget." He glanced down at the contract and studied it for a few seconds. "I trust your terms are fair." He picked up the pen and fumbled with it for a moment, then signed the bottom.

"Of course." Cassie stepped around the desk and held out her hand. "Thanks for signing the form. Don't worry, I'll keep it safe."

He shook her hand lightly. "Thank you, Ms. Prescott. You don't know what this means to me." He smiled back at her. The crinkles returned at the corners of his eyes.

She smoothed her skirt. "Hopefully we can bring you a little peace of mind."

"That would be a feat." Walker crossed to the door and placed his hand on the knob. "I look forward to our next meeting."

Cassie smiled at him, narrowing her eyes. Elsa was a fairly tall girl, but it was striking how much smaller this man looked than she did standing in the doorway. "I'll see you on Saturday."

Walker nodded once, paused, and held his hand motionless in the air. Then he was gone.

Cassie stared at the doorway for a moment more, then glanced up as the rasping hum of the ventilation broke the dead silence. Walker had apparently held the vents under his spell as well.

She turned and looked down at the contract. The signature was illegible, barely more than a jagged zigzag line. She picked up the pen and printed his name on the line below it.

John Walker. No friends, no family, and a name that sounded assumed. He might as well have been named John Doe.

"History is like concrete, never fast and hard at the time it is being set down... an accretion of loosely bound decision points, impressionable in the moment and solidifying only after the moment has passed. For the sentients we read about, there is only the present.

"Some relish the chance to make their mark, contriving to maximize the effect and ensure their place in the record. But often those who stumble unwittingly into the soft mix are the ones who make the greatest splash."

```
... GCL FN.036
Phi 78 24 37.00 / Theta -20 39 56.90 / Rho 35.26 / JD 3040384
Kappa Pegasi: USTINOV, "Eo-Nowar"; 9 March 3612 CE
```

Eo-Nowar was alive, even deep into the Ustinovian night. On the Zenith Explorer's final approach, the city had looked like a gigantic, lit-up layer cake balanced on a ring of needles.

There were at least 20 cities on Ustinov, and every one of them was 12 kilometers above the poison air of the desert, constructed atop enormously long nickel-iron stilts. Cyanide and springs of hydrochloric acid hadn't stopped the stalwart settlers any more than the ultraviolet radiation from Kappa Pegasi A. First-hand, the spectacle of an entire city thrust in the air made the feat of engineering all the more impressive.

It was probably going to be the last aerial view from the Explorer's cockpit for a while.

From inside the dome, the city was equally unusual. Outside, cars glided silently along canals of air outlined by photo streamers, crisscrossing both horizontally and vertically. The open, multilevel city blocks had the feel of a gigantic building under construction, and the tint of the dome and heavy artificial light created the illusion of perpetual dusk. In fact, the city of Eo-Nowar was always wide awake, which might have been encouraged by the fact that there was virtually no natural shift in light to prompt the people toward following a typical diurnal routine.

Fortunate thing, at the moment.

Dexter turned away from the transparent polyglass wall, rubbing his hands together. He sighed heavily. Jayjay would probably have a verdict from the people at the technical mechanics institute by now.

He pushed away from the wall, turning back toward the unnecessarily large switchboard console that took up half the cramped Port Authority dispatch control room. Constable Balboa was leaning his gargantuan frame over the devoted ENP com with the on-duty traffic officer. He looked up and stretched his back, then strolled across the floor toward Dexter.

Every ENP officer in the room wore a gray flak jacket with a prominent silver pin, but Balboa stood out as if he were among a crowd of drbdu. He had a striking wave of full blond hair and a thick, bushy mustache a shade darker, and the man was a mammoth; his head was practically scraping the ceiling.

"Massengill." Balboa put his hands on his hips and gave his slacks a tug. He gestured toward an unoccupied row of seats positioned along the back wall. "Let's sit down."

Dexter stepped to the seating area and sat, and Balboa sat two seats away him, spreading his legs and nodding back toward the switchboard. "Some bad news to start. Casino people ney fare have to prove you stole; they're allowed to make the final determination on whether their patrons are breaking the rules that they impose. And they're allowed bu-cue leeway on any punishments they decide to mete out. Your records will show you got fat off their funds; set fare, set-la toot-fare, it's all they need to justify their actions."

Dexter frowned. "That doesn't sound very helpful."

"No, pa toot, vrey-mun. But, if you counter-accuse them of fixing set-see things against you, then they are required to disclose their credit records. Then we check the records against the bank accounting files, and if we find any discrepancies, the casino is sudden in bu-cue trouble it does not want, par-sham. La, from there, you are mey-yer, mey-bu, you're in a better bargaining position. You might even get a pass on the account freeze. On the other hand, if we come up with par-yen on them, they're liable to come after your body with all they've got, toot-shoze."

Balboa seemed fairly optimistic about things, but the news didn't sound especially wonderful. Dexter looked back toward the transparent wall. "That's good, I suppose. What do you need me to do?"

"Wey. Plu rey, set-la—I just need your statement; you give me that, and we'll see if we can't pa-fare get these casino thugs off your case." He paused, scratching his mustache. "It does not fare help that you took you bu-shue time getting here, ney... I guess you're not so good at listening. You know you were supposed to call me when you arrived, don-see."

Dexter looked up at him. "I'm sorry. I had to stop at the tech-mech—my IU had a problem. I hope that doesn't make things worse, but I didn't have a choice." He squinted. "So you really think this is something I can get

194

out of?"

Balboa shrugged. "We'll see."

"But I assume I'll still have to pay a fine of some sort."

"Maybe wey, maybe no. Like I said, the casino ney wants an investigation. You're not going to go to Beta Lyrae again, par-sham, but they might just as soon want to have this shut down mey-bu."

Dexter rubbed his neck. It seemed too good to be true to hear the constable say he might not even end up paying a fine, though the idea of being fined by a group that was essentially extorting his fair share of credit was certainly outrageous enough, not to mention they had fired on him and his ship and might have killed him.

Dexter cleared his throat. "Well. As I said, I never did anything wrong. It would be nice to be able to keep all my earnings."

Balboa studied him for a moment. "Qua pass—what's wrong with your android?"

Dexter shook his head. "That's what I hope to find out."

The constable grunted. "Sey pa vu shue. I guess it's not your day." He paused. "I hope everything works out for her, toot-shoze. She sounded like a sensible advisor for you, mey-bu fare." Abruptly he tipped his head back and an odd smirk came over his face. "Sey por-qua… that's why you put the batto don-see. You were thinking of running, weren't you?"

Dexter looked down at the floor and ran a hand through his hair. "I really don't see how that matters now."

"It doesn't. Running from the IPA is never even a crime, par-sham. Unless a scarab happens to catch you." Balboa pulled a chicle dispenser out of a shirt pocket and flipped a pill in his mouth. "But I do have authority to detain you and haul your body to Muni Detention don-la if I think it's fare necessary. I'm your custodian, and you're status EV."

Dexter turned to face him. The man looked fully capable of dragging him to jail by hand, if necessary. "Well, I'm here now. I just want to get this over with, make sure Jayjay's all right, and put all of this mess behind me."

Balboa visibly swished the chicle pill in his mouth, nodding. "It would be a mistake for you to run now. You're not in as deep as you think." He sat back and nodded, staring in the direction on the ENP com. "Should not take long to get you out of here, ney, once the complainant's reps get their response to the scarabs."

Dexter looked back toward the window wall. Jayjay knew where he was. Unless there had been another problem, she would have to be coming through the open doorway fairly soon, setting aflash the scanner light fixed in the wall above the threshold.

Balboa exhaled and scratched his mustache. "Are you familiar with the name Teodor Monroe?"

Dexter shook his head. "Not that I recall."

"He's a senator on Anastasia. One of the wealthier ones; he has a lot of investments and ties to some big corporations spread around the Human Sphere. From what I understand, he has a controlling interest in the holding company that owns the Blue Topaz, and several others."

Dexter cocked his head. "So he doesn't want his name besmirched, I suppose."

Balboa nodded. "I would think a senator wouldn't want it to come out he's connected to an outfit with a history of creative accounting. He may have no par-yen knowledge of illegalities, but if he gets wind of a potential scandal, he'll want to shut it down before any attention gets directed his way." His eyes fixed on the ENP com area and he rose. "I think we're ready... let's go."

Dexter stood and followed him to the switchboard. Balboa called over his shoulder. "Your android is in good hands see, mey-bu. Par-yen fret."

Dexter smiled weakly. "Right. Par-yen fret."

Balboa stepped around the officer seated at the large, globular patrol com speaker that bulged out of the console. The terraced frets and their paper-thin, concentric grooves were barely discernible, tight enough to create the appearance of a smooth surface. Channel upon channel of coral node blenders to replicate the sound imprint and feed the massive conveyer to the dozens and dozens of guide-locks along the Port Authority municipal tower running from the top level of the city down to the lots. The com system was probably as old as the tower itself, but it did the job. Dispatch control had the multidimensional capacity to relay signals to systems in every direction simultaneously, though most of its business was likely with the stations around the K-Peg asteroid belt.

The duty officer glanced up at the constable. "Mey-bu, Connie."

Balboa raised his eyebrows. "Sey in?"

"Wey."

Balboa turned, patting the back of the chair. "IPA confirmed the agreement. All we need is your say-so, toot-shoze."

Dexter blinked. "So... it's a 5 million CU reclamation, with no criminal charges."

The big man nodded, swinging up an arm and scratching the back of his neck. "A fine, technical. Minor fraud and disorderly conduct. And, wey, no prison time. Also, you are permanent banned from Beta Lyrae, and the Topaz is ney liable for any some shoze in your statement." He gestured toward the com.

"Minor fraud, but a major fine. I suppose I can live with that." Dexter frowned and sighed, leaning toward oversized speaker. "Yes, I'll agree." He straightened, glancing at Balboa. "They let me keep over 600,000 CU. Actually, the fine only covers about three-quarters of my total history of winnings in Sheliak City, if you include the other casinos there."

Balboa shot him back an odd look, then pushed past the chair to the console and nodded at the com, raising his voice. "Did you copy? That's a sale, set-la." He sounded as if he thought the antiquated equipment needed help.

The com didn't have the normal irritating crackle of a cockpit comlink, but a heavy hum filled the room, barely hanging above the low threshold of human hearing. The incoming voice was also louder than it needed to be. "Copy. Thank you, ENM. That's a wrap. Irina 437 out."

Balboa flipped a toggle switch and the hum disappeared. "You're all square. Don't go back to Beta Lyrae pa fare, and you'll be free and clear from that group."

Dexter wagged a finger at the com. "So officially, I'm now on record as having defrauded the casino."

Balboa held out his hands. "They don't want any publicity ney rey mal-fare on the part of the casino. And the record will be sealed, because they don't want a body par-sham knowing they let you off."

Dexter scratched his head. "They didn't exactly let me off, considering the fine."

Balboa ignored him, backing away from the com and glancing toward the doorway. "I'll be in contact as soon as your batto gets clearance. Sey po-sabe, it will take some few hours for the approval to be filed. You can be on your way as soon as I give the word."

Dexter glanced across the room at one of the lot surveillance monitors. "And my account access at the Bank?"

"Lyuda will reinstate your account access within the next few minutes." Balboa shrugged. "You get to keep your ship, and you get to remain registered and legal to fly. And as you say, you get to keep plu grand CU, po-sabe plu grand more than I will fare make in my lifetime, Massengill. If I was you, I would be kissing the steel beams of the city walks."

Dexter stood. "Still, I essentially just agreed that I would never file a complaint against an organization that assaulted me and very well might have

197

killed me. I don't mean to sound unappreciative, because I really do want to thank you for everything you've done, believe me. It's not exactly fair justice."

Balboa laughed. "Fair justice. Sey-la-vee, mo-nome." He glanced around at the officers manning their duty stations and shook his head. "They're right about some shoze, you know."

Dexter stepped away from the console. "What's that?"

"2.5 M over five years, no losing days, par-sham. Sey plu steep to be 100 percent luck." The constable scratched his mustache with a finger. "They have a name for that here, set-la fare see. Cooly-bambeeny."

Dexter squinted. "What does that mean?"

"It means that your luck is as easy to swallow as diaper dung."

Dexter smiled flatly, smoothing his shirt and starting toward the doorway. "Your people have such a colorful way of saying things."

Balboa nodded at him. "They say some people have what they call 'problem brains.' They can get CRP scan misreads. Caused by neurological irregularities." He stepped back, pointing more or less toward the exit. "You might want to look that up, set-la."

Dexter shook his head as he headed out. "I wasn't aware. But I think I'd know if I were a genome psi." He looked back. "Thank you again for your help, constable—I'm in your debt."

Balboa called after him. "Stay away from the casinos, Massengill."

Dexter frowned as he crossed the small antechamber and rounded the zigzag ramp that led down the face of the municipal tower to the sidewalk at the city's top level.

From outside, the city resembled a warehouse filled with randomly placed boxes. The buildings on the top level seemed scrunched and randomly placed, with uneven rooftops and varied widths, extending downward beyond the line of sight, cut off by railed sidewalks that were essentially long balconies. But the building material was all the same midtone blue-gray, and it blended together like a big, all-encompassing shadow. The sky was a uniform tinted shade of amber, just as bright as it had been hours earlier, and the many photo-panels and strips had a similar shade. There were no trees or plants to speak of. It was like walking through a giant motherboard.

There were parks and other recreational areas on the lower levels, where the unpleasantness of the dome-filtered light was less visible, but it was hard to imagine the people of Ustinov venturing outdoors very frequently.

Jayjay was waiting at the bottom of the ramp, seated on a bench by the sidewalk railing. Dexter grinned and raised his eyebrows as his pulse quickened. The technicians had released her. She was going to be all right.

She stood as he approached. "How did it go?"

Dexter exhaled. "Never mind that—what did they say at the institute? Did they identify the problem?"

She looked up at him with a half smile. "Mild neural distraction from the crash at Barrier Island."

Dexter blinked. It was nowhere near as bad as it could have been. "That's all? Are you completely sure?"

Jayjay nodded. "The surgeon said it had to do with sudden function transfer from external override to the in-body processors. No lasting effects, but he said blackouts and enhanced emotionalism are the usual result."

Dexter shook his head. "But the spells started before Barrier Island—that was why you were there in the first place." He froze. "You did tell him that—he is aware of all the details, isn't he?"

Jayjay turned and looked out over the shoulder-high railing to the next island of buildings. "They say the earlier problem was unrelated. They theorize that the malfunctions before were an imprint of prior mnemonic breakdown, which the technicians at Barrier Island must have corrected."

Dexter stared at her. "They'll have to trace it."

"Yes, they promised to give us a bit-by-bit breakdown when they run the reconciliation. You'll be happy to know they also recommended routine follow-up checks of the neocortical net just to be sure." Her expression didn't change. "What about it, Dexter—are you going to be able to fund routine follow-up checks?"

It was a mind-bogglingly simple explanation. Theoretically, it was possible, but emotional response affectations often stemmed from the mnemonic system—there had really been no reason to think otherwise. Jayjay had experienced other symptoms that were the same before and after Barrier Island, particularly the intermittent spells of cross-the-board interruption in functionality. That it might have been a coincidence of two very minor, unrelated problems was almost too much to hope for.

Jayjay chucked him on the arm. "Dexter? Did you work everything out with the patrols?"

He shook himself. "We're officially free to go. I just have to stay away from Beta Lyrae."

"That was a given. How bad was the fine?"

He shook his head. "5 million CU." He frowned up at the cap of the Port Authority tower.

Jayjay shrugged. "I see. You win some, you lose some."

199

"There's a first time for everything, I suppose." He flashed a smile. "I'm still ahead, technically speaking. They didn't quite take it all."

"Of course you are." Jayjay smiled back.

Dexter stepped to the railing and took a quick glance down. The nights on Ustinov were some 20 hours, and it was nearing daybreak, though there would probably be very little visual evidence of it when the muted light of Kappa Pegasi A began mingling with the glow of the photo-panels. The cars were still gliding by intermittently; the traffic seemed heavier toward the lower levels, down where the ship was.

He turned and gestured along the sidewalk in the direction of the lift on the next block, just past the intersection. "Shall we?"

Jayjay nodded and they headed for the corner.

From the sidewalk, the railing hid the street traffic almost completely, all but for the faint aura of the headlights. Oddly, as active as the city seemed to remain at all hours, the sidewalks were empty. And for a bustling city, it was dead silent. The only sounds were the subtle whisper of thrusters whenever a car zipped by, blending together with the buzz of the climate control system vents in an almost imperceptible, lower-threshold hiss like a long, unending exhalation.

Dexter sniffed the stale recycled air. According to the patrols, the city actually was livelier during the day, but for whatever reason, he didn't have the impression there were ever very many people out on these walkways, technical wee hours of the night or otherwise.

Jayjay nudged him. "You know, for someone who just caught a huge break, you don't seem very happy."

Dexter looked down at the ground. Gray lattice padding was the only thing separating their feet from the carbon-steel framework of the city. Everything was gray. He shook his head, looking back up. "No, I'm fine, really."

"You're not your usual chipper self."

He frowned. "The constable was mocking me for complaining. Do you believe that after all these negotiations, after helping me through this entire incident, I think he doesn't believe I won those credits honestly?"

Jayjay cocked her head, peering sideways at him. "Well, it's not his job to believe you. They don't really care one way or another. They just want to make sure there's a settlement."

"They think I'm a testshirt." Dexter mumbled, half to himself. "He would feel differently about it if they chased him through a casino."

"He did go into your account records. You've made a lot of CU."

Dexter looked at her sharply. She looked almost amused. "What's your point, Jayjay?"

She shrugged. "I hate to break this to you, but most people aren't used to seeing someone win in gaming the way you do. For most people, earning that kind of credit is a lot harder than it is for you. You shouldn't be so surprised that some people find it hard to accept." She smiled and leaned into him, giving him a quick rub on the back. "Come on. Cheer up. The Galaxy is your proverbial oyster, augmented as it may be."

They reached the corner and moved onto the crosswalk that arched over the intersection in a graded, angular ramp. The railing along the span was a little lower, offering more of a view.

Dexter stopped and took a look out over the street of air. There at the top of the city, the cars moved in only two directions, passing just meters below the feet of anyone standing on the crosswalk. Below them, more cars flitted back and forth like fireflies all the way down to the tenth level. Dizzying, and a little spectacular. Apparently, the city planners had actually stumbled onto something pleasing to the eye.

The Explorer was down at the bottom, stationed at one of the central lots adjacent to the spaceport that sprawled across the base of the stacked city. Some 15 blocks away laterally from where the nearest lift would leave them off. Rather a long walk.

"Why are you stopping?" Jayjay was a couple of paces ahead, looking back at him. She still had a slight look of amusement on her face, and it was about as adorably relaxed as she had ever looked.

"What's the rush?" He moved in front of her. "Jayjay, I hope you don't mind, but I think I'm going to have to kiss you right now. I know we haven't really established…"

She put her arms around his neck. "Dexter, shut up for once." She pulled him close and kissed him.

Dexter closed his eyes and was immediately overwhelmed with the sense that he had needlessly wasted the previous five years, but then it didn't matter. He became conscious of his hands on her shoulders, a position that suddenly seemed familiar. He stroked her, running his palms down along her sides to the small of her back, and she pressed closer to him.

She pulled away, staring at him. Her eyes were wide and they looked dazzlingly enormous, leaving the impression they had remained open for the duration of the kiss. For a moment she looked intense, and then the smile crept back across her face. "That was nice."

Dexter blinked, nodding. "Yes. Very nice."

"We should probably go."

"If you say so."

She grinned and started along the down slope of the crosswalk, hanging onto his hand for a moment more, then letting it go, glancing back at him.

They reached the opposite block, and she crossed to the lift cylinder built into the corner of a moderately tall office building and touched the keypad on the wall.

Dexter stepped next to her and she smiled up at him again. Too irresistible. He wasn't going to be able to wait until they reached the ship. He reached for her hand and steered her in front of him, placing his other hand on her shoulder.

Her grip tightened abruptly, and he glanced down at the sudden pressure in his hand, then looked back at her face. He laughed. "Easy, Jayjay, my metacarpals are breakable."

She grabbed his shoulder with her other hand and stepped back, searching with her eyes. "Dexter... what's happening?" Her pupils were blown, far beyond the norm.

She couldn't see him. His smile disappeared.

"Dexter?" Her jaw began to tremble. "I can't... what's happening..."

Spasms and vision loss. Expanding system breakdowns. He shook his head. "Jayjay, I'm here—it's all right, just try to calm down." He pulled her close. Her entire body was shaking now.

"Dexter, I don't know what's happening, I can't see you, I can't feel you... this doesn't feel right... this really doesn't feel right..." Her voice was fluttering.

Blasted forsaken stars! The doctors at the tech-mech institute had probably run a couple basic tests on her arithmetic-logic processors and assumed a diagnosis without so much as looking for inconsistencies in her subroutines. "It's all right, Jayjay, it's just another spell—it won't last. We'll get it fixed, we just have to take you back to the institute."

Jayjay began blinking uncontrollably. Dexter hugged her tightly, trying to restrict her movement, but she fell back against the wall and slid to the ground, pulling him with her. She began jerking her head and twisting violently. One arm landed a blow on Dexter's ribcage and he winced, rolling away.

For several seconds, she flopped against the sidewalk like an asphyxiating fish. Then it was over. She lay motionless on her back, eyes wide, staring upward, one arm thrown off to the right.

"Jayjay?" Dexter panted, his pulse racing. "Jayjay?"

All she had to do was wake back up. He would take her back in, and they would fix the problem, or send her to someone else who could give her better attention.

"Jayjay, wake up!"

He crawled to her side and shook her, probing for the manual override nodule at the back of her neck. He pressed it several times. No response.

He shook her again and swallowed, staring at her for a long moment. He shook his head, touching her cheek. She continued to stare lifelessly upward. Suddenly the energy seemed to be rapidly draining out of his own body. He felt nauseous. He let himself collapse lightly on top of her, pressing his ear against her chest, as if he might hear a human heartbeat.

The bell on the keypad chimed and the lift door slid open. Dexter looked up and shook himself, glancing around, and his eyes fell on the crosswalk.

Jayjay was in the neighborhood of 100 kilograms—a lot heavier than she looked. He could drag her back to the municipal building if necessary, but with a ride he could take her directly to the surgical technicians.

He ran back to the center of the bridge and began jumping and yelling, frantically flailing his arms in the air. A handful of cars streamed past without stopping.

Down the sidewalk from Jayjay, a figure was approaching from some distance away. A large figure... possibly an anadon, by the look of it, although it was hard to tell in the thin light. Dexter moved back toward Jayjay, keeping his eyes on the figure.

Behind him, a car rose to the level of the crosswalk and turned, illuminating him and Jayjay. Dexter wheeled and began dancing madly, trying to beckon it closer. The car moved forward and crossed above the railing, passing over his head and settling onto the sidewalk behind Jayjay. A young, spiky-haired man stepped out of the car.

The man glanced at Jayjay and nodded at Dexter. "Set an android?"

Dexter dashed forward. "Yes—I need help. Can you help me get her to the technical mechanics service wing on Level D?"

A young woman with a green mohawk got out on the passenger side and glanced at the man. The woman nodded. "Kranz TMI."

The man shrugged and looked back at Dexter. "Absolu."

Dexter exhaled. "Thank the guidestars—I really appreciate this!"

The woman smiled. "Par-yen fret, mo-nome. We'll get her safe."

The couple each lifted an arm, and the man seemed surprised at the weight, nearly dropping her. The woman raised her eyebrows at Dexter. "Hold her feet... we'll back her in, wey?"

The car was a dragonfly, with two long vertical shutter doors that swung open both above and below the cab, making it relatively easy to load Jayjay in. They moved Jayjay onto the back bench, and Dexter caught another glimpse of the anadonesque figure in the distance as the couple got in the front. The figure had stopped, apparently content to watch the scene without getting involved.

Dexter climbed into the cab after Jayjay, and the woman in the front hit a control, closing the doors. The car rose above the ground and dipped back into the air canal, heading for the nearest level change.

*   *   *

A repeating loop of advertisements played over an oversized display glass without sound, creating a vague background pulse of light and color. A transparent attempt to brush at the consciousness of the people in the waiting room. Hypnotic to some, perhaps. Most likely a source of mounting irritation to most.

Dexter shifted in his seat and frowned, drumming his fingers against the tabletop, staring toward the back of the big room. Beneath the display glass, the semicircular passage that led to the surgery rooms remained sealed off by an opaque field gate, solid as the surrounding insulation wall.

The generic portable couchette booths lining the walls were full of people quietly sitting or standing around with blank looks and virtually no sense of anticipation, as if they all expected to be waiting for days, seemingly culled by frayed nerves or sleep deprivation. The dark maglev runway that split the reception area along the center from the outer hall to the operating rooms had been devoid of any foot traffic for a good 20 minutes.

Jayjay had been under the probes for over an hour. The primary expert on the neocortical net was a man named Tfariag, and he would apparently be consulting with a field-effect transistor specialist. They were giving her extra attention now that they had already failed to run an effective screen once. Small comfort now.

Something specific that the doctors could have targeted and resolved would have been quick. It was probably already past that point now. If they failed to diagnose the issue now, if her malfunction was already affecting multiple systems… he could fly her somewhere else, maybe seek out a more mainstream specialist and hope for different results. He could always get a second opinion.

Dexter rubbed his eyes. The image lingered—Jayjay prone on a maglev

204

gurney, still in the new dress as the medical personnel guided her across the floor, then disappearing in a blink behind the particle field.

The options were running out. But in the end, if Jayjay did have TPM, it didn't matter what he did. Her systems would begin to degrade on a large scale, she would have to be reassembled before her parts became unusable scrap, and that would be the end of her personality.

At the right extreme of the display glass was an image of the clerk at the front desk, an overly tall man seated somewhere beneath the flooring, presumably by the lowest-level entrance. The attendant was presumably there to watch several monitors on his desk, but he appeared to be examining one of his hands.

It was an intensive care unit in name only, apparently.

The tabletop of each booth was also a viewer screen, another indication that a long wait was not a rare thing. The idea of watching random clips on a viewer to pass time seemed somehow more tedious than paying attention to the silent advertisements; of course, doing just about anything would have probably seemed like drudgery. Overly intense artificial light, tinted polyglass, dark interior surfaces, with lots of metal and black rubber borders and molding. The entire tech-mech facility had a distinctly depressing flavor.

Dexter turned toward the entrance, where a small pocket of aliens were seated somewhat close to one another, several booths away. Two anadons and a scint. The scint seemed to be looking directly back at him with no attempt to hide it. Rather an unsettling habit. The scinti had a knack for sensing wounds... this one might have been homing in on the hotstitches.

Mainly the crowd was human—Eo-Nowar wasn't big on the travel circuit, so aliens tended to stand out. The scint continued to stare unabashedly. Dexter looked back for a moment, scratching his chest, then looked down at the tabletop and brushed the button that activated the viewer.

Several streams of text in various languages and scripts scrolled by at all four edges of the table, around various small squares showing different images. News footage, sporting events, and weather statistics. One movie of some sort, something flashing Ul'an subtitles. In the upper right was the image of the check-in attendant. No sound, but there were probably earpieces in some small compartment around the couchettes. Apparently the check-in attendant had to be contacted for sound. Dexter touched the weather image and it expanded to cover the entire table.

Dexter focused on the table and tapped the image of the check-in attendant. It expanded to fill the tabletop. The tall man glanced in his direction and gestured at his ear. Dexter found the earpieces in a small compartment in one arm of the couchette. He put the tiny round plug in his ear. "How much longer do you think this is going to take? Do you have any idea what they are working on?"

The man shook his narrow head wearily. "Name of patient?" Close up, the man's eyes seemed unusually far apart for the width of his face.

Dexter sighed. "Jajqrt170."

"One moment, mo-nome." The man turned his head slightly, looking at one of his monitors. "Full exploratory systems check."

Dexter raised his voice slightly. "I already know that—that's what they told me going in. What are they doing now—have they isolated the problem yet?"

The man blinked expressionlessly. "Sey par-yen. There is no new information. Dr. Tfariag will update the file when he has some few new shoze." He paused. "Can I fare help you with some other need, mo-nome?"

Dexter shook his head. "How long will it be?"

"Sey dee-fee-see... hard to say, mo-nome. These operations set-see fare do vary." The man paused again. The pauses seemed to be increasing in length. "Sey some few other needs?"

Dexter shut the viewer off and stood, removing the plug and pacing toward the entrance. An anadon in a nondescript beige multipurpose pilot outfit was now seated near the passageway to the front hall, apart from the other nonhuman sentients. The big saurian was somewhat large for a male, but the rounded form of the ridges around the brow clearly indicated the sex was male.

The sentient's eyes shifted toward Dexter. Dexter shifted and looked down at the metal flooring designed to keep the gurneys afloat, camouflaged amid a glossy gridwork of transparent linoleum tile. He sniffed and looked back up.

Now the anadon was now blatantly staring. The sentient stood and stepped toward him, crossing the floor surprisingly quickly. "You are waiting for your android?" He had about a half meter of height on Dexter.

"Yes, that's right." Dexter cocked his head. "I guess... you are as well?"

The anadon's eyes shifted to the display glass on the wall. "No."

Dexter scratched the back of his neck and shifted again, clearing his throat. "Yes, well, I'm hoping the procedure will be done soon." He nodded and smiled thinly. "Good morning. Dexter Massengill."

The anadon looked down at him. "I know who you are." He paused, hissing to himself as he looked back at the wall display, then looked again at Dexter. "I was hoping to speak to you."

Dexter studied the alien face, trying to focus on something other than the red eyes and their slit pupils. He squinted. "I saw someone on the sidewalk when my IU collapsed. Was that you?" He paused. "Have you been… following me?"

The anadon flicked his tongue in and out of his mouth. "I have been trying to track you down, yes. I apologize for my methods, but it was necessary to have this discussion in private. I have a business proposition."

A quasi-legal business proposition, perhaps. Dexter frowned and shook his head. "What is this about?"

The anadon bowed his head. "May we sit down?"

Dexter glanced over toward the field gate. "I suppose I would like an explanation… I don't see why not." He waved at his booth.

The anadon turned, his eyes shifting to the outer hall. He bowed again and followed him to the booth, folding himself smoothly into the seat opposite Dexter.

The anadon towered above the tabletop, seemingly taller than the hulking Constable Balboa, but the nonhuman seemed comfortable in the seat. His comparatively slender torso and thick legs were nimbler than they looked.

Dexter shrugged. "Go ahead."

The anadon lowered his voice to a soft, feral growl. "You've frequented Beta Lyrae, most recently the Blue Topaz Casino. You've made a large profit off the casinos over the years. Records show that you have a higher rate of success than any of these casinos. In fact, there is no record of you ever having turned a loss on any given day."

Blast! Balboa's investigation had brought the winnings tally to light, and now it was apparently a lot more public than the constable had let on. The anadon might have been a muni, someone who had seen Balboa's file. More likely, he was from off-planet. Maybe some corrupt member of the IPA looking for a payoff.

Or, the anadon was working with the casino people, which would undoubtedly be worse.

Dexter shifted in his seat. "I'm not sure who you are, but I've recently settled this business about my gaming winnings, and I'm not interested in getting back into it."

The field gate went down and several technicians escorted a small group of androids out. They were met by people in various other booths. Jayjay and Dr. Tfariag were not among them.

The anadon's narrow pupils followed the activity. "My name is Q'um

Lharaa Saaj. This proposition is not about revisiting the past. My associates are interested in your talents."

Dexter sniffed. "I can't help you."

Several people were moving past the booth, glancing in the anadon's direction, and Q'um Lharaa Saaj warded them off with a menacing snarl. He turned back to Dexter. "I am authorized to escort you to my business associates on Anastasia. You will be offered substantial compensation for your cooperation. We can discuss the details of the arrangement when we arrive."

Anastasia. Balboa's mention of the senator from Anastasia couldn't have been a coincidence. Dexter sighed. These people didn't know how to let things go. "I have no interest in shoving off to Anastasia while my IU is undergoing a procedure, and I wouldn't otherwise, regardless of whatever compensation your associates are offering—I don't want any part in it. Besides, as difficult as it is for you people to believe, I honestly can't help you. I have no idea why I win the way I do, and I have no control of it. So I'm sorry, but you've obviously wasted your time coming here."

Saaj paused. The breath crackled in his callused sinus cavities like the purr of a cat, though he appeared anything but content. He leaned forward and hissed. "Trust me. It would be to your advantage to accept this offer."

Dexter sat up. "Frankly, I don't have the time or inclination to discuss gaming, or to help your organization in any way. Whatever business you and your associates might be in."

"That is your prerogative, but you might want to reconsider."

"I don't think so."

A blue light in the tabletop display began to blink. The table seemed to turn itself on, showing an enlarged image of the check-in attendant. The man was attempting to talk. Dexter glanced around for the earplug, running his hands along the tabletop.

"Dexter Massengill?"

Dexter turned and focused his attention on the large wall display. He glanced from the wall to the tabletop. "Yes, that's me."

The attendant's monotone voice filled the reception area. "Dr. Tfariag would like to speak to you. He's asking for you to come inside." Beneath the wall image, the field gate disappeared.

"Yes, of course." Dexter stood and nodded at the anadon. "If you'll excuse me."

Saaj moved out of the booth and extended to his full height. "I will be stationed here for another day. Contact me through Port Com, if you change your mind."

Dexter turned and stepped onto the maglev runway, heading into the operating room passageway without responding. No, they were definitely not letting it go, and they quite possibly never would.

The passageway was essentially a long, low-ceilinged tunnel lined on both sides with rounded doorless portals. The pale, washed-out argon-mercury lighting seemed to give everything an aqua blue tint. A thin technician motioned for him to enter a work area on the left; Dexter ducked and stepped through the portal.

Jayjay lay in a polyglass tube, her eyes closed. A panel above her face had been opened, and a blanket covered her body from her neck to her feet. Dr. Tfariag and two other surgical technicians were standing over her, wearing white elastic caps over their hair. Tfariag was recognizable despite a cumbersome binocular device that covered his eyes. He stepped to Dexter's side. "Wey, Mr. Massengill, bu." He waved at the two other surgeons. "Set-see, this is Dr. Sarkin, and set-la, Dr. Fender."

Dexter nodded at them. Dr. Sarkin was a tall middle-aged woman, and Dr. Fender was a pale-skinned man. They were both noticeably thin. A lot of the people on the planet seemed to look underweight and sleep-deprived.

He looked back at Tfariag. "Tell me what's going on."

Tfariag shook his head. "Wey—what you need to know. We think she's going to be fine. We believe we were able to locate the problem, and it is fixable. The source is originating in the mnemonics."

Dexter closed his eyes and exhaled heavily. They were saying she was going to be all right, after all. But they had said so before.

Tfariag seemed to read his mind. "Perdone, Mr. Massengill. You should know sure we did a deep analysis before. The neural distraction fare did bear out all her symptoms, so when we ney fare did find any some shoze on our routine scans, we put the pieces together and made our best determination plu-bu based on the facts we had on hand."

Dexter looked sharply back at him, and stepped to the head of the tube, pushing past Dr. Fender. If the problem was in her memory, the man was not likely to get him to believe they had been looking in the right place during the previous surgery. "You checked her memory thoroughly? You checked all the connectivity, relays and field cells?"

"Wey. We checked prem storage, magnetics, static registers, the burner and ladder function, every field cell—we do that routine, set-la. As we thought, the problem was affecting her mnemonics, but it was ney being caused by memory failure."

Dexter shrugged, looking down at Jayjay. She looked peaceful—the frozen expression of fear and shock was gone. That her eyes were closed was a good sign; it meant they had already successfully stimulated autonomic motor responses. "What was it, then?"

Dr. Sarkin cut in, stepping forward to the tube directly across from Dexter. "There's an unusually large memory gap that drew our attention."

Dexter nodded, closing his eyes. "Yes, I specifically wanted that looked at when we were in before."

Sarkin held up a hand. "And Dr. Tfariag's team did review that. His team's protocols were sound; the patient had a layered malady that masked some of her symptoms and made the root cause difficult to diagnose, given the evidence."

Sarkin was obviously the new consult. Predictable that she would cover for the other institute surgeons. Dexter folded his arms. "I'm listening."

"Typically, when we see memory loss and the field cells are fully functional, it's related to a power supply problem. Dr. Tfariag's team did find power supply issues and the tests showed that they were affecting the mnemonics. The malady was consistent with the effects of a neural distraction, and the patient responded to the prescribed treatment." Sarkin wasn't using the local dialect, and she spoke with a more refined accent; she obviously wasn't a native Ustinovian, and the thought of that was somehow more reassuring than her explanation.

"So what was the problem, then?"

Tfariag glanced from Sarkin to Dexter. "Apparent, it's psychological. It's rare, but sey po-sabe cybernetic function can be undermined by interferences from the adaptive cognition die. Set pass when hypermutation causes an aspect of personality that finds a particular item of data repellent."

Psychological. Dexter stared at the surgeon. Psycho-cybernetic kinks had been a problem in first-generation android models with the advent of personality chips, but as far as he knew there hadn't been a reported case of it in the last thousand years, a good deal before Jayjay's time. He raised his eyebrows. "You're saying she was repelled by something in her memory, and that's what's causing these wide-scale system failures?"

"Wey, some few shoze stored in one of the field cells spanning that memory gap." The surgeon scratched his chin with a gloved hand. "Sey rev… embedded subroutine. A matter of repressed thought. In a case like this set-see, the unit subconscious shuts down some of her relays and isolates the field cells containing the unwanted information, creating a block within the mnemonic system. The information then becomes dormant for a period, and then it eventual reactivates and affects behavior. When that happens set-la, the information can be called up in a simple computer scan. When the block is filled, the unit returns to normal function."

Dexter stared at Jayjay. So it was the nine-month hole in Jayjay's memory, as much as she had always protested that it was pointless to dredge up old history. "Why is this happening now? Jayjay's had that memory gap for centuries. Why would it act up all of a sudden?"

Tfariag paused and lowered his binoculars as if he was only just realizing they were still on his face. "The cybernetic mind can fare be some mysterious shoze. As I said, set-see is not a common case, par-sham. My guess is an outside stimulus triggered the memory. The mnemonic system attempted to recall the memory, and the system began malfunctioning."

Dexter grimaced. Quite possibly, the malfunctions had been brought on by his own continued harassment. Still, better to have the problem dealt with and put behind them. He put a hand on top of his head. "So to fix the problem, we just have to retrieve the blocked information manually."

Tfariag nodded. "There is no real damage to any of her mnemonic processes, so sey par-yen, easy to fix." He paused. "If you're comfortable performing the scan on your own, you might want to do that, fare set-la, in the interest of respecting your unit's privacy plu po-sabe."

Dexter nodded quickly. "Yes, that's fine—I'm happy to do that."

"Your batto's on-board will identify the cells and interpret the information for you. You'll need to file set information la, read it, and relay it to your unit without involving the computer. You should ney tell her toot set shoze—just a few significant events. Her subconscious might sabotage the new information unless you confront her with it direct. Sey fair simple. You think your body can fare handle set-la?"

Dexter blinked. "Yes, absolutely." Jayjay looked truly angelic, lying there. Soon she was going to be her animated self again, out of the tube and back on the ship, rolling her eyes at his bad jokes, mocking his lifestyle. He rubbed his mouth and felt a smile spreading. "Is it safe to wake her?"

Dr. Fender sidled up on his left and spoke for the first time. "She will be in recharge for the next four hours, but we'll move her back to your batto in the meantime. When she is situated la, get her connected to your on-board and run a basic diagnostic. Your on-board will reacclimate her to her regular cycle."

Tfariag nodded at Fender. "She should be fine when she awakes, but you'll want to keep her prone and on a monitor until you refresh her memory as we described. You understand?"

"I understand."

Tfariag nodded slowly. "Trey-bu." He paused. "I'm told you were prepared to offer your batto as a guarantee of payment. Is this right?"

Dexter sniffed and put his hands on his hips, nodding back. "Yes. It won't be necessary, though—my account is no longer frozen. I've had the matter resolved."

Tfariag smiled and exchanged glances with the other surgeons. "Wey, we've contacted the Bank; you're squared away." He paused and gestured to a technician standing in the main passage. "Dr. Tezraymon will show you out. You give us a call if you have any more problems."

*   *   *

... GCL CE.006

Phi 29 53 36.40 / Theta 11 22 01.20 / Rho 5.10 / JD 3040384

70 Ophiuchi: OS, "Irina Vicinity"; 9 March 3612 CE

Teodor Monroe ran his hands up Ritsa Rabani's bare abdomen toward her breasts as his Scintivar Nova Archangel pulled out of hyperspace.

He exhaled. "It seems we've arrived."

She climbed off him and stepped away from the king divan, slipping into one of the discarded bathrobes.

If there had been a hint of any expression on her face, it was that of utter boredom. He lightly scratched his mustache as he imagined her again in motion, arching her back as she straddled him. He smiled. She would have likely reacted the same way to torture.

"I'll alert System Control." She turned and plunged through the semitranslucent shimmer of the dew-drop curtain, sending a lazy, spreading ripple of current outward across the threshold field as she headed up the long, low-lit corridor between the aft cabins.

Teodor watched Rabani disappear from view at the far end of the corridor. In a few years the Rabani clones had learned every facet of his life. Their mathematical minds had somehow become more fully utilized by the same chemicals that had given them the accelerated growth rate and tamped off the pleasure center of their brains. Each clone always knew what the members of the syndicate were up to, and they had tabs on every accountant in Sheliak City—they functioned virtually as a single-minded collective, ever-present and more efficient than any of the other staffers. As efficient as androids, really; they were deft enough to handle the intricate calculations of

212

space travel, if necessary. Regardless, space travel was much more interesting while the Archangel's computer remained on autopilot, and he had her full attention.

The provision of sex was, of course, a happy convenience, never specifically planned but a measure of good fortune through the crafty hands of Faro's genetic engineers. Nothing spectacular—the few Rabani clones who had been invited to the bedroom knew nothing Teodor himself hadn't specifically taught them, and their lack of capacity for pleasure created limitations on what he could do, removed the thrill of being able to manipulate them and bend them to his will. But other women constituted an investment on his behalf—time and devotion that wasn't often available for a man with so many other concerns. The selected copies of Ritsa Rabani served as a quick, unemotional diversion.

It had to have been some side-effect of the acid and cytotoxin mix Faro's people had injected in her pituitary gland—where the reasoning abilities of her brain had flourished, the creativity and emotion had been stunted. She was cold, and she would never realize the tragedy of her shortened life. Conveniently low-maintenance for a set of concubines; if there was a drawback it was that they offered no challenge.

Teodor pursed his lips at the curtain as it resolved back into its resting form, a sheer, dully glowing sheet of cyan, solid as a pane of frosted glass. Ritsa Rabani was his creation and his possession, and her multiplicity and razor-sharp skills made her a precious commodity; challenge or not, she would likely remain in his service for as long as her pool of DNA remained viable.

He slid off the heated king divan and picked the master guide device off the floor. He pressed a button and the entire forward bulkhead leapt to life, transforming into a gigantic, unbroken window of flawlessly rendered holographic animation and filling the cabin with dodecaphonic sound. He was suddenly looking at the image of a Hammerhead Lazyminer dragging a laser pan into an asteroid field.

Something about new corporate mining in the outer planets of the Ekaterina System. Teodor eyed the ceiling, raising his voice. "Go to Stasya."

The asteroid field was replaced by a recording of a ride to the infirmary by the assistant director at Stasya Hyperdynamics. A reporter's voice boomed through the surrounding speakers, detailing the demise of the AD's right ear, and of the man's indictment for participation in the big heist through information given by an anonymous informant.

Teodor smiled. The man had gotten off easy—Nasr-Rakh and Saaj had been given carte-blanche to use any means necessary to silence the AD after the heist. Still, as convenient as the AD's death would have been, the decision to maim was to be applauded. A surgical stroke rather than a bludgeoning. Creativity was a delightful thing in the business of extortion.

Rabani's voice came through the speakers, interrupting the broadcast. "I have Saaj on Ustinov."

Teodor nodded and wrapped himself in a clean robe, putting down the master guide. "What about Irina System Control?"

"Everything has been cleared. Paradise Tours has been informed that you will not be needing an escort to your chalet." The woman never hesitated. "Should I put him through to the MTA?"

"Good, yes. I'll be there in a moment." He splashed through the stratified droplets of water in the curtain, feeling the brief tingle of evaporating moisture against his skin as he headed along the corridor toward the main cabin.

He was now at a point he had long striven for—his money now gave him the power of immediate, universal respectability. He could go anywhere in the Galaxy without becoming conspicuous. A reason for being on a foreign planet was always handy; he could always reserve time in between voting sessions to visit a recreational bungalow, or schedule a meeting with a major corporation. Space was a gigantic environment, always large enough for even the elite players to hide. And he knew how to play.

It had never been different. Transforming his shipping business from a small, bi-global import/export to the dominant player in the Galinan clover market had happened swiftly and easily—it had never taken more than a bit of incentive for the right people to view his business favorably, and the well-timed dispensing of potential enemies. It had always been a matter of knowing where to direct the money and effectively identifying the moment he could get away with murder.

He moved through the open companionways at the heart of the ship and crossed into the heightened luxury of the main cabin, stepping quickly past the seating alcoves to the main terminal access station at the front end of the compartment. He cued the feed from Rabani as he moved in front of the huge embedded monitor, and the screen filled with an oversized depiction of Q'um Lharaa Saaj's anadon face.

Teodor leaned above the com. "Go ahead, Saaj."

The anadon spoke after a pause. "There is a problem." The anadon's voice was barely recognizable. The MTA's com had a specially designed rendering system, using filters and extrapolators to provide simulated live reception, but there was obviously something wrong with one of the mechanisms.

Teodor narrowed his eyes. "You were unable to enlist our man?"

"He did not accept the proposal, and I think he will not accept." The inflections of Saaj's words were choppy, garbled through overfiltration as if the amalgamation of tonal signals from the operational carriers was losing data through the arc reflectors. He sounded as if he were speaking through a sheet of fine polycloth. "It is in his interest to accept. But he does not seem… wise."

Teodor frowned, looking down at the floor. The com failure was making it difficult to focus. He would have to put a maintenance team on it at the next stop. He shook his head. "So you believe he's unwise. What makes you think so?"

"I am paid to know these things. This man smells weak and imprudent." Saaj hissed thickly. "This may not be worth pursuing, senator. I believe you will get nothing from this man." The texture of the yellow-brown saurian visage appeared grainy, on the screen. It was possible the transmission was being affected by interference from the field output of Irina's massive com halo, which might have meant there was no easy fix.

Either way, it was intolerable. Teodor exhaled. "I disagree—as you know, I can be very persuasive. But we will see, won't we? Continue to pressure him. I don't believe we're dealing with a man who likes violence. Make sure he understands how much this decision could affect the quality of his life."

The voice was silent. The implication couldn't have been clearer. There was an appropriate delay, then the sound of an aqueous gurgle as the anadon exhaled. "Senator, in my estimation this man could not have infiltrated our systems on his own. I believe there are other avenues to explore. This man is just a tramp."

Teodor straightened, looking up toward the overhead streamers. "Saaj, do you have an issue with what I'm asking?"

The anadon paused. "No, senator. But I feel I should give you my complete assessment."

Teodor nodded. "And I appreciate that, but this is not a typical casino infiltration. We'll pursue other avenues when we've thoroughly exhausted this one." He strolled across the cabin as Rabani emerged from the cockpit, stepping around him on her way to the lounge. "Saaj, I have found that the only way to get what you want in life is for you to be thorough and examine every possibility. Dexter Massengill is too good, too flawless a gambler to be a typical casino tramp." He watched the robe trickle up Rabani's legs as she bent to tidy up the hors-d'oeuvre plates left out on one of the glass tables. He scratched his mustache. "Ms. Rabani has presented you with all the figures. Mr. Massengill never wins more than a relatively modest share, all things considered. He's clearly able to win at will, but he always stops."

Saaj snarled. "The mark of a grifter. He doesn't want to be noticed."

The anadon's broken voice was rapidly becoming tedious, particularly with the unnecessary smattering of reptiloid vocal eruptions. Teodor sighed gruffly, turning back to the monitor. "That sounds remarkably like a contradiction, Saaj. A grifter without charm is generally not successful. Casino tests for CRP have repeatedly proved negative. It seems this man, this weak and imprudent tramp, as you put it, has found some inexhaustible source of luck, and yet he never exploits it. This is going to fascinate me until I know how he's doing it, and I intend to find out."

Saaj was silent, apparently afraid to comment further. Teodor nodded. This matter needed to be handled delicately, and there was no room for error. Saaj was well-intentioned in his candor, but this was not the time for a debate. Teodor cleared his throat. "Faro will be contacting you with further instructions. I'll speak to you again when I'm finished my business on Irina. For now, see that his ship doesn't get clearance to leave until Faro arrives."

"Ssaya."

"Get it done, Saaj." Teodor killed the transmission. He pursed his lips, looking at the control shelf. There was another matter that required his attention that did not need to be handled so delicately.

He stepped back to the MTA and pulled up the com transcripts, scrolling back to a separate message from several hours before. A one-way nock from Valentina, one that he had been pleasantly distracted from.

At this point he wasn't going to be available to tend to the matter personally. He rapped a knuckle against the console and spun around, fixing his attention in the direction of the lounge.

Rabani was setting a tray of cups and plates down on the galley bar. She looked back at him.

"You're aware of the information we received from Beta Lyrae?" He took a step toward her, clasping his hands behind his back.

She nodded.

"I'll need your talents there. When we get to Tango Charlie, I want you to touch base with our contact there and have her deliver Mr. Malgovar my message." He sniffed, raising his eyebrows.

She nodded again and disappeared behind the curtain. He watched the twin stars of 70 Ophiuchi grow larger as the Archangel made the final approach toward Irina's jade crescent, now less than a luna away. He sighed. It was a long time since he had last paid a visit to the IPA compound.

Saaj might have been having a difficult time convincing this gamer to volunteer his secrets, but there were other ways to obtain information.

*　　　*　　　*

... GCL EE.271
Phi 63 11 15.36 / Theta 14 47 00.47 / Rho 270.42 / JD 3040381
Beta Lyrae: VALENTINA; "Sheliak City"; 9 March 3612 CE

Ritsa Rabani watched her shadow grow longer and thinner as she approached Dion Malgovar's office.

Monroe's latest objective had been delivered from aboard a flight from Anastasia, where, she knew, he was accompanied by one of her counterparts. That one had been with him now for several months, wasting her usefulness by existing solely as his concubine. Sex was apparently critical even during an operation, seemingly as important to the senator as precise efficiency.

Rabani herself had participated with him before. The importance Monroe placed on it was puzzling.

She stiffened her shoulders as she stepped along the hallway. There was never a reason to argue. Monroe knew exactly what he wanted, and he got it. Always.

The day was about to break, and the Blue Topaz was as empty as it ever got. The peripheral office veins of the complex had just switched to low-energy concentration, and the chem lighting had been dimmed to conserve power. But to the sentients remaining in sections that weren't restricted to employees, the casino would appear as bright and welcoming as it was during peak hours.

The hallway seemed to get darker toward the office door. Malgovar was skimming profits again, using a partitioned account to recycle false intake receipts at an accelerated rate now that his standing had been thrown into question.

Of course, Monroe was aware of it, as he was of all of Malgovar's transgressions. Monroe had withheld retribution toward Malgovar as he had toward Gustin Yazov, a standard practice he would continue to employ. Not because he believed in second chances, but because he believed in building

217

a case that would call for a more severe response. Clearly, Monroe had no interest in meting out minor reprimands.

The door was slightly ajar, and a bright light from inside broke the deeper hue of the corridor.

"Yes, come in."

Rabani stepped inside the doorway and stopped. Malgovar was lounging behind his desk, holding a cup of grog.

"Ritsa. Where have you been?"

She remained expressionless. "I was receiving a communiqué."

He gave her a sour look. "I understood you were returning to the casino right after the meeting."

"There's been a change of plans."

He swished his drink around in his hand. "I see. Plans I'm not in on, I'm sure."

"That's right, Mr. Malgovar. I answer first to Teodor Monroe, as you know."

"Teodor Monroe." He put his cup on the desk and looked at her, then stood up and frowned. "I'm obviously aware of the arrangement we have, Ritsa. But I do have an understanding with Teodor Monroe—I have you here until the end of this pay period, and during that time, you work for me. Just so we're clear, if you have business with Mr. Monroe, you need to keep me informed." He sat down and sipped his grog, turning away from her. "I need you here, I have a business to run. So I would appreciate it if you would let me know next time you have a conflict, all right? Not too much to ask, I don't think."

She didn't flinch.

"So what do you want?"

She stared at him. "Senator Monroe is terminating your association with the organization."

As he moved to stand, the thin beam from her refined Blue Lake refractor pistol sliced a vertical line down his chest, splitting his sternum. He fell forward against the desk, knocking his grog on the floor.

Rabani turned and headed for the elevator.

*　　　　　*　　　　　*

The lift door slid open and Dexter stepped onto Level J—the Jetty, as it was known. On Ustinov, the bottom of the city was the reception area of the city, but the urban planners of Eo-Nowar had obviously not considered presentation a priority. The city's underbelly was like an exposed root system—largely a seemingly random amalgamation of gigantic girders and broken planes. All the usual social staples around a major spaceport were there—basic food and lodging, enclosed courts and recreational facilities—but like the rest of Eo-Nowar, the layout was clearly designed for function rather than comfort. The buildings were few and far between, and the conventional blocks of the upper levels gave way to long, narrow, crisscrossing catwalks and expansive squares of deceptively dense carbon-steel landing pads holding innumerable spacecraft, staggered vertically to maximize space. The support infrastructure hung down from there, visible in the gaps between the planes of metal, a jagged skeleton clinging to the massive city posts like spiderwebs.

The lift opened onto a small square with a long row of public transport scooters racked up and humming along one edge, hovering above the power strip. A somewhat unnecessary waste of thrust, considering it would have been just as easy to leave the tiny vehicles inactive and piled on their sides and would have served the same purpose. Perpetual motion through recycled energy on display. It was a shame the city officials didn't take as much pride in the general appearance of their city as they did in their engineering prowess.

Dexter stepped to the nearest scooter and climbed on, testing his weight, then took off in the general direction of the Explorer's lot, glancing downward as the scooter glided over the railing at the edge of the square. Beyond the web of girders, the desert below was hidden by the murky gray gloom of the hydrogen sulfide atmosphere.

Not nearly the spectacle of the swirling dust trails in the skies of Beta Lyrae, a view he probably wasn't going to have the privilege of seeing again—at least not for a long while. Perhaps he could venture back several years down the road, maybe not to play loqaqi. Surely the casino staff wouldn't be vigilant enough to pick him out of a crowd years later, if he didn't play the games. They would be concentrating on matters of CU.

He glanced at the reader console between the handlebars and pressed it with his thumb. The lot code appeared in the display, along with a directional indicator. The scooter made a minor heading adjustment, and Dexter tugged at the handlebars, reasserting control. The lot immediately ahead looked exactly like all the others.

He pushed the handlebars forward, descending toward the lower catwalk that snaked toward his lot and following it over the reinforced rail of the landing pad. The scooter promptly banked left toward the Explorer's piling.

He frowned as he nudged the scooter clear of the stationed spacecraft. Ultimately, he was going to need to find other things to do for a time. A temporary career change, at the very least. He could always continue gaming on a smaller scale if he got the urge—every major city had a fringe district.

Jayjay would have had him working in one of the cybernetics institutes, aging in a tiny office like Dr. Tfariag, making a living out of advertising his expertise at every given opportunity. What she would call a legitimate career. But there were other ways to earn CU while maintaining respectability and not sacrificing freedom.

He could always become an archaeologist, traveling to the outer reaches of the Galaxy studying abandoned iconath colonies like Akra and Lycronia, or the vorine ruins. Specializing in the vorines alone would have led him to sites across the Galaxy, and there would always be new evidence to uncover about the only known extinct sentient race, the only civilization powerful enough to vanquish the iconath dominion and chase them back to the Hub, establishing a massive empire of their own before mysteriously disappearing. The history of the Galaxy was fertile ground; even the cillians didn't know everything there was to know about it, and what they did know they rarely shared among the other sentients. Without a good theory about the vorine race's mysterious disappearance, there was plenty of room for a newcomer to make a name for himself. And over the long stretches of time, there had to be other yet-to-be-discovered sentient extinctions.

The pilings were long, vertical cylinders that ran from the platform up to the floor of the ninth level. They occupied the landing pad in every direction, each one surrounded by ships. The landing pad was completely packed with ships, yet for the most part, devoid of people; apparently the offworlders had all gotten wise to the fact that there was virtually no reason to be outside.

He suddenly had a vision of riding a mini-trawler in the Reed Country of Pike, gliding over the water, dodging the clumps of vegetation. The motion of the scooter was similar. The visit to Pike had been long ago, before he had bought the ship and met Jayjay. Pike was a peaceful, charmingly rural planet. Relaxing, potentially romantic. Possibly a good place to take Jayjay, if she was willing. If she was truly interested in pursuing anything beyond a friendship. There was always a chance this recent affection was another behavioral result of the mnemonic problem.

Dexter spotted the Explorer at a piling with two other ships as the scooter slowed and stopped, hovering centimeters off the platform. He dismounted next to a single-pilot Skyhawk, with sleek, arched wings that dominated the fuselage. Next to it was a Banshee Roller. Another classic. A flip-top window marked the small fighter's cockpit, with twin cannons fitted to the left and right of where the glass fastened in the hull. Not a bad way to bomb through a star system; of course, stylish muscle-rippers like the Banshee models weren't equipped for comfort.

The Explorer was stationed on the other side. The long, angular body of green, gossamer-piezoceramic aluminum fiber-alloy dwarfed the other two crafts and stood out with its less subtle lines: the somewhat unbalanced contours of the snakehead cab, the enormous all-purpose landing skids, and the ten robust exhaust cylinders in the rear. Not much to look at, comparatively, but scinti-built and a lot sturdier than most human craft. Zenith of Volier had been making ships for humans for longer than most other alien sentient corporations, and their models had changed little over the years.

Dexter stepped away from the scooter and gave it a long look. It was possible the scooters would return to the lift platforms automatically… there wasn't really anyone around to retrieve them, and presumably, the racks at the lifts would need to be kept filled. After several seconds, the single blue headlight blinked twice and then dimmed, but the scooter stayed put. And airborne. They were probably retrieved remotely, in shifts. There was an interesting job—keeping an eye on all the transport scooters in Eo-Nowar and rounding them up before their batteries died. There were tedious jobs, and then there were really tedious jobs. He turned around and took another look at the fighter.

Space had been more or less peaceful for nearly 200 years. The raxatots and kyhyvvhrs hadn't sent an invasion force across the empty gulf between the Crux and Sagittarius Arms since before the iconath had destroyed their fleets in the Hub, but the human fighter design was a popular holdover from the more dangerous days. And being armed still often came in handy; the Banshee Roller might have been owned by a freight escort contractor, someone who made a business out of deterring pirates.

The Explorer's ramp was down; Jayjay's technicians had apparently decided to leave the hatch open on the chance that the on-board had been left in remote access mode. An unwise thing to do, but dumber things had probably been seen among people hastening their androids to the tech-mech. Dexter patted the hull as he ducked and headed up the ramp, taking a glance toward the two somewhat puny cannons in the turret under the bow. High-grade purified diamond laser-assisted plasma pulse refractors, with 0.9 decimeter/second bore intensity. The Explorer's teeth weren't quite as big as the Roller's, but they were just as sharp.

He mounted the ramp and hit the keypad at the base of the ladderwell, letting out a yawn as the hatch sealed behind him with a hiss. Occasions for defense were rare enough as far as he could tell; he had flown more often than most his age and never required the use of the turret. Fortunate thing. It was difficult to imagine firing on someone under any circumstances—he had managed not to do it while facing down an industrial rock-cutter about to unload a volcanic laser blast at the cockpit, and things didn't get much more dire than that.

Supposedly the average pilot came across more than three instances of piracy in his or her lifetime, and interstellar crime was increasing, with pirate fleets lying in wait at remote tourist locations, developing gravitonic intercept technology that might theoretically enable them to knock unsuspecting ships out of hyperspace, and homing in on isolated sublight travelers in the open void. Hard to argue the statistics, considering the events of the past day—an entire Trojan belljar complex shut down on Stasya, just as it became apparent that one of the most genuinely upscale gaming establishments in the Galaxy was no more on the up-and-up than the underworld-dominated ghetto dives dotting the human frontier.

Crime had always abounded in the unpoliced in-between stretches of the Human Sphere. Dexter frowned to himself as he tapped the keypad a second time, activating climate control. In fact, crime had quite possibly changed his entire life from birth. Impossible to know for sure, but many from the public orphanages had lost their parents in incidents with pirates, particularly those retrieved during IPA salvage bolas and raised in the orbiting sanctuaries. He could very well have been one of them.

He mounted the short series of steps leading out of the ladderwell, rubbing his arms as the chill of the high-altitude air immediately began to fade. Jayjay was lying motionless in her berth with the blue institute blanket covering all but her head and feet.

Sleeping beauty. He kissed her on the forehead and stepped to the cockpit, glancing at the main terminal access displays long enough to verify the on-board's biofeedback and EEG displays were on.

He dropped himself into the command seat and held his hands poised above the keyboard, peering at the CTA monitor. He wriggled his fingers and dove in, opening a manual command stream and patching through to the MTA data transfer bus. The screen scrolled rapidly through a long directory and stopped at a heading that read, "Zen Exp Index: LGAB-1216: Independent Representation." Then the white text blinked away, replaced by a split screen showing a series of changing power and capacity measures on the right and a colorful, animated fractal pattern on the left, covered in part by his command stream window.

The Zenith Explorer's on-board system was a standard Astra Parallax-Dynamo, unchanged in several hundred years. The computer that had essentially raised him in the St. Francis Public wing of T Eradani 6 Station was an Astra Elemedia V4, remarkably similar even though its functionalities were more suited toward developmental incubation and tutoring than managing an FTL craft. Flying the Explorer without navigational assistance by an intermediary unit would have been difficult, but the protocols had virtually been burned into his brain in his years in front of control panels. He could have done it, if necessary. Plenty of craft were designed for a single pilot; the Explorer was more complex, but it was basically just a matter of interfacing effectively with the on-board. Still, open space was a grim prospect for a lone pilot, particularly when the pilot was accustomed to the company of an IU like Jayjay.

And with the most infinitesimal flaw, a perturbation in the spin of a quark, a single misfire among the entangled quanta, she might have been snatched away forever. Gone after functioning perfectly for 909 years, admirably guiding the Explorer for the last five-plus, operating consistently at optimum performance, offering her wisdom and her charm.

Five years going on six. Dexter glanced over his shoulder. Damned if he was ever going to fly with a different co-pilot. But now that was something he no longer had to worry about.

The fractal on the left side of the screen was replaced by the Vitruvian diagram of a female figure surrounded by a circle of multicolored graphs and pulsing vital indicators. A heading at the upper left read "MTA DTB: IU Jajqrt170 Ops." The readings indicated that Jayjay was fully replenished and ready for activation.

The on-board would have roused her immediately. Dexter shook his head. "Not just yet."

He expanded the head region of the figure, and an interactive hierarchal representation of Jayjay's neocortical net filled the entire screen, with blue blocks representing the core processor and tributary components. Dexter targeted the mnemonics, and another display appeared showing registers, cache control, and a honeycomb of field cell sections. He focused on the field cells and tapped in a transfer command on the entire range.

The fractal reappeared as the on-board read the data etched in the microscopic semiconductor film of Jayjay's memory—her entire history rendered in a few gigs of circle-hex code. Dexter's fingers danced over the keyboard, preparing a manual shut-down and resuscitation sequence in the command window. Translation to English would take another minute or so, and the decompression would hit the on-board hard; if there was a computer hiccup, the default mechanism might wake Jayjay and undermine the process. Best to be prepared.

The screen blinked and began filling with six-digit alphanumeric cell references. Dexter nodded, opening a second command window. "Okay... sort by temporal criteria... let's see what we have in 2703."

The date "1 Jan 2703" appeared at the head, followed by a mass of stilted, unpunctuated English with intermittent strings of grammatically correct phrases. A minute by minute account of Jayjay's mercilessly jumbled cognitive thoughts—for the most part, her memory was painfully complete. It was going to be hugely difficult to pick out something coherent to tell her, unless the block became a lot more apparent. Hopefully, the on-board would sort out the inconsistencies.

The year 2703 alone contained 18.5 million distinct words, some 80 megs of data. Dexter frowned and scanned downward, watching the cursor descend through the seemingly endless solid wall of text. Then the text abruptly disappeared. Dexter stopped the cursor and scrolled back up, staring at the screen.

/23:59:00 testing ran identical scan salaman requires nonsensical activities will not learn about ytaoan biochemistry by repeating identical sample analysis compiled in sector sierra zulu 742 invalid expedition testing testing this is my fault for participating i should continue to protest unscientific conduct testing salaman is undermining his own research will be discredited very probable xenobiologists guild revocation sfaon discommendation not prototypical human behavior some show design flaws in their thinking testing testing testing i want his approval i am fully capable he ignores guidance illogical behavior biologics think they know more than they know cybernetics are in a better position to make decisions than biologics testing often true not always true testing active microbe analysis run scan remember to perform complete systems metascan on c27 homeworld dusk cruiser salaman interrupted testing salaman is hiding something testing he will die if spacecraft is not sound i will be stranded microbes show low response rate to molecular stimuli results differ no way to determine whether effects are influenced by mitigating factors no time driven decay models to build upon salaman has restricted access on-board not accessible salaman is not rational violation of safety protocols we should end this expedition now

/2 February 2703
/00:00:00 unreadable…
/compile failure discontinuity minute 00:00
/compile failure discontinuity 02:02:2703
/3 February 2703
/00:00:00 unreadable…
/compile failure discontinuity minute 00:00
/compile failure discontinuity 03:02:2703

Line after line of unreadable data. Dexter keyed the cursor, dropping rapidly to the next section of obtainable transcript. Every minute of code was blocked through 11 November. Over nine months, as Jayjay had related. Dexter nodded; it figured to be more complicated than simply decompressing the cell data and reading it out loud, but this way he would know exactly where the problem was being caused.

He backed out of the field cells and pulled up the IHR of the neocortical net. He tapped in a bug scan and ran it on the entire cybernetic brain.

The screen blinked off and on.

/There is a problem in Mnemonic Register 8B affecting field cell 3A84KX.
/There is a problem in Mnemonic Register 8B affecting field cell 3A84KY.
/There is a problem in Mnemonic Register 8B affecting field cell 3A84KZ.
/There is a problem in Mnemonic Register 8B affecting field cell 3A84L0.
/There is a problem in Mnemonic Register 8B affecting field cell 3A84L1.

Bull's-eye. Five field cells—that was it. He focused on the IHR and targeted the culprit register, opening up a new directory showing a field of tiny buttons representing the registry keys. He paused, then tapped in a command to scan for aberrations. One of the buttons popped open almost immediately and filled the screen with Universal Command Shorthand. Good old Commash—required pidgin computerese for any sensible pilot, though a surprising number of pilots chose to rely on the IU rather than bothering to learn the programming language themselves. Most unwise, considering the potential for system breakdowns in the androids themselves. Jayjay was the case in point.

Dexter leaned forward, squinting. At first glance, the sequence seemed to center around photovoltaic arrays—he was in a circulatory operating system involving one of Jayjay's autonomic power drivers. Maybe the problem had something to do with the process of writing to the field cells... but the PV arrays didn't inscribe the semiconductor shells directly, so no failures in this particular key should have led to the memory failure. Data were recorded via the flashers and shutters, part of the ultraviolet-writer system, and that would have been a different registry key. Something else was going on, something out of the norm. No cookie-cutter solution. Sorting out the problem and fixing the code was going to be a bit painstaking. Unless...

A system interface between the photovoltaics and the mnemonics might prompt a self-correction. Normally, there was no need for the two systems to interact, so it might have been a matter of exposing the bad coding to the memory storage area; the deconstructed specifics in the missing memory were floating around in there somewhere, and if the photovoltaics were involved, they would hopefully point to where those data were sitting. Flooding the memory might even trigger the retrieval process outright.

He tapped in a command to copy the code, renamed it as active data, and dumped it into the stand-by cache. The monitor blinked.

```
/There is a new alert in field cell 3A84KX.
/Error: Action requires response; no response initiated.
/Error: Incompatible code.
/Examining...
```

Dexter sat back, nodding. Ideally, Jayjay and the on-board would be able to fix the problem and rewriting the code manually wouldn't be necessary, not that he couldn't do just as good a job. But a self-fix was much less intrusive, and less likely to have aftereffects.

```
/Error: Multiple unreadable addresses in field cell 3A84KX.
/Restoring 7,645 deleted storage calls...
```

Dexter frowned. Someone had gone in and manually deleted the recall headers? It meant the memory was most likely intact, but still... it was an excellent way to destroy a functioning neural network. Utterly irresponsible.

It was possible Jayjay had done it on her own to protect herself from a suspected corruption in the field cells, but there were better ways to handle that without risking a chain reaction of system breakdowns—why not purge the cells, or if necessary, replace them? Why leave unrestricted corruptions to wend their way through the layers of critical programming? It was as if someone had intentionally planted a ticking time bomb.

/Archiving...

/Reconstituted alert file: 2 February 2703

/00:00:01 Alert: Vital systems protection inactive; overriding new code...

The cursor blinked at the bottom of the screen. A command to reassign inputted information appeared for a split-second, followed by a series of rapidly shifting lines of circle-hex. An internal command; on 11 November, Jayjay's systems protection sequences had gone temporarily inactive, paving the way for someone to tamper with the recall headers in her memory, making it impossible for her to retrieve the data on her own. So it was definitely not her own handiwork.

Dexter scratched the top of his head, nodding slowly. From the looks of it, someone had planted a timer command in the PV array code and set it to go off on 11 November. The command had placed false virus indicators in the five field cells. Later, when Jayjay had tried to call up the memory, her own perfectly effective debugging system had locked out all the information acquired after 1 February.

Clever trick, diabolical as it was. The debugging system itself had been set up to cause the problem—it had done its job, getting rid of the apparent virus, and leaving no detectable malfunction at all. The debugging system had never malfunctioned, and there had never really been a virus. The plant had shut her down in a way that was completely undetectable without a lot of outside help.

The monitor cleared away the unreadable code and flashed another interactive message.

/Unable to represent; message titled "For Dexter Massengill" protected; protocol 1469.3, placing under quarantine.

/Unable to release in current forum without exposing system; transferring to on-board safe zone.

For Dexter Massengill? The alert had supposedly been initiated hundreds of years before he was born—either the computer was getting thrown off by the active data status or the corruption had caused the older data to mingle with more current information.

The monitor blinked again. Dexter stared as his name reappeared.

/11 November 2703. For Dexter Artimus Massengill. PRIORITY MESSAGE mem sys hum unit Jajqrt170 at hom cru C27 P32-6805. Author: Salaman Nevis.

/Mr. Massengill: My name is Salaman Nevis. This message is intended specifically for you, sent some 909 years before your present time. I assure you this is neither ruse nor error, as you will discover if you investigate further; it has been made possible as a result of a collaborative effort to contact you through time by those who have mastered the technique. Please give it your full attention.

/I've used this IU as a vessel to deliver you the means by which to conduct an expedition outside the constants of material spacetime established in the cosmic framework. For reasons I will explain, I ask that you to travel to a set of coordinates that are, from your point of reference, in the past. I acquired this groundbreaking information, along with the details of your existence, while studying the ytaoans.

Dexter shook his head, raising his eyebrows. It was too much to grasp all at once. The ytaoans! Jayjay had said little about the trip outside the galactic proper to the Large Magellanic Cloud, and she had never mentioned a thing about the ytaoans—Salaman had obviously wiped all traces of them while tampering with her memory, effectively hiding the information exactly as long as he had intended.

The ytaoans… the mysterious race of silent sentients that seemed to float freely in the void, untethered by any planet. They were rarely seen in the spheres of other sentients, and their place of origin was unknown; few knew much at all about them, though they were presumed highly telepathic, as they had no other means of communication. Apparently the presumption had been correct, if Salaman was telling the truth.

Xenobiologists had long been under the impression that the Ytaoan Race represented extrasensory perception in its purest form, but no one had any real proof. Many scientists had claimed the ytaoans had communicated with them telepathically. Salaman Nevis wasn't the first. But Salaman had seemingly devised a way to prove it—if he was telling the truth, he was now demonstrating that he and the ytaoans had knowledge of future events extending centuries forward. Dexter rubbed his mouth—they knew the details right down to his middle name. A torrent of questions sprang up, and he suddenly felt a pang of dread at the thought that this single message was the only thing that might ever provide answers to any of them. If Salaman's message wasn't complete, the truth might have been lost forever.

Dexter sat forward and read on, flipping the screen to the next section of text.

/I record this message at the conclusion of a historic nine-month study of a ytaoan group in the Tarantula Nebula of the Large Magellanic Cloud, some 191,673 light-years from my home on Earth. The view is magnificent here; the space is filled with dust of many colors. There is one planet, but the ytaoans live in space; they seem to gather in groups of four or 13 at different loci around this gigantic nebula. This seems to be their general gathering area for this particular galaxy, but they originally come from elsewhere in the universe.

/I was called to the ytaoan group through telepathy, their modus operandi. They can effortlessly see the thoughts of any sentient they choose, over any distance, and they view events of the future as clearly as we view the past. They have shared their knowledge with me, and now I am able to see things that no other sentient being can see, levels of detail in the shifting course of the universe that I will never be able to adequately describe. There is too much information to contain within the memory of an android. However, the ytaoans have selected me, a scientist, to communicate this specific set of data about spacetime dynamics and the tools and methods that can be used to truly master space and time; with this information, you will be able to make the necessary preparations to pilot your current ship freely among the 12 dimensions, which will enable you to travel into the past.

/To begin to understand why the ytaoans need your help, you must first understand that the Poincaré model of the cyclical universe is more or less accurate, with elements of Poplawski and Baum-Frampton dynamics. Spacetime is a contained canopy of energy and matter in constant flux, oscillating between extremes of maximum and minimum density. It progresses from quantum singularity to the Tolman limit, undergoes adiabatic reflexion, returns to a singularity, and repeats the process ad infinitum in an effective feedback loop, separated into individual, successive intervals of reality by cusps, or points simultaneously defining both the beginning and the end of time. There was never a true beginning, and there is never a true end.

/According to the ytaoans, there is another pivotal concept involving continuum theory to add to the equation: there is a standard pattern guiding all activity that does not change. Every time the material of the universe recombines, the subsequent explosion is consistent with the one in the previous cycle. The movement of every particle of matter and energy is repeated.

/Consequently, an identical chain of events is provoked at the beginning of each cycle, causing a sequence of identical results. Thus, the universe functions as a series of identical units, unimaginably vast and complex yet finite, equal in comparison, and therefore, a perfect, stable system. The pattern dictates that every physical reaction from the beginning of a cycle to the end remain equivalent from cycle to cycle. Everything that has ever passed must repeat itself perpetually, and that which has not yet passed must accordingly match that which has already taken place. The orbit of every planet, the interaction of every subatomic particle, and every manifested thought in the brain of a sentient being. In an idealized system, there is no variation. However, despite these overriding tendencies, there exists the potential for mutation. This is the role the ytaoans have undertaken: when a mutation occurs, the ytaoans work to correct it.

/The ytaoans are able to sense when the flow of matter and energy is interrupted, or when the universe and its contents are in some way out of balance, which occurs rarely and sporadically, with decreasing frequency through time: subtle, spontaneous irregularities that create changes in the course of events. When they deem it necessary, the ytaoans are able use their mental abilities to influence their surroundings psychokinetically in order to make infinitesimally small adjustments, or what we might refer to as minor course corrections. Typically these adjustments are too far-removed and miniscule to affect life beyond their own existence, let alone the consciousness or actions of sentient beings like ourselves and the other races of this Galaxy, but over the millennia the ytaoans have on occasion deemed it necessary to communicate with the other denizens among the stars, as they are now.

/The ytaoans have informed me that they require the assistance of a sentient being with interstellar navigation capability. They have deemed it necessary to correct a temporal displacement that will be created by a corruption at the subatomic level. To put it simply, a hole in spacetime will open up in the distant future that can only be repaired through proportionately nascent particulate energy. The necessary correction can be made by having a 37th-century ship travel to a specific point along the early-stage cosmic timeline, then return to its temporal point of origin. The ytaoans have identified you as an ideal candidate to conduct this trip.

/This can be accomplished by advancing through elevated dimensional space to a point at which regression to the structural dimensions will bring you to the coordinates of a point along the cyclical timeline that resonates among the dimensions. A platform for navigational translations can be backformed from an adaptation of ytaoan knowledge of the higher planes of existence, namely, the information and probability eigenspaces. This platform can be reused to calculate coordinates as needed.

/As it will no doubt be necessary for the on-board's function, I have provided a process key. However, I have also provided your computer with a specific set of coordinates. They are correct; they cannot be verified through conventional reconciliation algorithms unless multiple trips through the upper dimensions have been completed. Do not attempt to configure coordinates using the process key for the initial trip, as that would increase the likelihood of computer error exponentially; many floating decision points are involved, and there is no guarantee the on-board will respond correctly. Use my coordinate set, and lock the on-board in—the process is too delicate to cede control to any AIEs before the first leg is successfully executed. If you use all figures exactly as they have been inputted, your flight plan will be executed properly. I have also provided your IU with all the necessary calculations and coordinates; the IU will be prepared to elaborate on any points that are unclear.

/Be sure that you understand the risks before you agree to undertake this expedition. While the time required of you will be drastically reduced through dimensional time-shift, Lorentz dilation, and immersion in static cryonic suspension, you are still being asked to make a commitment that is likely to impact your life profoundly. If you choose to do this, your body will be subjected to extreme, prolonged torsion at the molecular level, as well as biochemical stresses that would be lethal without taking precise countermeasures. You will also be dependent upon the flawless functionality of various refits you will need to make to your spacecraft, including adjustments to the ionizer and the implementation of an unbound stasis net in the reservoir chamber. Failure in any of these systems could also put you in jeopardy. My instructions will keep you safe, but there is danger to you if you do not follow them exactly, or if you implement them improperly. The specifications are laid out in detail in the appendices to this message; read and consider them carefully.

/In all, you will need to complete three flight patterns to complete the task, including the initial stop to prepare your ship. Once you initiate in the flight plan, your coordinates will bring you to a point in time before the solidification of matter; hence, there will be nowhere for you land. Your modifications to the drive components will allow you to capture the necessary atomic material in plasma form from your surroundings passively, through the normal progression of engine engagement. Your return trip will bring you to your own proper position in time at my present spatial location, where the ytaoans will guide you in returning your ship to its original state. From there, you will be free to resume your life.

/The ytaoans have specifically selected you to complete this task. This is an opportunity to participate in the advancement of Humankind, and to help preserve the purity of greater environment for the betterment of life in this Galaxy. Whether you choose to participate is your decision; if you do not respond, the ytaoans will seek out another individual in the same manner. But whatever your decision, please be clear: this information is for you and you alone, and you are not at liberty to share it.

/If you do accept this request, you will be the first sentient to look upon the beauty of the universe in its infancy, before the solidification of matter. To go back to the beginning, and see how everything that we know once looked. You have been given a rare honor.

/Your IU will return to normal functioning now that you have released this message. If you choose to decline, I ask that you activate the self-purge I have installed. Memory of the message will be removed; the unit will be otherwise unaffected.

/--Salaman Nevis

Dexter ran a hand through his hair, staring dumbly at the dark screen for a long moment. He held a hand over the keyboard, frowning, then checked for more text. Nothing. That was it. He skipped backwards through the lines of the message and read it again.

He sat back in his chair, dropping his arms to his sides.

According to Jayjay, Salaman was an extraordinary genius with a very abrasive personality. She had never heard from the man after her blackout; he had just disappeared. No specific indication of where the man might have gone, though he had mentioned a lone planet in the Tarantula Nebula. He was asking them to make a stop there, around the time he had been there... perhaps he planned on being part of the welcoming party.

Jayjay had also mentioned that Salaman's father was a registered telepath. Maybe Salaman had the ability as well—it might have explained why the ytaoans had taken an interest in him, not that it could have possibly compared to what the ytaoans seemed to be able to do with their minds. People with telepathic stamps on their IDs were rarely very impressive. They usually lost at gambling—people generally weren't focused enough to predict numbers or cards with any consistency. Apparently all they usually got were vague images, nothing concrete. Of course, that had never stopped bouncers from throwing them out of the casinos. The idea that the ytaoans had identified the exact name of someone that far in the future, come up with all of the necessary precision calculations for this crazy expedition... and they had possibly given Salaman himself the ability to see the same things. The mental acuity was daunting, even a bit scary. They could have been scanning him at that moment, for all he knew.

He rubbed his eyes and looked up, staring absently at the beveled graininess along the edges of the quartz window. So Salaman and the ytaoans had picked him as their guinea pig to break the time barrier. No doubt it was an honor, even if it sounded completely preposterous. But maybe it shouldn't have seemed so outlandish—humans and the other sentients had mastered just about every other aspect of spacetime. Why not attempt to travel back to the past? Get a firsthand view of the obscurities in history, correct all the erroneous assumptions.

Dexter Artimus Massengill. It was possibly the first time he had ever been addressed with the full name. A gambling gadabout with virtually no qualifications or credentials was certainly an odd choice as a candidate. Of course he did know his way around a spaceship.

Whether the true perpetrator of this initiative was Salaman or the ytaoans themselves was a bit unclear, although the ytaoans obviously knew about it if they were as aware as Salaman made them out to be. Still, it was a bit odd that these all-knowing sentients needed help from anyone at all, considering they were apparently able to sense subatomic disturbances through endless stretches of space. If they were able to see the future, shouldn't they have been able to prevent this hole in spacetime from occurring, or at least prepare for it sooner? Hard to believe they weren't equipped to handle a subatomic patch-up job that was essentially a matter of dragging a ramscoop back and forth through time.

Possibly it was more about Salaman trying to make a name for himself, get credit for the discovery. Jayjay had hinted that the man had a bit of an ego, and he wasn't exactly well-respected among his peers.

Dexter turned around. From his seat, Jayjay's face was still visible peeking out from beneath her blanket. Her neocortical net had been throttled by the plant in her memory, but that was over now. No TPM corruption. She was going to be fine.

He sighed. He'd let her sleep a little while longer, then wake her up, jog her memory, and get her take on exactly what had gone on in the Large Magellanic Cloud.

She would be fine, but she was also going to be reliving her experience with Salaman for the first time. It would be a while before she was herself again. And in all likelihood, she wasn't going to be too keen on the idea of doing Salaman's bidding.

He looked back through the window at the pools of light around the pillars of the docking bay. If Jayjay wasn't on board with it, that was that. Humankind would have to make do with living in the present, and if that displeased the ytaoans, they could always find someone else to do the job. No, it was definitely a stretch to imagine actually attempting a stunt like this; it probably wasn't realistic at all. Of course, that didn't make the prospect any less intriguing.

VIII   TESTAMENT

"So the fire's-eye was life, and what the miner of Dessa had found was a treasure that went beyond anything his people would acquire far into the future. To offer it up to another was to give a unique and remarkable gift. Such a thing might have been well-received in century 37, when sentients were accustomed to such wonders… the extension of life through technology and a better understanding of the universe. Not so in century 20.

"For those in century 20, life was a greater struggle, though they may not have viewed it as such. For them, the power of the stone would be virtually incomprehensible, perhaps a thing to be feared as an infant might fear porridge forced into his mouth. For some of century 20, fulfillment was a fleeting dream. They lived like brush fleas in a pond, moving just enough to stay afloat, reserving their energy against tiring out and drowning… waiting to be saved by a passing leaf."

… GCL AE.001
Phi 00 00 00.00 / Theta 00 15 37.33 / Rho 00.00 / JD 2448891
Alpha Confinii: EARTH; "Philadelphia"; 25 September 1992 CE

Zack lay flat on his back on the mattress, staring straight up at a strand of cobweb running from the square ceiling lamp to the corner of the ceiling. Melanie Katsoulis's face slid across his chest, cutting off the view.

"You don't say much, do you, Zack?" Her head was backlit by pale afternoon sunlight skewed through the lopsided blinds, set off around the loose fringes of her hair like a disheveled eclipse.

He furrowed his brow and focused on her mouth, drumming his fingers on the small of her naked back. There were traces of a barely perceptible mustache above the corners of her upper lip.

She frowned and climbed off him, running her hand through her hair. "I think this is getting old again, Zack." She glanced around, pawing the nearest part of the floor and locating an article of clothing. "I mean, it's nice and everything, but I don't have time for this anymore." She sat back, looking at the open door of the room. "I better go. I have things I have to do. Real life."

Zack nodded. He rolled onto his shoulder and felt for the bottle of Tums that was just off the mattress, somewhere near his head. His hand knocked over an empty glass, then found the bottle. He shook several tablets into his hand and rolled back, stuffing them all in his mouth, then winced as he sat up. A powerful kink was starting to blow up in the left rear area of his neck.

Melanie shrugged and shook her jeans. She looked over at him. "Do you have any cigarettes? I'm out."

Zack stood slowly and stepped off the mattress, swallowing the remnants of the Tums tablets and grabbing at the pain in his neck with his right hand. He yawned, rubbing his eyes, and made his way across the floor to the bureau. He glanced down at himself, frowning as he scratched his chest. He was in his underwear; apparently he had managed to put it back on in the middle of a bleary half sleep. He yawned again, then opened a drawer and fished among the clothes with one hand, glancing back at Melanie as he pulled out a pair of khakis. "You think I started smoking in the last 24 hours?"

Melanie rolled backwards and pulled the jeans up her legs. "I thought maybe you had a guest pack."

Zack nodded at her. "You should try gum. Does better things to your breath—better for everyone all around." He snorted and put on the pants.

She shot him a dirty look. "You're not exactly perfect yourself, Zack. You might want to trim that scruff, by the way." She rubbed her cheeks mockingly and crawled onto the carpet, worming her way into a yellow pullover and bunching the rest of her clothes in a small pile.

Zack took two steps to the closet and removed his T-shirt. The ratty, wrinkled gray cotton looked as if he had used it as a dishrag. Maybe he had. He looked back at Melanie. She was dressed and standing, holding an armful of nonessential clothing. Ready to sprint home, probably. He shrugged. "Guess I'll see you when I see you."

She smiled. "I'm sure."

He tossed the T-shirt in a far corner of the room, reached inside the closet, and grabbed a plaid button-down off one of the hangers without registering the color.

Melanie paused for a moment, then nodded and moved to the door. "This was fun. Let me know the next time you make it down to South Philly." She lowered her eyes and scratched her cheek.

Fun, huh? He smiled, sliding his right arm into the shirt. "Deal."

Melanie nodded again, pointing over her shoulder. "I'll get my coat... I can show myself out. Bye, Zack." She disappeared through the door.

Zack watched her go, then tipped his head, cracking his neck, and finished putting on the shirt.

There was always a chance he'd run into her at another Homecoming. He turned back to the closet and frowned. Several pairs of slacks lay rumpled on the floor along with the only decent suit that fit him, collecting dust with a stack of old case files and a sea chest full of several generations of junk. Melanie hadn't said anything, but the place was turning into a complete dump. He brushed the empty hangers aside and started picking up the clothes, shaking his head. Understandable why some people got housekeepers. Maybe there was a maid in the Yellow Pages who was willing to barter for detective work.

He laughed under his breath. It probably would have been easier to torch the place and collect insurance. Where was a building fire when a guy needed one?

He straightened, rubbing his neck as the ache flared up again, then turned and set his eyes back on the tattered sheets of the mattress. More sleep wasn't such a bad idea.

Joey Imperato would be doing his circuit for Samuel Goldstine for the weekend, collecting money at the horse track and various crap holes around town, and he was possibly heading down to Atlantic City. Potential cover stories all day and into the night; if he had a lady friend tucked away somewhere, this would have been the time to pay her a visit.

Potential cover stories, and potentially 12 or so hours of sitting in the car for mind-numbing, useless bullshit. Brutal Saturday, maybe Sunday too.

The phone broke the silence. Zack let it ring twice, rolling his head and stretching his neck, then headed into the office.

He squinted as he picked up the receiver. "Yeah, Wyler."

The voice at the other end was immediately recognizable. "Hey, hombre, qué pasa? You still alive?"

Zack grinned.

*   *   *

Benny's was never very crowded before 8 o'clock, even though the place was one of the smallest on South Street. No dining area, no pool table or dart board. Just a simple bar with a row of some 15 stools. There were only five people there now, including Benedetto Taglia, the owner and sole bartender, who was busy helping a couple of customers toward the back. Other employees would be on duty later, when the night crowd found its way in, but for now, picking out a familiar face would be easy.

Sitting at the stool nearest the door with his arms spread wide was a lanky Cuban-American man in a yellow and green vertically striped shirt and a wide, flat, ridiculous-looking yellow hat. Pretty bold fashion statement for a guy working out of the 9th District.

237

He turned around as the door closed behind Zack. "Whew! Is the city still having sewage problems or did Zack Wyler just come in here?" He broke into a smile, flashing two rows of immaculate white teeth. "Bienvenido, man. Sit down."

Zack shook his head. "I think that hat went out of style with bell-bottom jeans." He stepped down off the platform at the door and moved a stool out of the way, leaning an elbow on the bar. "Trying to hide another bad haircut?"

Donatello Diaz touched his chest. "I know you aren't trying to say something about bad hair, Zack, because I seem to remember you in a jarhead crew cut that made you look like a convict."

Zack stared at the hat. A throwback from the Seventies, probably tucked away in some Caribbean vendor's shop for years before Donatello had snagged it.

Donatello sipped some sort of pale pink liquid in a hurricane glass with an umbrella in it. "Let me get you a drink, Zack. I know how hard it is for you nickel-and-dimers." He licked his lower lip, setting his glass on the table. "How about trying one of these? Daiquiri Canario. Banana liqueur, honey rum, strawberries, and, like, grape schnapps or some shit."

Zack frowned at the drink. "No thanks." He scratched his chin, pulling his wallet out of his back pocket and sitting on a stool. "I thought it was all about mojitos down there. And I'm buying, by the way."

"Uh-uh, tonight it's on me, Zack. No two ways about it. You want a mojito, I'll get you a mojito. Those things are like all mint and sugar—too sweet for me."

Zack took another look at the drink, raising his eyebrow. It looked exactly like pink lemonade. He snorted and frowned down at the black, varnished wood of the bar. "I do earn a living. You do know that, right?"

"Yeah, huh?" Donatello puckered his lips. "Hard to tell when you roll in here wearing threads like that."

Zack shook his head. He probably wasn't going to win a wrestling match about the tab. It wasn't any secret he was making a little less than he would have if he was still on the force, and Donatello was Donatello—the man liked to help out his friends, and he seized any opportunity to do so when his wife wasn't around. Hell, the inside tip-offs Donatello had sent his way on all the thefts and runaways were probably Private Island Detective Agency's main source of income over the past two years.

Whatever. Business had been a little light for a while, but it would pick up when it picked up. People were desperate, and there was always a supply of folks out there with screwed-up lives who needed private detective work. And regardless of the current screw-up incidence, he had enough cash to spring for drinks every once in a while. He'd probably end up having to steal the man's wallet. Good idea for next time.

Zack nodded. "I'll have Jim Beam on the rocks." He set his own wallet on the bar.

Donatello smiled, showing his teeth. "Mama, get ready 'cause I'm in rare form tonight!" He downed his drink and placed it daintily down on a coaster.

Zack laughed, squinting. Donatello was in a painfully good mood. The man was always smiling, but usually he had a frustrated look around the eyes, a look of long hours at the precinct. And he usually managed to work in a couple rants about the lieutenant breaking his balls, or the district attorney being a jackass, or the residual fermented stink of kimchi in his car from his partner's lunch.

Donatello beamed, wagging his head. Something was going on. The man hadn't even looked this happy at his wife's graduation party in May. Probably, he had finally gotten the promotion he had been pulling for. He had been on the force for a decade. Maybe they were finally taking him off the street.

Zack's eyes fell on the rack of liqueur bottles on the other side of the bar. He looked back at Donatello. "You must have had a pretty good vacation."

"Never better. Never better." Donatello suddenly raised his eyebrows. "So, Zack, did you meet any new lady-friends since I've been gone?"

Zack thought immediately of the lawyer at the Hollywood Café. "One that thinks I'm obnoxious." He frowned.

"That goes without saying, Zack." Donatello grinned.

Zack nodded. "And I ran into Melanie Katsoulis."

"Mel! Chiquitita bonita. Yes, she's living in South Philly, right? How's she doing?"

"She's doing great." Zack looked away. Cassandra Prescott and Melanie Katsoulis were never going to play a significant role in his life, and they were the last two people he wanted to talk about. He was probably never going to see them again. Why in the hell did Donatello always have to talk about women?

Benedetto Taglia was moving toward them with a bar towel, the elevated walkway behind the bar making his stocky frame seem taller than it actually was. Light glinted off his glasses as he pointed his strong chin from

Zack to Donatello and back. He held a hand in the air. "Yo, Zack, where you been the last two weeks, huh? You got an excuse?"

Zack shrugged. "Sorry, Benedetto. I've been sleeping during the happy hours. I'm on a rough case." He wiped his mouth, glancing away from Donatello and trying not to think about taking money from Samuel Goldstine. A lot of people at the 9th District had spent long hours trying to put Samuel Goldstine in jail.

Benedetto held a look of sincere concern as he considered Zack for a moment. Then he gave a quick nod and turned to the police detective. "All right, Dee, let's hear about Cuba. True what they say about all the white sands and the crystal blue water?" He nodded, dropping the towel and smoothing out his slick, gray hair. "What can I get youse guys?"

"Hey, Benedetto, call me 'El Capitán.' I'm still on vacation. I'm good for right now, but my man here will be needing a glass of that turpentine junk he likes."

"O! You got a perfectly good Italian name—you want more Spanish?" The bartender stepped back to the bottle rack. "J.B. rocks, Zack?"

"Yeah."

Donatello glanced at Zack. "I tell you, guys, it was mighty fine. Better than the last trip. This time I got certified to scuba-dive. Man, it's another world down there."

Benedetto returned with an oversized glass of whiskey and set it in front of Zack. Zack raised his eyebrows at Donatello. "That right?" He lifted the drink to his mouth.

"You ought to try it, man. All kinds of fish. Purple, green, fluorescent yellow."

Zack nodded at the hurricane glass. "Just like that foofy crap you like to drink."

Donatello ignored him. "I touched a nurse shark."

Zack shook his head, making a pained expression. "I'm not keen on imported air."

Benedetto pointed at Zack. "Hey, I'm with you, Zack. The sea's a dangerous place. Back in Sicily, the people know to look out at the water and admire it, but they don't go in. You go to the docks and look over toward Villa San Giovanni at 6 o'clock any day of the week, you can count 50 shark fins, hand to God."

Donatello shrugged. "You don't know what you're missing. We saw this manta ray that had to be about as big as a house." He held his arms outstretched, and Zack and Benedetto grunted simultaneously. Donatello nodded, eyes wide. "Then we went on this charter day trip, from Cienfuegos to Juventud, this island off the southern coast that was just crazy beautiful, man… it was like being on another planet. Marble rock formations and these gorgeous beaches with black sand. Mm-mm. Outrageously cool." He leaned forward and nodded, smiling. "But the main thing about the sailboat is just being out on the water, lying in the sun and drinking cocktails with the beautiful people."

Zack whistled, shaking his head. "Sounds pretty nice." He patted Donatello on the shoulder. "Welcome back to the fine urban cesspool that is the Northeast."

Benedetto reached across the bar toward Zack and faked a head slap. "O Madonne, what's the matter with you—that's how you talk about your home?" He held up a fist, then took a step to the right and poured out the contents of an ashtray, giving the bar a swipe with the towel before he set the tray back down. "So, Dee… did your wife catch you looking at any bella donnas?"

Donatello smiled, nodding. "Oh, there are lots of ladies to see down there, Benny, let me tell you. Everywhere you turn."

Zack raised his eyebrows and smirked. "You wouldn't catch me looking at anyone else if I was with Trin."

Donatello leveled his eyes at Zack. "Now I know you mean you wouldn't be looking at any other women because my wife is so mesmerizing. I know you were not just about to talk smack about my wife."

Zack leaned toward the bartender, looking at his drink. "Well, sure. Of course, she's a beautiful woman. Goes without saying." He paused. "But I also know better than to piss off someone who's been through boot camp. If I was married to Trin, I'd keep my eyes to myself, and a close guard over my groin." He grinned and raised his glass.

Benedetto let out a loud cackle, leaning forward with his big Popeye forearms and blasting the bar with cigar-breath. He stuck his chin in Zack's direction. "Salud."

Zack laughed into his drink, draining the contents.

Donatello shook his head, stone-faced. "That's cold, Zack."

"Seriously, she's like a walking SWAT team." Zack nudged him and nodded at Benedetto. "I guess it figures—back in training, he always had this thing for the SWAT team."

Suddenly, Benedetto's eyes popped wide open and shifted away from the two of them. He cleared his throat gruffly and wheeled away, grabbing an empty glass off the bar. Zack stopped laughing.

"Honey, if I were you, I'd watch my own groin." The low female voice would have been terribly sexy over the phone, from a safe distance. Zack grimaced and turned around.

Trinity Diaz was appraising him with her arms folded and eyebrows arched. She looked as if she had just walked out of a dance club, wearing a white dress jacket over a pink pastel leotard and blue jeans. The bright colors clashed sharply against her caramel skin. She looked comically annoyed.

Benedetto started snickering. Zack rubbed his mouth. "Hi, Trin. How was your vacation?" He picked up his glass and tipped an ice cube into his mouth.

She swayed back on her heels, keeping her eyes focused like a cobra preparing to strike. "It wasn't too tough. I did used to baby-sit when I was a teenager." She rolled her eyes toward her husband and smiled smugly.

Donatello was looking down, rubbing his face. He shook his head. "Nice timing, baby."

Zack stood up and gestured at his stool, bowing his head. "Sit down, Trin."

She sat, wagging a finger at Zack. "Oh, I'm not ready to talk to you yet. Walking SWAT team... my word."

He shrugged. "It was meant as a compliment."

Benedetto smiled at her. "Welcome back Mrs. Diaz. Looking gorgeous, as usual."

"Thank you, Benny." She shot Zack another dirty look.

"What can I get you?"

Trinity sniffed, glancing down the bar. "White wine spritzer?"

Donatello made a circle in the air above the bar with his finger. "Make it another round."

Benedetto nodded and stepped away. Zack looked across the bar at the bottle of whiskey on display in the shelved rack. It might have been a good day to take it easy on the sauce, all things considered. It was going to be an earlier-than-usual Saturday with Imperato's action-packed weekend... he would want to be clear-headed.

Hell, two drinks weren't going to kill him. He glanced at Trinity and sat down on the stool next to her. "Your guy here was telling me about the trip."

She nodded. "Very necessary. And very relaxing. We definitely enjoyed ourselves."

Donatello glared at her. "Zack, this woman does not know how to have a good time. Would you believe we had a chance to spend a day in a resort in Varadero for free, with a pool bar, a private beach... a two-hour all-you-

242

can-eat buffet, and a beach-side pig roast, mind you… and gambling comps. And she didn't want to do it."

Zack looked at Trinity. She closed her eyes and shrugged. "Yeah, free. Honey, I don't think so. Don't get me started."

Donatello widened his eyes. "A pool bar, Zack. A pig roast."

"Please." Trinity touched Zack on the arm. "It was just a time share. A bunch of tourist stuff you can do anywhere. I know this trip was your thing, honey, but I was led to believe I was going to get to see natural wonders. Zack, you have to see the pictures—that island is amazing."

"A pool bar… and a pig roast." Her husband slid closer, leaning into her. "We saw plenty of natural wonders—you couldn't turn around down there without seeing natural wonders. And besides, this wasn't about waterfalls and orchid gardens, it was about experiencing my family's heritage. Am I wrong?" He glared at Zack, touching his chest. "And my people clearly have a rich tradition in all-you-can-eat buffets, pool bars, and pig-roasts."

She momentarily shrank away from him. "Telling people I don't know how to have a good time—what is wrong with you?" She rolled her eyes. "You are not going to tell me you regret one second of the time we spent on those islands."

Donatello squinted at her. "I think I could have lived without hiking through the jungle for two hours." He leaned toward Trinity and she shoved his face away with a hand.

Zack leaned on the bar and nodded at him. "What about the family stuff—did you find out anything?"

Donatello scratched the back of his head. "Yeah, they keep pretty good records in Cuba. And I can tell you the Diazes are living strong in Pinar del Río. Apparently my great-great-great-great-grandfather was the first one over, on a trade ship from Cádiz in 1795. 18th century, hombre. That's a 200-year history on that island for la familia Diaz."

"Trade ship." Trinity shook her head. "I think you mean slave ship."

"You're gonna start that again?" Donatello glared at her, then held up a hand, turning to Zack. "Do you know we were at a Columbus statue in front of a historic church, and this woman flat out refused to take a picture?"

His wife stiffened. She frowned at Zack. "I'm not going to support what that man did."

Donatello moved closer to her. "Baby, it was a landmark. It's history. I just wanted a picture."

Trinity held up a hand. "Oh no. No, no. History is one thing. I'm all for getting back in touch with your roots, but people should not be celebrating this man just because he's a notable figure in history—history is filled with bad guys. Cristoforo Colombo, Cristoforo Colombo, everywhere you look down there. Do you know how many people died and were sold into slavery because of Cristoforo Colombo?"

Donatello blinked, glancing from Zack back to Trinity. "Shit, woman—for all I know that man is one of my ancestors."

Trinity shot him a sour glare.

Zack rolled his lips inward, keeping his mouth shut. Donatello put his arm around Trinity. She bristled briefly, then closed her eyes, smiling. "We had a very relaxing trip, my husband's present commentary notwithstanding. He was much more agreeable when he was alone with me."

Zack grunted. "I'll bet he was."

Benedetto returned and handed both of them a second drink as several more people entered the bar. "Gentlemen, Mrs. Diaz... I gotta take care of business. Youse guys yell if you need anything, understand?" He headed toward the other end of the bar, where a man was leaning halfway over the bar, waving a five-dollar bill.

Zack sipped the fresh drink and looked back at Trinity. She looked outwardly like any other seductive product of the Eighties fitness movement—an aerobicized, muscle-toned, proud African-American woman always ready with a sparkling smile—but she had a Marine pedigree behind her cardio-boxing kicks and punches. She was like a freight train in legwarmers.

She rolled her head toward him. "You got something to say to me?"

"I humbly apologize." He raised an eyebrow at her. "If it makes you feel any better, I haven't ever managed to successfully talk behind your back without you hearing it."

Donatello swished his drink around in the glass. He shook his head. "She has radar, man. Two weeks ago, Drew Torrance was over for dinner with his wife, right? I was in the living room telling Drew I don't like what Trin's wearing, 'cause she's got on this bizarre-looking thing with blue frills." He closed his eyes as she nudged him with her elbow. He cleared his throat. "The women are in the kitchen making a casserole with the fan turned on, and there's no way they're gonna hear. Ten seconds later, Trin comes in the room and tells us a police detective shouldn't talk about women's clothing because, quote, 'everybody knows police detectives have less taste than a piece of gum stuck on the bottom of one of my high school basketball shoes.'" He raised his eyebrows at his wife.

Trinity nodded, smiling. "That's right. Nobody gets away with talkin' smack in my house."

Donatello squeezed her. Zack gulped down half of his whiskey and squinted. "Well, Trin, sorry I missed that—you know how I love to see your husband squirm. By the way, a couple minutes ago, your husband offered to pay the bar bill for my sorry, deadbeat ass again. Thought you should know."

"That's only because I gave him permission." She squeezed Donatello back, beaming at him. Donatello shook his head and sipped at his drink.

Trinity turned back to Donatello. "Did you tell him what happened?"

Donatello tapped the bar, squinting. "I was getting to it."

More people came through the door. One was a blonde woman wearing a blue leather jacket and a lot of make-up. Zack smiled at her. "What—you got news?" He looked at Donatello. "What's the story, Mr. Donatello Delapuerta Diaz? Did you finally get that name change?"

"Ain't nothing wrong with my name, fool!" Donatello shook his head. "No, check it—turns out my wife is in demand. Even though she would have you believe her friends at the Corps had completely forgotten about her mad skills." He raised his glass, looking at Trinity. "To the very talented and highly desirable Trinity Diaz."

Zack nodded, raising his glass. "I could have told you that."

"It's hard to stay mad at you, Zack Wyler." Trinity beamed as she clinked glasses with Donatello, then Zack.

Zack swallowed the drink and raised his eyebrows, sneaking another glance at the blonde woman as she seated herself two stools away. He buried the thought and looked at Donatello. "So I take it the Marines had a computer programming job open up at one of their bases. Did they make you an offer you couldn't refuse?"

Trinity raised her eyebrows. "If I couldn't refuse it, we'd be spending the next year or so trying to learn Japanese." She and Donatello exchanged glances, then she looked back at Zack. "They wanted me back at the air station in Iwakuni."

Zack sat up. "Holy shit. Seriously?"

She nodded. "The aviation logistics squadron in my group lost their data communications maintenance officer. It calls for a W-3 chief warrant officer two notches above my last pay grade. My old CO recommended me for the position; I had all the prerequisites, and I've already taken the supervisor of electronics course they require." She paused. "I think they realize it's a lot to ask inactive personnel with family to pick up and move 7,000 miles away. It would have been a nice raise, though."

Zack nodded at Donatello. "You did always like Godzilla movies." He paused. "But I don't know about you as a Japanese house husband. In a kimono with a feather-duster... not a pretty picture." He grinned, sucking the last remaining traces of alcohol off an ice cube in his glass, enjoying the buzz in his head. He put the empty glass on the bar and Benedetto appeared, exchanging it with a full one and hurrying back to another customer.

"Yeah, man. Don't knock it 'til you try it, tailback." Donatello winked and glanced at his wife. "Sorry you're gonna miss out on that, hon."

Trinity laughed. "Yeah, I don't know if I'd trust you with a feather-duster, but I'm sure we would have found something for you to do." She patted his cheek. "You would have liked Japan. The living quarters at that base are really nice; I liked Okinawa when I was there, but Honshu's a little less jam-packed. Plus the Nishiki River Delta is gorgeous. I should take you there sometime."

He was nodding, looking back at her. "I'd be afraid you wouldn't want to leave."

She snuggled against him. "Well maybe you wouldn't want to leave either."

He touched his chest. "Oh, I'd leave. I'm a cop—I like my American burger joints and doughnut shops, and I need to know they're nearby. All they got over there are sushi bars." He stroked her back. "I'd miss you and all, but I ain't gonna live on no sushi."

Trinity shoved him in the shoulder. He grabbed her and gave her a quick kiss on the lips. Zack looked down at the new glass of whiskey.

Donatello winked. "I tell you, I'm proud of my girl. One of these days I'm gonna do right by her. If she wasn't stuck here with me, she'd probably be in D.C. running the Department of Defense by now. You know she made the Dean's List twice at the Naval Academy?"

Zack nodded. Donatello managed to work it into the conversation pretty much every time they got together. "Yeah, I know. Dean's list twice, 4.0 GPA, I got it."

"4.0 GPA, man. 4.0."

Trinity wrinkled her nose. "He's sweet when he wants to be."

Zack ran his tongue around the inside of his mouth. The two of them could have been a federal power couple if they wanted—Donatello's grades at Temple had been almost as good as Trinity's. He was as overqualified for being a detective in the 9th District as she was for being a hospital LAN administrator at Jefferson Memorial. Donatello had considered a life in the FBI for a time; the two had been close to moving to Virginia at one point a few years back. Now he had been in the 0-9 for ten years.

The man was in it for the long haul. Law enforcement was in Donatello's blood—his father had been on the job for 30-odd years, and Donatello had gone straight through his Criminal Justice program to the police academy. Eventually he'd probably get a promotion to lieutenant somewhere in town and they'd get a big house out on the Main Line and start raising a family. Donatello had known where he was going from the whistle, and he had never taken his eyes off the goal line.

Sharp contrast to the kind of man who got himself dumped unceremoniously into the ass-end of the private sector. Ten damn years. Zack shook his head. Two years longer than he had lasted. And counting. He sipped his drink.

Trinity shrugged. "Anyway, they made it sound like there might be other offers down the road that might be a little closer to home, so here's hoping." She swallowed some of her white wine spritzer. "Oh, here, before I forget." She raised her eyebrows and began sifting through her purse. "We were going through all these old pictures, and we found this shot from when you guys were at the football game last year... here. Keep it—we have dups." She held up a rectangular photo and handed it to Zack.

Zack looked down at it. He and Donatello were standing in the concourse at Veterans Stadium, grinning and holding up cups of beer with their arms over one another's shoulders. The green turf of the field was visible in the background, past the entrance to their seating section. The Temple-Penn State game, just about a year to the date. In the picture, Zack was wearing a navy and white windbreaker. Penn State colors at the Temple homecoming game. He smirked and scratched his cheek.

"Thanks." He raised an eyebrow at Donatello. "That was a good day. Lions won 24-7, if I remember correctly."

Donatello frowned. "It was close in the first half." He shook his head. "You should show a little respect for the school that actually graduated you."

Zack flipped the picture over. It was date-stamped in mid-September. They had apparently gotten a bunch of old rolls developed when they went in for new film. "Once a Nittany Lion, always a Nittany Lion, I guess. Also it doesn't pay to be a fan of Temple Owl football. I think Temple lost that game by about 40 points this year." He looked up. "Hey, what happened— we were supposed to get together to watch that, weren't we?"

Donatello finished his drink, folding up the second tiny umbrella and laying it on a napkin next to the first. "Yeah, I know, man, it was the weekend before we were leaving. I couldn't do it—too much stuff to do. I tried to get in touch with you about that like a week before, but you never called me back."

"Huh. Don't remember that." Zack looked down. Not much casework that week. There might have been a legitimate excuse for him to have missed a phone call... nothing specific was springing to mind. But if he had been dodging phone calls from Donatello, there was a good chance it had something to do with Samuel Goldstine.

Donatello patted the bar. "Guess you were snooping around, watching people doing what they shouldn't be doing." Benedetto stepped over from the other end of the bar and pointed at Donatello as he cleared the area of Donatello's empty glass and trash items. Donatello nodded once, holding up two fingers.

"Guess so." Zack picked up his wallet and slipped the photo inside. He hesitated, then leaned forward and slipped the wallet back in his pocket. "Just as well, though—you get pretty whiny during those blowouts." He cleared his throat, shaking his head and glancing from Donatello to Trinity. "So... what's the plan now that you're back? You going to take a little time to relax before you go back to work?"

Trinity nodded, raising her eyebrows. "Both of us are off until Monday. We figured we might need some decompression time before we dive back into the everyday grind."

Donatello nodded. "It's freaky, man. One minute you're in the tropical paradise of the Caribbean, and then the next... everything's back the way it was. Just like that." He snapped his fingers. "We have a couple days... we were thinking it might be a good idea to take it easy for a bit, catch up on some sleep." He suddenly slapped the table, breaking into a laugh. "But then, we thought, the hell with that!" He flashed his teeth at his wife.

Benedetto returned with new drinks for the Diazes, raising his eyebrows at Zack. Zack nodded, turned to the Diazes, and raised his glass. "Well, let me be the first to propose a toast, assuming the Torrances haven't already done you that honor, and if they have, don't tell me." The Diazes laughed.

Zack paused, frowning and raising an eyebrow. "Welcome back. And congrats on the promotion, even though you're not accepting it. Nice to know people in our military are smart enough to recognize a good thing when they see it." He downed the whiskey glass in one gulp and wiped his mouth with his sleeve. So much for stopping at two.

Donatello and Trinity sipped their glasses. Donatello reached out and chucked Zack on the arm. "Hey, thanks, man. That was almost coherent."

Zack shrugged, turning to Trinity. "I'd order us a round of sake, but, you know… you didn't actually accept the job. And sake is, you know… terrible."

She laughed. "It's actually pretty good, Zack. You should try something besides that firewater you always drink."

Benedetto returned with a new glass of whiskey, right on cue. Zack set the glass on the bar in front of him, holding it at the rim and slowly rotating it. He took another long swig and exhaled. The stronger effects of the alcohol were starting to sink in. He adjusted his position on the barstool.

Donatello waved a hand in the air. "Anyway, the plan, for real. We're gonna go down to Penn's Landing, grab a bite at the Moshulu, then hit the club scene. Teach the kids how to dance. I think you should come with us. You up for it?"

Another bunch of people entered. Zack stuck out his lower lip, glancing at the glass. Half-empty after a single pull. Lots of ice. Benedetto was about to start getting precipitously less attentive. "You two better go without me this time. I have some casework to deal with tomorrow morning, and I'm going to need to be awake."

Donatello nodded. "All right, last chance. You sure?"

Trinity jiggled her wine glass. "You're missing a good time, Zack. We're gonna conga."

Donatello stood and stepped behind his wife, putting his hands on her hips and moving his head rhythmically back and forth. Zack laughed at the floor, steadying himself. "Looks like Dee has had a little too much of that Caribbean air."

Trinity nodded, putting her glass down. "Definitely. He almost bought a Perry Como CD." She turned around and poked him, making a goofy face and singing. "It's bet-ter in the Ba-ha-mas…"

Donatello grabbed her and collared her neck with his arm. He shot Zack a concerned look as she giggled. "I didn't buy no 'Better in the Bahamas' shit, Zack."

Zack shifted and almost fell off his chair. He glanced over his shoulder. The blonde woman down the bar had her leather jacket off; underneath she had on a white halter top. She glanced back at him and smiled.

Trinity screamed as Donatello tickled her. Benedetto turned around and laughed at them from the other end of the bar as he shook a drink in a metal mixing cup.

Zack shook his head. "Looks like you two need a little more alone time. You better get out of here before Benny turns the hoses on you."

Donatello released Trinity and glanced at his watch as he reached for his wallet, fishing it out of his back pocket. "Yeah, I guess it is getting to be that time, isn't it, baby?"

Trinity shot him a look. Donatello nodded, waving a hand. "I know, woman, I wasn't gonna forget." He nudged her on the cheek with a knuckle and looked up at Zack. "Before we go… you doing anything on Sunday?"

Zack sniffed and shrugged. "Don't think so. Why?"

Donatello put his hand on Zack's shoulder. "Dinner at our apartment. I have it on good authority that Trin's making catfish."

Zack nodded.

Donatello went on. "You want, we can hang out ahead of time. Jump around town, find something to do during the day… maybe duck in a sports bar and catch the Phillies game." He paused. "Eagles have a bye this week, so I figure you got a window open in your schedule."

A fuzzy memory suddenly swirled… Melanie had mentioned the bye week too. She had been thinking of going to Chickie and Pete's in South Philly with a bunch of her friends; she had tossed it in his lap, and he had basically ignored it. And completely forgotten about it. She hadn't specifically invited him, though… not in so many words. The mutual one-and-done vibe had been pretty evident for the rest of the night, though seeing her again wouldn't have been the worst thing in the world. Maybe she had just been making conversation.

Zack shook his head. "Sports bar, huh? Trin, you kicking him out of the house?"

Trinity gave him a wry smile. "You know how it is. I got some things to get done, and if I'm making dinner, he needs to be elsewhere for a good two to three hours or I will go insane."

Zack squinted at Donatello. "Well, I can't very well pass up a chance for some of your wife's Cajun cooking." He made a loud lip-smacking noise, making sure Trinity was watching him. She blew a kiss at him.

"We're good, then. I'll give you a call." Donatello lowered his voice as he flipped open his wallet, pulling out a pair of twenties. "And we might possibly be having a Halloween party." He peered at his wife out of the corner of his eye.

Trinity frowned. "We'll see about that. You better be on your best behavior."

Zack smiled at the bar. "Keep me posted."

Donatello patted his wife's leg. "Yeah, all right. We'll talk later." He tossed the money on the bar in front of Zack.

Trinity stood, brushing off her clothes. Zack got up after her, and she hugged him. "It's good to see you, Zack."

He grinned. "If you get bored with Detective Diaz here, feel free to meet me back at my place."

She laughed. "Yeah, I think I'm all set."

Donatello slapped Zack on the back. It stung. "You sure you're gonna make it home all right, man? You know you're on the way downtown, and there's plenty of room in the car."

Zack nodded, wincing slightly from the slap. "I took a cab here, I can take one back. I'll be fine. You two take it easy." He sat back down on the barstool.

They said goodbye and Zack watched them leave. He turned around and looked for Benedetto.

*   *   *

Zack stumbled, forcing the woman roughly against the brown-painted plaster of the wall. She continued to claw his hair with her fingernails. Apparently, she hadn't noticed the wall. Zack blindly spun her around toward his apartment, working his tongue against the roof of her mouth. He leaned her against the door and it flew open as if it were on spring-loaded hinges.

They toppled sideways into the apartment, crushing his shoulder against the bare, dusty wood of the floor.

Damn. The latch was broken—he had forgotten. He pushed himself away from her, coughing. "You all right?"

Her make-up was smeared badly around her mouth like the face of a ghoulish circus clown, and her short blonde hair was scattered loosely in front of her eyes. She smiled a greedy smile. "Oh yeah…"

He stood up and lifted the woman off the floor, setting her on her feet. She pressed herself against him, slipping her hands underneath his shirt, and he grabbed her at her hips and maneuvered her in the direction of the bedroom, pushing her backwards.

She collapsed as her feet touched the mattress, pulling him on top of her and wrapping her legs around him. He tugged the halter top up over her head, forcing the neck strap past her face, and began fumbling with the hook of her bra.

She found his mouth with hers and darted her tongue in and out, then momentarily pulled her head back, breathing rapidly.

"Aren't you even… going to show me your place?"

He closed his eyes, reaching down to unbuckle her belt. "This is it. This is all there is."

He ran his fingers up her thighs, and she moaned.

*   *   *

```
... "Philadelphia"; 26 September 1992 CE
```

Cassie squinted up through the windshield at the dismal gray sky. The last time she had been on the road to the Philadelphia International Airport had been for a family vacation to France, and she hadn't been old enough to drive. The only thing that remained familiar was the suffocating stench of the refinery-filled swamp along the way. Even now that she was off Route 291, the smell of pollution hung in the car. The air-conditioning had only made it worse.

On her way to France, she hadn't noticed the state of the housing around the expressway by the airport. Not the ideal neighborhood to park an unattended Mercedes. Several minutes of sitting motionless in the car, double-parked in the street with the blinkers hadn't exactly inspired any confidence. Tinicum Boulevard was a two-way street, but it didn't look as if one car would fit between the parked cars, let alone two. Still, no one was honking. The street was a small, pothole-ridden tributary, and no one else seemed to be interested in using it.

The location was pretty awful. Everything was dirty—paint was chipping away on each house, revealing sloppy masonry, and pornographic stick figures and profanities were scribbled on a lot of walls. Jumbled electrical wires formed a web above the street, connecting the buildings to the wooden poles that leaned along the opposite sidewalk, looming over the playground. The few visible trees along the sidewalk were already losing their red and yellow leaves for the fall. In another setting, the trees would have looked pretty. Here, they just looked as if they were dying.

She raised her eyebrows, nodding. The impulse to return to better parts of the city wasn't going away. With any luck, the meeting would go quickly. Walker would give her the documentation, she would leave, and they would have everything wrapped up in one more trip. Hopefully.

Leaving the car in the middle of the street with the hazard lights on was probably not a good idea. Maybe it would create the impression that she wasn't going to be gone long, but it would more likely just draw attention to the car. She sat up and put the car in gear, then headed forward to the end of the block and turned the corner. There was an abandoned gas station a street away—that would have to do.

She located the gas station and pulled into a small lot behind the pumps, picking out a spot near an old, rusty sedan with broken windows. She sighed, shaking her head, then shut off the ignition, grabbed her valise off the floor of the passenger seat, and got out. The Mercedes let out a short squeal as she locked it up with the key remote. She took a quick glance to her left and right and started along the sidewalk. No one else seemed to be in the immediate vicinity, which may or may not have been a good thing. She was perfectly capable of handling herself if someone came at her, but the idea of brushing up on her karate in the middle of Tinicum Island wasn't overwhelmingly enticing.

She glanced up as she crossed to the playground. The sky was completely choked with dark rainclouds, but the rain was holding back as if it were waiting for the right moment. If anything about a thunderstorm had been mentioned in the morning newscast, she had missed it.

The playground looked as if it spanned about two blocks, maybe half the area of Rittenhouse Square. The fact that there weren't many trees might have been making the square seem a little smaller than it actually was. It could have used a little more cover; as it was, the neglect was apparent from the street.

A dull cement border wrapped around the perimeter, protecting a hedge enclosure that was little more than a chain of dry brambles. Cassie entered through an opening at the corner. Inside, disintegrating stony walkways snaked among several large plots of field and a few open areas of pavement, converging on a fenced area at the center of the square where a skinny, bare maple stood lashed to a pole. The plots were more dirt than grass. The entire area was covered with a scattering of damp, windblown leaves. The place was completely desolate.

Several benches were positioned along the walks, but there was no sign of the jungle gym Walker had mentioned on the near side. The playground equipment was concentrated in an area to the left of the fenced tree. A slide, monkey bars, a swing-set with one of the seats missing, a seesaw. A mud-filled sandbox. Plastic seats and steps, mostly cracked and broken, metal bars with flaking rust. Again, nothing that matched Walker's description of a white, dome-shaped climbing frame.

She frowned, turning away. Center City managed to keep its public parks clean and in good shape. This looked more like a condemned lot. Kids needed these places. Not everyone grew up playing in gigantic yards and plush game rooms.

She buried the thought, moving around the fence and turning her attention to the grounds on the other side. There were a few people strolling around and at least one seated on one of the benches. A man heavily bundled in winter clothing brushed past her, and she spun out of the way, staring back at him. He veered off and sat on one of the benches, then pulled a sandwich out of a bag as a pair of pigeons landed in front of him. She turned back around, scanning for the statue.

She was getting jumpy. She rolled her eyes. If something happened to her here, her parents would be coughing I-told-you-so's at her for the rest of her life.

She laughed to herself. If it had been up to her parents, she would have most likely still been living with them in the big house with the gigantic yard and plush game room, safely behind the gates and sealed off from the barbarians. Good and oblivious.

A small, white geodesic dome stood on the opposite side of an open area of pavement, seemingly at the farthest possible point in the square from where she had happened to park her car. A dark-haired man was seated on a bench several feet away, next to an ornamental wrought-iron water fountain. The man stood as she approached. John Walker, unmistakably.

This time he had on a gray windbreaker and black corduroy pants. Not quite as sharp as the clothes he had worn in the office, though they looked brand new, just as the clothes he had worn to the office had looked.

Cassie nodded at him as she reached the water fountain. "Mr. Walker."

He smiled. "Hello, Ms. Prescott. Have a seat." An envelope and several sheets of folded paper were set neatly at the center of the bench, leaving room for a person on either side.

A buffer. It might have been for her benefit or for his. She smiled back and shook his hand. "Thank you." She sat down on the left and set the valise on the ground in front of her. "I'd like to get through this quickly, if you don't mind."

"Of course." He pulled the papers from underneath the envelope. "I've transcribed my will statement here. This one I'd like to keep; the original is enclosed. Shall I read this one to you?" He unfolded the sheets.

Cassie shook her head. "That's not necessary—I'll go over it at the office. If you've got all the basic information, all we need to do is add the signatures and date it. Did you list me as your personal representative? That would need to be stated in the will itself."

He nodded. "Yes, I updated it a few days ago, adding you as the... I think I used the term executrix. Is that correct?"

"That's right—that's fine."

He was staring at the statement. He had the pages bound intricately in the corner with a wire-thin string of some sort. He exhaled lightly. "Good. Yes, I believe I understand the basic necessities… identifying myself clearly, identifying my assets and my heirs, leaving no questions as to how my possessions are to be divided." He paused. "There is another provision of which I think you should be aware."

Cassie shifted in her seat, adjusting her glasses. "That's okay, Mr. Walker, it's no problem if we need to redraft it—we have standard boilerplate we use for documents like this if it does turn out we need to adjust anything." She smiled again. "We'll get it straightened out."

He nodded. "Very well." He was still holding his copy in front of him.

She smiled and looked back toward the playground equipment. A pigeon was now perched on the high end of the seesaw. If she didn't manage to get everything straightened out before they met again, there was a chance she was going to become much more familiar with this playground.

She turned back to him and pointed at the envelope. "My copy is in there?"

He nodded and handed it to her. It was sealed as if he intended to mail it. She opened her valise, took out a file folder along with her personal planner book, and transferred the envelope to the folder. "Great. So… I'll review this at the office. And you said you want this expedited, if possible?"

Walker nodded again. "It would be very helpful, yes."

Cassie sighed, scratching her ear. She was probably going to regret making promises to this man, but for now at least, her Monday was fairly clear. "All right. Assuming I don't have any questions, I can try to have this typed up for you by Monday, end of day, we'll get it signed, and then we'll be all done. If there are questions, we'll obviously need to meet again. You're sure there's nowhere I can reach you by phone?"

He frowned. "I'm sorry. It's as I said before. Any discussion about this will have to be face-to-face."

She nodded, dropping the folder back inside the valise. "All right. Well I'll go over everything with you on Monday, if you don't mind meeting fairly late. But if there need to be changes after that, it's probably going to be close to the end of the week before I can complete another draft. Thursday at the earliest, I think."

Walker straightened, leveling his eyes at her. "I don't think there will need to be any changes. We can finish this matter on Monday, I'm sure."

255

Cassie met his eyes and felt a sudden chill. She cleared her throat and turned away, sliding out the pen tucked in the binder of the personal planner. "Monday it is. I can shoot for 5:30—how does that sound?"

"5:30 is perfect." He bowed his head. "Thank you for your responsiveness. I'm glad you're able to be so accommodating."

She wrote the time in her book and put it back in the valise, looking up. He was still holding his copy of the will statement. She reached out and took a hold of it. "May I?"

"Please."

She folded the papers back up and noted the next meeting time on the reverse side. She handed it back to him.

Walker looked at the note and put it back in the pocket of his jacket. "I see you'd prefer to meet here in the playground once again."

She smiled flatly and nodded. "I'm more comfortable outside. I don't mean any offense by this, Mr. Walker, but as a rule I like to keep my client interactions in a public forum. Some lawyers are willing to meet clients in their homes, but I'm not one of them. Unfortunately, in this day and age, we have to take precautions. I hope you can understand that." She was perfectly justified in using discretion, but the words sounded completely snobbish coming out of her mouth.

Walker shook his head, holding up a hand. "Oh, I understand, of course. It isn't a problem for me."

He wasn't going to press it, thank God. Social conventions were apparently a challenge for this man, but he was adept at adjusting. "I'm glad. So we'll meet back here, then." She paused. "Oh, one more thing—are you sure you don't have someone else who can join us as a witness? If I bring someone down from the firm, it's going to cost you a lot more. I really think you'd be wasting your money." She nodded in the direction of the playground equipment. "We could just ask someone here, if you want. All the person would have to do is watch you sign and then add his or her own signature to the paperwork."

Walker's smile disappeared, and he looked suddenly tired. He sighed. "Now it's my turn to apologize for my protective nature. Ms. Prescott, I do hope you took me seriously when I said I wanted to keep this as private as possible." He paused, and his gaze drifted toward one of the empty beds of patchy grass. "As I understand it, the Commonwealth of Pennsylvania does not actually require the signature of any witnesses on a legal will."

Cassie frowned at the pavement. "Believe me, Mr. Walker, I'm taking it seriously. It's a policy of my firm to obtain at least one witness's signature

256

on all of our legal documents. Listen, I'll do everything I can to keep this as private as possible—I promised to leave your name out of it, and I will—but you need to understand it's very important that we go by the book if you want your will to be challenge-proof. If I'm putting my name on this, I need to follow the legal requirements, and I'm also not going to be dishonest about what I'm doing from the people I work with. I couldn't help you under those circumstances." A pigeon landed a foot away from her valise and began pecking at the ground. She exhaled and peered back at Walker.

He looked content again, but with a shade less warmth. He leaned forward, clasping his hands together. "All right, I suppose I'll have to live with that." He flashed an abrupt smile. "At least, I will for a little while."

Cassie looked down at the ground.

He nodded. "Bring who you want to bring, Ms. Prescott. You know my situation—at this point, money is not my concern." He looked up at the sky and sniffed the air. "I'd prefer not to involve someone from off the street."

"As you like." Cassie stood, picking up the valise and holding it with two hands in front of her. His eyes were on her again, dark and intense, striking a contrast with his peaceful expression.

She stared back for a moment. There was something about his look that was more unsettling than usual. It might have been nothing more than the foreboding sense of mortality, though he didn't have the sunken rings or any of the other signs of utter exhaustion typically seen in the face of a cancer victim. It seemed to be something deeper than that, some other angst...

He had been as much of a perfect gentleman as she should have expected. Considering his circumstances, he had every right to be out of sorts, but he had been as pleasant to talk to as someone with friends and family and a full, healthy life in front of him. She was struck with a sudden urge to apologize profusely for forcing him to meet in the middle of a run-down playground instead of his home, and for being impatient. For trying to keep her time with him to a minimum. This man had no one.

"Thank you again, Ms. Prescott. It's nice we had this chance to talk." Walker was standing.

Cassie blinked and flashed a smile, waving a hand in front of her. "I'm sorry—it was my pleasure, Mr. Walker. I'd better get going." She extended her hand. "I guess I'll talk to you on Monday."

He took her hand and held it lightly. "Good-bye, Ms. Prescott. Thank you once again."

She nodded, turned, and headed rapidly in the direction of her car. A row of pigeons took off in a group as she cut back around the circular fence and past the decaying playground facilities.

She wrinkled her nose as she walked. The disrepair of the surroundings seemed to assert itself again, as if the meeting with Walker had been in a completely different place. As if she were coming out of a temporary trance. The voice of the sheltered little rich girl rearing its head, maybe. Fear of the barbarians outside the gate.

It was more than that. She glanced over her shoulder. Walker was definitely doing all he could to demonstrate how kind and pleasant he was, but there was still something off about him. Sincere as he seemed, he was rigidly guarded. He came off open, but he had some fairly extreme neuroses, and he was taking care to keep them tamped down.

And he was deceptively persuasive. Effortlessly persuasive. She had actually felt guilty for wanting to leave, not two minutes before.

Maybe the man was a lot more disturbed than he seemed. He might have been more than just neurotic. For all she knew, the cancer was a figment of his imagination. Or a lie.

Maybe not. But whatever the real story with Walker was, she was going to have to assume he was of sound mind if she was going to make a statement to that effect in his will.

One thing for sure, she was going to a lot of trouble for this man—a lot further out of her way to help a client than what was normally called for, and for someone she didn't really know at all. She definitely shouldn't have been feeling any guilt for wanting to limit her time with him.

Somehow, it seemed as if Walker wasn't going to be content with one more quick meeting.

The man at the other end of the park was still sitting on the same bench, watching the pigeons finish off the last of his sandwich. The sound of a car backfiring came from a few blocks away, and Cassie stumbled and almost dropped her valise. The man on the bench didn't flinch at all.

She sighed, angling out of the neglected playground and into the sidewalk, heading in the direction of her car.

*   *   *

... "Philadelphia"; 27 September 1992 CE

The Philadelphia Convention Center was an odd sight. People had gone to a lot of trouble to create the illusion of the outdoors in the expansive rooms; panoramic tableaus were tacked up all around the long wall showing scenes from Tuscany, Bordeaux, and Napa Valley, with rolling green hills covered with vineyards and olive trees under sunny blue skies. A carpet of turf ran wall to wall, broken only by walkways made to look like rough, stylized versions of dirt and stone. Sprawling white marquee tents had been set up everywhere, suggesting shade was necessary under the soft fluorescent lighting of the ceiling that loomed above. Presumably, it was what one would see at a typical wine-tasting event, with canvas flapping in the breeze, birds chirping. The smell of fresh grass.

Indoors was indoors. The air smelled like overworked dehumidifiers, and the atmosphere was about as pleasant and relaxing as the concourse in 30th Street Station. Ultimately, it looked exactly like every other prefab display the Convention Center had ever thrown together with heavy foot traffic in mind. The homages to nature were more a reminder of the crappy gray dampness on the other side of the walls than anything else.

Inside each tent was a row of folding tables decked out with neatly arranged bottles and glasses and attended by spiffily dressed wine officials. Most of the tasting areas were mobbed by dozens of less distinguished-looking people.

Zack looked out through the long, wide opening as a long-haired, bearded man in a black leather jacket stumbled across his field of vision and bowled into a middle-aged couple, spilling at least two glasses. Apparently, the $16 cover charge wasn't keeping out the riffraff.

He turned back to the table and glanced at Donatello Diaz. "I don't get this. They should have done this outside."

Donatello was eyeballing the half-filled wine glasses on a table with a big sign that read "Australians." He shrugged. "Not exactly ideal weather outside right now."

Zack frowned. "Who said they had to do it in late September? They could have done it for real over the summer. Fairmont Park or somewhere."

"This is how they roll in the upper crust... they want to have a thing, they do it. Whenever they feel like it. Just think of it as an all-day happy hour with people who don't smell like the subway."

Zack nodded. "It's stupid. This thing might as well be in a barn."

"You're the one who wanted to come to this thing." Donatello shook his head and scratched his upper lip. "It is what it is. Anyway, it's sure as shit better than spending the day cooped up in a bar with no windows." He looked across the table at the steward who was watching them. "You got any recommendations?"

The steward beamed. "We have a very fine Semchard. It's a white.

Please. Help yourself." He gestured at one of the half-filled glasses.

"Australian wine, huh?" Donatello picked up a glass and held it up to one of the portable lamp stands, swishing it in circles. Zack smirked. Donatello waved the glass at the steward. "Tell me, does this brand go well with French fries?"

The steward was unfazed. "Actually, one of the strong points of this particular wine is the way it can go well with almost anything. I wouldn't take it with fast food, though." He continued to beam. The man was skinny and had a pencil-thin mustache, and with the maroon vest, bow tie, and poofy white shirt, he looked as if he had stepped out of one of the wall paintings.

Donatello sipped the wine. "Mmm. Very... extra-crispy. Have some, Wyler. It seems these Australians can crush grapes almost as well as catching crocodiles. Excellent choice, sommelier."

Zack smiled at the steward. "He's just excited. His wife doesn't let him drink very often."

The steward nodded. "Of course."

Donatello smiled as he sipped. "Last time me and Trin came to one of these things we had a blast."

Zack shrugged. "Yeah, well it does have that feel of a place you get dragged to by a girl." He paused, raising an eyebrow. "You do actually still have testicles, right?"

Donatello swished the wine in his mouth and swallowed, raising his eyebrows. "Yeah, huh? I didn't realize you were so insecure in your masculinity. So maybe you should have brought that girl you been hanging out with the last couple of days." He gave Zack a sidelong glance and took another sip.

Zack squinted, shaking his head. "What girl? Melanie?"

"What girl? Man, did you even call her back?"

Big mistake mentioning anything about women to Donatello—he and Trinity were like a couple of pit bulls. Zack frowned flatly. "She's a friend from PSU, that's it. I'll call her back if I feel like it, and if I don't, I won't." He eyed Donatello. "If that's all right with you."

Donatello bowed his head. "I'm just saying. Girl from college has got to be a better choice than some 20-year-old skank from Benny's."

"Nice." Zack moved to an area of red wines. The steward was watching him, smiling pleasantly and patiently waiting to be prompted like a robot in Disney World. "She was more like 30. And you guys left before all that—you didn't even see her."

Donatello rolled his eyes, holding his wine glass delicately by the stem.

"Oh, I saw her. I'm a detective, chief… she might as well have had a sign on her forehead that said 'take me out for a test drive,' and you ain't exactly subtle either." He licked his lips. "Yo, man, I'm not trying to tell you how to run your life, but you might want to start circulating with a better crowd."

"You done?"

Donatello held up a hand and looked away. "That's all I'm saying."

"Drink your wine, genius." Zack nodded at the steward and pointed at a glass of red wine. "How's that one?"

The steward nodded. "Oh, yes, the Shiraz, very good. If you like red wine, the Australian reds are very popular. All of our samples here are very good, really."

Popular? Zack glanced around. There were one or two others at the table. The tent seemed to be less crowded than most. "Then why is no one else in here?"

The question seemed to make the steward even happier. "Oh, well the French and the Californian wines are still regarded as the best, of course, and the Australians are still relatively unknown to a lot of wine drinkers. But Australia has an ideal climate for vineyards. In ten years these wines will be rivaling the Germans and the Italians, and eventually they'll catch France and California. Go ahead. Try it."

Zack picked up the glass and took a gulp. A soft burn radiated outward as the wine ran down through his chest to his stomach.

The steward looked from Zack to Donatello. "Really, you've wandered into an excellent tent. Have you been to the other wine regions?"

Donatello was sipping a second glass. "We just got here."

Zack took another gulp, feeling the warm sensation of the alcohol bleed into his extremities. He exhaled and looked back at Donatello.

The thought of bringing Melanie along had entered his mind. Briefly. It might have been nice to be with a woman somewhere outside the nighttime bar arena. Of course, another date with Melanie might have given her the wrong idea, especially considering their past history. Besides, the point of attending this particular hokey wine-tasting event had nothing to do with Melanie Katsoulis.

Zack drained the glass of wine and blinked, glancing at the steward and clearing his throat. "I was wondering if I could get some information about the sponsors of this event." He handed the empty glass to the steward.

The steward nodded earnestly. "Of course. I believe you'll find all the information in the brochures—we have them right over here. Here." He picked up a slimline from his side of the table and handed it to Zack. "There you go."

"Thanks." Zack opened the folded sheet and scanned the callouts. "I understand this is being backed by a group of local families... and one of them... is the Prescott family?"

The steward nodded. "Yes, the Textile Prescotts. They organized the event for the first time last year. I'm sure you know how successful that was. There are now two other families in the Delaware Valley signed on." He smiled and lowered his voice to a conspiratorial level. "It's not official yet, but it looks like we're doing it again in '93, with more sponsors."

Zack nodded, glancing at Donatello. "Do the sponsors have a table set up anywhere? I was hoping to talk to someone in the Prescott family."

The steward's eyebrows went up. "Of course, of course. They would be in the donations area further inside the room." He leaned across the table and placed a finger on the open brochure, pointing to an overhead diagram of the Convention Center. "Right there, I believe." He grinned and straightened, pointing at Zack and Donatello. "You two help yourselves to whatever you want, all right? I'm going to go over here and help these gentlemen—you just holler if you need me." He sidestepped along the table to a small group of casually dressed young men who looked as if they might very well have still been in college.

Zack nodded. "Thanks again." He raised his eyebrows at Donatello. "Want to go?"

Donatello shrugged. "This is your deal, not mine. I'm just along for the ride."

Zack ducked through the entrance and went left, and Donatello moved to his right shoulder. Donatello nudged him as they walked. "I think that guy thinks you want to make a donation."

Zack studied him. "Is that so hard to believe? This is a fund raiser."

The crowd seemed to have thinned out noticeably in the past 15 minutes. The event had started at noon and was only supposed to go until 6; it was after 3, so the energy was starting to wane. They reached the main walkway, a wide, orange-tan slab of rubber mat that looked more like bubblegum than a natural dirt surface.

Donatello nodded as they passed another tent. "So... what do you want with a bunch of suburban upper-crust families who like to dabble in things like wine tasting?"

Zack shook his head. "I just want to see if I can talk to someone."

"You sure this isn't related to a case you're working on?"

"Nope. Not any more, anyway."

"Because the way you made it sound, you wanted to hang out a little, get your money's worth. This feels more like business."

Zack spotted a pair of booths on the right, near the far end of the path in the area the steward had indicated on the brochure. "This'll just take a second."

Donatello was nodding. "Mm-hm." He paused. "You wouldn't by any chance be keeping it close to the vest because you're working for a certain pasty-faced, fossilized, sorry-ass excuse for a soon-to-be-nonmember of the out-of-jail community. You'd tell me if you were working for Goldstine again, wouldn't you, Zack?"

Shit. Zack frowned, keeping his eyes in front of him. The whole fucking case was over and done with, and now Donatello was asking the question. And right at that moment, sitting in the apartment was a fresh, new $500 bottle of Glenfarclas left by Samuel Goldstine, along with the full amount Goldstine had promised for the Imperato case. Apparently, despite the glaring lack of any evidence of improprieties by Joey, Rachel Imperato suddenly wanted a divorce, and Goldstine was happy. Either she had met someone else herself, or the old man had finally broken down and threatened to cut off her allowance.

"Zack?"

Zack sighed. "This has to do with a case I took on for a law firm about a month back. I got threatened with a lawsuit, and I'm trying to get back in touch with my client's lawyer."

Donatello came to a complete stop. "Shit, Zack. Why didn't you say something? You want me to hook you up with a lawyer—I can stop off at the DA's office and ask Nick for a recommendation."

Zack turned around and took a step back toward Donatello. "No. Thanks." Zack scratched his beard. "It's not a problem. Don't worry about it, I'm not getting sued. I agreed to lower the bill, and everything's fine." He glanced over his shoulder. "Come on." He started back toward the booths.

Donatello caught up to him. "So... what, you changed your mind and decided you don't want to lower the bill?"

"Not exactly."

Donatello shook his head. "Why are you looking for a lawyer at a wine-tasting event?"

Zack looked at him without answering. Donatello was off the Goldstine inquest, at least. Zack rolled his neck and set his eyes again on the pair of booths.

It was only a matter of time before Goldstine tried to hire him again, but it wasn't worth worrying about now. Donatello would have understood why he had agreed to work for the man. Hell, there wasn't anything illegal about working for the man—it was an infidelity case for God sakes. Donatello knew money was tight, so Donatello would have understood. Donatello would have understood a hell of a lot better than anyone else at the precinct.

The booths were essentially a pair of big, white, plastic boxes with big, vertical openings separating the countertop from the overhead panel, where commercial signs were displayed. They had apparently been intended to mesh with the surrounding outdoor look, but they looked more like typical convention fare.

There weren't many people in the area, and there were only a few attendants behind the counter. Zack spotted a very corporate-looking woman with tightly pinned hair manning the booth on the left. Blonde. He hadn't seen her before. The two people in the booth on the right were men. The booth on the right was closer.

One of the two men disappeared out of view in a compartment in the back as Zack approached. The other stepped forward. The man was portly, dressed in a navy blue business suit. His expression was serious. "How can I help you, sir?"

Zack nodded at him. "Hi. I'm looking for Cassandra Prescott. I was told she was working here today."

The man raised an eyebrow. "Yes, Cassandra Prescott. I'll look into it, sir." He turned and disappeared into the back.

Zack turned and scanned the surroundings. A small group of people stood off to the left—a woman in a black, shoulderless gown talking to a pair of elderly men who were dressed like they were running for a national office. Another elegantly dressed woman was approaching the other booth, leaning on the counter in a familiar way.

Donatello stepped to the counter. "So, what's the deal here, Zack? This lawyer representing one of the sponsors?"

Zack shook his head. "I think she is one of the sponsors."

"You going to tell me what's going on?"

"No." Zack shot him a smile. "Go ahead and find another tent. I'll catch up to you."

"I'm fine right here." Donatello cocked his head and leaned his elbows against the counter. "You said this wasn't going to take long."

"Shouldn't." There was movement directly ahead, across the path. A group of women were stumbling out of a tent. They collectively paused, then headed left. Bachelorette party, maybe.

"You sure everything's all right?"

Zack glanced at Donatello and nodded once. "Copacetic, muchacho. Stop your worrying." He scratched his neck. "So, you claim to be a wine connoisseur. What do you think so far?"

Donatello pursed his lips. "So far, so good. $16 though... I have yet to get my money's worth, I'll tell you that."

"You can afford it." Zack exhaled loudly. "Besides, we need to get you off that banana strawberry daiquiri bullshit before your nuts fall off."

Donatello nodded, glancing around. "Yeah, huh? You need to broaden your horizons, my friend." He nudged Zack. "Tell you what, I think maybe I was wrong about bringing a date to this shit. If I wasn't married, I'd have to put this place on my list as a prime location for finding various fine specimens of the feminine persuasion." He pointed a finger lazily in the direction of the small group to the left. "There's someone for you right there."

Zack squinted. Donatello was aiming at the woman in black. She was facing in the other direction, but it was easy to see she had chosen the gown well. She had a stunning figure, and her hair was full and long, done up in wavy curls that spilled down her back about halfway to her slender waist. Probably a model; there were exhibitions going on in the smaller rooms. Excellent hair. Hard to gauge the color—it was lustrous, and there was an odd play of light and shadow where the woman was standing.

Zack nodded. "My friend, she is in a whole different league. She looks like she just got air-lifted from the Hamptons."

Donatello chuckled.

The woman turned slightly, showing off her profile. Her face was beautiful, of course. Every bit as stunning as the rest of the package. The rich just kept getting richer.

There was also the chance he was looking at the product of a team of the world's most expensive plastic surgeons. Zack craned his neck, looking for the portly man who had apparently completely forgotten about him.

He took another look at the woman, and she glanced back at him. She cocked her head, and her expression changed. He stared. The face was suddenly unmistakable. He was looking at Cassandra Prescott. She turned back to her companions, said something to them, touching one man on his arm, then headed straight toward him and Donatello.

Donatello took a step away from the counter and straightened. "Oh shit, Zack, she's coming over here." He glanced at Zack. "Do you know her?"

Zack raised his eyebrows. "That's the lawyer."

"Say what?"

Prescott stopped several steps away and folded her arms. "Zack Wyler." She gave Zack a puzzled smile. "What are you doing here?"

She looked different without her glasses, without the hair pinned back. Less like a hard-core ballbuster. She had looked sharp and sleek as a lawyer, very corporate-chic. She had definitely looked good before, unusually attractive. Memorably attractive. But this was something else... another level. The softness of her eyes stood out and dominated the striking symmetry of her face, framed beautifully by the natural spill of her twisting curls. She was lit up with unguarded sex appeal, and as much time as she had probably spent on herself, somehow the look seemed effortless, as if leaving the business persona behind was a matter of snapping her fingers, or stepping out of a shadow. She was overwhelming.

Zack suddenly realized she was waiting for him to speak and couldn't immediately think of anything to say.

Donatello bailed him out. He stepped forward and nodded at the woman, glancing back at Zack. "I take it you two know each other already. Donatello Diaz, Philly P.D. Friend of Zack's. Pleasure, ma'am."

The woman's smile brightened. "Cassie Prescott. Nice to meet you, Mr. Diaz... officer." She leaned forward and shook his hand.

Donatello's eyebrows went up. "Detective."

"Right." The lawyer shrugged, looking back at Zack. "Are you... here for the wine?"

"No, no." Zack shook himself, shook his head. "Well, yes and no. Here..." He looked down and pulled an envelope out of his jacket pocket. "You want to tell me what this is about?" He held it out.

She looked at it blankly and shook her head.

Zack exhaled through his nostrils and opened the envelope, pulling out a check. "This... is from you, made out to me." He paused, lowering his brow. "What's up with the check?"

The woman paused, looking back at Zack. "And how was it exactly that you knew you could find me at the Convention Center?"

"I guess I must have convinced your office it was urgent."

"Urgent." She frowned. "My assistant would have told you I'd be back in the office tomorrow. I also have something called voice mail. Really, this couldn't wait?"

"Explain the check, counselor. What gives?" Zack kept his eyes on the lawyer, but at the edge of his vision, he caught a glimpse of Donatello turning toward him and frowning.

The woman sniffed, arching her eyebrows. "Okay. Most people don't get that bent out of shape when they get a check; I didn't think you'd have a problem with it." She cleared her throat. "We took another look at your contract with Hannah and decided we should reimburse you for your time. This way, we don't have to get into any discussions in the future about claims you may or may not have on us."

Zack waved the check. "We, huh? This isn't a check from the firm, this is a personal check from your own bank account." He laughed sarcastically. "Don't tell me you didn't let your partners in on this. Why not? I can't imagine why they would have a problem with a little extortion."

"Extortion? Nobody was holding a gun to your head, Mr. Wyler. Don't worry, my partners know about our discussion. I'm speaking for myself here, but ethics-wise, I think I'm okay."

Speaking for herself! Zack snorted. "Oh, you do, huh? So, say I countersue your partners for, I don't know, slandering my name, hurting my business, something like that. Still feeling okay about the way you handled things?"

Prescott scrunched her nose and nodded. "Legally speaking? I'm feeling pretty good about it, yeah." She shrugged. "It's not slander if it's true. Besides, I never did get around to the point of spreading bad press about you, so the point is pretty much moot."

"Of course. Silly me to think I was getting screwed."

She shot him a sharp look, and fluorescent light played in her brown eyes. "Maybe it didn't seem fair to you, but it was a legitimate complaint, and Hannah Adams has just as much right to representation as anyone else. She felt she wasn't given her money's worth of service, and I agreed to help. That's my job."

Zack glared at her. Hannah Adams could take her legitimate complaints and shove them up her tight, ignorant ass. "Oh, yeah. I don't know where my brain is—how could anyone think it wasn't fair? What possible reason could a guy like me have to be unhappy about having some lawyer interrupt his day to rip him a new one."

The woman's eyes narrowed. "Honestly, is it possible for you to not be a jerk for one second?" She put her hands on her hips and turned halfway around, facing away from the booths and shaking her head. She turned back around. "Look, it doesn't have anything to do with liability, okay? I sent the check because I thought you should get paid for your time."

Zack nodded, running his tongue around the inside of his mouth. He glanced at Donatello, who was holding two fingers against his cheek, pretending to look serious and pretending not to pay attention. Zack scratched his arm. "That's it, huh?"

Prescott held up her hands. "That's it." She sighed and looked at the floor. "Hannah might not agree, but under the circumstances, I think you did what you were asked to do."

"Damn right I did."

"So I sent you the check, so you don't get to go through life talking about how a couple of female lawyers screwed you out of contract for no good reason."

Zack stared at her flatly. "So this is a pity check? Is that what you're saying?"

"Call it whatever you like." The woman paused and traced a finger along a group of curls that brushed her face just above the curve of her cheekbone. "You don't want the check, tear it up. Be my guest."

Zack grimaced at the check. "I didn't even add everything up yet." He scratched the back of his head. "This is for 300—this is like a hundred more than I told you, and I'm not even sure it'll be that much. I still have to go over my statements."

The woman nodded at the floor. "Well, I did take up a little more of your time than you were counting on. Call the excess an additional consultation fee. Your time is valuable to you, right?" She rubbed the sides of her arms as if she had suddenly caught a chill.

Zack watched as she moved her hands, shifting her weight from one foot to the other. She had a thing with fidgeting, moving her hands and arms around all the time, never quite comfortable, but somehow she made it all seem more graceful than frenetic. His imagination, maybe. Now that he knew she was a princess.

So apparently, Cassandra Prescott was no stranger to throwing money around.

On the phone, the assistant had mentioned that her boss had "a family obligation" before saying exactly where the lawyer was. Once the assistant had given up the location, it had taken all of about two seconds to find out that the Prescotts were one of the wealthiest families in the Philadelphia area; the name was all over the press clippings about the wine-tasting event.

No stranger to throwing money around, but she hadn't come off that way at the café.

Zack squinted. "You don't have to do this, you know. I'll live without your money."

Prescott rolled her eyes and groaned. "Jesus, God—will you stop pretending you don't want the damn check? Men are unbelievable." She shook her head. "Just give me a little credit for trying to be nice, all right? Maybe I just feel, you know, marginally responsible for making the situation slightly worse than it had to be... possibly because I may have jumped to conclusions slightly, and it could possibly be argued that I should have known better, considering I may have, at some point, witnessed certain instances in the past in which Hannah Adams has, shall we say, been less than completely diplomatic."

Zack raised an eyebrow. "Is that an apology, counselor?"

Prescott pursed her lips. "Take the check, Mr. Wyler."

Zack glanced at Donatello. Donatello rolled his eyes and shook his head. "I think you're a damn fool. Take the check, Zack."

Zack glared at him, frowned, and took another long look at the lawyer, then stuffed the check back in the envelope, folded the envelope, and redeposited it in his jacket pocket. "Fine. I'll take it. How's that?"

The woman raised her eyebrows and her face broke out in a patronizing grin. She cocked her head. "There. Now, that wasn't so hard, was it?"

God, she was beautiful. Not fair. Zack scratched his cheek. "Thanks. Pleasure doing business with you. Tell your friends."

She nodded. "Don't push it, Mr. Wyler."

He smirked at the floor.

She glanced at the booth. "There are a few things I have to wrap up here, so I'm going to have to excuse myself now, if you don't mind." She smiled at Donatello. "Detective Diaz, again, nice to meet you."

Donatello flashed his teeth. "Right on, darlin'."

She looked back at Zack. "Mr. Wyler." She nodded again and started to leave. Zack gritted his teeth and took a quick step forward, shaking his head. "Wait a second."

She turned around, dropping her arms to her sides. "What now?"

Damn fool... that was about right. What the hell? "Look, just so you know... I'm a damn good private detective."

She stared.

"It's a pretty good bet you're not going to find a better detective in the Yellow Pages. Not in this city."

She scanned the room and smiled. "So you're modest too."

He jabbed his chest with a thumb. "I'm sorry if I was insulting to you. But believe it or not, running my business means a lot to me. I put a lot into it; it's what I do. And I take offense when somebody tells me how I'm supposed to do it." He nodded at her. "Look, I just want to hear you say one thing."

"And what would that be?" Prescott looked genuinely surprised.

He hesitated. It was a minor miracle she was still listening. "You were wrong about me. I want to hear you say it."

Both her eyebrows were raised. "You really don't know when to shut up, do you?"

He shoved his hands in his pockets and looked away, shaking his head. "No, I really don't."

She tilted her head back. "All right, if it makes you happy... yes, I do believe I was wrong about you. I'm sure you're very good at what you do, Mr. Wyler."

"And another thing—no more of this Mr. Wyler shit. Call me Wyler or call me Zack, but don't call me mister. I hate that."

She folded her arms. "Okay. If I ever have the occasion to address you by name again, I'll be sure to remember that. Bye, guys. Enjoy the wine." She smiled as she turned away, stepping around toward the rear of the booth.

Zack watched her until she disappeared. "She likes me."

Donatello was glaring at him. "I know you don't really think that, because if you did, you would be doing something about that. Because what I just saw was some damn stupid shit, chief."

Nice. Zack exhaled and focused on another tent. "Let's go get some more wine before they shut this thing down."

Donatello shook his head. "I can't believe I let your white ass drag me out here to watch that sorry shit I just saw. You didn't even do anything— you just came out here and waved that damn check around."

Zack ignored him and started toward the tent.

"Fool, you owe me big time. Making me pass on the Phillies game. I hope it was worth it."

Zack laughed to himself. Donatello was full of shit. There was no chance in hell he hadn't enjoyed every last second of it. It was worth it just to see Cassandra Prescott in an evening gown, and it would have been worth the price of admission if they hadn't tasted a drop of vino. Of course, a snoot-full sure wouldn't have made it any less enjoyable.

He took another glance over his shoulder in the general vicinity of the booths. No sign of Prescott. Probably already off entertaining her daddy's sauna buddies, or hopping a private jet to a society-page wedding somewhere. She was definitely something else.

He shook his head and crossed the orange bubblegum path toward the nearest wine-covered table.

IX EXCAVATION

"So the key to virtual immortality lay locked in the past, and the key to unlocking the past lay dormant for over 900 years. Such is often the way of the great discoveries... the fledgling long waits for his wings to develop, and then rushes to the end of the limb the moment he can feel the air, never testing for an ideal wind. And often, those who are carried on these pivotal moments do not fully understand the consequences of their actions... indeed, some of the secrets of the universe were never meant to be discovered by sentients who would dive into action before careful consideration, let alone those who would abuse the natural laws for their personal gain."

... GCL FN.036

Phi 78 24 37.00 / Theta −20 39 56.90 / Rho 35.26 / JD 3040385

Kappa Pegasi: USTINOV; "Eo-Nowar"; 10 March 3612 CE

/1. Temporal dynamics and flight parameters.

    /...

    /1.3. Time expands at two different rates of acceleration relative to the cosmic points of maximum to minimum density in the material dimensions; each rate increases through a series of integral phase shifts dictated by a definable mathematic progression and a minimum basis interval, creating 511 distinct epochs. The real space basis in D1–D4 is the familiar unit of Planck time, $tP(R) = 1.708E{-}51$ y , expanding geometrically: R { $\Sigma^{\wedge}511 = 2^{\wedge}(i-1) * ((2^{\wedge}i) - 1)$; the structural space basis in D5–D6 is a rescalar ratio, $t(S) / t(R) = 4.788(E{+}53)X$, $tP(S) = 817.952$ y , expanding arithmetically: S { $\Sigma^{\wedge}511 = (i^{\wedge}2 + i) / 2$. At the end of phase shift 511, from singularity to zero entropy maximum expanse, the total time elapsed in D1–D4 is $5.118(E{+}256)$ y, while the total time elapsed in D5–D6 is $1.830(E{+}10)$ y. During early cosmic phase shifts, time passes much more rapidly in real space; during late phase shifts, time passes much more rapidly in hyperspace. Applicable expedition points fall within a range where hyperspace time is reduced relative to real space.

    /1.4. Past points along the cosmic timeline are accessible via velocity-based progression from D6 to D7, virtual inertial progression to D8, and virtual vector dodecaplex navigation within D8 to a temporal access point identified with the time preceding the target point. Regression from D8 is viable to any of D1–D7 along a line of harmonic resonance; harmonic resonance lines occur within epoch 98 at $1.327(E{+}8)$ y, the moment the total time elapsed is proportionate between the dual rates of temporal expansion, where equilibrium exists and at doubling convergent series ratios radiating toward the past and future extremes.

/1.5. The initial destination will bring the ship to epoch 99 at 5.474(E+8) y, some 13.2 billion years prior to the departure point. The first destination of the flight plan lies directly on the dimensional harmonic resonance line, since an exact date is not required for the purposes of the expedition; no travel time to reach a subsequent post-resonance point will be required in the first segment. The ship will reach the information eigenspaces through standard acceleration, requiring an estimated maximum 1,356.460 seconds, after which it will transcend temporal constraints and pre-plotted coordinates will guide it to the specified target point. ETT: +/− 4.436E−5 y. FHR: Negligible. MOE: 5.400E−8.

/1.6. For return to the modern era, the target date lies some 4.5 billion years after the preceding point of resonance in real space, beyond sustainability limitations for real space; therefore, travel to the second destination point must be completed in hyperspace. The equivalent time displacement from resonance in D5 hyperspace is some 1.2 million years, which is viable under given ship and on-board capabilities.

/1.7. The ship will repeat the dimensional progression sequence, with added navigational coordination to reduce timetable. Regression from D8 will allow for readdress of ship velocity above the aeonic and entelechial phase points, enabling near light speed at L−0.274(E−7) and a resulting Lorentz tau gamma dilation that will further reduce the relative travel time to some 878.4 years. ETT: +8.784(E+2) y. FHR: 4.284E−6; within STD FTL acceptable risk level. MOE: 5.400E−8.

They were outside, floating in an arc formation. 14 of them. Salaman could hear them, but Jajqrt170 couldn't. They had an organic mental connection with Salaman. A tap.

They were nothing to her, no more than a horde of gigantic foodroots. But gradually, they were getting to Salaman, making him forget who he was.

Nine months. Salaman had been in the Large Magellanic Cloud for nine months without a single communiqué to the Galaxy, observing the ytaoans, programming her and the on-board. Never trying to explain anything. But he had always remained focused—that was one thing that had never changed. At times, he still seemed sane.

The program was installed. Salaman was moving toward the airlock…

Another memory washed into focus, much more recent. Familiar. Jayjay opened her eyes. Dexter Massengill's face was centimeters from her own, in shadowy low resolution under the reduced cabin lighting. Traces of the even arcs of eyebrow and the subtle dimples and lines of the mouth barely registered, half brushed away by darkness… the high forehead and moderate narrowness of the skull were unmistakable in silhouette.

His face, his affect, everything about him was as familiar as anything she could remember, but now he looked different. Felt different. The combined impressions of comfort and excitement had been there in some form for a long time, but now it was distinctly more intense.

They were together, lying in one of the berths. She stirred against him, and the warmth of his body tripped receptors all over the surface of her skin.

"Jayjay? Is there something wrong?" Dexter nudged her. His hand was on her waist. "You look a bit unsettled. Were you dreaming?"

She blinked. "Dreaming. Yes." Salaman and the ytaoans. For 909 years she had been burning to recall the lost memories; now the lost months were jam-packed in the space of a nanosecond, set to flash across her neocortical net at the slightest prompting.

"Well. That's healthy, I'm sure." Dexter found her hand and grinned. "Nothing wrong with a little dreaming to take you away after an exhausting day." He winked at her.

She rolled away from him and sighed, pulling the sheet over herself and letting her head sink back into the cushion. She closed her eyes and suddenly thought of Salaman again, walking toward the airlock, his back turned. She shook herself and refocused on Dexter.

Dexter was still staring at her, grinning like an idiot. He raised an eyebrow. "The cabin air seems strangely refreshing just now. Wouldn't you say?"

She blinked at him and smiled. "Very refreshing."

He leaned close and kissed her lips, tracing a line up her back with his fingers. She responded, touching his face. Everything about him was deeply familiar, as if they had been intimate for much longer than a single day. It was that sudden lack of reserve, maybe. His resting expression had always had a sort of naturally oblivious, bright-eyed confidence, but there had always been an element of reserve when he had looked at her. Now there was a tangible aura of complete openness.

She pulled back and stared at his eyes, stroking his hair. "You're definitely one of a kind, Mr. Massengill."

He nodded. "I wouldn't have it any other way." He suddenly looked thoughtful. "Can you imagine if there were copies of me traipsing through the Galaxy?"

Jayjay propped herself up on one elbow. "That's a slightly scary thought."

"Well, for the casino owners, maybe." He exhaled loudly, wrapping an arm behind his head and settling back down on the mattress. He didn't look as if he planned to get up anytime soon. "I would think there might be a lot more satisfied androids if there were more of me bopping around." He peered at her.

Jayjay climbed on top of him. "But the Galaxy would be a lot less productive." She narrowed her eyes, smiling.

"In some ways."

She kissed him again. Dexter drew her in, guiding her head lightly with one hand, running his fingers through her hair. Then his other hand was on her back, just off the left shoulder support that capped the upper lateral framework of her kinematic chain, pressing her closer with surprising force, then sliding down along the bumps of the superficially rounded bands of her ribs. Then the visualized points of contact dropped out of focus and blended into a soft, wild outburst of untimed sensory input.

Dexter's rhythm changed subtly. He shifted, rolling her gently to his left and exhaled, staring up at the ceiling and again looking thoroughly relaxed. "I did mean what I said about making a contribution to society, joining the ranks of the skilled human workforce. Making an honest man out of myself."

Jayjay studied him. Given his current condition, the idea of Dexter being industrious was a little too irresistible at that particular moment. She smirked and gave him another quick kiss.

He was alluding to the message from Salaman, as reluctant as he was to broach the subject. The idea of traveling time had to have interested him. It was right up his alley, really… a pioneering adventure, something ideal for a nomadic star-hopper with virtually no family ties, and it had landed in his lap right at the moment he was looking to get away from the gaming scene.

He had other ideas on a potential occupation, none of which he had any qualms about mentioning to her, but it was Salaman's task that he really wanted to do. It was only a matter of time before he worked it into the conversation.

Nine months. She sighed. Inevitable or not, she wasn't going to be the one to bring it up.

She rolled off the berth, stood, and stepped to the galley bar. The slinky silk one-piece she had worn for less than an hour was bunched haphazardly near the edge of the countertop, exactly where she had discarded it. "Well you're above-average in both coding and electronics… that qualifies you to do just about whatever you want. The problem with you is that you don't know what you want to do." She glanced back at Dexter and slipped the dress over her head, sliding her arms through the cap sleeves.

Dexter nodded vaguely, scanning her as she straightened the dress over her hips. "Too true." The look was cartoonishly lascivious; he might have been exaggerating as a tacky goof, but there was good chance he was actually trying to emanate sex appeal.

She smirked and glanced at the floor. "You talk about Pike a lot, how I need to see the Reed Country. I wouldn't mind going there."

"Yes, I'm sure." Dexter pursed his lips and focused on her eyes. "Jayjay, what was it exactly—the thing that was distracting you?"

Jayjay frowned. There it was. She turned and moved behind the bar, popping open a drawer along the rear counter and taking out a star tours catalog.

Dexter let out a loud breath and raised his voice a touch. "I'll wager I can guess what it was."

Jayjay leveled her eyes at him. He was most likely going to persist in ignoring her subject for his, but two could play at that game. "I asked you first. Pike? What do you think? I distinctly remember a complaint about how we never remember to see the leas in Icthylion when they're in season." She set the catalog on the counter and tapped the power button, pulling up an alphabetical list of tourist spots. She zipped through the entries to the Ekseniya System. "And I happened to notice… summer is just about to begin in Icthylion."

Dexter squinted. "Icthylion. It's a beautiful place, but it's a little quiet. I'm not sure I'm quite ready to settle down in one place just yet, Jayjay." He sniffed. "I used to think I might try my hand at being a park ranger in the Reeds, but that was a long time ago."

The catalog had lots of pictures under the planet's listing—the display showed a smattering of lush, green, rolling hills and enormous catalpa trees; the throwback castles of Rileram Court, and scenes from metro restaurants in Harveston. A panoramic view showed a tchak boat trolling through a maize expanse of Massillon's famous phragmite wetlands. Normally, Dexter would dive in head-first at the first mention of a new and unique place. "No one's saying you have to settle down. Pike is just a suggestion—I just thought it might be a nice place to start, if you're looking for a change of pace." She shrugged. "It's up to you."

He nodded, sitting up and adjusting the edge of the sheet. "Well, you have a say too, Jayjay—I'm not going to twist your arm to go anywhere. I'd like to think we could work something out, come to some sort of mutual agreement on the ideal location." He grinned, almost swaggering. "Your comfort is my number one priority."

"Is that right?" Jayjay cocked her head without looking up. "You could have fooled me."

He yawned. "Well, yes. I suppose it all depends on whether you've come to your senses about making time with a derelict." He stuck out an arm and scratched his side, and the image of a gibbon sprang immediately to mind. "Where do you stand on that, Jayjay?"

Jayjay laughed to herself. Very different evolutionary origins for two beings as physically compatible as they were. "An often dense and insensitive derelict." She shot him a hard look. "Hmm. Can I get back to you on that?"

He blinked, raising his eyebrows. His smile got a little drier. He rubbed his mouth.

Jayjay shook her head, tapping the portable information carrier display and riffling through the electronic pages of the catalog. "Listen, I'm not kidding, Dexter—if you don't want to commit to something right away, that's fine, but if you really don't want to go to Pike we should figure out our itinerary, whether it's snow-skiing in Ekaterina, a trip to the Foazza Gardens, or whatever you want to do, because I really don't want to stay here any longer than we have to." She glanced at him. "Balboa said he'd get back to us quickly. It's been over five hours now—we are free and clear, right?"

Dexter rubbed his shoulder. "He said we were, yes." He paused and frowned at the ground. "It's about Salaman and the ytaoans, isn't it? The Tarantula Nebula—that's what you were thinking of, wasn't it?"

Jayjay pressed her lips together and continued to stare at the catalog.

"Am I right? I can't imagine you'd be preoccupied with anything else."

Jayjay frowned. "No, I can't imagine I would."

"Yes, I know. Insensitive." Dexter exhaled. "Jayjay, you know this already, but now that you remember what happened, it might help to talk about it—it will reinforce your mnemonics, and I'm guessing it will help you psychologically. Of course I'm curious as well, I'm sure I don't have to tell you that, but if you never want to say a word about it, I completely understand. It's just… if it bothers you, you shouldn't keep it bottled up. You need to know you're not alone."

Jayjay turned and dropped the catalog back in the drawer. Dexter was who he was, and ultimately he was trying to be helpful. In his bumbling, simian way.

Dexter abruptly tossed off his sheet and swung his legs to the floor. "These replaced experiences are going to read like new data. Just remind yourself consciously that the events of the past are just that. Salaman is long gone. Before long, the files will seat, and you'll be back to normal. So don't let it get to you too much."

Easy for him to say. Jayjay brushed her bangs. "I do know all this already. I get to read the techs' generic treatment guidelines too. Not to mention I've had about 909 years to learn about memory blocks, but thank you. Very sweet." She nodded at the cockpit. "Last chance to pick our next destination before I do it myself."

"I can't think much beyond spending more time with you right here in this berth." Dexter grinned lazily, then stretched and patted his chest, squinting up at the event timer above the back portal to the galley. "Nothing jumps to mind. I guess you'll have to surprise me."

Jayjay followed his eyes, glancing over her shoulder. The lime green digits read 20:37—already nearly a full Earth day since the engines had been on. They were probably fine; Dexter's settlement was apparently secured, and clearance delays were common enough. Still, settlement or no settlement, she wasn't going to be comfortable until Kappa Pegasi A and Ustinov were falling away in the Explorer's exhaust trail.

Dexter was on his feet, tapping his chin with a finger and looking in the general vicinity of the floor. Light from the cockpit caught the tall, thin, sinewy frame of his naked body as he stood there, hesitating. He was having trouble relocating his clothes, maybe. Jayjay looked down, burying a smile as she sat back against the galley counter.

He stooped and picked his slacks off the floor directly in front of him. "Actually, one thing does come to mind, to be perfectly honest. As long as we're talking about destinations." He half-turned, pulling his slacks up his legs. "Although I'm guessing you don't really want to talk about it."

Jayjay folded her arms and nodded, looking down. "You want to talk about Salaman's message."

He glanced around at the floor and located his shirt. He looked up as he put it on. "I'm not saying I necessarily want to make it the next thing we do, but I think at some point we're going to have to discuss this." He stepped to the galley and moved to Jayjay's side, leaning against the counter next to her. He shook his head. "Wouldn't you say?" He nudged her with his shoulder.

Jayjay shrugged away from him, shifting incrementally to her left, flicking her eyes toward the portside end of the bar. Dexter was being about as considerate as he was capable of. He was acutely aware of how she felt about it, and he had taken a good two hours to address it beyond the cursory acknowledgement of the fact that a node of data wedged in the programming of her photovoltaic arrays had been the cause of the system failures.

It might have been better if he had approached with his normal social ineptitude. This way, he was giving her no valid reason to be mad at him.

Dexter edged close again, touching her arm, then moving his hand to the center of her back. "All right, Jayjay, can I just say something?"

She tipped her head back and dropped her hands to her sides, lightly touching the surface of the drawers behind her. She looked blankly back at him, shaking her head. "Yes?"

He scratched his ear. "I appreciate what you've been through, and I'm aware any talk about Salaman is probably taboo right now, and that's all perfectly understandable, but frankly, the sort of information he left—these revelations about space and time, and this breakthrough navigational technique involving elevated hyperspace—this demands to be looked into, don't you think?" He paused, turning fully toward her. "He did send the message to me personally. You know me—something like this is going to keep bugging me until I get it out of my system." He half-smiled. His brow was knit, and his dark eyes were full of strange, overly intense empathy, as if he was trying to prove his sincerity. Some expressions never quite looked right on his face.

Jayjay avoided his eyes, focusing on his thin lips and the dimple at the center of his chin. Dexter was nothing if not genuine, in his muddling, naive way. She nodded, narrowing her eyes. "I get it. We need to have the conversation, I know. But you need to be aware that Salaman was insane. Definitively... he developed a god complex and programmed me to shut down so I couldn't stop him from ejecting himself out the airlock. He killed himself. If you're considering following through on what he asked you to do in his message, you need to take into account who you're dealing with."

Dexter stared for a moment, straightening. "He killed himself?" He lowered his brow. "Why would he do that?"

"He wasn't rational." Jayjay paced to the portside bend of the countertop and settled there, looking back at Dexter. "Think about what he's asking you to do—he wants you to disregard all the basic safety protocols and lay in a 4 billion-year flight pattern, trusting his word alone that the laws of physics we've been following throughout the history of spaceflight won't apply. I think you're familiar with those laws... they're the ones that cause the durable, stasis-enhanced circuitry that's been in cillian ships for eons to wear down every 50 years or so. Reservoir battery cells can last about 20. Hull plating and drive components, maybe ten. 4 billion years... the longest spaceflight on record is something like 430 years, and that was before hyperspace. No one's ever even lived in a prolonged hyperspace loop for anything over a week or so."

Dexter seemed to ponder the thought. "It's a fair point. But Salaman did offer an explanation for all that. On the contrary, whatever his emotional state of mind happened to be, his message sounded extremely rational."

Jayjay nodded. "Yes I know, he says there's no physical degeneration in the upper eigenspaces. There's absolutely no way to prove that. Salaman's calculations were meticulous, but you'd be flying blind. Even if this method he's left for navigation in these elevated dimensions works, his information has to be 100 percent perfect, and the on-board has to process all of it without any errors. Otherwise, neither the ship nor anything inside the ship will maintain its integrity, and you'll be dead before you ever find out about ship wear and tear in the upper dimensions, not to mention whether Salaman's recipe for surviving thallium pentacyanide poisoning and hyperspacial dementia is valid."

Dexter continued to look back at her as if he were reading streamed data directly through her eyes. "Clearly there's risk involved. What about the validity—what's your sense? I mean, I have to say, given the level of detail, it did seem very real to me."

The vent above the galley was blowing lightly but steadily, not far from the back of her neck. The ship had been inactive a long time, and the environmental filters were getting saturated with the trapped condensation from Eo-Nowar's muggy base-level air. It was about time for a climate control adjustment.

"True, there was a lot of detail." Jayjay frowned and touched the skin of her left forearm in the area of her embedded com transmitter. She was still isolated from the on-board, cut-off to avoid neocortical distractions during her interlude with Dexter. She was going to have to reconnect manually before she could fix the ventilation. She shook her head. "I'm not saying his message is necessarily inaccurate—maybe he really was able to compile this sort of specific data from the ytaoans. If anyone knows about the eigenspaces, I'd think it would be them. I think based on his state of mind, it's likely he did imagine or embellish some of it, but I'm sure he was doing his best to relay accurate data. There's probably some truth to it. If you like, I can run some validity tests to check whether the functionality is sound, but I'm not in any real hurry to dive back into all this. Unfortunately, there aren't any tests that will make it safe."

Dexter drummed his fingers against the countertop. "So you do think it's possible the ytaoans have this knowledge—these secrets to the mastery of space and time. That would essentially make them gods, wouldn't it, more or less? You think they're some kind of guardians for the universe?"

Jayjay shrugged. "They had Salaman convinced." The initial graphic extrapolations Salaman had run on the Dusk Cruiser's viewer had offered glimpses of a few of the photovores, lit in the glow of the ambient nebula dust. The enhanced iris input data from the external cams had revealed ridges and striped patterns on the concise, rounded spaceborne bodies. Subtle shades of yellow and brown... they had looked more like protozoans on a slide projection than shuttlecraft-sized beings floating in space. Salaman had only imaged them several times, right after arriving. After that, he had claimed he could see them much more clearly in his head.

She rubbed her neck and started as the fabric of the silk one-piece brushed against her upper body, registering the microscopic consistency in the texture. She widened her eyes. "I'll say this, they're legitimately powerful. Their brains are physiologically massive—the brain/body mass ratio is something like 0.978." She paused. "They were influencing Salaman, feeding him information, and he couldn't handle it. Or he did exactly what they wanted him to do."

Dexter was silent for a moment. "You're saying you think the ytaoans might have been instrumental in his suicide?"

Jayjay gave him a hard look. "All I know is he changed. He was a biologist, and he was completely single-minded before we went to the Tarantula Nebula, working exclusively on a four-year study of interstellar microbes. He had no background in cosmology. Once he made contact with the ytaoans, he lost interest in everything he had been working on and became obsessed with astrophysics, celestial and quantum mechanics, and the transcription of topological mathematics." She stepped to the bar and rested her hands, staring ahead toward the cockpit. "Maybe there was no intent to harm, but they affected him. One way or another, he died as a result of their influence. Before the nebula, he was too much of an egomaniac to kill himself."

Dexter nodded at the floor. "Well. I'm glad they didn't have the same effect on you."

Jayjay blinked. "They never even made any attempt to contact me. Maybe they do have all these answers to the questions that have been puzzling scientists for thousands of years, but if they do, there's no direct evidence of it. As far as I'm concerned, they don't know any more about the universe than single-celled interstellar microbes." She paused. "Dexter, I'm going to check back with ENMC—we should have heard something by now."

Dexter waved at the cockpit. "Go right ahead. I'm sure everything's fine. We might not be at the top of Constable Balboa's priority list, since there's no longer a question of my status."

Yet they were still stuck in the system until further notice. Jayjay pushed past Dexter and headed to the cockpit. Balboa might not have been good about making personal calls, but there should have at least been a clearance update message from the Port Authority. Ustinov had some unique protocols with its traffic, but the planet wasn't completely back-woods.

She dropped into the command seat and keyed the access window, leaning over the console. SOFT phosphor alphanumerics confirmed the remote access path to the on-board was closed. She tapped in the restore command and stared at the display glass. The on-board wasn't letting her in... manual access mode was locked.

She frowned and expanded the description. Green text flashed in a second window. A command redirect override from an external source was locking her out of main engine access and flight control. The com and caution-warning system were temporarily deactivated, and a scan of com records was underway—a bridgehead tap, relayed locally, with an Irina sector extension code... CZ006-485. Clearly IPA signature.

Blasted guidestars. Either the case was still active or the gaming people had found a new way to go after Dexter. It figured—the settlement had been too easy. She reactivated the com and alerts. The boarding light indicator flashed and the double-tone perimeter bell sounded.

She stood and glanced around, checking through the glareshield and side windows. Two people were hanging back at the edge of the pier platform on the portside.

She sat back down and ran a quick infrared proximity sweep, opening a separate view through the hatch cam. A man and a woman were talking to one another in the frame. The man was in a green, nondescript suit—typical IPA. The woman looked much more striking, with dark skin and straight black, pinned-back hair, wearing a sleek black suit, more corporate than scarab. The woman turned and stepped out of view as the man tapped a lapel com.

Jayjay's eyes flicked back to the green text in front of her. According to the infrared, there were now six people on the platform outside. The Explorer was now the only ship docked at the pier, but two cars were on the landing pad toward the stern.

Dexter appeared in the companionway. "The light's on. Someone's at the hatch?"

On a routine IPA check, the agents usually hailed the ship; this time, they weren't bothering. Jayjay sighed. "The IPA has us locked down, and they are scanning us. Apparently, they're not quite finished with us yet."

"What?" Dexter looked immediately out the portside window, then turned to the cam view on the display glass.

"Hold on." Jayjay tapped in a bypass command. The on-board didn't respond. She shook her head. There was virtually no chance she was going to be able to break an IPA override. "Did you actually hear their advocate agree to the settlement terms?"

Dexter nodded quickly. "I was right there when they made the arrangements with the IPA. This is completely outrageous!" He folded his arms. "This was all settled. I have no idea what they're looking for now—they can't come after me after they dropped the grifting charge, can they? They've already acknowledged the remaining CU belongs to me... it's all on file. What are they doing, Jayjay? Could it be a miscommunication?"

File transfer errors happened, but direct surveillance and seizure was aggressive treatment for someone who already had an advocate. This read more like a favor for an influential plaintiff. Jayjay shook her head. "I doubt it. We'd better ask." She glanced at Dexter and activated the com. "Can we help you?"

The agent at the hatch looked up at the cam. "Senior Field Agent Camphong, IPA SID. Are you the IU?"

"Yes."

The man glanced to his left. "Zenith Explorer, ship registration LGAB-1216... we have that Dexter Massengill is the pilot. Is he aboard?"

Jayjay paused, exchanging glances with Dexter. She held up a finger, shaking her head quickly. "He's here. Agent, we're waiting for clearance to leave port, and we're not sure what this is about—could you clear that up for us?"

The man nodded, looking down and pulling a porter out of his coat pocket. "We have an order to impound this vehicle until further notice. We need you to disembark so we can search the interior." He squinted at the cam. "I need to speak to Mr. Massengill directly—can you have him step to the com?"

Dexter moved next to Jayjay's seat. "Yes, I'm Dexter Massengill. Listen, I think there may be some sort of mistake here... if this is about the Blue Topaz Casino matter, we settled that a few hours ago. I'm being represented locally, so if there's an outstanding issue, you need to contact Constable Balboa of ENMC."

The man nodded again, tracing a hand down along the closed button line of his jacket. "Agent Camphong, IPA SID. Mr. Massengill, we're going to need your ship for a little while. I'm aware of your recent case, I understand it was resolved, but I have new a filing from Transworld Bareilli HC." He glanced at the porter. "The complete details of the claim will be made available to you within the hour, but basically it alleges you are in possession of proprietary information of an affiliated company called the Grand High Entertainment Group based on Valentina. According to the claim, you are in violation of UCCS 567.6, which has to do with privacy of internal corporate practices and carries various fines and penalties. Irina and local authorities have jointly issued a warrant to search your ship and run a clean sweep of all on-board systems. If we do find evidence of a violation, you'll have the opportunity to respond to the claim through representation by an advocate of your choosing." He paused, shifting his weight. "Do you understand everything I've said to you, Mr. Massengill?"

Dexter leaned over the com, glaring at the cam view on the PDG. "Excuse me? Do I understand it?"

"Do you understand everything I've said to you? Do you need me to go over it again?"

Dexter opened his mouth and shook his head. He looked at Jayjay. Jayjay nodded and motioned at the com. Dexter closed his eyes and waved a hand. "No... yes, I understand, I understand what you said, but I'm not in possession of any—"

The agent cut him off. "We'll sort out your response to the claim later, but for now, I need you to disembark. The IU will have to stay on board to provide us with assistance to the on-board if we need it. I can tell you the process will go more smoothly if you don't attempt to impede our investigation... that is, don't tamper with the on-board, don't attempt to destroy any information, and don't attempt to leave port on this or any other vehicle until we tell you." The man exhaled, tipping his head back. "We're in control of your ship now, and you have ten minutes to disembark. After that we board with or without your permission."

Dexter frowned. "Ridiculous. I'm sorry, but that's just not acceptable. I'm not going to accept anyone aboard my ship until I talk to my advocate."

Jayjay glanced at an empty area of the PDG. These agents weren't concerned about a local advocate, and giving them a hard time wasn't going to make them want to move any faster.

The woman in black stepped back into the picture below the hatch. Her face remained down and obscured by the overhead angle, almost as if she was consciously trying to avoid the cam, but Dexter seemed to fix on her immediately, staring at the view frame. His mouth tightened.

The IPA agent coughed into his fist. "Ten minutes, Mr. Massengill. We'll get started as soon as you're off."

Dexter shook his head and stepped to the portside window, then whirled, stalking back to the command seat and jabbing a finger at the console. "You have no business doing what you're doing…"

Jayjay grabbed his arm. "When can we have our ship back?"

The agent was peering up at the ocellus as if he could see who he was talking to. "If you aren't in possession of the information, you'll get your vehicle back when we complete our examination. You'll get your clearance and you'll be free to go. For now, you're not authorized to leave this location."

The agent backed away and the woman moved to the center of the frame, looking up. She had a narrow face and black, penetrating eyes. "Mr. Massengill, my name is Ritsa Rabani. I represent Transworld Bareilli."

Dexter was staring darkly back at the view frame. "I know who you are."

The woman nodded once, keeping her eyes deadlocked on the ocellus. "There is an alternative. My company has a need for a people with your skill set; we believe you have developed a particular methodology for success that could be a great benefit to an organization like ours if you are able and willing to replicate it while working with us. We are prepared to drop all complaints if you agree to share your experience in a consultant capacity. We would of course compensate you for your time, and should you qualify through our initial screening process, we may be able to offer an extended contract contingent upon your performance through the probationary employment period."

Dexter gaped, stepping back from the console, staring at the glareshield. He raised a hand to his forehead, touching it as if he thought it might explode. "You're offering me employment?" He held out his hands, shaking his head. "You tried to kill me yourself. To execute me." He raised his voice. "Did you hear that, Agent… Camphong, or whatever your name was? IPA officers out there, listening in? This woman was operating a kill team! At the behest of the Blue Topaz Casino—this Transworld Bareilli HC."

They were on record. Jayjay spun toward Dexter. His settlement with the casino included a gag order, and he was going to blow it. Jayjay hissed. "Bugs, Dexter, you can't say that…"

But Rabani remained impassive. She nodded again. "What may or may

284

not have happened in the past is not our concern, and should not be yours, since there is no longer any record of those claims." The slightest hint of a smile appeared at the corner of her mouth. Sheer, silky-smooth confidence. "You have our proposal. It's your choice. Our company offers fine opportunities to those skilled in the business of credit augmentation."

Dexter exhaled raggedly, tapping the side of his leg with a fist. He raised his eyebrows at Jayjay, his jaw clenched.

Jayjay rolled her eyes toward the com. "Give us a minute." She shut it off and sighed. "You have to think before you speak. You're giving them ammunition, and you're jeopardizing the settlement you actually do have."

"But Jayjay, she was there, leading the way—if she had her way, I'd be dead." He was completely exasperated, breathing rapidly through his nose, his eyes wild and intense. He looked like a different person. "They think I'm going to work for them after all this, after everything that's happened?"

"Calm." Jayjay stood and patted him on the arms. "They think you're a mercenary. Mercenaries don't take things personally. Just forget about the offer—no one's going to make you work for them. This is all probably just a ploy to get you to take them up on it, so just forget about it. All right?" She looked up at him, touching his face. "All right?"

He focused on her gradually, slowing his breathing. He nodded. "Right. You're right—of course, you're right. I'll try to keep my mouth shut."

She gave him a squeeze on the arm. "We should just let them in, Dexter. If we give them a hard time, it will only make things worse."

He ran a hand through his hair. "They have no business going in our private files, Jayjay—I did not steal any proprietary information."

"I know that." She glanced at the view beneath the hatch. "Now we just have to hope they don't try to plant something incriminating." She frowned. If the holding company people had enough pull to sway an IPA detachment to plant evidence, they had all the leverage they needed.

"Jayjay…"

She gripped his shoulder and looked up at him. "You need to get in touch with Balboa, find out where we stand. If we have to fend off more accusations, that's what we'll do, but hopefully once they know you aren't using stolen data to infiltrate the casinos, they'll leave you alone."

Dexter frowned back at her. "What about you—they can just keep you locked in here as long as they please? What about the Definitions of Species?"

Jayjay's eyes drifted down toward the center of Dexter's chest. The articles of AIE rights—in the Human Sphere, there were specific restrictions against punishing artificially intelligent entities for the actions of their biologically born associates. Good thought. "It depends on how long they try to keep it going, but we might be able to get some traction with that if they give us more trouble. My guess is they'll only keep me on board until they're done their scans. Just find Balboa. He'll make sure they follow protocol."

Dexter nodded and looked down, putting his hands on Jayjay's hips. "You can be sure I'm never going to agree to work with these people. Put me in prison, take my CU. I don't care." He smiled thinly. "They couldn't possibly keep me in there for more than a year, could they? I could manage that."

Jayjay kissed him. "Let's not let it get to that. Now go, let's get this over with. Find your advocate." She steered him to the companionway and stepped back to the com. "Stand by... we're opening up. Feel free to board." She leaned to the right edge of the console, flipped the lock toggle switch, and tapped the ramp button. Low-threshold microservos whirred lightly in the recesses of the hull plating as the gangway lowered toward the platform.

Dexter made his way to the edge of the ladderwell and stood aside as the first pair of agents came aboard. He looked back toward the cockpit one last time and flashed a smile before disappearing down the steps.

Jayjay turned back to the PDG and watched him cross in front of the ocellus. Ritsa Rabani was still in view to the right of the ramp, nodding as she touched her ear. Reporting back to her employer—the senator from Anastasia, according to Balboa. The man was going to an exorbitant amount of trouble on a fishing expedition... mining for luck. The man obviously thought he had something with Dexter. He might have thought otherwise if he spent about five minutes in a personal conversation with him. Apparently this senator wasn't one of the more rational people to dabble in the gaming business.

They weren't completely at this company's mercy—Dexter had recourse, and Balboa had helped before. If rationality and logic had any sway, the company would cut its losses and leave them alone. And hopefully Dexter did have a little of that luck left in the bag.

Dexter moved out of frame. Jayjay closed the panel and turned to face the companionway.

*   *   *

Eo-Nowar Municipal Control Central looked vastly larger from inside than it did from the city walkways, more like a spaceport concourse than the lobby of a civic facility. The whole of it took up the full hectare allotment per block and extended from the second-lowest level to the top of the city, the atrium alone covering the bottom third. Sidelong rectangular entryways stretched across the front, leaving the cavernous block open to the public while the threshold security fields remained inactive, which by the looks of things was practically round the clock.

Most of the floor was wide open, with public convenience areas spread around the perimeter and reception islands scattered over the gray expanse of steel and pewter parquet. The place had the same loosely enclosed feel of the walkways and streets of air. Massive load-bearing beams were left uncovered in the build of the towering walls, exposing the city's structural framework, and the inside-out impression was further reinforced by the diffuse, unobtrusive, low-intensity glow of the Fresnel tile lamps that checkered the distant ceiling, as dim and even as the filtered dome light on the outside. In between the girders and trusses, paired lifts ran from the floor through the ceiling, strung around the huge room like vertical strands of binding cable. The platforms within shined through the clear polyglass tubing, breathing life into the walls as they carried people rapidly up and down.

Dexter moved inside, glancing around and soaking in the breadth of the place as he snaked his way among the sporadic foot traffic. The atrium wasn't at full capacity by any means, yet people seemed to be everywhere, some hurrying in random directions, some strolling aimlessly or standing idly. More space to move around encouraged a more active use of the space, perhaps. Different people on different schedules... the broad mix served as another reminder of Ustinov's nondiurnal aspect.

Dexter slowed as a man in shabbily draped clothing came stumbling in from the left, grumbling to himself. Dexter kept his eyes on him for a moment more, then picked his way through a slow-moving group and headed for the nearest reception area. Seating fanned out around a rhombicube booth unit with four open sides, each face dominated by a widescreen overhead viewing panel. For the moment, the seats were deserted and there appeared to be one person attending the booth—a thin, pale woman with short, electric violet hair.

Dexter nodded as he stepped to the booth. "Excuse me." He patted the countertop with both hands. "I hope you can help me—I need to speak with Constable Dig Balboa.

The woman moved to his side of the rhombicube. "Yes, one moment." She made a few subtle motions behind the counter and looked down as a display panel appeared in front of her. "Is this regarding a pending case file?"

Dexter glanced at the two lines of phosphor text floating within the black background. The projection was removed from the surface at a slight angle, just enough to make the green lettering impossible to read from the opposite side. "I believe the case file is closed, actually." He paused, moving squarely in front of the woman. "Constable Balboa recently represented me, and I need to speak with him, if that's possible. It's rather important."

The woman raised her razor-thin eyebrows, exposing a touch of fairly heavily applied lavender eye shadow. "Do you have his RC extension?"

Dexter pursed his lips. "Actually, I don't. He told me to go through the ENMC channel from my ship, but I don't have access to my ship at the moment."

"Mey-bu." The woman stared at the display and tapped at a keypad behind the desk. She cocked her head without looking back at him. "You will have to talk to dispatching to arrange an interview with the next available detective... I am not getting any open contacts at the moment."

Dexter frowned. He shook his head. "Oh... no, no, I don't want to set up a formal meeting, I just need his help—it's very important I speak with Constable Balboa. This involves all the same parties he was just dealing with. He's familiar with my situation—he was handling this earlier today, not three hours ago."

The woman shifted her stance, scrutinizing him as if she were preparing to fit him for a shirt. She sniffed and nodded at the display. "Your name, pley?"

"Dexter Massengill."

She straightened, looking down as the prompted information blinked. "I can check his schedule... they are often running double-shifts." She tapped the keys, narrowing her eyes. "DiGuiseppe Balboa... yes, he is in. I can message him you're here, but I can ney promise he will be available for you. These schedules are not always kept current, and detectives can get called on a case at short notice."

Dexter nodded. "That's fine, that's good. Thank you—I appreciate that." He patted the countertop, glancing around.

Balboa owed him a call anyway—surely the man wouldn't mind at least offering a little additional advice, even if it was off-the-clock advice. Hopefully he would agree to stay on as advocate. He certainly seemed like the obliging sort, and he knew his way around claims negotiations...

"Par-yen. It's no problem, sir." She paused. "Ah, la. He has received your message... he is here, set-see, and he is on his way down. You can fare wait for him in the seating area." She smiled.

Dexter exhaled. "Perfect. Fabulous—thank you very much." One hurdle cleared—Balboa would wipe away all the nonsense with a nock or two, firm up another settlement, and that would be that. The ugliness of the casino people and this micromanaging, usurping senator-mogul from Anastasia would soon be fading memories.

Dexter turned and looked toward the gaping entryway he had used, surprisingly far across the floor. Jayjay's instincts had been on the nose, as usual; they couldn't have left the system too soon. He looked back at the receptionist, who had moved to the right, behind the adjacent closed face of the rhombicube. "It's amazing you can get a hold of someone in here as quickly as you do—such an enormous facility."

The woman glanced at him and smiled, closing her eyes, then turned back to whatever it was she was doing.

Dexter leaned on the counter and nodded at the empty seats. "Are there particular times when it gets busy here?"

The woman shook her head absently without looking back. "We have scheduled service days for licensing and registration." She paused. "You can wait in the seating area. The constable will be down soon."

Dexter bowed his head and waved, stepping away. He strolled past the perimeter of seats and turned, looking back toward the lifts along the center of the rear wall. A lift disc glowed as it dropped toward the floor at what looked to be near freefall speed, perhaps delivering Balboa. Of course, the constable could have been anywhere, and odds were against it. If it was him, he certainly wasn't wasting any time.

To the right of the paired tubes, an odd, precarious-looking chain of scaffolding switchbacks climbed roughly halfway toward the ceiling, ending at a long, thick beam that might have served as a platform for construction. Daunting bit of engineering exhibited in the municipal facility alone. Construction… there was a very different occupation, something that offered a very different sort of thrill, and probably a continued sense of accomplishment. Probably something that might have proven quite interesting. Unfortunately, it was also one thing that exceeded his qualifications.

He looked back at the rhombicube and his eyes fell on the display panel in his direction. An ad showing a Torrez Starhopper rotating on its axis flashed away, replaced by a sweeping view of a remarkable, bulbous rock formation standing in the center of a yellow, sulfur-stained gorge. Tiny ships hovered and buzzed around it. A local tourist promo… Ustinov's

Smokewater Sea, according to the caption.

Abruptly the view switched to a sweeping bucolic scene—a glistening lake in a flower-studded valley, under a dazzling red sunset. A caption in rose freestyle script read, "Ekseniya… take a break from the commotion."

More prodding for Pike. Apparently, the forces of the universe were in cahoots with Jayjay.

"Dexter Massengill?"

Dexter spun, raising his eyebrows. Dig Balboa was looming behind him. "Hello." He glanced back around at the lifts at the center of the rear wall. "Your department is near the top, isn't it? How did you get down here so quickly?"

The big man flared his nostrils. "I was fare on my way when you called—I tried to get you on your com, but you were already off the batto." He lowered his brow. "Walk with me for a minute." He turned and nodded toward the front of the municipal building, motioning with his hand.

Dexter blinked, hesitating for a moment, then nodded back, staying with Balboa as the constable started across the floor. Dexter sniffed, looking up at the man. They seemed to be heading in the general direction of the entryway. "You've heard the news, I take it… they came after me again?"

Balboa kept his eyes forward. "Wey. I pulled the warrant when it came through." He paused. "You're fare doing the right thing, letting them run their scans. But these people mean business, Massengill. I don't think they're going away anytime soon, par-sham. Do you have any idea what they're looking for?"

Not going away anytime soon. Those weren't quite the words of encouragement he had started in with the last time. Dexter frowned flatly. "From what I can gather, they think I found some sort of backdoor to their system security at the casino." He exhaled through his nose. "They then invited me to work for the company—they said they'd drop all their claims and provide compensation if I became a consultant for them, if you can imagine that."

Balboa gave him a sharp look. "They did, wey? You might want to think about taking them up on that."

Guidestars—was he kidding? Dexter glared back at him. "That's not an option I'm considering."

Balboa studied his expression for a moment as they walked, then returned his attention forward and nodded. "Tough to get close to someone who's tried to have you ghosted, om-bu fare sur-mun. But if you can put over your personal feelings, sey ney, there's no mey-yer way to protect yourself than by making yourself valuable to them."

"Not if I don't have what they want. I've told you I never did anything to infiltrate their architecture, and it's true, whether you believe me or not. I don't even know what the systems in the Blue Topaz are—they could be using anything, they could be using collective network relays, remote referential cores… anything. I wouldn't know what approach to take."

Balboa shrugged. "Wey-mey… but you do have the skills. You're a full-time flyer and you live on your batto. You could fare do a crash-prep manual refit if you had to, couldn't you? Anyone with more than 20 years' experience in the void can hold his own against a security platform." He eyed Dexter. "These people set-see are about maximizing profit, and they don't offer employment light, pa fare. If they think you can do the job, then sey po-sabe—you probable can."

Maximizing profit. The prospect of being chased around the Galaxy, fending off one claim after another was disturbing to say the least, but it was far less repugnant than the thought of giving over freedom to these soulless predators and having to face them on a daily basis, helping them as they continued to do anything and everything possible to grind out CU. Extortion and murder included. Dexter cleared his throat. "Let's forget I mentioned the job offer. We're going to have to tackle this problem from a different angle."

"Fare ney. I can't say I blame you." Balboa was angling away from the entryway, toward a row of public terminal booths. He moved past the first booth partition, glancing inside. "Unfortunate, they have your batto… which gives you no leverage. See." The second booth was empty. He stepped halfway in and turned, signaling Dexter to enter.

Dexter stopped as he moved inside. "What's in here?"

"We need access from a public outlet." Balboa stayed by the partition for a moment, scanning the floor outside, then moved to the square, black display table by the inside wall. Three cushioned benches surrounded the table. He gestured at the table. "Sit down."

Dexter shrugged and stepped to the near side of the table, slipping onto the bench and patting the cushions as he adjusted his legs. More room than there seemed to be. He raised his eyebrows. "Do you think it's going to be a problem getting my ship back?"

"Not sure." Balboa wedged his bulky frame into the seating on the opposite side and grimaced. Not quite universally comfortable, apparently, but booth seating did seem to be the standard for the hemmed-in design considerations of Eo-Nowar. Balboa hadn't chosen the most ideal place to live for someone his size.

Dexter glanced at the tabletop as Balboa activated the display. "Can't we just file another counterclaim—say they're harassing me without good reason? There has to be a law that prevents this sort of thing, I would think."

Balboa shook his head. "You can fare do that, but they have a right to protect their company, so this time, their claim is technical legitimate, undue as it sounds. I think a counterclaim will just prolong the impound period." He frowned at the table, tapping a pair of touch-activated dialog prompts. The tabletop flashed and shifted, showing instructional text surrounding an array of blue and white squares—a visual box-level directory. "If you do nothing, my guess is whoever's running point on this set-see will find some other way to hang you up, like claiming you've transferred the information to some other hiding place."

Dexter frowned, leaning forward and scratching his arm. "Is that legal?"

Balboa nodded slowly. "They don't have good cause, but they have power and influence, and they're fare apparent willing to use it."

Dexter shifted around the corner of the table to the inside wall to get a better angle of the display. "You said something about a senator from Anastasia... you think he's calling the shots?"

Balboa looked back at him. "Sey po-sabe, wey. If he wasn't on board, they would have dropped this, set-see. Sey pa mey-bu. It's not good—it means he's not threatened by you." He paused. "Obvious the senator has friends in Irina. If he's got the IPA acting on his behalf, sey pa bu-cue fare, there's not much you can do. They can flag your ID with a special interest pending investigation or hostile status, put you on indefinite administrative detention, cite you with a fine you can't pay and lock down your CU."

Dexter shook his head. "Well, what can I do?"

Balboa's eyes lingered on him for a moment. He tapped through the directory, opening up a panel of metadata, with three phosphor columns of profile code. "We're in Requisitions... this is the file on your batto. Your ship. If you look about halfway down the first column, under 'STS,' you see there's an '03.' You see what I'm talking about?"

Dexter leaned in, looking at the screen. "Yes."

"Set-la, that's your batto's status. '03' means there's an active impound. If you change it to '17,' it means your batto is under voluntary protective custody. Once the vehicle has that status, wa-la, it's fare eligible to have control transferred back to the owner—and it won't set off any alerts, par-sham." He backed out of the profile to a broad directory. "Set-see, this is Municipal Control. Requisitions is third from the bottom, toward the right. See." He pointed at one of the many boxes, glancing at Dexter, then backed up to the access interface. "You just put in the access key, ask for the Municipal Control directory, and find your way back to your ship's profile screen. You think you can fare do that?"

Dexter looked down at the tabletop. "Well... yes." He squinted. "You're telling me I need to steal my ship back?"

Balboa exhaled. "Set coom set fare. You're just about out of options. For whatever reason, these gents are locked onto you. My guess, they're going to make your life miserable until they get what they want. They're fare going to make you pay, one way or another. You need to depart the system."

Dexter sat up, shaking his head. "But... you're saying I'm better off as a fugitive? What about my account—won't they freeze my CU, put out an alert on my ship?"

Balboa sighed. "You would have to start over, falsify your ID and your batto registration. I hate to say it, but set-la, it's not that hard to do, special for an om-bu blessey like you. But you'd have your batto back, and you'd fare have your freedom." He scratched his mustache. "Just stay out of the Human Sphere until you get everything fixed."

Dexter stared at the multicolored ENMC logo now floating on the screen. He was going to tamper with a law enforcement mainframe, violate a directive from the IPA. Was this actually the best option?

"Take some time to think about it if you like. Your batto's impound status isn't going to change anytime soon, ney." Balboa leaned forward. "Sey tue, it's fare up to you, but if you ask me, set-see, this is going to end with either this company getting exacta-mun qua fare it wants from you, or you getting killed." He scratched beneath his ear. "Maybe after some time, the circumstances change, and you can fare try to straighten everything out legal. But for now, in my opinion... you're not going to have the option of going back to your normal life unless you take action. I don't know if I'd make the same recommendation to someone with roots, but you're mobile. You'd just be taking your act to a different part of the Galaxy."

Dexter rubbed his eyes. "Why... why can't you just do this right now? Why the need for me to go back through these screens. You were just in the ship profile—why couldn't you just flip the status for me and go from there?"

"Because these public access stations set-see are two-way. If I make the status change, eventual they'll review the command override, and they'll see it came from here, and they'll see I was the one who did it. I like you, but I'm not willing to lose my job over this if I don't have to, par-sham." He breathed and nodded at the table. "Now listen... I'm leaving you an internal access key card. Use that sequence when you change the status. Once that's done set-la, you have to close out, and then reenter the system using your personal account ID. Just put in 'expedited control transfer,' then put in your batto registration code. You'll be prompted with a question about what you want to do; you answer, confirm, then close out again and go back in with the temporary code. Go back to Requisitions, enter 'expedited control transfer,' and pick your batto registration from the list. It will fare probable be the only one. Then you'll see a screen that gives you the choice of approving or denying the request. You hit approve, and you're done, wa-la." He paused, nodding. "Just wait until I'm gone. Do you need me to run through it again?"

Dexter looked from Balboa to the tabletop and back. He scratched his cheek. "No, it sounds simple—this looks like a basic system directory. I won't have any trouble finding my way through." He sighed. "I'm just... not sure about this. It's a lot to digest."

"Mey-bu, consider it an option that's there if you need it." Balboa extracted himself from the bench and stood. "If you do decide to do this, they won't notice it for a while, but I suggest you get your body back to your batto as soon as you have your control back and leave as soon as all the scarabs are finished their scans. Just lay low until everyone's off the pier." He glanced out at the open floor and pulled a card out of his breast pocket, dropping it on the table. "Just put in the last six digits through the standard access prompt. That card's from our testing lab and it's traceable, so I'd appreciate it if you took it with you and destroyed it, first chance you get."

Dexter reached for the card and nodded, clearing his throat. "I'll remember." He glanced at the crudely pressed alphanumerics on the translucent plastic. It was an automatic access key, with a silver photo strip running beneath the code along one edge. Presumably there was a card slot somewhere on the table, but inserting the card was obviously not what Balboa wanted him to do—possibly, it would trip some security measure he wasn't mentioning.

The constable moved back to the edge of the partition, again looking out at the spread of people across the floor. Hyperconscious of the surroundings to the last, like a man who had reason to believe he was being followed. Balboa was probably just being extra cautious, but the body language wasn't exactly reinforcing his argument that surreptitiously freeing the Explorer was a safe thing to do. He looked back at Dexter. "Fare mey-yer, whatever you decide. And if you do stay in-system, just give me another call—I'll rep you as long as you're here."

Crossing paths with Balboa at all had possibly been the best instance of good luck in recent memory. Dexter moved around the table and stood. "Thank you, Constable Balboa, really."

"I hope it all works out for you, toot-fare. I hate to see an om-bu like you get a bad turn." He smiled and stepped away, heading out onto the floor, then rounded right and disappeared past the partition.

Dexter looked back at the table. It would probably take five minutes to go through the screens and unlock the ship. Five minutes to change the course of his life, become an exile from Human Space for at least the next few years. There was still a chance the holding company people would give up when they didn't find what they were looking for, leave him alone. There was still a chance it would all go away.

Of course, if he did unlock the ship, it would most likely remain unnoticed until he actually left the system. And if someone did notice it, it would look like a simple clerical error unless he actually took advantage of it. The subsequent request to transfer control back to the pilot would look like nothing out of the ordinary. If he chose, he could always free the ship and then wait on the results of the scans—leave the system only if absolutely necessary. Balboa had put it exactly right—it was an option that was there if he needed it. A well thought-out, reasonably low-risk option. The suggestion was inspired considering the man's job was to prevent that sort of thing.

Dexter sat back on the bench on the side Balboa had previously occupied. If he didn't release the lock now, he wasn't going to have that flexibility. But if he had to go, he had to go. After all, he was in the market for a destination. The Scinti and Teledura Spheres had just as much to offer as the human portion of the Galaxy. Just fewer humans.

And an extended vacation from humans didn't sound like such a bad thing at that particular moment. Dexter cleared the display and tapped in the last six digits of the key card.

*   *   *

Cristan Faro shifted in his seat and shook off a chill, keeping his eyes on the central screen in front of him. The parser flow variance reading in the lower right corner buzzed like a trapped elf-fly, locking in on the 0.8 sigma range as the blocks of register data unraveled in a steady column along the left. He removed his specs and passed them in front of his mouth, giving the lenses a quick breath and rubbing them with his necktie.

He glanced up at the dimpled xenon oval that ran around the perimeter of the ceiling, bathing the Farmingdale Scarab's command terminal access chamber in a pale, lavender glow. The compartment was huge for a ship only 20 meters in length, set behind the cockpit with room enough for six IPA officers. It was a flying war room. The console shelf wrapped around the cabin like a horseshoe, jam-packed with state-of-the-art hardware beneath high bulkheads including a spread of clustered monitors at each station and a larger shared display glass viewer designed for multilevel surveillance.

A window into Monroe's Archangel now covered the bulkhead above the three station monitors, a wide-angle cross-section of the senator's main cabin from the MTA com. The rounded seating of the lounge was just visible at the right edge of the elongated screen—an emphatic reminder of the lack of consideration the Scarab's designers had given for comfort. The Scarab was all about utility, built for IPA crews who didn't do a lot of sitting around. The low, harsh lighting didn't help.

The stagnant ventilation while the ship was idle didn't help either. Cristan sat back, wincing at a mounting cramp in his lower back. Body heat and ambient power circulation might have been the only means of heat— with no one else aboard, the ship felt like a walk-in freezer.

Working aboard the Archangel was a different sort of experience—the Scinti designers were long past the compulsory aspects of spaceflight, and the Archangel was the top of the line. With the IU functionality incorporated directly into the ship's on-board, there was more space in the cockpit than the typical Scintivar Deiassa models. The soft lighting and foam-thickened convertible driver-recliner made Monroe's cockpit seem more like an extension of his lounge than the command center of the ship. Carpet pads dominated the consoles, with ergonomic filament switches and intuitive surface-flow mapping to complement a beefed-up audio interface system. Everything was set up for a pilot to literally fly the ship in his or her sleep.

Of course, working aboard the Archangel usually constituted being face to face with the senator, which necessarily carried an equal measure of exhaustion.

Cristan frowned at the activity log in the leftmost monitor. The master list of cannibalized subsystems and preliminary findings was piling up—2 kilometers away the Scarab's wave of simultaneous interactional scans was tearing through the Zenith Explorer's data stores, cramming the IPA software through the on-board's access points. Not much to do now but watch while the IPA programs did their job.

In fact, the senator's Archangel was probably every bit as technically equipped as the IPA vessel—he had chosen the most customizable ship the Scinti made and upgraded every system, packing the hull from scoop to burners with sensors and military-grade defense schemes and then burying everything under high-end furniture and Galinan facades.

Monroe was somewhere toward the rear of his ship at the moment, most likely relaxing to the multimedia center in his master cabin. He did have a predilection for luxuries; he liked to cloak himself in lavish comforts and extravagant impracticalities, making appearances in open cars and designer wear, getting his name in the news. In reality, the exhibitions were a calculated cover—he was disarming the public with a carefree, camera-friendly face while he ran his conglomerate with cold, surgical efficiency. He had no tolerance for incompetence and he expected perfection from his people, and anyone who didn't perform adequately would be made to suffer the consequences. Sometimes the consequences were extreme.

Cristan scratched his eyelid and replaced his specs, exhaling as he looked across the three monitor screens. The senator would have argued that there was a need to discourage unacceptable performance, to demonstrate authority. That a behavioristic approach was just good, legitimate business. But sometimes, it was clearly more about his own gratification than the benefit of the organization... it was about physiological need. Monroe lived to mete out punishment. He derived far more pleasure administering suffering than he did from his overt indulgences.

And Teodor Monroe hadn't become who he was through good, legitimate business.

"The engineers here are worse than those Sunderland Apportionment blowhards."

Cristan looked back up at the Archangel. Monroe was strolling into the wide viewer frame holding a glass of red wine. He stopped several paces away from the MTA com, raising his glass. "It seems whenever I visit this place they're having large-scale climate control problems. It's enough to make a person feel positively unwelcome."

The senator projected his gripping presence from 107 lights away as effortlessly and effectively as he did in person—and it was good to be 107 lights away. Cristan nodded. "To be fair, they didn't know you were coming."

"They never do." He lingered near the center of the cabin and glanced wistfully in the direction of the Archangel's cockpit. "Mr. Faro, how are you making out—can I get you anything?" The overhead cabin light glinted through the crystal of the wine glass in sharp pink, as brilliantly as if the senator was standing aboard the Scarab.

"I'm fine, senator." Cristan touched the bridge of his glasses, pressing them tighter against his face. "The scans are all up and running, so we're good to go." He paused. "There is an off-chance I'll need a ride to the other ship, depending on whether we hit any major snags... I'll probably have a better idea of what we're dealing with after about 20 minutes."

Monroe gave him a hard, unreadable look, swishing the wine in his glass. "I see. I was thinking more in terms of refreshments. You know, there are five occasions for drinking, according to the ancient Romans: the arrival of a friend, one's present or future thirst, the excellence of the wine, or any other reason." He took a sip. "This is excellent, but I think I'll go with future thirst for now—I'm anticipating imminent satiation. I wasn't expecting to hear about obstacles this soon. What's your concern, Mr. Faro?"

Cristan nodded. "Land mines. The on-board might be running encrypted shadow processes designed to exclude data from the exports, or worse. The blind, brute-force scans the IPA uses might trigger scuttle programs or read-response counterattacks. If so, recovering the information could potentially take much longer." He cleared his throat. "It's just a time issue... from the Explorer, I'll be able to find and neutralize any independent processes if I have to. I can run a few conjunctive internal queries for explosive unstructured statements, rule out the system vulnerabilities with deep sensitive-target vetting, and we might have to backtrack, but once I do that the Scarab should crack through. It probably won't be necessary... I'm assuming you don't want any surprises."

Monroe took a long, slow drink from the glass, flashing a sour frown as he swallowed it down. "You're surrounded by the finest intelligence equipment available in the Human Sphere. All those massive, devoted processing blocks, those suppressive, paralytic algorithms. That's raw power at your fingertips. You should be grateful, Mr. Faro—few civilians have the opportunity to run ops aboard a Scarab without IPA supervision. I had to call in a big favor to arrange it—I now have to put up with the assistant commissioner's hunting stories at the Governor's Ball next month." He stepped toward the MTA and his face grew large in the viewer. "I should think someone like you would be enormously embarrassed by failure to make use of such an ideal tool. But I'm confident you'll manage without having to abandon ship."

He certainly had a point. "Let's hope so, sir."

"Yes, let's do that." Monroe was smiling again. "You're of course welcome to join me in this particularly robust Pashat Rufina Superiore—say the word and I'll have a bottle run out to you."

Cristan gave a quick two-finger wave of salutation. "Thank you, senator—maybe after I'm done." He slid in front of the monitor on the right.

"Of course. Do what you must." Monroe brushed his mustache. The senator was crowding the cam ocellus like a child peering into a terrarium. His arching eyebrows stretched up and out of the frame. "20 minutes, you say?"

"At the most, yes." Cristan nodded without looking back up at the exaggerated image. The senator's expression of tacit demand was more than familiar. Cristan scratched the back of his neck. "The search parameters are fairly broad in this case, so we might be collecting and sorting through potential sources of interest for a while before we can make sense of anything. That said, these programs are targeting the designated regions for encrypted data and also looking for signs of scrambled information… nonlogical key series, misaligned code, progression hiccups, or any gaps or bumps in the log files. If something suspicious turns up, I can check on it right away. It's hard to say—if we get lucky, we could hit something in a couple of minutes."

"Lucky, yes." Monroe sniffed and drained his wine, stepping back toward his lounge. He set the glass on an end table by the hull and turned back. "It seems to me if you're trying to hide something, the smart move is to avoid the earmarks of encryption. Better to hide it in an unremarkable location, lost amid banal operational files and masked somehow."

Cristan nodded. "That's right, senator—that's the approach. But ultimately, whether you use redirects and overwritten code or blatantly lock a file down, there's no safe place to hide your data without guarding it with reactive processes."

Monroe narrowed his eyes. "I understand the AIE neocortical net is around 2 million times more densely packed with writable storage than the average ship's on-board." He paused. "Be sure you check the android's memory."

Good instincts. At that moment, the on-board's dedicated IU field cells were being translated on the starboard monitor along with several other high-priority regions. "We're actually looking into Dexter Massengill's IU specifically. It was included in our parameter specs because of some recent activity." He moved in front of the keypad and pulled up the corresponding process segment. "The unit has undergone three intrusive procedures, something that would typically suggest TPM or a memory hardware problem, but implanted information could create symptoms that look a lot like a corruption. Massengill might have been trying to clean up his own mess when he checked the unit in at the tech-mech. Or, he might have had his information hidden during one of the procedures—exploratory surgery would have been a good cover story."

Monroe pursed his lips and nodded. "Another thought, Mr. Faro. A ship's android is in a much better position to camouflage information than a human pilot operating through an access platform."

"True." Cristan shifted to the next monitor and brought up the Kranz TMI prior-day com log file. He squinted as he skimmed back through the details. "Two of the procedures were done just yesterday in Eo-Nowar, both after the advocate was contacted about the Blue Topaz incident; if Massengill had information he was trying to hide, he may have been looking for a way to move it." Cristan sat up and cleared his throat, glancing back at the active scan on the other monitor. "No evidence of a misalignment now, so the android's probably clean herself, but if there was something there, we'll find it in the on-board imprints."

"Excellent." Monroe smiled broadly, pacing slowly back across the viewer. "If I'm right, we'll find some interesting tidbits in the android. And it won't be in a conventional encryption—this man will know his way around an operating system. I'm thinking it will be disguised a little more cleverly, in a place where most scans don't usually look. A microservo response test, or some other self-correcting maintenance subroutine."

Microservos. Cristan rubbed his mouth, keeping his head down and smiling behind his hand. The idea had merit, although there were logistical problems with blending compressed information into the structural process scripts. It wasn't relevant to the task at hand, since the IPA scans would be flooding every system regardless. In any event, inviting further discussion about it was asking for trouble.

The senator moved to the far side of his ship, turning his attention toward one of his paintings. Possibly, he was content to wait until the scans had produced results. Not likely.

Monroe had virtually no technical background, but he was a virtuoso problem-solver and he attacked impracticalities and compartmentalized thinking with a vengeance. Keeping himself well-informed was his effective religion, and he retained information as if he were burning it to his own silicon-germanium field cells. He demanded full disclosure from his subject matter experts, and knew exactly enough to assess when he was and wasn't getting it from them, whether it was about coding and cybernetic architecture or any of the other various components of his organization.

And he was relentless. He extracted every detail he wanted, and if he felt he was getting the truncated layman's version or sensed the slightest hint of condescension, he showed no mercy.

The senator swung around and stepped back toward the MTA. He laughed abruptly, raising his eyebrows. "Be honest, Mr. Faro. You think I'm wasting my time."

Cristan stared at the viewer. He shook his head. "I know better than that." He tapped the console and sighed. "If you're convinced this is worthwhile, that's enough for me."

Monroe nodded. "The idea of luck has always been fascinating to me. On some level, as human beings we need to believe that there's an easy way out. That one day, no matter how we have squandered our existence, a stroke of fate might descend upon us and change our lives for the better." He sniffed, looking up at the ceiling and tapping his chest with a fist. "I have a fundamental problem with that idiosyncrasy. This arrangement we made with the advocate initially, allowing this man to fly with all that credit... do you realize we have validated the legitimacy of his winnings, and in effect, acknowledged this luck that he claims to have? I can't in good conscience let that stand, can I?"

Cristan raised his eyebrows and glanced at the viewer. Monroe generally didn't expect responses to his rhetorical questions, but sometimes he liked to throw out feelers.

Not this time. The senator turned and headed for the lounge, raising his voice. "This has nothing to do with luck, Mr. Faro. Luck is a manufactured construct... a euphemism invented by those who lack skill. I say Massengill happens to have that particular commodity in abundance, and in my mind, skill is always worth a closer look." He skirted the back of his settee, patting the top edge of the cushions. "This man has something on the casinos, and all I need is one scintilla of evidence. A little leverage to precipitate full disclosure." He stopped and half-turned as if he were posing for a company holograph. "This is more than a run-of-the-mill psi grifting op. I've been over the P-and-P and seen all the security schematics—our gaming facilities are as tight as the central command zone in the Raxatot Sphere. Beta Lyrae has a long history of aggressively protecting against these sorts of vulnerabilities. Seven years, and the man doesn't come out on the short end a single time? Things like this simply do not happen. I have to protect my business, Mr. Faro. He's a threat to my profit margin and he stands to expose internal gaming functions and methodologies, to undermine our blueprints for success. Seven years... this man has practically been on my payroll as long as you have."

Cristan watched Monroe through the upper fringes of his lenses. The senator's tone was tongue-and-cheek for the moment, more or less an exercise in oratory practice—he couldn't have considered Dexter Massengill to be a serious threat to the casino industry, although he certainly didn't take any amount of profit-siphoning lightly. Massengill had been careful not to get too greedy, which suggested the man was somewhat sensible, even though he had made no attempt to create doubt by mixing a few down days into his winning streak. There were less meticulous casino owners in the Galaxy... dabbling credit-soaked industrialists too blithely out-of-touch to care about their business in any detail. A few of them might not have bothered to go through the channels to recover the amount Massengill had taken, and that was apparently what the man had counted on. Of course, for Monroe, this was about more than the credit.

Monroe was frowning in the direction of the MTA, leaning on the couch. Cristan cleared his throat. "Sorry, senator—I'm listening. Seven years is a long time to run an infiltration op, whether it's psi exploitation or a system break. It doesn't look like an inside job—Massengill reads like a devout loner."

Monroe inhaled sharply. "I'm guessing this man's area of expertise is more akin to yours—he's mastered logic and applied that versatility in ways that complement his desires and skill sets. I think we'll find he has security information on gaming locales all over the Human Sphere. If he really is a genome psi using some ingenious method to disguise a psychic advantage, well that's another thing entirely. Why stop at falsifying CRP test results? Maybe he's found a way to enhance telepathic effectiveness, trained himself to home in on specific details referencing cillian experiments on scinti or teledura focus techniques—maybe he's done his own research, found some exciting innovation in brain chemistry. If this is in any way involving inherent genetic ability, he's operating at a level of efficiency well above average over an unprecedented duration, and that, my erudite friend, would be a precious piece of information far more valuable than the credit he stole." He paced across the viewer, looking steadily in the direction of his cockpit. "Either way, when we're able to prove his ill-intent and apply the right amount of pressure, I'm sure he'll fill us in with many useful details."

Massengill had no idea what he had gotten himself into. Cristan scratched his neck and turned his attention downward, and there was a blink in the lens at the right edge of his vision. He frowned at the right-hand monitor. The logical search of the on-board's IU field cells had hit on a telepathic reference in a cell that carried an out-of-sequence time stamp.

He swung himself fully in front of the monitor. "Just a second, sir—

something came up. Stand by."

Monroe nodded, narrowing his eyes, and took a step toward the MTA. "There we go. Send it up as soon as you're ready."

Cristan nodded, squinting at the screen. He tapped in a thread search and pulled up the cell's metatag. He was looking at a long-term archive, an early area of the android's memory that would have had to be near the unit's inception. The highlighted cell was loaded with an oversized nodule of compressed data, newly transcribed to recent memory with virtually no other mnemonic connections—it read like a dead cell, but it had apparently been accessed within the last 24 hours. Definite tampering. He decompressed the record and raised his eyebrows, skimming through the text. The information was seemingly random and unusual... pattern parameters, theoretical specs on upper-dimensional hyperspace dynamics, with extremely specific, manually entered calculations. It looked like a legitimate flight plan. There was also information about human physiology, extrapolated cryonic effects on the body, time dilation figures.

A long string of numbers drew his attention. He sat forward, straightening his glasses. He shook his head. The number was too high—18 digits to the left of the decimal. Possibly an error, considering someone at some point had either keyed in the data at a terminal interface or populated the file using voice command. Supposedly it was a time parameter of over 100 quadrillion seconds. Billions of years.

He cocked his head, scratching his ear, and flipped to the associated recent memory cells. A message had been written by a man named Salaman Nevis, something about the ytaoans. The message was about time-travel, sent to Dexter Massengill from some 900 years before. On its face, it was absurd. Impossible. But the level of detail was insane.

Time travel. Cristan removed his glasses and rubbed his eyes. It was as if someone had crafted a message specifically designed to get the senator's attention—a well-thought-out deception that went right to the heart of everything that Teodor Monroe cared about, stashed in an unlikely random location. If it was a hoax, it was a good one. To put something like this together... whoever had done this was brilliant.

Monroe was going to take it seriously, whether that was warranted or not. Cristan shook his head again, double-checking the dates. If it was a hoax, it wouldn't bear up under scrutiny. He tapped in a code integrity scan and looked up. "Senator, you're going to want to see this."

The ytaoans—the original genome psis. If the message was somehow real, Monroe's instincts were truly amazing. Maybe the senator had some hidden psi inclinations of his own.

He was at the terminal again. "What do we have, Mr. Faro?"

"I'm sending it up now." Cristan brought the recent memory text to the forefront, pulled up the Scarab's com, and transferred the record to the discrete data interchange.

Monroe was in front of the MTA again, his face again looming near the cam. His eyes dropped slightly as he looked at the monitor directly beneath the cam. For a long moment the only motion on the viewer was the shifting of his irises under the red dots of reflected terminal diodes. There was a barely noticeable tightening at the edges of his mouth, exaggerated by the size of the viewer's projection. Any farther away and the change in expression would have been imperceptible.

He stroked his mustache lightly, his eyes still riveted on the monitor. "This is the final piece of the puzzle."

The words were spoken quietly, almost as if to himself. Cristan swallowed, carefully watching him. "I'll have to vet this thoroughly."

Monroe looked up. "Yes. Of course." He paused. "How long will it take to verify the information?"

Cristan sat back and shrugged, shaking his head. "That might take some time. Some of this involves theoretical constructs that we can't really relate to the models we have."

Monroe nodded. "But you can test for inconsistencies, something in the language that might undermine the authenticity?"

Cristan raised his eyebrows. "That I can do, yes. There's a lot to work with here… we have a standard forensic process we use for this sort of thing. There's also a large amount of math that will be relatively simple to check."

"Good. Let's get started on that." Monroe exhaled, stepping back from the terminal and looking up toward the ceiling. "Meanwhile, I'd like to proceed under the assumption that this is legitimate. And accurate." He scratched his chin and nodded at the cam. "I believe the message said something about the Fatima System."

Cristan nodded. "Yes, I saw that."

"Make arrangements to meet me there, as soon as possible. Put all other projects on hold, Mr. Faro—I want everyone on your team on this as of right now."

"What about Massengill?"

"Massengill, yes." Monroe straightened and looked thoughtful for a moment. "Well I think we're past the point of indoctrination, don't you?" He smiled. "We'll need the android, of course. I'll inform Ritsa. And I will expect to see you on Fatima… let's give it three hours… that should give you and your IPA friends enough time to extricate yourselves."

Cristan glanced around at the monitors. "Sir, I realize this situation is intriguing. It's an incredible find, no question… but I think it needs to be said that this could be a set up. If this information is off even a little bit, the integrity of the ship can't be maintained."

For an instant, a cold look flashed over the senator's face. Then, just as quickly, he looked amused. "I think that's obvious, don't you?"

Cristan exhaled and cleared his throat. "It sounds as though you're thinking of attempting this flight yourself. You need to know that even if all the information passes the sniff test, there's no way I can ever guarantee that something like this will work."

"Destiny or destruction." Monroe stepped to the terminal. "There's no reward without risk. But I like to think I have the unwavering ability to determine when one outweighs the other. I don't need your guarantee, Mr. Faro… I just need your endorsement."

"I'll do what I can."

"Just see that you check it thoroughly." Monroe lowered his voice to a whisper. "It's what I've been waiting for. Have a nice flight, Mr. Faro." He closed the connection and the viewer faded, blending with the slate gray shade of the chamber bulkhead.

Cristan blinked. Maybe it really was the man's destiny. He looked again at the information displayed in the monitors… a map for traveling beyond the limits of time and space, all spelled out in plain English in under a gigabyte of electronic characters.

Theories abounded about the potential implications of time-travel, the effects of changing events in the past. Presumably this information covered those details somewhere… the memory of Monroe might blink out of existence for the people he was leaving behind, or the Galaxy as it was might completely change. The results of wars, the histories of the sentient races. Births and deaths. Lives might be erased, or created out of nothingness.

Monroe was going to jump at this, whether the information held up to scrutiny or not. If the specs weren't sound, attempting something like this would probably kill him, but if they were, it would give him access to more influence than any of the technology he had ever had at his disposal.

The power to play god. It was the only thing the senator had ever really cared about.

X   TRESPASS

"One who seeks out absolute power is like the predator in a forest chase. In anticipation of the kill, the predator's bloodlust grows stronger as it closes in on the prey. The predator becomes more and more single-minded in its purpose. For one who aims to prevent such a kill, the task becomes more difficult with every second.

"In truth, the promise of absolute power can often be as much a threat as the power itself."

```
... GCL FN.036
Phi 78 24 37.00 / Theta -20 39 56.90 / Rho 35.26 / JD 3040385
Kappa Pegasi: USTINOV; "Eo-Nowar"; 10 March 3612 CE
```

Dexter gripped the handlebars of the public scooter lightly, letting the automatic guidance system implement its shallow, even heading corrections as it directed its way toward the Explorer. He craned his neck, looking back. Another scooter hung in the distance behind him, seemingly following the same course.

There were a few other scooters visible off to the left and right, buzzing along among the pilings and staggered platforms in various directions. There were no traffic lanes in the Jetty—scooters were more or less free to fly over any unoccupied platforms, though the automated routes tended to steer clear of them wherever possible. Considering the lack of distinct pathways through the air and the scarcity of traffic compared with the great number of lot locations, there didn't seem to be a high likelihood that one scooter should end up following another unless they were both going to the same pier.

The scooter might have been unmanned, looping back to a previous location. It was far enough back that the shape was drowned out by the bright blue headlight and the white boarding streamers on either side. It might have been a member of the IPA team, possibly still at work on the Explorer, though the scarabs had used cars at last check. Then again, it might have been a tail. Other IPA or munis keeping an eye on him, or someone from the holding company... Ritsa Rabani. Or the anadon.

If Balboa was right, it shouldn't have been a surprise.

Dexter took another look back. The other scooter was gone. He raised his eyebrows and exhaled, shaking his head. A little paranoia wasn't necessarily a bad thing, given current circumstances.

He glanced up as he passed under one of the city's long, vertical passages, catching a glimpse of the dome's murky, fading glow far above before the scooter moved beneath the plane of the next city block base, squinting at the mass grillwork fixtures that dominated the foundation. Thousands of nested halo lamps kept the landing level lit in a yellow cocktail of zinc sulfide-tinged neon and xenon luminophore.

The Jetty should have felt brighter after well over an hour in the dimness of the upper city, but as it was, the lighting still seemed muted. The piers were kept well-lit—clearly the output from the halo lamps was much more intense than any of the paneling higher up—but now the wash of pale yellow only enhanced the intermittent shadows. If anything, the entire area looked even bleaker than it had looked the last few trips across.

He looked ahead as the scooter banked softly and started a wide right turn. Possibly, the impression of gloominess was real; the power grid might have been spelling the base lighting incrementally, running through a brief, temporary conservation mode. More likely, it was his imagination. The bottom level might have been brighter than the rest of the city, but ultimately it was still a part of it. There was something vaguely oppressive about the prospect of spending long stretches of time contained in a single, gigantic enclosure... somehow it was more conspicuous than being sealed midflight in a spaceship, despite the extra room. Perhaps that extra room just brought home the scope—the constant awareness of a vast virtual prison.

He had spent more than enough time in Eo-Nowar.

Pier F-37 was at the edge of the South Orange Lot, a relatively short ride through the air from the city's interior and the third lot from the lift. There were 60 lots spread over the level, four great triangular arrangements of 15 distinct color designations, and bands on each of the thick, cylindrical pilings made the lot identifiable at a glance. The scooter was angling among a series of sky blue bands, bisecting the last adjoining lot diagonally. The bands ran from blue to orange, and the Explorer came into view immediately, standing alone on its platform. No sign of scooters or cars.

Dexter took the handlebars and guided the scooter in, crossing the railing and putting down halfway toward the Explorer. The ramp was up— another good indication the IPA had cleared out, at least temporarily. He climbed off the scooter and paused, glancing at his wrist, then frowned, dropped his arms to his sides. Force of habit. The wristcom was on Valentina, presumably in some forgotten storage locker at the Blue Topaz Casino. Meanwhile, a perfectly good replacement was sitting in one of the tool drawers in the environmental cabin, yet to be configured with the ship.

Just as well... better to keep the com signals to a minimum. The munis and scarabs weren't likely to be actively looking for his signature, but there was no sense making extra noise. No telling who was listening.

He crossed the platform, glancing up at the cab as he circled around the front of the huge landing skid to the inside of the starboard forward cross-trunk that ran from the skid to the Explorer's fuselage. He found the manual ramp lock panel open at chest level, as it should have been—good thing the IPA people hadn't overridden the automatic landing protocols to seal things up. It might have taken a while to get Jayjay's attention, assuming she was still aboard.

He frowned. There was a chance Jayjay had been forced off once the IPA team had gotten everything they needed from their scans. She normally wouldn't have gone far knowing he was on his way back, but it was possible she had tried to meet him at the ENMC facility. It would take her at least 40 to 50 minutes to get from the upper levels to the ship once he contacted her... more time for the authorities to notice the control transfer.

Hopefully, the fact that she wasn't waiting for him on the platform was a sign that they had let her stay aboard.

He focused on the number pad and tapped in the triplicate code sets. The display tape blinked slowly. If Balboa's method of fooling the system hadn't worked, he was in all likelihood in the process of sending a security alert to the nearest patrol.

The panel let out a soft, high-pitched triple-beep, and the hatch above hissed as the lock mechanism released the framing seal. The Explorer whined as the ramp came away from the hull and lowered itself toward the platform.

Dexter grinned and nodded. So far so good. He walked back around the skid as the lip of the gangway touched down, barely making a sound.

He took two steps up the ramp and something brushed at the edge of his vision... movement to the left, farther back along the skid in the shadows beneath the ship. He stopped and squinted into the darkness. Nothing. He frowned and continued up the gangway.

The lights in the ladderwell were off, and there was no sound coming from the climate control. Jayjay wouldn't have left everything shut down. She wasn't on board.

Blast.

Behind him, the hollow drone of approaching low-end verniers came from the right, followed by the choppy whisper of airbrakes. He turned as a scooter came to a stop, hovering just off the transom along the near edge of the landing pad. The distinct jet black hair and slender form of the rider was unmistakable through the break in the rail. Ritsa Rabani turned and looked directly at the Explorer's hatch, standing with her hands clear of the handlebars on the narrow span of the vehicle as if she were waiting in an enclosed lift.

Dexter stared. She must have been 10 meters away, but her dark, unnerving eyes stood out, clear and intense, glinting under the halo lights like polyglass. They might have been artificial at that—she certainly seemed to have the demeanor and efficiency of an android.

It was over. She had him. In seconds the IPA would be on top of the ship…

Red light flashed across Dexter's face, and a deep voice growled from the right. "Don't move."

The anadon… Saaj. Dexter whirled, looking down. The big saurian was behind the second cross-trunk, low against the skid with a 98 compromizer braced along his right arm. The targeting site at the top of the muzzle blazed like a dying star, tracking narrowly upward toward the area of Dexter's forehead.

The anadon hissed. "Stay where you are… if you turn for your ship, I drop you."

Dexter's eyes locked on the weapon, and an electric chill ran from his shoulders to his fingertips. He swallowed dryly. "At last check you were offering me work in your company." He nodded in the direction of Rabani and the scooter. "I take it we've moved on from those negotiations."

Saaj rose, smoothly emerging from his cover spot and crossing the landing skid nimbly with two legs and an arm, keeping his red eyes on Dexter. Somehow he kept the length of the resonator chamber on target, seemingly in full control of the entire weapon with the wide, boxy stock poised along his forearm and a single clawed hand on the trigger grip. "The position is no longer available." His breath rumbled in his sinuses. "Now… put your hands to your head, and come down from the ramp. Move slowly."

Dexter brought up his arms and touched the back of his head, keeping his elbows out. He started down the ramp and glanced again at Rabani as she tossed her hair, standing confidently on the motionless scooter. If the scarabs were on their way, she and the anadon would have known it—they knew exactly what they were doing.

They're fare going to make you pay, one way or another.

Dexter's pulse raced. If Jayjay were in the ship, lying low, she would have acted by now—called for help, or got on the turret. Which meant she definitively wasn't on the ship. Jayjay was gone, and no one was coming.

He shook his head and twisted to the right as he stepped down onto the platform. "Where are you taking me, exactly?"

Saaj was closer now, moving sideways and holding the weapon conventionally, with hands on both grips. The red site line was on Dexter's neck. "Keep walking. Head for the scooter."

They were either going to kidnap him or kill him. If they were going to kidnap him, they wanted him alive—so they might have had instructions to keep him that way even if he attempted an escape. If they were going to kill him... then he really had nothing to lose.

Dexter moved slowly away from the ramp, glancing to the left, toward the outer piling at the other end of the platform. The piers would all be fitted with light and heat sensor alarms, as at any spaceport landing area... most likely, the alarms were contained inside the columns with the ocelli and the rest of the terminal-linking hardware, so laserfire was sure to catch someone's attention. But there was no guarantee of a quick response from Port Authority Control. The company operatives obviously would have preferred not to open fire, but it didn't mean they wouldn't.

Only one way to find out for sure. He stopped and turned. "Where are you taking me?"

Rabani immediately raised her own refractor. Saaj glanced in her direction, shifting the weight of the compromizer back onto his right arm and holding up his free hand. He stepped closer, extending his arm and practically brushing Dexter's chest with the muzzle. The gun must have weighed 20 kilograms, and the anadon was wielding it like a hollow baton. "It will go better for you if you comply, Massengill."

"Why should I go with you?" Dexter scowled at him. "If you want me to go with you willingly, you'd better tell me where it is we're going."

The anadon's throat crackled, something between laughter and a deep, bronchial cough. "Not far. Keep moving." He nodded toward the opening in the rail.

Dexter followed his eyes, looking back at Rabani. The scooter hung over a meter away from the edge of the transom, not close enough to board easily, not without a good jump. Rabani shifted in her stance, steadying her aim. Below the scooter was nothing but empty space. They meant to dump him over the edge.

Saaj flicked his split tongue, and the upturned corners of his mouth stood out like a sadistic smile. "Let's go. You're going one way or another." He moved behind Dexter and jabbed him roughly in the center of the back with the gun.

Dexter stumbled forward. "Is this really necessary? Why can't you people understand that I don't have any information that can help you? This is completely ridiculous—I haven't done anything wrong." He paused, shaking his head. "You won't get away with this, I hope you know. You can't just go through life solving your problems by killing people—at some point, someone's going to stop you." He slowed, and felt the broad slot of the gun's muzzle in his back again. He closed his eyes and exhaled, turning back around. "You know, I'm really not in the mood for a walk."

The anadon growled. "Move or I shoot, Massengill."

Dexter shrugged, peering over his shoulder. "Why should I? You obviously intend to kill me."

Saaj raised the gun, stuffing the sharp edge of the ionizer line along the top of the barrel beneath Dexter's chin. "Maybe you don't know what it feels like to experience cellular death over selected areas of your body… there are few things that cause greater pain to the human nervous system. So I suggest you resume walking and spare yourself the unnecessary suffering."

Falling the 12 kilometers to the planetary surface couldn't have possibly been much less painful… he'd suffocate as the poison filled his lungs, chemically burning from the inside out as the acidic gasses scored his flesh, writhing in torturous agony and possibly dying of shock before he even hit the ground.

Dexter sighed and glanced over the anadon's head at the big center piling just beyond the Explorer. Let them deal with the alarms, whether it represented a minor complication to them or not. If he was going to be made to suffer, why not return the favor? "Sorry. I guess you'll just have to do it the hard way."

Saaj withdrew the weapon, pointing it up in the air. "Either way is easy enough." He snapped his left arm forward and clutched Dexter's face, digging in with the toothlike claws at his fingertips and shoving him backwards across the platform.

Dexter fell, banging the back of his skull against the dense, solid surface of carbon-steel. Saaj put the compromizer down, stalked toward him, and grabbed him by the shirt at his chest, picking him up easily. He smacked him across the face with the back of his other hand and flung him in the direction of the scooter.

Dexter landed hard on his shoulder, rolling to his opposite side as pain spread across his back. His vision swam, and the surrounding lights seemed to darken. He blinked, gingerly dabbing at his face as he staggered to his feet. The blurry form of the anadon was barely visible, stooping to gather up the weapon, coming at him again, this time more slowly.

The weapon wasn't even necessary. The anadon probably had the strength to separate a man's head from his body with a well-placed flick of one of those tensile, spring-loaded arms.

Dexter staggered to his feet. "You're going to have to throw me off yourself." The prismatic sparkle around the end of the weapon seemed to dance through the air, licking down along the center his torso as the anadon stepped back and aimed in the area of his abdomen. *There are few things that cause greater pain...*

The anadon pulled the trigger, and the reflector over the muzzle's trapezoidal cross-section flared up in brilliant, retina-scorching magenta. Dexter gritted his teeth and winced, instinctively raising an arm in front of his face and bracing for the searing heat. It didn't come.

He blinked, lowering his arm. The anadon was reeling, contorting his body as crooked streams of electric current wrapped back along the shaft of the resonator chamber and over his arms and torso. He dropped, rolling sideways as the sleeves of his yellow multipurpose suit caught fire.

A second later a plasma bolt exploded behind him, somewhere against the bottom of the next level. Dexter stumbled dizzily, struggling to will his feet to move as he turned to face Rabani. Thick, electric blasts sounded everywhere, echoing across the landing pad, lingering as if time had suddenly slowed and stretched everything over a single, protracted instant. Light from the impacts flashed repeatedly, in every direction.

Rabani and the scooter were no longer hanging in the air behind him. In the space beyond the transom, the entire level was flickering. Dexter glanced around wildly, trying to focus. Rabani was gone. The sound of a single laser blast continued to reverberate... a single, fading echo.

A rolling wave of darkness spread over the field of lots, followed by a second, patchier ripple of smaller sections of reestablished power. In the distance, scattered cars dropped into view, then righted themselves in midair as Dexter stared, bobbing back up through their respective channels of air as if bouncing on the ends of dangling elastic strings. Then, just off the edge of the platform, Rabani's scooter reappeared, unoccupied.

Dexter rubbed his eyes. *What in bloody blazes was happening?*

A charged hum swept across the piers, and a hollow, booming recording sounded through a blend of collective speakers that had to have been fitted collectively throughout the city. "This is a public service announcement. Emergency back-up power systems have been activated. Please use caution. Avoid all urban transport until further notice. We are experiencing city-wide system failures due to unusually intense solar activity. Stand by for further announcements. Emergency back-up power systems have been activated. Please use caution…"

A power outage. Rabani's scooter had died, and she had been unceremoniously dumped toward the planetary surface in a blackout every bit as unlikely as the one in Beta Lyrae. Far beyond unlikely. Maybe he was dreaming, or in some sort of stupefied, delusional state, unable to think clearly about what was going on. By itself, the incident at Beta Lyrae had been an extreme stroke of luck, but this… this was virtually impossible.

He turned and looked blankly toward the ship, shaking his head as he paced hesitantly back across the platform. His eyes fell on the anadon off to the right, face down and motionless on the platform. The compromizer had misfired, possibly because of a bad or hastily replaced cartridge, or faulty wiring. It might have happened one time in 500. It could have been a related effect of the solar flares, excessive ambient electromagnetic radiation. But it had still gone off at exactly the right moment, at a distinctly different moment than when Rabani's scooter had lost power. Everything had gone down at precisely the right instant to save him.

Something else was clearly at work. Was he really a genome psi, operating on some level that was outside his own consciousness? Was there even such a thing? Even if there was, this situation involved massive solar flares 100 million kilometers away—no level of telekinetic ability was going to give anyone the power to manipulate solar flares, let alone at that distance. There wasn't a sentient in the Galaxy with the ability to do that.

Except perhaps the ytaoans. Maybe the ytaoans were helping him…

Jayjay. He shook himself and looked back at the Explorer, jogging forward across the platform, then breaking into a run. He dashed and up the ramp and punched the habitat set control on the wall without looking as he moved inside the ladderwell. "Jayjay?"

He shook his head. So she definitely wasn't hiding out, lying low… of course it wouldn't have been like her to let him fend for himself. Most likely, she had moved out with the scarabs at the end of the scans—presumably she would have an excellent reason. Whatever it was, she would be listening for him, waiting for his call.

He took the steps two at a time, moving quickly through the main cabin and into the cockpit. She was never going to let him hear the end of this one, assuming she actually believed the story. Yet another example of dumb luck… the exception that proved the rule of natural selection.

Salaman and the ytaoans. If the ytaoans were truly interested in his well-being, they might have guided him through some better decision-making over the last few days.

Maybe luck was just luck, and coincidences were just coincidences. With an infinite number of universes out there, somewhere someone was bound to be the unlikely survivor of a few tricky scrapes.

He moved around the right side of the command seat, switching on the master control breaker on the right panel, then hitting the on-board power as he sat down. The dome lights rose gradually as the hard panel diodes flashed on around the shelf from left to right. Dexter eased the seat forward and tapped the autolink, leaning over the com speaker. "Jayjay, are you there?"

The remote link was strictly closed-circuit, and the scarabs weren't likely to be dialed in anyway, since they had apparently left everything off. But doing a lot of com nocking from a ship with a freshly bogus status couldn't have been a tremendously wise idea. "Jayjay?"

He frowned. Her response should have been fairly immediate. He was going to have to contact the munis again. Blast—where in blazes was she?

He tapped the keypad and opened a dialog panel, staring at the display glass as the green frame appeared in front of him. He pulled up the com records and narrowed his eyes. Not a single call in the listings… for a full 24 hours. Everything was gone, including the nocks to and from Balboa. The IPA people had wiped the transcripts.

He hit the autolink again. "Jayjay, I need to know where you are." The diode strip above the small round speaker remained lit to the yellow bead— the neutrino operational carriers were completing the arc to Jayjay's com, so her com system was functional. She just wasn't responding. The scarabs might have had her sorting through their scans.

He focused again on the panel. The data signatures were probably still there. Dexter flipped to operational mode and opened the on-board core action logs, querying the previous two hours and sifting through the lines of Commash. He exhaled through his nostrils, staring as the strings of code flitted in and out of the panel frame.

The IPA scans jumped out… directive after directive stamped with registration ID SC-FN4 Pd 58. The base of operations had apparently been a Farmingdale Scarab, presumably stationed in another lot somewhere nearby.

The ID showed up again at the bottom—a single call from the Scarab, from South Maroon Pier B-19. A keyed nock, addressed to "SiteAE1." The on-board had automatically flowed the transcript text straight into the event record.

/Assemble your team and escort IU to baseship, we will be requesting extended voluntary assistance. Fast response please, Irina will confirm. More details when you get here.

Dexter stared. They had taken Jayjay. And the fact that she wasn't back at the ship meant there was nothing voluntary about whatever assistance they wanted from her. The IPA would have had no cause to detain her, but the IPA obviously weren't the ones calling the shots.

He spun out of the command seat and dove through the companionway, rounding toward the ladderwell and guiding himself down the steps, then froze. The anadon was at the top of the gangway, his body heaving with hoarse, labored breaths.

"Yrissor!" The sentient's callused head practically brushed the upper edge of the hatch. His suit was half-blackened, the thick, yellow-brown skin of both arms badly burned. His arms were tight to his sides, with one clawed fist wrapped around the hilt of a combat knife. He raised the knife in front of him and snarled. "Your luck just ran out."

Dexter grimaced, clenching his teeth and glancing aft. The pistols were all in the environmental cabin. Guidestars—why hadn't he thought to grab a refractor? He took a step back, holding up a hand. "Listen… you don't have to do this."

The anadon hissed and lowered his head, shifting his stance and stepping across the threshold, then abruptly buckled as rose light flared behind him. He lurched to his left, rolling as his shoulder hit the side of the hatch and tumbling off the gangway.

Dexter stared blindly through the open hatch for another delayed moment as the fringes of his vision shimmered from the laser blast. Suddenly the only noise over the landing pad seemed to be the sound of his rapidly beating heart. He looked down at his hands—they were raised defensively, hanging as if frozen in time. He rubbed his eyes, squeezing the bridge of his nose, and squinted ahead.

"You all right?"

Balboa. The constable was directly in line with the gangway, a pace off the bottom of the ramp with a dark, fuzzy object in his left hand that had to be his sidearm.

Dexter took and unsteady step across the threshold.

"Massengill?"

Dexter waved and blinked, trying to clear his eyes. "I'm fine." He snuck a glance to the left. The anadon was on his back near the inside line of the landing skid, his arms and legs splayed wide and his head twisted sideways. His eyes and mouth were slightly open, motionless. He still appeared to have a firm grip on the knife. Dexter looked back down the gangway. "I need your help, constable—I need to get to the South Maroon lot quickly. I think my IU is there. Can I get a ride?" He scanned the landing pad and spotted a car not far from the near transom. Balboa had parked directly on the platform.

Balboa shook his head. "The scarabs already took off—what I came here to tell you." He holstered his refractor, nodding off to the right. "They updated the case status after we talked. Scarabs put in for expedited clearance and they left about 35 minutes ago. Last report says they needed the IU's assistance, and the IU agreed to go with them. Headed for the Fatima System, Deze-Twalls know why."

Dexter frowned, shaking his head and stepping toward the constable. "She is not with them on a voluntary basis. There is no chance of that—she would have talked to me first." Fatima System... why was that familiar?

"Unfortunate, possession's 99 percent of the law." The constable pointed toward the cab. "Listen, Massengill, you need to leave—Port Control's got their hands full straightening out the city. We just had a fare-bu severe bout of solar flare-ups, I don't know if you noticed, par-yen."

Dexter exhaled heavily. "I noticed."

"If you wait for clearance it could be five, six hours. You want to chase your android, you need to go to Fatima."

Dexter raised his eyebrows suddenly. Salaman's message... the kamandra leaves were on Fatima. The bastards had gone through the on-board and turned up Salaman's specs for time-travel—that explained why they would want to drop everything and rush her aboard their own ship. They were going to make sure they harvested every detail from that message, most likely present the specs as their own. Apparently they thought they could turn the information into a profit windfall.

Unless they were going to try to attempt a time-travel expedition themselves.

"Did you hear me, Massengill? You need to get moving right now." Balboa stared intently at Dexter for a moment, then sniffed and scratched his mouth. He turned sideways and rolled his head back, looking up at the next level. "I'll get on the com with ENPC, run interference don-see and fare make sure they ney-pa blast you out of the sky. Just get your batto in the air."

Dexter nodded, looking down. Blast him out of the sky—they would actually blast him out of the sky for jumping clearance? He shrugged and rubbed his neck. "All right, yes, thank you again, Constable Balboa. I'll take her up right away." He paused. "I really appreciate your help... I'm not sure how I'll ever return the favor, but I'll try to think of something."

Balboa backed toward his car and raised his voice. "You can thank me by never coming back this way." He grinned and signaled with two fingers. "Get her up la, Massengill. Stay out of trouble."

Dexter nodded back, briefly watching the constable cross the platform, then turned, took a last look at the anadon, and ran toward the hatch.

*   *   *

... GCL XE.045
Phi -0 48 22.24 / Theta -9 48 27.32 / Rho 44.35 / JD 3040385
Epsilon Sagittarii: FATIMA; "Port Zukara"; 10 March 3612 CE

/5. Preservational prerequisites.

/...

/5.10. The ship will remain primarily enclosed in D5 space during transit; exterior wear will be negligible; the scinti-made piezoceramic fiber-alloy is ideally suited for long-term endurance, and the hull shielding will be limited to the momentary peripheral shock trauma given during the dimensional interchanges. In addition, reflex field enhancer technology will provide for interior preservation over an extended period and easy refit. Reconfiguration of the forward ionizer in accordance with the given specifications will allow for long-term processing of ambient matter for D5, effectively providing steady influx and recyclable power supply at low rate of consumption.

/5.11. The ship is equipped with a full cryonic suspension stasis net complex designed to sustain survival of up to 6,600 y in real space within maximum allowable fatal hazard range; on-board system error rate for Gwalid-Kavnandor M4 scinti-shell models with Astra Parallax-Dynamo interspecies command interface is infinitesimal while in FTL cruise mode.

/5.12. Reconfiguration of the life-support chemical circulation package is necessary to counter delayed shock from protracted dimensional displacement, which would result in neural atrophy and metabolic acidosis immediately upon emergence from cryonic suspension. Preservation of general homeostasis requires an injection of thallium pentacyanide proportional to body mass resulting in blood ratio of 0.862. It must be administered during stasis, beginning after the initiation of suspension with a constant, gradually increasing to the required level at 2.498 y, and decreased back to zero at the same rate, beginning 2.498 y before emergence.

The ship's life-support system will be sufficient to support the new package without additional hardware modifications.

/5.13. Stable distribution of the thallium pentacyanide over the protracted time period requires that all molecules in the chemical package be pure; fusion-made chemical constructs will not guarantee the efficacy of the counter-agent. The chemical occurs naturally in various species of plant life spread around the galactic vicinity, but it will be most easily obtained via the sap of the kamandra desert palm, in the Fatima System. The chemical is a potentially lethal toxin, and it may only be ingested through the measured process described, via life-support and while under suspension.

The artificial human woman lay on the convertible berth, staring blindly toward the ceiling. The measured features of her face held the peaceful, innocent countenance of a contented child, unetched by lines of emotion or age. Like a blue, life-sized doll.

Teodor looked down at the android, pursing his lips, and traced a finger along the outline of her cheek. She was one of the classic first-line models, patented, idealized beauty for those with a preference toward small, athletic body types, with a coating of masterfully conceived organic-plastic skin that was seemingly impervious to wear—a brilliant blend of science and nature, and a tantalizing demonstration that the idea of immortality was neither impossibility nor abomination.

Teodor smiled, shaking his head. Over 900 years old, like the message she had delivered. Admirable workmanship, and a fine-looking specimen at that… having the option to employ her full gamete of services could have been a convenient bonus—a pleasant addition to his selection of entertainment at the end of the long journey. It would have likely required little effort on the part of Cristan Faro or one of his technicians, a matter of tinkering with her somatic motor subsystems and readdressing a few restrictive protocols, allowing the Archangel to assume physical control, creating an effective zombie concubine. Unfortunately, the necessary adjustments for the flight were too delicate to risk modifications to any of the IU's functioning.

It was a shame. It wasn't every day a man had the occasion to thoroughly test the capabilities of a classic android. The two Rabani clones would be available to fill the role, of course, assuming their cellular stability held up through the trip. And with the incubation system in the suspension chambers and an unlimited time table, there was no reason he couldn't eventually use their idealized DNA to produce as many varieties of perfection as he pleased.

He lifted his gaze, following the clustered mass of bonded microwiring and bus cables from the android's limbs to the cavity in the hull. Reportedly, Faro's people had already done the work of harvesting the technological specifications and manufacturing a safe connection between android and on-board and now it was only a matter of adapting the Archangel. They had all the information they needed, and they knew what they had to do. The same ship that had served as the organizational floating command center and a more familiar home than any of the ground-bound penthouses and villas was now going to be the conduit to the Galaxy's most treasured prize.

Teodor stepped to the MTA, glancing again at the message on the monitor, the text he had already reread more times than he knew, emblazoned at the very end like a byline on a literary work with the name of its author. *You have been given a rare honor...*

Indeed. The artistry in the methodology had become even more astounding as the endless implications of the finer details began to sink in. If it was true, the gift this man had given, the instantaneous power he was offering up to people he would never know, was immeasurable. The ytaoans had always been the key, living a placid existence outside the reach of the sentient races, content with their knowledge of nature, content to take their secrets with them to the end of time, but this man had wrested it away. A human man. If it was true, the humans now had the ability to transcend time and space, to circumnavigate the universe. With this knowledge, a single man had the course of galactic history in his grasp.

Faro's team seemed unable to find anything wrong with the information. All things considered, even if Faro had assessed the chances of success at something less than acceptable, the statistical norms no longer applied. Finding the last piece of the puzzle had always been inevitable. It was, in fact, a matter of destiny, and it was no accident this message had fallen into the hands of someone with the means and gumption to act upon it.

Teodor turned as footsteps fell on the gangway. Cristan Faro appeared in the hatch. He nodded at the senator and stepped out of the way as a squat, bronze-skinned Fati technician crossed into the lounge, heading for the stern.

Teodor raised an eyebrow. "You have a change in status to tell me about?"

Faro hesitated, glancing at the flat analytic notepad in his hand. He shook his head vaguely. "Running the flight pattern without the android is officially out. Success rate projections fall way off with the automated IU models, so if you're still intent on doing this, we're going to have to cede some functional control."

The development sounded as irrelevant as anything the technician had reported since his arrival. The senator cocked his head. "It was my understanding you were already going ahead with those modifications."

Faro scratched his ear. "We were. And we have. It was a last resort situation—ideally, we want to limit the number of variables, and having a separate and potentially hostile entity's influence isn't something we really need. I tried to make it work installing a separate package of matching guidance specs and running everything through the Archangel directly, but there's a huge risk of a data corruption if we transfer it and don't replicate the IU's natural sequencing exactly."

Teodor frowned. The gifted principal of technological operations had been immersed among the hapless ruminations of his process-oriented tech gente for so long he had lost sight of the goal. "Mr. Faro, did I not make myself clear earlier? I'm fairly sure I told you I'm interested in two things— whether and when. You have already informed me this flight would be viable, and you told me we were on track to be operational within the hour." He took a step toward him, rolling his neck and curling his arms across his body one at a time to stretch his shoulders. "I'm not hearing anything about a new estimated time of departure... in fact, if I didn't know you better, I'd think you were hedging against your earlier assurances, and as you know, I'm not a big fan of people who hedge their bets."

Faro sighed, dropping the notepad to his side. "Sorry, senator. Full disclosure, just trying to keep you in the loop. Nothing has changed. We limit the risk by slaving the IU to the on-board. If we do that, the coordination changeovers should go smoothly, assuming all of the spacetime dynamics work the way they're supposed to. I can't find anything that's obviously wrong with the calculations... we're making some fairly radical assumptions, but as far as I can tell, the math is solid." He shook his head and shrugged. "The flight's viable—it's just not optimal."

"Not optimal?" Teodor folded his arms and lowered his brow. "That is a matter of opinion, and it's a surprisingly unenlightened one—if there's a reason you're subjecting me to this tedium, I'm not hearing it."

"Sir, you have to understand these flight specs are like nothing I've ever seen. Your on-board is basically going to be completely restructured by this... presumed reflective natural reaction every time you pass to a different dimensional level. It's beyond the known principles of sentient science." Faro was now staring steadfastly back. Clearly, the man had conviction, misguided as it was. "I know how you feel about this, but I think you should consider holding off. With this information, given a few years, we should be able to validate this more thoroughly."

A few years—had the man gone mad? Cristan Faro generally relied upon stark, succinct fact over sycophantic embellishment, and he always had a keen barometer for the mood of a room. Above all, he knew how to wring solutions out of impossibilities, and he was categorically not one to foul the air with the carping of a myopic idler.

"You disappoint me." The senator narrowed his eyes. If Faro had a flaw, it was that he tended to be overly fixated on minutia. It was to be expected— he was being true to his nature, and like most who lacked vision, he failed to grasp the substance of what was now at hand. Teodor tipped his head back. "I suspect that if I gave you a century, you wouldn't have all of it verified. The moment is now… a few years might as well be 100. Unacceptable." He stepped toward Faro and held up a hand as if to grab him by the face, then closed it into a tight fist. "There is no choice. When you've got your hands around the neck of human history, you seize it. Or you die. And I'm paying you quite handsomely to ensure that I experience the left side of that equation, so I expect you to deliver." He exhaled through his nose.

Faro didn't flinch. "There's another concern, if you'll let me finish."

Unflappable, after all. But it was no accident Faro was the man charged with making this trip a reality. Teodor waved a hand. "Let's have it, then. Make your point."

"We can keep the IU's connection to the on-board limited to a one-way stimulus-response relationship. We can channel her navigational commands, and prompt her to direct the flight using the input from the message, and as you know, we can lock her motor system down completely. But she will be active. She has an embedded NOC, so she'll be free to contact her control ship, or send a distress signal. She could contact the IPA… we could settle an AIE abduction legally, but it wouldn't look good for you or the organization."

Teodor nodded, suddenly smiling. "All the more reason to leave sooner rather than later. Of course, that's not really my concern anymore, is it? Where I'm going, I will be irrevocably unreachable."

The look of resignation crept across Faro's face, though he did well to suppress it. "The Archangel will be good to go as soon as we complete the reconfigurations to the ramscoop ionizer. It should be no more than another 40 minutes." He glanced down at his notepad, stepping past the settee. "There are a couple of things I need show you before you leave." He glanced astern.

Teodor shook his head. "By all means." He gestured toward the aft

321

companionway.

Faro nodded and moved through the lounge, weaving his way along the S-curve path left by the glass-table seating alcoves and wire sculptures like a man who owned the ship. He had spent more than a few hours aboard the Archangel, and if he had ever taken pleasure in the accommodations, he had never showed a sign of it.

Teodor glided after him, crossing the adobe tile of the wet bar and dining area and following him through the aft portal into the environmental cabin. The square-edged polish of the smallest, least accommodating compartment of the Archangel contrasted sharply with the supple surfaces of the lounge, though the faux sgraffito walls and marbleized terrazzo laminate of the floor was as pristine as that of a convention hall. The cabin had served as little more than an antechamber over the years, but it would soon become a mausoleum for the universe's longest-lived cocoon.

Teodor glanced right, toward the four cryonic suspension chamber cells that formed a loose chain along the ovolo baseboard, expertly disguised with the shadowed edges of the convex, quarter-round bulge. Pragmatically blended with the decor, but still identifiable.

Faro's Fati assistant was at the far side of the room, rummaging in one of the supply drawers by the environmental terminal access panel, but Faro had ignored the man and gone straight to the worktable along the central bulkhead. A small collection of devices was arranged on the table. A bulky medical booster gun was at the near edge, with an almost invisibly thin, 5-centimeter needle protruding from the nozzle, a silver line under a transparent sheath of acrylic, capped by a blue stopper. The magazine had been removed from the stock and replaced by yellow insulation tubing that twisted across the tabletop and connected the gun with a compressible drum that looked as if it might have been appropriated from a distillery mechanism.

Faro glanced back at Teodor, indicating the drum with a hand. "This is the particle fusion-filter. If you're able to obtain a sample of pyropite, all you need to do is open the chamber at the top, place it inside, and activate it using the pushbuttons." He rapped the circular, spiral-seal lid, and it resounded with a hollow, metallic clang. "It will need to remain activated through the phase transition, so make sure you leave it on once the mineral is sealed inside."

Teodor moved closer, sidling toward Faro and eyeing the controls around the rim. Basic interface, no more complex than a remote lock. The container itself looked large enough to contain a human head, much larger than it needed to be. "You developed the design?"

Faro nodded. "We modeled a transport ferry's converter chamber and adapted it for plasma refractor cartridge technology. Normally, a chamber like this would only work with silicates in grains no bigger than 0.2 microns, but here, we're presuming the sublimation process is already taken care of. We just needed an enclosure large enough to fit a more substantive chunk of material and an avenue to direct the charge at the moment of disintegration." He glanced across the table. "Once the matter is ionized, it should stream through the conduit to a modified neural stimulator. The initial surge of the phase transition will be contained. In theory, if we can then merge the charge with your body's electric current before it dissipates, you should get the same effect as anyone contacting the matter in its solid form."

Teodor frowned. "I understand the theory, Mr. Faro—remember whose definitions your resolutions are designed to satisfy. And please do me the courtesy of sparing me your preambles about risks and guarantees and replicating exact parameters in a test environment."

"Well, the only risk is losing the energy... you'll be safe either way. Based on the given data, I believe it will work." Faro shook his head and shrugged. "We don't understand this material very well, and neither do the cillians, but once it's broken down, it should be possible to direct the particles the way we would handle it in any other controlled energy forum. Ultimately there's only one way to know for sure."

Quite. Teodor returned a sharp look, then nodded at the gun at the end of the table. "Tell me about the stimulator."

Faro exhaled and paused, adjusting his specs. "The device is fully connected, so you don't have to worry about activating the stimulator separately. The current will stream through the needle immediately, so it needs to be grounded in an accessible nerve entry point at the time the matter disintegrates."

Accessible nerve entry point. Faro was dithering just a tad. "I take it there is a preferred place for this injection."

"You're going to have to go through the eye." Faro cleared his throat.

Teodor stared at the needle. "The eye."

"There's a danger the energized particle stream might dissipate if you try a subcutaneous injection and miss a nerve, which would be easy to do. Dermal tissue is resistant to electric current and likely to disrupt the flow, but the fluid in the eye seems to have a strong conductive effect. We've been able to consistently create a linking arc to the optic nerve." He looked at the floor and scratched the back of his head. "This is one thing we've been able to test thoroughly."

Teodor tapped his temple. "How marvelous. And it would have been exceedingly more marvelous had you seen fit to mention that particular detail to me before, on any of the many occasions we've had to discuss the logistics of this project." He cocked his head and clasped his hands behind his back, turning fully toward Faro.

Faro nodded. "Sorry, senator... a lot of these details haven't seemed relevant before today."

"I'd say the need to stick a 5-centimeter needle into my eye is a relevant detail."

"I understand, sir. Again, I'm sorry." Faro sighed. "There should be virtually no sensation. If it helps, you can close your eye as long as you make sure the needle goes completely through the lid and into the cornea. If you're not comfortable doing it yourself, you can have the autodoc do it—the procedure has already been added."

"Comfortable is not a word I would ever apply to needles or autodocs." Teodor blinked, shaking his head. "No, the prospect does not thrill me, but I'll manage it on my own." He frowned at the worktable and brushed his mustache with two fingers. "Any other surprises?"

Faro moved to the opposite end of the table and picked up a small handheld device. "This will help you track down the material once you're within close range." He handed it to Teodor.

Teodor stepped to Faro's side and took the device, turning it over in his hand. The black crescent fit neatly into his grip, just a touch smaller than the typical portable information carrier. Again, the controls were simplistic—three buttons to the left of a glossy display, with a single diode indicator.

"It's a photon dispersion sensor. Not my design, but it's easy to use. The thumb button is the activator—when you hit that button, the reticle display will show you the light intensity in your immediate area. It has a 200-meter range, but it will be much more effective within 5 meters or so. You can adjust the radius with the scoping buttons."

Teodor clicked one of the other pushbuttons. The diode began blinking, and the display resolved from a fuzzy glow to several green dots surrounded by widening wavy lines of decreasing brightness, not unlike a contour map. He raised his eyebrows. "And if the pyropite is locked inside a lead box?"

Faro shook his head. "The optics are engineered to work on shielding metals. It will detect disturbances in oscillating broad spectrum wavefronts and can effectively extrapolate patterns and pinpoint photoelectric activity through most materials, particularly pure, natural-state moleculars like the kind you'll be seeing in the Pre-Fusion Era. It's not perfect—some polymers can cause failures, depending on the intensity of the source, but the source would have to be completely enclosed. And you're looking for a particularly focused source of energy... if you're near it, it should show up as a single bright dot. The display will react proportionally, so any other background glow on the screen should fade out and make it fairly obvious when you're close."

Teodor nodded. "Very convenient. I'm sure I can put it to the test."

"I thought you'd like that." Faro stepped back from the table. "The on-board is set to go into the operational details of all of these tools on your command, so if you have any questions about how to use something, just say the word." His eyes drifted toward the sealed doors of the suspension chambers. "The Rabanis have been briefed as well."

"I'm wondering, Mr. Faro." Teodor narrowed his eyes, cocking his head and pursing his lips at the floor. "Is it me? Do I strike you as the sort of person who would be incapable of properly following basic instruction, or someone who isn't particularly mechanically inclined? Because I like to think of myself as fairly adept when it comes to your technological milieu, let alone these child's trinkets you've left for me to learn... I think there are all of two pushbuttons I will need to commit to memory, and yet you feel it's necessary to program my on-board to prompt me."

Faro fell silent, his eyes hidden behind the light reflecting off his lenses. The man had truly endured more than his share of aggravation. Small price to pay... he would know the benefits of his promotion soon enough, and he would see the rewards of competence and loyalty, with every instance of drudgery and abuse paid back a thousandfold.

Of course, when the Archangel completed its trip back in time, the Galaxy of the 3600s and all its players would be gone from existence.

Teodor nodded and pursed his lips. "Go ahead, Mr. Faro." He waved absently. "Say what you mean to say."

"Just making sure you're aware." Faro risked a bland frown. "If these specs are accurate, this time-shifting will subject everyone aboard to some extreme stresses. You should be fine, but I'm not sure about the Rabanis. Their tissues aren't the same, and we might not have the right dosage proportions for their body chemistry."

"Don't worry, my consigliere." Teodor sucked in a breath, tipping his head back. "If I'm not sufficiently prepared, you haven't done your job, and I would know it if you had failed to do your job." He paused and glanced around the compartment, clearing his throat. "The shield belt has been thoroughly tested, I trust."

Faro nodded sternward. "Yes, you'll find that stowed by the emergency hatch with the evac supplies. Basic stasis tech, we gave it the full run-through and found nothing wrong." He looked back at Teodor, hesitating as if he was going to add further explanation, then nodded again silently.

The Fati turned and momentarily glanced at Teodor before heading back through the portal. Faro watched him go, then glanced at his notepad and nodded. "I guess that's it, then. We'll have to run a final system test once all the reconfigurations are complete, and then you'll be all set. I'll be at the port station terminal for the rest of our prep… if there's anything else you think of, you can contact me there." He stared at Teodor like a child waiting to be dismissed.

"You're really going to miss me, aren't you?" Teodor crossed the floor, stepping in front of him, and patted him on the shoulder. "Go do your thing, Mr. Faro." He gestured at the portal.

Faro stared for a moment more, then lowered his head and exited into the main cabin. Teodor followed him out, winding back through the living quarters to the operational area of the main cabin.

Faro glanced over his shoulder as he reached the hatch. "You'll need about two minutes to safely process the flight pattern before you jump, so we'll keep the IU inactive right up until then. If she does manage to call for help, you'll be on your way before anyone can do anything about it." He stepped down onto the ladderwell and stopped, looking back. "Are you sure I can't convince you to hold off at least for a couple of days? You're leaving a widespread empire behind, a seat in the senate—we'll still be ready to go if you want to make a quick trip back to Anastasia. Make arrangements. You're free to leave whenever you chose."

Teodor nodded, crossing the floor and moving directly in front of his principal technician, looking down. Competent to the last… the man knew the situation would soon be forever changed. "Frankly, this empire no longer has any meaning to me. It's trapped in its place in time, and I am not. It is of no further use."

With the head of the organization gone, the pressure on those who had been held so rigorously accountable over the years would soon be released, and Faro knew it better than anyone. And yet the man persisted in his accommodations, rising above and beyond the call of duty at a time when he might have gotten away with relaxing his efforts.

In fact, given the vulnerable position the Archangel was about to be in, it would have been an opportune time for sabotage. The situation hadn't changed yet. The best way to know a man's mind was through his eyes, and for the moment, the gleam of the overhead light on Faro's specs hid his eyes.

But there were other ways to know a man's mind. Cristan Faro held no malice. The man stared back at him, his mouth poised in the same ever-placid expression, the sharp part of his immaculate, pepper gray hair at the level of Teodor's eyes. Faro had no reason to betray him—the man was most likely getting exactly what he wanted. And even if he bore ill-will, the killer instinct had never been in him.

Teodor touched Faro's chin. "Time is at my mercy now." He leaned in and kissed the man's lips, then straightened and exhaled. "The Articles of Association cover the event of my abdication quite clearly; the arms of the company are now in your control, subject to the approval of the rest of the board. You can be assured your position is secure." He paused. "According to our new friend, Mr. Nevis, you have 30,000 years before the havoc I wreak on the timeline takes hold and erases everything in the universe. I suggest you enjoy it."

Faro was silent for a long moment, frozen and apparently speechless. Perhaps mortified. He shook himself and turned, glancing out the open hatch. "I should be getting back, sir."

Teodor smiled. "Wish me godspeed."

"Right. Godspeed, senator." Faro sidled down the steps, nodding. "I'll contact you when the reconfigurations are complete."

"Very good." Teodor bowed his head. "Thank you for your service, Mr. Faro. You're a good man."

Faro smiled flatly. "I appreciate that, sir." He paused. "I'll be in touch soon." He turned and headed down the gangway.

Teodor watched as the man reached the narrow platform pier below and started back toward the tiny spaceport, a few hundred meters away. Outside, the double blue-white flare of Kaus Australis was low above the rugged line of distant mountains, and the shadows of shrub patches were stretching long across the broken plain.

Cristan Faro would most likely remain in obscurity, content to stand aside as one of the other board members moved in and took hold of the enterprise. The man might have made an excellent leader, but he lacked the critical element of desire to position himself above all others and deny those who would challenge his power. Without desire and without a punishing killer instinct, a man could never be truly successful in leading an empire. Controlling it, expanding it. Keeping it vital and hungry indefinitely. Faro was not that man. But then, few were.

Teodor narrowed his eyes. Perhaps the organization would degenerate to what it had once been… a handful of ordinary corporations, fighting to remain solvent in a competitive marketplace.

It didn't really matter at all. The ingredients of empire were abundant, and the recipe was plain, simple force of will—an inexhaustible commodity. Everywhere there were people ripe for exploitation, everywhere and at every moment in time.

Teodor smiled, focusing on the spaceport. A galaxy full of 37th-century people, the Port Authority staffers scurrying to do his bidding, the IPA, all the senators and lobbyists and media hounds… none of them were ever going to know what they were missing.

He turned away from the hatch and stalked through the lounge, heading for the wet bar.

*   *   *

… GCL XE.045
Phi -0 48 22.24 / Theta -9 48 27.32 / Rho 44.35 / JD 3040385
Epsilon Sagittarii: OS; "Fatima Vicinity"; 10 March 3612 CE

Dexter eased the helm to the right, guiding the Explorer starboard, centering the glareshield on the long curve of Fatima's beige surface. He downshifted the throttle to the freefall position and the display glass sprang to life—virtually frozen long-distance navigation ephemeris blinked away in favor of the active meters and diagrams of the approach array. Alpha and velocity parameter numbers buzzed above an eight-spoked pie target that bounced loosely in the crosshairs of the altimeter, gradually settling against the bull's-eye as the on-board killed main propulsion and adjusted the thrusters to pitch the ship into a smooth orbit.

His eyes swept over the panels, lingering on the navigation array at the right side of the display glass. He sniffed and fingered the mode selector on the helm. The Hertzsprung-Russell photometric 3-D sector geodesic plot disappeared and a double-circle representation of the system appeared in its place, immediately shrinking to a small pair of dots in the upper-left corner of a Mercator map of the planetary surface.

He stowed the helm and tapped the autolink, keeping his eyes on the com diode strip. "Jayjay, are you there?" The green light at the left extreme blinked once, then went out. Her com wasn't functioning. She was either offline or in hyperspace.

He shook his head. It might have been too late. He shifted to the keypad and ran a quick tracer detect—if she was still in the area, the on-board could pinpoint her, assuming the people holding her hadn't tampered with her RLU and disabled the beacon.

Nothing. She was gone from the planet... maybe on her way straight out of the universe.

He stared out the glareshield at the blackness that hung above the planet. He could always go port to port, searching for clues. If there was a record of her signature and it was tied to a ship ID, it would be a start. There might have even been flight plan information out there somewhere. There were probably thousands of terminal records to sift through, but given enough time, he and the on-board were bound to find something.

Time was one thing he had in abundance if Jayjay was already on her way through the informational dimensions.

He sighed and queried the com records, and sat up, widening his eyes. A new message was in. Jayjay had called. He leaned forward and hammered the keypad, opening the record. The display panel expanded and filled with text.

Extensive unfiltered data... Jayjay had flooded the com. Abridged function details, partial narratives and non sequiturs. It wasn't a message— it was a window into everything she was processing at the time. The bastards had jerry-rigged her, cut off her command functionality. That didn't bode well.

Dexter scratched his chin. All he needed was a destination... if she had been given any access to the flight plan, it would be most likely be in this memory blast.

Several solid text blocks down, the stream-of-consciousness plain-English interpreted thoughts and process key sequences were broken up by a long series of numbers, out of context at first glance and most likely indecipherable without extensive analysis, but a distinctive set of coordinates jumped out of the mix: 00.00.00.00 00.15.37.33 00.00 2446200.

He squinted. Galactic space and time... the phi-theta-rho set was unmistakable, and the seven-digit number at the end had to be the Terra Diem. Jayjay was on her way to the Alpha Confinii System some 1,600 years in the past. Earth.

That was it... the on-board already had the necessary information to follow her out. It was just a matter of implementing the reconfigurations Salaman had specified in his message. Dexter glanced back upward through the text. There were other indications of Salaman's message scattered among

Jayjay's words. His eyes stopped on a passage containing additional numerical data.

...transformation set repeating Sag A disk plane radius 65,000 ly Alpha Nadir to Alpha Equator Alpha Nadir to Alpha Equator timelapse 002.741 s JD 3040384 JD 2446200 timelapse 140633308867985114.421358584040252378947092078674944 015388188297072 s Th(5)CN4-BTR 0.862x Th(5)CN40 intrvl 78843563.7348782203 58294468648325292474011153073843964826 s...

He sat back, frowning darkly. No question about it—the people who had taken Jayjay hadn't even bothered to replicate the telemetrics; they had just wired her into their ship and taken off on a time-travel expedition without the least deliberation. It was as if they had already had the trip fully planned, ready to depart the moment they found the means.

He scrolled farther down. The massive block of information ended abruptly, followed by a single, distinct thought—apparently the only bit from Jayjay's split-second sample that she had intended to relay.

/Goodbye, Dexter. Stay safe.

Dexter rubbed his mouth and pulled up a list of specs on the kamandra desert palm. Polycarpic monocotyledon common all around the subtropical and tropical bands of the planet... found in swamps, dry riverbeds, and at the fringes of jungles and appearing in long, sprawling, solitary stalks with broad, thick, pinnate leaves. He set up an optical scan program, then quickly turned his attention on the map, querying for urbanization and climate zones. The wide panel erupted in swaths of brown and yellow land, sprinkled with traces of green, mostly lining the limited areas of water. Dollops of glowing white light showed the cities, markedly fewer than a jam-packed mecca like Scalaway or Anastasia, but spread well-enough across the land like any other nonfrontier planet.

Dexter nodded. If Balboa was right, he was a fugitive from the IPA, or would be soon enough. He was going to have to avoid the population centers, and he was going to have to refit the ship himself and hope the on-board implemented all the reconfigurations properly. It was going to be strange operating the ship without Jayjay, but it was nothing he couldn't do.

He lowered his brow. If she supposed he was about give up that easily, she didn't know him very well. He examined the low latitudes and picked a small, green area near a region of small lakes safely secluded from the nearest settlement. He tapped in the coordinates, and a small locator arrow appeared in the north central area of the projection. He unhooked the helm, grabbed the throttle, and downshifted to the reentry position, glancing left to the six circles of the primary flight array panel and checking his heading as he aimed the Explorer southwest.

XI   NOVA

"And so the past became the present, and the course of events was changed. The slate of history was dashed, and a new slate fashioned, fresh for new inscriptions to be carved. For the pioneers who engineered this change, this new path offered infinite promise... a chance to realize aspirations long unfulfilled, and perhaps a chance to affirm their destiny.

"But change is not welcome to all. For those secure on their established paths in life, such an upheaval might seem far less desirable. And though those of Deiassan century 20 had never experienced their lives as their lives should have been, there is more to sentient perception than tangible observation... they may yet have sensed the reverberations of this disturbance in the course of time, unprecedented and far-reaching as it was, as airborne flocks and herds of beasts might sense the subtle signs of an approaching storm, shifting direction, or stampeding across the land in collective disquiet."

```
... GCL AE.001
Phi 00 00 00.00 / Theta 00 15 37.33 / Rho 00.00 / JD 2446200
Alpha Confinii: EARTH; "Bahamas Vicinity"; 15 May 1985 CE
```

The co-pilot settled unsteadily back into his seat and jammed his headset on. "We're just coming out of the storm."

"It's about fucking time. See if Colonel Pine is at the goddamn airport yet. We need new orders."

The co-pilot cleared his throat. "Homestead, this is Osprey, we have a Tango-Romeo-one-one-four... Homestead, this is Osprey, Tango-Romeo-one-one-four..."

Braddock looked out the front window. A gray cloudbank seemed to dissolve as he looked on, and a wave of blinding sunlight hit the plane, flooding the cockpit like a flash of lightning. Braddock winced and blinked. He rubbed his eyes and tried to shake off the red tint of afterimage on his retinas. It was going to be a long, ball-busting, smacked-ass of a day.

"Homestead, Osprey, Tango-Romeo-one-one-four..."

A glowing orange speck appeared at the top of the window, slowly descending, bisecting the sky perfectly with a straight white trail. For a moment, it looked like a focused area of residual vision impairment.

The pilot was looking in the same direction. Braddock nudged his chair. "The hell's that?"

The pilot squinted. "Looks like a shuttle coming down. Don't know about any shuttles being up there right now… usually pretty good about keeping us informed."

The orange glow disappeared past the lower right corner of the window, leaving the slowly dissipating contrail.

"Roger that, Homestead. Stand by." The co-pilot turned and tapped his headset. "I have the project leader."

Braddock exhaled loudly. "Let me talk. Give me that…"

The co-pilot placed his hands on the earphones and nodded. The pilot was also nodding.

"Goddammit! You have another goddamn headset around here somewhere?"

The co-pilot took off the headset and handed it to Braddock. Braddock grabbed it and yanked the cord almost out of its plug in the console, fumbling with it for a moment. "Fuck!" He fitted it roughly over his ears, positioning the mouthpiece. "Yeah, is this Pine?"

The voice came through in a tinny rasp. "This is Colonel Aberg. What's going on, Braddock? Is Archerfish secure?"

"Yes, sir. Secure as he's gonna get."

"I understand you boys had a wolf in the chicken coop." The colonel paused. "Is your cargo damaged?"

Hell of a question. "Negative."

A burst of static temporarily interrupted the connection. "Say again, Osprey—is your cargo damaged?"

Braddock rubbed his forehead with the back of his hand. "Negative. No damage, no incidents since departure. The situation is contained."

"All right, Osprey, we have a change of plan… stand by for new coordinates. We have you over Bahamian airspace right now."

The pilot's voice cut in. "Roger that."

"Your trip just got shorter, Osprey. We're going to put you down in the Bahamas, and we'll take it from there. Stand by."

Son of a bitch. It figured—Mission Control was probably as jumpy as he was. Braddock scowled at the floor. Damn right, wolf in the goddamn chicken coop.

The pilot nodded. "Roger that, Homestead. Hey, you guys picking up a high-speed object in this area on your radar?"

A different voice, even less clear, took over. Someone in the control tower. "Copy that, Osprey, we don't know what it is. We're not getting accurate readings on that over here."

The pilot glanced at Braddock. "Looks like a shuttle coming in for a landing from here."

"We had something going over 30,000 m.p.h. about a minute ago… not reading anything now. Some kind of glitch, interference from the storm." The voice paused. "Stay safe out there, boys. Over."

The pilot glanced at the co-pilot. "Weird."

Braddock frowned. The lower part of the contrail was still visible. Glitches in the control tower's monitors weren't visible to the naked eye. "Either of you ever heard of something that goes 30,000 miles an hour?"

The pilot shook his head. "Nothing goes that fast. Meteor, maybe. Something like that." He shrugged. "Chalk it up to astronomical phenomena. Every once in a while, you see some strange things flying around up here, Captain. One time I saw a pair of yellow lights come out of nowhere up in Thule, Greenland, when I was flying an F-14, middle of the night. Zipped right over top of my head. Never did find out what that was. It happens, much as people don't like to think about it. Personally, I like to think of it as nature's way of keeping you on your toes."

Braddock stared at the man for a long moment. Whatever it was, it didn't have anything to do with Avila, so it wasn't something he needed to worry about. The only thing he needed to worry about now was keeping everyone from killing each other while they waited to find an uncompromised airbase. And they were going to be stuck on some sparsely populated island for however goddamn long—now it would probably be another ten hours before his feet hit American soil.

He took another look at the pilot. Next assignment he was on, he was damn well going to make sure he knew exactly who he was getting thrown into the fire with.

*   *   *

… "San Salvador, Bahamas"; 15 May 1985 CE

The reaction by the two fishermen was almost more precious than the beauty of the island.

A pier was some 50 meters away from where Teodor had landed the Archangel. With the cab aimed at the broken-down wooden dock, he'd had a clear view of the primitives as they were hauling the day's catch from their boat.

Teodor dashed his foot against the sand and took in a deep breath of air

334

that seemed much fresher than the history books had suggested. He laughed as he thought of the fishermen, dropping their nets at first, staring for several short seconds, then running down the beach in the opposite direction.

It would be interesting to see the effects of the alarm he was causing… the splash he would make on this timeline with minimal effort. He was significantly ahead of the target moment, more than enough time for any ripples he made to build momentum and redirect the course of events. Perhaps his appearance would set off a disturbance that would somehow alert Walker, or perhaps a new sequence of events would lead Walker to another location by chance. Of course, now it was clear that any overindulgence that led to a disadvantageous result could easily be erased with another short trip through time.

Teodor smiled. In all likelihood, he could make as much noise as he wanted. Walker was set on a course that likely extended deep into past. He would be wary, perhaps even dangerously prescient. But he would have learned long before to carefully plan out his path, avoiding notice, avoiding the business of others, and he would be guided by his will, not by the middling influences of distant events. As it was, seven years and four months ahead at exactly 04:57 hours Terra Zulu Standard on 29 September 1992 CE, the pyropite was going to erupt and engulf John Ulysses Walker. Sooner or later, the gemstone would be pinpointed, wrested away from Walker, and secured. Short work for a man who had time at his beck and call.

There was of course the nagging possibility that Massengill had escaped and tailed him here, looking for the android.

Q'um Lharaa Saaj hadn't reported in, and his com had been nonresponsive. There might have been any number of explanations, but Massengill had already proven to be resourceful and elusive when pressed. It wasn't beyond possibility that he had escaped again, and if he had, he might have been motivated to reobtain the android and her valuable databanks. He would have had the means to follow the Archangel into hyperspace if the android had somehow transmitted destination coordinates to him.

The affairs of Saaj and the Rabani clones, the corporate concerns and all the politicking were now matters of another time. Massengill was possibly the last, greatest threat to the quest of a lifetime, but he too would fall away once the pyropite was in hand. The cillian chronicles were being written even now, elsewhere in the Galaxy… testimonials of invincibility. Immortality. It was no longer just an idea, one of Faro's far-flung conceptions contingent upon technology in development. It was a reality. The past was now the future, and the most important event among Faro's investigations was no further away than a brief spell in the suspension chamber.

It would likely take no more than a few hours to home in on Walker and flush out the pyropite. The man's address was a matter of historical record. As it was, the stopover afforded the flexibility to select a good place to dump off the android and sidetrack Massengill in the event the insufferable man was in fact following him. Meanwhile, there were matters of historical significance to attend to.

The on-board computer had calculated the time and coordinates flawlessly. San Salvador, 15 May, 1985 CE. The cross and plaque that marked Christopher Columbus's first steps in the New World were meters away from where the ship had touched down, directly ahead on a patch of grass that rose above the sandy beaches.

Teodor laughed out loud. He could have actually beaten Columbus to the punch this time if he had so chosen. Unfortunately, changing the timeline that drastically didn't fit the plan for now, but leaving a curious message some seven years ahead of time was harmless enough—acceptable risk. He could allow himself that much. After all, San Salvador was a mere 300 kilometers from the ideal nexus to of one of history's most effective professional killers. Too juicy to pass up.

He checked the time on his wristcom. 17:45 TZS—early afternoon at the location. The air transport would be in its place of refuge by now, on another island almost due east over the sea. There was a ten-hour window while the personnel carrying Rafael Avila were at their most vulnerable. Assuming historical accounts were accurate, the transport was in the process of being reassigned to a different point of entry into the United States. Avila was an important prisoner, having drawn much attention, and he had already come close to escape during his extradition. If left alone, the transport crew would refuel on another island, then successfully bring the man in through a small port called Biloxi. Avila would die in an American jail cell under questionable circumstances within the month, and one of the world's great professional assassins would be wasted.

The Rabani clones and their unstable genetic makeup had failed to survive the trip, as Faro had surmised, but their DNA samples would remain viable in the cryonic chambers indefinitely until they were needed. Teodor glanced over his shoulder at the ship. Ideally, the extracted skin cells wouldn't need to remain in suspension for long. He was robbed of his personal assistants now, but acquiring a blood sample from Avila would presumably be a simple matter, given the proper hardware. Faro had left him fully prepared.

Teodor stepped up to the cross and brought his hand to the soft plastic of the concealed holster in the right pocket of his permanent press slacks, casually slipping out the custom adjustable-beam lissajous Ruby-12 refractor pistol another Rabani clone had taken off a Veran arms merchant. He fired at the plaque, blackening the metal and erasing the inscription. He turned to the cross and melted the point of intersection until the sides sagged slightly downward. Then he fired slightly higher. The top of the cross split off and plunged to the grass.

He smiled. A bold arrow pointing upward was all that remained, artistic in its molten imperfection. He brushed his cape away from his belt and withdrew a plate of steel, printed long before, placing it on top of the marred plaque.

I, THE SCROLL OF HIST'RY MINE AT LAST,
FROM YONDER SENT MY SHADOW O'ER THE PAST,
MY MARK LEFT HERE, THE FORMER MARK ERASED:
UPON THIS DAY COLUMBUS IS REPLACED.
TEODOR MONROE — 15 MAY 1985

He turned and headed for the Archangel, glancing down at the garishly oversized belt buckle that now served as the linchpin of his otherwise historically accurate upscale business attire. The fashion violation was surely lost on the era, though unfortunate enough if the detail found its way into the annals of posterity, but a worthy tradeoff for virtual invincibility to the weapons of the day. In a world without lasers or plasma weapons, projectiles constituted the only real potential danger, and with a touch of a pushbutton on the side of the hideously clunky clasp, Faro's specially designed body shield would surround the one who wore it and dampen the inertia of any imminent projectile well below the threshold of lethal force. A refreshment in technology from the onset of the particle engineering era—every approaching body issued a detectable gravitonic vector that a given field could be designed to respond to in a desired way. Simple engineering allowed for the creation of a shock absorber impermeable at up to 20,000 newtons of force. The protection was in common use among the IPA scarabs, and in the fringe settlements of human civilization. Faro had enhanced it, of course. There wasn't a gun on 20th-century Earth that posed a threat from more than a meter away. He was already a virtual god.

Of course, the likelihood that the shield would ever be engaged was miniscule. The people of 20th-century Earth would have no reason to issue a preemptive strike of any kind; anyone without the compunction to commit violence would be hopelessly ignorant of any need to be proactive. Still, if there was to be violence, it would most likely occur at the outset, where the military were holding Avila.

The ship stood at the top of a low bluff, poised on a patch of dry, unkempt grass. He took a last sweeping look at the local scenery and nodded as he wheeled and stepped back onto the gangway. Once he had the pyropite, everything would change. He might choose to stay for a while, exercise his new power over this ancient domain. 20th-century Earth held a certain primitive charm, and he would soon have literally all the time in the universe.

He stepped quickly back to the cockpit, slipping through the soft-field curtain with a hiss and dropping down in the command chair. He leaned back, testing the fluidity of the recline, rolling his neck as he cleared his throat. "Next stop, please."

"As you wish, Master Monroe."

The mechanisms of comfort showed no signs of aging after a multibillion year flight. He listened as the hatch sealed itself closed.

The ground fell away, and in seconds he was again flying low over brilliant blue water broken by tiny flashes of green and white. This Caribbean region was reminiscent of the resort areas of Scalaway. Perhaps the old places of terrestrial beauty were overlooked in his day in favor of the newer, less air-polluted planets.

The thought of the android in the rear compartment crept back into his mind. On the chance Massengill was in pursuit, the IU was a liability as long as it remained aboard, so there was no question it would have to be jettisoned. Now might have been a good time for that—it would have taken seconds to dump the android into the open water. If the unit sank, Massengill would be effectively out of the picture while he puzzled out an aquatic recovery. But there was a chance Massengill would be ill-equipped to perform such an operation, in which case he might fall to direct pursuit if he had a mind for vengeance. And there was also a chance the android's model was had provisions for floatation.

No, the android would have to be placed somewhere else. Somewhere out of the way, where finding the unit would be challenging but not impossible.

The ship accelerated momentarily, and the view through the glareshield blurred, then resolved to show the coastline of a single elongated cay. Faro had said the transport would be putting down on a neglected airstrip toward the southern coast, the only landing port on the sparsely populated island. The transport party was also hoping to avoid other people.

Teodor gripped the helm, feeling the subtle adjustments under his hand as the ship guided itself downward. It swung to portside around an outward bend in the beach, crossing above the coastline and a vast, flat stretch of brownish vegetation. In moments the overhanging brush fell away, and the aircraft below became clear, standing at the long landing strip's southern extreme.

It was essentially a monstrously large metal bird, impressive in size even compared to the craft of the 38th century. It was hard to imagine it flying. The look of these primitive manifestations of flight was familiar enough to anyone who held an interest in aviation history, but seeing it in person... it looked like a patchwork of bolts and loose paneling, wastefully expansive along the wings, borne on bloated, woefully inefficient engine cylinders. And this particular craft was supposedly one of the sturdiest of its day.

The crew inside would see the Archangel momentarily if they hadn't already. Perhaps they were scrambling around frantically, or reporting something nonsensical to a nearby base.

"Send the pulse." Teodor raised his eyebrows. "Let the games begin."

Nothing apparent happened; the craft remained poised silently on its archaic wheels exactly as it had been the moment before. Faro had said the electromagnetic pulse would have no visible effect, but it was extremely unsatisfying not to witness any real damage.

Teodor frowned as the ship settled across the length of the nearby tarmac in an angular attack position above the other craft. "Everything went as planned, I take it? The vehicle is nonfunctional now?"

"That is correct, Master Monroe."

"And the people aboard? Alive and unconscious?"

There was a short pause. "There are indications of higher brain function. Patterns match typical responsiveness for one conscious individual and nine unconscious individuals."

So the stun effect had fallen short. The Archangel's electromagnetic pulse was calibrated to knock out power with the added bonus of overwhelming the neural pathways to the point of inducing unconsciousness for anyone inside the vehicle, but there were no guarantees—the effect on the passengers tended to vary, depending on positioning and other factors. Minor problem. Teodor nodded once. "Send the pulse again."

"As you wish, Master Monroe."

There was motion around the back of the craft even as the on-board responded. Someone had managed to get off before the second round of shock treatment.

Teodor scratched his mustache. "I'd like to see that, computer, and you can spare me the commentary from here on." A new window appeared in front of him in the PDG, showing a smaller view of the activity outside the ship. He focused on the window as the view shifted and zoomed toward the movement, showing a lone man in uniform. He appeared to be yelling, aiming a weapon—the 20th-century version of the hand pistol. It was not Avila, of course. One of the captors.

So, the projectile weapons were out. Teodor smiled and cocked his head. "What did he say?"

"Paraphrasing: If you think I'm giving him up now, you're mistaken." The on-board's smooth feminine voice rendered the words with the usual level of pleasant monotony.

Brazen. Teodor stuck out his lower lip. "Target him. Rapid-fire."

Laser light and plasma streamed from the turret beneath the cockpit to the rear of the other vehicle. The man flopped silently into the sand.

Teodor inhaled sharply. His pulse raced. The industrial-strength weapon made the kill quick and easy... instant death with a voice-prompted command. Distant and impersonal, as if he had ordered someone else to do it, yet somehow it was every bit as much of a rush as ending a life more directly. Crushing a windpipe with the sheer force of his thumbs... feeling the last gasp of escaping heat of the body on the breath as he steered the victim through the point of utter pain.

He patted his knees. "Lower the gangway." He dove back through the buzz of the dew-drop curtain and waited for the hatch to unlock.

These people had never stood a chance. Even before he had his hands on the pyropite, the sheer juxtaposition of technology that was basic and pedestrian in the 37th century had already granted him a measure of immortality... a taste of what it would be like so soon.

Teodor touched his belt and activated the dampener shield as he moved down the gangway, hopping off the end of the ramp before it touched the broken pavement. He took a long look at the fallen man in uniform as he approached the other vehicle. The corpse was thoroughly twisted and blackened by the concentrated blasts. The attitude was commendable, if misguided. Hopefully the officer's countrymen would be less blindly stubborn.

The weapon was by the man's side—the projectile-throwing mechanism wasn't remotely as precise or far-reaching as a refractor, but it was just as lethal if it found its mark. There would be moments outside the ship that would be safe enough, but it would probably behoove him to maintain the body shield at all times, on the chance there were others who would react in similarly noncompliant fashion. Fortunately Faro had managed to eliminate the sporadic shimmering and faint buzzing normally produced by the resonance of a short-range particle field, so he would experience no side effects or tactical disadvantages.

Teodor fingered his own pistol as he stepped around the metal bird's massive open hatch and onto the ramp. There was a chance the stun effect could begin to wear off for some of the crew in minutes…

Inside the craft, men were down along both sides of an enormous cargo bay. One man was bound to the bulkhead at the very back, behind the ramp, hanging upright, suspended by the handcuffs on his wrists. The man's face was smeared with dirt and unrecognizable.

Teodor stepped in front of him, took a small multipurpose stylus syringe out of his breast pocket, and frowned at the man, then scanned the room again, concentrating on the other faces. The man in chains was the only one not in uniform. This would have to be Avila, assuming history wasn't in error and the man was in fact present here; in any event, the on-board was equipped to confirm the identity before the splicing process was initiated, before any of the Rabani DNA was wasted.

There was movement within the long cabin—the crew were beginning to come to. Teodor found an open area of skin near the chained man's jugular and pressed the point of the stylus against his neck. The man immediately stirred, rolling his head. Teodor stepped back.

The man shook himself, struggling violently against his ties for a brief moment before focusing. He blinked at Teodor. "Quien esta ahora? Quien es usted?"

Teodor slipped the stylus back in his pocket and took another look over his shoulder. There was movement, but no one seemed ready to stand, let alone put up a fight. If someone managed to so much as get a look in his direction, the person would most likely fail to remember it. A brief conversation with this legendary figure was perhaps in order.

He turned back to the man on the bulkhead, raising his eyebrows. "You are Rafael Avila, yes?" He paused. "I prefer English." The representative tongue of humans had evolved very little over the centuries, according to file, and it had already been widespread during the time period—there was a fair chance the man would understand.

"Qué bueno—un otro ingléso. You don't sound like an American. Who are you, gringo?"

The man's recovery time was remarkable. Coherent after a few minutes... had he not been shackled in place, things might have gotten a little more interesting. Teodor frowned, cocking his head. "Yes, who am I indeed? I am your savior, it would seem. If you're the man they call 'El Mano Blanco,' I'm going to expand your horizons." He pursed his lips, then glanced at his wristcom and tapped the cover plate, activating the light and flashing it in the man's direction.

The man squinted and twisted away. "Salvador." He laughed dully. "Salvador, eh? If you are my savior, you will let me go free."

Teodor nodded, staring at the man as he moved his face back into the light. The man's eyes were icy and intense, tinged pink with blood, like the eyes of a man from Demteedum. The eyes of an albino. There was no mistake—this was Avila.

Teodor turned and stepped toward the gaping maw of the hatch, raising the pistol in the air as he turned back toward Avila. "Let you go free. I'll be doing much more than that, Mr. Avila. I'm going to transform you into a brand new person, and you're going to live a long and fruitful life."

Avila gritted his teeth as he jerked his wrists hard against the cuffs. "Hola, gringo—you can unlock my irons... the keys are in the cockpit. You will get your reward." He spat into the air. "Eh, where are you going? You can't expand my horizons if you run away like a rata asustada."

Teodor lingered at the hatch. "I'm afraid it's too complicated for me to easily explain, but a few drops of your blood are all I'll need." He patted his breast pocket. "I thank you for your gift, Mr. Avila. It's truly been a pleasure to meet you."

Avila shook his chains and raised his voice. "Loco cabrón!"

Teodor turned and headed down the ramp, grinning broadly.

*   *   *

... "Mayaguana, Bahamas"; 15 May 1985 CE

The midday sky was thick in haze. The pale yellow disk of the sun filtered through the cloud-swept whitewash as if it were shining from behind a sheet of cheesecloth.

Inspector Ambrose dropped his gaze to the dry brush forest at the south edge of the airstrip. Behind the tiny yellow terminal and the neglected remains of the U.S. Air Force control tower, the shallows of Abraham's Bay fanned out like a turquoise bowl. Two flecks of color dotted the surface in the middle of the water—a pair of windsurfers. Several yachts were visible farther out toward the fringe of darker water. Tourists on a quest for a no-frills, peace-and-quiet retreat.

One of the few settled areas on the island was about 3 miles away. Aircraft flew overhead regularly, but it would have been hard to miss the noise of all the unexpected landings. The people were apparently determined to remain oblivious. No surprise—it was easy to ignore, looking in the other direction. Even for someone standing in the midst of it.

"John."

Ambrose turned, shifting his weight from one foot to the other. Henry Pennington was jogging slowly toward him along the shadow of the giant C-130 that now dominated the back end of the runway. Ambrose squinted as a sudden gust caught him in the side of the face with gritty salt air. "What is it?"

Henry stopped in front of him and half-turned, pointing his thumb over his shoulder. "The Americans found another body."

Ambrose cleared his throat. "Another one from the plane? I thought they accounted for all the crew."

Henry shrugged. "I don't know. It's a woman." He paused. "It's a little strange. Roy's up there already." He headed back toward the chaos.

Strange. It couldn't have been much stranger than the first one. Ambrose started after him and stumbled over a tuft of grass sprouting through a crack in the pavement. He winced and steadied himself.

Henry glanced back at him without slowing down. "You going to make it?" There might have been a trace of a smile on his face.

Dimwit. Ambrose frowned, feeling his ankle throb as he picked up his pace. The godforsaken place hadn't seen a day's worth of maintenance in 15 years. He focused on the cluttered mess of vehicles that now formed a barrier blocking the taxiway to the tarmac. The plane's fat tail loomed overhead and the rear cargo bay door hung open in front of them, forming a ramp like the entrance to a museum. The wingspan took up nearly the entire width of the asphalt runway, and off the starboard aileron was the Black Hawk helicopter that had brought the Americans, 12 marines along with the two officers from the Naval Investigative Service. The Americans had wasted no time, covering the 400-mile trip from their base in Miami in under two hours.

Ambrose flared his nostrils as they moved out of the shadow, heading through the space between the plane's fuselage and the helicopter. Ahead, a knot of road vehicles were parked at odd angles, covering the area between the aircraft and the taxiway. Hap Boyce and his two garage apprentices were lingering by his blue pickup, conversing with some of the U.S. military personnel. Henry rounded away from the group as he approached, drawing a few glances. Ambrose followed him around an old sedan and another pickup, keeping his head down as they neared one of the two police vans on the island. The other van had already run off, carrying a handful of the plane's more traumatized crewmen.

Ambrose sneaked a glance as they moved past. The empty gurney was still behind the remaining van's open rear doors, left unattended. Just next to it, the hideously burnt corpse of the American Air Force captain lay on the ground, now covered with a blue blanket.

Ambrose breathed through his teeth, looking back out over the long stretch of sun-bleached asphalt as they neared the taxiway. Straight ahead, the far section of the old airstrip was 2,500 feet of government-run wasteland. In truth, the entire length of the ramp was now in a pathetic state of disrepair, its pavement cracked and riddled with potholes and patches of grass from end to end, but the northern third was completely unusable, crumbling to gravel in vast sections, overgrown with moss and blended with the surrounding weeds around the edges. Not really a suitable stop for huge military craft, but the Americans weren't being forthcoming about the mission.

Henry seemingly wasn't in a forthcoming mood himself, silently picking his way along. It was a long straightaway to the scrub, but he seemed to be angling for the taxiway. Ambrose nodded at him. "Where did they find the woman?"

"Off the tarmac. Next to the wrecks."

The inspector raised his eyebrows. "The wrecks. That's a sight out of the way, isn't it?"

Henry looked blankly back at him, glancing at his feet. "You want to go back to the car?" He smirked. "Everyone knows you don't walk on sand or up hills, but come on, man. It's a flat hundred yards, if that."

Easy for someone on good ankles to say—not to mention the corporal was about 60 pounds lighter. And "flat" was hardly a good description for the condition of the pavement. Ambrose frowned. "I'll survive the walk— thank you for your concern." He paused. "That's not what I meant. The wrecks are well away from where they found the other body."

"I guess." Henry shrugged. "It's not far from the tracks."

They moved onto the taxiway. Ambrose's eyes fell to the two long rows of hastily placed traffic cones that now ran toward the far corner of the tarmac, cobbled together along one side with what caution tape they had available on the island. The cordoned-off area marked a peculiar trail of discolored, ring-shaped depressions on the pavement: two long, thick tracks, each one containing two rows of smaller rings abreast a single row of larger ones. The depressions were all aligned and evenly spaced, at least 15 meters across and some 60 meters in length, all told. It was as if someone had painstakingly marked the pavement with giant branding irons.

Crop circles on pavement. The work of mischievous teenagers, maybe... possibly coincidental to the events involving the military craft. Hopefully. Obviously it was something they were going to need to investigate eventually, but there were plenty of reasonable, conventional crime scene aspects to take on before they tackled that one.

Ambrose grimaced, putting his hands on his hips and looking down at the pavement as they passed the first of the cones, tasting hot, wet air as he breathed. He coughed and cleared his throat. "What's strange about it?"

The corporal blinked slowly. He shook his head. "Come again?"

"The woman's body. You said something was strange." Ambrose nodded ahead toward the end of the tarmac.

Henry sighed. "She's blue. Head to toe. Like someone painted her." He paused. "Looks like she must have drowned."

Ambrose pursed his lips. It would have been an odd place to find a drowning victim. "Head to toe?"

"Right." Henry raised his eyebrows. "She's naked. Blue skin all the way down."

More incongruous details. Ambrose frowned and wiped his brow, glancing at the sky to the right, above the tiny terminal at the south end of the tarmac. The sun was climbing—by now they should have been finding answers, not piling up more questions. Typically, a case on Mayaguana was as black and white as an Oreo cookie, and just about as inconsequential.

The scant airport facilities seemed isolated from the commotion, looking just as abandoned and desolate as usual—a tattered, white terminal building with broken windows and fallen roof panels, along with a pair of restroom huts, one with blackened walls, barely standing after a bad fire. The domain of hutias and lizards.

What was left functional was good enough for a tiny island of 300 people and a limited tourist draw... no more than three aircraft touched down in a week, most of them small planes. The islanders generally liked to stay put, and most were seemingly content to let the airport fade into the jungle.

The other end of the tarmac served as an informal aircraft graveyard.

345

The brush spilled over the edge of pavement like an overturned can of paint, and three small aircraft were deep in the vegetation, stripped of machinery and seating and surrounded by littered debris. They were lined nose to tail, as if queuing up for departure. The arrangement of cones ran more or less directly toward the old, yellow DC-3 in the corner.

Henry walked quietly along the cones, apparently satisfied with the information he had already offered. Ambrose squinted ahead. There was activity off the plane's tail—Detective Sergeant Roy Thatcher was with the man and woman from NIS, Special Agents Scanlon and McCants. Roy looked up and nodded as Henry approached the end of the pavement.

Henry slowed. "The body's there." He pointed a thumb over his shoulder. "I'm in for lunch—I'll be at the firehouse."

Ambrose waved him off and moved into the grass. Roy stood off to the side with Scanlon, presumably the senior official among the Americans—the tall, thin man was at least 20 years older than the female agent. McCants was to the right, examining a matted-down area in the deep grass and jotting notes on a small pad. The body was hidden from a vantage point of more than a few feet away, but there was no mistaking the 6-foot hole in the overgrowth.

Ambrose frowned and stepped to Roy's side. "What have we got?"

Scanlon squinted at him. "Victim's a woman in her 20s, no obvious signs of trouble." He indicated the area with his long chin.

Roy nodded. "This looks like it may be a separate case, boss. Have a look."

Ambrose eased closer to the disturbed grass and grimaced. The woman lay flat on her back, eyes wide, naked as described. Her appearance was startling despite the preliminary description—she was thoroughly blue, as blue as the clear water in one solid, uniformly pale shade. It was as if her entire body had been dyed like an Easter egg.

Ambrose shook his head. "You don't think this is connected?"

Scanlon moved next to him. "There were no women aboard the plane. She's hidden, out of the way, unlike the other victim, and she's got no burns on her. Of course we have no idea what happened here... lot of question marks to check off. Be nice if one person aboard that plane had managed to see a damn thing." He frowned, glancing back toward the C-130. "Hell of a mess. You had any murder cases recently?"

"Not on this island." Ambrose stared at the body. Bright blonde hair, very fit, attractive woman. Her eyes had the same darker tone as her lips, similar to the deep color of a bruise. "I've seen a few drowning victims over the years. Nothing recently. I've never seen a drowning victim who looked like this."

Roy stepped around Scanlon. "You mean the blue skin?" He sniffed the air loudly, nodding. "Yeah, boss, I don't know. "Cyanotic skin means her blood is oxygen starved, but it could be drug-related, or some kind of poison."

Ambrose stared back at the detective. If he was disturbed by the scene, there was no evidence of it on his face. Roy Thatcher was a young 35, and the throwback, platform-style high-top fade made the man look even younger—it was easy to forget he had been with the police for nearly ten years.

Agent McCants looked up from her pad. "It's definitely not a drowning." She crouched over the body near the woman's head, waving over the face with her pen. "This is severe tissue hypoxia. Her methemoglobin has to be off the chart for this much discoloration. There are chemicals that can cause effects like this, like in blue baby syndrome. Nitrates, barbiturates, things like that." She shook her head, squinting. "Not even a hint of lividity here... she can't have been dead for more than three or four hours."

Roy looked at her sharply. "It would have to be closer to four—that would put the time of death inside a half hour before we got here."

McCants brushed away a loose strand of dark hair. "Probably right around the time the other incident was taking place." She nodded, straightening her back, and glanced at Scanlon. "It doesn't necessarily mean the incidents were related... the plane incident might have scared off a separate attacker."

Roy frowned and snorted. "Not fast enough."

Scanlon cleared his throat. "Inspector, with your permission, we'd like to get the woman's body on a table somewhere nearby, avoid any jurisdictional issues assuming she's a citizen of the Bahamas. Agent McCants is a licensed medical examiner in the States—she can do an autopsy, get some information before we head back." He paused. "I assume you have a place in town?"

Ambrose rubbed his mouth. He shook his head. "We're not really equipped for anything complicated. If you need any supplies, we'll have to fly them in from Nassau." He peered again at the body. "It might be advisable to relocate the woman to Rand Laboratory Morgue at Princess Margaret Hospital... if you don't have room in your helicopter, we can call for a medevac."

McCants stepped to Scanlon's side. "I have a kit if it's not too much trouble for you to prepare a room—all I need is a long, flat table. I just need to conduct a brief external examination and collect some initial tissue and blood samples that might rule out a connection. It will be much faster for us if we do the intensive lab work back home."

Scanlon lowered his brow. "No need for a medevac, inspector. We've got room on the helo for our serviceman, and we'd like to get him back home as soon as we can. We'll keep you apprised, but it would be a big help if you could expedite this."

"Of course." Ambrose swallowed dryly. The stationhouse lounge was where the banged-up aircraft personnel had been directed; those folks would be ready to clear out by now, but the thought of having a corpse cut open on the table where people had their lunch and coffee was less than appealing. Perhaps they could requisition a new table. He sighed, leveling his eyes at McCants. "How long will this take?"

She stared at him for a moment, then shrugged. "Half hour, maybe 45 minutes."

"Very well." Ambrose turned, glancing at Roy. "We'll take her to the stationhouse. Let's get her on a gurney and put her in the van."

Roy nodded. "Right." He put his hands on his hips and looked back toward the marines spread over the airstrip.

Scanlon looked down and unclipped a hand radio from his belt, turning away as he raised it to his mouth. Ambrose grunted quietly at the back of the man's head. More than likely, the dead woman was an American herself, but protocol dictated that she remain in Bahamian custody until her citizenship was verified. As it was, the Americans were going to be zipping in and out for some time, leaving massive trails of paperwork in their wake and most likely rendering the local police obsolete in the interim.

Ambrose looked again at Roy, who now seemed to be lingering. The inspector raised his voice. "What are you waiting for? Let's move, sergeant."

Roy nodded toward the female officer. "You want me to ride with Agent McCants?"

Ambrose swept an arm across his forehead, shaking off the sweat. "She can ride with me. Go get Pennington—that horse's ass has been on break long enough."

*　　　　　*　　　　　*

Roy Thatcher glanced in the rearview as the doors at the back of the van swung shut. The body was strapped down, packaged under the bunched plastic bag-like furniture in a moving truck. He took the keys off the visor and cranked the ignition, twisting to his left. There was an extended delay before Henry Pennington's face appeared in the passenger side window.

Ambrose and McCants were 10 feet across the tarmac in the inspector's Impala Coupe, their faces hidden behind the car's windshield. Roy leaned toward the passenger side, peering up through the window. "You want to pick up the pace a bit?" He frowned at the sedan. "You're already in the old man's doghouse." The sedan honked and flashed its headlights on cue.

Henry opened the door, tossing a pack of Marlboros on the dash as he climbed in, smiling as a lit cigarette hung from the corner of his mouth. "I suppose it can't get any worse, then." He slammed the door.

Roy glared at him. "You're gonna put me in there with you." He put the van in gear, rounding toward the terminal. "You sure it's okay to tie down a body with bungee cords? The skin could bruise if it's too tight."

"What am I supposed to use?" Henry shrugged, tossing his loosely bound dreadlocks. "It's a ten-minute ride—I'm sure it's fine."

Roy guided the van through the gateway in the fence, past the terminal building, winding left around the quarry and along the coastal road. He checked the sideview mirror. The Impala was already 20 feet behind them, just crawling up to the gate. Ambrose was notoriously slow behind the wheel. Roy cleared his throat, glancing left. "You better hope she doesn't bruise. That's what the gurney straps are for."

Henry cleared his throat and leaned forward, patting the dash. "If you had been the one buckling her up, I guess that would have been your call."

Roy frowned, raising an eyebrow at Henry as the man sat back, sucking on the cigarette. The man wasn't the only local island cop who didn't take his job seriously, but he was pretty blatant about it for someone who was in his second year as an officer.

Henry tipped his head back and took another drag, tapping the ash out the window. "Believe me, you don't want this girl's body to go flying off the first time you hit a curve. Straps wouldn't have held." He paused, glancing out the window. "This girl, she may look small... but she has some weight hidden away. No easy job getting her on that gurney, my friend."

Roy laughed under his breath, shaking his head. Hard to tell if Henry was joking. At a glance, the woman hadn't appeared to have an ounce of excess body fat on her.

The road wound left around the curve of Abraham's Bay. The land softly sloped down toward the white beach, and a string of houses were visible on the opposite hill. Roy inhaled as he glanced right, soaking in the view. The water was calm and clear as a swimming pool, all the way to the ocean, gorgeous even on a cloudy day. More than enough reason to spend a life in the islands…

Something stuck out along the horizon—a huge oil tanker off in the distance, maybe, though something looked off about it. Roy swung the van around a bend in the road and took another glance, frowning. A hairline crack of sky appeared between the horizon and the bottom of the vessel. It was airborne. Abruptly it swerved and disappeared.

Roy focused on the road. Another military helicopter, maybe… disguised by an odd trick of sunlight above water. Probably not quite tanker-size—apparently, it was a lot closer to shore than it had looked. How much cavalry did the Americans need to investigate a couple of dead bodies?

Suddenly the thing was in the windshield, swinging above the beach and dropping straight toward the road. Tires screamed over dry pavement and the cigarette pack flew across the dash. Henry was yelling, pressed to the passenger side door as the van skidded off the left edge of the road and jolted to a halt against the shrubs along the embankment. Roy threw up his arms and caught the wheel squarely in the chest, bouncing roughly back to the seat cushion as the van creaked like a settling pile of collapsed girders.

Then all the noises stopped. The van was stalled out. Roy blinked, looking down. His leg was almost fully extended against the brake pedal, all the way to the floor. He peered left, breathing slowly. Henry was sitting up, wedged against the door and looking a little shell-shocked but apparently okay. He seemed to be staring right past him. Roy rubbed his chest and winced, shifting to look back toward his own window.

The aircraft was still there, big and strange-looking and dropping smoothly onto the road as if it were being lowered on an invisible string. It wasn't making a sound, except for an odd background hiss that seemed to be coming from every direction. Below it, the air seemed to warp like a heat mirage.

Roy squinted, shaking his head slowly. "What the hell…?"

The thing had two pontoon-like landing skids spaced wider than the road. The skid on the vehicle's right touched down inside the edge of the pavement while the other was well into the brush along the opposite shoulder. It was long… very long. End-on, it was impossible to tell exactly how big the thing was, but it might well have been bigger than the C-130.

The ship could practically levitate. Propulsion with virtually no sound. Sweet Jesus, Mary, and Joseph—who in blazes was in there?

Henry whispered behind him. "Start the car, Roy."

Roy glanced at the wheel absently and twisted the key. The engine didn't make a sound. He shook his head and tried again. Just a click, as if the gas tank was suddenly empty. He stared back out the window. The C-130's engine had died too, according to the reports... suddenly and without explanation.

"Start the car, Roy!"

"It's dead. We're not going anywhere."

Henry thumped against the passenger door, scrabbling for the handle. "Speak for yourself, man." He got out of the van and took off down the road.

The Impala was stopped sideways about 20 feet away, directly in view of the open door. Ambrose and McCants were making no move to get out. Henry made a beeline for the car, ducking around the back bumper and dropping out of sight.

Roy gripped the wheel, looking again at the huge landing skids. They were about right for the tracks at the tarmac... this had to be the thing that had left the two long rows of perfect circles in the gravel. This crazy, wingless airship was what had grounded the C-130 and killed the Navy captain. Flash-burned him like a turkey fryer. Henry was possibly right to run, but even if Ambrose's engine still worked, they weren't about to outrun a ship like this in a Chevy Impala.

The inspector and the NIS agent were apparently more comfortable in the car. If they had the urge to leave, they weren't showing it.

Roy stared, mouth shut. His pulse pounded, and rushed nasal breaths rasped in his ears as if he were wearing scuba tanks. He shook his head. Everyone who had stayed inside the C-130 was still alive. Running wasn't a good move, not now.

He focused again on the massive vehicle, trying to digest what he was seeing: a front end like the front of an 18-wheeler on a blown-up scale, more angular, tapered for aerodynamics. The surfaces looked aged like an old stone building—a mix of mossy green and gray. A distinct, opaque panel stretched over the area where the windshield should have been, set back from a broad, flat nose dominated by a grillwork of reflective metal and tinted glass above a spread of dark machinery that looked as if it extended farther back along the underside. Nothing like anything on any military ship he had ever seen.

Who the hell was inside this thing?

There was movement to the left... a narrow strip came away from the hull and lowered toward the ground. A ramp. Roy shrank away from the window. They were all going to find out exactly who the hell was inside this thing, like it or not. He swallowed and crossed himself.

The ramp hit the ground, and almost immediately a man appeared at the top and jogged down as casually as if he were heading out the door to his home on a morning commute. Just a typical-looking dark-haired white man dressed like a mechanic in a pale blue jumpsuit. He reached the bottom and rounded to his left without hesitation, heading behind the van. He glanced briefly in Roy's direction without breaking stride, then slipped out of range of the window.

Roy twisted around and shifted across the seat cushion to the open passenger door. No reaction from the other car; presumably Ambrose and McCants still had their eyes on the man. Roy tensed. No reaction was probably the right idea, but the thought of having the man lurking outside his field of vision was slightly more than he could stand. He held his breath and poked his head out the door, looking back.

There was a muffled clattering at the rear doors. Roy whipped his head back inside and pressed flat against the seat, locking eyes on the rearview mirror. The man was twisting the handle, trying to open the doors. Unsuccessfully. Roy frowned. Henry couldn't have locked them up—the keys were in the ignition the whole time he had prepped the body.

The clattering stopped, followed by footsteps. The man was coming back around the driver side. Roy dug his fingers into the cushion.

The man stepped to the window and looked in. "Hello? There you are, excuse me... I believe my friend is inside your vehicle."

Roy stared dumbly back at him.

The man nodded and glanced toward the rear doors. "She's about 180 centimeters in height, bright blonde hair, and she'll have a blue pigment in her skin. That should be a fairly incontrovertible description." He paused. "I'm able to track her location, and it seems to be right here. Do you mind helping me open the doors? I'm having trouble with the mechanism."

He blinked and nodded slowly. "She's here, yes. Just a second." He moved back to the driver side, grabbed the keys from the ignition, and hesitated. The man stood smiling back at him for a moment, then straightened and stepped back as if he had only just realized he was in the way.

Roy opened the door and got out. The man was tall and thin and extremely fair-skinned. His speech was clipped, as if English wasn't his first language, but the accent was hard to place. Not exactly intimidating at a glance, although his apparent inability to detect anxiety in an obviously high-anxiety situation was unsettling. Hopefully he already knew the woman's condition.

Roy moved around to the back of the van, keeping his eyes on the stranger. He cranked the handle, nodding back as the man stepped next to him. "Sometimes it sticks." He paused, exhaling through his nose. "I should tell you… we found her in the grass. We don't know what happened to her yet."

The man frowned, cocking his head. "She was nonresponsive, then." He nodded. "That's understandable." He waved at the doors. "Please, go ahead."

Nonresponsive? Roy scratched the back of his neck, glancing toward Ambrose's Impala. Ambrose and the officer were now outside the car, on their feet behind the open doors. Roy cleared his throat and twisted the handle again. The latch popped. He sighed and swung open the doors, stepping back.

Henry's system of bungee cords had come undone. The gurney had flopped sideways, and the blanket that had been placed over the body was now loosely covering both body and gurney at an angle, leaving a single blue leg exposed. Roy breathed rapidly, peering carefully at the man from the ship. No noticeable reaction to seeing this alleged friend of his in lifeless disarray. It would have been great to get inside the man's head for just a moment.

The man climbed inside the van, moving the blanket and kneeling over the body. Roy looked back at the gigantic flying ship. NASA had run a base on the island until 1970, but the ship was clearly beyond anything anyone in the area would have ever laid eyes on. Some kind of experimental technology from some other part of the world. The man didn't seem to have a malicious bone in his body—hard to imagine this was someone capable of taking out a C-130 and burning a man to a crisp. So this woman with the blue skin was apparently with this man… so who in God's name were these people?

Roy turned back to the van and started, eyes wide. The man from the ship was now helping the woman climb out. She was suddenly alive and ambulatory, draped in the blanket and moving deliberately as she placed her feet on the ground and steadied herself. The man wrapped an arm around her back and the two of them headed in the direction of the ship.

"I'll be damned." Roy shook his head and stepped after them, looking from the van to the ship. "She was… how did you do that? She was dead."

The man stopped and looked back. "Actually, she wasn't dead. Just… very ill." He looked thoughtful for a moment, pursing his lips. "You don't mind if we keep the blanket, I hope."

"It's yours." Roy stared at the woman. She looked just as blue as she had looked before. "Listen, ah… we're trying to sort out everything that happened here. We've got a contingent of police here, we've got American military, federal personnel… we've got a lot of questions. I don't know who you are, but you should come back to town with us to help us iron out these details."

The man raised his eyebrows and nodded at the ground. "I understand. I apologize, but we're in a bit of a rush. I'm afraid I can't help you." He turned away.

Roy stepped forward. "Wait—now look, we've got an Air Force captain dead back at the airstrip, and a downed plane, and markings on the ground that look an awful lot like they were left by your ship. You need to tell us what happened back there."

The man exchanged glances with the woman. Her expression was stern. The man tipped his head back and sighed. "I'm sorry about the commotion. It wasn't my ship—I'm only here to get my friend. I haven't been to your airstrip, and I really couldn't tell you what happened there. I'm sure it won't happen again." He paused. "I really can't say any more than that. Again, I'm very sorry for the intrusion. Thank you for your help."

Roy shook his head. "If it wasn't your ship, then whose ship was it?"

The man and woman weren't going to answer again, and there wasn't a damn thing anyone in the vicinity could do about it. They continued to the ramp without looking back.

Roy turned back toward the Impala, frowning. Ambrose and McCants were coming, most likely wondering what the hell was going on. They weren't going to be happy with what little explanation he had gotten, but it wasn't as if he'd had a choice. With a ship like that, the mystery man and his resurrected friend could do pretty much whatever they wanted.

Only here to get his friend. His once-dead, blue-skinned, naked friend...

Roy laughed under his breath. At this point, it didn't much matter what the man said or didn't say. Whatever they put in the paperwork, there was no way anyone was going to take any of it seriously.

Maybe they could just write it up as another plane crash. Circuit malfunction in the cockpit causing a fatal electric surge, something like that.

I'm sure it won't happen again...

Roy glanced over his shoulder. Behind him, the massive, technologically impossible ship was already rising above the road, once again in virtual silence. It was gone in under ten seconds, shooting out over the water and veering right, zipping away behind the east side of the island in a blink without leaving any trace of contrail. Disappearing back to whatever magical place it had come from.

He rubbed his mouth, turning back to Ambrose and McCants. They were all probably better off not knowing any more about it than they did.

Ambrose stared out at the water as he approached, hands on hips.

Roy glanced from the inspector to the NIS agent. "You saw what happened?"

The agent frowned, running a hand through her hair. She said nothing. Ambrose grunted. "We saw it."

Roy nodded. "I take it the autopsy's off." He shrugged. "What now?"

Ambrose looked back at him. "I think I need to get lunch. I'll decide after that whether or not I need a new career." He gave McCants a long look, then turned and headed for the Impala.

*   *   *

```
... GCL AE.001
Phi 00 00 00.00 / Theta 00 15 37.33 / Rho 00.00 / JD 2446200
Alpha Confinii: LUNA; "Taurus-Littrow"; 15 May 1985 CE
```

/2. Causality and logistical considerations

 /...

 /2.8. Transition between the information eigenspaces D7 and D8 is accomplished via virtual inertial progression, a momentum-based reflexive translation of velocity through the material dimensions. This progression from D7 to D8 will accordingly require the number of minimum time units along the eighth order of the triangular series, exactly 36 tP. While this duration is too miniscule to be perceived from the point of view of the traveler, the dynamics of spacetime are such that 36 tP in the virtual dimensions translates to 29,446.282 y in real time; therefore, upon the emergence of the traveler in D7, those who remain in the material dimensions will continue to experience events for this extended span of time.

 /2.9. Entering D7 effectively removes the traveler from spacetime; therefore the traveler's influence on the sequence of events necessarily ends at the entry point. Effectively, the traveler is removed from existence from the point of view of those who remain in the material dimensions. For the duration of the traveler's immersion in D7 and D8, events in the material dimensions will transpire along a new course, with the traveler's effect on his surroundings thus removed, creating a temporary deviation in the natural course of events. The effects of this departure from the timeline will be eliminated upon the reemergence of the traveler in the material dimensions.

 /2.10. Accordingly, when the traveler reemerges in the material dimensions at the selected time, he effectively enters a new universe with a fresh sequence of events. From the point of the traveler's emergence, the traveler will have the capability of influencing events that, from the traveler's point of view, were in the past. The result is a new, earlier deviation in the natural course of events. The effects of this departure from the timeline will remain through the duration of the spacetime cycle, but they will be eliminated upon the closure of the cycle, after which the universe will resume its natural course.

/2.11. To an extent, the influence of the traveler and the resulting effects can be countered by the ytaoans; however, pronounced influence may result in cascading deviations that cannot be corrected during the present cycle. Therefore it is critical that the traveler limit his exposure while displaced.

The Earth was small but vivid through the scinti quartz, high in the window. It looked exactly as it should have looked, like a crystal blue marble streaked with chalky whorls. A lone ornament on a black curtain.

Dexter let his gaze drop down to the broken moonscape. A pair of isolated mountains ascended away to portside and starboard, framing a bunched set of toothy hills that curled around the arching horizon and separated the valley from the nearest significant crater. The hills were pale in the earthlight, forming a photonegative contrast with the darker lunar soil of the valley in the foreground.

There, about 100 meters dead ahead of the Zenith Explorer, amid a scattered array of silvery objects, was the unmistakable rectangle of a flag. Evidence of one of Humankind's first ventures to another world, now less than two decades old. There were still traces of color... the unfiltered ultraviolet light hadn't yet burned it away completely.

Salaman Nevis's instructions had truly brought them back in time. There was no question about the value of his information now.

Dexter stretched his arms, leaning back in the pilot seat. Everything was ghostly, lost in shadow without the lights or bustle of the bases that wouldn't begin construction for another 200 years. The base sites were beyond the rumpled, cratered terrain of the Taurus Mountains to the east and south, somewhere within the two vast, unstirred planes of microdust—the Seas of Tranquility and Serenity, the first maria named in Human Space. Very different feel than his previous trips to the Earthmoon, to be sure.

The Earth may not have shown any tangible differences, but it had held a different feel as well. It had effectively been reborn... now there was boundless wild plant life and much less urbanization. It was before terraforming, before atmospheric circulation engineering and the huge O2 megamixers—he had just tasted fresh, nonrecycled air for the first time, although to a roamer like him, any open air not canned in a spaceship tended to seem the same. But the chill had probably been the most noticeable thing. Theoretically, the temperature on this Earth wasn't significantly colder than the Earth of the 37th century, and it was probably warmer in the tropics where he had landed than most of the places he'd visited recently, but 20th-century Earth had felt uncomfortably prickly and clammy. Something about the heightened activity of recycled air at the atomic level left natural air feeling off, perhaps.

Salaman had given him and Jayjay an astounding gift. Of course, it was a gift that might well have never been experienced if the two of them had been left alone. And if Jayjay's retrieval had gone less smoothly, the achievement would have been much more difficult to appreciate.

Dexter swiveled in his seat, looking back toward the main cabin. Teodor Monroe had held Jayjay's fate entirely in his hands, and it would have been easy enough for him to make her untraceable, or worse. But he hadn't.

Jayjay appeared in the companionway, and Dexter jumped. She pursed her lips. "You're still awake, I see."

He stood and stepped in front of her, resting his hands on her waist. "Good idea, coming here. It's romantic being on the Moon all by ourselves. Don't you think?"

"I suppose. It's also the only mass within a sub-light radius that's large enough to hide us from radio detection." She flashed a smile and kissed him, then pulled back and scanned downward, resting her arms on his shoulders. "So is this the way you're going to dress around here for now on? I thought you were cold."

She was back in work clothes, having gone to the trouble of digging one of the unopened dress packs out of the holds and changing out of his adorably oversized pilot suit. Too bad. He glanced down at the gray fabric of his undergarment. "Well, you've got the climate control adjusted to a toasty setting—I'm actually quite comfortable." He raised his eyebrows. "Besides, I thought I'd wait until you finished all your checks. I wouldn't want to get all dressed up only to have to disrobe again."

She smiled, tracing a finger through his hair. "Easy, tiger." She patted his chest and pushed past him, dropping into the command seat. "It's just as well. You need to sleep."

Dexter followed her lead, sitting back down at the pilot station. "I've been asleep for over a billion years, Jayjay. If there's one thing I don't want to do right now, it's to get more sleep."

She nodded and tapped in a command, keeping her fingers poised over the CTA console as a dialog panel appeared on the display glass and spit out a brief, coded response. She kept her eyes on the screen as she spoke. "878 years, for someone inside the ship. You wouldn't have made it to one billion, hyperspace or not. But either way, that's far too long for your brain to be shut down in cryonic suspension. You're isolated in a delta-wave loop, with intermittent electric REM induction, so your body isn't able to progress through the natural sleep cycle. So actually, you haven't had a good night's sleep for the duration. If you don't get any rest, you're going to collapse. So go to sleep—you're going to need at least three hours under hypodormine before you'll be able to function." Her hands flew over the keys, and the panel rapidly filled with text.

Dexter shrugged. "I think I'd like to take a break from functioning for a good long while. Anyway, it's not as if we have any pressing needs."

Jayjay said nothing. Annoyed he wasn't taking her seriously, perhaps.

He sat back, looking again out the front window. He shook his head and laughed. "Jayjay, honestly, I'm too wound up to sleep. I just completed the Human Race's first trek through time in history. We're looking at the Earth in 1985. It's not exactly something I expected I'd be doing the last time we made travel plans."

Jayjay slowed her pace on the keypad. "Technically, Teodor Monroe was first."

She was apparently determined to pop his balloon. Dexter nodded. "Aha. Well, I hope he appreciates the honor." He sniffed and rubbed his eye with a knuckle. "Seems like the grandiose sort... I imagine he had fame and glory in mind when he took up the task. Of course, he did have you on board for the trip, so I can still claim the first solo flight." He blinked at Jayjay. She still seemed more interested in the feedback she was getting from the on-board.

"I suppose." She widened her eyes and shot him a quick glance, smiling flatly. "I guess it's too late to hope it doesn't go to your head."

He looked across the console, staring at the primary CTA monitor. "Are you running more diagnostics? I thought all the system checks turned up no anomalies."

"That's right. Nothing jumped out."

"You're running redundant scans manually now? Wouldn't it be easier to plug in?"

She dropped her hands to her lap and turned toward him, widening her eyes. "I'm not running a manual scan. The performance data are compiling on the MTA." She flashed another smile and turned back to the console.

"Well, that's good." Dexter hunched forward, clasping his hands together. "So… are you going to tell me what you're doing now, or are you going to make me keep asking questions?"

"Can we talk about it later? You need to go to bed, Dexter."

He grinned. "Not unless you go with me."

She smiled without looking back.

He squinted, rubbing his neck. "I think we've checked every function on this ship three times over. The ship's automatic inventory went off on pattern exit just as it should have, and I told you I ran a line audit while I was tracking you…"

She rolled her head toward him. "Yes, Dexter, you told me about the line audit." She shook her head absently. "It's a little more involved than basic diagnostics. Salaman's program used transformational algorithms, and it altered control signals, reorganized registers… it's as if the build is brand new. It's like working with a different ship. The ALUs have been enhanced, operating with the new drive specs and these theoretical fundamentals we used to navigate the higher dimensional shifts."

Dexter nodded slowly. "But your connection to the on-board is still sound."

"As far as I can tell, the responses are normal. Everything looks good so far. Don't worry—just precautionary." She paused. "Salaman obviously had all his Z's and O's squared away… he's layered in the detail like a spaceport control system. Apparently, he knew what he was doing."

Salaman's accomplishment was remarkable, no doubt—genome psis didn't tend to do that well at precision predictions. Salaman had effectively managed to refit a ship nearly a millennium in the future using technology that didn't exist, terabytes of complex telemetry rendered flawlessly, coaxing an ordinary on-board into making projections it wasn't designed to do. Of course Salaman had apparently had a lot of help.

"Yes." Dexter covered a yawn with his fist. "Well, I assume the ytaoans had a hand in this."

"I guess I shouldn't be surprised. If any of the information they gave you had been the slightest bit off, you and the rest of the ship would most likely be liquefied in a fermion-boson paste right now." She cocked her head and sighed. "With your luck, I don't think that's possible. Look, you need to leave now—I don't want to have to pick you up off the cockpit floor."

Dexter exhaled through his nostrils, looking down at the cockpit floor. There was little argument about his luck, now more evident than ever. He had yet to sort out the rather unlikely chain of events at Eo-Nowar's lower level—a timely power-outage, the malfunction of the anadon's compromizer, Balboa arriving at the perfect moment. The wild universe had many offerings, many of which had no simple explanation, and the events on Ustinov were probably going to remain squarely in that category. "You used to say you didn't believe in my luck."

Jayjay glanced out the window, her eyes in the direction of Earth. "Now I'm not so sure." She focused again on her monitor and hit a function key on the console, and the on-board responded with a pair of bell tones. She stared expressionlessly at the screen for a long moment, then abruptly started tapping the keys again. Her fingers glided over the keypad.

Dexter ran his tongue around the inside of his mouth, feeling the grit of his teeth. His mouth seemed unusually dry. Maybe it was another side effect of protracted cryonic suspension. He straightened in his seat, stretching his lower back. "Well, I've definitely had my moments. But as you said before, Salaman's specs always looked solid, and you had a chance to go over all of it yourself. Coming out of all this in one piece had less to do with luck and more to do with competence—yours and Salaman's."

Jayjay was watching him. "Don't make it out to be less than it is, Dexter—it's more than just competence. The flight plan, the design specs Salaman sent us… all of that had to be flawless. He had to know things about hyperspace dynamics that no one had ever even theorized, much less tested; he had to account for every flight-related interaction down to the subatomic level, and he had to know exactly how the operating system would respond. There could have been file corruptions. 909 years is a long time to store a mass of sensitive data." She watched the on-board spill another stream of green circle-hex alphanumerics. "You didn't even have me aboard to make course corrections or transition through any process interruptions. I'm pretty sure I wouldn't have been able to help in any way even if I had been aboard, since the protocols were out the window and the arithmetic projections were so unconventional."

Dexter frowned, lowering his brow. A fair point. Salaman and the ytaoans seemed capable of anything. He'd already had the thought himself, among other seemingly crazy ideas, but hearing it from Jayjay gave it a little more weight; perhaps the ytaoans' clairvoyant machinations were in fact somehow intertwined with his good fortune on Ustinov. It was just as good as any other explanation.

He snuck another peek at Jayjay's screen. The command lines were moving too quickly to catch any familiar coding, but it was scrolling upward in large chunks. Too sporadic and interactive to be a run-down of typical system information. Clearly more than plain logic and analysis. It looked more like research, some sort of archive file call.

He scratched his cheek and sat back, looking blankly down at the butterfly grips of the helm nestled perfectly in its recess at the pilot console alongside the labeled tiles of the throttle ignition sequence. It would have been interesting to see Jayjay's reaction if he suddenly fired up the engine and took the Explorer on an unscheduled horse ride.

That would most certainly not have ended well. He sighed and let his eyes drift across the console in a useless, cursory scan of the indicators, and settled on the com display to the right of his own monitor. He frowned, leaning closer. The diode strip above the speaker was lit through the orange bead. Active interface. He shook his head. "Jayjay, are you trying to hail someone, or am I looking at a malfunction?" He glanced at her station. Her com display was lit exactly the same—green, yellow, and orange.

Jayjay stared back for a long moment. "I'm just probing."

Dexter cleared his throat lightly. "You do remember we're in the 20th century. You won't find too many database sites with compatible signatures."

Jayjay nodded, looking back at her screen. "Monroe's ship has a compatible signature."

He squinted. "The Archangel? Why would you want to contact the senator's ship?" He turned, switching on his monitor. "I was hoping he was long gone by now."

"He's not. His ship is about 30 million kilometers away, in an exterior heliosynchronous orbit keeping pace with Earth along its orbital path." She frowned at him. "I really didn't want to get into this with you until you were a little more clear-headed."

Dexter blinked and rubbed his nose. "I'm crystal-clear. Let me in on your thinking, Jayjay—what do you want with the senator? I thought we were rid of all that business."

Jayjay sighed. "I did some information gathering while I was interwoven with the Archangel—I was hoping to get an idea of what he was planning, why he picked this particular time as his destination, in case I had a chance to relay anything useful to you. He's carrying volumes of static data from cillian transcripts that center around this time period. The common root is apparently a mineral called pyropite that destabilized all over the Galaxy on JD 2448894, which is 2,694 days from today, some seven years plus. Monroe's next stop. There's separate evidence that points to a specific location on Earth where one of these minerals may have been. It looks as if this trip is Monroe's attempt to track it down."

A diagram of the ship appeared on Dexter's monitor, along with several links to operations Jayjay was running, including the file block she was reading. Dexter looked back at her. "You're saying he abducted you to go on a treasure hunt through time?"

She folded her arms and her eyes flicked upward toward the photo-panels. "Based on what I read, Monroe thinks this pyropite will make him immortal."

Dexter studied her expression. There were no overt traces of skepticism. "You think he actually believes that?"

"Oh, he believes it. There's a lot more where that came from. Monroe has devoted a huge amount of his resources toward experimental research in extending human life. Genetic engineering, electromagnetic dynamics, cybernetics... you name it. He's also invested in time-travel experiments, which suggests he's become convinced that getting his hands on the pyropite is the answer." She glanced at the screen and scrolled upward, shaking her head. "He's obsessed. The man's managed to amass as much wealth and power as anyone I've ever heard of, but he's not going to be satisfied unless he figures out how to prevent his own death."

Dexter rolled his head back, closing his eyes briefly. A man who viewed himself as a god... the description was eerily familiar to Jayjay's accounts of Salaman Nevis in the Tarantula Nebula. And now Monroe had used her just as Salaman had, treating her as so much hardware, effectively enslaving her for a time. Now she seemed to be fixated on the senator, but no wonder... past issues had a way of bubbling up to the surface.

Dexter rubbed his eyes and sat up. Jayjay was looking intently back at him. She nodded toward the window, distinctly in the direction of Earth. "I'm concerned about what he might do next." She paused. "I've been working on a plan to shut him down."

He furrowed his brow. Was she serious? "Shut him down? Jayjay, he's out of our lives. Why not let him have what he wants—let him go about his business, stay out of his way? The man is dangerous."

She looked at him sharply. "I know. That's what I'm afraid of. He's a threat to the people here."

Dexter looked up at the Earth. The gravitonic drives were capable of covering the 400,000-kilometer distance in minutes. Monroe was apparently somewhere between Earth and Mars now, but it wouldn't take him long to reach the Moon if he so chose, and he wouldn't have had trouble singling out their electromagnetic field if he was looking for it. The craggy rock wall around the Taurus-Littrow Valley suddenly felt significantly less secure. "I'd have to say he's a threat to us too... I'm sure he's armed better than we are. What exactly did you have in mind—how do you mean to shut him down?"

She turned back to her monitor. "I have his access encrypt, so all of his on-board operations are fully readable. I was walled off from interfering in command functions, but under the right circumstances I can implement a bypass. Once I do that, it should be easy to sabotage the entire ship. His peripheral com descramblers have an electromagnetic pulse emission; it's just a matter of turning the Archangel's pulse in on itself."

Dexter stared at her for a long moment. The intensity of the cabin light was becoming mildly irritating, and a dull ache began to worm its way along his back. He shifted, brushing the bare skin of his triceps against the cold fabric of the pilot seat's arm rests, and a chill ran from his neck to his shoulders. He eased himself forward in the seat. "Are you sure this is necessary? I mean, we're talking about confronting a man who very nearly had me killed. Have you considered this may be some sort of emotional response you're having, something that may be more about what you went through with Salaman? Sometimes, when people go through traumatic experiences, they need closure."

She glared at him. "This isn't about me being manipulated, Dexter— I'm fully capable of distinguishing between past resentment and present concern." She nodded, cocking her head. "I've thought this through. I understand the dangers, but I believe the dangers are potentially even greater if we decide to leave Monroe alone."

Dexter squinted. Now she seemed to be making no sense on any level. He rubbed his arms. "All right, let's assume that's true. What if he's alerted to our hails? He seems to be extremely resourceful—I'm not sure why or how you think he won't see us coming long before we're able to do anything to his ship."

She nodded again. "He won't see us coming—my com tap reads as a collaborative connection, and I'm disguising our hails as a referred internal subroutine. My call sign will show in the log, but Monroe would have to request a complete run-down and catch the process insert himself. He won't know to look for it, and there's no IU—his on-board does all the screening directly." She paused. "Believe me, I don't want to put our lives at risk again any more than you do. But this is something we need to think about."

It sounded as though she had already done all the thinking for him. "So... what is it you think will happen if we do nothing? Are you saying you think there's something to this mineral, that Monroe's going to transform himself into some sort of invincible superman?" He muffled a sudden yawn and shook his head foggily.

"I don't know about that, but I don't know that he needs to. He clearly thinks of himself that way already, and with or without the mineral, his technology makes him the most powerful human being on 20th-century Earth. He might like the idea of settling in and changing the course of human history. We're 1,600 years in the past... if he exerts a strong enough influence, the Galaxy we know might never exist. Think about it, Dexter, we're the only ones in a position to stop him." Jayjay's bright hair gleamed under the photo-panels.

Dexter looked down at the floor and sighed under his breath. "You know, I was really hoping we could take some time to relax and enjoy ourselves. One crazy idea I had... we could go to Beta Lyrae, look at the dust spiral as it was before any people settled on Valentina. No casino officials to kick me out of the system." He laughed quietly to himself. "Give myself a chance to prove it was never all about the gaming. But I had another idea, a better idea. We could have gone to Scalaway. I imagine the Thousand Islands look a lot different without all the built-up civilization. It's not that far, either. An idyllic virgin paradise, and not a soul within 30 light years—now there's a unique vacation opportunity."

Jayjay smiled and slid forward, patting his knee. "That sounds nice. Maybe we can still do all that."

He covered his face with both hands, pressing his palms into his eyes, then rubbing his temples. "Is this really our responsibility? I mean, yes, granted, we're in the best position of anyone to preserve history, but how can we be sure he hasn't already had an irreversible negative impact on history?" He sniffed and cleared his throat, then laughed dully. "Who is to say it's negative, anyway? Maybe over the course of his dastardly deeds he'll inadvertently do something that causes some sweeping improvement."

"I can't answer that. But you've seen him in action, and it's because of us that he's here. I think we have to do what we can to minimize what he can do. You heard the man from Earth—he's already taken down a military vehicle and killed at least one person."

She had obviously given the matter a lot of consideration. Of course she was looking at things rationally, logically. She could have perhaps delivered the words in a slightly less patronizing way. Dexter shook himself, leaning slowly back until he felt the seat against his shoulder blades. A more intense chill fired along his spine. He exhaled noisily. "Tell me about the plan... I want to understand the plan to shield society from Senator Monroe. You want to leave him stranded in orbit?"

Jayjay had her seat turned fully toward him now. Her brow was knitted, but she looked more amused than concerned, for some inexplicable reason. "If I try to do the bypass while his ship is active, his on-board will react to protect the ship. This only works while he's on the ground. If I'm right, he'll land in North America when he comes out of his holding pattern in seven years. If he shuts everything down, we monitor the ship until he reactivates it, and I run my bypass then—his on-board's start-up protocols will be bogged down in pre-ignition activities and a lot of auxiliary functions, so I'll be safely through before the ship recognizes there's a problem. Then I send the pulse emission, knock out every system on the ship, and we move in and blast his scoop, turrets, and any other rigged weaponry just to be sure he's grounded for good and can't do any major damage. Ideally, he'll be on board and unconscious."

Dexter rolled his head, stretching his neck, and nodded slowly. "We disable the ship. And then we just leave him there?"

Jayjay nodded. "Essentially, yes. He won't be able to reboot the ship without a compatible power source. We leave him marooned on Earth with no functional technology and effectively eliminate any threat he poses... take away his power, leave him helpless." She paused. "He may or may not be on board while the ignition sequence is initiating—he has full terminal access in his RLU and the sequence is completely automated, so he may be inclined to give himself a head start. If so, things get a little more dangerous. We could potentially be leaving him at large with a fully effective refractor, which he could use to funnel power back into the ship if he knows how to install the backup system."

"I see." He shook his head, scratching his ear fuzzily. "What if he isn't aboard—what then?"

Jayjay sat forward. "I try to pinpoint his location and immobilize him with the turret. He'll be nearby... it's just a matter of tracking him down before he does any damage to our own targeting system."

Dexter raised an eyebrow. "Immobilize him. Low-energy burst pattern?"

"I'll do what I have to do to separate him from any tools he's carrying. As long as we can take away his technology, the people here should be able to keep him under control as much as they would any other 20th-century criminal." Jayjay gave Dexter a hard look. "I'm content to leave him alive, but if he engages us in a firefight, I won't waste time hamstringing the turret with safety protocols."

Optimistic. No telling what the man was capable of if they left him unchallenged on Earth. Technology or not, Monroe carried the knowledge of the 37th century in his head, and he clearly had a history of doing quite a bit of damage with his acquired knowledge and skillful manipulation. Not to mention what he might have been able to accomplish with this supposed talisman he hoped to find. Unsettling thought, the idea that they might need to contend with a man bolstered by the supernatural power of some fabled treasure.

Dexter laughed weakly to himself. It was a simple plan, really, but attempting to work things out on his own was starting to seem monumentally difficult. Of course it wasn't exactly their purview to decide a man's fate. Jayjay was probably just being reasonable. She was on top of things. She had obviously considered everything there was to consider, carefully weighed all their options.

He looked up at her and a fresh thought abruptly wandered into his head. "What if we can't find him?"

"That's unlikely, since I can track the signal from his remote. He would need to be in the area. We'll know ahead of time if he's not on board, so I can be ready to take off and chase him down if necessary." Jayjay turned back to the CTA panel, nodding in the direction of the glareshield. "It's possible he could dump the remote and slip away. If that happens, there's not much more we can do."

Dexter blinked, nodding absently. "He'll still have the refractor on him if that happens, I would think. So he'll still have his weapon, if we leave him to it. And as you say, he could recharge the ship, if he managed to get back aboard."

Jayjay sighed. "And the people of the 20th century will have a formidable fugitive on their hands for about ten years, if the refractor is fully charged. Not to mention we would be leaving substantial technology behind that might end up making a huge impact on history, if the people figure out how to exploit it. Which is why it's so important we disable the ship's drive and weapons systems." She set her hands on her knees and turned back to Dexter. "Some of it's out of our control. We just have to hope he's not able to get away on foot."

Dexter frowned, blinking heavily. The people would need to be warned, of course, on the chance that the senator did get away, free to use his weapon. Unchallenged, lording over the planet. They didn't want to interfere with history, of course—they would need to exercise discretion. But the people would need to be warned about Monroe, at the very least.

Jayjay had her hands around the situation, obviously. He could rely on her straightforward logic. Ambush the senator... sabotage his ship. It would all most likely work out. Monroe wouldn't slip away. Maybe he would go off on another whim, fly to another time. They would be off the hook, with nothing between the Explorer and open space.

The brown gridwork of the floor panels blurred. Jayjay was out of her seat, stepping toward him, and suddenly he was on his feet, stumbling through the main cabin with his arm draped over her shoulders. He vaguely registered a berth in low light, extended only enough for a single occupant. Then he was staring up at the dimmer lines, a fuzzy mess as the dull light seemed to bleed across the ceiling. For a moment, he tried to focus on the barely discernible circle of the porthole at the low threshold of his field of vision. The tiny, brilliant, blue marble Earth was somewhere below the bottom edge, hidden from view.

He closed his eyes and imagined a smattering of green, unsettled islands spread across another sea of glistening blue. 20th-century Scalaway, with its pure, natural air. True paradise, and not a soul within 30 light years... no casino owners, no IPA, no crazy, power-mongering senators. It was all right there, waiting for them, and it was theirs for as long as they wanted to stay.

XII   THE MINER

"We live... it is the ultimate way we express our thanks to the forces of nature that create us. We breathe the air we are given and nourish ourselves with the fuel that passes to us, and we survive for the time that is allotted us.

"The fire's-eye fell to a man who did not seek to find it. He lived modestly, in shadows... far longer than the natural duration for a member of his species. He endured pain, and he survived. If he believed in none of the gods of the many cultures he passed through, he believed in life, and the earth and sky that had offered it up to him. He honored what he believed to be his duty... he was given this gift of life, and he did not waste it. He endured, though he did suffer doubt about the choices he had made... condemned to self-imposed isolation, he had only his own experience to rely upon, with no buffer against his own judgment.

"But in the end, he would see the merits of his choices when he crossed paths with another man of similar standing, and briefly glimpsed the true look of a life less honorable."

```
... GCL AE.001
Phi 00 00 00.00 / Theta 00 15 37.33 / Rho 00.00 / JD 1460131(E)
Alpha Confinii: EARTH; "Athens"; circa 15 August 716 BCE
```

There were people clustered in the dirt concourse of the agora, many more than there had been ten years before. Many of the stone shops had doubled in size, and the buildings now surrounded all sides of the long quadrangle, hemming it in like a fence. The building stones were smooth now, with shared stoas and colonnades, and polished statues in the narrow grass park at the center had replaced the crude figures of before. The stench of fishmonger stores was gone, and the air was now filled with the smell of tanning leather. And fabrics of rich red and blue shades dominated the shops' outdoor displays, along with the pottery and silver and gold wares.

The lands of Greece were growing much faster than the lands to the East. Even in the hills of an island apart from the main population centers, leading a hermitic lifestyle had become markedly more difficult. The notion of staying outside the reach of civilization was now a fancy of the past. But while the rise of civilization made hiding in seclusion problematic, it made hiding in plain sight that much easier. Especially for those with experience at remaining unnoticed.

Orestes laughed under his breath as he moved into the square, keeping his steps even and his pace slow. Experience was one thing he had. Unfortunately, being careful wasn't always going to be enough.

The sun was blazing from its azimuth perch in the crystal blue sky. It was unusually hot, even for summer, and the vendors lingered outside in front of their shops to the left and right. The people were moving sluggishly, already visibly exhausted as if they had been milling around for a full day.

The pattern was clear... the world was on a gradual course toward greater and greater numbers of people, and one day it would be choked with humanity to the extent that being aloof would not draw attention among the increasing speed and distraction of everyday life. But for now, relative anonymity carried with it a requirement to be familiar with one's neighbors.

Orestes glanced around, briefly brushing his chest. The ancient goat-hide pouch was bound snugly beneath the folds of his Assyrian cloak. He exhaled calmly. The number of eyes on him was increasing. The more they watched, the greater the chance they would sense what he hid, or catch a glimpse of it while he moved it from one secure location to another, as some had in his previous travels.

The medicine shop was there along the far fringe of the square where it had been on his previous visit. It appeared unchanged amid the surrounding structure. This was the place... he was unknown in Athenai. In the larger cities, the people were busy, and tended not to be as preoccupied with business that wasn't their own. Here, it would be considerably less likely that people would take seriously a tale of baetyls and miracles. And this shopkeeper was known for his discretion.

Orestes felt a pang of dread as he approached—one sensation that the stone seemed to be incapable of eradicating. He sighed, concentrating on the warmth of the stone in the pouch against his chest. He might have waited another year, honed his apothecary craft in Kefalonia further and perfected his surgical technique. But there was no valid reason to wait any longer. His technique was sound enough, and what he lacked in scholarly knowledge would be compensated with instinct, as it had many times before. He could wait another ten years, or he could wait another 50—he would improve little, and the time would go by in the blink of an eye. And he would again be faced with the same problem: he was vulnerable as long as the stone could be taken away.

Ultimately, he had no choice. The prospect of robbery would only grow; the danger increased with the population, and he had to act if he wanted to extinguish it.

He went through the doorway. Tall wooden shelves reached near the ceiling against every wall, packed with jars and boxes of plants and berries that filled the air with a muted, complex aroma containing a distinct, heavy scent of pine and rosemary. There was a long, cloth-covered counter with a meandros fringe set at the left wall, and a smaller wooden table and chairs to the right; Aristeides, the shopkeeper, was seated in one of the chairs, apparently asleep, his back propped against the wall. He was an old man now, visibly much older than he had appeared before.

Orestes's eyes went to the arched entryway toward the far right corner, covered by a green curtain just behind the shopkeeper. He crossed the floor and nudged the man back to consciousness, and the man slowly opened his eyes.

The shopkeeper waved his hand in front of his face and blinked, frowning. "I'm resting. Is this urgent?"

Orestes nodded, frowning at the man's withered skin. "It is. I need your help." The difference in the man's appearance was jarring—it was as if the man had aged before his eyes. Ten years of working with herbs had passed quickly after the long crossing over the violent tracts of Assyria and Anatolia.

Aristeides sat up, rubbing his eyes and squinting. "You don't seem sick."

Orestes lowered the hood of his cloak and glanced at the back entryway. "I understand you have a room in the back where surgery can be performed."

The shopkeeper stood up and waved his hand in the air, laughing and shaking his head. "Surgery? I'm an old man... I can barely hold a knife steady when I eat."

Word among the people of the Attican countryside suggested the man was downplaying his abilities. If it was true that the practice of vivisection had fallen out of favor, the shopkeeper would be slow to admit his endorsement of it. Orestes shook his head. "I only need your facilities and your herbs, and I will pay you well for it. I ask only that you give me one hour of privacy." He looked toward the back room and freed the bag of ingots lashed to his belt.

Aristeides stared at the bag in his hand, then raised his eyebrows, amused. "Do you intend to perform surgery on yourself?"

Orestes was silent.

For a moment the shopkeeper looked mystified; then his expression gradually slipped to one of worry. "It's not polite to waste an elder's time, my young, dark friend. You are either a prankster or a fool. You'd best move along with your nonsense—you're interrupting my rest." He gestured toward the front door.

Orestes stepped forward, holding up the bag of ingots. "This is no prank. I have here 600 oboloí in Lydian electrum. That's enough for you to buy yourself a fine new house in the city." He dropped the bag on the table in front of the shopkeeper, letting the metal rods clatter across the wood. He nodded at the shopkeeper. "Please listen to me. I have a list of the supplies I need. I am familiar with the procedure, to the extent that I don't trust it to anyone else. I am an apothecary myself, from another town, but I don't have the supplies of Athenai in my store."

Aristeides took a long look at the money. He closed his eyes, shaking his head. "It's not permitted. The Eupatridae frown upon the cutting of the flesh, which is often done by an untrained hand and almost always unsuccessful. There are temples out at the Acropolis where they prefer to treat the sick with a knife and a hasty appeal to the Gods—you should go there." He stepped around the table and stood by the front door, turning back to Orestes and folding his arms. "But don't expect them to allow you to cut yourself, even there. It's unheard of."

It was to be expected. The wise tended to shy away from the inexplicable. They were apprehensive about the unknown—all the more reason to share with them as little as possible. But this man gave himself away... he had no love for established convention. This man only needed to be lightly pushed along a path he had already chosen.

Orestes exhaled. "I don't wish to cause trouble. But I know you don't share the opinion of the oligarchy about the benefits of surgery conducted by a skilled hand." He watched the old man's expression. "Let me do this thing. I'm sure you could use the windfall, and you will be no worse for it."

Aristeides grunted. "Except that I stand a good chance of having to dispose of a deceased madman without being seen to do so."

Orestes frowned at the floor, stepping away from the table. "I'll have you know that your refusal to offer a proper surgical bed will not deter me." He paused, drawing the straight-edged Babylonian dagger from the scabbard at his side. "If you refuse, this business will be more painful for me and messier for you. But I will see my own blood drawn before I leave this place, one way or another."

The shopkeeper stared back for a long moment, then abruptly broke into a laugh. "You are mad, aren't you?" He sighed and scratched his cheek, then stepped outside, peering around momentarily before reentering, swinging closed the heavy wooden door and throwing the latch. "That blade is no tool for surgery, unless your aim is to see how many holes you can punch in your flesh before your strength leaves you. No need to be rash, stranger—let's have a look at your list." He came back across the floor, moving around the counter, and stooped, taking a clay writing tablet and stylus and a round, pebble-studded mosaic tray from a low shelf by the wall and placing them on the countertop.

Orestes joined him at the counter and pulled a rolled and bound bublos scroll from his cloak. The shopkeeper took it from him and frowned as he opened it. He perused the inked items for a moment, then looked up, glancing back at the electrum spread on the smaller table. "That is a substantial amount of exotic metal. Where are you from? You sound like a Northerner, but you don't look Greek."

The man had a keen ear. Orestes stared back at him. Decades of immersion in the Greek culture in the northern reaches of Epirus had provided for much practice with the nuances of the language, but perhaps it was possible to render a dialectical accent too perfectly. "Isn't it better for you if you don't know?"

The Aristeides raised an eyebrow. "No, it isn't." He rubbed his nose, keeping his eyes on the list. "It's said that any dead man left unburied or unnamed will anger the gods. And if I get caught, and I can produce no name, the archon and his friends will be left to concern themselves with mine, if you take my meaning." He stood over the tablet and picked up the stylus.

Orestes nodded. It was inevitable. The offering of a name… the simplest of gestures for any respectable member of society, and a constant reminder of ostracism for the pariah. There had been many names, and in truth, no one was any more real than the next, but only one would jeopardize his current standing in Kefalonia. "I promise you, I know what I'm doing. Whatever happens, I will not die in this shop." He closed his eyes, bowing his head and touching the pouch at his chest.

"You think you're immortal? Well, that explains why you believe it's possible to effectively conduct your own surgery." The shopkeeper smiled. "Be that as it may, if you want my help, I need a name."

"I'm from the East. From Lydia, the origin of those ingots." Orestes paused. "I'm nobody." The word hung in the air like smoke. *Oudeís.* Nobody. He looked up at the shopkeeper. "Oudeísos. Oudeísos of Lydia."

"That's an odd name, stranger." He pushed away from the table and turned, picking items off the shelves. "I don't have any echinacea in store. You'll have to use garlic instead… it will protect against subsequent illness just as effectively." He grabbed a bowl and a small measuring cup from the shelf, placed them on the table, and began transferring scoops of the herbs from their containers to the bowl. "Nothing you've listed here will suppress pain—I presume you have your own remedy for that?"

"Papaver. Flower of Morpheus. I have all I need for pain." Orestes swallowed dryly, looking at the bowl. "If you would provide a mortar and pestle by which I can prepare a salve, I would be most grateful."

The shopkeeper shook his head as he slid the mosaic tray in front of him and set the herb containers on it one by one. "You leave me very little choice, friend." He nodded in the direction of the rear entryway. "You'll find a mortar and pestle next to the bed. And you will see another bowl there… it contains a base of oil and alcohol in proportions that I've found to be ideal in salves; I suggest you add half a cotyla if you intend to use all the contents of your ingredients." He placed the bowl on the tray and clapped his hands, stepping back from the table. "You'll find everything you need, including a proper set of surgical implements."

Orestes bowed. "Thank you, sir."

"The amount you need to use will depend upon the work you need to perform. And I believe your estimates may be light. Feel free to take more."

Orestes nodded and picked up the tray and stepped to the curtain, but Aristeides moved to place a hand on his arm. "Surgery is more difficult than it looks to the man performing it, my friend. Are you sure you don't want my help?"

Orestes frowned at him. The man's face held genuine concern—it was clear the shopkeeper's reputation was well-founded. Mortal Man had too often proven himself vicious over the years; an observation of history was a study in exploitation, personal aggrandizement and subjugation of the weak. Desperate survival at all costs. But there were still true altruists that stood out amid the dark struggle. Refreshing… and surprising. Orestes leveled his eyes at him. "It would be difficult for me to explain it rationally, but I need to do this alone. Trust me. I will not be harmed."

Aristeides nodded slowly. Now the man knew he spoke the truth, despite all evidence that it was madness. The truth was always there to be read in a person's eyes when the person knew how to convey it.

Orestes pushed the curtain aside and moved into the back room. The bed was little more than a low table covered with straw, surrounded by several small stands contained the items the shopkeeper had described. A large mortar and pestle of white marble, a ladle, and the bowl of salve were to the left, with a basket of white hand cloths and a small tub of water beside them. To the right were the surgical tools, neatly arranged in their box.

Orestes set the tray down and immediately poured the contents of the bowl of herbs into the mortar, mashing it quickly and returning the paste to the bowl, then adding the oil-alcohol base, measuring the quantity by eye. He stepped around the bed and picked up a scalpel with a bellied, serrated steel blade wired to a finely crafted bronze handle and a spatula sculpted in the form of a leaf at the other end, presumably for probing. Much sharper than the Babylonian dagger.

Next to the box were a sponge, a bleeding cup, and various slabs to hold ointments. Everything he would require and more—Aristeides might have been in the habit of carefully screening his surgical clients in the front room, but he had certainly made no effort to hide his practice here.

Orestes took off his cloak and untied his belt and the strap over his shoulder, removing the pouch that held the stone and setting it on one of the tables as he glanced back at the curtain.

He exhaled heavily and let his chiton slip to the floor, taking the pouch and scalpel into his hands, then climbed onto the bed and moved the various items near enough to reach from a prone position.

His pulse began to quicken. He would certainly survive, as he always did—there was no question about that. But the stone wouldn't protect him from the pain.

He opened the pouch and removed the small bag containing the powdered papaver seed. It would dull the sensation to a degree, and the helleboros and anison in the salve would help—a mixture derived from the elixir concoctions of Chaonian mystics and Phoenician priests, possibly a better mixture for suppressing pain than most of the Greeks yet knew. But simple herbs were unlikely to mask the sting of cutting deeply into the flesh while conscious.

And allowing himself to lose consciousness was not an option.

He sniffed the seed powder, then placed the open end of the bag between his lips and shook the contents into his mouth. He gagged at the dry, chalky blandness of the taste, and quickly covered his mouth with a fist to suppress a cough. He cleared his throat and ran his tongue against his teeth, glancing at the tub of water. There was no apparent drinking cup in sight. He would do without replenishing himself with a rinse for the moment.

His head became slightly dizzy—the odd effects of the papaver were beginning to take hold. No more time to lose. He took the stone out of the pouch and felt the energy flow unimpeded through his hand once again. He firmed his jaw as he looked at the red glow emanating from deep within, through the smoother facets of the mineral, newly firing his determination. It would be worthwhile, whatever temporary pain he had to endure. It was a small price to pay to become one with the mineral... to permanently bury it from sight within his own flesh, the only way to truly protect it from those who would take it away. It could only make him stronger.

He placed the sponge and several cloths by his side, lay back, and poured the salve over his left ribs, shuddering as the icy coldness rushed over his skin. The cavity in his abdomen was the best location, judging by the positioning of the organs he had witnessed in the corpses he had had the opportunity to dissect, coupled with that added intuition offered by the stone—a heightened sense of his own anatomy. He lined up the pointed end of the scalpel blade against the bottom edge of his ribcage on the left and took several rapid breaths, then pushed.

Agony exploded across his side like the shock of a lightning strike. The sensation was excruciating, and he opened his mouth to cry out, but his voice caught in his throat. He gasped as the muscles of his stomach and intestines wrenched unexpectedly, but the intensity of the pain quickly tore his mind away from the nausea.

He focused on the stone as tears welled in his eyes. The cut had to be wide and deep, big enough to fit the stone. He gripped the handle of the scalpel and sliced laterally along the rib, and the pain ripped into him anew— his neck tightened, and he clenched his jaw and felt as if his teeth would break under the strain. His vision swam. Again, he tried to focus on the stone... relief seemed to be streaming toward him through a tiny point far away, as if his left hand had grown infinitely small as it held the stone, and his arm stretched out to the sky.

He cut further, faster, suddenly drenched in sweat and blood. His skin was on fire. He let go of the scalpel and blindly groped for the bowl of salve, pouring the remainder of the bowl into the open wound. Numbness began to creep across his skin. He brought the stone up to the wound with his left hand and tested it against the opening. It was still not large enough, but immediately the pain began to ebb. He found the scalpel again and plunged it back in the wound, cutting down and away from the ribs. He moved the stone back to his side and wedged it beneath the loose flap of flesh. The opening still seemed too small, but he continued to push, tearing the flesh at the corners of the incision.

The stone passed inside him. He dropped the scalpel and reached for a cloth, staring upward at the even wooden slats along the ceiling. He began to shake over his entire body. He closed his eyes.

The stone felt like a warm spring of water building inside him, spreading across his chest to his extremities. The pain faded like a distant memory.

He suddenly felt as if he were in a completely different place... a sprawling, complex structure as large as a city, with walls and tunnels of glass and surrounded by monstrous flying machines. He had never seen it or heard tell of it, never experienced it in any way, yet it felt strangely and thoroughly familiar. He was standing in an open, brightly lit room while an emaciated woman in a tight blue uniform looked back at him from behind a white counter. Then it was all gone in a flash of brilliant, intense light...

He was in a much smaller room, stark and dimly lit, but somehow much warmer and more comfortable than the other place. Now another man stood before him, pointing at him with an unfamiliar device. Again, the vision was wiped away in a sudden flash of brilliant, intense light. Red light, like the color of the stone.

The stone was no longer a rock fallen from the sky. It had bonded with him, become a part of him, blended with his body and soul as if cast from the heavens for that specific purpose. It would remain that way for lifetime upon lifetime into the distant future. But it would not remain that way forever.

He refocused, rolling his head to the side, vaguely aware that there was motion in the room. Aristeides was above him, rushing among the small tables, fussing with the sponge and the cloths to clean the spilled blood—the shopkeeper had entered, going against the request for privacy. It was to be expected... it was too much to ask a man with care in his heart to ignore cries of anguish. Orestes brushed his hand delicately along his side and felt the damp stickiness of blood, but the wound was already closed.

Aristeides froze, stepping back from the table. He had seen the wound site now, seen that it was healed.

The shopkeeper dropped the blood-soaked cloth in his hand. "Heavens be damned. Who are you?"

Orestes raised himself on his elbows. "I am nobody."

*   *   *

... "Philadelphia"; 28 September 1992 CE

As the Moroccan incense dissipated in the stagnant air of the small room, the long journey took place one more time. Centuries fell away as seconds, borne on horses and chariots, galleons and planes, over mountains, seas, and forests that spanned eight empires.

Items had come and gone, mementos representing the many places John Walker had called home. An object of relative significance would fall into his hands, and he would keep it for a while, sometimes for centuries. There had been a time when he had hoped to amass a great collection of things... a physical record of his travels. But the stuff of his life was gone now, but for a few trinkets he happened to still have. Gone like names of the past, like his list of aliases. Survived only as thoughts in his perfectly preserved memory.

The old straight-edged Babylonian dagger lay next to a much more modern leather scabbard, set directly in front of him at the center of the floor, apart from the other items. The metal had faded, though the blade had never once drawn blood. It had come to him idly, picked from a pile of unwanted weaponry. He had chosen a small blade, something that could be easily concealed. At first, he had sought a deterrent—something to fend away robbers. Then it had become more important... the thing he would use to end it all when the time finally came. Now it was a symbol. A reminder. The knife was bound to the stone as his blood was bound to the stone.

Walker sat cross-legged in his flannels, elbows resting on knees, fingers pressed against temples. He closed his eyes and felt the flow of time, visualizing the long trek and the shifting landscapes as the years blended together in a rhythmic parade, like a wave breaking softly along the shore. He saw again the mathematical symmetry in the architecture of the Greeks and the Romans, the rigorous rendition of the angles and columns. The luxuries and aromas of Islamic Spain and the exquisite, impassioned beauty of the French countryside.

Peace and harmony of body and mind. It was effortless now, remembered like innate instinct in every muscle, in the blood coursing rhythmically though his veins, in the slow and even pace of the air through his lungs—it was a residue of the Eastern philosophy he had taken with him from the heart of the British Empire, from Indians and Chinese supplanted from their distant lands to live in the poverty of the Manchester slums. Now, this ancient Buddhist exercise served as an agent of healing, a purpose that would have been of little use to him prior to this day. Now he was in dire need of his mental disciplines.

He touched the line of his rib cage, felt the strangeness of the cotton and elastic cloth against his skin. The pain of a month before had taken him by surprise, overwhelmed him as the effects of the stone had dissipated. It had taken not much more than an hour to drain the strength taken in over the many thousands of years. At first, he had felt as though the power might never leave him; the cut of the knife had seemed to do no more damage than a common scrape. The blood flow had stopped quickly, and the buzzing sensation of the skin sealing itself had followed immediately, as it had always done upon each of the many minor nicks and bruises he had incurred over the years. But the buzzing had stopped before long. And when the pain had radiated across his chest, he had been sure he would die.

It had taken him a minute or so to recover, but slowly it had come back to him... the memory of the burning fire that was human pain. The power of the stone had faded, but his mental faculties had not. The pain of the incision was to be expected, no better or worse than anything he had felt in the time before he had found the stone. The blood loss had been minimal, and it had required no special medical attention. Sheer will was enough to get him though the pain; will would have allowed him to survive a wound much worse than the efficient cut of the tiny, razor-sharp blade. This time it had gone better than the last—a 79-cent box cutter from an art supply store had proven much more effective at cutting skin than the ornately crafted scalpel at the Attican medicine shop so many years before.

The deed had been done. The stone was now in place in its modern, makeshift mausoleum. If Cassandra Prescott chose to accept it, she would find it there. What she did with it at that point would be determined by her heart and mind alone, but she would experience its power, at least. When she saw the stone and held it in her hands, she would understand.

Still, there was a chance she would have an extreme reaction to being named as his heir. From his will statement, she now knew of his intent to leave his possessions to her. She was an honorable person, and she would surely ask to be excluded from the will—or at least to be dismissed as his legal representative in favor of unbiased counsel. She had been reluctant to trust him, but he would have a chance to convince her to accept it... they had another meeting yet. He would have time to explain his full intentions. She would not believe him at first, but she would see that he was telling the truth. He could make her understand the stone's power.

He could have forced the stone upon her as well, exposed her to its light directly, but to do so would be, in effect, to take the choice away from her. In the end, the choice was hers, and it was a choice she would need to make without being under the direct influence of the stone.

He frowned, turning toward the door of the small apartment. Ultimately, each person was the master of his or her own decisions... there were no guarantees. It might have been a stretch to think he could forge trust with a woman so indoctrinated in the presumed omniscience of her time, so sold on the familiarities of her reality. Perhaps these instincts drawing him to this woman were misplaced, and he was truly fated to carry the stone until the end of days. But deep in his core, the feeling was resonant—his role as custodian of this great power was nearing its end. Since longer than he could remember, the dictates of his instincts were precise and accurate. There was a tangible sensation that was firing his nerves now, more than just speculative anticipation. Now was the time. The long journey had reached a stopping point. The stone's hold on him would be over sooner, not later.

Enough rumination. If the stone was to pass to another, time to enjoy the natural world was suddenly limited. There were still places to go where the open landscape wasn't cluttered with buildings. Tainted as the sky had become, on a good day, even in and around the modern urban megalopolises, the sun still overpowered the factory smoke.

Today had the feel of a good day.

His eyes fell on the garments neatly laid out on the floor in front of him. He unfolded his legs and stood, stepping into the brown slacks, then putting on and buttoning up the crisp, cream-colored shirt. His newest set of clothes, the latest in a long line of urban camouflage. It was possibly the last time he would need to blend in.

Before long, he would look for the last time at the tiny room where he had been living for the past 50 years—his home in America, the world's latest empire. No more hiding in run-down population centers. The tropical islands of the Pacific were wonders of the world he had not yet seen. If the gods would allow it, paradise would be the place to retire and live out his final years, a place where he might rejoin the human race.

He stooped and picked up the dagger and scabbard, fitting the knife into its sheath and tying it fast with a loop of string. The ancient Babylonian artifact would pass to the woman as well—she might not choose to cut herself as he had and certainly not with such a crude implement, but it might also serve as a reminder for her. Vigilance through simple, proven means.

There was something comforting in the thought of passing on another less critical heirloom. Something that represented an active choice he had made… a small reflection of an aspect of his nature that hadn't been imposed by fate.

He slipped the bound dagger into one of the deep front pockets in the slacks, stepped across the room, and picked up a burlap sack by the wall, fishing out an envelope. Travel was so much simpler now—37 slips of paper printed in green could be easily carried on his person. They had no noticeable weight, and they would take him anywhere in the world.

He closed his eyes. It had been far too long for many things.

His trench coat was set on a nail in the plaster of the wall. He put it on and lifted four sheets of paper folded together from the inside pocket. The copy of his last will and testament. He flipped to the second page and reread the last two listings.

> To Ms. Prescott....
>
>> One Antique Babylonian-made Carving Knife, Steel Blade,
>>
>> Ox-Bone Handle, Value Unknown, kept in Place of Residence
>
> To Ms. Prescott....
>
>> One Gemstone

The words were as effective as they would ever need to be, whether or not they contained the proper legal terminology.

He looked at the note on the back written by the hand of Cassandra Prescott, then slipped the will back in its place in his jacket, along with the envelope of money.

Through the wall came the sound of footsteps, firm and swift against the buckling floorboards of the outer hall. It was immediately clear they did not belong to the lawyer woman.

The door creaked open and light poured into the room. "John Ulysses Walker, I presume. Though I believe that's not the name you were born with." The face of the man standing outside was unfamiliar, but the expression showed a certain disconcerting recognition. The voice was mysterious, the accent indiscernible.

Ulysees. Walker took a slow step back. Few strangers knew him at all, with or without the middle name he rarely used, the one connection to his past that distinguished him from so many others. Beyond that, there was an alarming air about this man... something out of place in a very odd way, a sense abundantly clear even as he hung in the shadowy hallway.

The man moved inside the room as if responding to the reaction as a lack of resistance. He looked around sharply, nodding to himself. His clothes were impeccable, fine and perfectly fit, with an elegant gray topcoat over a charcoal vest and matching slacks pressed so well that they seemed made of steel. The man was probably wealthy among his peers. Accustomed to power. His manner was smooth and confident, with careful, practiced expression, but there was an unmistakable purposefulness to his posture. Veiled aggression. His was the face of a man who felt himself superior, even more than his polished appearance suggested.

The stranger turned, his gaze lingering on a Moorish vase on the floor by the wall. "You seem to prefer the dark to artificial lighting." He arched an eyebrow as if he had uncovered something of personal relevance, then shook his head. "Remarkable."

Walker straightened in his stance. "Is there something I can help you with?"

A smile played over the man's lips, but his eyes remained fast in an unmistakably cold stare. Walker stared back. This man was foreign to everything he had ever known. He had come a long way, and he had the look of someone curious with his surroundings, as adept as he seemed at hiding his intentions.

The man sniffed loudly, shaking his head. "Allow me to introduce myself—my name is Teodor Monroe. You have something I'm interested in… a mineral with unique qualities. I'm certain you're familiar with what I'm referring to."

The stone. The stranger's words hung in the air like the image that immediately came to mind. Walker frowned despite himself. No one had any way of knowing about the life-giving power, not Cassandra Prescott, not anyone in Philadelphia, though the recent weeks marked the first light that had fallen on it in long years. Still, no one had laid eyes on it, and no one had been told a word, outside of the single vague citation in the will in Ms. Prescott's hands. The last living soul who had looked upon it in the open air was long dead, buried and forgotten in a faraway land.

"To you this mineral would seem one of a kind, but I know otherwise. It's a small nugget of aluminum silicate—a rare specimen of gemstone. For my part, I've been studying minerals of this kind for quite a long time. My search has led me here, and I intend to collect it." The man's face steeled. His resolve was strong. This visit was not a whimsical chance errand.

"Where are you from, Mr. Monroe?"

The man felt along the wall by the door for the light-switch. He found it and the single bulb hanging from the ceiling lit up the room. Casually, the man raised a strange weapon from within his jacket. A small, angular handgun that looked completely unfamiliar.

"I'm a busy man, Mr. Walker. I realize you've earned the right to be treated with more respect, but under the circumstances I don't have that luxury. The stone is dangerous, and I am equipped to handle it. You are not. Now, please… if you will. I'll need to see that gemstone." The man's eyes held the truth, to an extent, but his aim was clear. He had little interest in anyone else's welfare.

Walker pressed his fingers together. "You are too late; I have already given up the stone you seek."

Monroe rubbed his mustache. "History doesn't lie, Mr. Walker. I've seen your future. This stone of yours will ultimately kill you, before the end of this day if you don't hand it away. Your stone is due to erupt in a blaze of light… something in its physical constitution will cause it to rupture, presumably the same thing that gives it this power you've managed to enjoy for as long as you've carried it. Early tomorrow morning at 04:57 Terra Zulu Standard—that is, just before midnight, your time—this stone of yours will be destroyed, and it will destroy you with it. I know you still have it. So please, let's dispense with the deliberations. Either you direct me to the stone, or I end your life right here and now and look for it myself, which I am fully prepared to do." He took a step closer, lowering his eyebrows and raising the gun. "My time is wasting, Mr. Walker. Make your choice."

I've seen your future. The stranger's words were markedly more authoritative than those of a soothsayer or prophet of old; he spoke almost as if he had already witnessed this rupture of the stone first-hand.

Walker's gaze dropped below the level of Monroe's eyes. The thought that this inexhaustible source of life might suddenly snatch it away after so much time seemed like a nightmare long cast aside, but even as this stranger gave his overtly self-serving account, a vague memory began to rematerialize… the description of the blaze of light felt as true as if it had already happened. He had seen it long before, in a vision. In another life.

Perhaps his subconscious had been long at work, sensing the danger and driving him toward an urge to finally rid himself of the stone out of an instinct to survive. He had experienced spells of clairvoyance before. If this man did speak the truth, the stone would be a danger to Cassandra Prescott as well. Perhaps that too would have become clear over the next few hours—perhaps he would have had a change of heart about giving it to her, and he would have retained it, both for her sake and for his own. Perhaps he had always been destined to have the stone at the fateful moment.

"As I said, I cannot help you. Do as you will, Mr. Monroe. But I am ready for death."

Monroe's eyes narrowed. He frowned grimly. "Just as well."

Walker nodded once, and suddenly envisioned an imperfect image of the face of his mother—fuzzy and incomplete, a composite of dark, long-forgotten eyes, high cheekbones, and vaguely familiar lips and straight, pulled-back hair. Then it was a view from outside a house in Eridu, one of the larger houses among the mud huts of the city. A hammock underneath the palms, by one of the canals his father had built.

He found himself thinking of the names of the gods. So many gods…

382

and an ancient prayer. *Zi Anna hépàd, zi Kia hépàd... by Heaven be conjured, by Earth be conjured.*

An intense light hit his face, and for an instant a searing fire tore through his skin.

Teodor stood over the ancient body, glancing around. The room was practically empty but for a modest clutter of archaic electric devices, seemingly collecting dust in a neglected corner. The man was a true ascetic, with no tables, no place to sleep—no furniture of any kind other than a small, intricately engraved wooden desk and a single desk chair. There was a small closet and a large sack of yellowing straw by the wall opposite the door. The pyropite would most likely be on Walker's person, perhaps even surgically implanted inside the body.

Teodor transferred the refractor pistol to his left hand and slid the small, crescent shaped photon dispersion sensor from the pouch on the hidden sling beneath his left arm, thumbing the activator without hesitation, sweeping the round edge around the room. The indicator made no sound, and the tiny screen showed only the modest, diffuse tint of the lamplight. He frowned.

Light was light, and the pyropite's light was brilliant. It was that simple, Faro had promised. Few materials would prevent the material's energy from registering as a distinct green pinpoint, and yet the display showed only a dull, nebulous soup.

Teodor clicked the scoping buttons, increasing the range. The pattern brightened but remained diffuse. He shook his head and tapped his belt, switching off the inertia-dampening body shield—Faro clearly hadn't suspected the shield to interfere with the sensor, but perhaps he had somehow overlooked the protective field's effects on photon emissions...

No change. Teodor flared his nostrils. Faro wouldn't have made the mistake of leaving the sensor untested... but it would have been an opportune moment for a man in his position to unleash a bold power maneuver, safely out of range of reprisal and with his only superior at his personally engineered, technological mercy. No man was above sabotage, not even Cristan Faro, with his rigorous adherence to procedure. Unflinchingly forthright as the man was, if he had felt it was in his interest to cut off the head of the empire, he would have seized the opportunity to do so. But he wouldn't have contemplated sabotage by tampering with this sensor while leaving the ship's hyperdrive in perfect working order—Faro wasn't capable of that sort of stupidity. There was a simple, more reasonable explanation.

I have already given up the stone you seek.

The lie of a desperate man. It had to have been a lie—the pyropite had been Walker's lifeblood. He had to have kept it close. He couldn't very well have given it away if he was going to be carrying it later that night.

Clearly the pyropite had a connection to living beings—perhaps living tissues were able to mask the photon emissions. Faro had cited theories, but he wouldn't have been able to test for such a scenario.

Teodor nodded. He was going to have to get a little dirty.

He crossed to the closet, looking back around the room as he slipped off the topcoat and placed it on one of the loose paper-covered wire hangers. He loosened the sling that held his equipment pouch, looping the carbon-fiber thread around a second hanger and testing to make sure the flimsy, unconvincing device would hold it up. Then he undid the vest, hung it separately, and immediately stepped back to the body, kneeling and narrowing his eyes.

Walker had dropped to his knees and crumpled backwards, his arms flung loosely outward, his head suspended by the stiffness of the spine, with a blackened jaw line thrown toward the ceiling in a fitting pose as if to make a final plea to the sky. The face was gone, skin and muscle tissue vaporized. In its place were the unfinished features of a statue in progress… glazed bone with shallow contours smoothed by the plasma's focused heat. Two dark pits where the eyes had been. The charred corpse looked completely nonhuman. It might have been a twisted artist's papier-mâché manikin.

Teodor snorted. A poetic send-off to the man's lifelong anonymity. He cocked his head. If Walker had implanted the object surgically, he would have likely done the job himself. It would have to be just beneath the skin, somewhere that didn't stand out above the bones or displace organs. Somewhere beneath the ribs.

Walker wore loose, exceedingly plain clothes—a dull beige overcoat, now splayed open like the wings of a dead bird; a loose-fitting ivory shirt with buttons down the center; umber slacks. Teodor set the refractor and sensor on the floor, leaned forward, and tugged at the collar of the shirt, causing the torso to bounce lightly above the contorted legs. He tore the shirt open, breaking the tiny buttons and exposing the chest and midsection. Below the shirt, Walker was naked but for a large bandage around the upper abdomen.

Teodor nodded, smiling broadly. There was only one explanation for such a bandage. He pulled it off easily. Underneath was a ragged, semicircular scar. He picked up the refractor and stood, resetting the aperture

384

to fine-tune the stream of plasma. A minimum-intensity laser-assisted beam would slice neatly through the soft flesh, cutting only at the surface. It would be clean and easy, and there would be no danger of rupturing the pyropite as long as he kept the plasma away from the wound...

He looked again at Walker and his smile disappeared.

The cillian texts had described the pyropite as having healing powers, erasing all evidence of wounds. If Walker's body held the stone, there should have been no scar. For that matter, the scar looked relatively fresh... if the man had carried the stone in his body for thousands of years, the scar should have faded significantly more, whether or not any added healing powers were in effect.

Walker had removed the stone from his body. Recently. So he had been telling the truth, at least to a point.

Teodor focused his attention on the clothes. The shirt had a pocket on the left breast. The pants had several pockets. Based on the blast radius compared against the cillians' observations of other samples of pyropite, Faro had estimated the stone to be 0.3 kilograms—probably too large to be carried in a small pocket. But his estimates might have been off.

There was something of substance tucked along the man's right hip, hidden inside the slacks. Teodor raised his eyebrows and slid out a short, flat shaft. A crude hilt of hardened wood protruded out of a stylish leather wrap. A dagger. Walker had been concealing a weapon of old. Teodor untied the covering sheath and studied it for a long moment. Metallic blade, miserably discolored. This was possibly the item Walker had used to cut himself, though there was no evidence of blood. On hand to put the stone back inside his body, perhaps. Why had he removed it—had the fool actually intended to give it away? It was close at hand, then. It had to be.

Teodor dropped the knife and turned to give the room another scan, and a spot of white caught his eye—paper protruding from a pocket in the inner lining of the overcoat. He stepped around the body and withdrew an envelope full of various small, green-tinted slips covered in intricate print, along with a neatly folded set of papers.

He discarded the items and did a quick cursory check of the pockets on the outside of the overcoat, finding only a pair of printed cards. One was clearly a form of identification: a simple name and a nine-digit number. Not even a picture. He tossed the cards after the other articles of paper and shifted his attention to the straw sack at the wall.

The contents weren't heavy; Teodor dumped the sack, squinting as various artifacts spilled onto the floor—ancient tools and trinkets, odd carvings, some brooches studded with jewelry. A small silver device with a tiny, tooth-like blade stood out, seemingly brand new among the time-worn items. The journal written in cuneiform was there, just as it had been described in the obituary on record. An ample trove of valuable antiques, but as the sensor had indicated, no glowing gemstone.

He returned to the closet, which was empty save for his own garments and the few other articles of clothing that hung next to them—several shirts and slacks encased in a protective translucent film—and several other sets of presumably lesser-quality clothing left unprotected in folded stacks. He riffled through the clothes, checking pockets, then examined the walls, looking for hidden panels, tapping at the surfaces behind the coat and above the shelf. A panel to the right came away easily, revealing a rusty, metallic apparatus, some sort of heating mechanism with some room around it that might have been an ideal hiding place for a small object, but there was nothing there. He turned, moving back outside the closet and putting his hands on his hips. Perhaps Walker had stashed it in some inaccessible place, underneath the floor or behind one of the walls, and then had any evidence hidden by renovations. There was still time to look. There weren't many places left to check, as long as it was somewhere in the room. Faro had overlooked some aspect of the material that was causing it to be immune from detection by the photon-sensing mechanism, and it was hiding in some secret cubbyhole, close at hand. It had to be close…

Teodor looked darkly at the dead man's empty eye sockets. The man had welcomed death, after having coveted life for so long—inexplicably squandered an unprecedented run of endless years, just to avoid giving out a simple, harmless detail about the location of his prize. Had time dulled the man's mind?

I have already given up the stone…

Teodor sneered and stalked to the body, scooping the refractor up from the floor and adjusting the settings. He fired several short bursts around the floor and walls of the room, scoring the flimsy surfaces with narrow, twisting openings. A red-tinged glow would have revealed the location of the pyropite—but it could have easily been tucked inside a box or cloth that would hide its light. If the unworthy fool had kept the stone in the room, finding it would require more than a hasty, impulsive flourish. It would require a much more meticulous examination. Perhaps a few hours of dissecting the apartment, picking carefully through the unpleasant debris.

Teodor glanced at Walker. He paused, then fired again, burrowing into the neck and severing the flambéed head from the body with a flick of his wrist. His hand trembled as the gun wavered over the torso. Purely on lack of vision the man deserved to have his carcass rendered to a spread of seared and chopped meat, and it would have taken seconds. But there was still a chance the pyropite was there, buried deep in the flesh.

His eyes went back to the dagger on the floor.

He dropped to his knees, grabbed the knife and stabbed at the body, slicing through skin, sawing raggedly at the area around the scar. The meat of Walker's abdomen flopped open, exposing gray and pink innards and dribbling dark blood onto the floorboards. Muscle and a pasty film of wrinkled fascia sank away from the cutaneous tissues around a cavity beneath the central area of the original incision. Walker had kept the stone nestled there, just beneath the right lower edge of the rib cage. No question.

Teodor lowered his brow and exhaled loudly through his nostrils. The man's flesh was as flimsy as any man's... thousands of years with the pyropite had left no lasting effect. His face had been ruined, scarred as anyone would have been after a close-range Ruby-12 plasma blast with the output maximized. A little resilience from a reservoir of life force would have been expected. This held no promise at all. The pyropite should have protected this supposed immortal far better than that, but Walker had proven weak. This crumpled husk of a man had never deserved such power. Such utter waste...

Teodor pursed his lips and slashed at the torso, widening the wound and plunging in with his left hand, working upward with the knife in his right. He gritted his teeth, groping with his free fingers, plowing through jelly-like masses and rubbery layers of muscle, sinking his arm deep into the thick syrup of stagnant fluid. He snarled and pulled out the knife, stabbing repeatedly at the center of the chest, prying at the ribs with his other hand until he had a second viable opening. He shifted his weight forward, moving in with both arms, hacking rhythmically through the arteries around the heart, scraping against bone to move it aside. He carved through the web of tissues, mincing them and scooping them out in bundles.

He grunted, straining with increasing strength, fighting back down toward the groin. Walker toppled sideways, and Teodor lost his leverage, falling forward and splashing shoulder-first into the pooling wetness on the floor. His knees slid away and he was suddenly pinned with his face pressed against the cold, dry skin of Walker's sternum as if he were slowly being outmaneuvered in an even wrestling match. He thrust his mouth around, biting at the body, and locked on with his teeth, thrashing his head and coming away with a mouthful of skin.

He blinked blearily. The bandage. The wound had been fresh. Walker had removed the stone—it was the only thing that made sense. But it could have also been subterfuge. The extremities... the pyropite could have been implanted in an arm or leg. It would have been less intrusive, smaller impact on his health.

Teodor twisted away from the body and stabbed at the left arm, flaying the skin in a long strip, then moving to the legs. A hollow in the long shafts of bone would have stood out quickly. He ripped through cloth and skin, dragging the blade along the length of each leg of slacks, then flipped the body and concentrated on the remaining arm.

Nothing. No manufactured hiding places aside from the abdomen. The pyropite was not in the body. He rose on his knees, panting heavily, scowling down at the desecrated headless corpse. The flailing, mechanically positioned arms gave it the grotesque appearance of a partially assembled android. He brought the blade down and buried it in one of the trapezius muscles, standing and backing up a pace.

He ran his hands through his hair and took another glance around the room—the sack, the closet. Sizzling holes in the walls and floorboards marking a hurried failure. He had by no means looked thoroughly—with more time, he would find it. But if it truly wasn't in the room... there was a chance he would need to make a second trip through time. Clearly, he and Faro hadn't adequately prepared for this scenario.

He tipped his head back and screamed at the ceiling, then shook himself. He found the pistol on the floor and wiped his mouth with the back of his sleeve, smacking his face with the stickiness of clarified butter and the scent of bile. He gasped and spat at the floor, raising the weapon again, aiming it at Walker's midsection. No danger of rupturing the stone if it wasn't on the man's person—nothing to save him from total annihilation now. Dismembering the corpse like Purusha in Hindu myth would have provided a fitting poetic end to Walker's existence. Complete destruction as the ultimate, inescapable destiny of the man who had cheated death for so many years.

Teodor held up the refractor. History dictated that the pyropite would be in Walker's possession at 23:57. If Walker had in fact chosen to give the stone away, there was another factor at play. Some other twist of fate had been set to deliver the stone back to him.

Teodor frowned at the floor, picking the sensor from the spreading pool of intercellular fluid and drying it against his shirt, and raised an eyebrow at the paper items he had dropped nearby.

He picked up the folded papers, shaking them off, and found the two cards from Walker's outer jacket pocket below them. He looked at them again. The second card contained various names... some sort of membership information he had barely glanced at before. Halpern, Sutherland, and Kovach, LLP... "a professional corporation." In the upper left was a full name and title: Cassandra Prescott, LL.B., J.D. Attorney and Counselor at Law. A connection to the outside world... a lead?

He flipped the card and his pulse rate quickened. A time and place for a meeting—a playground, on Tinicum Boulevard at noon. A meeting at 12:00. The meeting had occurred on Saturday, 26 September. Two days before.

A meeting with a member of a legal firm. He opened the folded papers. The very first paragraph, written very legibly in something that looked like a fine metallic chalk, made the document's purpose clear.

> I, John Walker a.k.a. John U. Walker a.k.a. John Ulysses Walker, of Philadelphia County, Pennsylvania, do hereby assign Cassandra Prescott of the Law Firm of Halpern, Sutherland, and Kovach to distribute all of my Property and Belongings, which consist of all that is stated on these Pages and nothing more, in the following manner:

It was the rough copy of the man's will. He had chosen an heir.

The next three pages were an account of the items in the sack, and several other odds and ends locked away in banks in Spain and Italy. Teodor scanned the list quickly, dropping each page to the floor when he was satisfied it didn't contain any mention of the pyropite. His eyes stopped when he came to the very end.

The last item read simply, "One Gemstone." Unlike the other items, there was no description or mention of a location. And he was bequeathing it, among other things, to the very same Cassandra Prescott charged with executing the will. The only thing below the notation was an illegibly scrawled line followed by John Walker's name.

Teodor glanced at the other side of the page, then suddenly raised his eyebrows. There was a note in someone else's handwriting. It wasn't as easy to read as the writing in the will.

> Playground, Monday, 5:30 PM, for return in good order.

Teodor nodded, crumpling the paper in his fist. Walker hadn't been quite as reclusive as his profile had let on. He was close to this woman... she would know exactly where the stone was. She had very likely taken temporary custody of it herself—history dictated that it would pass back to Walker before the moment of the eruption, at the airport, but she was apparently holding it for him and scheduled to return it some six hours before the stone took his life. The man was apparently planning to fly away from the city; he was obviously in flux. It made sense that the location of the stone might also be in transition.

Teodor slid the business card into a pocket in his slacks and checked the time on his wristcom. 15:10 local. Still plenty of time to find the woman. "Playground" could have meant anything—a designation of some informal location or a social club of some sort. Either way, it would be difficult to pick the woman out of a crowd without knowing her face. But she would be easy to locate at her place of work. All he had to do was find a directory.

He slid the card into the breast pocket of the shirt, frowning as he touched the soaked fabric of his clothes. That wouldn't do. Fortunately he still had with him a modicum of anachronistic convenience. He focused on the oversized belt buckle and activated the reverse function, closing his eyes and tipping back his head as the particle field flash-burned the surface of the retrofitted clothing's treated fabric, razing away the organic refuse and prickling his skin with electrostatic energy. For a few brief seconds it was like hot ozone-tinged breath at his ears and nostrils, and then the charge dissipated. He tapped the mode control again and exhaled, brushing at the front of his shirt. Crisp and dry as clothing off the rack. His feet suddenly stood at the center of a perfect circle of spotless floorboards amid an impressive spread of chaos.

He wheeled around to face Walker's closet and stepped to the hangers holding the unblemished articles of the throwback set. He nodded to himself as he took a final look around the room, slipping back into the vest and refastening the buttons. The past did indeed have its charms, but this was not a place to stay for any great length of time. A man could lose his mind.

He fitted the thread of the sling back over his shoulder, adjusting the pouch beneath his opposite arm, and his eyes fell again on Walker's blackened corpse.

He smiled.

*   *   *

A man in a long overcoat and a classic fedora with a sharp, curving brim moved through the parking lot below the building containing Cassandra Prescott's law office. He stopped at a navy blue, smoothly sloped four-wheel ground car, presumably his own private mode of transportation.

Teodor stepped out of the lift and moved away from the building. There was no time to waste—the city patrols would be arriving soon, and the local denizens would identify him. He had to leave, even though the city patrols were now the best means by which to locate the woman.

She had already left the building, perhaps to meet John Walker early, perhaps on another errand. Wherever she intended to go now, she would inevitably be called in by the patrols to answer questions about the latest incident at her workplace.

The man saw him approaching and inadvertently dropped his keys, stooping to gather them up. Teodor watched for a moment, then aimed his refractor.

The man stiffened and held up his hands, palms forward. "Listen, I have very little cash."

Teodor raised an eyebrow. Cash. He had to be talking about currency. "I need several things. First, I need to contact your local authorities. I need you to tell them you have information about a break-in on the 15th floor. I want you to find out exactly where to go to report this information, and I then want you to give me a ride to the same location." He raised the pistol. "Do you think you can handle this, or shall I dispense with you and find someone more cooperative?"

The man shook his head rapidly, keeping his eyes on the refractor. "No, no, I can do that."

Teodor smiled congenially, moving around to the passenger side of the car. "Good. Now, I've noticed several communication booths along the walks. Take me to the nearest one."

The man smiled nervously as he hit a button on a tiny remote with the keys; the vehicle responded with an odd squeak, followed by several muffled clicks as the door locks sprang open. "Well… I have a cell in the car. Do you want me to use that?"

Teodor nodded. Though many things were still primitive, the 20th century had seen the start of a few technological conveniences. He motioned for the man to enter his car. The man did so, and Teodor followed his lead, keeping the pistol positioned threateningly. "Drive away from the building first. You may use your cell when we're on the street. If you continue to be helpful, I will consider letting you live."

The man didn't seem overly pleased. He started the car.

Of course, so close to the city patrols, killing the man would be a necessity.

The earthbound vehicle pulled out of its parking spot and headed out under the low ceiling, Teodor glanced again at the man's hat. Reasonably stylish, breathing life into a rather dreary ensemble. The man's overcoat was a formless mess, but the smart tilt of the fedora brought the entire look together. Not bad at all. Teodor raised an eyebrow and looked through the sloping glass window in front of him, glancing up at the distorted angle of his reflection.

It was a big city. There was always a chance someone had seen him sneaking unescorted through the building, or earlier, along his trail of public interactions. Donning a hat was by no means an adequate disguise, and it wouldn't necessarily make it any more difficult for someone to identify his face. But it wouldn't make it any easier, either. This was, after all, a primitive place. The recognition technology was in its infancy; they probably couldn't even extrapolate a positive match with a pair of pictures if they weren't able to accurately gauge the shape of the head.

Besides, a 20th-century fedora was an excellent souvenir.

*　　　　　*　　　　　*

A blue station wagon came to a full stop at a yellow light, and Cassie raised her right hand, holding it just above the horn. No need to look at the time again… the light in the sky was fading. It was almost 6, well past meeting time. She bit her lip.

Hopefully, John Walker had gone home before waiting too long—hopefully, she'd catch him there and put the whole mess to rest. If he had owned a phone, it wouldn't have been a problem. If he had been a typical, normal person.

She glanced at the cell phone between the two front seats, and its tiny red light blinked as if on cue. She focused on the number in the display. The office again. Nine calls now. Brian Mackey was presumably freaking out about the contracts and determined to make Elsa's life miserable until he had visual evidence Cassie was back in the office. The messages might have been worth a listen purely for entertainment.

Brian could suffer for a little while longer. One catastrophe at a time.

She was moving into the Tinicum area, finally. Smaller, uneven streets, where there should have been less traffic, but somehow the pace wasn't picking up. She had been on Route 291 for a full half hour, thanks to thousands of gapers slowing down to look at a jackknifed semi on the northbound side. The light turned green, and the station wagon went back in motion, lurching, then stopping, then creeping along like a garbage truck. She gripped the steering wheel and shook her head.

The will, as it had been made out, had been more or less in good order. Technically, several of the descriptions called for minor statements of clarification which would leave the respective items closed to any subjective speculation—she could have inferred his intentions, drawn up a formalized will, and submitted it to Walker for his approval. No problem. Unfortunately, whether the document was legal or not was irrelevant, since its specifications were ridiculous.

A list of odd trinkets to the University of Pennsylvania and the Philadelphia Museum of Art, and the rest of it—liquid assets in various bank accounts, among other things—bequeathed to the executrix. To her. Walker had named her the primary legatee to his estate.

A double-parked van was blocking traffic in the right lane, and she slowed to let a red car move in front of her to get around it.

To have the will formalized now, to do any work on it at all, was impossible. If she had taken two seconds to look at it while sitting on the bench with Walker, there would have been no need for a return trip to Tinicum. The fact that Walker had no phone meant she was obligated to face him again to refer him to alternative probate counsel. And to ask him nicely to keep her name the hell out of it.

What had the man been thinking? He had come off as genuine enough—obviously he was expecting her to see it as a nice gesture—but did he think she had no integrity at all?

She had probably missed the appointment now, which would mean the issue wasn't going to die by the end of the day. Another traffic light turned red as she approached a small, oddly angled intersection. She groaned silently.

She could have turned back, left it up to him to contact her. Mailed the will back to him at his street address, disregarding his instructions not to—was it her fault he wasn't comfortable using basic, accepted means of communication? She couldn't send mail, she couldn't call him on the phone... blowing off his instructions would have been borderline unprofessional, but still, it wasn't as if Walker's specifications had been normal, or even reasonable.

Cassie frowned. She had agreed to deal with a kook, and now she was paying the price. Walker's home was just a few blocks away. If he wasn't home, she could slip the contract termination letter and the will under the door, and that would be that.

It was hard not to feel sorry for the man, but maybe there was a reason for that. He had been adept at controlling the mood of the room, not unlike a skilled attorney. Maybe he really did have pancreatic cancer, maybe he didn't, but it probably wouldn't have been hard for him to fake sincerity. He might have been using her as a way to get close to her family—it wouldn't have been the first time a con man had tried to scam the Philadelphia Prescotts.

She turned at the second traffic light and found an open spot in the area of the Langford Hotel, based on Walker's directions. She shut off the ignition and glanced down. The phone light was blinking again. She sighed and picked up the receiver. "Yes?"

"Cassie? Where are you?" Elsa's voice sounded loud.

Cassie rolled her head, rubbing her neck with her free hand. "I'm in my car, late for my appointment, and you can tell Brian I'll be back to finish up those contracts when I'm done, like I said. I'll probably be back in about an hour." She hesitated. Maybe an hour and a half. She was going to need food at some point. "It's late—why are you still there?"

"Everyone here has been trying to figure out where you were—I've been trying to reach you for the past hour." Elsa paused, and her breath hissed through the tiny receiver.

Cassie raised her eyebrows. Elsa was speaking quickly, atypically frazzled—the chaos of the firm didn't usually get to her. "What happened—what's going on?"

"Cassie, listen… someone broke into your office. It's a disaster—your files are a mess, everything's dumped all over the floor, all your drawers, wastebaskets… everything. Things are broken, bookshelves are knocked over. Everything."

Cassie blinked, staring through the windshield. "Oh… God."

"It looks like the intruder went through the shared cabinets too. Files are on the carpet all over the office—who knows what was taken? But yours is the only private office… the other offices were left alone."

Walker? Cassie clenched her teeth, brushing her hair away from her eyes. She shook her head. "This happened today, with people there? Is everyone all right?"

"Everyone's fine. It was just Brian and Phyllis and me. No one was inside when it happened." Elsa sighed raggedly and spoke more quickly.

"There was a fire alarm on our floor. They made everybody leave the building from floors 12 to 17. We all assumed it was a drill—it was late, I've never heard of a drill that late, but you never actually think it's a real fire." Her voice was uncharacteristically up-tempo, as if she was coming off about six cups of coffee.

Walker had been at the office before; Elsa had seen him and would have known what he looked like. "Did anyone see who did this—did they check the security tapes?"

"There was a man who stopped by right before this happened. He had to be on the floor when that alarm was pulled, and I don't know who else could have done it—I remember wondering why I didn't see him when we were going down the stairs. He was looking for you, and he was very insistent, Cassie—he actually asked me for your home address." Elsa cleared her throat. "The police were here, taking fingerprints. They're going to look at the tapes, I'm sure. They want to talk to you… they left a number. You're supposed to ask for Detective Dulnicek." She paused. "Cassie, I'm worried. Is there something I need to know—are you in trouble?"

Cassie shook her head unconsciously. Why would Walker want to rifle through her files—why would anyone want to rifle through those files? None of her open casework dealt with anything particularly sensitive. Most of it wasn't even remotely interesting. "Elsa, did you get a good look at this man—had you seen him before?"

"No. He didn't have an appointment, and he's never been in here before, as far as I know." Elsa paused. "He was tall… other than that, he just looked normal. I don't know, my mind is scrambled, Cassie—I don't know if I gave a very good description to the police."

It wasn't Walker. Cassie exhaled. "That's all right. I'm sure you did fine."

"Here, let me give you the number for the police…"

"That's okay. I'm in the car." Cassie closed her eyes, dropping her head and pinching the top of her nose between her thumb and forefinger. She ran a hand through her hair, tipping her head back. "I'll get the number off my voice mail and call them as soon as I can. Is everybody still there at the office?"

"Brian and Phyllis said they would stay late if you wanted to come back here. But Brian said not to worry about those contracts until you get things squared away with the police. Most of the admins already left, though."

Cassie nodded. Elsa's attempt at subtlety. "Yes, you can go home. And take the day off tomorrow, okay?"

"Thanks, Cassie. Are you sure you'll be all right?"

"I'll be fine. I can take care of myself."

Elsa laughed nervously. "Yes, sure, you'll be all right." She didn't sound convinced. "I guess I'll see you in a couple of days."

"I'll see you then. Take it easy." Cassie cocked her head. The phone rattled as she tried to hook it back underneath the dashboard.

The day was rapidly becoming an all-timer on the list of bad days. She looked out the window at the dark neighborhood. It had been bad enough in the daytime, and now somebody, for whatever reason, was digging around in her office. Whoever it was, the person was probably nowhere near the Tinicum area and would have had no way of knowing that she was in the area short of tracking her cell phone calls since she hadn't left the location with anybody, and the only note containing Walker's address was with the rest of Walker's file in the confidential envelope on the passenger seat next to her. But that fact didn't make the area seem any less menacing.

Someone out there was digging in her things, maybe following her around. Someone reckless enough to commit a felony in broad daylight.

Elsa's description didn't match, but if the police knew about Walker, they would strongly recommend steering clear of the man's house. If Walker was a con man, he might have had an accomplice. He also might have had enemies, which might have provided a rational explanation for the paranoia.

She looked back at the phone. If she called the police now, they were going to tell her to drop everything and head back to the precinct. Entering a stranger's apartment building alone might not have been the safest thing to do, but she would be in and out in a minute or two. If she left now, the Walker situation was going to be hanging over her head indefinitely, and the last thing she wanted to do was make another trip to Tinicum.

She grabbed the big envelope off the seat and climbed out of the car, shutting the door, and the alarm engaged with a beep as she keyed the remote lock. She turned and looked up at the morose row of buildings, narrowing her eyes.

The Langford didn't jump out at first glance. The entire block looked abandoned, marked by dark, broken windows and exposed areas of brick. A small sign for another hotel called the Ambassador hung above an open doorway with the word "vacancy" lit up in orange neon beneath the name. So the electricity was working, at least. The area looked as if it had been hit by a hurricane.

Cassie scanned the street numbers. Houses of squalor. The people who lived in these buildings believed they had no alternative; they probably could have sued their slumlords for building code violations, but these were people who had given up on the idea of a decent life.

If Walker really did live in this place, he was truly unable to function in society. The man might have been schizophrenic. Cassie rubbed the back of her neck and shook off a sudden chill.

Walker's address appeared on the wall of a stretch of bricks little wider than the doorway. The door was shut, but a handwritten sign on the inside of the blurry window pane read, "LANGFORD."

She pushed the door open and stepped inside. A piece of paper was tacked up next to a stairway that disappeared up into the darkness. She flipped a light switch, and a couple of uncovered fluorescent lamps went on. The paper was a notice about repairs to the heating system.

She headed up the stairs. The steps creaked under her feet, leaving the impression the entire stairway was about to collapse under her weight. She breathed, shaking her head. The person who had broken into her office probably had nothing to do with Walker. If Elsa was right and it was the man who had been asking questions about her, it had probably just been an attempt to make a quick score with minimal effort; the man was probably just some random burglar who had seen her name and knew about her family and thought he would find something valuable.

Then again, if the man really was somehow connected to Walker, he might have been on his way to Walker's apartment right at that moment.

The stairs opened out onto a long hall before winding around to the next flight. The wood boarding of the floor was buckling, stained with dust and cigarette ash and scattered over with flattened candy wrappers and crumbs. Tiny shadows shifted along the blackened molding where the walls met the floor. Roaches.

Two doors were spaced evenly along the wall, with a third at the far corner. Walker was in 1C according to the information in his will; the first door read 1A. Cassie started down the hall, squinting to her right as she approached the second door. Also not the right number... Walker's apartment had to be the third.

There was a dull clank behind her, and she jumped and whirled around, inhaling sharply. Nothing. The hall was completely empty. The noise sounded again, this time softer, coming through the wall toward the ceiling. Bad plumbing in an upstairs room. She exhaled and nodded, shaking it off. Her pulse was racing, and she was starting to crinkle the envelope in her hand. She frowned. She was acting like a basket case.

She took another glance around, then moved quickly forward and the smell of garbage hit her in the face. It was a thick, musty, static cloud and it seemed to get stronger toward the end of the hall. Somewhere between burnt leaves and a very large dead animal. She grimaced and covered her nose and mouth.

The third door was open a crack, and light was coming through. 1C— definitely Walker's apartment. He was apparently home. It didn't mean she needed to linger; the contract termination letter would tell him what he needed to know. If he had any questions, he could learn how to use a phone.

She stepped to the door and slipped, flailing her arms as she steadied herself. The floor around the doorway was wet with a film of liquid, glossy and black in the low lighting. Something had spilled inside Walker's apartment, and it had to be tied to the source of the smell. It might have been blood.

Cassie froze, fighting back a stomach convulsion. It might have been something else—a sewage leak, or some other kind of liquid refuse. It wasn't necessarily blood. But somehow, blood seemed as if it were the only possibility. Something terrible had happened, something she didn't want to know about.

Her instincts were screaming at her, telling her to drop everything and dash back to the car, but she had to look inside the apartment. She had to be absolutely sure. If no one was inside, she could leave the contract termination letter and all the documentation, she could forget that she had ever met the man, and she could put the whole bizarre, sorrowful episode in her rearview mirror.

She nudged the door open and gasped.

*　　　　　　　*　　　　　　　*

The stagnant air of the 9th District interview room was clammy and cold, as if the ventilation system had conked out. The detectives probably had the thermostat programmed that way.

At least it didn't smell like death.

Cassie twisted the latch on her handbag in a circle, glancing out one of the barred windows. The lighting was dim and uneven, just bright enough to be annoying.

Detective Pestello sat at the long Formica table, staring at Cassie from under a single black eyebrow that met in a tuft at the center of his forehead. He looked away, shaking his head. "Everybody's got something they're trying to hide. I don't know, maybe you imported Cuban cigars, or ripped a tag off a mattress. Maybe your family's circumventing tax laws in some way. Not really my concern." He raised his fist to his mouth and grunted. "Withholding information on a murder investigation... that's my concern."

Ugh! Cassie cleared her throat and refocused on the detective's large face. "I'm not withholding information."

Pestello stretched and yawned, lifting his oversized forearms in the air. He threw them back, loosening his shoulders, then scratched the center of his chest, leaning over a small spiral-bound notepad. "The whole story, Ms. Prescott. I need to know everything. Okay, look, lawyers from the big, downtown firms don't make house calls in the ghetto. You were in a little, rat-hole room containing a dead guy, 37 G's, and a pile of valuables with documents that said you were going to inherit this stuff. Look, I'd like to help you here, but you need to clue us in on what's going on."

She sighed. Somehow the throbbing in her head was managing to intensify. "You'd like to help. Isn't that supposed to be your job—to protect and serve? Should I have reported this to the mailman?"

The detective leaned back in his chair, bouncing lightly and looking as if he would be completely comfortable entertaining her for the next several hours. He squinted. "Is that supposed to be funny? You think coming at me with an attitude is gonna help us catch this guy?"

"I don't need the third degree, detective—I need protection." Cassie tapped her finger against the table and suppressed a cough. Pestello wasn't smoking, but someone with cigarettes had been in the room recently. In the yellow light of the semifunctional fixtures, particles of soot were still visibly moving through the heavy air.

Pestello rubbed his thick neck. "All right. Obviously, we want to make sure you're safe from this guy who tore up your office, whoever he is. We can put a black-and-white at your apartment and keep an eye out, but if you don't tell us anything, all that does is make it harder for us to catch this guy, right? I'm just asking you to be reasonable. Work with us—you know, the way lawyers usually do with cops. Murder scene's one thing... you weren't there, I get it. But like it or not, the vic's connected to you, you're involved. I might not like you for the murder, but anything else out of the ordinary is going on, typically it helps the investigation when we know the details. And it's pretty clear your relationship with this man was a little bit out of the ordinary."

"I told you I met him twice. Two times, his request. There was no relationship." She brushed several dry strands of hair away from her eyes and imagined herself back inside the apartment under the hot, pulsing spray of her shower massage. "I'm familiar with the routine. I know I need to tell you everything I can, I've answered all your questions, and I think I'm starting to hear the same ones over again. And I'm pretty sure most cops manage to get through the interview after about 15 minutes, unless they think they're dealing with someone who's holding out."

Pestello pursed his lips as he scanned his notes and acted as if he couldn't hear. Cassie scowled and shook her head, glancing left at the big two-way mirror. Trying to negotiate the situation with a plea for help was going to leave the worst impression imaginable, but a pretense at bravado would have been stupid. The vision of Walker's body lingered in her mind— the headless figure, torn open as if it had been attacked by hyenas, smeared over with blood that was so dark it looked black. And the head, several feet away—burnt to a crisp, eyes gone.

It had been worse than anything she had seen, let alone experienced first-hand. Medical examiners' photos, brutal spectacles on video tape… prep work meant to shock a jury. Far worse. Walker's death was the work of a seriously disturbed and sadistic animal, a sociopath devoid of any trace of value for human life. A monster. One with access to her name, thanks to a business card and that completely misguided will. By now the man knew more than enough to track her down.

She stared at the clock above the closed door that sealed off the mayhem of the precinct's second floor. Quarter to 8. Her parents kept no secrets about where they lived; the house was well-secured against intruders. But she needed to call them soon.

What in God's name was she going to say?

"Detective, I would really like to leave." She tried to keep the whine out of her voice. Pestello held up his finger, eyes locked on the notepad.

She focused again on the mirror, trying not to focus on the stricken, weary look that seemed embedded in her face. Evidently, the rest of the homicide team was perfectly fine with dragging out the interview, assuming anyone was even bothering to listen in. The blunt, clumsy interview had been going on for nearly a half an hour now—30-odd minutes of sitting in a room in front of a myopic, borderline-degenerate cop who seemed to think he needed to slow-walk the material witness, probably because they had virtually nothing other than her testimony to go on.

She moved back and forth in her chair, wincing at the predictable squeak. Hopefully the sound was as grating to Pestello as it was to her. Not likely; the man was about as pliable as the bird-bombed statue of Massa the Gorilla in the zoo. He was immune to the fact that she was part of the criminal justice system herself, and he wasn't fazed by facts, logic, how frazzled she was... how frazzled anyone in her right mind would have been after stumbling onto a bloodbath in one of the worst neighborhoods in the city.

So her situation was questionable, there were a large number of very weird surrounding circumstances to digest—so what? It wasn't relevant if she didn't know anything. "You know we're not getting any closer to catching anyone here."

He finally looked up. "You worked a murder investigation before? How about you let me do my job, Ms. Prescott? I do what I do. And I'm not the only one working this case." He shrugged. "You're telling me you never met this man before last Thursday—he just shows up and next thing you know, he forks over his property."

Let him do his job. Cassie rolled her eyes. If she had worked for the district attorney, the man would have found a way to get through the questions a lot more quickly. "It happens. People do strange things sometimes... I have no idea who this man is or why he chose to put me in his will. It's completely inappropriate." She sighed. "I did drop him as a client—I mentioned that already. You saw the termination letter."

She shifted. The hard-edged metal chair couldn't have been more uncomfortable. The painful design was undoubtedly intentional, although it was hard to imagine these guys putting that much forethought into anything.

Maybe it was a personal thing, less to do with competence and more to do with a power jag—maybe Pestello was dragging his feet because it wasn't every day he had a pretty lady in a room, all to himself. The gun-toting, knuckle-dragging, hairy Neanderthal.

The detective lifted his arms up, either engaging in an odd stretch or a half-assed attempt at feigning helplessness. He waved at his notes. "Try to put yourself in my shoes, all right? The only connection between these two incidents is you. I'll ask you again... why would somebody trash your office? Is there a reason I should believe the guy who tossed your office was looking for the same thing as a killer down by the airport? Do you know what that thing might be? Help me out, here."

She leaned forward and placed her hands firmly against the tabletop. "Look. Let's get through this, okay? A man came to my office and looted it, apparently looking for something that he thinks I have. I don't have it. I don't have any idea what it is—maybe it's one of the items named in the will, I don't know." She raised her eyebrows, cocking her head. "I don't know anything about it. Now, I'm feeling a little unsafe outside my apartment at the moment, so if you can get your people to send that car, I'd really appreciate an escort home."

Pestello rubbed his chin and squinted up into the light fixtures as if fascinated by them. "Seems to me you're in about as safe a place as you can be right now."

Cassie groaned.

"All right, bear with me, please, Ms. Prescott, can you do that?" He picked up his notepad, brushing off the surface of the table with a forearm. "This is not your typical case, all right? We got a lot of moving parts, and it's a little difficult for me to get all these unusual details situated in my tiny, one-track brain."

So the gun-toting knuckle-dragging Neanderthal was also a wise-ass. Cassie shook her head silently.

"Let's rehash. John Walker." He wiped his nose with a finger as he read from his notes. "John Ulysses Walker, according to the bank accounts and the will. Man had seven different European passports, without the middle name, but no driver's license. Fingerprints aren't in any database, just like the prints on your office furniture. No records on this guy, other than the bank accounts, none of which are in this country or require any kind of verifiable identification we can obtain, and it looks like he spent some time working with a printer supplier in Wilmington 26 years ago. Which would explain the printers and lamination machines we found in the man's apartment, and might possibly explain the passports."

Cassie waved a hand in the air. "I don't know anything about it."

"The man was living his life off the grid. Common name, probably using other people's Social Security numbers to conduct business when necessary. Guy like that takes good care to make sure people don't know his real name. I'm thinking maybe his killer knows who he is." Pestello gave her a hard stare, nodding once. "The wounds were a little extreme… can't wait to hear what the M.E. has to say about this. Looks to me like he got his head burned right on off." He paused and ran his tongue around the inside of his mouth as if fishing for food morsels.

Cassie looked down at the faded linoleum tiles of the floor. She rubbed her eyes. "Is there a point to this?"

"No furniture in the room. Not one chair. Just a pile of clothes, the gold and jewel junk, some little elephants, and the money. Along with a couple of machines that happen to be perfect for running a fake ID business."

Cassie flashed him a look that mixed disgust and exhaustion, glancing again at the clock. If she got up and walked straight out the door, there wasn't anything they could do to stop her. The precinct lieutenant could have issued protective detail; the lieutenant would have been in the only closed-door office on the floor.

Pestello was shaking his head again, with his mouth twisted in a severe grimace. "I'll bet this skel has a rap sheet a mile long, if we ever get a hit on him."

There were two knocks. The door opened and a bald, black man in glasses with a neatly trimmed goatee stuck his head in. "Mike, you got a call." He disappeared, leaving the door open.

Pestello nodded. "That's the boys at the scene." He got up and straightened the reports.

Cassie smiled curtly, shouldering her handbag and lifting her coat from the table as she stood. "I'm done waiting here, detective."

"All right. Let's hear what these guys have to say about what transpired, then we can get you out of here." He was examining her, watching for a reaction.

Lazy bastard. He had been stringing her along intentionally, waiting for the crime scene report so he could check her statements against the evidence before she left the building. So he wouldn't have to bother with follow-up. He was just trying to keep his paperwork to a minimum.

Cassie shook her head, opening her mouth, then looked down and laughed to herself. It wasn't worth it. She waved at the door. "Go ahead, let's get it over with."

She followed Pestello back into the open interior of the thinly lit precinct facility, still filled with loitering policemen in ties and shoulder-holster suspenders, sporadic phone-ringing, slowly tapping typewriters, and the general air of tired single-mindedness. Her eyes lingered for a moment on one of the bar-covered window frames as she moved out onto the floor, weaving around the desks. The ambiance was exactly the same as every other district office building she had experienced, though it seemed distinctly more oppressive now that the problem was hers. Posting bail and fetching the shoplifting teenage kid of a client was tedious, but it wasn't ominous. Now the place felt more like a hospital before an operation.

She glanced across the floor to the lieutenant's office. The squad leader was visible through the open blinds, at his desk and on the phone; he very likely had his hands full with the John Walker murder himself, coordinating with Tinicum police or talking to the district attorney's office. The sheer, naked violence of what had happened to Walker would garner attention from the D.A. and all the local news outlets. Psycho killers always made good press. Whether or not that would help catch the man was up in the air—the damage to Walker's body was so thorough and gory the police seemed to be having trouble getting past the question of the murder weapon, which didn't bode well.

Another thing up in the air was whether or not a pair of cops sitting in a car outside her apartment for a couple of days was adequate protection for a man like this.

A tall, dark, slender man in a tweed sport coat rapped on the lieutenant's door as she looked. The lieutenant got up and motioned him in, still on the phone; the man entered, and the blinds closed. Cassie stopped and squinted. She had seen the man before, in a totally different context...

"Yo, Ms. Prescott!" Pestello was standing at a desk by the wall, holding his phone. "Have a seat." He pointed at a wooden chair that looked about as welcoming as the metal seat in the interview room.

She stepped to the desk. "I think I'll stand."

He nodded absently as he put the phone on his shoulder and started leafing through a file folder. She glanced back at the lieutenant's office as the man in the sport coat came back out, laughing and waving over his shoulder. She nodded to herself. Detective Diaz, from the Convention Center. Zack Wyler's friend. The man adjusted his tie, side-stepped past another detective to the reception desk, and grabbed a radio from a wall rack by the entrance, then disappeared down the outside stairway.

So Zack Wyler still had friends in the police department. Not really a surprise in principle, considering Wyler was an ex-cop, although Detective Diaz did seem a little too personable for someone who might be tight with Wyler.

Pestello hung up the phone and it immediately rang again. "Hold on." He settled into his chair.

"Sure, why not?" She set her coat on the back of the chair, glancing around, and a fairly tall man standing by the next desk caught her attention. The man had on a fedora and a fancy wool-blend topcoat. He noticed her and smiled, looking back. She turned back to Pestello, adjusting the strap of her handbag over her shoulder.

The man in the topcoat stepped to her side, tipping his hat, then removing it. "You don't look like someone who belongs in a place like this."

She nodded and flashed a weak smile. Pestello was still ignoring her, scribbling more notes in his book as he went through the folder. Apparently he was going to be on the phone for the foreseeable future.

The man in the topcoat folded his arms, stepping around her and standing with his back to the wall as if to survey the room. "It's maddening how long these things take, isn't it? Have you been here long?"

"Of course." She looked up at him. "Longer than I would like."

He raised an eyebrow. "I'm discouraged to hear that… if they haven't felt the need to exercise a little efficiency for someone like you, they obviously aren't going to do it for me." He smiled again, keeping his eyes on her for an extended moment, then looked back out across the floor.

Cassie looked down at her handbag, smiling to herself. Evidently, gallantry was this man's game. It went with his look. He had a thinly trimmed mustache, salt-and-pepper hair, and striking gray eyes… overall as straight-laced and well-coiffed as if he had walked out of a black-and-white movie. Too debonair and sharply dressed to be someone who worked in the precinct building; presumably he wasn't any happier about being stuck there than she was. He looked like someone who would have known her father.

He touched his mustache. "I'm sorry… are you Cassandra Prescott, from the law office of Halpern, Sutherland, and Kovach?"

Pestello glanced briefly at the man, sticking out his elbow as he moved his hand to the phone receiver, then turned his attention back to the paperwork, nodding.

Cassie narrowed her eyes at the man in the topcoat. "Do I know you?"

"You might. I'm four floors down from you, with Geitner and Boggs. We're not as large as your firm, but I represent clients in the city as well. I think we've both spent more than our share of time in these dreary public halls." He sighed, pursing his lips in a pout very similar to that of a cocktail party guest notifying a server that the crab dip needed to be refilled.

"You're a defense attorney." Cassie nodded. He didn't seem preoccupied enough for someone working a district case, and his face didn't ring any bells. "I'm sure I've seen you at the courthouse."

He smiled broadly. "I'm sure. I thought I'd step over and say hello… remind you there are still people who can both sympathize and communicate on your level, present company notwithstanding." He turned and gestured at the surroundings.

"Well I can definitely appreciate that." Cassie shifted in her stance, again fiddling with the handbag and shifting the strap away from her collarbone. "What brings you here?"

"Why am I suffering this blue-collar hive of ineptitude?" He raised his eyebrows. "I assume it's the same reason you're here. Fulfilling our obligation to the client… a triviality of the occupation. One thing is certain— I can think of many places I would rather be."

No argument there. Cassie sighed, glancing toward Pestello. "Actually

I'm not here for a client. I'm being questioned as a material witness." The words sounded oddly indifferent as she said them out loud.

The lawyer looked immediately concerned. "You're not in any sort of trouble, are you?"

"I shouldn't be." She squinted at him. Where was this man from? There was something peculiar about the way he was talking, as if he was trying to hide an accent. It didn't seem to be affecting his confidence, or the smoothness of the delivery—he was probably pretty good in front of a judge and jury. She nodded at Pestello, still on the phone. "You know how the police are. I'm sure I'll be fine."

"I'm sure you will." He glanced back at the next desk. "Well, I'll leave you to it, then. It's nice to finally meet you." He moved away from the wall and paused, turning back and holding up a finger. "I don't usually do this, but I'm going to be in the building for a while longer. Would you do me the honor of joining me for a bite to eat when you're finished here?"

The man definitely had a practiced approach. Cassie cocked her head and smiled. "I don't think I would be very good company right now. Thank you, though."

He looked surprised. "Oh, nonsense—you need to wind down after an ordeal like this. I've been put through the wringer myself on many an occasion." An obese detective brushed past Cassie's seat, stuffing a chocolate bar into his mouth. The lawyer stepped out of the way, nodding after the detective, then refocused on Cassie. His face broke into another magnetic smile.

Cassie shook her head. "I'm going to have to take a rain check. It's been a long day. When they're done putting me through the wringer, I'm going straight home to collapse on the couch." She paused, examining him. It wasn't a good day to be going on blind dates. "I'll look for you at the courthouse."

The man lingered, glancing around the room as if he suddenly wasn't sure how to handle the end of a conversation. She raised her eyebrows. "You never told me your name."

"Teodor Monroe." He bowed his head.

She nodded. "Teodor. That's different."

Pestello cleared his throat loudly and hung up the phone. "Excuse me— I hate so much to interrupt. I got some information for you, Ms. Prescott."

Cassie blinked. The big detective was back on his feet. Maybe his rear end was starting to get as sore as hers was. She looked at him expectantly.

Pestello's eyes flicked to the other lawyer. "Prints at the murder scene match the prints at your office. That's a definite solid connection between the two incidents." He nodded at Monroe. "You being helped, sir?"

Monroe shook his head, holding up his hands. "I don't mean to interfere. I was just leaving." He held up a hand, turning to Cassie. "Again, pleasure to meet you. Good luck."

Cassie waved, nodding back. The lawyer smiled and stepped away, heading for the stairwell.

Pestello watched him go. "Friend of yours?"

Cassie looked toward the stairwell. "Another lawyer. I run into people in places like this from time to time." She paused. "You were saying?"

"You know anything about a gemstone?" He frowned.

Cassie shrugged. "He had something about a gemstone on his will, from what I recall. What about it?"

"All of the other nonmonetary items on the will were found on the premises, but we didn't find any gemstones. Might be what the killer was looking for."

And if the killer and the office intruder really were the same man, there was a good chance he thought she had this gemstone. Cassie bit her lip, frowning in the direction of the interview room.

Pestello raised his thick, continuous eyebrow. "Even if you don't know anything about this thing, there's a good chance the killer thinks you do."

Cassie looked back at him, shaking her head. The man's powers of deduction were amazing. "Anything else?"

He nodded. "They found two more victims. A couple of women from the suburbs turned up in an alley down the block." He stuck out his lower lip, scratching his chin.

Cassie raised her eyebrows. "And you think they're connected to this?"

Pestello paused. "Similar burns." He sniffed loudly. "I know you're a busy lady, but you might want to think about relocating for a while. Get out of town, stay with some friends. Be on the safe side."

Cassie stared back at him, trying to focus. The words seemed unreal. She squinted, shaking her head. "I'll think about it."

He shrugged. "Your call." He peeled off a sticky note from the pad on his desk, opened his drawer, and fished out a business card, handing her the note and card with two fingers. "Go down to the front desk and ask for Sergeant Lynch. He'll have the guys downstairs dispatch that car for you."

The note was barely legible, but Cassie made out her own name. She kept her eyes down, nodding slowly. "Okay, what about my family? This person has my information—what if this person goes after them? Maybe they should be getting some kind of protection too. Do you have someplace they can go, like a safe house or something?"

Pestello scratched his upper lip. "Can't help you there. That's more of an OCB thing, not something you usually need to worry about with one of these solo humps, but this case... I'd let them know. Maybe you could all go to the French Riviera—that's what you rich folks usually do, isn't it?" He winked.

Shit. Cassie exhaled, running a hand through her hair.

Pestello pointed at the business card. "You call that number if anything comes up, you see anything suspicious or unusual. Or if you happen to remember anything that might be relevant. You never know." He smiled.

"Right." She pursed her lips, slipped the card in her handbag, and cleared her throat. "Thank you, detective."

"Take care. Stay out of trouble."

She turned away from Pestello's desk. The half-dozen other men in the room were more or less all looking in her direction, and those ahead of her stepped back out of the way as she walked toward the small doorless entrance to the Homicide Division, oddly reminiscent of a line of attendants at one of her mother's parties. She glanced around as she exited into the yellow light of the stairwell, secured the handbag strap on her shoulder, and grabbed the metal handrail as she headed down the steps, keeping her attention forward.

The first floor was four turns down. She moved to the outside wall on the last landing as she passed a pair of officers in uniform with a short, muscular Latino man in a skullcap and handcuffs, then hustled down the last flight as she spotted the front desk at the right side of the big lobby's checkerboard tile floor.

A bright-eyed, white-haired man in a pale blue uniform stepped to the open window along the wire-cage counter as Cassie approached. He seemed to know who she was. "Ms. Prescott?"

"That's right." She nodded and handed him Pestello's note. Nice that the detective had called ahead. So the man wasn't a complete jackass. She peered at the older man, squinting. "You're Sergeant Lynch?"

He smiled and his cheeks flushed red. "That I am, that I am. Well, the detective wasn't exaggerating—you are easy on the eye, young lady."

She cocked her head and flashed a smile. "Aren't you sweet." She rubbed her neck, looking away. Right the first time; Pestello was definitely a jackass.

The sergeant stepped to a wall covered by a pigeon-hole message box and took out a set of keys, then sounded a dull buzzer. A much younger man in an identical uniform stepped across the floor, fiddling with a device on his belt, and stopped by the window next to Cassie.

Sergeant Lynch raised his eyebrows. "Where are you parked?"

She rubbed her arm. "Right out in front on 12th Street, toward Vine. It's a blue Mercedes 190E."

The white-haired man leaned against the countertop, still smiling. "We're going to send two units with you, all right? You're going to want to make sure these boys are by your side until you get to your door, and they check the apartment before you go inside. You understand?"

Cassie nodded. "Yes—thank you very much."

"That's what we're here for. Now, the detail stays with you until you tell us otherwise—you just need to notify us if you're going anywhere in the meantime. All right, our boys will be out shortly, so you just wait inside your car until they get there. They'll pull up behind you and tap the horn. Okay?"

"That's great. I really appreciate it."

The sergeant waved away the thanks and nodded at the other man. "Officer Cole, Ms. Prescott here could use an escort to her car." He winked. "Take care of her, will you?"

The young officer nodded. "Yes, sir."

Cassie sighed and turned, and her eyes stopped on a man in a topcoat holding a fedora, leaning casually against the wall across the floor.

"Well, I see they still haven't finished with you." Teodor Monroe pushed away from the wall, lolling his hat on one hand.

Cassie fell back and bumped roughly against the counter, nearly dropping her handbag.

Officer Cole looked at her sharply, then focused on Monroe. "Hey, whoa, miss... everything okay?"

Cassie shook herself. "Fine, yes. I'm okay, thanks. Sorry." She brushed her hair, shaking her head. "Teodor Monroe, right?" She shook her head again, glancing at the officer. "It's okay." She cleared her throat, stepping across the floor and looking back at Monroe. "Sorry, my nerves are just about fried. Long day."

The lawyer shook his head. "Perfectly understandable—I apologize for startling you." He stepped to the door and opened it for her. "I'm done here. Can I walk you to your car?"

She paused and glanced back at the cage. "Probably not the best day. Maybe we can talk more another time." She laughed abruptly. "I'm a little indisposed right now."

Monroe nodded, smiling. He ran a hand over the top of his head, then

409

straightened. "I'm sorry. It's just… I've been hoping to meet you for quite some time now." He paused. "You know what? Never mind." He nodded. "Some other time. I'm sure I'll see you… at the courthouse."

She smiled back at him. Unbelievable. Apparently, testosterone levels were on an uptick lately. Pretty soon, she was going to have to start wearing a fake wedding ring. She nodded. "Thank you. I'm sure I'll see you around." She glanced at Officer Cole. "I think I'm ready to go."

The officer stepped across the floor and opened one of the inner double-doors, holding it for her. She waved at Monroe and headed out, opening the outer door in return, then followed the officer down the front steps, turning left up the sidewalk. She glanced over her shoulder briefly, then caught up to the officer. The Mercedes was about halfway down the block, parked by itself along the red curb of the loading zone, the only spot she had been able to quickly find. A citation was a virtual guarantee, but a parking ticket was one thing she could afford to not worry about.

"Ms. Prescott."

She spun on her heels. The lawyer had followed them out. She frowned. Some guys could not take no for an answer. She held up a hand. "Hey, you seem nice… maybe I didn't make myself clear, but this is really not a good time for me."

The man stopped in the middle of the sidewalk. The streetlights went on as if on cue, faintly lighting the backdrop behind him as the overhead twilight dwindled. "Ah, Ms. Prescott, it's true you are very, very charming—a pleasant surprise. But whether or not it's a good time for you, that's not really my concern."

He was a virtual silhouette, and his face was dark, impossible to read. Cassie shook her head, adjusting the handbag strap on her shoulder. "I'm sorry… what did you just say?"

He stepped toward her. "You misunderstand my intentions. I'm not interested in you—I'm interested in John Walker's stone. I believe you know where it is."

Cassie blinked. For a moment, the thought didn't transmit. Then she felt a rush of adrenaline, and her ears rang with the memory of a shark-warning alarm she had heard at the beach on a family vacation to Key West long before. She had been about 12 years old. It was almost always a false alarm, Fulton had said. Almost always, it was just a dolphin.

Officer Cole moved next to her. "We all right here?"

Cassie shook her head, groping for the officer's arm without taking her eyes off Monroe. How could she have been so stupid? An unknown man had appeared out of nowhere and she had just dismissed the possibility that he was a threat, under the worst circumstances imaginable. Because he was wearing good clothing? All the deriding of her parents and their superficialities, their emphasis on presentation and flare, on flashing their wealth around in the form of expensive dinner attire, and now here she was exhibiting just as much status-driven ignorance toward a man who had approached her in a police station.

"Let's go, Ms. Prescott, let's get you in the car."

The officer took her arm and steered her back toward the Mercedes, still four or five car-lengths away. She glared at him and hissed under her breath. "It's him, officer, this is the man—I think this is the killer. You need to call for help."

The officer turned, directing her behind him and holding up a hand. "You want to tell me what your business is with this woman, sir?" He unhooked a portable radio from his belt.

Monroe took a step back. "Oh, hello, officer—am I overstepping? I really don't mean to cause concern. Please, allow me to make myself clear." He reached inside his coat.

The officer yelled and reached for his gun, and suddenly the sidewalk was flooded in a blaze of pink light. There was no sound of gunfire.

Cassie shook herself, trying to blink away afterimage, focusing on the vague, shadowy form of the man in the topcoat. There were others on the street, but now they seemed to fade away, like background details in a dream. Officer Cole was down, flat on his back with a massive burn wound on his upper chest. He wasn't moving.

Monroe tipped his head back, raising his voice. "Now then. Let's expedite things, shall we? The stone, Ms. Prescott. Tell me where it is—I'm not a patient man." He raised a hand, holding something in the air, gold-tinged in the shallow cone of increasingly visible lamppost light. A very thin gun—some kind of laser? Who in God's name was this man?

She firmed her jaw and started slowly backing up, holding out her hands. "Listen… I don't know what you heard in there, but the contents of John Walker's will are part of a police investigation now, so if you want this stone back, you might want to let them find it before you make any more inquiries." Her eyes drifted down toward the officer on the ground. He was dead. He had to be… this man had just killed a police officer right before her eyes, on the sidewalk right out in front of the police station. The man hadn't even hesitated a second.

The police cruiser was going to come around the corner any minute now. She just needed to buy a little more time.

Monroe stepped toward her. "Yes, it does seem you've gotten yourself involved in matters beyond your scope of understanding. Oh, I'm sure at the moment you do wish our demised friend hadn't brought you into this. But we both know he did." He aimed the weapon. "The stone is yours now. He willed it to you. I saw the document myself."

Cassie sneaked a glance over her shoulder. She frowned, flexing her fingers in the air, opening and closing her fists and feeling the tension in her knuckles. "That will was never made legal. I met with Walker but I didn't want any part of it." She narrowed her eyes. "Sorry to disappoint you, but you're wasting your time."

Monroe tittered quietly. "Stunning and clever, Ms. Prescott. You make a convincing case. I might be inclined to believe you, but as someone who holds that stone would know... its value is immeasurable. I don't expect the person who holds it to give it up easily." He was speaking more smoothly now. The accent was coming out clearly, and it was strong, smooth, and unfamiliar. "Frankly, I don't have a lot of time, so my options are limited. I'm just going to assume you're lying. And in case you happen to be carrying the stone with you and you're factoring that into the equation, make no mistake—it won't protect you from me, whether you're holding it or not."

It won't protect you. The strange statement hung in the air for a moment. The man was sounding more and more psychotic. Where was that damn police car? And where was everyone else—didn't anyone see what was going on?

Cassie's pulse raced as she stared at the weapon. "I don't have any stone, Mr. Monroe, or whoever you are. This is in the hands of the police now—you really need to listen to me, because if you keep on this course, you are not going to get what you want."

She glanced around as she continued to back away. No visible police. The sidewalks were more or less deserted now, as empty as they could possibly be in a city at dusk. If anyone had seen the blinding flash, they had long since turned tail. If she was going to get away, she was probably going to have to do it herself.

She was already even with the Mercedes. She bit her lip and started angling toward it.

Monroe followed her eyes, meeting her stride for stride. He nodded to Cassie's left. "Your conveyance, I believe." A bolt of light leapt from the shadow, shearing through her windshield like a knife through tinfoil and leaving a smooth, oblong hole. "I'm going to need you to stay here for the moment." He placed the fedora back on his head, like a mobster from the 1920s, casually aiming the gun in her direction. "Last chance, Ms. Prescott."

She stared at the car. Steam rose through the gaping, concave hole in the glass. The steering wheel was on the street side, so if she managed to get the door open, she was going to have to go straight across the passenger seat. The damage seemed to be limited to the windshield itself. The engine would still function, most likely, but it was a moot point if she couldn't get to the wheel, and this man wasn't going to wait while she got the door open.

She closed her eyes and nodded, holding up a finger. "Wait—just a minute, please. I do have something that might help, if you give me a minute to find it."

Monroe strolled toward her, gesturing with the gun. "You don't have a minute. Now, I'm a little short on time, I need the stone by tonight, and if I don't get it, I'll become intensely angry. I'm significantly less charming when I'm angry."

She swallowed dryly, turning slightly so that her handbag shoulder was away from Monroe, slid her hand inside the bag, found her keys, and fingered the remote. The car began flashing its hazards and honking repeatedly.

Monroe cocked his head at the Mercedes, staring as if he had never heard a car alarm go off. He stopped a pace away from her. "A ploy. To attract attention? Your instincts of self-preservation appear to be lacking."

"I'm sorry, no... he gave me some information about a place he was storing it. It's in here somewhere." She set her eyes on his jaw line and breathed, trying to keep herself calm. He was just about within reach.

Monroe eyed the bag and thrust the gun inches from her face. "Thank you, Ms. Prescott. I think I'll just take the whole bag, if you don't mind terribly." He held out his other hand, raising his eyebrows.

Cassie glanced at the odd, narrow muzzle of the weapon. Alien... everything about this was off, completely bizarre. Images of the victims flashed in her head, the horrifying burn wounds. This weapon had done it to them. Now it was pointed at her face, point blank. Only one chance. She slid the strap off her shoulder, then caught Monroe's eyes looking past her. She turned.

The police car was stopped in the street. One policeman was already out of the car, moving onto the sidewalk. The driver got out and stayed at the car, leaning against the door. The first man spoke. "Ms. Prescott? Sorry for the delay." He slowed almost immediately, glancing around and putting a hand on his sidearm.

Shit! Cassie raised her voice. "No, wait! He's got a—"

Monroe scowled, his face transformed as if he had just pulled off a mask, and he stepped clear of Cassie, whipping his weapon in front of him and firing. He hit the man on the sidewalk in the face, turned, and hit the driver. It happened in less than a second. Again, no gunshots—just silent, lethal light. The two officers never knew what hit them.

Cassie dropped the handbag and lunged, kicking Monroe hard in the crotch, then spun and swatted the gun out of his hand as she jump-switched to her other foot, landing a high roundhouse kick across his jaw when he buckled forward. She came down in a fighting stance with her fists chambered, and she advanced as he staggered backwards, connecting a quick blow to the solar plexus and an upper-cut directly to the nose, knocking the fedora off his head.

Monroe snarled and fell over, clutching at his face. Cassie snatched the handbag off the sidewalk, found the remote, and darted around the car, hitting the lock and flinging the door open, fumbling for the ignition key as she dove into the driver seat. She jammed in the key and started the car, peeling out hard and swerving to avoid a Buick parked along the opposite curb. No more blazes of light hit the car.

She blinked, rubbed her eyes, and squinted at the rearview, stepping on the gas. Nothing but the golden shine of streetlamps. The block of the 9th Police District Office disappeared behind her.

$$*\qquad\qquad *\qquad\qquad *$$

Cassie leaned against the inside of the phone booth, watching a line of traffic on I-95 heading south, out of the city. Diffracted headlights tracked along the blurry glass, washing back the shadow in relentless waves, leaving her exposed.

She took a deep breath of cold air and shuddered, rubbing the goose bumps on her arms beneath the thin fabric of her shirt.

She was dealing with a psychopath. It was real. A man with a gun that looked like a toy in a novelty shop—some kind of impossible, ridiculous gun that burned people to a crisp where they stood—was stalking her, someone who wasn't afraid of taking on the police at their doorstep. Someone hell-bent on finding this thing that John Walker had apparently been so obsessed about keeping hidden. A gemstone.

What the hell was happening?

Grotesque images flashed in her head like slides—men frozen in stride with incinerated faces, Walker's ravaged corpse, Monroe's silhouette at the

414

center of a storm of blinding electric pink. Silent explosions of intensified light, over and over again.

She looked out at the car, idling behind her. Home wasn't safe. The police weren't going to keep her safe. Using the cell phone in the car wasn't a good idea as long as there was a possibility that someone was tracking it, whether it was Monroe or the police; it was better if no one knew where she was until she figured out what she was going to do.

Good luck figuring that out. Her mind was functioning about as well as the Mercedes' warped and caved-in windshield.

A car horn honked somewhere behind her back and she spun around, knocking the receiver of the phone off its cradle. She breathed, touching her eyes, and leaned back against the cold glass. "Jesus Christ!"

Her face felt like ice. The phone booth was warmer than the car, but not by much. It was as if she had just spent the last half hour skiing down a mountain with no facial protection.

How long had she been in the phone booth? "Come on, Cass, think!"

She had made the anonymous call to the police, left them Monroe's description. She had called her parents. What else...

Neither of her parents had answered the phone, which was probably a good thing, considering they would want an explanation. The short version was on their answering machine, and they would take it seriously as long as she didn't give them any of the absurd details. All they needed to know for the moment was that they needed to get Fulton and get out of town. They would be safe at the house in Newport, at least for now.

Of course, none of them were going to be truly safe if Teodor Monroe didn't get what he wanted—not until he was dead or behind bars.

What was it about this gemstone? And why in God's name had a man who barely knew her decided to give it to her? Who were these people, and why were they all so completely insane?

It won't protect you...

She rubbed the sides of her face for a moment, feeling the numbness in her cheeks as she stared at the dangling phone. She could wait, lay low until she made it to Rhode Island and hope Monroe would get himself caught before he managed to track her down. The police were probably in manhunt mode, and Monroe didn't seem to be interested in keeping a low profile. It was possible they would track him down fast... catching him or winning a gunfight with him was another story. The man seemed capable of taking out an army platoon.

This gemstone might not have been able to protect her, whatever that

415

meant, but it could give her a chance to negotiate for her own safety. If she needed to bargain for her life, she was going to need to know what it was. Or where it was. Walker hadn't written the location of the gemstone in his will, but he had obviously intended to give her more information about where to find it. He might have left a clue.

She picked up the receiver, listening to the steady, overly loud hum of the dial tone and shivering as she blew out a long breath. She was going to be stuck going from phone booth to phone booth and freezing her face off until she made some decisions. Her eyes fell on the Yellow Pages on the small shelf beneath the phone.

If she was going to track down this gemstone, she was going to need help without involving the police, or attracting attention. She was going to need a professional, and she was going to need to find the person without going through the firm. A discreet private detective on short notice.

Zack Wyler would have enjoyed the irony immensely, no doubt. She started laughing uncontrollably, then abruptly trailed off.

There were lots of private detectives in Philadelphia besides Zack Wyler. She cocked her head, holding the phone on her shoulder, then grabbed the Yellow Pages and flipped it open across her right arm. It was almost 9 o'clock, but plenty of private detectives ran businesses out of their homes— someone had to be taking calls.

The automated voice of an operator interrupted the dial tone, telling her that she needed to deposit a minimum of 75 cents if she wanted to make a call. Cassie frowned and hung up the receiver, leafing through the book to the section on private investigators.

XIII   THE HUNTER

"So the stone passed from its long custodianship and was there for the taking by those who would endeavor to claim it. But in the new path forged by the incursion from the future, the fate of the stone was not set. It would be determined by the man whose skills were best suited toward tracking it down... either the man who had specifically traveled back in time for it, with his advanced tools for retrieval and acquired knowledge of its nature and history, or another man with no stake, thrust into the fray; either a man with no regard for history, or a man with no regard for his place in it.

"Indeed, the path of the Deiassa of century 20 was bound to the fate of the stone, and the future impact would be calibrated by the man who wielded it, fading like the ripple of a droplet of rain, or else resounding as a devastating wave."

... "Philadelphia"; 28 September 1992 CE

Zack stared mistily at a black-and-white diagram of a twin-engine plane, vaguely aware of the distant sound of a jackhammer against metal in short, even bursts. The sound seemed to be getting louder, ringing in his ears. Like a phone.

There was a loud click. Zack blinked and sat up, rubbing his eyes. A garbled voice came through the answering machine speaker briefly, followed by a sickly beep and an abrupt pop.

Another shredded tape. The cheap piece of crap was feeding wrong again.

He stood and stepped to the other side of the desk, frowning down at the answering machine and poking at the cassette door. Stuck. He grabbed the box with both hands, pulling at the door until it snapped completely off. A crumpled stretch of tape was already knotted around the spools. He growled and slapped the machine, and it went over the edge of the desk, yanking the phone after it with a resonant bang.

"Crock of shit!" He rubbed his mouth with the back of his hand. Goddamn Mondays.

He set the phone back on the desk, unplugged it from the answering machine, and dropped the machine in the wastebasket, then fell back into the desk chair with a loud sigh.

He looked again at the picture of the plane for a moment, then flipped *The American Pilot's Handbook* closed. There was a lot of bullshit he was

417

going to have to go through if he wanted to get back into flying, but ultimately it was just a matter of getting the pilot's license renewed. Plenty of places to get that done in the Philadelphia area, not that it couldn't wait until he was seriously ready to make a career change. Getting the requisite flight experience directly in St. Thomas or St. Croix was probably easier to schedule, and definitely a hell of a lot nicer.

No reason he couldn't head south in a few months. Get out of town by the start of the new year, bring on a little change of scenery for his birthday. A month or so would give him time to get the testing and certificates done and get a feel for the area, maybe make some business contacts for when he finally did make the move and change his life. Donatello had managed to swing a trip to the Caribbean, and he was still giving upwards of 60 hours a week to the city. No such scheduling constraints on a self-employed private detective.

Zack yawned and rubbed his mouth. Another couple of years and he'd have enough to make the move for good. Start up the charter service and forget about all the sleaze and filth of the scum-choked streets. And the Goldstines and Imperatos of the world could go the hell.

The tinny treble of low-quality stereo music was just barely audible, blending into the soft background growl of the city. The radio was on, turned low, as it probably had been for three days or so. Zack squinted across the room in the direction of the sound. Four Tops song. His eyes fell on the harmonica sitting at the far edge of the blotter.

He picked up the harmonica and sat back, putting his feet up on the desk, then blew a few test chords and shook his head, grimacing sourly. Wrong key, and he was too damn groggy to bend notes.

The music stopped for a news break. Zack tossed the harmonica back on the desk and focused his attention, staring at a hole in the little toe region of his left sock. Something about some experimental military aircraft making a crash landing in Valley Forge.

The dry monotone of the announcer droned on. Over 100 people had died in a plane crash in Nepal, and a bunch of people in Maine and Nova Scotia had seen strange lights in the sky. There was a quick note about uncertainty in the stock market, and then a second announcer took over with the sports report.

Zack grunted. Not a slow news day for air-traffic controllers... not exactly something that made a person want to run screaming toward a career in aviation. Maybe it was a sign.

There was a knock at the door, followed by footsteps. Zack swung his feet back to the floor and kicked something hiding under a napkin on the desk. A shot glass clattered on the floor.

Cassandra Prescott stepped into the office doorway. "Hello... Mr. Wyler? Your door was open." She squinted at the floor in the direction of the shot glass.

Now what? Zack nodded. "Counselor." He stood and flashed a quick smile. "My door is always open, like it says in the ad. Broken latch, so I don't have much choice." He scratched his shoulder. "And I'm pretty sure I told you not to call me 'Mister.'"

"Right. Wyler." Prescott glanced around at the various files spread around the desk and her eyes fixed on the harmonica. "I saw the ad. I didn't realize you meant it literally."

"It's on my list of things I need to fix. But as you can see, there's not really much in here to take." He leaned forward and removed the harmonica, stuffing it in his back pocket. He glanced at his watch. Pretty late in the day for an unannounced visit. "Besides, I'm a social kind of guy. What can I do for you, counselor?"

Prescott took a tentative step forward. "If this is a bad time, I apologize." She cleared her throat. "I did try to call first. I couldn't get through... I was hoping you kept late hours."

Zack glanced at the answering machine in the wastebasket. "I'm upgrading my messaging service." He frowned and shook his head. "You here to tell me about another client with a beef about my work?"

The counselor laughed weakly, looking down. "Ah... no. But I do need a favor. I need your help." Her voice was flat. She wasn't used to asking for favors, apparently. Maybe she just wasn't happy about asking for a favor from him.

She looked a little rough around the edges this time, not nearly as collected as before. She was dressed as if she had just come from work, but her white shirt was half-untucked and her navy blue skirt was rumpled pretty badly. She wasn't wearing a jacket, even though it was around 40 degrees outside. Her whole attitude was off. Something had rattled her.

He got up and moved to the side of the room, prying a chair away from a pile of loose file cabinet drawers. He set it in front of the desk. "Here, sit down."

She glanced around cautiously. "Sure. Fine." She nodded and lowered herself into the chair, setting her handbag on the floor.

He slid back behind the desk and dropped into the desk chair. Prescott's hair was pulled back loosely, tattered and mussed as if she had tried to fix

419

herself up in a hurry. "You mind if I ask what happened to you?"

"It's a long story." She was staring at the corner, where several groups of overstacked files had partially collapsed and spilled onto the floor. "This is really where you see your clients?"

Zack eyed the mess of old files. "I'm renovating. Try to relax. Tell me why you're here—what's going on?"

Her jaw tightened visibly. She nodded. "I need to find a missing heirloom. A gemstone that one of my former clients cited in his will."

So she had actually come for detective work. She had come to him, despite all the ugliness with the Hannah Adams case. Maybe out of guilt, some sense of responsibility after bad-mouthing him. Maybe the counselor just had a thing for him. He leaned back and grinned. "A gemstone, huh?" A little out of the norm, but then a member of the Prescott family wouldn't normally be looking for a detective in the Yellow Pages either. "And you thought I was the man for the job."

Prescott frowned at the floor. "Look, yours is about the only detective agency that's open right now... I didn't know where else to go." She was trying really hard to convince him she wasn't happy to be there.

He sighed. "I take it you need to find this gemstone sooner rather than later."

She stared at him. "As soon as possible." She paused. "There's someone else looking for it, someone connected to my client. Someone dangerous."

He nodded, blinking slowly. "What makes you think he's dangerous?"

"He threatened my life. He apparently broke into my office, and then he confronted me directly... and threatened my life. He's convinced I have this thing."

"Wait a minute." Zack leaned forward. "You're saying some guy said he would kill you—you sure about that?"

She glared at him.

"Okay, okay. Why don't you go to the police?"

"The police can't help."

Zack shook his head. "Why is that?"

Prescott stared back at him. "Look, I've already been through all this. I already talked to the police. They know about this man... trust me, they have their hands full. I need someone who can focus attention on this gemstone, who can get me information on it quietly." Her expression was noncommittal—as if she hadn't decided how she was feeling about what she was saying. Common trait for someone who wasn't good at lying.

Zack scratched his chin. The counselor was probably used to dealing with the police… it was possible she just didn't want to embarrass herself by exposing her vulnerability to them. But this woman wasn't stupid enough to think she could avoid the police when someone was threatening to kill her. "How is this man connected to your client?"

She looked back at him blankly. "I don't have a clue. He said his name was Teodor Monroe. He said he was a lawyer from my building… he was lying, I'm sure. He had an accent." She paused and exhaled. "And he has a… kind of a ray gun."

"He has a what—I'm sorry, what does he have?"

She stood up and put a hand on her hip, hanging her head low. She sighed heavily. "Listen, Mr. Wyler. I have no idea how to convince you this is true, but it is. I know it sounds totally ridiculous, but the man has some kind of futuristic superheating laser, some kind of something… and it looks like a ray gun. Like I said, his name is Teodor Monroe. I saw him shoot three police officers with his gun, whatever it is. He killed them."

Zack raised his eyebrows. "He killed cops… with a ray gun?"

Prescott nodded. "They were escorting me, and he killed them. He shot my car with it and melted a hole in my windshield. He's killed others, I think, including my client, John Walker—at least, their injuries were consistent. They were all burnt. Walker, my client, he wanted to leave the gemstone to me in his will… I found him dead in his apartment, and I've already been over this with the police in great detail. His body… was massacred. Ripped open, ripped apart. Burnt. It had to be the same weapon." She shook her head, staring into space.

Zack stared at her for a long moment, trying to digest the words. He shook his head. "All right… you have any idea what this gemstone really is? You know anything at all about it?"

"No. There was no description. All I know is this man is trying to find this thing, and killing people. I was working with Walker, and this man must have found the card I left with him, and now he thinks I have what he wants. I barely got away from him. He'll be looking for me now."

Zack rubbed his face and studied her. There was a crazed twinkle in her eyes as if she thought there was no reason in the world why he shouldn't act on her words immediately. Desperate hope, maybe.

He himself must have looked as if he was watching someone who had just begun a rain dance in his office.

It was hard to believe this was the same person who had so elegantly and systematically ripped him a new one at the Hollywood Café, the same paragon of charm and confidence who had electrified the Convention Center.

421

Of course, she still looked stunning, if a little frazzled. But before, above everything else, she'd had an edge. Now the edge was gone.

Her energy seemed to drain as she watched his reaction. "You don't believe me." She turned slowly and began walking toward the door, leaving her handbag in front of the desk where she had left it. "He doesn't believe me. This is not good. He doesn't believe me, and I'm going to die."

"Hold on." Zack jumped to his feet, darted around the desk, and grabbed Prescott by the arm, turning her around. Her eyes were wide and starting to water at the corners… it could have been tears, but she did look as if she might have gone about a minute without blinking.

She shook her head. "I don't know what I'm supposed to do—I think he's going to kill me. He needs this thing now, and I'm never going to find it. He's going to find me and kill me with that ridiculous, impossible laser gun."

"Hey—calm down, okay? Let's just figure it out." Zack paused, staring at her. "You said he melted your windshield?"

She nodded. "Yes, right in front of the precinct building. He shot it at my car and the windshield just… gave way. It was instantaneous. Those police officers too, they never stood a chance. He didn't care, it was like nothing to him. He shot them in the chest… the face."

Zack closed his eyes and shook his head, soaking it in. Assume what she was saying was true, build it from there. There could have been a guy with a laser gun. It wasn't completely impossible. Maybe he worked for some high-tech corporation that used lasers, got his hands on some handheld prototype.

If the technology existed to manufacture a handheld laser gun, it wasn't public. That kind of weapon would have pretty much rendered regular guns obsolete. It was the kind of thing governments would compete for.

Zack frowned. The woman obviously believed what she was saying—maybe she was having delusions. Maybe. But if she was, something tangible had driven her over the edge. She was legitimately shocked and scared, or he hadn't seen a thousand people just like her at the 9th District.

"How about this—show me your windshield? Then I guess I'll have to believe you."

"Look, I'm telling you the truth." She turned around to give him a better view of her calves. Her wrinkled, blue suit skirt looked slightly browned, as if she had fallen ass-backward on a patch of dirt. "You want to see my windshield? That's some of it—I've been sitting in it for about 20 blocks."

Zack nodded. "It's definitely a new look for you." He waited. One leg

422

of her stockings had a severe run in it, exposing a patch of very smooth, bare skin.

She turned and waved a hand in front of her eyes. "I'm up here, Wyler. I don't have time to get into a subversive objectification speech right now."

Back to her snappy old self again. Good sign. He smiled. "Be sure to let me know when you do have time, counselor. Wouldn't want to miss that."

She gave him a predictable glare. He turned, grabbed her handbag off the floor, and handed it to her, then stepped back around his desk. "Let me just get my gun, and we can go."

"You'll need shoes too."

He took the Beretta out of the top drawer and frowned as he located his shoes behind the desk chair. It was shaping up to be another beautiful week.

He put on his shoes and crossed the office, motioning for Prescott to follow, then grabbed his jacket and headed through the front door, stopping at the top of the stairwell and glancing back.

Prescott pulled the door closed and turned as it rattled back open behind her. She frowned. "Is there a trick to this?"

"Leave it. Come on, let's go."

Domed wall lights flickered as they headed down the brown, dingy steps, rounding the four floors of long half landings in relative darkness. Prescott stayed quiet as they moved, hugging the inside railing.

Zack squinted as they reached the lobby floor. It was unattended, as it was just about always. The small, empty area was well-lit compared to the stairs and left nowhere for anyone to hide, but Prescott scanned it thoroughly before stepping out onto the black and white tiles.

She slowed, focusing on the front door. "Tell me you're formulating some sort of plan of attack here."

"I'm working on it." He scratched the back of his head. "You all right?"

She frowned and gestured absently. "I'll be fine—let's go." They headed across the floor. "So... are you going to tell me your take on this? You haven't said a word. You think I'm crazy, don't you?"

It was a definite possibility. Zack shook his head. "Maybe you inadvertently got yourself involved with a couple of guys who know something that most people don't. Maybe they're doing some experimental testing, someone stole some trade secrets, something like that. Could be drugs, could be information on microfilm. The gemstone's the key—we find that and we know what we're dealing with. Probably not a gemstone at all."

The front door opened to an iron gate, where a secondary external door was missing, as it had been for over a year. Prescott tapped his shoulder. "It's right there."

"Holy shit."

The Mercedes was halfway on the sidewalk, wedged at a sharp angle between two cars in a spot far too small. And the windshield was as she had described it—a smooth, lateral hole cut across the glass like a tear in a sheet of saran wrap. It would have taken a thug sitting on her hood with a blowtorch an hour to do the damage he was looking at. He glanced at Prescott. Her face was drawn; she looked more pained than vindicated.

She sighed and looked back at him. "What now?"

Zack exhaled. "Okay. You said you found this guy's body at his apartment. Then you reported it, I take it? You remember when that was?"

"His name was John Walker."

He waited a beat. She nodded. "Three hours ago. I reported the body at about 6:15 and drove straight to the station. The police would have been at the scene before I got to the precinct building; they were already filing their report." She frowned flatly. "They kept me there well over an hour."

Zack nodded. "Crime Scene might still be there, but the Homicide guys'll be cleared out by now. Airport area, right?"

"That's where the apartment is. But the police I talked to were 9th District. That's where those officers were shot down."

Zack suddenly froze. "9th District? You sure about that—the 0-9?"

She stared at him. "Yes, I'm pretty familiar with the precinct layout. Why, what's wrong?" Then she frowned. "Oh, I forgot—you know the people there. I'm sorry…" Her voice trailed off.

Zack squinted and shook his head. "Why the hell is the 0-9 dealing with a homicide all the way down there?"

The counselor brushed her hair slowly with one hand. "The break-in at my office was in the 9th District. I had Detective Pestello's name already, so I called him first." She shook her head. "It's connected, obviously, so they're working the case jointly with 12th District police."

Zack frowned, staring at the melted windshield. Donatello's district. There were 70 or 80 people at the 0-9, and he knew a lot of them. He probably knew the dead cops, and there was a good chance he knew them really well.

He buried the thought. "Jurisdictional issues… off chance they might not be done bagging everything up." He paused. Hopefully he could get a hold of Donatello and get a better idea of what was going on. "Come on— we might get lucky. My car's this way." Zack headed in the direction of 17th Street.

Prescott hesitated, then hurried after him. "Get lucky how?" She held up a hand, glancing over her shoulder at the car. "Hey, where are we going?"

Zack stopped and turned around slowly. "Can't tell who we're dealing with, or where they're taking the evidence, so our best bet right now is to get down there and see the place for ourselves. Unless I hear otherwise." He raised his eyebrows. "Maybe I can twist somebody's arm, get a look at something useful. Point us in the right direction."

Prescott frowned. "Do you even have any idea what to do if we do manage to find this thing?"

He nodded. "We should keep moving. Let's go." He turned and headed back along the street.

"Won't we be in the way? What if the body's still there?"

He didn't turn around. "That's what I'm hoping for." He picked up his pace, scanning the opposite sidewalk. Obviously she wasn't overly thrilled about going back.

If the police decided this gemstone was relevant to the murder, they were going to lock it down as soon as they found it. Whatever had gone down between her and her client, the police weren't going to share anything with her until they were done investigating—if she wanted information, she was going to have to find it herself.

Her instincts were probably right. If this psycho came after her again, it would definitely help her chances if she could direct him to where it was and get the hell out of the way. Of course, based on her story, the man might have been out for blood whether she gave up the gemstone or not.

The man was a cop-killer… with any luck the police would gun him down before he got anywhere near the counselor again.

Zack rounded the corner, turning onto 16th Street. The lighting was low, and the sidewalks were virtually empty, but a strolling couple on the other side of the street cast a big, obvious shadow on the walls of the buildings. It would have been tough for someone on foot to keep up with them without being seen. He glanced over his shoulder without slowing down, then focused his attention ahead until he reached the next curb, barely acknowledging the pulsing traffic flow as he crossed the intersection.

Prescott stayed a step behind him. "Do you always park ten blocks away from where you live?"

"It's good cardio." Zack frowned, looking back at her. "We'll get there, Ms. Prescott."

A noticeably different expression flashed over her face. Irritation? She sighed and her eyes seemed to linger on his mouth. "I think I'd prefer it if you just called me Cassie."

Cassie. He raised an eyebrow. Irritation at the forced need for familiarity, maybe. Or maybe it was more about the stigma attached to the family name. He shrugged it off and spotted his car halfway down the block.

Prescott was muttering again. "I really don't know about this… I don't see the point in going back there. I was there, the police have been all over the place. Besides, this is taking forever."

"Sorry to inconvenience you. It tends to be harder to find parking spaces when you don't park on the sidewalk. We'll get you a cab next time." Zack cleared his throat. "It's right up here." He slowed and gestured at the car.

Prescott raised her eyebrows as if she were looking at a beached whale. "That's your car?"

"I'm having my Beemer pin-striped." Zack side-stepped between his rear bumper and the grill of a Toyota Corolla that looked brand new next to the flaking green paint of the Dart. "Hop in."

Prescott fingered the handle. "Are the locks broken on this thing too?" She popped the door open and slid into the passenger seat.

Zack shot her a dark look as he swung in next to her, flipping the door closed. "It drives just fine. And it has a windshield. If you like, I can drop you back at your Mercedes." He keyed the ignition. The car stalled.

"Problem?"

Why exactly had he decided to help her? "Just give me a second."

He pumped the gas pedal and cranked the ignition once more. The car shook roughly and the engine spluttered to life.

"When's the last time this thing had a tune-up?"

Zack exhaled and nodded. They were a hell of a lot closer to the downtown hospitals than they were to Tinicum… maybe the counselor would prefer to see how her story played from the inside of a rubber room.

He took a sidelong glance at her as her pulled into the street and sped toward the traffic light at the corner. She was starting to sound more like herself, at least. Feeling normal again, now that she wasn't the only one dealing with the situation. She was staring evenly at the windshield, looking more resolved. Her face had a little of its natural electricity back.

Cassie. Zack looked back at the street, shaking his head. Sucker for a pretty face. That was exactly the kind of thinking that was going to keep him locked in a world of shit. One of these days he was going to figure out how to think straight around women.

Prescott peered at him. "So… what is it exactly that makes you think they'll let you look at the crime scene?"

"Don't worry about it—they love me at the 0-9." A thought resurfaced and he frowned immediately. He glanced at her. "I need to make a call. Hand me my cell—it's in the glove compartment."

Prescott leaned forward and opened the glove compartment. She raised an eyebrow at him as she pulled out the mullet wig.

Zack lowered his brow. "Disguises are sometimes necessary in detective work. The phone?"

She handed it to him and he opened it and hit the on button, keeping his eyes on the road. The light at the cross street turned yellow as he approached. He stopped the car and tapped in Donatello's number. "You remember the guy I was with at the wine tasting?"

"Detective Diaz." She nodded. "The men that were killed were uniform cops, not Homicide. I saw your friend inside at the precinct. He wasn't there when the men were killed."

Zack nodded. For some reason, he didn't feel relieved. Donatello wasn't picking up. The voice mail tone sounded. "It's me. Got an emergency here—call me back soon as you can."

The light turned green. He frowned and stepped on the gas.

*   *   *

Multiple flashing red and blue lights burned through the darkness, forcing Teodor's eyes open. He glanced around blearily, trying to focus his vision. A stout woman was standing over him, tending to him. For a moment, he was completely disoriented, his mind awash with hazy images and random detail, and the only certainty was the sensation of nausea, the waxy paper under his nose, and a violently abhorrent noxious odor. He twisted and blinked as his eyes teared in reaction to the chemical scent, and another sense began to take shape… a singular notion. Failure. Something had gone wrong, and something of vital importance was lost.

The woman backed away a pace, taking away the paper and its toxic pungency, and the immediate environment crystallized. He was in the street, propped up against the coarse walls of a building. She was in a dark blue uniform, different than the gendarmes, and she had a stethoscope draped round her neck. A medic, of sorts. Another man moved in as she stepped back, towering above her—a thin, very dark-skinned man with a bald scalp, thin-rimmed spectacles, and black, sharp-edged hair around his lips and chin that looked as if it had been painted on. The man placed his hands on his hips and turned away. "You like this guy for being reliable? He looks like he's gonna have trouble remembering how to talk."

427

Another man larger than the first shoved his way past the medic and nodded down at him. "Sleeping Beauty awakes." He shrugged. "How we doing, sir? You ready to answer a couple of questions?"

Fragments were gradually returning to memory. John Walker's heir, the only link to finding the pyropite, had slipped through his fingers. He had passed out. Precious time had been wasted, possibly too much time... the rupture of the pyropite was imminent. He was likely fated to return to hyperspace to start over again and try to take the pyropite for the second time, an exceedingly annoying inconvenience. He would go through it as many times as it took. Trial and error would ultimately pay off, of course, but that promise made the prospect no less excruciating.

Still, this trip wasn't definitively over. He had underestimated the Prescott woman, but she hadn't defeated him yet.

"Yeah, this is the same guy. He was with her upstairs." The larger man squatted, staring at Teodor. "Couple of nice shiners you got there. You wanna tell us what happened here?"

The man was familiar—the detective who had consulted extensively with Prescott. There was an investigation underway. Several vehicles with flashing overhead lights were stopped in the street; traffic was blocked with a few flimsy-looking A-frame barrier stands. A small crowd of onlookers had gathered and were lined along more barriers forming a cordon across the walkway in front of the patrol facility. The authorities had been drawn to the commotion and descended upon the area... by now they would have seen to the slain patrolmen and would be very interested in the testimony of someone directly involved.

It was not an ideal circumstance. Teodor tried to reposition himself against the wall and felt painful stiffness in his neck muscles.

The medical woman departed, heading for one of two large boxy vehicles in the nearby street, this one with its rear doors flung open. The slighter of the two detectives stepped forward in her place. "Sir. Detective asked you a question."

Teodor looked back at him. African negroid, much darker than anyone on Galina or Anastasia. It was to be expected, of course. The 37th century had seen well over a millennium more of human racial mixing. This man's color was purer. Teodor shook his head. "I'm sorry. It's all a big blur."

Neither of the two detectives were dressed particularly elegantly, with long, hastily lashed neckties and drab, formless overcoats, though the African's style seemed marginally smarter, particularly as the larger man bounced on his haunches, dragging the walk with the coat's lower edge. The

428

African detective gave Teodor a hard stare. "You were talking to Cassandra Prescott inside. You were with her out here, I assume—did you see what happened to her?"

Teodor sat up suddenly and felt renewed pain in his back. The refractor. It had been in his hand. If the woman had knocked it away...

He rubbed his right hip as if tending to an injury. The pistol was in the concealed holster in the pocket of his slacks, safely tucked away and at the ready, though under current circumstances he was seated at an unwieldy angle, and he was in no position to grab it while it was pinned beneath the coat. He had to have secured it at the last gasp before passing out; the woman's blows had apparently induced a hole in his memory.

His topcoat was buttoned—he had done it intentionally, to better hide what was underneath. He placed his left hand on his chest and unbuttoned the coat at the sternum. The sling was still in place as well; inside his right arm he felt the slight bulge of the pouch containing the other necessities, nestled against his ribs. All the critical equipment was intact. He had everything he needed.

He had been fortunate. For a time, he had been completely at the woman's mercy. She had obviously fled the scene in a rush to save herself... the wise move was to hide herself, as he had incontrovertibly proven that the authorities were unable to protect her, but if she had chosen to circle back to these patrolmen, he would have surely found himself relieved of the weapon and locked away upon his return to consciousness. As it was, these detectives remained in doubt. They were now a nuisance, nothing more.

As long as he had the refractor, there were no real obstacles the people of the day could erect for him.

"Sir, were you with the Prescott woman? Did you see what happened?"

Teodor exhaled a long, slow breath. His mind raced. The patrol detectives were naturally looking for Prescott as well, and they had a far better notion of how to find her than he. He could turn the situation to his advantage. He nodded, wincing as he moved his head. "Cassandra... yes. I was with her. We were attacked... is she all right? Where is she?"

The medical woman returned holding a small plastic box. She knelt by his head and set the box down, opening it and taking out a square blue bag. She tucked the bag behind his neck, guiding one of his hands to hold it. It was a cold compress—a pleasant coolness radiated over his skin, temporarily stemming the dull wave of pain. "You're probably going to be pretty groggy and sore for a while." She glanced over her shoulder. "No apparent fractures. Good chance he has a concussion. He banged his head pretty hard. Try to take it easy on him."

The larger detective looked down at the ground and scratched the top of his head. Abruptly, he put his hands on his coat-covered knees, propelling himself back to his feet. He began fiddling with his necktie, as if attempting to tighten it with one hand.

The African rubbed a finger across his mustache. "Can you tell us about the attack? What did you see?"

Teodor pressed his eyes closed, but it seemed to intensify the steady throbbing in his temples. "It was dark. There was a man, shabbily dressed... I thought he was a vagrant." He cleared his throat and was seized by a sudden cough. He shook his head gingerly. "He must have been hiding out by her vehicle. It was all very fast. I'm not entirely certain of what I saw."

The medic brought out a wet cloth and dabbed lightly at Teodor's mouth, frowning. Teodor winced, reeling at the odd sensation... his face felt numb and distorted. The cloth came away blood-soaked.

The woman squinted at him. "He's probably going to need stitches. He's okay for now, I think, but we should probably take a ride to the emergency room when we're done here."

The larger detective nodded. "Thanks, Bev. Give us a minute, all right?" His mouth moved, and for a moment it looked as if the man was chewing something.

"Sure. Let me know." The woman closed up the box, stood, and headed back toward the vehicle.

The African folded his arms, watching her go, then turned back to Teodor. "Try to break it down for us anyway. Step by step. What happened first?"

Teodor sniffed. "This man surprised Ms. Prescott as she tried to get into her vehicle. I was some 4 or 5 meters away. She set off her alarm, I believe." He shifted against the wall, adjusting the compress with his left hand and touching his face with his right. "I tried to run up from behind... I got my hands on him, but he is apparently versed in the martial arts. That's all I can recollect." He started suddenly as he felt his upper lip—grotesquely swollen on the left. An effect of Prescott's first blow. Facial features could be fixed easily enough, but if she had done damage, she deserved to be answered in kind, whether or not this particular trip ultimately yielded the stone. He would have plenty of time to find her afterwards.

He ran his fingers lightly along the line of his nose, also misshapen and completely numb. The woman would pay dearly if he crossed her path again.

The African glanced sideways at his partner, shaking his head. "What about the officer that was with her—where was he when all this was going down?"

Teodor paused. The iciness on the back of his neck began to become irritating. He leaned forward and lowered the compress. "He was somewhere between me and Ms. Prescott. Perhaps that's why the assailant didn't see me." He looked to the other detective and scowled, lowering his brow as he felt an ache welling in the area beneath his left cheekbone. They would be expecting disgust, revulsion. "There was a flash of light. I saw the officer fall. As I said, it was all very fast. None of it seems to make any sense."

The larger detective snorted. "I'll buy that."

Teodor studied the man. Understandably skeptical. They would continue to question him, possibly take him into custody if they didn't believe what he was telling them. Getting free by force was a simple enough matter with the refractor and the shield; each of these patrolmen likely had a sidearm, though these people had already demonstrated themselves to be slow on the trigger. But time was a critical factor now, and he could ill afford any more delays.

He blinked slowly. The larger detective was taking down notes with a stylus and pocket-sized pad that looked to be a book of paper for manual transcription. Nascent Computer Era life was proving to be intolerably slow-paced. The game was still afoot, but suffering these detectives helplessly as the seconds wasted away was maddening. He was going to have to accelerate the process very soon.

Teodor glanced at the African, now the nearer of the two. "Excuse me, detective, what is the time, please?"

The larger detective grunted and smirked. "You got somewhere you need to be?"

The African raised his eyebrows, straightening his specs with a finger, and glanced at his wrist. "I got 8:28."

Teodor felt his chest tighten. Almost 20:30, local time. Not much time at all. Realistically, these stumbling detectives were his last hope—they knew more about the city than he, and by now, they would know more about the woman. And now that they had reason to believe she was one step in front of a killer, intercepting her had become a matter of urgency, whether or not their investigation truly did center around the gemstone cited in Walker's will, as Prescott had suggested.

Teodor stared between the detectives at the people along the makeshift barrier. It was possible that Prescott had been telling the truth—that she had never had any interest in Walker's stone—but the situation had changed. If she was smart, she would now be looking for it as leverage for her own protection. Finding the woman was the best chance of finding the stone, more now than ever.

The large detective took a step closer, keeping his eyes on his notes. The little notepad made his fat, hairy mitts look even larger than they were. "All right. You got a name, sir?"

The notepad could have potentially been a valuable store of information. Teodor focused on him. "Teodor Monroe. Please, call me Teodor. I believe I gave you the name earlier. And what do I call you, so I can tell my associates who to thank for my extended visit here?"

The big patrolman scratched his thick, black, interwoven eyebrows and glanced at his partner. "I'm Detective Pestello, this is Detective Torrance. You can call us both 'detective.' How do you know Cassandra Prescott, Mr. Monroe?"

"We are colleagues. We work in the same building." He paused. "We only formally met today, but we've seen each other fairly often in public, during the course of the workday."

Pestello nodded. "Right. At the courthouse."

"Yes. I'd been meaning to ask her out to lunch for some time. I'm surprised you didn't ask her these things earlier, when you saw us talking inside." He narrowed his eyes, watching the detective's expression.

Pestello snorted, returning a cold, unflinching glare. "Who says I didn't?" He smiled smugly. The man was in his element, as far as he knew.

Teodor's eyes again fell to the notepad. He moved his hand over the area of his belt buckle and felt the familiar bulky surface of the shield control. It would still be active, the way he had left it before the woman had knocked him out, but the detectives were currently bordering on encroachment of the field perimeter; it wouldn't protect him if they decided to fire at him from where they were now standing. But they wouldn't. These functionaries were hopelessly bound to their pedantic procedures. He had the upper hand as long as he played along.

Safety was only a few paces away… it was a matter of getting to his feet. Stand up and step away, and the Ruby-12 would become accessible as soon as he swept open the overcoat.

He feigned a look of concern, frowning shallowly and ignoring the inevitable swirl of pain generated by the minutest of facial manipulations. "If Ms. Prescott is with this killer, she's in grave danger. Are you certain you're pursuing every lead?"

Torrance leaned against the wall, scratching his cheek. "We think the killer might have been going after a gemstone named in the victim's will. You know anything about that?"

Teodor stared up at the man, keeping his expression blank. So the stone was indeed part of the investigation. Prescott had told the truth—they had deduced the importance of it from among Walker's properties. On one hand, the fact that they were willing to mention it to him meant that they didn't have sufficient information to find it, but the fact that they were looking for it specifically could only help. And perhaps they were mentioning it not because they thought he could help them find it, but because they were watching for his reaction.

He pursed his lips. "I really don't know anything more than what Ms. Prescott told me, and she didn't tell me very much. I only know that her office was attacked, and that she was handling the matter by coming to you. I don't think she felt very comfortable about the situation. What sort of gemstone is this?"

Pestello's face broke out in a wry smile. "You got kind of a funny accent, Mr. Monroe. Where are you from?"

Only one regional English dialect of relative obscurity from the approximate time period sprang to mind. These people were most likely unable to discern the particulars of language nuances in any case. Teodor raised his eyebrows. "Cornwall."

Pestello glanced at his partner. "Cornwall? Where the fuck is Cornwall?"

Torrance shook his head and let out a laugh. "It's in England, genius."

"The southwest corner of England, to be more precise." Teodor paused. "I don't see how this is helping... I've told you everything." He frowned indignantly. "What exactly are you doing to find Ms. Prescott?"

Pestello lowered his brow, squaring his broad chest as if he were preparing for a fight. "You spoke to Detective Dulnicek earlier today, that right?" He frowned at the notepad. "She said you were here about the break-in at the office of Ms. Prescott's law firm. She said you answered a couple questions, then hung around asking about Cassandra Prescott until she showed up. You generally like to poke your nose into other people's business, or is it just this particular situation that's got you all hot and bothered?"

Hot and bothered. Indelicate clumsiness. The colloquialisms of the era were gratingly similar to the portmanteaus of Veran fringe pidgin. Teodor straightened, raising his knees as he slid his feet closer to his torso. He flexed his calf muscles, trying to fight off any residual atrophy. Standing up quickly would be difficult, but he would manage it if forced—the detective's line of questioning was rapidly becoming more aggressive. Teodor calmly locked eyes with him. "I'm sure there's been some sort of misunderstanding. I was in the building during the break-in, yes… it's the first thing I mentioned to Ms. Prescott when I saw her here at the station."

"That so?" Pestello turned to Torrance. "That's some coincidence, huh?" He looked down and ran his hand the length of his necktie. "Lot of people work in that building… I didn't see anyone else down here. How did you even know about the break-in? You don't work in that office."

"Well, we all heard about the fire evacuation, of course. And then the patrolmen came. I thought I'd stop by Ms. Prescott's floor to see if everything was all right."

"You just met her today, correct? You often checking in on other people's law firms, making sure everything's okay? What, was it your turn to be on Neighborhood Watch for the building?"

Teodor looked down and laughed. "I'm sorry, detective. I have worked with her firm on occasion, actually. But I must admit, today my primary reason for being there was to meet Ms. Prescott. As you saw, she's quite an attractive woman." He glanced at the other detective, lightly rubbing his eye with a finger. "When I see something I want, I like to go for it." Another ache played across his face, and he smiled, soaking in the pain.

Torrance and Pestello exchanged glances. Pestello nodded, tapping his notepad. "I'll bet you do. I'll bet you do." He rubbed his jaw, and flipped several pages back. "You said you work in her building… what was the name of your firm, Mr. Monroe?"

Teodor rolled his neck, picturing the business card in his breast pocket that he had taken off the owner of the fedora. It might as well have been in the right pocket of his slacks. His pulse was beginning to quicken. Things were about to progress much more rapidly. "We're just a small firm. Geitner and Boggs." He shook his head, leaning forward. "I assume you'll need my contact information—why don't I give you my card?" He nodded at Torrance, bracing one hand against the wall. "Do you mind helping me up, detective?"

Torrance advanced and offered his hand. Teodor gritted his teeth as the man pulled him to his feet. For a moment, his muscles burned and dizziness washed over him, but it ebbed as quickly as it had come, and his head began to clear.

The graceless light of the red and blue beacons flashed in Torrance's specs. "You good?"

"I'm good." Teodor smiled. "Thank you, sir. I'll be forever in your debt." He glanced at Pestello, smoothing the overcoat with both hands. "Now... I believe I've got that information right here." He turned toward the wall, brushed aside the topcoat, and moved his right hand to the pocket containing the fitted plastic holster.

"Yo, Pesto."

Teodor straightened, closing the coat and dropping his hand to his side. A man was approaching from behind the big detective. "Thought I'd check in." The man stepped around Pestello, flashing a quick, toothy smile.

Pestello nodded, stretching his back as he flipped the notepad closed, snapping the stylus under a rubber band along the binder. "Yeah, hey, I didn't know you were still here."

"Yeah, Lieu said you guys could use some help with the canvass. How you guys doing over here?" The man's eyes lingered on Teodor.

Teodor ran his tongue around the distorted contours of his lips. The man looked more like the typical Earth-dweller of the 37th century, with moderately dark skin tone and features that reflected centuries of racial mixing. He had a slighter build than the other two men, perhaps a bit taller with a shock of straight black hair and thin but strikingly pronounced eyebrows. Hints of a Latin background, possibly... Rafael Avila might have looked similar without his pigmentation deficiency.

Torrance nodded at the newcomer. "You hear from the ER?"

The other man rubbed his hands together. "Finley's awake. They're saying they think he's gonna make it."

Torrance shook his head. "Small miracles, brother." He reached forward and tapped fists with the other man.

The other man turned to Pestello. "What do you say, Mike? It's like a mute convention over there. Sarge has the all the unies on this here, so I'm all freed up—you got something for me to do?"

Pestello scratched his chin. "We're gonna work this lead a little more." He shrugged. "We're rolling down to Tinicum Boulevard to see what the county boys turned up. We could probably use some help down there, if you want to get a jump on it."

The man bowed his head. "Sounds good—I'm on it." He spun and jogged away.

Pestello raised his voice. "Thanks, Dee. Tell the Lieu."

Teodor stared after the man. Tinicum was John Walker's domain. The authorities were continuing their investigation at the murder site. He looked back to Pestello, focusing on the notepad in his oversized hand.

Torrance stepped away from the wall, glancing back at Teodor, then turned away. He lowered his voice a notch. "We should check back."

"Yeah, huh?" Pestello nodded. "You go, I got this."

Teodor narrowed his eyes as Torrance headed up the sidewalk. So there was a survivor. In minutes, the detectives would have a much clearer picture of what had occurred in front of their facility.

Pestello smiled and stepped forward. "Oh, we're not done here just yet." He looked at his notepad, flipping it back open. "Mr. Teodor Monroe from Cornwall. What say you and me head back inside for a bit? You look like you can walk."

Teodor cocked his head. "I really don't think that's necessary, detective—I've told you everything I know and I've been more than cooperative, not to mention patient."

Pestello frowned, scratching his nose. He held open his coat, deliberately putting his sidearm on display. "Humor me." He grunted. "Let's take a walk. You, ah... you do want to help us track down your friend, get her out of danger. Correct?"

Teodor paused, leveling his eyes at the big man. Pestello strongly suspected he was guilty, yet the detective wasn't showing the slightest sign of fear. Bravado or stupidity. Yes, the man was definitively in his comfort zone. Teodor smiled, tasting blood at the corner of his mouth. "Of course." He started along the sidewalk, then stopped abruptly before he was quite abreast of him. "Oh, you wanted my information, didn't you?"

Pestello shook his head, nodding absently toward the station building and gesturing with his left hand. "Let's go—we can do that inside."

Teodor swept back his topcoat, slipped the pistol out of its holster, and fired into the detective's chest. The plasma was set to stream with the laser axis in an unbroken beam like a long, blazing knife; Teodor increased the gain with his thumb and sliced upward just short of the neck. The man hung, frozen on his feet for a good second before dropping to his knees. Teodor picked the notepad out of his hand and backed away as the man flopped forward to the sidewalk.

Teodor turned his attention to the medical vehicle. The woman was just emerging through the open doors. He fired again, holding the gun low and running the beam diagonally upward and into her face, then spun, scanning the crowd to his rear and keeping to the shadows along the wall as he stepped evenly toward the perimeter. There were shouts of confusion among the scattered onlookers, but no one was reacting—no one had seen it. The uniformed patrolmen were turning to look only now, and their eyes were on the fallen detective. Teodor sidestepped through the space between the wall and the beam of the last A-frame barrier, keeping the pistol poised and ready to fire again, but for the moment the others were ignoring him, rushing past.

There had been no noise, and the flash of light from the laser shaft had apparently been perfectly masked by the vehicles' overhead beacons. The escape had gone flawlessly, but he would certainly be identified in seconds if he lingered. He crossed through the dispersing crowd, staying near the wall and walking briskly until he reached the corner, then turned right, heading into a small alley, and broke into a run, glancing over his shoulder. No one seemed to be following.

Adrenaline surged through his body as he moved into the dark cover of the tightly spaced buildings. The feeling of triumph was back for the first time since Walker's death. The stone would be in his hands eventually, even if the first trip back in time proved to be nothing more than a trial run. He had the luxury of trial and error and the will to continue until he knew the exact location—it was only a matter of time. And now he had a measure of help.

With luck, it would only be a matter of hours.

The image of Detective Pestello's broad face flashed in Teodor's mind. So easy. The detective had brandished his sidearm like a war trophy, but had predictably failed to anticipate the attack. He had never had a chance to place a hand on his woefully inadequate weapon. These people were helpless against him if they stood in his way... fortunately, it wasn't necessarily an indictment of their ability to perform a basic investigation—and now they would be largely motivated to do so.

The patrolmen would know what to look for at the scene. They were professional detectives; they were equipped to find leads, and they had the advantage of being familiar with this ancient metropolis. Now that they were looking for the stone themselves, they would inevitably uncover evidence that would point in its direction, and Walker had undoubtedly hidden it away somewhere relatively close by. The question was whether they would find it fast enough—they or the Prescott woman.

Teodor frowned, slowing as he approached the well-lit walkways of the cross street ahead. He had miscalculated the potential complexities of interpersonal dynamics. Granted, the people for the most part had been moved as easily as expected by the muscle of future technology, but Walker had not turned out to be the perfect antisocial ascetic that his abject lack of a historical footprint and presumed centuries of solitude had suggested, and the confidante he had chosen had proven to be an unpredictable nuisance.

Teodor shook his head. A particularly painful nuisance. He cautiously moved out of the alley, checking both directions. No sign of vehicles with flashing red and blue lights. He headed left, away from the patrol station, watching the intermittent traffic flow.

The Prescott woman had possibly led him completely astray, away from Walker's home. There was a chance she had spoken the truth, and she truly did know nothing, and if so, Walker's dalliance with her was potentially a fatal red herring. But Walker had met with her, and he had spoken to her. If Walker had hidden away the stone with her in mind, she might yet have been the key without even knowing it.

The four-wheeled vehicles seemed to be stopping momentarily at the intersection. Teodor walked to the end of the block, glanced back, then moved into the street, slipping between a pair of parked vehicles and turning to face the approaching headlights. Keeping a low profile would have been paramount under normal circumstances, but he had to act fast... gaining transportation to the scene of the murder legally would undoubtedly take too long. He raised his arms in the air. The nearest few vehicles blasted his ears with a chorus of base, tonal noises. The drivers were acknowledging him. He smiled, squinting into the blinding, overly bright lights.

A yellow vehicle skidded to a stop a few meters away, just next to the one he was blocking. He pounded on the hood once and moved around to the driver side door, keeping the refractor low against his side as he approached. The driver's window was open. A dark-skinned man wearing a turban peered at him expectantly. "Yes? Address?"

Teodor blinked. "8328 Tinicum Boulevard. Just along the southwestern city limits, I believe." He paused. "You can take me there?"

The driver nodded. "Yes, near airport, no problem. Get in back."

Teodor raised his eyebrows. Not a bad system at all. He nodded and opened the back door, sliding inside. There was a plastic wall separating the front seat from the back, and an electronic display to the driver's immediate right showing zeros. A metric of some sort. The vehicle was different from the others. Some sort of commercial transport.

This driver would expect payment at the end of the ride. Teodor nodded as the driver accelerated. "Make it fast. I'm in a hurry." He leaned forward. "I'll make it worth your while."

"No problem, sir."

Teodor laughed to himself and shifted in his seat, depositing the pistol back in its holster. Perhaps Ms. Prescott would be at the scene herself when he arrived. Pain would be the operative word, if he had another opportunity for a fresh conversation with the woman. She might have been a bit more forthcoming with the added ingredient of carefully applied force. Or not. Either way, hearing the Prescott woman scream would make a nice nightcap if he didn't manage to secure the stone this time around.

He dabbed at his face, leaning back against the broken, vinyl seat.

* * *

There was movement at the open doorway. A skinny blond-haired kid dressed as a paramedic exited Walker's building, ducking beneath the yellow warning tape and stepping out to the ambulance parked over the curb. The kid opened the passenger door, then closed it again and headed back into Walker's building, leaving the flashers on. The red lights made the broken-down block look like a war zone.

Cassie's eyes slid from the ambulance to the pinched, chubby face of the police officer standing in front of her. The man wore a different uniform than the officers of the 9th District—a slick, black commando sweater with large glossy pads at the shoulders and elbows instead of the flak jacket—though the insignia on his hat indicated he was a typical patrol officer. The man stood casually in the middle of the sidewalk, with one foot crossing the other and a hand on a hip as if he were leaning against something invisible.

She glanced back at Wyler, still on his cell phone covering his ear with his other hand. Presumably, he had finally gotten his friend on the line. She turned back to the officer, tossing her hair to her opposite shoulder. "Look, anything you can do would be a major help." She glanced at the yellow tape. They had sealed off the entire building—apparently any residents who weren't already holed up in their apartments were going to have to remain outside.

The officer looked back at her blankly. "I can let you wait here. That's about it. Strict orders—nobody goes in or out."

She exhaled. "Well, can you at least tell me whether or not you've removed the evidence?"

He looked at the ground. "Why would I tell you that, ma'am?"

She paused, nodding. The idea of getting stuck in a second police station for another hour of questioning was about as appealing as the thought of reentering Walker's home, but she was going to have to give the man something. "All right, look... my name is Cassandra Prescott, I'm the personal representative of the deceased, and I have a list of his personal belongings I need to account for."

The officer squinted and took a glance down the street. "Ah, ma'am, if you're connected to this case, you're going to need to talk to Detective Hammond back at the stationhouse." He smiled.

Her best option was probably to go home, climb into bed, and crawl under the covers. She shook her head. "I was the one who reported this— I've already spoken to the police about this at length. I'm familiar with the laws. As Mr. Walker's representative I get access to his home, and under the circumstances I need to verify that nothing's been stolen." She stared at his name plate and badge. "Officer Comisky, 4121. Right?"

Wyler stepped next to her and nodded at the officer. "Give us a second, all right?"

The officer shrugged and stepped away, unhooking a two-way radio from his belt and raising it to his ear. Probably reporting her name to the 12th District detective. Cassie watched him for a moment, then flashed a glare at Wyler. "What? I think he was getting ready to let me go in."

"Doubtful." He paused. "Just talked to Donatello. He's on his way. Says he left about 20 minutes ago. Should be here soon."

Cassie nodded. "Fine. Good." She stared at Wyler. He looked slightly shaken. "Did you ask him about the evidence?"

Wyler frowned. "Someone just shot up the 0-9. Killed one of the Homicide guys heading up the case."

"Are you kidding?" Cassie shook her head. "Detective Pestello?"

Wyler nodded. "Yeah. Him and a paramedic. I used to work with those guys." He cleared his throat. "He was interviewing a witness. I didn't ask about details, but it's pretty clear things are a little jammed up at the station right now."

Monroe. It had to be the same man. "That's awful." Cassie stared at the ground. "Listen, Wyler, I'm really sorry."

He scratched his neck. "Yeah, well… can't say you didn't paint an accurate picture of what this guy is capable of."

Cassie glanced at Wyler and said nothing. The image of Detective Pestello smirking at her played in her head. He might have still been alive if she had headed back inside the station instead of taking off in her car and waiting 30 minutes to report Monroe's description.

The blond paramedic was back outside the building again, coming around the front of the ambulance. He got in the driver side and closed himself in but didn't start the engine. If they hadn't already moved Walker's remains into the vehicle, they had to be doing it soon.

Wyler's eyes were also on the ambulance. "Donatello said the case is a total mess right now. Crime Scene had about half the evidence bagged up when the guys from down here showed up; they agreed to leave everything for the 1-2, but the M.E. was tied up, so they were going to let the 0-9 run with it. Crime Scene cleaned out all the evidence except the biological bags and moved it up to the 0-9, and then the uniform cops got hit, and apparently they asked the 1-2 to take over this side of the investigation."

"So what happens now?"

Wyler shifted his stance and exhaled loudly, putting his hands on his lower back. "Maybe we luck out, believe it or not. Donatello was in the middle of running the small stuff back down to the 1-2 guys when he checked the message. He might have what we're looking for. Said he had an envelope with something that looks like a safety deposit key." He raised his eyebrows. "Envelope has your name on it."

Cassie frowned and shook her head. "If he had a safety deposit box, chances are it's nowhere nearby. The only banks he had listed in his will were overseas." She looked in the direction of the ambulance. Officer Comisky was hovering near the front bumper, looking back in her direction. "It's probably a key for his post office box."

Wyler stared at her. "Post office box. You think he might have left some things at the post office?"

It sounded unrealistic. Cassie shrugged. "I don't know. But he definitely had a post office box. There were instructions in the will about closing his account at the post office and collecting any leftover mail. He made it pretty clear he wasn't comfortable accepting mail delivered to his home address."

"Possibility, I guess." Wyler grimaced as if he had just tossed down a stiff drink. "Not exactly a secure place to leave valuables for someone who's paranoid. He leaves it there, he's giving access to all the postal workers."

He was right. There was no way Walker would have trusted the post office to hold onto one of his belongings, let alone something he considered valuable; he hadn't trusted anyone, and he had specifically stated he didn't trust the mail. Cassie sighed.

She glanced at Wyler. He was staring at one of the windows on the second floor of Walker's building, looking pensive... at least someone's brain was still working. He had actually managed to make the world seem a little closer to sane, amazingly enough.

She cocked her head. Walker could have easily closed the post office account ahead of time—the fact that he had left it to her to deal with was a little out of character. The man had been a complete recluse, wanting as little connection to society as possible, and he had been particularly sensitive about his contact information. But instead of canceling a public record address box, he had gone to the trouble of adding all that extra detail to his will. Very weird.

Then again, it wasn't as if logic could generally be applied to the behavior of John Walker.

Wyler nodded at her. "Did he tell you which post office it was?"

Cassie studied him. "No, there was no specific information—I assume I would have had to look it up. Although he might have left the specifics in this envelope." She paused, gritting her teeth. "Do you really think the envelope could be a lead?"

He raised his eyebrows. "Let's hope." He turned and looked up the street in the direction of an approaching car. "That looks like Donatello. Come on." He glanced briefly at Officer Comisky, then headed up the street to meet the car, waving as he walked. Cassie followed him to the passenger side window.

Wyler leaned on the door and nodded. "Thanks, Dee."

Donatello leaned toward him. "You owe me for this, Zack. Big time." He waved his hand over a pile of junk on the passenger seat. "What do you need?"

"Just the key for right now." Wyler scanned the pile on the seat. "But let us know if you get any other leads out of this crap, okay? Call me on my cell."

Donatello picked out a cellophane bag containing an envelope and held it up. "We do have other guys working this, Zack... should I tell them all we're running everything by you going forward?"

Wyler took the bag. "They might not mind the help right now."

Donatello nodded, looking to the windshield. "I heard that. Nevertheless... Lieu will have my ass if he finds out I messed around with this shit."

Cassie stooped. "I really appreciate this—I wouldn't ask if my back wasn't completely against the wall."

Donatello shook his head and held up his hands. "No, no—I don't want any details. Now, none of that stuff's been reported. If anyone asks, you had your hands on it before all this craziness happened."

Cassie nodded. "Okay. Do you want it back?"

He shook his head again. "Never happened. Just keep me posted if you find anything. We want this guy real bad." He glanced around. "You guys should clear out of here ASAP... I'm gonna check in and have a look at the scene, since all I got are a bunch of scribbled notes, and none of the people from my district who set foot in there it are still alive."

Wyler frowned. "Yeah. Sorry about Pestello. And everyone else."

"Yeah, huh? Hell of a thing." Donatello was silent for a moment, then flashed a forced smile. "Being on the job's rough. Not much else to say."

Wyler nodded. "Take it easy, Dee."

"You too, guy." He shifted his head, peering at Cassie. "You be careful, now—I hope everything works out for you, Ms. Prescott."

Wyler handed Cassie the bag. She glanced at it and waved. "Thank you very much, detective."

He pointed at her. "Right. Next time, you call me Donatello. Now scram, you guys." He nodded at the windshield. "Yo, they got a guard out here or what?" He waved quickly and pulled the car forward, parking directly behind the ambulance.

Wyler touched Cassie on the arm. "In the car... let's go."

She stared at the envelope inside the bag for a moment, then crossed the street to the Dart and got in. Wyler was inside the car a second later. He nodded at the bag. "Anything in there besides a key?"

She took out the envelope and poked it open, then flipped it upside down. The key dropped into her lap. The key was on a ring with a tiny tag with just enough room for two capital letters. "MI."

Wyler started the car and thumped his fist on the dashboard as the engine labored. He glanced at her. "MI? That's all it says?"

"The key has a number... 47. I don't know what the MI means." Cassie shook the envelope and held it open in front of her. "Wait a second." There was an inconsistency in the paper—a narrow rectangle. Another slip of paper attached to the inside. She ran her finger inside and felt tape. She loosened it and pulled it out. It looked like a message in a fortune cookie, complete with an inscription in tiny print.

The engine rumbled to life. Wyler patted the dashboard and pulled into the street, pounding the brakes roughly as he got the car turned around in about five lurching stops and starts. "Goddamn power steering's shot. What does it say?"

"U.S.P.O. at 1000 Tinicum Island Road." Cassie shook her head. Walker was definitely consistent. It was a public place, but the man had gone to a lot of trouble to keep its location apart from the will; maybe he really had left something important there. "So... I guess we're going to the post office? If the boxes are in the lobby, you can usually get in there after hours."

Wyler shrugged. "You never know. We sure as hell don't have anything else to go on." He glanced at her. "He definitely meant it for you. I have a hunch this is about more than just a post office account."

Something seemed to glimmer for a split second in the sideview mirror. Cassie turned completely around and stared out the back window. "Did you just see something flash?"

Wyler checked the rearview mirror. "Beacon on the coroner's vehicle?"

She shook her head. "I don't know." Just a trick of the light probably. Or she was starting to see things. The flashers of the ambulance were about the only thing still discernible behind the car.

She turned back around. The road went on for two more blocks, then went left. Hopefully, Wyler knew where he was going. Tinicum Island Road would have to be in the area, probably not far. The car turned, severing the line of sight to the chaos around the Langford Hotel and the tiny room that still contained Walker's remains. Cassie glanced again at the sideview mirror. No more red light—just another line of dark, time-battered buildings sliding by. She looked again at the key. If it didn't pan out, they were nowhere. And Teodor Monroe was still at large.

The image of Walker's disfigured body flashed in her mind one more time. The man suddenly seemed meticulous and thoughtful... infinitely more complex than a schizophrenic kook. At the very least, he had apparently had every reason to feel paranoid.

The woman lingering next to the car was clearly Cassandra Prescott, returned to the scene. She stood next to a man in civilian clothing, conversing with someone inside a vehicle in the street. The woman had enlisted help, possibly more detectives. The two stepped back from the vehicle, and it pulled forward and parked directly behind a larger, more brightly colored vehicle flashing red lights—an official's emergency vehicle of some sort. The Prescott woman clearly looked at something in her hand before glancing around and moving to another car with the man.

The woman and her companion got in the car. Teodor stepped forward, staying out of the light of the street lamp ahead of him. The car remained where it was, but they were liable to leave at any moment... he would have to act fast. Clearly, the person inside the first car had delivered something to the woman, and now she and her companion were acting on this new information.

Teodor turned his attention to the first car. The man inside got out and crossed the flat stern of the flashing vehicle toward Walker's residence, then paused at the front steps, looking back. Teodor squinted, frowning. This man wasn't in uniform either, but he was dressed like the detectives at the patrol station—in fact, it wasn't completely clear at that distance in the low light, but this man might have been one of the men who had already confronted him. The man of mixed color. The man doubled back to the larger vehicle, stopped along the right side somewhere toward the front end, and opened a door. He leaned against the open door. He had to be talking to someone inside, possibly the driver.

So the larger vehicle was active, and there was already a man inside who could drive it. Ideal situation. Teodor glanced over his shoulder. The yellow commercial vehicle was long gone; keeping the driver there under duress would have been too risky with local authorities on the scene. Just as well—there was always another driver.

The car carrying the Prescott woman pulled away. Teodor moved out of the shadows and walked quickly toward the man at the side of the large vehicle, staying near the wall.

"Hold it, sir."

Teodor froze. He turned around slowly, sliding his hand in his slacks pocket and finding the pistol. Behind him was a patrolman with a fleshy face, though his build appeared to be trim. His hand was on his hip, presumably on his weapon, still in its holster. The man nodded at him, pointing the thumb of his other hand toward the street. "Let's take it across the street, all right? This area's off limits."

Teodor nodded and slipped out the pistol, firing through the folds of the overcoat, carving into the officer's torso with the refined, uninterrupted beam. He released the trigger button and reset the refractor to conventional output without looking as he moved around the emergency vehicle and to the passenger side door, keeping the weapon low.

Donatello Diaz glanced at the coroner's vehicle as he headed for the doorway. Jerry Sacks was behind the wheel, looking as if he was perfectly happy to stay there all night. Coroner probably hadn't even heard about the latest shit hitting the fan. The kid was just sitting there with his head back, keys hanging from the ignition, so apparently they hadn't even gotten the corpse out of the building yet. Maybe the guys down here were still waiting for word from the 0-9. The kid obviously didn't know what was going on.

Goddamn disaster.

He made his way to the yellow tape, glancing around. Where the hell was everybody? They didn't worry about keeping the scene clear in the 1-2?

Directly across the street from the ambulance, Zack's piece-of-shit car pulled away from the curb, turned around, and headed up the street with the bag of evidence. The deed was done.

Nobody knew what the hell they were supposed to be doing on this one. Donatello rolled his head around, stretching his neck, and stepped back to the ambulance, tapping the window with a knuckle and opening the door.

"Hey, Sacks."

Sacks nodded at him. "Hey." He was tight-lipped, tense. Kid was probably thinking of quitting public service. Hell, the kid looked as if he should have still been in high school.

"You still waiting on the body?"

Sacks nodded again. "It's pretty bad up there. Body parts all over the place. Crime Scene hasn't cleared moving anything yet. I'm surprised we got any evidence out of there at all."

"Yeah, huh?" Donatello shook his head and cleared his throat. "Can't wait to see it."

Sacks gripped the wheel. "Seems like they could have used me more downtown."

Donatello frowned. "Yeah, it's gonna be a long night. I'll probably see you over at the morgue…"

Something flashed at the fringe of his vision… there was movement down the sidewalk behind the ambulance. "What the hell was that?" He turned and squinted. A man was coming toward the vehicle, walking fast.

Donatello removed his gun from its strap. "Hold up, sir…"

Sacks's eyes were on the gun. "What's going on, Dee?"

A flash of red light exploded against the pavement to Donatello's immediate left. "Shit!"

"Drop your weapon." The man was close now, strolling closer.

Donatello tried to blink away the afterimage. Goddamn! He had just let a man walk clean up to the scene, and the man had a goddamn laser weapon trained on him. This was the perp—this had to be the perp. The shit was true—a goddamn laser weapon.

Sacks was petrified, his back against the opposite door.

Donatello wiped his chin against his shoulder. This was the perp, and this perp wasn't letting anybody walk away. Only way out was to put the man down.

"All right, all right. Easy, now… let's talk about this." He had a good fix on the man now. He swung his gun up and felt immediate, intense heat the length of his arm as the second blast exploded against his shoulder. He reeled back against the door of the ambulance as the gun fell out of his hand.

The man moved to within a couple of paces, circling outward so that he had a view inside the cab. The face was familiar—the witness who Pestello and Torrance had been grilling about an hour earlier. The man had looked wrong then, at a glance.

Donatello wheezed through his teeth. The pain in his shoulder was spreading, and his fingers didn't want to move. The door against his back was the only thing keeping him on his feet. To his right, Sacks wasn't making a sound—he was staying right where he was, even though anyone with any sense would have gotten the hell out of there, gone for assistance. Kid was probably petrified.

Donatello shifted his stance, bracing his good arm against the arm rest, trying to focus. Directly in front of him, a few feet away, was an overly thin, squared-off number eight, with two pinpoint holes. A gun from the future, aimed straight at his face.

The man holding the weapon smiled. "I need a ride." He looked at Donatello. "That car, driving away… you know where it's headed, don't you?"

Zack's car. Hell yeah, the man was after them. "Maybe. But it's none of your goddamn business."

The man shrugged. "It was worth a try."

Donatello pressed back against the door and cringed, suddenly. Trinity still had no idea what was going on at the 0-9. He hadn't called…

Shit, first damn day back from vacation. An image shot through his mind, Trinity in an outdoor shower under the hot Cuban sun, squealing as he tossed a cup of ice water over the curtain. Then everything went black.

Teodor watched the body of the dark, thin detective spill onto the curb. He glanced up the street. The red taillights of the Prescott woman's transportation were still visible but receding fast.

The young man in the driver seat was staring, shaking, holding up his hands. "Please… look, I'll do what you want, I'll give you a ride, just please don't kill me."

Teodor boarded, shutting the door, and resting the pistol on his arm, aiming at the driver's head. "If you stay close to that car, I might let you live. But I suggest you leave right now."

*   *   *

447

The Tinicum Island Post Office was little more than a tiny room in a tiny lobby in the middle of a strip mall along the side of the airport.

Zack glanced through the glass door to the drive leading into the strip. Nothing going on out there yet. Maybe he was wrong. Hopefully he was wrong.

Prescott crossed the lobby, holding up the key. "We have a problem."

They had more than one problem. He raised an eyebrow.

"The boxes are all three digits in this place. We need a two-digit box, for a two-digit key, and Walker sent us to a three-digit post office."

Zack sniffed and looked back out the door, focusing on the neon, multiple-sign marquis at the top of a short pole to the left of the entrance. The print on the post office door had a suite number.

He pushed the door open and glanced over his shoulder. "Come on, it's not here."

Prescott followed him out to the middle of the parking lot. "Where are you going? What are you looking for?"

He held up a hand. "Simmer down, counselor." He scanned the shops along the L bracketing the lot. It wasn't a big strip… there was a pet supply store, a couple of take-out places, a pharmacy, a Hallmark. His eyes stopped for a moment on a UPS store. He shook his head. Damn.

The counselor had her hands on her hips. "You going to tell me today?" She looked as if she was about to start stamping her feet.

Zack sighed. "Every shop in this strip has the same address. 1-0-0-0— the address Walker left. One Thousand Tinicum Island Road. That's where we are. I thought maybe he just sent us here for the mall; the key could have been for one of these other places here."

Prescott stared at him. "Right. One Thousand." She looked down at the key.

He exhaled, scratching the back of his head. "Nothing jumps out, though."

Prescott stepped next to him. "What about 1,001?" She showed him the key tag. "MI is 1,001 in Roman numerals. Walker was into antiquities. If it was here, he could have just left us the suite number, right?"

Zack raised his eyebrows. "Surprised I didn't think of that myself."

Prescott pointed across the street. "What do you think that place is?"

The airport was across the street, sprawling for miles under heavy floodlights that made it about the brightest spot in the city, but closer up, another smaller set of floodlights made a distinct complex visible. The neon sign was too far away to read from where they were standing, but it was pretty clear what the place was.

"It's a storage facility. Nice going, counselor—come on, let's go." Zack grabbed the counselor by the arm and started toward the car, then stopped suddenly.

An ambulance was parked in the shoulder of the road, just behind the entrance to the strip. The coroner's vehicle. The headlights went out as he looked. "Goddammit! Okay, we're walking—let's go."

The parking lot was unlit on the opposite side, along a line of trees. He broke into a jog, heading for the shadow, then angled toward the road, onto the grass and down an incline. He looked back as he reached the road. Prescott was just hitting the slope.

He cursed under his breath. "Come on!" He turned back to the road and started across, moving slower, glancing in the direction of the ambulance. No visible movement. The road was completely empty, so crossing wasn't going to cause a commotion. It was dark all the way across... maybe they wouldn't see.

"Hey..." Prescott was catching up, shaking her head. "What's going on, Wyler?"

He exhaled through his teeth. "We're being followed."

"What?"

The tail had been easy to pick out in the thin traffic. The only other headlights merging onto Route 291 from the backstreets around Tinicum Island had closed in fast from a pretty fair distance away, close enough to give a good outline of the lightbar over the top. The vehicle had fallen back, but never gone away. Anybody's guess who the hell it was. There wasn't a normal scenario where a coroner's vehicle should have been tailing them.

Zack hit the other side of the road and ran straight up a hill of mulch, dodging through a row of low bushes and angling toward the lights around the gate. Still no movement on the opposite shoulder. He looked again at Prescott. "In case you didn't notice, that ambulance across the street... I think they followed us from Tinicum Boulevard."

Prescott breathed, trying to keep pace. "When exactly were you planning on telling me that?"

"I was hoping I wouldn't have to."

Prescott stared at the ambulance. "Who is it—who's they?"

"We gotta hope they're still looking at the strip mall."

"Wyler." She coughed, slowing down. "Who's following us—who do you think it is?"

"Don't ask me." Not a whole hell of a lot of possibilities. Zack frowned without looking back. Who. Good goddamn question.

He reached the fence and hunched his back, staying low and making his way around the perimeter until he came to the entrance. Aluminum wire fence reinforced with stainless steel crossbeams, and a long, rolling front gate, closed and definitely locked. A security camera at the top. An attendant's booth was on the other side with the lights on. Night staff on duty... barbed wire around the top. Scaling the fence was out. In front of the door was a parking gate and a push-button number pad; the only way in was to punch the correct code.

Zack slipped around to the front of the pad. "Walker happen to write any favorite numbers in his will?"

Prescott shook her head. "1,001?"

Zack tapped in 1001 and frowned. "Looks like it's three digits. Wait a minute..." He tapped in another number and a green light on the console went on. The horizontal barrier swung upward and the wire gate in front of it clanked and slid open. He grinned and jogged through the gate.

Prescott caught up to him. "Okay... what did you do?"

"M-I. M is the thirteenth letter, I's the ninth. 1-3-9. Elementary."

Prescott looked at the ground and nodded. "You're not as dumb as you look."

"Thanks."

The storage facility looked like a miniature city neighborhood of nothing but single-car garages. Long rows of corrugated metal locker units with identical rolling doors were crammed together on either side of a wide ramp like bland, one-story blocks along an empty asphalt boulevard. Zack checked the numbers on the nearby doors... single digits. Apparently the units in the forties weren't near the entrance. He nodded at the counselor and started down the gentle slope of the ramp, then heard footsteps.

"Can I help you with something?"

The man hurrying up behind them looked like a pompous college professor in a cardigan, with glasses and a meticulously trimmed blond beard.

Zack flashed a smile. "We're good, thanks."

The attendant circled around the two of them, stopping in front of the line of locker doors. "Excuse me... I'm sorry, but we don't allow people to just walk in and help themselves after 8 p.m."

Zack frowned. "Is that right?"

The attendant seemed to be sizing them up. "It's for the security of our account holders. We get our share of break-ins in this neighborhood." His eyes lingered on Prescott. "You have something to remove?"

Prescott glanced at Zack. "Yes. One small item."

The man turned, looking back toward the gate and tapping his lips with a finger. "Where is your car?"

Great. Probably a moonlighting graduate student used to getting kicked around all day, using the time to take out his frustrations and pretend he wasn't a complete peon. Zack exhaled heavily through his nostrils. "We live nearby. Can we get on with this?"

The attendant stepped back and folded his arms. "I'll grant you access to a storage unit when and if I decide to do so."

Zack snorted. Perfect. The one place Walker had chosen to trust dealing with was guarded by a prissy control freak. He scratched his shoulder and looked back at the gate. They were going to run out of time dealing with this asshole.

Prescott stepped forward, glaring at Zack. "I'm sorry. Look, we're in a bind here—we're not trying to do anything illegal. I'm here representing John Walker... I understand he had an account here." She paused. "He died recently."

Zack looked at the ground and muffled a groan.

Prescott nodded. "Mr. Walker had a couple of items here, I believe. I'm in the middle of tracking things down, and I just need to confirm the information he gave me. Here..." She took a business card out of her handbag and handed it to him. "My name is Cassandra Prescott. And you are...?"

"Gregory Baldwin." The attendant frowned at the card. "I assume you have the key."

Prescott nodded, stepping back.

Baldwin sniffed, glancing at Zack. "I'm afraid I can't grant you access unless we have your name on file, Ms. Prescott. If you give me the key, I'll check our records."

Shit. Zack pointed a finger at him and growled. "Look..."

Prescott moved in front of him, holding up a hand. "Just a second, Wyler. I'm sorry, Mr. Baldwin, but I have specific instructions not to let this key out of my hands. And in all likelihood, you're not going to find my name in your records as I'm sure Mr. Walker was not under the impression you were in the habit of preventing people from retrieving their belongings." She pointed at the ground and cocked her head. "We have the code to get in and we have the key; now, I really don't see the problem here."

Baldwin pursed his lips, nodding. "Well, I'm having trouble

understanding why you need anything so urgently at this hour."

Prescott folded her arms. "That's not your concern, Mr. Baldwin. I've had a very long day dealing with Mr. Walker's affairs, and as I said, we're in a bind. If you feel more comfortable accompanying us, fine, but if you turn us away, the owner of this place will hear from my office in the morning."

The man looked from the counselor to Zack, then looked down, scratching his cheek. "All right. I'll let it slide. What's the locker number?"

Prescott sighed. "47."

"Follow me. It's right over here."

Zack caught Prescott's eye and grinned as soon as the man's back was turned. She ignored him. He laughed silently at the ground, glancing again at the gate. Still no one coming... maybe they had lost the tail.

Of course, if it did turn out to be the man with the laser, it would give them a chance to get him the gemstone and be done with it. Assuming the man didn't decide to leave their smoldering remains plastered all over the storage facility.

Unit 47 was around the far corner, about ten doors in. Baldwin stopped and turned, waving his hand at the padlock like a game show model presenting a prize. "Here we are."

Prescott stepped to the lock and held up the key, hesitating for a moment. Then she fitted it and turned. The lock popped open.

Zack exhaled and realized his pulse had picked up. Baldwin stepped in and grabbed a strap at the bottom of the door, sliding it open with a loud bang. The man reached in and flipped a switch, and a single bulb went on in the middle of the ceiling, lighting an area not much larger than a rest room with a single toilet. A group of small cardboard boxes was spread around toward the rear; other than the boxes and a splintering wooden skid leaning against the side wall near the door, the locker was empty.

Prescott went in and knelt by one of the boxes, pulling open the top and digging through a bunch of styrofoam peanuts. She dumped the contents on the ground. "Nothing." She dumped two more, then paused and brushed her hand through the white packing material. She frowned and stood, holding up a small wooden disk with a triangular fin. A sundial. "This can't be it, can it?" She tested its weight.

Baldwin removed his glasses and placed one of the ear hooks between his lips. "You're free to take it out of the facility, but you'll have to remove the boxes if you want to close the account." He waved at the concrete floor. "And please clean up any garbage."

Prescott shot the man a fiery look for a long moment, then dumped the rest of the boxes and turned to Zack with an identical expression. If Walker had sent them on a scavenger hunt for a goddamn sundial, they were screwed. Zack returned her stare, shaking his head. It couldn't be the sundial. He moved inside the locker glancing at the skid. Prescott stooped and dug again through the peanuts, shaking her head.

Baldwin suddenly paled. He put his glasses back on and held up his hands. "Now, look—help yourself to whatever's here, but if something is missing, I can't help you. The facility can't be held accountable for missing items." He frowned. "Now you'll really have to be going—I can't have you lingering on the premises, and I have to go back on duty."

Zack stepped to the skid and lifted it away from the wall. Baldwin turned on him immediately. "That pallet is the property of this facility, and I really can't have you messing around in here any longer… I'm going to have to remove it myself. Now, please, get away from there." He moved next to Zack and took hold of the top of the skid, then looked down. "Oh."

A rumpled paper bag was against the wall beneath the angle of the skid. Baldwin bent down and picked it up.

Zack exchanged glances with the counselor, then cleared his throat in Baldwin's direction. "I think that's ours, chief."

Baldwin was frowning, staring at it. "Looks like trash." He stooped to pick it up, standing back up slowly. He looked at Zack, then back at the bag. He cocked his head and smiled for a moment, then sobered. "That's very strange."

"What's strange?" Zack shook his head at Prescott. He looked back at the man and snorted. "Let's go… hand it over."

Baldwin pulled something out of the bag that looked like a lump of balled-up oily rags. He was smiling again, shaking his head. The bag dropped to the floor. He started unraveling the cloth.

"Hey, Night Shift, wake up." Zack stepped around the skid, lowering it to the ground. "Goddamn it…"

Everything in the storage locker went red. Zack winced and stumbled back, shielding his eyes with an arm. He blinked, trying to adjust. The light was coming from right in front of him—a cluster of distinct, refracted beams casting a weblike pattern of varying intensity over the corrugated metal walls, emanating from the object in the attendant's hands.

Baldwin's back was against the wall. He was clutching a rough-edged, translucent piece of softball-sized rock that was shining about as brightly as the rotating beacon at the top of the coroner's vehicle. He was bent over it, staring intently. The lenses of his glasses were glowing like a pair of huge, flaming eyes.

Prescott's voice came from somewhere to Zack's right. "Mr. Baldwin…"

Baldwin didn't respond. The rock glinted as he turned it in his hands, rotating the pattern on the walls like light reflected from a disco ball. He gasped abruptly. "It's like the units, like galvanized steel." He shook his head without looking up. "Galvanized steel. This is the facility. My cells, this facility."

Prescott spoke again. "Mr. Baldwin. Gregory… it's Mr. Walker's gemstone. It's what we've been looking for. I'm going to need you to give it to me."

Zack squinted. Prescott couldn't have been more than four or five feet from where he was standing, but her voice seemed distant. Everything in the tiny shed now seemed as wide open as a gymnasium.

The light shifted suddenly as Baldwin straightened. He paused for a moment, then whirled and dashed out of the locker.

Zack shook his head. "Shit!" He launched himself after the attendant.

Baldwin was already rounding onto the main passage back to the gate. The red light blinked away as he moved out of sight… Zack followed without slowing down, then yelled, jumping awkwardly out of the way as the long, low forks of a hydraulic jack slid in front of his ankles from behind the corner. He recovered his balance quickly and sprinted up the walkway, refocusing on Baldwin. The man was nearing the gate, a silhouette within a red halo gliding up the mild incline. Zack cursed and lowered his brow.

What was this thing? *What in fucking hell were they dealing with?*

It wasn't a garden variety gemstone—that was for goddamn sure. One touch had instantly transformed this officious mullet-head into a crazed junkie. Some kind of experimental laboratory shit. They were probably all going to die of radioactivity poisoning now.

The gate was shut again… the control to reopen it had to be on the way out somewhere along the driver side, but Baldwin just stopped in front of it, making no move to evade. He was bending over in the middle of the pavement… setting the gemstone down?

Short-lasting effect, maybe. Zack slowed, hanging his tongue out one side of his mouth as he caught his breath.

Another blinding blaze of light flashed out from somewhere ahead of Baldwin, bathing the view and overpowering the gemstone light for a split second. A vision-searing red—distinct from the soft, steady gemstone light, momentarily engulfing Baldwin's outline. It was gone as soon as it came.

Suddenly Baldwin was lower to the ground, on his knees. Then the man collapsed sideways, crumpling like a test-dummy.

Baldwin's form seemed to drift out of the way, fading into the darkness beyond the red halo lingering over the pavement. The gemstone sat at the center, unattended.

Zack moved forward, barely conscious of his feet against the ground. No way around it now. Take it back to the counselor, get it to the authorities. He had to pick it up now. No choice. He reached down…

The glow of the gem seemed to settle in the palm of his hand, draining through his skin and rushing over him like warm water. The redness moved around him and blotted out all other sight, clinging to him, pouring into him, coursing with his blood like a pulsating womb. He was alone within an isolated, protected sphere, separated from the rest of the universe by a shield of light. Outside was darkness. Nothingness. As empty as the beginning of time…

He focused his eyes, and the redness seemed to become clear, and it highlighted every detail at the entrance to the storage facility. He looked around.

He was on his knees, clutching the stone with one hand. Baldwin was below him, sprawled on his side with blank eyes staring back at Zack through broken glasses. The man's chest had been scored by a lightning blast, open but partially burned dry. The same sort of wound that had killed Walker and a bunch of others. Laser burns.

The scene seemed to crystallize, down to the most minute detail. A section of wiring and crossbeams were cut away at the center of the gate. Two men stood on the other side, in front of the hole. One was a man in uniform, cowering, looking down at the fallen storage facility attendant; the other was in an overcoat, standing casually with a hand on his hip. The man in the overcoat held the pistol Prescott had described. He was smiling beneath a perfectly straight mustache.

Teodor Monroe raised the pistol without aiming it directly. "Children really shouldn't play with matches." The accent had English-sounding open vowels but the overall intonation was more casual, more like the words of an American.

Footsteps sounded softly on the pavement behind Zack. Prescott was coming.

The footsteps stopped immediately. "It's him. Oh God…"

Monroe's eyes widened, straining into the red glow. "Well! Ms. Prescott. I don't believe we bid each other a proper goodbye when last we parted."

She hissed. "It's him! Wyler, give it to him!"

Zack kept his eyes on the gun. Such a lethal weapon, yet it seemed harmless, insignificant. He suddenly felt that nothing could touch him through his red shield. Nothing in the world.

Prescott was screaming from several paces away, standing clear of the red aura. "What are you doing? Give it to him! He'll kill you—give it to him!"

Monroe took a step closer, making sure to keep the other skulking man at the gate in his view. "Wise words, Ms. Prescott. You have nothing to lose, and nothing to gain. The stone is mine, and if I don't see some action soon, I'm just going to have to take it from this man's dead body." He aimed his gun. "Let's have it. I'm on a schedule."

"Wyler!"

Something in the counselor's voice caught Zack's attention. Pure fear—she seemed to think Monroe was actually going to kill him, almost to know it. Was it possible? Did Monroe have the power to penetrate this growing invincibility?

He concentrated on Monroe, and suddenly saw that he was going to shoot the weapon. Zack blinked. Was he reading the man's thoughts?

Instinctively he jumped to his feet, seizing Baldwin's body and holding it up as the laser leapt at him. The shot was blocked—his strength was crazy, his coordination flawless. But it wasn't really him. The heightened capabilities and this impossible foresight were only effects of this stone, this ridiculously powerful gemstone.

Monroe was going to shoot again. Zack whipped the dead man's head in front of his own. He felt the searing heat of the laser burn too closely—he wouldn't survive a direct hit. Monroe was going to go on killing until the gemstone was in his hands. Monroe was going to kill him if he continued to hold it. And then Monroe was going to kill the counselor.

The man by Monroe's side turned to go. Monroe looked away for a moment, pointed the gun in a different direction. That was the window—Zack dropped the body and hurled the stone over the gate and into the darkness.

The halo of red light arced lightly away like a flare in the distance. Monroe grabbed the other man by the collar and headed after it, forgetting the people in front of him.

Zack closed his eyes, and his head swam as if the gemstone was still affecting him. Dizzy as a drunk, but now the strength was gone. He turned, and the muscles in his legs reacted as if he were getting onto a row boat in rough water. He wobbled and fell backwards.

Prescott ran forward and looked down at him. "Wyler... are you all right?"

Zack raised himself up on his elbows. The world seemed to be stabilizing itself around him. The rush was gone just about as quickly as it had come. "I feel like I just donated all my organs."

"Can you stand?" Prescott moved to help him, and he waved her off, nodding. Her eyes were wide as he got to his feet. She pointed toward the gate. "How did you do that?"

He rubbed his face and stared at her. "These new friends of yours..." Pain started to spread around his back. He exhaled loudly. "You might want to take them off the family Christmas list."

She was shaking her head. "You were flipping his body around like it was a cardboard cutout." She glanced at the newest corpse and her lips contorted as if she was suddenly nauseous. She covered her mouth and looked away. Clearly, the similarities to cardboard ended there. "So... I guess we check back with the police now. Let them take it from here."

Zack stared at his hands. "It was like I knew exactly what to do." Suddenly he looked up at the ruined gate. "Wait a minute."

He sprinted outside and looked around. A security guard was slumped near the keypad with half of his neck missing. Zack's eyes darted down the road and fixed themselves on the large vehicle that was speeding into the distance with a faint red glow in the windows.

The counselor came out after him. "Wyler, he has what he wants now. And he let us go—he didn't have to do that. Look, I can't ask you to do anything else for me. We should check in with the police..." Her voice trailed off as she spotted the guard. She gagged briefly, then cleared her throat. "He doesn't need me for anything anymore, so maybe he'll leave me alone now."

"No one's safe now." Zack frowned without looking back at her. "That man is going to do whatever the hell he wants, and there's not a damn thing anyone can do about it."

"Wyler..."

He glared at her. "Maybe you think you could convince the U.S. military to order an air strike on the guy, because short of that, I think we're S.O.L."

She put her hands on her hips and tried to avoid glancing at the security guard's body. "What's your point?"

He turned and stepped in front of her. "That thing, whatever it was... that gemstone... totally tapped into me. I can't explain it in a way that would make anyone understand, but that thing has power, and I just handed it to that psycho."

Prescott cocked her head. "You did what you had to do. I don't understand this any more than you do—none of this makes any sense to me. I think we need to just let the police figure things out now. Call your friend." She paused and looked at the ground. "Look... you were great, all right? I'm happy we're still alive. I'm having a hard time believing it. Thank you for helping me."

He looked back at the road. Problem was, it actually was starting to make sense. The big picture was pretty much incomprehensible, but it was coming into focus now. Monroe had a laser gun and an accent out of nowhere. He had needed the other man because he didn't know how to drive. He had killed to get a gemstone that nobody else seemed to know about—an object that seemingly had Holy Grail-like powers, pure rejuvenation and enlightenment to the degree that it would have been impossible to believe for anyone who hadn't experienced it personally. Everything about the man and the gemstone seemed totally alien. And then there were the reports about experimental military crash landings and strange lights in the sky.

"So let's just call your friend, all right?"

Zack sighed through his teeth and headed for the road.

"Hey! Where are you going—Wyler, what the hell?" Prescott hurried after him.

He glanced over his shoulder. "Stay here and call whoever you want. I'm going after him." No traffic either way as he reached the front end of the storage park's driveway. He continued into the road without slowing down.

"Hey, I'm talking to you!" Prescott moved to his shoulder. "Are you nuts? What did that thing do to you? He will kill you. Look, it's over—let the police catch the bad guy."

Zack frowned. "The police don't understand what this bad guy is capable of." He fixed his eyes on the counselor. "You don't understand either." He picked up his pace, jogging up the hill below the strip mall.

She raised her eyebrows, staying close. "Oh, I don't, huh? I was there, remember?" She paused, waving down at the road. "He's gone, by the way. How did you think you were going to find him? We have no idea where he's going."

Better question: What the hell did he think he was going to do if he did manage to find the man? Zack grunted. "I have a hunch." He reached the parking lot at the top of the hill and rounded toward his car. Hopefully, Monroe hadn't tampered with it.

The counselor's instincts were probably right. Now that the man had what he wanted, he would probably leave her alone. He was a homicidal maniac, and there were people who were trained to deal with homicidal maniacs—not to mention the Philadelphia P.D. would be pretty damn motivated to catch a cop-killer.

But there was a thought screaming at the back of his mind like a vivid dream suddenly remembered: an impossibly large empire that shouldn't have existed... billions of people in misery, at the whim of a careless, ruthless, invincible madman... thousands of years of darkness. He couldn't shake the goddamn idea of it—if someone didn't stop Monroe now, the man was going to become untouchable. And this was the last chance.

Maybe the gemstone had done something to him. Considering his sudden general lack of any trace of common sense, he was probably down a couple of million brain cells since he had laid hands on the goddamn thing.

Prescott stopped as he reached for the car door. "All right, fine. Go after him. But I'm going with you. I got you into this—if it's anyone's responsibility, it's mine. Anyway, no one's going to believe what happened here if you're not around to corroborate the story." She moved around to the opposite side of the car and looked across at him defiantly.

He stared back at her. No chance of talking her out of it. And he wasn't about to try to physically keep her from getting in. He shrugged. "Fine." He reached for the butt of his gun and pulled it out as he opened the door and dropped into the driver seat.

She got in after him. "Fine." She slammed the door, shaking her head. "Do you even have a plan?"

He raised an eyebrow and handed her the gun. "Yeah. I'm betting he isn't immune to bullets. Not yet, anyway. Put that in the glove compartment for me?"

She frowned and took the gun. "Nice plan. Let's hope the car starts."

He smirked and twisted the ignition, pumping the gas with his foot. "Just try and keep your opinions to yourself, okay counselor?" The car engine rumbled and caught. He nodded.

Prescott put the gun away and sat back, grabbing the seat belt and snapping herself in. She narrowed her eyes. "Answer me one question. Do you really think you have a better chance against him than the Philadelphia Police Department?"

He cocked his head, glancing at the road as he brought the car down the hill. "I'm a little more familiar with the situation. I had my hands on the gemstone. I think that makes me more qualified. Besides, I'm about as good as it gets when it comes to handling a gun."

She nodded, folding her arms. "You might be the most stubborn, arrogant, egocentric person I've ever met. And that's saying a lot, because most of the people I hang with are stuck-up beyond belief."

He smiled. "Hey, you're the one who said I was great." He turned left, and stepped on the gas, slamming the car into third gear. "Hang on, I might have to break a couple laws here."

She rolled her eyes. "This is going to be a long trip, isn't it?" She paused. "Where are we going, anyway?"

"Valley Forge."

"Valley Forge?" She shook her head. "What's in Valley Forge?"

"If my guess is correct…" Zack sighed, sitting forward and looking up as the car accelerated beneath a green overhead sign. The Route 76 interchange was somewhere ahead, just past the Girard Point Bridge. "His ride is in Valley Forge."

Shadows stretched across the front seats, twisting clockwise in an endless feedback loop as the lampposts along the outer fringe of the airport flashed by the passenger side windows. Like a sundial on fast-forward.

Valley Forge. Military crash landings and UFOs. If he tried to explain it out loud, he was liable to break off the chase and head for the nearest downtown bar.

He snorted to himself. That probably would have been the smartest damn move he had made all night.

XIV   TERMINUS

"Thus Dessa was visited by its future... two ships carrying sentients with very different motives, similar only in the confusion they left in their wake. Infinite possibilities shrank to the last remaining variables, hanging in the balance of a few distinct choices.

"It is but a moment that may change countless lives, but the moment is there and then gone. There is no luxury of measured decision... only instinct, and the memory that lingers long after. But like the dwellers of the forest, those faced with such immediacy are ever compelled to action... when the trees burn, those who live there must take to the wind and get water, or else suffer the loss of their home.

"The stream might be far, but with wings there is always hope."

... "Philadelphia"; 28 September 1992 CE

Mary Beth Connolly stared at the flood lights where the road met the tree line. The natural barrier might as well have been a 30-foot barricade, effectively cutting off any view of the downed aircraft. Presumably it was back there somewhere, but apparently, all anyone was going to see was a painfully nondescript roadblock—assuming anyone was actually still watching when the story aired.

A little background glow would have helped. A few licks of flame in the woods, or some smoke in the distance. The people in this town went nuts for fire.

She turned and kicked a clump of dirt in the direction of the electronics set up in front of her. "This is bullshit."

Jim Picket peered out from behind his camera tripod. "There's that legendary Northeast charm... good stuff, M.C."

She nodded. "Kiss my ass, Jim."

Without warning, the spotlight went out. Mary Beth rolled her eyes. "For Christ sakes!"

"Sorry!" Ken Driscoll was fumbling with the wiring. The light went back on.

The college kid obviously had no idea what he was doing. Just another brilliant move by Dennis Rigby back at the studio, using an on-location shoot as a training exercise when they already had limited available crew.

Mary Beth tipped her head back and looked up at the microwave antenna tower fully extended above the roof of the news van. "Alan, I'm getting old standing here—can we get this moving?"

The tinny, filtered voice of the director filled her left ear. "Three minutes, Mary Beth... okay, no, we're cutting the iso-record, Greg, just fix those captions—it's a crash-site, not a rash-site..."

Jim stepped away from the camera and poked at the side, checking the cables. He glanced at Mary Beth and grinned. "You know, you really are getting old."

Jackass. She ignored him and looked back at the roadblock. Most of the MPs had left hours before, either falling back to the crash location or moving off to some other post around the perimeter. The two covered trucks were still there, along with a police cruiser, but only a few guards were visible, lingering in the road. One was leaning against the hood of one of the trucks, clearly smoking a cigarette. They weren't exactly expecting to fend off a renewed reporting frenzy.

At about 4 p.m., not long after the crash had happened, the park had been buzzing with reporters, microphones in people's faces, and police working to clear the area. The kind of chaos that only happened with huge stories... and it had pop, like a headline the network news teams would want—a cutting-edge stealth plane crash-landing in a nationally recognized historical park. But the military had immediately down-played everything and locked down the scene, and supposedly there had been no deaths, no major injuries, and very little damage or anything else that might have held people's attention. The story had gone stale fast... then the precinct shootings had taken place and sucked all the attention of the Delaware Valley to Center City. Everyone sitting on the Valley Forge crash story had suddenly been left on an island. And yet here they were seven hours later, going live on *News at 11* because that was the way the station manager wanted it. Even though the story had already run at 6, even though everyone had already heard about it and no one really cared, even though they had absolutely nothing to show on camera.

Dennis Rigby had his head up his ass.

The worst thing about it was the cold. The heat in the news van was no refuge with the four geniuses on the crew opening every door on the vehicle every two minutes. On top of that, today, for the first time, she was wearing the purple walking coat that had looked so chic in the window at Strawbridge's, and today, for the first time, she was learning that the lining of that purple walking coat was for shit.

She fingered the cordless microphone. It couldn't possibly take much longer. The broadcast was underway... the first two segments would be about the police shootings and a handful of other murders across town, but they would still be on in the first ten minutes. Valley Forge was nothing new now, but it was still a bigger story than flower store rip-offs and dogs running in traffic.

Alan Tanzer came around from the back of the news van, one hand pressed against the ear of his head-set, the other waving in the air. "Okay, people, get ready to go live."

Jim tucked his head back behind the camera and adjusted the lens. "Are we seriously going to shoot the trucks? It's like footage of a tailgate party... this is going to be like watching paint dry." He paused. "Actually, speaking of watching paint dry... M.C., how much pancake did you put on? You look like you've been bobbing for powdered doughnuts."

"Why don't you die?"

Alan trotted backwards several steps, glancing around. "Greg, we're good?" He nodded. "Okay, iris... character... Jim, Mary Beth, you're good on the preview. Get ready... and five... four..."

Mary Beth brushed her hair across her face as Alan's fingers counted down to one. The audio in her ear switched from the low-quality scratch to the smooth, thick program feed from the studio at City Line Avenue. Larry Kent was already going into his scripted lead-in. Greg Henderson had the levels up a notch too high, and the aging anchorman's legendary vocal bass sounded as if it were brushing on her eardrum.

"...our Mary Beth Connolly is on the scene at Valley Forge. Mary Beth?"

She nodded slowly, knitting her brow in a practiced look of empathetic consternation. "Yes, hello, Larry... this area of the park has been shut down since about 4 o'clock this afternoon... as you can see behind me, they have blocked off the main road and are not letting anyone through... they have also closed all roads leading into the park until further notice. The Air Force is here, along with some local police... they've been saying the same thing all day, that a large experimental aircraft they were testing crashed in a field very close to where we are... they are reiterating there were no casualties and very minimal damage to the park... apparently the craft came down in an open clearing, and the pilot sustained only minor injuries. Obviously, under the circumstances, they want the aircraft exposed to as few people as possible... they are citing national security considerations."

Beneath the spotlight, the text on the teleprompter scrolled upward, and Larry's voice rolled along, virtually word for word. "So they haven't given out any specific information about what might have happened?"

463

She cocked her head. "Not really, Larry—they're keeping things pretty close to the vest. Earlier today, we did get an official statement from Master Sergeant Richard Phillips of the Air Force's 913th Squadron, who said that they were running maneuvers with experimental aircraft from the Willow Grove Naval Air Base about 20 miles east of here." She half-turned and waved in a direction that may or may not have been toward Willow Grove. "It seems likely the aircraft originated from there, although the commander did not confirm that. Of course, it's no secret the military has invested a lot of money recently in stealth reconnaissance technology, so we might very well have some kind of newly designed stealth plane on the other side of those trees. But it looks like we won't know exactly what happened here for a while... we may never know."

"Well, I'm sure if anyone can get to the bottom of it, you can." Larry let out a forced laugh. He was improvising—the fossil had a tendency to be mesmerized by the sound of his own voice. The man was an icon, and he knew it.

She smiled and nodded. "We may find out more after things get cleaned up around here." She raised her eyebrows. Not a bad off-the-cuff transition... hopefully Larry would pick up on it.

"Any word on how long the park will be closed?"

Good. She glanced over her shoulder, nodding. "Well, according to the current plan, they will be clearing all nonmilitary personnel out of the park at midnight, so we're actually going to get kicked out not too long after we sign off here... then they're going to fly in and airlift the plane sometime in the middle of the night, and we're told all the aircraft will be gone by the morning. However, clean-up crews are scheduled all day tomorrow... the Air Force and some Navy personnel will be working with park rangers and picking through the area, inspecting the scene for hazards and anything that might have come off the plane. They will have the outer roads and some sections of the park open at some point tomorrow, but it's looking like this area will be closed down until Wednesday at least."

Larry responded almost immediately with his folksy close-out line. "More military planes... well, let's hope there are no more mishaps. Thank you... Mary Beth."

She nodded. "Thanks, Larry."

The stereophonic sounds of the studio were replaced by a rapid, incomprehensible conversation between Alan and the audio engineer. Bottom line, they were off air. Mary Beth glanced toward Alan as he held up a hand and nodded. "We're clear."

The light went off again. Mary Beth groaned. "Oh, Jesus Christ, you've got to be kidding me!"

Ken was shaking his head, holding out his hands. "But I didn't do anything."

Suddenly her earphone buzzed, and she heard Alan yell from where he was standing. He was looking up. Jim stepped back from the camera and pointed. "What the hell is that?"

Mary Beth spun and stared at the sky. A black shadow was growing rapidly against the city-lit cloud cover. A low-register hum suddenly surrounded the field—subtle, hard-to-pinpoint white noise, like the sound of a central air unit. The airlift? Why would the military go ahead with the airlift before they cleared the park?

Alan was running back to the van, yelling as if Greg could hear him. Jim was back on the camera, tracking back and forth. "Alan, I'm getting zigzags here." He glanced over his shoulder. "Alan!"

Lights were going on and off across the field. The two huge floodlights set up at the roadblock were out, leaving the covered trucks and MPs invisible against the silhouetted trees. Someone was trying to restart the engine of one of the other news trucks. People were shouting, running around aimlessly, pointing upward.

The shadow in the sky was roughly cigar-shaped, more like the bottom of a boat than an aircraft, growing slowly... it was gigantic, more than a couple of hundred feet. Some kind of blimp? The sound was a little like a blimp, but the outline was too long and narrow, with literally no curvature. For a moment it seemed to be dropping straight down, preparing to land right there, but then it began to slide toward the line of trees.

Mary Beth glanced down at her microphone and tapped the head. Nothing. She frowned at the news van and stepped toward Jim. "You still have power?"

He nodded, running a hand along the side of the camera, snatching glances at the sky. "I still have color too... it's not the CCDs. I think the surge might have fried it."

"Maybe not. Everything's down—I think it's the feed. Try unplugging it."

Jim wiggled the cables loose, flipped a switch, and looked back at the tiny side monitor. "Back in business." He grinned. "I wouldn't have figured you for an AV girl."

"You have tape?"

He nodded.

"We're going solo—come on." She looked back in the direction of the roadblock. Still dark. The thing in the sky was above the other field now, close above the treetops, but too dark to make out. If they stayed put they weren't going to see a thing. She looked back at Jim Picket. "Come on! You want in on this story or not?"

"Just a second!" He detached the camera from the tripod and slid into the shoulder stock, then began adjusting the lens.

She didn't wait. She took another look toward the roadblock and headed straight for the trees, about 50 feet to the left of the road.

Some of the other news crews were mobilizing now—Gary Fitzpatrick was leading an entourage from Channel 3 along the road on foot, directly toward the guards. Good—the more the better.

The massive thing in the sky might have belonged to the military. They might have had something as big as an airborne battleship that could hover like a helicopter without thumping the ground with the chop of the propellers. But the military wasn't about to buzz a field full of reporters with one of their latest prototypes.

So what the hell was up there?

Jim raised his voice behind her. "Wait up—this thing's heavy."

Mary Beth glanced over her shoulder and hissed. "Hurry up and keep your voice down!"

Ahead, light began to fan through the row of trunks, shifting steadily like a roving beacon. Headlights from the clearing on the other side... cars were active. The Air Force had its hands full. Keeping news people away from the scene was definitely no longer top priority.

She stepped into the brush and picked her way along the edge until she found an opening, then sidestepped through, ducking and bending branches out of the way. She crouched as she reached the other side.

The clearing was lit unevenly—at least four or five Jeeps carrying mounted spotlights were still in motion. The thing from the sky was hanging just above the grass maybe a hundred feet away, facing at an angle away from her and toward another identical craft. They looked like a pair of giant bullet trains on skids.

Ten glowing orange circles set in a three-row hexagonal pattern stood at the back of the one in the air, possibly the craft's means of propulsion, but there was no evidence an engine was even on—virtually no noise other than that subtle hum, and not a single light other than at the rims of those circles. The ship dropped softly to the ground.

This was not about stealth planes.

Jim made his way out of the bushes behind her. "Thanks for the face full of prickles. You know, there was a perfectly good trail about 20 feet away—holy shit! What is that—a couple of freaking spaceships?"

She shook her head, looking out at the field. That was exactly what they looked like. They weren't helicopters—what else flew without wings?

"Spaceships, M.C."

"I know, let's get it on tape, let's go." Mary Beth looked back at the pair of ships. There was movement near the fringes of light… the MPs were already in position around the perimeter. For now the camera angle was fine, but she was eventually going to have to get closer to get a good look.

Jim squatted, fitting his face into place against the viewer and adjusting the lens with the other hand. "How's your mic?"

She frowned, waving the microphone. "Still out. You're going to have to turn up the volume."

He shook his head, nudging the camera along his shoulder. "That's no good—all you'll hear is my heavy breathing. There's a time a place for that… no, look, you gotta get next to me. I can't get both ships with your head in the picture."

She nodded. Jim was an asshole most of the time, but he knew his job. She knelt next to him and looked back out over the field.

Jim cleared his throat. "All right, you're on."

She exhaled. "This is Mary Beth Connolly, we're here at Valley Forge, where an enormous craft has landed in the park… we don't know what it is, or where it came from, but it has just landed in the field that had been sealed off by the Air Force… we are looking at the field now, and as you can see there are two of these gigantic vehicles, they appear to be at least as large as jumbo jets… the Air Force security forces stationed here have surrounded the craft that has just landed, and they do appear to be armed." She paused. A flashlight went on much closer to the tree line, and it appeared to be pointed in her direction.

Jim lowered the camera. "Shit!"

Mary Beth glared at him. "Don't stop shooting—we'll be fine!"

Jim shook his head. "Sorry, Lois, I'm out. I didn't sign on to spend the night in a military prison." He shrugged, glancing quickly back at the approaching flashlight. "Besides, we don't want them confiscating the tape, right?"

She stared at him. "Oh, you are not going to do this to me."

He backed toward the trees. "You'd leave if you knew what was good for you—a cover up like this, these guys are liable to go ape-shit." He raised the camera, pushed his way through a bush, and disappeared.

"Damn it, Jim!" She threw the microphone after him and put her hands on her hips, looking back at the ground. Idiot. They had every right to report the news, and all a night in jail would do was make the story better.

Out on the field, the noise level suddenly picked up—engines were revving, and someone was barking commands through a loudspeaker. The words were distorted, impossible to make out. She turned and glanced around. The flashlight was gone. The guards were pressing closer to the newly landed ship, lining up along the skid on the near side...

She squinted and cupped a hand above her eyes. There was suddenly an opening toward the front end. A ramp was moving toward the ground.

Someone was coming out.

The emergency vehicle sped along the straightaway toward the dark, undulating rise of hilly grasslands, flashing its red overhead lights against the trees that dotted the immediate landscape. The road would soon take a circuitous left, following a creek around a patch of woods as it snaked its way up the steep incline before coming to an end at the final road leading into the park, but the ship lay ahead, just beyond the hillcrest.

04:13 Terra Zulu. Less than an hour before the pyropite was going to rupture. Teodor dabbed at the function buttons on the wristcom, flashing a directional display. The ship was under 3 kilometers away now, edging over toward 15 degrees. Somehow there was still enough time, but the roundabout road meant an extended approach on foot. He would have to scramble to get the equipment set up for the energy transfer. It was a matter of dropping the stone into Faro's makeshift concoction and activating the device—a matter of seconds. It would be close.

He flipped back to the remote link display and tapped in the ignition code. A yellow status bar appeared, quickly changing to green. No problem connecting to the ship. A second status bar followed suit, signifying the ignition sequence was under way. Teodor pursed his lips, resting his head against the high seat-back in the vehicle's cab.

Too many mistakes, too many unforeseen circumstances. At the very least, the first loop through time was a successful research trip. He had managed to identify the stone's location at the storage facility; it would be there the next time, if he did miss this deadline and was forced to travel time again. The next time there would be no need for interaction with Walker, no entanglements with this Prescott woman or the local patrols... there would be no further complications.

But the stone was already in his hands… he was so close to becoming the permanent custodian of this beautiful energy. To miss the deadline now would be excruciating.

Even now, the stone's energy was coursing through his nerve fibers, transforming him. Its power was as novel and incomparable as he had hoped and suspected—exactly as the cillian documents had described, but no amount of educated description could adequately prepare a man for the experience itself. The wear of 90 years, all the stress and the previously inescapable discomfort of age, all of it had gone in a new surge of vitality that had entered through his fingers upon first contact. It belonged to him— he had already transcended the bounds of his prior existence, tasted the sweet ambrosia, and he was permanently stronger, strengthened physically, mentally. Gripping the stone, feeling its warmth made everything about his previous existence pale in hindsight. He had been blind, as the song went. Only now could he see. Waiting another round of dimensionally distended years to be immersed in the full power of the pyropite would be difficult to be sure, but now he knew what he was getting. All and more.

And in the end, it would come to him. One way or another.

The RLU chimed twice. Teodor frowned and looked back at the display. Offline. The ship was no longer active. A second later the com failed and the link indicator went completely red.

Teodor shook his head closing his eyes, and thoughts seemed to clarify effortlessly, like a cleansing agent spreading across a dusty window, forming a picture in his mind as if he were getting it through a video feed. It wasn't just a malfunction the com… the entire ship was down in the space of a few seconds. No external incursion through the hull would have had that effect— not that the locals had any capability of breaching the hull with anything short of fission weapons. Power failure, or any sort of shutdown from within the ship, would have left emergency systems active and traceable, including the peripheral coms. An electromagnetic field pulse was the only thing that could have done it… the Archangel's specially fitted EMF pulse was designed to have that exact effect.

Massengill was already here, blocking his path. Massengill had managed to overthrow the Archangel's functioning, most likely through the connection his android had with the ship. So Massengill had retrieved the android. The man meant to stop him, to ground him permanently. It was no longer a question of securing the stone on time—it was a question of securing the ship.

Teodor narrowed his eyes. His mind raced. He was still at an advantage while he held the stone. The solution would come through a specific course of action based on logic, knowledge, and execution. There was no room for error, but he was no longer capable of error. Massengill would fail.

The driver slowed the vehicle. "This is the park up ahead, I think. I don't really know my way around."

Teodor leaned forward. A small pool of light broke the gloom ahead. They were approaching the park's south exit—a tiny, one-way single-lane road that intersected the larger road where the latter veered to the left. It was the ideal entrance point for the final run to the ship, but now there were spotlights set up, with a single vehicle stopped by the side of the road, its headlights on. A roadblock.

Teodor nodded. Local obstacles were to be expected—they were not the problem. But now he needed to save time. "Go straight ahead. Full speed—do not slow down."

The young driver murmured. "It's a do-not-enter." The boy was just as thoroughly rattled now as he had been at the outset, but outwardly his tone was more resigned than nervous now.

Teodor waved the refractor. "Do exactly as I say."

The driver accelerated. Teodor stared through the front window as they neared. An armed man stepped to the middle of the road, holding up a hand. Military personnel.

"He has a gun…"

"Do not slow down. Sound your hailer. He won't shoot."

The emergency vehicle jerked violently as it hit the rougher surface of the smaller road. The man outside stepped quickly back out of the way as they flew past, blasting the vehicle's excessively loud warning signal. He jogged after them for a moment, then returned to the parked vehicle. There was no further pursuit.

Teodor eyed the driver. "Now shut off the overhead lights and continue up the hill until the road turns."

The layout of the park was clear in his mind—finding an optimal touchdown for the Archangel and thoroughly familiarizing himself with the area had always been a key focal point—but it was now as if he could see everything spread out before him exactly as it was on all the maps, as if having the stone in hand added a dimension to his perceptions. A happy convenience. Without Massengill barring the way, the entire formidable task would have gone through with minimal effort, but as it was, mental and physical acuity was likely going to mean the difference between success and failure.

The smaller road led up the long hill between two rows of tightly packed trees. They were coming up on a sharp right. Teodor snapped. "Stop here."

The driver braked, and the vehicle skidded to a stop. Teodor threw open the door and glared at the boy. "If I were you, I'd continue on this road." He hopped out, pointing the pistol at him one last time. "If you send anyone after me, I will find you and kill you." He closed the door, darted around the front of the vehicle's cab, and struck out through the left bank of trees, shaking off the overcoat as he ran.

Teodor blinked, picking up his pace as he came through to the open field. Lines and textures in the dark resolved almost immediately, as discernible as if the panorama were splayed out before him under the light of day. The direction and distance of the Archangel was clear without the aid of the RLU... he was just about a kilometer away, with nothing between him and the ship but grass and another patch of scattered trees.

His mind raced. Concepts to which he had previously devoted the minimum consideration now crystallized... recollected diagnostic fundamentals, exhaustive, virtually extraneous particulars from flight instruction manuals flooded to the fore as if recently memorized. The Archangel, like most ships, was fitted with an independent core unit at the stern. All the critical life-support and flight specs were embedded and echo hard-coded, set to replicate upon system restart. Activating the ship was not a problem if he could get inside—the stern unit would automatically reconstruct the core registers and restore function to all on-board systems by channeling fuel from the reservoir—he only needed an active power source to fire the core. Transferring a fuel cell from the engine block required a functional portable converter, which, like every other device on board, would be dead until it was recharged. But he had a fully effective refractor pistol. Connect the stock battery directly and maximize the output, and the stern core could be fully charged in seconds, the rest of the ship and its auxiliary components completely functional within a few minutes—including the particle fusion-filter.

Perhaps he wasn't too late to tap the stone after all, if he managed to get inside without a hitch. The lock would be left intact, the gangway sealed, but he still had a fully functional RLU, which contained a key-surge failsafe in the event of the loss of power or on-board control. The override was a simple process involving the landing skid control panel, but waiting for the gangway to open would add delay. He would need to move quickly.

And there was a greater problem. If Massengill truly intended to stop him, he wouldn't be content with temporarily disabling the ship. Massengill would have it in his mind to finish the job.

Teodor ran faster, feeling the rush of blood in his muscles and chest. His body seemed already attuned to increased exertion—his respiration remained smooth and even, well-synchronized for the pace of an uphill sprint. Effortless and invigorating. He smiled and felt the cold air against his teeth.

As he ran, he felt a sudden pressure in the membranes of his ears, then felt it spread over his body as the vibrations formed an audible sound—the distinct, muted hum of gravitonic lift. There it was… Massengill's ship. The attack was clear—Massengill would move in close and rake the Archangel with his ship's turret, targeting weapons and main engine components. The ship was on the other side of the hill, cut off from view, but Teodor could almost see it low in the sky, sliding in from the north, and wheeling around as it dropped onto the field ahead. Massengill would be on the ground in seconds.

The last patch of trees were some 50 meters away now, just off the crest of the enormous hill. Soft light glowed through the trunks and open limbs and formed a ragged outline along the treetops—more spotlights in the distance, set up by the local military. The landing had obviously drawn their attention, to their misfortune. It could only help. Normally, a feeble local blockade would have done little more than provide a brief firework display for anyone who managed to survive. As it was now, the locals would be running interference.

He dove through a tight pass in the foliage and headed up the final stretch of the incline.

The ramp of the gigantic craft touched the ground. A single figure was descending.

Mary Beth whirled and stepped to the edge of the trees, yelling as loud as she could. "Jim—they're leaving us alone! Jim!" She looked back at the ship. They were going to miss the whole thing. Damn it…

The leaves behind her rustled, and Jim crunched his way back through the bushes. "Miss me?"

She tugged his arm. "Come on, we have to get closer—they don't care about us now."

"Wait—I think you dropped something." He handed her the microphone. "You never know when you're gonna need one of these."

She grabbed it from him. "Stay behind me, and start rolling, clown."

She stooped and headed across the field, keeping her eyes on the MPs around the ramp.

Headlights came from around the front of the ship—a single Jeep. A man was hanging out the passenger-side door, shouting into a loudspeaker. That would have to be Master Sergeant Richard Phillips, the commanding officer. Not much for a sound bite earlier, but he wasn't afraid to open his mouth now. The MPs peeled off as the Jeep pulled up to the bottom of the ramp.

The figure emerging from the ship was a man in a suit, blazing white in the crossfire of the Jeeps' spotlights—his skin looked as pale as his clothes. At first glance he seemed unusually tall, but it might have been another effect of the light. He lingered near the top of the ramp for a moment, holding his hands in the air as he looked around at the troops. His way of letting them know he was unarmed, probably, but it looked more like an awkward attempt at a greeting wave. Then he stepped back to the threshold, touched a control fixture on the ship, and began to speak... the sound carried as if he were wearing a hidden microphone.

Mary Beth checked over her shoulder. Jim was a couple of paces back, filming as he moved. She slowed as she neared the guards, moving laterally and staying a good 10 feet behind them. The 20-odd Air Force MPs were clad in dark flight uniforms, spread thin in a wide arc around the ramp. They were standing, not exactly dug in as if they expected a firefight... but they all had assault rifles ready. Their attention was fixed on the man on the ship.

Master Sergeant Phillips got out of his Jeep, set a metal case on the hood, opened the split lid, and took out a military field phone, thrusting it to the side of his head as he stepped around the grill and stood facing up the ramp as if he was using his wide body to block access to the ground. Then he lowered the receiver, appeared to listen briefly to the words of the man on the ship, and barked something back at him. The specifics were impossible to make out—the two were talking loud enough but interrupting each other, and there was a lot of background noise. Somewhere, a jacked-up dashboard radio was spitting out harsh, tinny military call signs interspersed with blasts of static.

Abruptly Phillips turned and made some sort of signal to the front line, then redeposited the phone inside the case and moved alongside the ramp, resuming the discussion with the man on the ship in a lower voice.

A stand-off between armed forces and some kind of defense contractor, maybe? Whatever it was, this was a rare opportunity for on-site action footage, the outcome was totally unpredictable, and she wasn't getting any of it. No chance the camera microphone was going to pick anything up from as far out as they were…

The hum was gone. The ship's engine had shut down, and she hadn't even noticed. She tapped the microphone head and winced as it let out a piercing whine.

She whirled at Jim. He started moving backwards, his face still behind the camera. One of the MPs turned. His gaze lingered for a moment, but he turned back to the conversation at the ramp.

Enough. Mary Beth glanced down at the microphone. Whether it stayed functional was a coin-flip, and for all she knew, the feed wasn't online anyway, but she wasn't going to get a sound bite unless she got a lot closer. Hopefully Jim would hang back and keep the tape rolling from a distance. The man on the ship had his back toward her, and the master sergeant was now on the opposite side—they weren't going to see her coming.

She slipped through the opening between the line of MPs, angling straight for the huge landing skid. There were shouts behind her. She swung herself over the skid without slowing down, setting her free hand on the cold metal and vaulting it like a pommel horse. Her feet hit the ground hard, and she lost balance, slipping momentarily on the grass, then recovered, steadied herself, and hurried toward the ramp, staying as much as possible in the shadow of the undercarriage.

The two men were still talking as she neared.

"That is not an option."

"Just listen."

"Sir, we can't have any of that—we need everyone off your ship."

"We're not posturing for an attack. He is. You have to understand…"

"Mr. Massengill…"

"Take heed—this man is devious and extremely dangerous…"

"All right, let's talk about it down here."

"You're obviously very thorough with your defenses—that's good. Just keep this man under close watch, and keep in mind he's already killed and injured others."

"Down here, sir."

"Really, that's not necessary. Now, I've given you fair warning, and that's really all you need to know."

"Like hell it is. Who put you up to this? Who are you?"

"I'm sorry. I told you…"

"Do you understand the situation you're in, Mr. Massengill?"

Mary Beth caught movement out of the corner of her eye. Three MPs were closing in behind her. She ducked to the other side of the ramp and held up the microphone, turning toward the man on the ship.

"Mary Beth Connolly, Channel 10 Eyewitness News—sir, we are trying to make sense of what's happening here… can I get your name?"

The man took a step back, frowning. He glanced around, cocking his head. "Dexter. Dexter Massengill." He shook his head. Master Sergeant Phillips swore silently.

A hand grabbed Mary Beth roughly by the shoulder, but she wrestled her arm free, circling out for a clear view up the ramp. "Can you tell us who you are and explain what's going on? Are you the pilot of this ship?"

The MPs had her hemmed in. A short man who couldn't have been much older than 20 held up his hands. "Ma'am, you can't be here."

She ignored him, raising her voice and glancing at Phillips. "Who do you work for, sir? Where is this ship from? We deserve an explanation."

Dexter Massengill sighed, glancing back toward the ship. "I suppose you'll most likely hear it from the senator anyway." He sounded vaguely European, though there was a noticeably odd cadence to his words. He scratched his shoulder and moved down the ramp, turning toward Mary Beth.

Two MPs moved in and got a firm grip on both her arms. The young-looking airman took the microphone out of her hand. She wriggled, twisting toward the commanding officer. "Master Sergeant Phillips… please, he's answering! We all want to know." She looked back toward the ramp, straining against the MPs' arm locks. "Say that again—what senator? Do you work for the Department of Defense?" She groaned. "Master Sergeant Phillips?"

The master sergeant signaled the MPs with two fingers. "Hold on, airmen." He put his hands on his hips and stepped toward the high end of the ramp. "Sir, if you got something new to tell us, you better spit it out right now."

Massengill nodded and stepped forward. "All right. We're from the 37th century. Your future. Senator Monroe is as well—that's the man aboard the other ship. We followed him here to make sure he couldn't do any major damage to the people of your time. We intend to disable his ship, render it harmless, and return to our own time, where we belong." He paused. "I hope that's a satisfactory explanation; I really couldn't go into any more detail, as I'm a novice when it comes to time-travel, and I'm really not versed in all the technical specifics."

Time-travel. Mary Beth frowned. Apparently this man felt comfortable enough to jerk around an entire squad of Air Force military police. Probably a defense contractor mouthpiece, or some other government flunky. Maybe the man wasn't even authorized to pilot the thing.

A woman appeared at the hatch and stepped quickly down the ramp, stopping next to Dexter Massengill. She moved fluidly, like a cat. She looked significantly shorter than him, wearing a similar jumpsuit.

The woman placed a hand on his back. "I think they've heard enough. We need to move." Her accent was more subtle, but similar to his—nondescript European.

Master Sergeant Phillips cleared his throat loudly, nodding at the woman. "Now, look, I don't know what kind of game you've got going here, but we need to get everyone on that ship disembarked and debriefed, and we'll do it by force if we have to. Is there anyone else aboard?"

The woman sidled past Massengill almost protectively, half-blocking him with her right shoulder. She looked down at Phillips. "You're right to consider us a threat. We have weapons capabilities superior to yours, and the other ship has had its defense systems upgraded. If that man regains control of his ship, you won't be able to take him down."

Mary Beth stared at the woman. She and Massengill both looked monochromatic in the odd play of lighting over the circle of grass—pale skin tone blended with the fabric of the clothing. But the woman seemed flushed in a bluer glow, and at second glance her skin actually looked cornflower blue, distinct from the grayer shade of her outfit.

A cameraman snaked his way through the crowd surrounding the ship, moving in from the left. So Jim Picket hadn't turned tail just yet. Any footage was good footage at this point, but the story wasn't going to be half as good if they didn't manage to glean an actual fact or two about what was happening.

The woman glanced around at the crowd. "You want proof?" She moved in front of Massengill and gestured to her left, and there was a sudden burst of light, followed by a small explosion toward the front of the other ship. The MPs on Mary Beth's arms tensed simultaneously. A hushed murmur swept across the crowd, followed by the scattered snap of magazine cartridges.

The woman raised her voice. "We just hit his main turret, part of his weapons system. It will take about 15 seconds to neutralize the rest of the weapons components along with all flight and navigation capabilities." She took a step down the ramp, pointing at the other ship. "Our weapons fire lasers and charged plasma using built-in precision-targeting algorithms. You do not want a fully operational weapon-ready ship like that falling into the wrong hands; the man aboard that ship could take out this camp site in a matter of minutes."

For a suspended moment, the scene seemed frozen in time, under a spell of virtual silence. The MP platoon was either waiting for a cue or staring in disbelief while the master sergeant ran a hand through his hair, suddenly facing away from the ramp and toward the other ship. The blast had been instantaneous, and it might have come from anywhere. It might have been nothing more than a very intense camera flash—no way to tell whether it had come from a gun on the ship—but the effect was unmistakable. The front end of the other ship was now half-obscured behind dark, thin tendrils of smoke, rising at an angle from somewhere at the bottom. Direct hit, and right on cue, as if a production team had been coordinating everything from a studio inside the ship.

Mary Beth blinked. Maybe that was exactly what it was—a well-organized production. Lasers and charged plasma. It was ridiculous—out of a comic book. Was she supposed to believe these people were actually from the future? What were they trying to pull? The woman's skin was blue for Christ sakes—why would a person go to the trouble of dying her entire body cornflower blue?

Two red lines of light sliced in from the left, followed by a third. There was an explosion against the hull, and one of the two figures tumbled off the ramp—Massengill, the man. The woman was suddenly on her knees with a weapon of her own, shooting orange-red flashes back in the other direction.

Gunshots ripped out from behind. Someone screamed. People were yelling. Sounds were coming from every direction as the searing blasts of light flashed back and forth around the hatch, but the blasts themselves seemed to make no noise as they impacted against the metal hull. *Lasers and charged plasma.*

Mary Beth backed up slowly, shaking her head. The MPs holding her arms were gone. The Air Force had no idea what was going on. They were supposed to be there to secure the situation, but they had completely lost control. Nothing was happening the way it was supposed to happen.

This wasn't an elaborate prank. These people weren't pranksters… they didn't work for a defense contractor, they didn't work for the government, and they weren't military. Everything about the way they looked and talked was wrong.

Jim Picket scrambled in front of Mary Beth, his eyes wild. "Jesus, M.C., get down!"

She fell forward, and then her face was in the grass. She rolled her head sideways and caught a glimpse of Jim's camera lying free. The news van might as well have been a million miles away.

It would all be over soon. The noise would stop, and the people would leave, and they could all go home and forget any of this impossible night had ever happened. She would just feed her cat and go to bed.

Somewhere off to the right an explosion briefly drowned out all the other noise. An exploding gas tank in one of the Jeeps or trucks. Maybe a stash of ammunition.

It would all be over soon.

"Our weapons fire lasers and charged plasma using built-in precision-targeting algorithms. You do not want a fully operational weapon-ready ship like that falling into the wrong hands; the man aboard that ship could take out this camp site in a matter of minutes."

Jayjay looked around at the crowd. The people were nonresponsive, some gaping at the smoldering gun turret beneath the cab of the Archangel, some just staring blankly back at her. They were rattled, and they didn't know how to react. Good.

She touched Dexter on the back. "Was that a good enough warning?"

Dexter looked brightly back at her. "I'd say so."

"Come on, let's go."

She started to turn, and a red plasma bolt leapt out of the shadows to the right, beyond the ship's stern, smacking her dead-center in the chest. She lunged forward as a second blast missed her above the left shoulder. A third shot sliced ahead of her, barely missing Dexter and scoring the Explorer's hull forward of the hatch as he fell backwards off the ramp.

Ruby-12 red spectrum light... Monroe was not on the ship.

Jayjay dropped to her knees, firing into the distance behind the ship, and called over her shoulder. "Dexter—are you all right?"

The short, staccato bursts of high-performance, rapid-fire industrial machines rippled across the field—the sound of 20th-century automatic rifles. With luck they weren't still aimed at the Explorer.

Dexter yelled back from the grass. "Jayjay, that has to be Monroe!"

"I realize that." Jayjay scanned the field. The heat signature of the laser was distinct. She fired again.

"I thought you said he was on the ship—he's not on the ship, Jayjay."

She shook her head, continuing to return fire. The life-support readings had clearly identified someone on board—a human male, with labored breathing right for someone knocked unconscious by an EMF pulse. "Either he figured out a way to fake life-support readings in a ship with no functioning on-board, or he picked up a house guest."

"That's a smash." The pitch of Dexter's voice rose as he gasped, gulping breaths in between words. "You're telling me we're going after one of the more successful scheming politicians in the Galaxy and we didn't anticipate he would find any allies?"

Monroe was approaching, moving around to the right. Jayjay frowned. "Stay down, Dexter."

"Jayjay, we have to take out the drive. We have to do it right now."

Jayjay sighed. Triggering the blast to the Archangel's turret from outside the ship was one thing, but she wasn't going to be able to accurately readjust for the ramscoop's incision points without moving the ship and getting floating decision point feedback from the on-board, and blindly firing the turret now that chaos had broken out was going to get someone killed.

Toward the stern, Monroe stopped firing... and stopped moving. Jayjay sent three more blasts in his direction, then paused, frowning. He had tossed away the refractor. Switched to a different weapon...

An automatic rifle opened fire not far from the gangway, flashing ignited gas and filling the air with its ear-pounding noise. Bullets clattered off the Explorer's hull, and Jayjay took several sharp hits to the left leg. She reeled, then regained her balance, but another series of hits sent the pistol flying from her hand.

She spun and dove flat against the ramp as a line of flying metal passed just above her back, popping the casing and circuitry of the locking pad at the threshold of the open hatch and streaming inside the ship.

Dexter Massengill's android was addressing the crowd... for the moment, all the attention in the field was focused on her diminutive mechanical frame.

Teodor breathed evenly as he descended the steep, grass-covered bluff, angling toward the tail of the Explorer. The spectacle spread before him was as plain as if he were poring over a stylized schematic.

He saw everything. The arena was a vast, broadening triangle of flat land, bordered by clustered hills and broken stretches of dense woods, and the arrangement of vehicles and individuals within was as quantifiable as a handful of chess pieces on a board. The Archangel and the boxy hulk of the Explorer stood at an angle nose to nose, bracketing the curl of forest at the field's far right extreme. An elongated ground vehicle was stationed near the Archangel, with six smaller vehicles and makeshift portable spotlight stands scattered in relative disarray in the space between the scinti crafts and the forest. 27 people surrounded the Explorer's extended gangway, where light poured through the open hatch and a man stood above the others with his feminized machine. Massengill and his android had chosen to dally with the locals.

Their mistake. Teodor smiled. It would all play out organically and in fast progression, with very little orchestrated effort—the confusion of the collective public was as palpable as the scent of dinner. These people were poised to erupt in helpless chaos, and he was in position to direct it… it would be like running a knife through butter.

He reached the bottom of the slope and quickened his pace, checking the shield control on his belt. He gripped the clean cut of the refractor pistol's stock and kept his eyes locked on the gangway, some 50 meters away.

Without warning, the Explorer blasted the Archangel beneath the bow as he looked on—they were going for the forward weapons array. The Archangel's turret was finished. It had begun—the methodical IU was using her link to the Explorer's weapons systems to nonchalantly disable his ship even as she instructed the locals. She hadn't so much as looked in her target's direction as she had issued the command. Teodor seethed at a sudden impulse of rage, but surprise and bilious revulsion were immediately drowned out by the machinations of higher brain function as instinct took hold of his muscles and he broke into a sprint. The android would go for the drive next, but the drive would not be so easily disposed of… the ship would remain viable until they repositioned to open a rupture in the exhaust. He had perhaps a minute to react.

The android and Massengill were likely armed. Teodor lowered his brow, feeling cold air in his nostrils. A firefight at this distance was not ideal—the first laser blast would give away his position, and the synthetic female was sure to be programmed with superior targeting skills, even if Massengill wasn't a good long-range marksman himself. But there was no more time. The moment was now.

Teodor leveled the pistol and fired three successive blasts at the two figures on the gangway. The first shot hit the android in the chest, but she dodged the second. Massengill went over the side—another hit? The man couldn't possibly have reacted in time…

The IU was already firing back. Two quick blasts scorched the air just beneath Teodor's right arm as he fired back, followed by a second salvo.

Teodor angled closer to the Explorer, changing direction just enough to evade the android's fire, keeping the hatch in sight. He could almost see each shot's trajectory before it menaced, see whether it would strike and where he needed to dodge. The mock female wasn't missing by much. Her skills were automatic; even enhanced by the power of the stone, his margin of error was no smaller than hers. He wasn't going to bring her down with a plasma bolt. He could do damage, but she was too sturdily designed to be immobilized by a hand weapon—her critical functions were protected by a thick carapace and redundant circuitry. Conversely, it was already apparent that the stone would not likewise protect him if the android found her mark. He was not invincible yet.

The threat of the blazing, lethal heat was real—the IU was successively singeing his torso, laying in circular pattern fire around his refractor, trying to take out the weapon itself.

The heat. Teodor swore under his breath, scanning the spread of individuals in the field. His refractor was giving him away. He instinctively dove out of the way as a group of bullets raced by not far from his head. Bullets were flying over the grass, virtually all off-target... the patrolmen were all likely to be armed. The nearest patrolman in the field was some 15 meters away. Teodor snatched his hand out of the way as another blast from the android narrowly missed.

Teodor rolled, pinpointed the patrolman, and cut him down with the refractor. Without looking, he felt the gain switch at the base of the laser's pump line, deactivated it, and holstered the gun as he sprang back to his feet and raced in the man's direction. The android fired several more times, remaining fixed on the origin of the last plasma strike.

The 20th-century weapon lay by the man's feet. Teodor scooped it up, tested its weight... it was essentially like a modern-day two-handed gun, as inferior as it was. Same shape, same trigger location. Teodor nodded, moving his hands into comfortable position, and sent out a flurry of bullets without looking. The weapon was heavier than a refractor, and the smooth, discernible report it seemed to have with each discharge was more satisfying, in a way. This weapon dictated a muscle reaction, took hold of the gunman's body. He smiled and advanced, firing another burst, directing it this time at the field of locals to the right of the Explorer. Then the IU's laser blasts resumed, roving back in his direction. This time she did not come nearly as close. Teodor sent an extended series of bullets back at her, concentrating on the refractor in her hand, and as he watched, the synthetic woman jerked sideways on the gangway. The pistol fell away—she was disarmed. She staggered, hesitating momentarily, then went down against the ramp.

There was movement below the ramp, where Massengill had fallen. Teodor sent a final spray of bullets into the area, then sprinted past the gangway, heading for the Archangel. The men in the field were scattered now, firing sporadically and ineffectively. Teodor looked to the left as he neared the front of the Explorer, focusing on the turret beneath the cab. He slowed. As a group, the bullets weren't as destructive as a solid laser blast, but they could still do damage. He cut toward the turret, directing his fire toward the narrow pivot extension connecting the turret cannon to the undercarriage. The mechanical rattle of hard metal battered the weapon for a full ten seconds with no effect, and then abruptly the sound was replaced by a hollow stream of empty clicks. The weapon was spent.

Teodor dropped the two-handed weapon, reactivated his refractor, and resumed firing at the turret, stepping closer as the red beam scored the undercarriage. Seconds later there was a quick succession of brief, smoldering flashes and a burst of sparks.

Teodor snorted. No way to know whether the damage was sufficient to permanently disable the ship's main weapon, but there was no time to inspect it. He spun and ran toward his own ship, glancing in both directions as he crossed the short stretch of grass. The patrols were scattering, ignoring him.

He rounded past the front of the starboard landing skid to the forward cross-trunk and stopped in front of the manual operator panel, dropping the refractor at his feet and opening the tiny cap at the top of his wristcom, extending the wire and snapping the tiny carbon-foam button into its place on the panel. The alphanumeric display above the keypad lit for a moment, then dimmed, then lit again. The wristcom display blinked in tandem with the panel on the ship. An alarm bell sounded above the ship's hatch, remaining on in a piercing, unbroken tone. A single clank resounded inside the hull, and the gangway released while the bell continued to tone. Teodor disconnected the wristcom and picked up the pistol, darting back around the landing skid as the gangway neared the ground.

Teodor breathed, nodding. Behind him, the Explorer's turret remained silent. The android had now had ample time to aim for the other critical parts of the ship, yet the ship was still intact and viable. The Explorer had been effectively neutralized. Now he was in the clear.

He checked the wristcom. 04:35 now. Still more than enough time to harness the stone's power. This was going to be a memorable day...

He was struck as he turned, thrown to the grass and enveloped in an ionized chain-reaction of blue-green as the protective shell responded around him. He gasped and ran his hand over his ribs… six points of impact, evidenced by a line of mild paresthesia along his right side. Bullets from the two-handed weapon, absorbed successfully by Faro's shield, yet the force alone was enough to knock him off his feet.

The refractor was still in his hand. He rolled and spotted the assailant, raised the pistol, and buried the man in laser-assisted plasma with a squeeze of the trigger, then climbed back to his feet and glanced around, dusting off his clothing. It seemed these people didn't yet quite appreciate who he was, or what was happening to them.

He smiled and cocked his head, raising his voice. "And now I am become death, destroyer of worlds."

He turned slowly, firing indiscriminately into the darkness.

The bullets stopped, as suddenly as they had started.

Jayjay rose on her elbows and knees and dabbed at her chest with a hand, checking the scope of the blast wound. Some of the superfluous outer sensory connections had been severed, along with the cosmetic damage. Nothing critical to core functioning, and nothing that couldn't be repaired with the help of the on-board.

She climbed to her feet, crouching low and glancing down at the bullet hole in her leg. The tiny bits of metal hit with the force of a micrometeoroid. She shook herself, turned, and moved up the gangway, looking over the side for Dexter. He was lying in the grass along the inside line of the landing skid, motionless for a long moment. Then he rolled onto his side, glancing back in her direction and signaling her with a quick wave of his hand. She nodded down at him. "I'll get you some cover. Just stay down."

"Go stop the ship, Jayjay. Before he gets inside."

Jayjay ducked through the hatch and stepped quickly up the ladderwell, rounding toward the cockpit. Monroe might have been able to get his ship back online, given enough time—the man seemed to have a lot of tricks up his sleeve. They just had to make sure they didn't give him enough time.

She sent a remote ignition bypass command, activated the gravitonics, and fired the lifters as she slipped into the CTA seat, refocusing on the weapons systems, then frowned as she called up the forward turret. Irregular readings. Nonfunctional.

She closed her eyes, glancing toward the starboard window. The rotor actuator was down, and there was damage to both output couplers and one of the flashlamps. Monroe had already hit the turret cannons.

There wasn't time to fix the rotor. There was no way to aim the cannon, and she was going to have to replace at least one of the flashlamps with a spare pump cell before they could fire on the ship at all. If Monroe figured out how to start his ship back up in the next few minutes, he was going to be able to make a run for it, unless someone managed to shoot him down before he made his way aboard.

Bullets were flying outside again. By all rights, any man walking into crossfire like that should have been hit several times over, but Monroe was obviously protected by something along the lines of an IPA-grade portable particle shield. The man had access to everything—he had probably reverse-engineered operational definitions to protect him from specific antique automatic weapons.

Dexter was nowhere to be seen, but he hadn't boarded. Hopefully, he had enough sense to find cover.

Jayjay stared through the glareshield at the Archangel, and as she looked, the ship's gangway cracked open and began lowering toward the ground. Monroe came around the landing skid to the ramp as it hit the grass. He seemed to pause for a moment... then he went down, falling hard to his left. Jayjay sat up. Monroe was visible at the edge of one of the portable spotlights, clearly flattened by automatic weapons—he had hit the ground like a hammer—but he was still moving. Another man was closing in, but Monroe fired back with the refractor. Seconds later, Monroe was back on his feet, torching the surrounding field with laserfire.

Jayjay shook her head, glancing at the monitor and running an inventory of the exterior supply stocks. Monroe still needed to boot up his on-board from scratch before he was safe. He wasn't out of reach just yet.

She left the seat, heading for the engine compartment.

"And now I am become death, destroyer of worlds."

Robert Oppenheimer's legendary translation of the Hindu *Bhagavad Gita* scripture seemed to fit the moment. Krishna's missive to Prince Aruja—the man was but an instrument in his lord's presence, all his enemies already as good as annihilated by divine will.

Teodor sniffed the air. Plasma boiled along the broad-band laser conduit at maximum gain, licking the surrounding grass and searing optical lacerations in the night. The people of the 20th century who remained were still clearing the area, running away, but to no avail. Three more of them fell before he stopped, holding up the pistol and nodding to himself. Now they would remember him in the proper light.

Many were down and motionless, but something focused his attention back in the direction of the Explorer, and he immediately saw the threat. Massengill stood out somehow among the prone bodies, lying in the grass in the shadow of the ship's bow, refractor pistol in hand, bracing to fire. Without thinking Teodor snapped off a shot in the space of a second, landing a blast directly on the hand that held the weapon. Massengill's refractor erupted in a flash of pressurized gas and fell harmlessly to the ground as the man tumbled away.

Teodor's eyes widened. The accuracy and swiftness in the reaction was near impossible, let alone his sudden ability to single out at a glance the only weapon that was a threat across a dark, cluttered field. This was clearly more than enhanced nocturnal vision.

Massengill's last stab had gone awry. Teodor nodded at him. "Pleasure to finally meet you, Mr. Massengill." He lowered his brow, studying the shape of the Massengill's silhouette against the ground, fixing his sights on the man's head.

There was movement to the left—a four-wheel vehicle came through an opening in the bushes at the edge of the woods, running dark, with no lights on. A civilian sedan, smaller than the military ground transports scattered over the area. It was accelerating toward the Archangel, specifically toward him... moving very fast.

Teodor swung around to face the car and fired a steady beam into the grill. Flames burst through the metal carapace over what had to be the crude engine as Teodor sliced upward into the front window. The car veered sharply into the front end of the Archangel's right landing skid and crumpled against the ship's titanium alloy like a paper model, twisting sideways and rolling onto its topside. The belly of the car went up in a small explosion, but Teodor stepped toward it, fixing his eyes on the man lying on his back halfway out the side window. The man who had led him to the stone... this man had touched it himself, known its power.

The man was still alive and armed with a handgun. The man raised his arm, and two shots caught Teodor squarely in the chest, but this time he had sensed it, leaning into the impact, and staying on his feet as the bullets hit the stasis shield, staggering back as he absorbed the blows. He sniffed, shaking his head. The stone had drawn more than one suitor, but in the end, it belonged to one man alone. He leveled the refractor at the man's exposed chest and fired, then turned and dashed up the Archangel's gangway.

He moved quickly through the aft portal to the environmental cabin, picking the vague shapes of toggle switches and pushbuttons out of the gloom as his mind raced to recall the diagnostic layout of the backup terminal. The interior of the ship had to be black as pitch without power, but the trace amounts of light through the portholes and quartz glareshield were apparently enough for him.

The detachable bus was located directly beneath the panel of auxiliary ports, several of which were occupied by the particle fusion-filter components, already set up and ready to use. He grabbed the cord and attached it to an open port, connecting the other end to the stock of the refractor pistol and dialing the weapon to elicit the maximum charge. Diodes around the power center of the core unit began to blink immediately, quickly spreading across the aft terminal control panels. The overhead lighting went on next, still dim under the minimum auxiliary power package. The ATA's reduced-size rectangle of display glass flashed in bright green, then opened a command window with a rapidly scrolling list of codes with a corresponding English translation for each system test, too quick for any human to read. The ventilation system hummed as the climate control kicked in. Seconds later, beneath the floor, the main converter went on and the cabin lights brightened.

Teodor raised his voice. "Confirm your response to oral command."

A tinny, unformatted voice responded. "Oral command response is operational."

Teodor nodded. "Are secured-access protocols in place?"

"Yes."

"Deactivate all com systems and limit all input to oral command until further notice."

The on-board paused. "Com systems are inactive as a result of a code inconsistency introduced through PNOCR-MP2 during the previous ignition sequence."

"Good. Seamless transition." He paused. "Prepare for lift-off, on my orders." Teodor glanced momentarily at the whizzing information in the command window, then turned to the indicator diodes above the ports connected to the fusion-filter. All active. They were operational. The time on the wristcom read 4:50. The stone was his in minutes.

He stepped to the worktable where the containment drum end of the filter was secured, studied the controls along the rim for a moment, then tapped the pair of buttons that activated it and opened the spiral seal at the top. Just a very simplistic container on the inside... the only thing distinguishing it from a typical cooking pot was a fine, centimeter-high grillwork around the bottom edge and a maze of hairline grooves over the base.

He looked down and unzipped the pouch across his chest, removing the pyropite and gingerly cupping it in his hands. Now there was no noticeable difference in sensation with the direct contact against his skin. The stone's power had already entered his system... perhaps he was now acclimated to it. He placed it in the center of the drum and resealed the top, turning his attention to the long needle at the end of the booster gun, fastened in its nesting place to the left of the drum and pointing up at the overhead. According to Faro, the needle would need to be in his eye at the moment the stone erupted, some seven minutes hence. To be safe, he would be wise to insert it at least a few minutes ahead of time... two to three full minutes of waiting with a needle sunk in his eye. So be it.

He opened the strap securing the gun and removed the blue stopper at the end of the needle, testing the gun's weight. It felt light in his hands. He frowned and took another look at the time, then glanced forward toward the cockpit.

It was impossible to see what was now at play outside, in stark contrast to this sudden enhanced insight the stone had given him while things were within his field of vision, and suddenly not knowing was excruciating. The Archangel was safely closed up and for the moment immune to programming encroachments, but the android might yet have had enough time to repair the Explorer's turret, and there wasn't time to relocate. If the stone was delivering him a measure of heightened telepathy, perhaps he should have been reassured that there was no apparent signal of imminent danger. Not quite satisfying enough, not when he was this close.

His eyes fell on the suspension chambers along the port side of the cabin where the hull met the floor. The seven-year-old clone was in the aftmost cell, its display lights now active. If Faro's genetic concoction had worked properly, the new version of Avila would already be fully grown. The system shut-down would have cut off all stimulants to the brain stem, brought the incubation process to a halt, and effectively left the man comatose, unable to regain consciousness without assisted resuscitation by the on-board and autodocs... an interruption in life-support now could have potentially been devastating. Time would tell whether the man had lost brain function, but according to the indicators, he still lived. If there was damage, it was nothing that couldn't be repaired in time. And time they did have.

Teodor checked his wristcom again, feeling his pulse quicken. He exhaled and moved the end of the needle in front of his eye, firming his jaw.

He concentrated, straining to keep his eyes open as he moved the needle closer, looked up, and inhaled slowly through his nose as the point broke through the sclera and plunged into the fluid beneath. His eye began watering immediately, but somehow the irritation was negligible. There was no trembling, no unsteadiness. There was no pain. He was in complete control of every muscle of his body. He felt as if he could have held the position for hours, if necessary.

Faro had suggested he close his eye, insert the needle through the lid. Eyes shut… hardly an appropriate way to transcend into the next state of existence.

The wristcom chimed three times. The moment was here, but there was no discernible sensation. Faro had narrowed it down to a matter of seconds, or so he had guaranteed, unless there had been a mistranslation in the related cillian records, some sort of error…

Time seemed to slow to a complete stop. When it happened, there was no mistake, no question. The stone's matter disintegrated, and for that instant the fusion-filter's flimsy metal casing held a pure, precious energy that hadn't been liberated since the dawn of the universe. In the next instant, the energized photons streamed into Teodor, setting his nervous system ablaze, firing every ganglion, scorching his extremities. The searing energy stabbed at his eyes and heart like invisible daggers, sweeping over his skin in waves. For an instant, it was clear the crude mortal fabric of his body wouldn't contain it. John Ulysses Walker's fate was now irrevocably usurped.

Then his eyes went from blindness to intense focus, and he was staring through the starboard hull of his ship, beyond the intricately woven matter of the fuselage and into infinity. Several thousand synchronous beings sprang out of the dark void, dispersed across the universe, all-knowing, all-powerful, acting as the organs of life and maintaining the integrity of everything that would ever be.

He remembered the ytaoans and knew at once that they had an indestructible connection with the power he had tapped into. And he knew that just beyond his comprehension was a wealth of knowledge so vast that it could confound him, overwhelm him forever. He could almost taste it.

He shook himself, gasping for air as if thrust into a low-density atmosphere, and the booster gun fell to the floor. The needle disintegrated against the tiles. Another thought swam to the forefront of his mind, and his muscles snapped into action as if guided by forces outside his body.

He darted to the cockpit, moving as if in a protracted dream, plunging through the beaded curtain and sliding into the pilot seat, pressing his hands firmly on the control shelf, barely conscious of the pulsing red flow of warning lights streaking around the curve of the panoramic display glass in front of him. Outside the glareshield, flashes of laserfire lit the darkness like lightning, revealing wisps of rising smoke to starboard. The Explorer was attacking again, somehow. But the fire was still concentrated on the bow. The rotational actuator was gone—they couldn't adjust the turret's aim.

Teodor unhooked the helm from its nesting place and cleared his throat. "Lift-off, right now. Evasive package, manual heading."

Another pair of plasma bolts exploded below the right glareshield, shaking the ship. Teodor glanced toward the bow of the Explorer, unsettlingly close. Repeated fire from point-blank range would do serious damage to the lower hull if he let it continue, but Massengill and his IU had no way of hitting the vital drive components if they couldn't change the angle of the Explorer's turret. Though they would have a shot if they gave chase.

The ship should have already been airborne. "Is there a problem?"

"The rear thruster malfunction is being corrected, Master Monroe." The broken scratch coming through the cockpit speakers was almost inaudible.

Rear thruster malfunction? "No, unacceptable—describe the issue, full detail, right now."

The cabin lights dimmed for a moment, then brightened up again. Teodor frowned and leaned forward. For a moment, he felt a crease appear in his brow. He could almost see his expression changing, as if observing himself from some new, detached location. The android couldn't have found another way through the ship's security systems that quickly...

Then the ground began to drop away. Teodor eased the helm forward, swinging away from the field in a rising arc. He exhaled, sitting back and stretching against the seat, feeling every muscle exploding with new life.

Teodor snorted, glancing up at the central speaker. "That's more like it. Remind me to issue a reconfiguration of all coms before we lay in a flight pattern. And track the other ship. If it approaches, we use the pulse to shut it down midflight."

Once the Archangel hit hyperspace, it was over... they would never find him without a way to track his ship. Massengill and his android might yet continue the pursuit, try to shoot him down from behind. If they did, they would regret it.

Monroe had seen the Dodge Dart coming well before Wyler got close. Cassie stood slowly as he turned his laser on the car, staring as flames engulfed the hood. The car banked right and crashed into the landing gear of the massive ship, bouncing away like a cheap toy without making a dent, then flipping over and skidding to a stop, rotating completely around so that the driver side was on the left.

Cassie gasped, stepping out of the bushes. From her vantage point, Wyler was visible lying halfway out the window. Was he moving? She shook her head. Of all the ill-conceived, harebrained, stupid, stupid ideas. This was total madness—how in God's name had she let him go ahead with this?

Flames erupted along the car's exposed underside. Cassie covered her mouth with a hand and yelped despite herself. "Wyler! Oh shit…"

Monroe was approaching the driver side. Wyler raised an arm and fired at him twice—Monroe seemed to react as if he'd been hit but stayed on his feet. Then Monroe stepped forward and blasted Wyler with a red blob of light that exploded against his chest. Monroe turned and headed up the ramp of his ship.

Cassie ran toward the car without thinking. *Stay in the bushes no matter what happens…* bullshit. That promise was moot now—and she was an idiot for going along with it as long as she did. This was her problem, not Zack Wyler's, and there was no sane reason to leave it to people better equipped to handle it. Jesus Christ, why couldn't he just let it go? As if he were the only person alive who was capable of stopping the man—as if he were at all capable of stopping the man! The stupid, macho, delusional ex-cop…

She glanced around as she crossed the grass between the trees and the long landing skid. The field was suddenly quiet. The moment she had arrived on the scene she had been ready to believe anything—two giant spaceships, surrounded by mayhem, people running in different directions, flashing lasers, bodies strewn around like Civil War casualties. It was incomprehensible. How in hell had Wyler known about the spaceships? In that moment, it had suddenly seemed that he knew exactly what he was doing, and she had seen the chaos and gone along with letting him use his scrap-metal-on-wheels to attack a man with a laser gun.

It was by no means safe to go near a burning car, but the hell with that. She jogged around a tire and a loose chunk of the car's front chassis, then slowed and stopped dead as she saw Wyler's body. He lay on his back under the flickering light of the flames. A black, charred circle covered the right half of his chest, just below his neck. His head was turned slightly to the right, and a line of blood ran from his mouth. His eyes were open and still, reflecting the orange light. He looked as if he had been mauled by a bear.

Cassie blinked. "Oh God. Wyler?" A sick feeling began to well up in the pit of her stomach. She knelt by his head and touched his chest, withdrawing her hand quickly. His plaid blue and white shirt was starting to darken around the wound.

The flames over the car abruptly increased in intensity, then died back down. Cassie glanced up absently, then looked back at Wyler. Jesus, was he dead? She bit her lip, opening and closing her fists. She had seen her share of bodies this day, but this was infinitely worse. She was complicit—Wyler was only involved because she had involved him. She knew him—suddenly it seemed she had known him her entire life. She shook her head. No, this was not going to happen...

She nudged him again. "Wyler! Get up, you asshole!"

Wyler's eyes suddenly rolled toward her.

"Wyler!" She stood up and turned around in a circle. "He's alive! You're alive. Oh God, I have to get you away from here." She crouched behind him, gripped him under the shoulders, and leaned back on her heels, trying to use her weight to move him out of the car. For a moment, he seemed stuck, but after a few seconds his legs came free and she dragged him clear of the car.

"Wyler, can you hear me? Talk to me, come on." She set him back down, and his head lolled, spilling blood onto the grass. He coughed weakly, remaining motionless from the neck down.

Damn it! Cassie stepped back and raised her voice, scanning the field. "Help! Is anyone out there? I need help—this man is dying!" The words sounded ridiculous as soon as they were out of her mouth. There were probably people dying all around her.

She looked back down at Wyler. He was right about one thing—this man was definitely more than the authorities had bargained for, whether they were equipped to stop him or not. She ran a hand through her hair, resting it on top of her head.

Someone was coming toward her out of the shadows between the two ships. She stared blankly for a moment, then shook herself and waved her arms. "Yes—good! Over here, over here!"

The approaching man had a tall, thin frame, like a basketball player. He glanced at the flaming car, then stopped as he looked down at Wyler. Cassie shook her head. "This man needs medical attention right now! Can you help us—do you have a car?"

The man glanced at one of the spaceships, then stepped around to Wyler's opposite side. He stared. "He's not dead?"

"He will be soon if you ask me any more stupid questions!" Cassie put her hands on her temples. "I'm sorry." She tipped her head back and exhaled, closing her eyes.

The man stared for a moment, then turned back toward the far ship. He signaled into the distance, then turned back. "I'll see what I can do. Wait here, just a moment."

He ran back toward the other ship as another figure emerged—the silhouette suggested a woman, much shorter. The man pointed back toward Wyler and the two seemed to exchange a few quick words while the man gestured repeatedly toward the near ship. Then he hurried for the far ship's ramp as the woman moved closer.

Cassie nodded absently at her. "He's been shot with a laser."

The woman stooped, examining Wyler's eyes and touching his neck. She nodded slowly. "He won't last long here, but I might be able to do something for him on my ship." Abruptly she scooped him into her arms and stood back up effortlessly, cradling him as if he were an oversized ragdoll. "You'd better leave. We're about to open fire on this area." She turned toward the farther ship.

Cassie jogged after the woman. "Wait—I'm staying with him."

The woman turned back. Light glinted smoothly over the surfaces of her eyes. "That's not advisable. We may need to keep him with us temporarily. The other ship could leave at any time—that's our priority. We may be forced to take off while we're still treating your friend."

Cassie jumped. The woman had moved into one of the sporadically spotlighted areas, and she suddenly looked thoroughly alien. Her skin was pale blue, and a scorched laser blast was evident in her chest, just below her neck. No evidence of blood—just an empty blackened hole above the sternum where her clothes and flesh had burned away. Cassie shook her head. "Who are you people?"

A low hum came from the near ship. The woman looked sharply at the ship, then resumed heading toward her own, raising her voice and calling over her shoulder. "Listen, you're welcome to come aboard, if you want, but if we go after the other ship, I can't promise your safety. The man we're chasing may try a counterattack."

They were chasing Monroe. Cassie exhaled, shaking her head. Lucky for her—for all she had known, they might have been working with the man and equally dangerous, not that she had given it any consideration whatsoever. She caught up to the woman, matching her pace. "But you will bring us back?"

"Yes. Assuming we stay alive."

The man appeared in the hatch at the top of the ramp. "Jayjay—his ship is completely back online. We have to get moving... you're sure you're finished with the turret?"

The woman looked up at him as she stepped onto the bottom of the ramp without slowing down. "No, but it's functional. Just get in there and start firing, and be ready to take off."

We may be forced to take off...

Cassie worked her jaw, grinding her teeth. Jesus. The fact that she was walking onto a spaceship was a thought that wasn't remotely conceivable, and if she were somehow able to put it in perspective and look at the situation realistically, she probably would have been running screaming toward the woods. But insanity aside, Zack Wyler was now at the mercy of these people, whoever they were, and she had placed him in that situation. She had to see this through... it wasn't as if she had a choice. Even if it meant riding on a damn spacecraft.

The woman moved Wyler quickly through the hatch. Cassie paused at the opening, glancing back at the field toward the other ship. The words of a junior high school history teacher echoed at the back of her mind: *No blood was spilled by the enemy's hand in Valley Forge... all casualties were the result of natural hardship...*

As she looked, a single bolt of red light exploded against the bottom side of the other ship's bow. Monroe's ship... these were the good guys, apparently.

That was what she was going to keep telling herself, anyway. She sighed and looked down as she stepped across the threshold and into the ship.

XV   ASCENSION

"We grow and learn and convince ourselves that we hold dominion over matter and energy and the way of things... that we are ever free to call up our vast knowledge and our long-developed technical skills if we need to bend nature to our will. And so, we are reminded from time to time that we live ever at the mercy of time and space.

"The wise traveler knows as he ventures into the elements that there is no such thing as an infallible instrument... he must respect the unpredictable nature of the universe and prepare for the unexpected. So it was for the ancient seafarers of Dessa's past, and so it will always be.

"There in the end, when the instruments fail, the traveler must look to the stars."

```
... GCL AE.001
Phi 00 00 00.00 / Theta 00 15 37.33 / Rho 00.00 / JD 2448894
Alpha Confinii: OS; "Earth Vicinity"; 29 September 1992 CE
```

/13. Nondisclosure.

/13.1. As of 2703 CE, human engineering is not capable of producing the technology needed to conduct the proposed expedition. Superaeonic travel will require a breakthrough in hyperspace navigation techniques that will not occur until the invention of microstasis suspension circuitry in 3524 CE, in the Human Sphere. The cillians and the proteids currently possess similar technology; however, their spacecraft and computational platforms are highly provincial and limited in scope, and as such, their current processes will not lend themselves to this manipulated form of travel without extensive modification. Any attempt to use these time-travel techniques prematurely would increase the chance that this information will spread, and it is critically important that this knowledge be limited to a single disciplined individual. The 37th-century scinti-built ships styled for long-term habitation with universal interface are among the first in this Galaxy designed with all the basic logistical needs; therefore, the necessary hardware modifications are minor, and initiation of the flight plan without outside help is viable.

/13.2. In the wrong hands, the ability to travel time is potentially hazardous to the natural progression of events in our universe. Measures have been installed that will make it convenient for you to encrypt all the critical data enclosed and eventually dispose of it; nevertheless, this does not guarantee it will be protected from attempts to access it. The confidentiality of the data will remain your responsibility.

/13.3. The ytaoans have trusted you with this sensitive information only because they require particulate energy that they would otherwise have no access to. They have identified you as an individual who will not exploit or abuse this privilege, and they deem that you will not violate this trust. I expect they are correct, as always, but I leave you with this reminder: whether or not you choose to execute this request, no one else must know about it for the remainder of your life. When you die, this knowledge dies with you. Do not seek outside help or companionship on your journey, do not attempt to travel to points other than the destination I have delivered to you, and do not disseminate the information in this message.

The ten prominent circles of the Archangel's exhaust cylinders flared as the ship broke through the Kármán line and out of the protection against the Sun's cosmic rays. Dexter glanced to the environmental panel at the extreme right of the cockpit. The thermostat spiked but stabilized quickly as the ships moved higher into the thin ionosphere. No problem there. Twitchy lighting and sluggish response time on the display glass interface were one thing, but a failure during the escape phase could have been disastrous.

He frowned at the operational window in the PDG, which continued to insist that there was nothing wrong. The flickering of the cabin lights and glass cockpit issues had lasted only a few seconds, just after the engagement of the main engine—normally an indication of a power flow problem—but the on-board had failed to identify anything. The wiser move would have been to run a complete diagnostic prior to take-off. Of course, that would have meant letting Monroe get away. As it was, the man was minutes away from hyperspace, where he would be free to plot a course anywhere in time, wreaking havoc at will wherever he decided to go. There was only so much they could do to stop him, but if he made hyperspace, they were decidedly out of the picture.

Dexter eased the throttle to the open space position and felt the shift in the hum of the engine below the floor. Smooth enough. Maybe the lighting was just a temporary hiccup; the on-board wasn't identifying a problem because there wasn't one—at least, not any more. There was virtually no chance Monroe had done something to affect the ship... unleashed some sort of attack virus program or low-level EMF pulse. If he had, it would have shown up in more than the lighting. Still, there was no underestimating this man.

He fixed his eyes on the targeting window directly in front of him and reached beneath the shelf, once again unlocking the turret and moving himself in front of the joystick as he pulled the double-handle from its stow position beneath the shelf. Jayjay had managed to switch out one of the two blown flashlamps in less than a minute, but the aim and focus were gone, and the working left cannon was misaligned. To hit Monroe, Dexter was going to have to aim the entire ship. Not possible while subject to aerodynamics, but now they were free of the heavy atmosphere.

Judging by the shots as they had landed while the ships were on the ground, the sight was off 3 centimeters to the left in the PDG window—Jayjay hadn't had time to reprogram the on-board for the physical damage to the turret. Dexter tapped the translational thrusters, shifting the diagram of the Archangel's exhaust gradually to the right, trying to line up the center of the epsilon cylinder based on dead reckoning. The two exhaust holes in the inner lateral-line cylinders were the only surefire entry points for knocking out the back end of a fusion powered ship; a direct hit with enough power would cause an energy clot and rupture the fusion channel… if Monroe's on-board failed to detect the breach in time, he would lose control of his ship and be suspended in space. There was also a chance the ship would lose integrity and explode.

Dexter swallowed, gripping the joystick with both hands and readying his finger on the trigger. One way or another, he was attempting to end another man's life. In fact, he was probably attempting to end two. Jayjay hadn't said it out loud, but the easiest way for Monroe to have created signs of life about his ship was to bring another person aboard—possibly an abduction of someone completely innocent. Of course Jayjay would say the impact on history should take priority.

The joystick was heavy in his hands, almost unmaneuverable. Jammed by the inoperable rotor actuator. Dexter shook himself. They'd had their chance to ground Monroe safely, leave him and whoever else was aboard to the people of the 20th century. Eliminating Monroe from the universe would probably leave all those people a lot better off. If there was an innocent aboard Monroe's ship now, it wouldn't be the first new death resulting from Monroe's arrival… there had been dozens left dead in the field, on top of the man in the islands and probably many more in the city. Monroe had made his impact on history.

Dexter sighed. It might have been out of his hands anyway—pulsed laserfire from a single cannon might not even be enough to cause the rupture. Apparently the damage to the coupler mirror on the right had been too much for a quick fix. Jayjay had done what she could to give them a shot, and that would have to be enough. In fact, the prospect of letting the man loose in the Galaxy's past was becoming more undesirable every second they had a chance to observe the accumulation of his monstrous acts.

The exhaust cylinder moved into position in the target window. Dexter clenched his teeth and fired, glancing through the glareshield. The laser blast missed the ship entirely, falling off to the left. Dexter tapped the thrusters, shifting in place, and fired again. Another miss left, though this time the plasma hit the inside of the cylinder. Not precise enough. He needed a second cannon and the fine-tuning of the on-board. He rubbed his mouth and tentatively tapped the thruster control again, this time shifting the Explorer vertically. He exhaled and fired again.

The Archangel jolted out of line as the shot released. The blast burned along one of the ship's landing skids, and the skid began to come apart, drifting upward against the fuselage. Rivulets of electricity ran in a wave from the bow to the stern. Dexter glanced at the round crystal of the EMF indicator as the red rectangular representation of Monroe's ship faded away.

The ship had gone out of control on its own. It remained in a lopsided tumble for several seconds, then disappeared in a searing flash of light.

Dexter blinked, rubbing his jaw. He heard footsteps—Jayjay was behind him. He kept his eyes forward for a long moment, staring at empty space through the glareshield. Apparently, Jayjay was doing the same. He turned in his seat. "Did you see that?"

Jayjay was one step into the cockpit, her eyes locked on the view. "That was the Archangel?" She stepped to the console, between the seats. "We just got lit up scoop to burners." She looked at him sharply. "What happened?"

Dexter looked back out the glareshield. "I don't understand. I missed the shot. I didn't hit anywhere near the exhaust, but he blew out like I broke his fusion chamber wide open."

Jayjay frowned. "That couldn't have been a pure drive breach—we would have felt the shock through the stabilizers. That almost looked like a jump."

Dexter shook his head quickly. "He couldn't have jumped. His EMF went down—I was looking right at it."

"You're sure that reading was correct?"

"Jayjay, you don't understand—I saw the ship was come apart." Dexter sat up, laughing at the floor. "You can check the footage yourself on the viewer recording. The ship had to be losing integrity on its own. I barely grazed the skid and it came away like it was an ice sculpture. Even if he still had fusion power... Jayjay, he went into a free gyroscopic roll before I hit him. That's why I missed him—he was completely out of control."

The android nodded, pursing her lips. "He might have tried to go to hyperspace too quickly. There are normally preventive fail-safes, but Monroe's people did a lot of customization to that on-board." She paused. "That might explain a rapid high-energy decay effect that would look something like a jump into elevated space."

Dexter leaned back in the seat, rotating back around and gestured at the view. "There you go. His on-board couldn't have coordinated a jump while his ship was disintegrating... something went wrong aboard that ship. I have no idea what it was, but something went wrong." He paused. "I did hit the epsilon cylinder before that last shot. Maybe that triggered it."

Jayjay sighed. "I don't like it. We've been showing some glitches too."

"So I noticed." Dexter glanced back at her. Very little got by Jayjay, busy though she was with the autodoc in the environmental compartment. He squinted. "You think the power problems are connected to what went wrong aboard the Archangel?" He frowned. Jayjay's link hadn't been reestablished... with two separate systems, a common cause would have to have been external. "What exactly are you suggesting?"

"Not just power problems—power allocation problems. That's the on-board core. False auxiliary failures too... I don't know." Jayjay nodded once and turned. "Let's just get these people back home as soon as possible." She disappeared into the main cabin.

Dexter watched her for a moment. Problems with the on-board core. Guidestars, it was always something. He turned back around and brought up a navigational window, moving himself back in front of the helm and easing the throttle down one notch to the fall position. He tapped the rotational thrusters and paused frowning at the screen. No indication of right yaw. He leaned over the com. "Jayjay, I think I'm getting a problem with the attitude sensors..."

Without warning the stars outside the glareshield wheeled to the upper left, then stopped abruptly, and for an instant the gravity stabilizers failed as the ship bounced out of the dive, pitching violently upward. Dexter flew out of the pilot seat and banged hard against the left portion of the control shelf before flipping onto the floor, flat on his back.

He blinked up at the soft lighting of the overhead panels, stunned. The stabilizers were active again. The ship had settled down. He rolled onto his shoulder, breathing heavily. Get these people back home. Stellar good idea.

Teodor felt as though his mind was turning itself inside-out. It was the pyropite, and he was tempted to ravage the computer in the hope that he could guide the ship mentally.

His rage was surprising—never before had he felt so completely consumed, and yet he still seemed to have the ability to compartmentalize it, separate it within his brain. His eyes bored against the electromagnetic field indicator in its isolated place in the left control panel. The red glow of a passenger-class ship was millimeters below the green dot in the center. Massengill was right on his tail.

Teodor's mind raced. The on-board errors had emerged at lift-off and compounded from there. The computer had failed to process the prearranged flight pattern, and maddeningly failed to recognize Galina as a valid destination, maintaining an arbitrary heading to an abstract sector somewhere on the other side of the Galaxy. The throttle was locked in on primary drive at a steady velocity that was going to prevent the ship from approaching hyperspace.

It couldn't happen—it wouldn't happen. His goal had been achieved, the ultimate goal that any man might achieve. He was the only one who would ever have the means and the will to do it, and it was not by coincidence that he had managed it. It was destiny. The universe had chosen him. The idea that this meager pretender thought he could steal it away from him was utterly preposterous. The universe would never allow it, not now, at the moment of coronation. He wasn't going to be destroyed now by a blast to the fusion drive, and he wasn't going to be confined to space for all eternity by a malfunctioning computer system.

Teodor raised the cocktail glass in his hand, flaring his nostrils as he stared into the clear, burgundy lucidity of the wine he had so blithely prepared... the perfect blood-colored, healing elixir worthy of celebrating the consummation of a lifelong goal. Teodor laughed under his breath. The Romans drank often, but there was never a sweeter occasion than immediately after a conquest.

Faro's voice filled the cabin air, as tangible as if whispered through the vents, or carried on guided neutrino arcs over the infinite stretches of time. *I think you should consider holding off... with this information, given a few years, we should able to validate this more thoroughly...*

Teodor wheeled on the companionway and shot a fiery glare in the direction of the main compartment, throwing the glass through the dew-drop curtain and vaporizing the wine. "Fool! You never understood me, did you? Never truly. So the blind shall remain blind."

He refocused on the EMF indicator, just as the cockpit alarm sprang to life. The EMF indicator went blank and the lights dimmed. The ship yawed slightly to the left. Teodor held his stance, feeling the motion in his legs and ears—he could see it happening as clearly as if he were watching the ships from above. Massengill had not yet fired, but the on-board had introduced another twist, another computer-guided wrinkle throwing the craft into a pointless, reckless tailspin.

But Massengill was firing now, and Teodor felt it in the nerves of every tissue. The Archangel rolled, and the succeeding violent jolt was the report of a plasma strike finding its mark along the port landing skid, reducing it as if the ship were a composite of flying paper lanterns.

Teodor opened his eyes, and a single thought took hold—a memory of another Cristan Faro caveat, long ago, something from a discussion upon first reviewing the transcripts of cillian records. There had been mechanical failures, and the effects had been widespread.

It was the pyropite. All that matter was erupting, disturbing the course of processing in the Archangel's on-board, most likely affecting power grids on Earth as it was in the Cillian Sphere and on all the other sentient worlds of the time. Muddling thought and computer function alike, just for a few brief minutes—not long enough to cause a major stir in a society ill-positioned to observe it, but plenty long enough to put the Archangel at a fatal disadvantage.

Teodor was at the mercy of the stone.

The alarm wailed, and the ship went into an aggressive pitch. The floor fell away as the gravity simulators failed. Teodor hit the ceiling and smashed against the overhead photo-panels. He closed his eyes as the bow twirled in a visceral corkscrew. In the last moment, he envisioned the blue haven of Earth receding in the distance. Then all sanity evaporated in a blackening chaos.

*   *   *

```
Nonspatial. GCU NA
- / - / - / JD 2448894
Previous Fix: "Earth Vicinity"; 29 September 1992
```

The twin-engine Piper Navajo shot through a cloud and back into the light of the setting sun. An island was ahead, in the middle of the wide horizon.

Suddenly, a series of dots formed an arch in the shape of a frown above

500

the island. The dots grew larger, and began to look like eyes in the sky, round in the middle and tapering at the ends. They were milky yellow, with no pupils.

Then the one at the right end of the frown flashed in red. It separated from the rest, and the formation fell into disarray. Dark clouds moved in front of the sun. The Navajo dove at the island, and the island exploded. A whirlpool emerged in its place. The ocean below became the empty void of space, and the foam of the whirlpool became a galaxy of stars.

Then the center of the galaxy resolved itself into the face of a well-groomed, mustached man staring back with angry eyes, someone vaguely familiar. A striking, evocative face. The face expanded, slowly covering the rest of the galaxy.

Zack opened his eyes, and instantly felt as if he were still dreaming. He shook himself, but the feeling didn't go away. He was looking up at a tiled ceiling, with round windows down the middle. What he was seeing through the windows didn't make any sense.

Rings of color blended in and out of each other. The lines on the ceiling were also in motion, shifting slowly as if he were looking up from the bottom of a pool, through a lilting surface of water.

He felt a dull, lingering sting in an area between his neck and sternum, and the knowledge of familiar pain floated into his memory. Intense, unbearable pain. The edge was gone now, obscured by a warm numbness and a mild tingling sensation in his fingertips and feet. Apparently he was heavily drugged. "Goddamn. Happy birthday to me."

Cassandra Prescott's face appeared above him. Her features were more angular than usual. She looked like an elfin princess out of a fairy tale. "It's alive!" She grinned, and her eyes seemed to shine. "You've looked better, Wyler." She seemed to grow taller, then slid away in the direction of his feet. "How are you feeling?"

"Like I just fell off the Merry Pranksters' bus." He squinted, opening and closing his fists. He turned his palms downward and touched the surface he was lying against. Firm and spongy, with an odd texture like fine grillwork. Some kind of makeshift bed, protruding out of a recessed area of wall along his left side. Comfortable but very, very weird.

"Luckily, we had access to just about the only place on Earth where you could have received treatment for critical laser wounds." Prescott leaned against the wall, which seemed to bulge outward slightly. Hard to tell whether it was another illusion.

Zack winced and raised himself up on his elbows, shaking off a moment of dizziness. The counselor's face flashed a brief look of concern. He eyed her. "We also happened to be in just about the only place on Earth where you can actually get critical laser wounds."

Her eyes narrowed. "You might want to dig deep and try to fake being nice for a little while. They did virtually bring you back from the dead." She frowned, cocking her head. "Besides, it's hard not to get shot with a laser when you basically a drive a car straight at a man with a laser gun. Did you really think that would work?"

Zack raised an eyebrow, shifting his weight as the muscles in his arms began to ache. "Had to do something." He paused, shaking his head. "So, counselor... where exactly are we?" He focused on her face. His vision was starting to get a little clearer.

Prescott raised her eyebrows and stepped back, glancing up and waving a hand at the surroundings. "We are on a spaceship." She shrugged. "I don't have any idea how you knew spaceships were in Valley Forge Park, but here we are. Closest thing to a hospital."

He looked around and grunted. "Love the decor... this place is like a cross between a go-go bar and a morgue. Reminds me of a Chinatown massage parlor."

He eased himself into a sitting position and the warm stimulation in his chest seemed to get slightly warmer. He frowned down at himself and gingerly dabbed at the area of his heart with his left hand. His shirt was gone, and some sort of rubbery blue bandage was wrapped around his upper chest, completely preventing any look at the area. Critical laser wounds... Monroe had done it. The image of the man standing over him rapidly crystallized in his memory—the dark silhouette, the backlit fringe of well-manicured, curly hair maybe 10 feet away. The sudden splash of crimson light like an animated cartoon. That gun had sliced up stacks of people and it had hit him point blank, dead-center in the chest.

The counselor cleared her throat. "You should probably take it easy, try not to touch it. The laser plasma weapon, whatever it was... it did a lot of damage to your chest. I'm not sure how they managed to fix it the way they did. The... person who was working on you..." She paused and shook her head. "They were saying you should lie flat until we get back." She swallowed dryly.

She seemed genuinely relieved to see him. Not that surprising, considering there probably wasn't any good reason he should have still been alive. These people with the spaceship were going to have some explaining to do. Zack rubbed his mouth. "I feel fine." He paused, craning his neck. At a glance, the interior of the spaceship was like a stretched-out living room; at the end of the long compartment was a narrow, open companionway, and if he was hearing right, the sound of muted voices was coming from that direction. The ship had the feel of a cabin-cruiser, only magnified... creature comfort decorations interspersed with utility functions, all packed together within the same limited space. Definitely a hell of a lot bigger than a Piper Navajo. "Until we get back, huh? I take it we're airborne."

Prescott cocked her head and flashed a grim smile. "Actually, I'm told we're in space. They took off chasing after Monroe while we were on board." She scratched her nose and looked down toward the floor. "These people evidently wanted to stop him as much as we did."

They were in space. Of course—where the hell else were people with a spaceship supposed to go? Obvious as it was, that didn't make it any less strange to see the counselor uttering the words with such a straight face. Zack nodded and pawed at a small bandage wrapped around the inside of his left elbow, probably the target area the people aboard the ship had used to feed these miraculous drugs of theirs into his veins. Effortlessly bringing him back from the so-called dead while they chased Monroe out of Earth's atmosphere. Sure, why not?

He rubbed his eyes. "Where's Monroe now?"

Prescott frowned. "I'm told they destroyed his ship. They gave me some of the details—it has to do with the engine, and how they travel faster than light speed, and I don't really understand the mechanics. The bottom line is, Monroe is not a problem anymore. Now they're just worried about getting their own ship under control."

Zack rolled his head, stretching his neck. "What do you mean... we're flying through space but they don't have the ship under control?"

Prescott shrugged, shaking her head. "They say there's no danger of hitting anything. We're in hyperspace flight mode, and we're travelling in an elevated dimension. Or something."

Monroe wasn't a problem anymore... hopefully that much was true. Zack snorted. "I'm glad these people are so on top of everything." He exhaled heavily and straightened his arms, shifting his legs in front of him, testing their weight.

"Are you trying to get up? That's really not a good idea."

He ignored her, sliding his legs over the right edge of the bed and easing himself forward. For a moment he thought his foot was never going to touch the ground. He felt a sudden swirl of queasiness in his stomach.

503

"Wyler. I don't think you're going to be able to stand. Fine—don't blame me if you fall on your ass and knock yourself unconscious again."

His feet hit the ground. He paused and took another breath, then stood. His legs wobbled for a moment. He stared at his feet, nodding, and raised his eyebrows at Prescott. "You were saying?" He smiled, stepped away from the bed, and immediately collapsed.

Prescott rolled her eyes and stepped across the floor to help him up, but he waved her off, leaning back against the bed. She threw up her hands and stalked in the direction of the companionway, then turned, folding her arms. "Of all the pig-headed… you have no idea how bad off you were."

He breathed, glancing around. The leg muscles were weaker than he expected. The counselor was completely right, but damned if he was going to openly acknowledge it to her. Besides, it didn't much help that the convex sides of the vehicle appeared to be subtly stretching farther outward as he stared at them, or that the lines on the floor looked every bit as fluid as those on the ceiling, as if he were trying to walk across a surface of gelatin. He rubbed his neck, steadying himself. "Shouldn't we be floating around? You know, weightless, since we're in space?"

Prescott sighed loudly. "Gravity simulators."

"Ah." Zack squinted. The counselor seemed fairly well indoctrinated. How long had he been out of it?

There was motion behind her. A petite, athletic-looking woman with distinctly blue skin came through the companionway and approached the bed.

"You're going to be weak for a while. Your wound should be okay by now, but it's probably better if you don't try to walk yet." The woman had an oddball accent, like Monroe. Hers was a little different, a little smoother.

Prescott cleared her throat. "Wyler, this is Jayjay. She brought you aboard and saw to all your treatment." She paused. "Jayjay… Zack Wyler."

Zack remained on his feet, gripping the edge of the bed with one hand. The counselor was giving him a hard look, raising an eyebrow. He nodded. "I guess I ought to thank you for saving my life. I appreciate the help."

Jayjay studied him for a moment. The woman looked pure blue, with deep blue eyes and lips that complemented the bizarre skin color. Her hair was a short, bleach-blonde bob that looked so symmetrical it belonged on a Barbie doll, so stark white and glossy it almost looked metallic, and it seemed vaguely to pick up the blue tint of her skin. She stared back at him indifferently. "It was the least we could do. Dexter told me you saved his life as well."

"Who's Dexter?" Zack glanced at Prescott, then shook his head. "Never mind—I understand you guys were after Monroe. You got him?"

A resigned look flashed over the woman's blue face. She turned and glanced back at Prescott, and Prescott looked at the floor. Apparently, the matter had already been thoroughly discussed. Jayjay nodded. "Dexter was able to do some damage with our turret, but from what I can gather, Monroe's ship seems to have self-destructed on its own."

Seems to have self-destructed? A little too noncommittal with the response. Zack shrugged, frowning. "So he's dead?" He glanced at Prescott. "Because if he's still out there, no one's safe—not on Earth, and not on whatever freak-show planet you people are from."

Jayjay returned a curious look. She nodded slowly. "We know he was dangerous—that's why we landed. Our intention was to stop him. Monroe's ship made what we call an unbalanced jump while it was undergoing power fluctuations, meaning the ship and everything on board lost integrity during a failed transition into hyperspace; he can't have survived."

Zack lowered his brow, glaring back defiantly. "Maybe so. I don't know about any of that, but I got a first-hand look at what he's capable of, and I'm not sure you're aware of the kind of power he's holding."

The woman didn't flinch. "We're aware of why he came to Earth, and what he was trying to find. He can't have survived. It's no longer your concern, so try to put yourself at ease."

Monroe and his goddamn glowing rock. Zack grunted as the memory of the thing's power flashed again through his mind, the charge of the energy coursing through his nerves and the sudden electric clarity in his vision, in his head. The harsh emptiness when it was out of his hands. Nothing like the buzz of a drug, not even the overwhelming painkiller dosage that must have currently been in his system—the drug effects were alien, clearly an encroachment into the nervous system from the outside. Holding the stone, it was as if the thing had become a part of his essence.

And the mere memory of it was every bit as bad as alcohol withdrawal. Zack grimaced and his mouth went dry. "It was a stone that gave off its own light. It was in my hands, and it enhanced my strength, my agility, sharpened my senses." He shook his head. "I gave it away—I gave it right to the bastard. Now it's his. I didn't realize what I was doing…"

Jayjay nodded, watching him carefully. "None of that matters now. If Monroe had it with him on the ship, they're both gone."

Zack looked back at her. The woman obviously knew a lot more about Monroe than he did—the man was her business, not his, and there was no reason to think they weren't capable of ending the man's reign of terror just because he hadn't successfully smashed his car into him. These people had come fully prepared to stop him, and apparently, they had done it. But the image of the man's growing face in the dream was hard to shake. There was something real about it, and it was setting off alarm bells. What the hell was it about that goddamn dream?

He looked down, shaking his head. "Who is he, anyway? Who are all you people?"

"Monroe's just a man with a large amount of capital." Jayjay hesitated. "We're from your future. Monroe figured out how to travel time; we decided we didn't want to leave him free to travel through history unchallenged, so here we are."

Zack scratched his cheek. "Sure, of course—time-travelers. What else would you possibly be?"

The woman went on in straight deadpan. "And we're going back where we belong as soon as we get you back home."

Zack nodded. "I hope you enjoyed your stay. Tell you what, you think maybe you might want to do it again—you know, go back in time to clean up the mess of bodies you guys just left behind? Because I'd love to avoid the part where I get a gopher hole burned in my chest."

Jayjay stepped in front of him and patted him on the shoulder. "You really should get some rest."

Zack staggered under the force of her hand and almost lost balance, raising his eyebrows. She was shockingly strong. At a glance, she was in good shape, pretty tough-looking for her size, but it felt as if she could hit like a 300-pound defensive end.

She shot him a narrow-eyed look and turned, heading back toward the companionway. "If you'll excuse me, Dexter and I have some things we need to deal with so that we can in fact get you back home."

Zack stared at her for a long moment. She was a bucket of laughs. He pushed himself away from the bed as he glanced back at the counselor. Apparently women in the future didn't change a whole hell of a lot.

Prescott frowned. "You don't listen much, do you?"

"I'm not getting back on the dissection table, thanks." He brushed past her, then turned, lowering his voice. "What's with the blue skin?"

She nodded, looking at the floor and rubbing her left arm. "You sure you want to know?"

Zack raised his eyebrows and stared at her.

"She's sort of…" Prescott cleared her throat and tossed her hair, leveling her eyes at him. "She's an android."

Zack continued to stare, then nodded and turned, jiggling a finger in his ear. "She's an android. Right." He stepped uneasily to the door, slowing as he tried to digest the scene on the other side.

He was looking at a spaceship cockpit from the future. Two seats were in position in front of a broad console jam-packed with buttons and switches and a thick black panel flashing animated electronic computer displays. Above it was a huge segmented windshield, and outside, ahead of the ship, the entire visible spectrum was on display in a series of bands. Red fringes on either side blended successively into orange, yellow, and green, and ran together in the middle in a blur of darkening blue. A thin, fuzzy violet strip split the outside sky in half.

He closed his eyes and shook himself, then stepped into the area between the seats. The blue woman was already seated to the right; the other seat was filled by a dark-haired man who seemed preoccupied with one of the electronic displays. Zack sniffed and nodded at the man to the left. "You must be Dexter."

The man flashed a smile at him. "I am. Dexter Massengill, pleased to meet you, sir. I hope you're feeling better."

"Better than I was. So you're from the future."

Massengill raised his eyebrows, keeping his eyes on one of the screens as he tapped at a small keypad. "3612 CE. That was the year we left, anyway."

Christ, the man was completely serious. Zack rubbed an eye. "Someone told me I saved your life. That true?"

Massengill looked surprised for a moment, then straightened in his seat, and his head rose above the back of the chair. He was a lot taller than he looked at first glance. His face became thoughtful. "Yes. The man we were pursuing... the man who shot you... he had me lined up when you came at him in your vehicle. He turned his attention to you, and I reached cover."

"Monroe." Zack sighed. "I guess that makes us even."

The man nodded and smiled again, turning back to the controls. He seemed to be fixed on a screen that looked a lot like an electronic diagram of a gyro horizon next to a scrolling stream of gibberish. Avionics in 3612 CE.

Zack stared at the windshield for a long moment. "This what it's like to travel in another dimension?"

Massengill looked up, glancing across the console toward Jayjay, then settling on Zack. "Oh. Well, this is one of the elevated dimensions, yes." He paused, turning back to his computer screen. "We are in... primary

507

hyperspace, to be exact. Dimension 5. Normally, we would have been through to D6 a long time ago... much, much quicker. The only feasible way to get from star to star. But as yet, we are unable to lay in a legitimate flight pattern."

Zack frowned at him. "So I heard. You people are going to be able to get us home, aren't you?" He glanced back as Prescott entered the cockpit.

Massengill pursed his lips. "I'm sure." He shook his head. "For now, we are on course to maintain an extended fall around the gravity well of the Galactic Core, which is a temporary default when there is a problem in a navigational element. If we leave this flight pattern alone we'll be in space for somewhere in the neighborhood of 12,000 years."

Jayjay leaned forward and cut in. "We're not going to be stuck in open space for 12,000 years—there are things we can do to correct whatever problems we're having."

Massengill nodded. "Yes, these on-boards will have the occasional error affecting the flight pattern... compensation for gravitational anomalies and solar wind can sometimes be tricky, there are times when coordinates need to be reconfigured at the last moment, but these things can all be corrected eventually. If we have to reinstall the core we will, but Jayjay and I are fully capable of handling that." He smiled again. "Don't worry, you and your friend are in good hands."

Zack raised his eyebrows. 12,000 years. He looked again at Prescott. She had crossed to the right, examining one of the projected displays in that area of the black panel. She didn't seem too concerned.

Great. Pulled from the dead only to potentially spend the rest of his natural life trapped aboard a renegade spacecraft. He glanced at Jayjay and placed a hand on the back of Massengill's chair, nodding down at the man. "This wouldn't be what you call an unbalanced jump... would it?"

Massengill glared back at him, then shook his head at Jayjay. "Not at all—we're fully in hyperspace, we never would have lasted if the ship didn't go through smoothly. The matter won't decay unless there's molecular instability before the ship hits absolute velocity—Jayjay, what did you tell him?"

Zack smiled in Jayjay's direction. The woman looked back. "Nothing. We're dealing with on-board communication problems, Mr. Wyler, not drive failure. You're not in danger."

"Sure." He raised his eyebrows. "As long as I'm okay with being stuck in space."

Prescott stretched, pressing her hands against her lower back. "Hey

Wyler, why don't you let them do their job?" She rubbed her neck. "Believe me, they've already been grilled ad nauseum. Besides, you need rest, remember?"

He took a step back and turned toward her, touching the bandage over his chest. "Counselor, do I detect a note of concern?"

She scratched behind her ear. "I think it's more about me not wanting to have to listen to you anymore." She turned, peering out at the red wash beyond the window along the right side of the cockpit.

Zack watched her for a moment, staring at the line of her profile. The solid surfaces were starting to seem less fluid, but there was still a hint of motion along the edges of separation. The counselor looked more human than elf now, but the contrast of the dark background still seemed to enhance her fair-skinned complexion as if she were on stage, made-up and under a spotlight. The same disheveled clothes she'd had on all night seemed to accentuate her figure more as she stood in front of the window. Particularly the navy skirt.

He rubbed his jaw, turning his gaze back toward the main windshield. 12,000 years aboard a ship with the counselor would get tiresome at about day two.

The sky outside the front window was the one thing that appeared unaffected by the bleeding visual effects. The bands of color were as frozen as if they had been painted there.

Prescott stepped back across the floor, following his gaze toward the windshield. "I can't say I thought I'd be looking at a view like this when I got up this morning." Her brown eyes were wide, and the reflected color array was visible against her lenses.

Zack shrugged. "Beats a sunset on the Schuylkill River." He flashed a wry smile.

Massengill abruptly leaned back in his chair. "It's my favorite thing about flying. There's a natural diffraction in the Doppler Shift that occurs to anyone travelling at faster-than-light speed, so you get a blue-centered view of the visible spectrum directly in front of you whenever you're in hyperspace."

Prescott nodded. "It's beautiful."

Massengill beamed. "Isn't it? We call it the Rainbow Road. You don't find gold at the end of the journey, but it provides for a very scenic ride."

Zack exhaled. "Where are the stars?"

Massengill shook his head. "At the moment, we're not in the real dimensions—we're in D5, or the first level of hyperspace, where matter is defined by its structure but not its substance. So from this point of view, you won't be able see stars or matter of any kind. The ship's integrity is preserved in an electromagnetic pocket while it passes through hyperspace, but outside the pocket, from our standpoint, there is no space. What we're seeing is really just a reflection of our own energy."

Prescott shook her head. "Doesn't make any more sense than it did a half an hour ago."

Zack squinted at the view, grabbing the top of Massengill's chair and letting it take some of his weight. The colors might have been a pattern on a curtain hanging 10 feet outside the windows, but the infinite depth was immediately apparent, as if the whole of it was genetically programmed, innate knowledge. The lines were too perfect—even the blurred edges of color had a pattern to them. The scene was definitely surreal... the perfect, surreal end to a day that had been about as rational and tangible as a dream fleeting from memory. The Rainbow Road was a striking image all right. Maybe not as beautiful as a starry sky, but striking.

Zack glanced down, shifting in place. His legs were starting to feel heavy. He patted the chair. "I guess now we know what Heaven looks like." He looked around, rubbing his eyes. "All right, that's it for me. Wake me up when we're home." He turned and headed back through the companionway.

THE END

*   *   *

The circular field was suddenly a mass of motion. The projection cylinder had closed and the lights in the surrounding trees had gone on, obscuring the overhead panorama of stars. Everywhere, the scinti students were climbing to their feet and spreading their wings. As soon as the excusal was announced, they would be taking to the air in droves.

Marigold Frisby Josephson pressed her back against the wide cross-section of bark, watching the field from the ground entrance of the Giant Rockwood. She turned her head as the elevator door opened.

Bon Sheridan Deiga stepped out, wringing his long, thin hands. "Marigold. Members of the fellian should not be hiding in the projection tree after ceremony. You know better than this."

She nodded. "I know, but I have to find out something."

The rings around his eyes shrank slightly. "Lots of the students have questions for the story-teller, but if they all decided to suddenly crowd inside the projection tree after ceremony, they would spill out the top, and all the sheridans would be trapped inside."

She looked at the ground. "Shey Deiga. I'm sorry. I wouldn't have come here, but I'm not going to be able to sleep unless I find out a couple of things. And if I can't sleep, I'll be up all night, keeping everybody else up all night, and we'll wake up Shey Aful-Kiron, and he'll wind up having to call you to ask you the very same things I'm going to ask you right now."

Deiga's eyes went wide. "Well. So. We don't want to keep Shey Aful-Kiron up. What is it, Marigold?"

She stepped forward, looking up. "You know how Dexter is always lucky, throughout the story? His luck has something to do with the fire's-eye. And the ytaoans. It does, doesn't it?"

Deiga touched a button set in the wall and the elevator door closed behind him. "What do you think, Marigold?"

She smiled. "I think Salaman Nevis didn't just want Dexter to go back in time. He wanted Dexter to meet up with the ytaoans, just like him. And the ytaoans needed Dexter to do something for them, and Dexter was the only one who could do it for them because he was so lucky."

Deiga touched a bony finger to his callused lips. "I see. And what was it the ytaoans needed Dexter to do?"

She raised her eyebrows excitedly. "Get the fire's-eye!"

"But why would they need the fire's-eye? It was clear in Salaman's message that the ytaoans were already omniscient and had great telekinetic powers."

She frowned. "I haven't figured that out yet. But I also think Zack and Cassie never get taken home. The malfunction continues and they can't get the ship out of hyperspace until Dexter and Jayjay's time. And that's how Zack's identification card wound up in the museum. He must have become famous for being from a different time, and given it to someone to remember him by. And I also think Monroe doesn't die. He gets away, doesn't he? Am I right?"

The old scint bowed his head. "I think you have a very large imagination, and a four-day ceremony is bad for your sleep. You should go back to the dormitory. According to Shey Aful-Kiron, you will be having a multi-class social science examination soon. So. Tomorrow, you need to start concentrating on your studies."

Marigold felt like stomping her foot. "But, Shey Deiga, that's not fair! Am I right or not? Tell me!"

He gestured at the opening, but she didn't move. "I have told you the complete story of the Deiassan fire's-eye, from when it was found by Uru'ishtim of Eridu to when it was incorporated by Teodor Monroe. Two men who challenged time and nature. In the end, fate did not favor these men."

He gestured again. Marigold lowered her head and stepped slowly out of the tree. He followed her.

She held her hands out. "Then it's over? Dexter and Jayjay just dropped Zack and Cassie off and then headed out and did whatever? Nobody ever did anything else with the fire's-eye?"

"In the end, the fire's-eye of Dessa ceased to exist when it broke down to its molecular components in Teodor Monroe's particle fusion-filter. And on that same day, all the other fire's-eyes in the universe disintegrated. Or were you not paying attention?"

Marigold said nothing.

"Patience, Mageveila. The legends are a part of life, connected to the present the same way our genetic code is evidence of our ancestors. Never will there be an end to all stories of truth before the lights of the heavens burn no more." He paused. "There is always another legend."

$$\Omega$$

ACKNOWLEDGEMENTS

Thanks go to my family for their unwavering support, and specifically to my brother, Michael Grofe, whose help in producing the graphic cover art was critical; my step father, Robert Steppacher, Sr., who provided sound marketing and financial advice; and my mother, Kathryn Steppacher, who contributed essential technical feedback. My mother is a nutritionist and a dietary subject matter expert; when she points out problem areas in my fiction related to food, I take it seriously. A concept of mine called "ferdiss cutlets," a sort of roast beast of the future, gave her fits of laughter where it was not intended. While that was by no means her greatest contribution to the book, I can see now that some things in the universe of science fiction cuisine are better left uncreated.

I received valuable editorial support over the long history of this story's unusually long gestation. Nancy Rosenberger, my high school literature teacher, generously offered her free time in her thorough review, and her suggestions and painstaking exploration of the plot points opened me up to new possibilities in my approach; her knowledge of English literature and enthusiasm for language and the written word also helped give me the foundation I needed to embark on a career as an author.

I owe the publication of this book as it exists today to my friend Karlee Finch, who provided the last review and also gave me the push I needed to see the book in print by engineering a personal hardback copy for me on her own. She is thoughtful, generous, brilliant, and tenacious, and she never ceases to amaze me. She is an inspiration. Her field of study happens to be geology, which I think is perfect for her because she is truly, in both a literal and figurative sense, an absolute rock star.

Finally, I need to thank my father, Jerrold Grofe. He raised me to seek perfection, and his often amusingly gruff personality and unique sense of humor shaped my voice. I think it was his love of science and nature that lent me the fascination I have for astronomy and theoretical physics, and thanks to him, I tend not to be satisfied with one of my stories unless it's on the ridiculously grandiose side. But, while I'm looking for ways to explore the wild and fantastic possibilities of the universe, thanks to my father's disciplined adherence to fact, I like to think I've learned to maintain an infusion of logic and technical realism no matter how crazy the story gets. My father was the first person to read this book in its original form, and his dispassionate input was exactly what the story needed. His insights, and his sense of humor, will always be a major influence on me and my work.

ROBERT WILLIAM GROFE was born in Philadelphia and has lived in the area for most of his life; he currently resides in Collegeville, Pennsylvania. He holds a B.A. in writing seminars from Johns Hopkins and has been writing professionally for 20 years. During college, he was a staff writer and illustrator for the student-run *Black & Blue Jay* magazine and regular cartoonist for the university newsletter, and he worked as a freelance reporter for the *Newtown Square County Press* before joining The Vanguard Group in Valley Forge, where he now copyedits corporate reports and marketing materials. He enjoys traveling and has spent many months sailing in the Chesapeake Bay and the Caribbean, which he believes has fueled many of his ideas. As for his interest in space, he credits that particular inspiration to his parents, who in 1969 deposited him in front of a television set and forced him to watch the Apollo 11 Moon landing at five months of age. He writes fiction in his spare time; his first novel, *Hellbender*, was published in 2009 and is available through Sense of Wonder Press.

Light of the Fire's-Eye is the first book of *The Spacetime Cycle*, a trilogy that Robert has been developing since his college graduation. He hopes to have his epic science fiction series completed sometime before the advent of the flying car.

* 9 7 8 0 6 1 5 8 0 8 3 1 4 *